THE VISITATION MONSTER

FRANK Peretti

THOMAS NELSON
Since 1798

NASHVILLE DALLAS MEXICO CITY RIO DE JANEIRO BEIJING

Published in Nashville, Tennessee, by Thomas Nelson. Thomas Nelson is a registered trademark of Thomas Nelson, Inc.

Thomas Nelson, Inc., titles may be purchased in bulk for educational, business, fund-raising, or sales promotional use. For information, please e-mail SpecialMarkets@ThomasNelson.com.

ISBN 978-1-59554-520-6

Printed in the United States of America

08 09 10 11 12 QW 5 4 3 2 1

THE VISITATION

In loving memory of Kip Jordon.

INTRODUCTION

I NEVER THOUGHT I'd get sick of being a Christian. I was practically *born* a Christian, raised in a Christian home, nurtured in church and Sunday school. If there was anything going on at church — special meetings, singspirations, Bible studies, vacation Bible school — I was there. I read my Bible every day, prayed regularly, witnessed to others whenever I could, and knew all the hymns by heart. I was a youth pastor, an associate pastor, a teacher, a preacher, a public speaker. I was on the right road, had plenty of approval, and no plans to change course.

But no one told me I was still growing up and that the time would come when all the familiar trappings of the Christianity I grew up with would no longer be comfortable. Like a child growing out of his clothes, I was having trouble getting things to fit— except for one T-shirt that said, BEEN THERE, DONE THAT.

No, I wasn't backsliding. Satan wasn't tempting me. I wasn't even disillusioned—well, not with God. Call it growing pains. I was beginning to feel the difference between *religion* and *relationship*. The more I longed to know God, the more fed up I got with all the Christian "stuff." Where was God really? Would I really find Him in all the religious trappings, my particular Christian culture that told me by word and example what a Christian ought to look like, act like, believe, and do? For most of my life I'd wrapped that world around me like a security blanket; I felt safe, like a child at home with loving parents.

But kids like us grow up and need our own relationship with God, forged in the heart through time and experience, not draped around us by the church we attend. We need to know God for ourselves, not secondhand.

Coming to that realization, that point of growth, can be a lonely time. You just feel so tired of everything: No, I didn't have my "quiet time" this morning, so arrest me. If I have to sing that chorus one more time I'll scream. Maybe I'll stay home from church this time just for some peace and quiet.

And you don't buy everything so readily: Maybe that was a prophecy to you, but to me it was bad acting. How do I know God really said that to Pastor? I didn't hear anything. Are we *really* going to vanish in the twinkling of an eye?

And everyone has a cure for what ails you: You need to read your Bible and pray more. You need to come back to the Lord. These are lies of the Enemy; speak in tongues and they'll go away.

Well, don't worry. I made it through. Jesus walked with me through every moment, and I could see Him so much more clearly on the other side. I have a wonderful church family, I like singing the choruses, and I still read my Bible and pray every day. But things look different now. My faith is my own, I like where the Lord has brought me, and I won't be going back.

Having been there, having done that, and having survived, I thought I'd write about it. Wherever you are in your own walk with the Lord, I'm sure you'll find some common ground between yourself and Travis Jordan, struggling out of all that religion to find the real Jesus.

— FRANK E. PERETTI
June 2003

PROLOGUE

THE HAMMER RANG against the nail, piercing skin, cutting vessels. It rang against the nail, piercing muscle, chipping bone. It rang against the nail, anchoring arm to rough-hewn wood. It rang. It rang. It rang.

And then the ringing stopped, and the young man hung there under the scorching sun, faint with pain, alone. He could not shift his weight, flex his knees, or even turn his head without feeling the fire of the nails. His wrists were swelling around the nail heads. His blood was drying in the sun, turning brown on the wood.

He cried out, but God did not listen. It could have been God who drove the nails, then put his hammer down and turned away, smiling in victory. It could have been God who left him to bake and bleed in the sun, unable to stand, unable to fall, as the sun marked the passing hours across the cloudless sky.

Stinking with sweat. Crimson with sunburn. Dried blood crackling around the nails. Pain the only reality.

He cried out, but in the cauldron of his sun-boiled mind he heard only the voices of his accusers and the ringing, ringing, ringing of the hammer—sounds that would forever haunt his memory and echo through his nightmares.

"You're a child of the devil," they said. A child of the devil who needed to be contained.

A child of the devil?

He cried out once again, and this time, a voice, a mind, answered and a power coursed through him. Suddenly, he could bear the pain and make it fuel for his will. With burning will, he determined he would live.

And living, he knew what he would do.

1

SALLY FORDYCE left the house as soon as the breakfast dishes were done, walking a little, jogging a little along Highway 9—a narrow, straight-as-a-string two-lane with a fading white line and an evenly spaced parade of utility poles. This was eastern Washington State, quiet and solitary. Wheat fields, spring green, stretched in every direction over the prairie swells. Straight ahead, the highway dipped and rose gently into the distance until it narrowed to a vanishing point at the far horizon. The sun was warm, the breeze a little biting. It was April.

Sally was nineteen, blonde, slightly overweight, and severely unhappy, mainly because she was no longer married. She had believed everything Joey, the trucker, told her about love, and how she was that girl silhouetted on his mud flaps. The marriage—if it happened at all—lasted three months. When he found another woman more "intellectually stimulating," Sally was bumped from the truck's sleeper and found herself coming full circle, right back to being Charlie and Meg's daughter living at home again. She had to keep her room clean, help with dinner and dishes, get home by eleven, and attend the Methodist church with them every Sunday. Again, her life was not her life.

She had tasted freedom, she thought, but she was turned away.

She had no wings to fly and nowhere to fly even if she did. Life wasn't fair. (To hear Charlie tell it, he and Meg must have made up a list of all the dumb mistakes they hoped she would never make and given her a copy. Needless to say, things were tense.)

Even before she tried Joey, the trucker, Sally used to find escape out on the wheat prairie in the stillness of the morning. Now she returned, even fled to this place. Out here, she heard no voice but her own thoughts, and her thoughts could say whatever they wanted. She could pray too, sometimes aloud, knowing no one but God would hear her. "Dear God, please don't leave me stuck here. If you're there, send a miracle. Get me out of this mess."

In all fairness, it was past time for Sally to feel that way. Except for those who had wheat farming in their blood and couldn't wait to climb on a combine, most everyone growing up in Antioch heard a call from elsewhere—*anywhere*—sooner or later. When they came of age, all the kids who could find a way out left—usually—for good. Sally had come of age, all right, but had not found a way out. Charlie and Meg would probably tell you that she was not the kind to look for one, either. She was still waiting for it to come to her.

The halfway point of her jog was a spreading cottonwood at the top of a shallow rise, the only tree in sight. It was monstrous, and had to have been growing there long before the roads, farms, or settlers came along. Sally double-timed her way up the rise and was breathing hard by the time she reached it. She'd developed a routine: Every day she braced herself against the huge trunk and stretched out her leg muscles, then sat and rested for a moment between two prominent roots on the south side. Recently, a short prayer for a miracle had also become part of the routine.

The stretches went easily enough. She had cooled down, her breathing had settled, she could feel the flush in her cheeks from the exercise and the cool air.

She rounded the tree—

And almost jumped out of her skin.

A man was sitting between the two roots, exactly in her spot, his back against the gnarled trunk and his wrists draped lazily over his knees. He had to have been there all during her stretching-out, and she was immediately curious, if not offended, that he had said or done nothing to indicate his presence.

"Oh!" she gasped, then caught her breath. "Hello. I didn't see you there."

He only chuckled and smiled at her with a kindly gaze. He was a remarkably handsome man, with olive skin, deep brown eyes, and tightly curled black hair. He was young, perhaps as young as she was. "Good morning, Sally. Sorry if I startled you."

She probed her memory. "Have we met before?"

He shook his head teasingly. "No."

"Well, who are you?"

"I'm here to bring you a message. Your prayers have been heard, Sally. Your answer is on his way. Be looking for him."

She looked away for only a moment, just a slight, eye-rolling gesture of consternation. "Be looking for who—?"

He was gone.

"Hey!"

She walked around the cottonwood, looked up and down the road and across every field, and even looked straight up the trunk of the tree.

He was gone, just like that, as if he'd never been there.

After one more hurried trip around the tree, she stopped, a hand against the trunk to steady herself, her eyes scanning the prairie. Her heart was beating faster than when she'd come up the rise. Her breathing was rapid and shallow. She was shaking.

AT OUR LADY OF THE FIELDS CHURCH in Antioch, Arnold Kowalski was busy dust-mopping the quaint little sanctuary, pushing the wide broom between the pews and down the center aisle, moving a little slowly but doing a thorough job. Arnold had been a soldier, a carpenter, a diesel mechanic, and a mail carrier, and now, since retiring, he had taken upon himself the unofficial title of church custodian. It wasn't a paid position, although the church did provide a little monetary gift for him each month as an expression of love and gratitude. He just did it for God, a few hours a few days a week, pure and simple. It brought him joy, and besides, he liked being in this place.

He'd been a devout member of Our Lady of the Fields for some forty years now. He never missed Sunday morning mass if he could help it. He never failed to make it to confession, though now at seventy-two the confessions were getting shorter and the penance easier. He liked to think that God was happy with him. He considered himself happy enough with God.

Except for one thing, one minor grief he had to carry as he moved slowly down the center aisle pushing his broom. He couldn't help wishing that God would pay just a little attention to Arnold's arthritis. It used to flare up occasionally; now it was only on occasion that it didn't. He was ashamed to think such a thought, but he kept thinking it anyway: *Here I am serving God, but God keeps letting it hurt.* His hands throbbed, his feet ached. His knuckles cried out no matter which way he gripped the broom. He was never one to complain, but today, he almost felt like crying.

Maybe I'm not serving God enough, he thought. *Maybe I need to work longer. Maybe if I didn't take any money for what I do here . . .*

What am I missing? he wondered. *What am I leaving out?*

He always took off his hat when he entered the building and blessed himself before entering the sanctuary. Right now, as usual, he was wearing his blue coveralls. Perhaps a tie would show more respect.

He pushed a little more dust and dirt down the center aisle until he stepped into a beam of sunlight coming through a stained-glass window. The sun felt warm on his back and brought him comfort, as if it were God's hand resting on his shoulders. From this spot he could look up at the carved wooden crucifix hanging above the altar. He caught the gaze of the crucified Christ.

"I don't want to complain," he said. Already he felt he was overstepping his bounds. "But what harm would it do? What difference would it make to this big wide world if one little man didn't have so much pain?" It occurred to Arnold that he had addressed God in anger. Ashamed, he looked away from those gazing wooden eyes.

But the eyes drew him back, and for a strange, illusory moment they seemed alive, mildly scolding, but mostly showing compassion as a father would show to a child with a scraped knee. Sunlight from another window brought out a tiny sparkle in the corners of the eyes, and Arnold had to smile. He could almost imagine those eyes were alive and wet with tears.

The sparkle grew, spreading from the corners of the eyes and reaching along the lower eyelids.

Arnold looked closer. Where was the light coming from that could produce such an effect? He looked above and to the right. It had to be coming through that row of small windows near the ceiling. To think he'd been attending this church for so many years and never noticed this before. It looked just as if—

A tear rose over the edge of the eyelid and dropped onto the wooden cheek, tracing a thin wet trail down the face and onto the beard.

Arnold stared, frozen, his mind stuck between seeing and believing. He felt no sense of awe, no overshadowing spiritual presence. He heard no angelic choir singing in the background. All he knew was that he was watching a wooden image shed tears as he stood there dumbly.

Then his first coherent thought finally came to him. *I have to get up there.* Yes, that was the thing to do; that would settle it. He hurried as fast as the pain in his feet would allow him and brought a ladder from the storeroom in back. Pausing before the altar to bless himself, he stepped around the altar and carefully leaned the ladder against the wall. Every climbing step brought a sharp complaint from his feet, but he gritted his teeth, grimaced, and willed himself up the ladder until he came eye to eye, level to level with the carved face.

His eyes had not been playing tricks on him. The face, only a third life-sized, was wet. He looked above to see if there was a leak in the ceiling but saw no sign of a stain or drip. He leaned close to study the image for any sign of a device or some kind of trickery. Nothing.

He reached, then hesitated from the very first tinge of fear. Just what was he about to touch? *Dear God, don't hurt me.* He reached again, shakily extending his hand until his fingertips brushed across the wet trail of the tears.

He felt a tingling, like electricity, and jerked his hand away with a start. It wasn't painful, but it scared him, and his hand began to quiver. Electric sensations shot up his arm like countless little bees swarming in his veins. He let out a quiet little yelp, then gasped, then yelped again as the sensation flowed across his shoulders, around his neck, down his spine. He grabbed the ladder and held it tightly, afraid he would topple off.

A strong grip.

A grip without pain. He stared at his hand. The vibration buzzed, and swirled under his skin, through his knuckles, across his palms, through his wrists. He lightened his grip, tightened it again, held on with one hand while he opened and closed the other, wiggling and flexing the fingers.

The pain was gone. His hands were strong.

The current rushed down his legs, making his nerves tingle and his muscles twitch. He hugged the ladder, his hands glued to the rungs, a cry bouncing off the wall only inches from his nose. He was shaking, afraid he would fall. He cried out, gasped, trembled, cried out again.

The electricity, the sensation—whatever it was—enveloped his feet and his scream echoed through the building.

SUNDAY, PASTOR KYLE SHERMAN prayed the prayer of benediction, the pianist and organist began playing the postlude—a modern rendition of "Be Still My Soul"—and the congregation of the Antioch Pentecostal Mission rose to leave. The after-service shuffling was the same as one would see in any church. Folks gathered up their coats, Bibles, Sunday school papers, and children, then formed slow-moving clusters in the aisles and doorways to joke and chat. Families, singles, friends, and visitors passed through the main doorway where the young pastor stood to shake their hands and greet them. Kids went as wild as their parents would tolerate, running outside after being scolded for running inside.

Dee Baylor was among the departing saints that day. A steady and constant presence at Antioch Mission, she was a robust, heavy-set woman in her forties with a prominent nose and hair that added measurably to her height. Short, mousy Blanche Davis and tightly permed, blue-rinsed Adrian Folsom were walking with her across the gravel parking lot as the three worked excitedly to keep the Christian grapevine alive.

"That's all he said?" Adrian asked.

Dee didn't mind repeating the story or any part of it. "Just that 'her answer was on his way.' And according to Sally he said *his* way, not *its* way."

"So who was he talking about?" asked Blanche.

"Maybe her future husband," Adrian ventured. "God told me I was going to marry Roger."

"So what about the crucifix at the Catholic church?" Blanche wondered.

"You can't limit God," Dee answered.

"No, you can't limit God," Adrian agreed with extra insistence in her voice.

"But a weeping statue?" Blanche asked, making a crinkled face. "That sounds awfully Catholic to me."

"Well, it's something a Catholic would understand."

Blanche considered that in silence.

"We need to be seeking the Lord," said Dee, her eyes closing prayerfully. "We need to be expecting. God has plans for Antioch. I think the Lord is ready to pour out his Spirit on this town."

"Amen." That was what Blanche wanted to hear.

"Amen," Adrian echoed.

Dee looked up at the sky as if looking toward heaven. The clouds were breaking up now. Patches of blue were beginning to show, promising a pleasant afternoon.

Adrian and Blanche walked and continued the conversation until they noticed they were by themselves. They looked back.

"Dee?"

She was standing still, clutching her Bible to her bosom and looking heavenward, her lips moving rapidly as she whispered in another language.

"Dee?"

They hurried to her side. "What is it?"

All she could do was point, then gasp, her hand over her mouth.

Adrian and Blanche looked quickly, afraid something might fall on them. They saw nothing but billowing clouds and patches of blue sky.

"I see Jesus," Dee said in a hushed voice. Then, raising one hand toward the sky she shouted ecstatically, "Jesus! I see you, I see you!"

Brother Norheim walked by. He was old, bent, and hard of hearing, but a respected church pillar. He knew how a church should be run and how the Spirit moved and how to properly wash out the communion cups so as not to offend the Lord. When he started "Bless the Lord, O My Soul" from his pew in the evening service, everybody sang right along whether Linda Sherman could find the right key on the piano or not. He could see the ladies were excited about something.

"What are you looking at?"

"I see the Lord!" Dee gasped, and then she broke into a song. "I see the Lord . . . I see the Lord . . . He is high and lifted up, and his train fills the temple!"

Adrian and Blanche kept staring at the clouds, hoping to spot something, making quick sideways glances at each other for clues.

Brother Norheim looked the sky over, smiling with three golden teeth and three gaps. "The firmament showeth his handiwork!"

"What do you see?" Adrian finally asked.

Dee pointed. "Don't you see him? Right there! He's looking right at us!"

Adrian and Blanche looked carefully, following the point of Dee's finger. Finally, Blanche drew in a slow, awe-struck gasp. "Yeeesssss . . . Yes, I see him! I see him!"

"Where?" Adrian cried. "I don't see him."

"Isn't that incredible!"

Adrian put her head right next to Blanche's, hoping to gain the same perspective. "Show me."

Blanche pointed. "See? There's the top of his head, and there's his ear and his beard . . ."

Adrian let out a crowlike squawk she usually saved for funny jokes and deep revelations. "AWWW! You're right! You're right!"

Now all three women were pointing and looking while Dee kept singing in and out of English. Brother Norheim moved on, glad to see the saints on fire, but others came alongside to see what the commotion was all about. Dave White, the contractor, saw the face right away, but his wife, Michelle, never did. Adrian's husband, Roger, saw the face, but found it an amusing coincidence and nothing more. Don and Melinda Forester, a new couple in church, both saw the face but disagreed on which direction it was looking. Their kids, Tony and Pammie, ages eight and six, saw Jesus but also saw several different animals on top of his head.

"Look!" said Adrian. "He's holding a dove in his hand, you see that?"

"Yeeahhhhh . . ." Dave White said in a hushed voice, his face filled with awe.

"He's ready to pour out his Spirit!" Dee announced with a prophetic waver in her voice.

"Eh, beats me," said Roger, squinting at the sky.

"He's speaking to us in these last days!"

"You're crazy," Michelle insisted. "I don't see anything."

"Hey Pastor Sherman!" Tony yelled. "We see Jesus in the clouds!"

"There's a rooster!" Pammie squealed.

"IT JUST KEPT GOING FROM THERE," Kyle Sherman told me. "The three women started seeing all kinds of things because the clouds kept changing. For a while Jesus had a dove in his hand, and then after that he turned into a door—you know, the door to the sheepfold, the door to heaven, whatever you want—and then—" Kyle looked toward the ceiling as he recalled the appearance of the sky. "Uh . . . a flame, I think." He drew it in the air with his hand. "Kind of wavy, you know, up and down like a pillar of fire."

Kyle hadn't used any names up to this point, so I asked him, "Are we talking about Dee Baylor?"

He nodded, looking abashed.

"Adrian Folsom and Blanche Davis?"

Kyle nodded again, a reluctant yes.

"Makes sense," I said, picking up my coffee cup and taking another swallow.

It was Monday, the typical pastor's day off. Kyle Sherman and I were sitting at my kitchen table with coffee cups and a bag of Oreo cookies between us. He was still in his twenties, dark-haired, wiry, a fresh horse ready to gallop. For the past four months, he'd been at this table in this little house several times, keeping in touch and trying to be a good shepherd.

And hoping to keep some strays from straying further, I surmised. I know I caught his attention the moment he arrived to take over the pastorate. I was still the official pastor until I passed my mantle to him, but I was conspicuously missing. Antioch Pentecostal Mission had a pastor—a *former* pastor—who couldn't go near the place.

Kyle immediately did the pastoral thing by coming after—coming to—me and becoming a regular part of my life, welcome or not. The minister in me understood what he was doing and admitted that, if I were in Kyle's place, I would have done the same. As for the rest of me . . . well, I'll get to that.

Today's visit was decidedly different from the others, however. I hadn't heard quite so many Praise Gods or Hallelujahs from Kyle today. I could tell the spiritual escapades of Dee Baylor and company were weighing on him.

"Dee seems like she's—" Kyle was either struggling for words or waiting for me to fill in the blanks.

I filled in the blanks. "Dee is a follower with followers. Meg Fordyce has a little prayer and praise meeting at her house once a week, and Dee gets out there pretty often. Just put it together from there."

I could see a light bulb coming on, but Kyle apparently wasn't comfortable with my drift. "I'm not sure I follow you."

"Kyle, it's simple. Meg told Dee about Sally seeing an angel. That means someone else is getting a special visitation from God that Dee isn't getting. You don't get something from God without Dee getting it too. She won't allow it."

Kyle actually looked disappointed. "So what about Sally? You think she made the whole thing up?"

"You can talk to Charlie and Meg about Sally. It's up to you, but no, I don't believe her. It sounds too much like the vanishing hitch-hiker." Kyle laughed. "You've heard about that, right?"

"Oh yeah." He paused. "So Dee's copycatting?"

"No, with Dee you get it back with interest. Sally saw an angel. Dee's seeing Jesus."

But Kyle shook his head, still unsettled. "They're excited, Travis. And not just Dee and Adrian and Blanche, but the Whites, the Foresters—"

"Excited about what? Jesus in the sky with a rooster on his head?"

"Pammie thought it was a rooster."

"Hey, you asked me." I set my coffee cup down on the table like a judge closing a case with a gavel.

"So what about Arnold Kowalski?"

I made a conscious effort not to roll my eyes. "Didn't a statue of Elvis start crying once?" I looked in my empty coffee cup and then at the coffee maker. There were still at least two cups in there. "You need a refill?"

"No thanks."

I got up and poured another cup for myself. "Maybe Arnold Kowalski is the Catholic version of Dee Baylor."

I could tell from Kyle's tone that he was getting impatient with me. "No, now come on, Travis. Kowalski went to Dr. Trenner down in

Davenport, and he took x-rays and the whole thing. He says the arthritis is gone."

I sat down, my hand still on the handle of my coffee cup, and just looked at him. "What do you want me to say, Kyle?"

He sighed. "Just say what you think."

"I've already said what I think."

He stared at his empty coffee cup, dragging it by the handle in little zigzags around the table. "But you don't suppose God could surprise us once in a while? You know, do something we weren't expecting?"

I leaned forward. "Kyle, what these people experienced, they expected. Trust me." I leaned back, sipped my coffee, and tried to come up with some closing comment. "If you want my advice, I'd say don't sweat it. This kind of thing comes and goes and the wrinkles wash out eventually."

"I just need to take a position on all this."

The very thought of someone else having to take a position gave me a dark little pleasure. "Yeah, you're the one who has to remain stable, aren't you? Well, it won't hurt to let the jury stay out a while."

"I think Dee and Adrian are watching the clouds again today—"

There was a knock at the front door.

"It's Rene," I said, then hollered, "Come in!"

She came in. "Hi, Trav."

Her blonde hair was pulled back in a ponytail and she was wearing her old green sweats, same as she did every time she came over. I introduced my big sister to the new pastor, and I took pleasure in another thought: Rene lived in Spokane, so she didn't have to worry about Kyle calling on her.

"Don't let me disturb you," she said, turning toward the bedroom.

"We were just finishing up."

"Uh—" Kyle fished around for his lost thought but apparently found another one. "Anyway, the ministerial's going to meet tomorrow morning to talk about all this. I think Nancy Barrons is going to be there."

"Great," I said. "Newspaper coverage. That'll put the fire out."

Kyle raised an eyebrow at me. "Hey, Travis, the whole town's buzzing about this. There's a lot going on out there and you're missing it."

I smiled. That made three pleasurable thoughts in a row.

Rene came out of the bedroom with my laundry basket. She was giving me a look, most likely a comment on how full that basket should have been but was not after a week.

Kyle was still talking. "Anyway, why don't you come with me? I haven't gotten to know all the ministers yet. You can introduce me, sit in and listen, have some input."

It was a ploy, pure and simple, and not the first time Kyle had tried to get me moving in the old church circles again. I gave a little disarming chuckle and wagged my head.

"It'll be at the Catholic church. We'll all get a chance to look at that weeping crucifix."

I made a face. I couldn't help it. "Get real!"

Kyle just raised his hands in surrender to logic. "Hey, you can bicker about hearsay or you can go straight to the source and see it for yourself."

"And sit down with all those ministers again? Not this year, thank you."

Rene walked behind me to the refrigerator and checked my supply of frozen meals and leftovers.

Kyle looked at me for a moment, and I knew I wouldn't like his next question. "Do they have something to do with it?"

"To do with what?"

"Yes," Rene answered.

I shot her a glance over my shoulder and she shot me one back.

Kyle had no fear of thin ice. "With you resigning your pulpit, sitting here in this little house all by yourself—"

"Never changing your clothes," Rene cut in, "not shaving, not cleaning up—"

"I change my clothes!" I said.

She looked at the laundry basket on the floor. "There's only one shirt in there. Have you worn that same shirt all week?"

I looked down at the shirt I was wearing. I couldn't remember how long I'd worn it. "I like this shirt." I turned back to Kyle. "And you're living in the parsonage now, with my blessing. You're welcome to it."

Kyle raised his hands to show a truce. "I didn't mean . . ."

"Trav, we're not trying to pick a fight."

No, they weren't picking a fight. It was just the same old dilemma: friends whose loving concern keeps stumbling into your raw nerves, with every irritating stab well meant. I stared at my coffee cup because I couldn't look at them.

"It's your life, I know that," Kyle said gently. "We just care about you, that's all."

Then you might come up with a solution I haven't heard already, I thought.

But I didn't say it out loud. We had already had that conversation and it got us nowhere. Instead, I just looked at him, managed a smile, and reminded myself that I really did love this kid—sorry, this man. This fresh new pastor, this up-and-coming man of God with the young, pretty, piano-playing wife and the two energetic kids. I reminded myself that twenty years ago I was sitting in his place. I was thinking the same things, offering the same solutions, excited for the same reasons. *Man*, did that feel like a long time ago!

"Thanks for the invitation," I said finally. "Not this time. Maybe later, when I've got something better to say for myself."

He returned my smile. "Okay." And to his credit, he dropped the subject. "I gotta get going. Give me a call if you change your mind." With that he rose, patted me on the back, and headed for the front door.

"Oh, I will," I promised almost jokingly.

After Kyle closed the front door behind him, I looked up at Rene, still standing by the refrigerator. She was in her late forties and looking great, though giving me a somewhat scolding look the way big sisters do. It had always been her role to run interference for me while reaching back to swat me when she thought I needed it.

"We're, uh, we're doing better, Kyle and me," I said. "We got along pretty well today, all things considered."

She shrugged. "One of these days you're going to give him a lot of credit just for coming back."

"I do already."

"You gonna let me cut your hair today?"

"Maybe next time."

"You're getting pretty shaggy."

"Next time."

She came around and sat in Kyle's chair, facing me directly. "I don't know when that will be."

I figured it would be a week, just like always, but I could read in her eyes how wrong I was. "You and Danny going on vacation or something?"

She sat back in the chair and sighed deeply. "Travis Jordan, I owe you an apology. I've been wrong."

"Wrong about what?"

She drew a breath and sighed it out. "Wrong about letting you just sit on your rear." This was Rene's characteristic bluntness, her tough love. "Trav, it's been ten months. You know Marian would be upset to see you like this. *I'm* upset. Danny and I have been talking about it, and he's right: I thought I was helping you by doing your laundry and planning out your grocery list and cooking most of your meals. But . . ." She looked away and drummed her fingers on the table while she built up to it. "I can't be your mother anymore. School's starting in the fall, and by that time you're going to have to be a clean, resourceful, responsible adult again. You're going to have to be an example."

"In other words, *get a life.*"

"No, you *have* a life. I'm telling you to get on with it. I mean . . ." She looked around the house. It was a small place. She could see the dining room, living room, and bedroom from where she was sitting. "When we were kids, Mom would never let us get away with a mess like this. We had to clean our own rooms, remember? Now here I am, cleaning *yours*. What's wrong with this picture?"

I looked around. This was a mess? I'd come to regard it as simply having everything I owned in plain sight and within easy reach at all times.

"I shouldn't even have done this, but I talked to Don Anderson yesterday, and he has a washing machine in stock that was damaged in shipping. It works fine, it just has a dent in it. He said he'll let it go for a hundred dollars. Travis, buy it. Hook it up and use it. Get yourself some rope and make a clothesline out back. The weather's warming up. You can dry everything back there. And did you try that meat loaf recipe I gave you?"

That meat loaf. "Uh, yeah. I think I cooked it too long."

"You used to cook when you and Marian were in California. I know; she told me. And you still have the makings for meat loaf in the freezer. Try it again. Try all the recipes again, and keep trying, 'cause after today, I'm out of here." She hurried around me and picked up the laundry basket. "I'll do this load, and then . . . you'd better buy that washing machine." She bent and kissed me on the cheek. "We're gonna talk someday. We have to."

"Sounds like we just did," I said.

"We will. I promise. Bye."

She smiled at me, turned, and went out the front door.

I heard her Bronco start up and drive off, and then the remarkable quiet of a small eastern Washington wheat town set in. Such towns have no ambient rumble of traffic. The only airport is a small strip for crop dusters several miles west of town. I could hear the electric whir of the clock on the wall and the intermittent drip from the kitchen sink. Somewhere in the neighborhood a dog barked. A breeze caused a dry leaf to skitter along the concrete just outside the patio door.

I sat motionless and intensely alone, ignoring the coffee growing cold in my cup and trying to get through my head what had just happened. It could have been the proverbial two-by-four against the side of the head. It sure felt like it.

I finally got up and stood in the archway between the kitchen and the living room, numbly scanning the disheveled state of the one-bedroom bungalow. The coffee table had disappeared under books and magazines I'd planned to read or been reading, most of them open to wherever I'd begun or left off. I had to assume that

I had flung my coat and hat over the chair near the door, but I sure couldn't remember doing it. I could probably blame the post-office for the newspapers and catalogs that were spreading like kudzu over every level surface including the floor. The cluttered kitchen counters were filled with dirty dishes and cereal boxes still stood around after a week of breakfasts. It suddenly occurred to me how embarrassing it would be if my landlord were to drop by.

I made my way to the bathroom and found something equally messy in the bathroom mirror: a graying, weathered, whiskered, forty-five-year-old former . . . *what?* Anything I had ever been, I wasn't anymore. I knew that much. A question from my ordination application came back to me: *Are you always neat and clean?* I stifled a laugh. Not today.

But Rene's point was well taken: Someone else was going to have to look at this face when September rolled around—a whole classroom full of sixth graders. I'd managed to regain a teaching position I held years ago, when Antioch Mission was a fledgling congregation—any small-town, small-church pastor can tell you the value of a secondary source of income. Because the job didn't start until September, it had always remained an abstraction to me. I'd shaved perhaps twice since the job interview, and never viewed the upcoming responsibility in light of the fact that I was a wreck.

Things will have to change, I told myself. *Pretty soon. Tomorrow, maybe.*

Enough of the face. I left the bathroom and looked out the bedroom window expecting to see the same winter-browned hill that rose just west of my place, with a tight grove of wind-battered cottonwoods at its crest.

There was somebody out there.

I stopped. I'd never seen anyone on that hill before. I wasn't even sure who owned that land.

But there was a man standing by the cottonwoods, resting an arm against one of the old trunks. He was facing my direction, and didn't appear to have anyplace else he needed to be.

Was he looking at me? I went closer to the window and shifted my head back and forth, squinting a bit. He was looking at me. He wasn't just looking west or looking toward the house. He was looking at me. I could feel my brow furrowing, and he responded with a slight smile and a nod.

There was something about those eyes that held me. From here, I guessed they were deep brown. But that gaze you didn't see every day. It seemed to say, without words, *I know you.*

Who was this guy?

His hair was long and black, parted down the middle, curling down to his shoulders.

He had a beard.

I looked away, catching myself, corralling my runaway thoughts. *Uh-uh, no Travis, don't think that.*

He was wearing a white robe, wasn't he? I looked again, and yes, he was. A white robe tied in the middle, open at the neck, with long sleeves that hung loosely from the arms. I couldn't see his feet because of the tall grass, but it was a reflex, a natural step to imagine sandals. I'd been to Sunday school all my life. I'd seen the pictures.

He was still looking at me, and seemed to be enjoying how awkward I felt staring back.

I finally shook my head and said, "No. No way."

He laughed, nodding his head yes.

I casually moved away from the window.

Then I ran to the patio door and bolted outside. Whoever this guy really was, I was going to know it within the thirty seconds or so it would take me to reach the crown of the hill. It was a gag, right? Somebody sent him to shake up the weird old former minister.

But now the breeze played across the deserted grassy slope and the cottonwoods stood stark against the sky all by themselves, just as one would expect on a warm April day. He was gone. Just like that.

2

JUDY'S EAT-A-LONG AND TAVERN was one of those low-budget enterprises you usually find associated with out-of-the-way towns like Antioch. It was a one-story, sagging structure with weathered siding and a neon sign atop the roof that used to say EAT before it broke nine years ago. Even without the neon sign, the building still shouted at passing motorists with the words *JUDY'S—Since 1955* painted across the front in huge white letters. Besides the three grain elevators immediately south and Bud's Shell station across the street, it used to be the first thing you'd see driving into Antioch westbound, and for that reason became one of the town's prime landmarks.

Judy Holliday ran the place and did most of the cooking, although she'd taken on an assistant fry cook so she could get off her feet a little more often. She had to be pushing seventy by now, but she still got up early and drove herself hard—that, she told me, was what kept her so young and attractive. Back when Antioch was the nearest and best place to store and ship grain, Judy cooked meals and brewed coffee for truckers, farmers, ranchers, and railroad workers. When the truckers switched to the interstate, she kept on cooking for the farmers, ranchers, and railroaders. When the farmers and ranchers sold out and the railroad abandoned the northern route, Judy cooked and brewed for whomever was left: the local folks, the small farmers at lunch, a few truckers who serviced Antioch on their way somewhere else, and people who still had trouble making meat loaf, like me. To hear her tell it, she had been too busy to notice any change in the amount of business. It was never that great anyway. As for the broken "EAT" sign, she said, "To heck with it. Nobody's gonna read it anyway."

Judy's was located on the east edge of town, and when I say "edge," I mean abrupt edge. Antioch has no suburbs, no outskirts. Like a model railroad laid out on a square table, the streets and buildings occupy a tight, one-mile square grid and do not extend beyond that. In this part of the country, there is land for building towns and there is land for farming and ranching, and the two never mix. If you stand in Judy's parking lot, you're in town. Take one step east and you're in a wheat field. Stand at the east end of Myrtle Street and look west, you'll see early postwar homes comfortably arranged along the quiet oiled streets without sidewalks. Look east and you'll see acres of plowed, featureless farmland as far as the horizon. The other end of Myrtle Street is easy to see, by the way. The street, like the whole town, ends abruptly at another wheat field only a mile away.

My rental house was at the end of Myrtle Street on the west edge of town, with a quiet neighborhood to the east and that once serene, now mysterious hill with the cottonwoods to the west. This evening I had to get out of there. I was still smarting from Rene's two-by-four, and somehow that messy little house only worsened the pain the longer I stayed.

I also felt a serious need to see and talk to some people I could be sure were real. I checked all around that hill and those cottonwoods for footprints, trampled grass, anything that would show someone had been there, and didn't find a thing. That scared me, not so much that I saw someone on that hill, but that I thought I saw someone. I needed some time in the real world.

Judy's was only a short hop over to the highway and then a one-mile drive through the center of town. I locked up the house for the first time since I'd moved in and drove my Trooper.

I passed by the old Methodist church, Kiley's Hardware, and the Baptist church, where a week-long revival was underway. What was that evangelist's name? I am not kidding: Everett Fudd. Once again I felt the strange sensation that I was viewing the town in a home movie from the '40s. Over half a century ago, somehow, this town materialized on the prairie, liked the way it was, and froze that way. Yes, some new buildings had appeared over the years. Our Lady of the Fields had a new brick structure, forced upon the congregation by a deep underground spring that swallowed up the old one. Every so often there would be a fresh coat of paint on a storefront, like that weird, Pepto-Bismol pink Don Anderson chose for his appliance store. But those were only minor changes to over a half-century of sameness.

Many things about the town were normal enough. We had our local Kiwanis club and Grange, our Amway dealers and Jehovah's Witnesses, our Cub Scout paper drives and youth group car washes. Our high school played other small-town high schools and our cheerleaders did silly fund-raisers like rocking-chair marathons and jog-a-thons. We had a parade every Fourth of July, and Amos Sjostrom always took part with his old hay wagon and Clydesdales.

Even so, you didn't have to live here too long before sensing it: Antioch was a town looking forward to the past. I used to notice it in the churches of Antioch, especially my own: *Do the old things again, just do them harder. Back out of the slump. Don't go forward, you've never been there. Replay the memory, it's always better. That old-time religion was good for our fathers and mothers and it's good enough for us.* I knew Brother Fudd was singing the same tune down at the Baptist church, just him and the same dozen people every night, "taking the town for Christ."

I don't know why all this began to wear on me after fifteen years, but suddenly it did.

For the entire fifteen years that I pastored, I never went inside Judy's. It was, after all, a tavern as well as an eating establishment, and there are places a Pentecostal Mission pastor in a small town like Antioch just doesn't go. I took the big step soon after I re-signed, however, for two simple reasons: I wanted to know what kind of people were in there, and I was hungry. I tried Judy's broiled chicken over rice with mixed vegetables and salad and found it quite satisfactory. I tried the twelve-ounce steak the next time, and the pasta salad the third. The barbecued half-a-chicken was good the fourth visit and a little dry the fifth, but four out of five good visits wasn't a bad score.

By then, I'd gotten word second- and thirdhand that the talk had started: The former pastor of Antioch Pentecostal Mission was backsliding and giving in to the world. I viewed it as a step forward. After all, I'd never been here before. I'd never gotten to know these people. This was new for me. And while I never even tried to develop a taste for beer, I liked Judy's coffee. All that to say, I became a regular customer and continued dropping in whenever the prospect of cooking my own sorry little meal seemed too overwhelming.

"Hey, Trav!" Judy called from behind the bar, her hair a white fright wig and her apron stained with gravy. She called me "Rev" the first few times I came in, but as soon as my ordination papers lapsed, I let her know. She and the other regular customers have called me "Trav" ever since and have acted more at ease around me, although I still get junk mail addressed to "Rev. and Mrs. Travis Jordan."

The interior of Judy's was just one more example of how Antioch was frozen in time. Back in the days before taste, a clever restaurant trendsetter must have bought up all the dark wall paneling and red and orange shaggy carpet in existence, sent sale announcements to every backward, small-town, greasy spoon restaurant in America, and retired with a small fortune. I'm guessing Judy was one of his first customers. She made no apologies, however. Her carpet displayed several darker shades after so many years of traffic, spills, and cigarette butts, but she didn't seem the slightest bit interested in replacing it or anything else. The dark walls were hiding the film and dirt just fine. The wood tables and booths were so solid she only had to replace the red-and-white checked tablecloths once a year.

The bar was in the back, well stocked, with ten stools. Five of the stools were occupied today. I got a wave of hello from Greg and Marc, the contractors, both wearing billed caps and flannel shirts—the back of Greg's shirt was torn wide open at the shoulder but he wore it anyway. For two months after they introduced themselves I thought they were half brothers, but finally Marc admitted that they didn't have the same mother either, and they had a real laugh over that. Two stools over from them was George Harding, the retired wheat farmer. He didn't talk much but he didn't grumble much either, so he fit in. Skip another stool and there sat Linda and Irv, local truckers somewhere in their early forties. They'd been living together unmarried for eighteen years. The sin of it aside, they'd put up with each other for so long I honestly felt the relationship would last. They said hi. Occasionally one of the five heads would turn toward the television hanging on the wall. Right now, there was a basketball game in progress with the sound turned low.

The rest of the place had a nice dinner hour going. I saw plenty of regulars and the jukebox was thumping away, just one big subwoofer in a gilded box. My favorite booth by the front window was empty, so I took it, setting my hat and coat beside me on the bench seat. Gildy, Judy's granddaughter, brought me a menu and silverware.

"Hey, Travis. Mind if I join you?" It was Brett Henchle, the chief of Antioch's three policemen. He was in uniform, wearing his gun and badge, and I figured he was on his dinner break. A Vietnam vet with shrapnel still in his leg, he was big enough for this or any job that required occasional head breaking.

I gestured to the bench seat across from me. "Have a seat. How you doing?"

"All right," he answered, and I could tell he didn't mean it. He sank onto the bench and then looked around the room, bothered about something, trying to work up to saying whatever it was. He didn't get there before Nancy Barrons came along. She owned and edited the Antioch *Harvester*, our local, twice-a-week newspaper, and I surmised from the cassette recorder and notepad that she was working. "Hi. Am I interrupting anything?"

Brett seemed thankful for the reprieve. "No. You go first," he said, scooting over.

"You sure?"

"Just let me hear what he says."

She slipped in beside him and set the notepad and recorder on the bench, out of service for the moment. That was like her. She was going to talk as a friend first and be a reporter second.

She was in her thirties, an independent sort, with auburn hair pinned up Katharine Hepburn style, single but dating a columnist in Spokane. She was into natural foods, a little yoga, and probably voted for Clinton, although she often took him to task in her editorials. We'd had our disagreements, sometimes nose to nose, mostly through her editorials and my dissenting letters to the editor, but it never got nasty. She won a few—I had to concede I only had half the story on Christopher Columbus. But I won some myself—she turned dead set against partial-birth abortion.

"How are things going?" she asked.

I wasn't about to go into the details of my afternoon. I only replied, "Strangely. How are things going with you?"

She laughed. "Strangely."

I noticed Brett smiling as if agreeing.

"Did you hear about Sally Fordyce seeing an angel, and the weeping crucifix at Our Lady's?" she asked.

My grimace and nod clued her in. "Kyle Sherman told me about it earlier today."

Nancy looked at the table as she asked, "See that couple over there?" I glanced discretely at a young couple in a booth across the room. "They came here from Moses Lake to see the crucifix for themselves. They believe in it."

"Did it weep for them?" I asked.

"No, but they still believe in it. They're going to get a room over at the Wheatland Motel and then spend the day at Our Lady's tomorrow, as long as Father Vendetti lets them stay."

"To . . . ?"

"To see if it'll cry again." Nancy lowered her voice. "She has leukemia."

I closed my eyes, sighed, and felt grief for them. "How did they find out about it?"

"His mother attends Our Lady's. She called them." She leaned forward a little, her voice still low. "Travis, I don't know what to think about all this. It sounds like something that should go in the paper, but . . ." She flipped her palms upward, at a loss. "You've been there and back. Any perspective on all this?"

"Are you skeptical?" I asked her.

She smiled. "As always."

I gave a little shrug. "So am I." I stole another glance across the room. "So I see a bit of tragedy."

"Tragedy?" She set her notepad in front of her and clicked her pen. "May I?"

I nodded, then mentally reviewed the names, the faces: Sally Fordyce, Arnold Kowalski, Dee and her friends, this couple across the room. I stopped when my own name came up. "This kind of thing reminds me that it's a crummy world out there, and there are things we have no easy answers for. When people are hurting, they start grasping. When the world hands you a pile of sorrow, you look beyond the world for some kind of relief, or at least an explanation. That's what a lot of religious experience is all about."

Nancy scribbled down my thoughts. "You think I should say anything about the cloud sightings?"

"If you write about any of this stuff, you may as well."

She smiled and nodded, understanding my point. "All the same thing in your book?"

"I'm not trying to be derogatory."

"Sure."

"I just want to emphasize that these are very *human* events. People are involved, and people have wants, wishes, fantasies, earnest desires . . . and pain. Lots of pain. Given that, people can be very creative. They can hear things, see things—you follow me?"

She nodded affirmatively. "Gotcha."

"Off the record . . ." I prompted, and she put down her pen. "I had a lady once tell me she saw Jesus standing right next to me while I was preaching. I knew another young fellow who claimed he saw a demon fly in his bedroom window. Also a little girl claimed to see an angel on top of her neighbor's roof. People have told me all kinds of things. It's nothing new."

She seemed a little nonplussed. "And you don't believe them?"

That question flustered me. I had to work a long time to come up with an answer. "It's a tough call; it's so subjective. You have to know the person. You almost have to be the person. The same thing applies here."

"So obviously, another witness to the same thing might help."

"Well, sure, if I saw . . ." I tripped a little trying to say this. "If I saw Jesus myself, then there'd be a little more, uh, credibility, I guess."

She picked up her pen again. "So, do you think this is going anywhere?"

The question made me laugh. "In Antioch?"

She winced and snickered. "Sorry."

"Well, to be fair, I think the people who've had these experiences are hoping it'll lead to something, that somehow it'll change things. You know this town. Somebody has to get restless eventually."

"But you don't think it'll lead anywhere or develop into anything?"

I felt cynical, which saddened me a little. "I've seen it before. It'll come, it'll go."

She clicked her pen and put it away. "Thanks for your time, Travis. You too, Brett."

"Think you have a story?" I asked.

She stood and had to think a moment before answering. "Well, it's interesting. Maybe that's reason enough to print it."

"Anything interesting is news in this town."

She laughed. "That it is. See you."

"Bye."

Brett Henchle watched her go out the front door, and then told me quietly, "You might be wrong, Travis."

I looked at him, expecting a punch line to reveal he was kidding. There was no punch line, only his troubled eyes boring into me. "What do you mean?"

"I'm not in pain. I'm not religious. I'm not restless. I like my job, I like living here. I didn't make up what I saw today."

That stopped me cold. Brett Henchle saw something? "You?"

"You want to hear about it?" he asked in a traffic ticket tone of voice. He was challenging my cynicism, I could tell.

I gathered my composure, pried my mind open again, and said, "Yeah. Tell me about it."

He glanced around the room, clearly on edge, and then spoke in a lowered voice. "For a while I thought I was going crazy. I was coming back from Spokane on Highway 2, and there was this guy hitchhiking."

Uh-oh.

"I was feeling pretty good, I wasn't in a hurry, so I figured, hey, I'll pick the guy up—if he doesn't mind riding in a squad car. He looked a little weird anyway, so better a cop gives him a ride than some innocent citizen—"

I interrupted. "Hey Brett."

"Hm?"

I held my hand up, just trying to keep the peace as I offered my question. "Did this guy get in the car, ride with you a while, say 'Jesus is coming soon,' and then disappear?"

I regretted the question the moment I asked it. *He's never going to talk to me again*, I thought. *I've insulted him, I've—*

He froze, his face turned pale, and he stared at me as if I'd told him Martians had landed. "How did you know?"

This just couldn't be happening. "I . . . uh . . ."

"Did someone else run into this guy?"

Now we were in a face-off, staring at each other as if each was waiting for the other to crack into a smile, confess the whole thing was a gag, and break the tension. Was Brett trying to outlast me? If so, he was an incredible actor playing a role vastly different from his nature. I finally broke the freeze-up by asking, "You've never heard that story before?"

"What story?"

No. Brett wasn't a Christian; he wasn't part of the culture. I could be reasonably sure he'd never heard that popular rumor that circulated around Christendom every few years.

"Well, we'll, uh, get to that. You say he looked a little weird. What did he look like?"

"Long blond hair, like a hippie, about five-seven, early twenties, wearing a white sweatshirt and jeans. He looked a little ghostly—you know, pale and skinny like he was sick. Couldn't have weighed more than 120 pounds. He got into the car, the passenger seat right next to me, fastened his seat belt, and rode with me for a couple of miles."

"Did he say anything besides . . ."

"He said he was coming to Antioch to visit some friends. He didn't say who. I talked a little bit about the town, the weather, you know, just making conversation, and then he said, right out of the blue, 'Jesus is coming soon,' and then—" He took a moment to watch the memory play through his mind. "Out of the corner of my eye, I thought I saw him make a quick movement. I turned and he disappeared. There wasn't any sound or anything. His seat belt was still buckled. He just wasn't there anymore. I slammed on the brakes and pulled over and checked every inch of that car. I looked up the highway, off the shoulder, drove back the way I came. The guy was gone.

"Then I talked to Nancy this afternoon—and listen, I haven't said a thing about this to anyone except you—and she starts telling me about people seeing angels and a crying crucifix and Jesus in the sky." He looked at me intensely. "Now that tells me I'm not crazy, but it also tells me there could be a blond, five-seven suspect in town that I need to question before he pulls this little stunt again."

I couldn't believe I was even having this conversation. "Have you talked to Sally Fordyce?"

"Is she the other person who offered this guy a ride?"

Oh brother. What could I say to that? "No. Brett, the story about the hitchhiker, it's a rumor, a legend."

"Was."

I stared. It happened to *him*—not to a friend of a friend who told a lady who was aunt to the woman who was married to the man who used to work for the guy who last repeated the tale. It happened to Brett Henchle, the man sitting right across from me.

"From what I understand, the man Sally saw had a totally different description."

That news did not cheer him. "Oh great. So there might be two." He thought aloud as if bouncing his theories off me. "He said he was coming here to visit friends. What friends? Who else are they going to play tricks on?" He sniffed in frustration. "You see the problem I'm up against? This whole thing is so religious, it's not going to look good for a cop to be poking around interfering."

Finally I thought of something worthwhile to say. "Brett, I understand the Antioch Ministerial is meeting tomorrow morning to talk about all this. Since it's a religious thing, if anyone is going to know the latest details, the ministers will. Maybe you ought to drop in and find out how extensive this stuff is and if anyone else has seen either one of these . . . whatever they are."

"Are you going?"

God works in wondrous ways. "Yeah, I'll be there."

I called Kyle when I got home, told him I would go with him to the ministerial meeting, then braced myself. To his credit, he didn't gush all over me as I feared he would. After four months, he was starting to learn.

IMAGINE A TIRED OLD DOG, lying in the road, suddenly finding itself wrapped around the axle of a speeding truck. That's how I felt my first five minutes with Kyle Sherman. I was tired and feeling old, I hadn't shaved, the place was a mess, I was planning on a quiet session of journaling. And suddenly, there he was.

"Praise God, brother! I'm Kyle Sherman! Just came by to share the love of the Lord!"

His greeting had the same effect on me as that soup kettle they used to bang on to wake us up at summer camp. He was standing on my front porch in brown slacks, tan sport jacket, blue shirt, and Looney Tunes tie, and had a big, gold-edged Bible in his hand. His brown hair was slick with mousse, he was grinning like a Cheshire cat, and he was in high gear.

I knew he wasn't a Jehovah's Witness; they always travel in twos and compliment you on your house.

He couldn't be a tax assessor because he wasn't carrying a clipboard with the plot plan on it.

He wasn't a salesman because he carried no samples.

But like all three, he hadn't called first. He just showed up. I wanted to kill whoever told him where I lived.

"You're the new pastor?" I asked. I wasn't curious. I was amazed.

"Guilty as charged, brother!" He was so jubilant, so on top of it, so young.

I let him in because it was the right thing to do and invited him to have a seat wherever he could find one. He stepped around the model airplane I was working on, dug a man-sized space in the magazines and newspapers that covered the couch, and had a seat.

"Nice place you have here."

I'd left the pastorate a month before and had not returned to Antioch Mission since. Call me picky, call me a grouch, but I expected Kyle Sherman to know there had to be a reason. The moment he opened his mouth I knew he didn't have a clue.

When I ate dinner at Judy's, nobody I met there talked about church. We talked about fishing, baseball, country music, cars and trucks, and the condition of the roads. We argued about politics and local issues. We even talked about religion and spiritual matters, which I didn't mind, not at all.

But we did not talk about Sunday school attendance, the church van, the outreach program, or the Blessing Barrel. We didn't haggle over the Sunday morning song list or whose job it was to change the sheets in the nursery. We didn't talk about the budget and the offerings or the need for an ongoing children's ministry, or whether we should allow Dee Baylor to fall on the floor every time we prayed for her. Potlucks and men's fellowships and ladies' Bible studies and the struggling youth program never came up.

But Kyle started right in talking about all that stuff as if I'd asked him for an update. I wouldn't go near the church, so he brought it to me. "The youth group's going to have a lock-in this weekend/Dave White and Brother Norheim showed up for men's prayer breakfast. Is it always just those two?/I'm thinking about painting the van/Bruce Hiddle still smokes. I wonder if he should be on the deacon board?/Emily Kelmer wants us to sing 'Swing Low, Sweet Chariot,' but I don't think that's a worship song/Did you know Jeff Lundgren doesn't want to do the Young Explorers anymore?/How often did you preach on giving?/We need to develop the children's ministry—"

He was out to cover everything. He talked fast, he talked loud, he got more and more excited, and I just sat there trying to gauge if my nerves could last longer than this seeming catharsis. I could feel a lingual tonsil starting to swell up. I began to feel a gnawing pain in my stomach.

Then it came: the one sentence predestined from all eternity for this moment, this place—exactly what it would take to set me off: "Travis, we're going to take this city for Christ!"

"*We?!?*" My voice came so loud and sudden it made him jump. It also made him stop talking. I leaned forward in my chair, so far I almost stood up. "Now you listen to me." I said it slowly, and I know I sounded downright vicious. "Have you even *asked* this town if it wants to be taken for Christ? Have you even met the folks down at Judy's or working at Kiley's Hardware or Anderson's Furniture and Appliance and gotten their input? I guarantee you, Kyle, I know some people around here who do not *wish* to be taken for Christ." He looked like he was about to interrupt, but I didn't give him a chance. "No one . . . has ever . . . taken a city for Christ. Not Paul, not Peter, nobody. Not even Christ took a city for Christ."

Now I did stand up, too upset to hold still. "You come cruising into this town throwing that big, glorious claim around as if it were some kind of mandate from the throne of God, but who's going to do all the work in the real world? I suppose you think everyone in town has his own transportation, so you won't have to organize a car and bus route and deal with people who don't want to come that Sunday but didn't call, or people who aren't ready on time so you have to sit there waiting for them while all the other people on the route are wondering where you are, and everybody ends up getting there late.

"And once you take this town for Christ, what are you going to do with all the kids? Is Judy Milton still breast-feeding Baxter right out in the open during the service?"

"I was going to ask you about that."

"Ah! Aha! That boy's old enough to unbutton her blouse himself. Want some more? Of course, babies don't just nurse. They scream too, and there are plenty of mothers out there who are going to sit there with that kid and let him drown out your sermon—during the most important part, I might add. You might ask them to take the kid out, and some might, but they'll be back with the same kid the next week. Either that, or they'll get huffy and not come back at all.

"Which brings me to the nursery sign-up sheet. Keep that puppy circulating or somebody's going to get stuck in there doing the job alone and forever while all the parents dump their kids on them. Same goes for children's ministry. Be careful you don't find anyone *too* good at it, because they'll get stuck with the job until they burn out. And then the parents will start to mutter about who's going to take charge of the kids, and maybe some of them will step forward to do something about it, and some of them will just go elsewhere.

"Youth ministry? It's the greatest, but don't you dare make a mistake. Because after you've done anything and everything to disciple those kids, it's your mistakes the parents will tell you about.

"How's your car running? Once you take this town for Christ you're going to have to visit every person, every family, until you run yourself ragged and your wife starts to complain that you're never home. You'll be so busy visiting that folks will start complaining that you never come to visit.

"In the meantime, you'll always have a contingent in the church that wants to dance in the aisles and fall on the floor and have battles of the prophets and insist that leg lengthening services are the answer to everything, and if you try to bring some balance to all that stuff they'll start their own faction and accuse you of 'quenching the Spirit.'

"When you take this town for Christ you're going to get all this stuff with it. It's all going to be right in your lap."

By now I was thinking I'd better stop before I outtalked the young man I thought talked too much. I took a breath. "Pastor Kyle Sherman, dreams and goals in ministry are fine and good, but spare me this 'take the town for Christ' stuff. I've been taking as much of this town as wants to go for the past fifteen years. I've been there, done that, got the tee shirt, and the town and I are sick of it."

He looked up at me from the couch. His face seemed so different, so tranquil, when his mouth wasn't moving. "You seem bitter."

Well, I could let this young buck start counseling me or I could get back to my journaling. "Thank you for coming to visit. I'm pretty tired." I moved toward the door, and to his credit, he followed my cue.

THUS ENDED MY FIRST MEETING with Kyle Sherman. I did not go out of my way to encounter him again, but it happened on several occasions anyway, either by God's hand or by Kyle's. As I've mentioned before, Kyle has no fear of thin ice.

That's one reason—among the others—that I accepted his invitation to go with him to the next morning's ministerial meeting. It was the first time I'd taken him up on any invitation to do anything, but I knew those ministers. If Kyle stepped out on thin ice this time, he was sure to break through, and there were sharks waiting below to eat him alive.

3

KYLE PICKED ME UP a little before ten the next morning and we rode together. In a town the size of Antioch there isn't much time to discuss anything while on the way somewhere, so I found myself talking fast.

"Morgan Elliott's the only female minister. She used to copastor the Methodist church with her husband, Gabe, but he was killed in a car wreck three years ago. Nice gal. I wouldn't call her a liberal, but she's definitely not a fundamentalist, either.

"Paul Daley's a kidder, and he likes being Episcopalian as much as you like being Pentecostal. He'd genuflect at a light pole if it had a cross piece on it.

"Al Vendetti is as Catholic as the Pope himself. His father was Catholic, his father's father was Catholic, his oldest sister is a nun in Philadelphia. I got into a religious argument with him once and he finished it in Latin. But listen, you respect him and he'll respect you. You get yourself into a scrape he'll be the first one there, and besides that, he plays a mean first base on the softball team.

"Bob Fisher's Southern Baptist, so he's sound and solid. Just don't get into a doctrinal dispute with him. He doesn't like being disagreed with."

There was no more time. We had arrived at Our Lady of the Fields.

Thanks to the underground spring that had undermined the old church, Our Lady of the Fields now had one of the newest buildings in town. It was sand-colored brick, traditional with its tall spire and arched, stained-glass windows. It sat on a solid foundation ideally located on the main thoroughfare through town. Father Al always posted the title of his sermon on the illuminated, covered sign that sat in the front yard.

As Kyle pulled into the parking lot, I recognized some of the cars already sitting there. "That's Morgan Elliott's Jeep Cherokee. And I think that Ford belongs to Sid Maher, the Lutheran pastor." There were plenty of other cars, including Nancy Barrons's Volvo and Brett Henchle's squad car. This meeting of the Antioch Ministerial was going to be unlike all the others: well attended. I kept telling myself I was only a visitor now, but that didn't take away the tremors deep inside me.

We walked along the sidewalk toward the front door.

"I haven't been in too many Catholic churches," Kyle said quietly.

"I've only been here once, for a funeral," I admitted. "I don't know that the ministerial's ever met here. But Kyle . . ." I stopped, he stopped. I had to get this said before we went in. "I'm never going to tell you to compromise your convictions. But remember what the Bible says about being sly as a serpent and harmless as a dove."

He wasn't quite getting my message, I could tell. He gave me a suspicious look. "What do you mean?"

"I mean . . ." Suddenly I found it hard to form an answer with him looking at me like that. "I mean, there's a time to speak out and there's a time to just listen and, you know, stay cool."

"Stay cool?"

Something else came to mind. "With this bunch, it's easy to get into a discussion that just goes around in circles, and take it from me, if you really want to go around in circles, it's best to find a merry-go-round somewhere, you follow me?"

"A merry-go-round." Now the look in his eyes had to be something he normally reserved for Mormons at his front door.

"Think of it as two gravel trucks going opposite directions on a one-way street. Sure, one of them is wrong, but both of them are going to get smashed when they hit, right?"

"You're not telling me to compromise?"

"No. I'm just telling you to be wise. Be discreet."

He thought about that a moment, and finally—*finally*—he relaxed and smiled. "Okay, Travis. I gotcha."

"All right. That's all I'm going to say."

The brass handle on the big paneled door yielded, and the door opened. There were two other men in the foyer, and the moment I saw them, I thought I'd seen everything. Howard Munson and Andy Barker were standing on either side of the sanctuary door, peering into the sanctuary like two kids sneaking a peek at something forbidden. They turned as we entered and recognized me at once.

"Travis!" said Howard, the older one with the balding head and wire-rimmed glasses. He offered his hand. "Great to see you again!"

I introduced him to Kyle and told Kyle how he pastored the Gospel Light Pentecostal Tabernacle over on the southeast corner of town, that little white chapel near the grain elevators.

Howard introduced Andy, a young wheat farmer with stern-looking eyes even when he smiled. Howard said nothing about the small, independent Bible study Andy led in his home, a little group that had split off from Howard's church over a dispute about—well, about Howard. I didn't tell Kyle about Howard having a strong, negative opinion about every other church but his own, but Kyle may have noticed my surprise to see these two together and within the walls of a Catholic church. Of course, neither had actually gone farther than the foyer.

Howard looked through the sanctuary door again, shook his head in pain and disgust and muttered to us, "Incredible. Just incredible."

The sanctuary was a comfortable, intimate place that could seat,

I figured, about a hundred worshipers. It was warmly colored, with dark wood pews, red carpet runners down the aisles, and brass fixtures. The crucifix was in its traditional location, on the front wall above the altar, illuminated by a ceiling-mounted spotlight.

There were at least twenty people occupying the pews toward the front. Some were kneeling, some were sitting, all were looking steadfastly at the crucifix. I recognized the couple I'd seen at Judy's the night before sitting right on the aisle.

"They're waiting for the crucifix to cry again," Andy whispered.

"Incredible," Howard repeated, shaking his head again.

The ladder Arnold Kowalski had used to reach the crucifix was still where he'd left it, and now a man sat next to it reading from a psalm book.

Howard leaned close. "That's some kind of lay assistant sitting up there. I understand if anything happens, he's there to maintain order and assist people climbing the ladder."

What was I feeling? Awe? Foreboding? Even in my skepticism, I couldn't escape the fact that, real or imagined, nothing like this had ever happened in Antioch.

"Where's the meeting going to be?" I asked.

"Uh . . . I think in the fellowship hall."

I could tell Howard didn't want to go into the sanctuary. He asked in a whisper, "Is there another way to get there?"

I pointed toward a door at one end of the foyer. "I think it's through there."

We went through the door and down a hall to a sizable, multi-purpose room. Most every church has such a room for wedding receptions, potlucks, and socials. At one end was a large pass-through into a commercial-sized kitchen, and coffee was available on the pass-through counter. Four folding tables were arranged in a square in the center of the room, and already the other ministers were mingling.

"Hey Travis!" Sid Maher, the Lutheran pastor, stepped up to shake my hand, and I introduced him to Kyle. He was tall, dark-haired, and bespectacled—a likable guy. His burden for unity among the pastors made him even easier to get along with, and he was glad to see me—with caution. "We're going to be sharing information and concerns, but I don't think we'll need to debate anything."

"I just came to listen," I told him.

He smiled and patted me on the arm, then turned to Kyle. "You have some tremendous shoes to fill."

"I think he brought a pair of his own," I quipped, and Sid laughed.

We helped ourselves to some coffee.

Burton Eddy stepped up to introduce himself. He was short, with black, horn-rimmed glasses, and wild brown hair. He pastored the local Presbyterian church and was, to put it mildly, a liberal. "Welcome to the booming metropolis of Antioch!" he told Kyle in his whiny, sneery voice. "How's the church going?"

"We're taking this town for Christ," Kyle announced unabashedly.

Burton gave him a fatherly pat on the shoulder. "You'll get over it." Then he turned to me. "Travis, I never got a chance to extend my condolences to you. Marian was a saint if ever there was one."

"Thank you. You're right."

He laughed. "On *that* we can agree!" He looked around the room, checking out who else was there. "And I trust we'll strive for consensus on other matters today?"

"I'm just here to listen," I repeated.

He gave me the same pat he'd given Kyle. "Good to see you."

Sid Maher was chairman of the ministerial and was taking his place at the center of one table. Kyle and I were headed for the table when a big-framed man with heavy jowls came up to greet us—effectively blocking our path to the chairs. He spoke to Kyle first and didn't even look at me. "And you must be the new minister at the Pentecostal Mission church."

"That's right," Kyle said boldly, shaking the man's hand. "Kyle Sherman."

"Armond Harrison," the big man answered. "Pastor of the Apostolic Brethren."

Kyle hesitated—digesting the church's name, I figured—before saying, "Okay."

"I understand you've brought a guest today?"

Kyle hesitated again.

"He's talking about me," I told him.

"Oh! Yeah, sure. Travis and I are together."

The big man weighed that for a moment and then gave a slow nod. Then he moved in closer—so close that Kyle had to shift his weight backwards—and peered at Kyle through his thick bifocals. "Of course, you were aware that this meeting is just for the ministers."

"I'm only here to listen," I told him in as pleasant a tone as I could muster.

"And Travis is my guest," Kyle confirmed.

Armond Harrison directed only the briefest glance at me, then spoke to Kyle. "I suppose each minister is free to bring a guest. Nice to have you here."

He turned away as Kyle and I took our places at the table.

"What was that all about?" Kyle whispered while trying not to look like he was.

"It's a great story," was all I said, sitting down. With one discreet glance, I saw Armond Harrison settle like a sinking ship into his chair directly across the square from me. He caught my glance, and his narrowed eyes sent a clear message back. It was just like old times.

Sid opened the meeting with a prayer and then made some opening comments. He thanked Al Vendetti, sitting to his immediate left, for opening Our Lady's facility to the other ministers—I think we all nodded in agreement except for Howard. "It's the first time we've ever met here, which is one historic note. The other might be the large attendance."

We laughed politely. I counted ten ministers. Nancy Barrons, Brett Henchle, and I brought the total attendance up to thirteen. Nancy had her notebook ready; Brett sat next to her, looking ill at ease and out of place in his uniform. Sid acknowledged their presence but only glanced at me and nodded.

"So . . . now . . ." He looked around the table. "If we can go about this in a somewhat orderly fashion, why don't we recap what we know so we all have our information straight? Al, perhaps you could start?"

Al Vendetti was dark and Italian, in his forties, with his Philadelphia roots easy to guess in the way he talked. He cleared his throat, quickly caught everybody up on what had happened to Arnold Kowalski, and then explained the people now sitting in the sanctuary. "We have pilgrims in town. One couple came from Moses Lake, three came from Seattle. There are some from Spokane and some from Ritzville. Word's getting around, and they're here just to wait and watch."

He looked at Paul Daley, the handsome, bushy haired rector of St. Mark's Episcopal, who took the floor. "Yes, I was telling Al that I've gotten some inquiries as well, mostly from Episcopalian friends on the west side who got wind of this somehow. Not being Catholic, I don't know what to tell them so I refer them to Al." Then he added with no change in tone or facial expression, "But they do seem fascinated that this time it's *Jesus* crying and not Mary."

Al realized Paul was teasing and laughed. "In any event, we're still investigating, and so far we've found nothing happening here contrary to faith and morals."

Sid gave the floor to Morgan Elliott, who began a recap of the whole incident with Sally Fordyce. As we listened, I couldn't shake the image I still had of her being a flower child of the '60s, maybe even a singer in an acid-rock band. Her silver-streaked hair was wildly curly and hung past her shoulders, she wore roundish, wire-rimmed glasses on loan from John Lennon, and her voice had a Janis Joplin rasp as if she'd been born perpetually hoarse. "Sally hasn't tried to embellish her story at all. I'm not even sure it would have gotten around town except for the other things happening. Bob . . ." She looked across the table at Bob Fisher, pastor of Antioch Baptist. "You were telling me about someone in your church?"

Bob Fisher, short and solidly built, eyed the gathering grimly as he related, "It's a member of my congregation who prefers to remain nameless."

Morgan piped up, "But you did say it was a *man?*"

She got a smile out of him. "It was a man."

"Just wanted to underline that little detail."

We all chuckled again, and the laughter took some of the edge off the discussion.

Bob continued, "He was fishing down by the Spokane River when he saw a man standing on the riverbank, just the same as Sally Fordyce saw. The man, or angel, or whatever it was, said 'Jesus is coming to Antioch,' and then he disappeared. It was that quick, that simple."

"Do you believe him?" Paul Daley asked.

Bob considered his answer for just a moment and then replied, "I believe he's sincere about whatever happened to him. I'm just not sure what happened to him. His account sounds very similar to a popular rumor that circulates every once in a while."

I stole a glance at Brett Henchle. He just sat there with a stern look on his face, silent as a stone. I could guess he wasn't about to stick his neck out, and I couldn't blame him. I wasn't about to speak up, either.

"Travis," Paul said. "I heard the people at your church are seeing Jesus in the clouds."

I smiled at Paul without saying a word, then leaned over and spoke to Kyle. "That's your cue."

"I'm not so sure," Kyle answered. "We had some folks who were seeing Jesus, but they were also seeing animals and a door and a flame of fire. Little Pammie Forester saw a rooster and then Bugs Bunny." That got a laugh from the group. "A few of the women came back on Monday, but the weather was too cloudy. You can only make out shapes when the clouds are scattered to broken. Overcast won't cut it."

Sid offered, "So for visions in the clouds you should get a weather briefing."

"Absolutely."

More laughter. Laughter was usually a good idea at these meetings.

"By the way, everyone, this is Kyle Sherman, the new pastor at Antioch Pentecostal Mission."

Good old Sid, always the bridge builder. Introductions went around the table and Kyle was off to a good start. I breathed a little easier.

Paul Daley offered, "A man in my church once received a prophecy from a cutthroat trout, but this could be a little different."

"What was your evaluation on that one?" Bob Fisher asked.

"Oh, the fish was delicious."

More laughter. Paul was good for loosening things up.

I couldn't be sure if Burton Eddy was really sneering or if it was just his usual crooked way of talking. "But we're starting to see a schematic here, aren't we? One supposedly supernatural occurrence breeds another, and then another, and before you know it, we have a real hysteria."

"So you don't think any of this is real?" Sid asked.

"Oh, it's real to those experiencing it, I suppose, the same as any dream or hallucination seems real. But this stuff catches on, and we'd be making a big mistake to cater to any of it. We'd only be feeding the frenzy."

Kyle added, "And there's always the possibility that these are demons we're dealing with."

No laughter. Burton just stared at Kyle.

"That's my concern too," said Bob.

"Whoa, now let's approach this carefully," Sid cautioned.

"Here we go again!" said Armond Harrison, glaring at me as if *I* was the one who said it.

Bob fired back, "Armond, it's only wise to be wary of deception. You can't believe everything that comes down the pike as though it's from God."

"Well if God does send anything our way," said Howard, "it's about time!"

Al was keeping cool outwardly, although his face looked a little red as he asked Kyle, "Are you suggesting that a demon healed Arnold's arthritis?"

"Well, just check the long-term results," Kyle answered.

"You mean, the much greater church attendance, or Arnold jubilant, walking about and rejoicing in what God has done?"

"No, I mean people turning their attention and devotion to an idol instead of to the Lord."

Armond's big jowled face was so red you could feel the heat clear across the table. "I see nothing has changed at Antioch Pentecostal Mission."

Morgan started laughing, wagging her head. "And the beat goes on," she said, then confronted Kyle *and* me. "There *might* be a good side to this. Don't condemn something just because it falls outside your religious paradigm."

Kyle tried to counter, "We're not condemning anyone—"

"*Let* people follow their personal sentiments. It can't hurt, really."

"Hear, hear!" said Burton Eddy, clapping his hands.

"After all, what is religion but—"

Sid raised his hands for attention. "All right, fine. Kyle's had his say, you've given your response, I think that should be enough—"

"No!" Morgan insisted. "We came here to share observations, and I'm going to share mine. Religion is a cry of the human heart for meaning. Every tradition has its myths and visitations, and this case is no different."

"You're saying this is all a myth?" Paul Daley asked.

"A myth," Burton said with a nod, his arms crossed. Then he added, "Not that myths aren't a legitimate expression of culture—"

"I don't want to get sidetracked on that," Morgan cautioned.

"Well isn't that what we came to determine," Sid asked, "whether we're dealing with myth or reality?"

"It doesn't matter."

"What doesn't matter?" asked Howard.

"What matters is what it all *means*. I don't want us to get into a big fight over whether this is God, demons, or myth and miss the deeper causes."

"But you said it was a myth," Andy protested.

She brought her chin low over the table and scolded him. "I did not say it was a myth! I said—"

"Arnold's healing is real enough," said Al.

"Well what *was* your point?" Sid asked, trying to help out.

"This is a *human* thing."

"A human thing!" Burton repeated with another nod.

"So Arnold healed himself?" asked Al.

"The pilgrims aren't visiting Arnold," Paul observed.

"*May* I finish?" Morgan's Janis Joplin voice was rising. The others backed off. "When people have religious experiences like these, I take that as the expression of a need. Now we can expend our time trying to attribute this stuff to God or demons—or myth— or we can look for the spiritual needs these occurrences represent and be ready to minister to those needs in practical ways."

"But you're totally overlooking the deception that could be involved," Kyle countered.

She shook her head emphatically. "It doesn't matter."

"It does matter! The truth always matters!"

"Whose truth? Yours or theirs?"

Burton raised his index finger and plopped it down. One more point for Morgan.

Al jumped in, addressing Kyle. "These people are not worshiping an idol! They are waiting and seeking the God the image represents."

"They don't need an idol to do that."

"It's *not an idol!*"

"They don't need *any* mediator save Christ himself!"

"Judging, judging, judging!" Armond Harrison bellowed. "Of all the arrogance!"

Sid was shaking his head, looking toward heaven. "Our Lord must weep."

Paul Daley looked at me. "Well Travis, what's *your* view on all this?"

"NO!" Sid shouted—and shouting was something he rarely did. "I don't think—"

"He's no longer a part of this ministerial!" Armond growled.

"Then let him speak as a layman," said Bob Fisher.

"You don't get it," Morgan lamented, still on her previous subject. "You just don't get it."

Burton Eddy said something about my prior record, but by now everyone was talking at once and I couldn't make it out. Armond heard it and bellowed out his agreement, but Paul was still harping on getting feedback from everyone present while Morgan was still trying to make her point, whatever it was. Howard and Andy had gotten into an argument that somehow drew in Bob Fisher, and Sid was trying to straighten out Kyle on what was and was not acceptable in a ministerial meeting. Nancy Barrons was having trouble taking notes.

I did hear Al Vendetti counter Sid. "I might like to hear what he has to say."

"Me too," said Bob, turning from Howard and Andy.

"If he speaks, I'm leaving this table!" said Armond.

"Now, now . . ." Sid tried to calm things.

"He's my guest!" Kyle objected.

"If *either one of you* says another word, I'm leaving the table!"

Kyle rose from his chair. I reached over and pulled him down again, but that didn't keep him from saying another word. "We are commanded by the Word of God to contend for the faith once and for all delivered to the saints, and if there are lies and deception—"

"So now we're all liars?"

"Has anyone seen Jesus?" I asked.

"In the latter days there shall be false christs and false messiahs showing great signs and wonders!" Kyle was preaching by now.

But Sid heard me. "What?"

Howard and Andy stopped arguing and looked my way. "What did he say?"

"In order to deceive, if possible, even the elect! Read your Bible! That's all I'm saying!" Suddenly Kyle noticed how quiet the room was and how everyone was looking at me. *He* looked at me.

Paul asked, "What was that, Travis?"

I scanned the room, a little jarred by the sudden silence. "I was just wondering, has anyone seen Jesus? That's what this is all about, isn't it?"

For a moment, they just looked at each other.

Morgan offered, "Sally's 'angel' spoke about the answer being on his way."

Al said with emphasis, "The pilgrims here *are* looking for *Christ.*"

Bob built on that. "My person said the angel said 'Jesus' was coming."

Suddenly, to the surprise of everyone, Brett Henchle spoke up. "That's what an angel said to *me!*"

Everyone's head turned so quickly I thought I heard some neck joints crack.

"You saw something?" Sid asked.

"A hitchhiker," said Brett. He quickly recounted the story and then said, "So there's one more side to this. It might not be God or the devil or myth. It might be some clever huckster moving in on the town, and he might have some friends in on this with him. Now I'm not here to downplay anyone's religion, but I'm not look-ing for some heavenly vision here, I'm looking for a suspect. You tell the people in your churches that if anyone sees these guys again, I'd like to know about it." He rose from the table. "Thanks for letting me sit in. It was interesting." Then he walked out, his boots clunking on the linoleum in the hall, his portable radio hiss-ing as he clicked it on.

"If *Jesus* shows up, then we'll really have something to talk about," I said.

Silence.

"Well, if I may change the subject," said Bob Fisher. "As most of you know, we're having a week-long revival with Everett Fudd. We expect the Lord to do some great things and we'd appreciate it if you'd pass the word around."

"What about the softball team?" asked Paul. "When does that start?"

EVERYTHING WENT WRONG on the way home. Kyle, emotion-ally wounded, kept bleeding all over me and making it sound like my fault, and I was sour and brooding about a conversation I'd just had with Bob Fisher.

"You just sat there!" Kyle huffed as we drove across town. "These are pastors, ministers, people answerable to the Lord for how they lead their flocks and they get off on this stupid, wishy-washy, tolerance stuff—that's Morgan Elliott's bag, right? She and that Burton what's-his-face. She's some kind of liberal, feminist, radical, politically correct female pastor type, and all the men in there don't want to stand up to her, right?"

"She's a widow, and she made sense."

"Not if she thinks the truth doesn't matter!"

"I was talking about the people-having-needs thing. She's concerned about people, and I think that's commendable."

"At the expense of the truth?"

"That's an entirely different issue."

He really turned on me. "It should bother you!"

I shrugged. "I've already been bothered."

He shook his head in dismay and disappointment. "Something's happened to you, Travis."

I muttered, "Sure it has."

"What'd you say?"

"Nothing."

"And who in the world is that Armond Harrison character?"

"He's a cult leader."

Kyle checked for traffic, jammed on the brakes, and pulled over. "What?"

I did not want to go into it. I didn't have to go into it. I don't know why I did go into it. "He came out here from Michigan with about thirty followers, and they have their meetings in his house over on Maple Street. Some of them work in town; I think a few commute to Spokane. They're just average, hard-working people."

"But they're a cult?"

I ran down the list—an old, wrinkled list ingrained in my mind through months of public and private discussion, debate, accusation, counteraccusation, and vitriol. It was a list peeled off a can of worms, and I would have loved to forget it. "The Apostolic Brethren deny the deity of Christ, don't know diddly-squat about atonement or salvation, and think they're all going to be christs someday because Jesus was just one of many 'christs' one of many 'sons' of God. They're into pop psychology—you know, deep meanings behind bodily excretions and private body parts and whether or not your mother breast-fed you. They consider the whole church one big extended family, so they move the kids around from family to family wherever Armond wants them to go. Armond usually requires the young women to live with him for a while so he can teach them about sex—whatever his view of it is, anyway. They, uh, they do things." I wanted to cut this short. "That's about the gist of it."

Kyle's grip on the steering wheel was so tight I thought he'd bend it. "And he's on the *ministerial?*"

"You have eyes."

"Why isn't anything done about it?"

"Something *was* done about it."

"But he's still there!"

"End of story."

"But he's a heretic! He's a pervert!"

"Nobody's asking you."

He yelled at me. "What?"

I tried to explain, even though I was pretty sure it wouldn't do much good. "Kyle, in the long, drawn-out scope of things, it's really none of your business what the Apostolic Brethren do and believe. You can preach the truth just as God called you to do, but what Armond and his bunch choose to believe is up to them and you're better off just leaving them alone. If you don't believe me, just try to break up their little church. See how far you get. After you fall flat on your face, you can thank God you live in a country where heretics like Armond Harrison can still roam free, because *his* freedom is *your* freedom."

Kyle shook his head. "I can't . . . I can't be on this ministerial!"

"Oh, you'll break their hearts."

"Travis, you're talking like you're in agreement with all this!"

I did not need or desire this conversation. I was looking at the door handle, seriously thinking of bailing out of the car. "Not in agreement. Just wiser, that's all. We *did* talk about that before we went in, remember?"

"So you just sit and let people like that on the ministerial? You just sit and let me do all the fighting, all by myself? You let me walk right into that wolf pack and don't lift a finger to defend the truth, to help me out?"

"I warned you."

He sighed a deep sigh, shook his head, and reiterated, "Something's happened to you, Travis. I mean, the things I used to hear about you, the great spiritual warrior you used to be. You need to come back to the Lord, Travis. You need to get right with God."

I grabbed the door handle and just about tore it off. "See you around."

"What are you doing?"

I flung the door open and practically leaped out. "The ride's over."

Kyle leaned over, calling to me. "Travis, I'm just trying to help you. You're heading down the wrong road."

I was already walking. "I know my way home, Kyle!"

"You know what I mean!"

I stopped and turned. "Yes, I know what you mean. I know the language, Kyle. I was speaking it before you were born. *I* used to lay that trip on people! But *you're* the man of God now, *Pastor* Sherman. Fight the good fight any way you want. The cause is all yours. Just stay out of my face!"

I turned and kept walking and did not look back, even as I heard him close the door I'd left open and drive off.

I SUPPOSE WE COULD HAVE AVOIDED our little spat if Kyle had been here two years ago, the first time Everett Fudd came to town to revive us at the Baptist church with a week of special meetings. At least he would have had a better picture of what was eating at me.

I wanted to help Bob Fisher out so I got on board and an-

nounced the revival meetings in my morning service. For three of
the meetings, I brought some of my choir over. Bob and I even
sang a duet one night while I played my guitar.

And every night we listened to Brother Fudd preach his long,
rambling string of jeremiads, railing against any and every sin, real
or imagined, and continually reminding us how backslidden, self-
ish, and cold of heart we all were. He came from the "to wake 'em
up, beat 'em up" school of preaching, the kind that gave rise to a
popular description of the Bible belt: "Punch a hole in the sand and
guilt pours out." I often looked around the room to view the
weathered faces of those being revived and wondered how much
of this stuff these people really needed.

Bob and I saw these same faces in church most every Sunday.
They were the regular people, the habitual church attenders who
viewed the fact that there was something to show up for as reason
enough to show up. God bless them, they were many a pastor's last
gasping reason to continue having a midweek Bible study or a
Sunday evening service, and now they were, at least in my mind,
Bob's primary justification for scheduling Brother Fudd.

They came every night, and every night Brother Fudd beat
them up. He accused and scolded them, then shoved their tattered
souls up against the sublime memories of the past for comparison:
the great revivals that happened in another place, another time; the
things that God used to do; the way it was when they first found
the Lord. Wherever they once were, they had strayed. Shame on
them. *Shame on them!*

And the altar call was always the same, a piano-accompanied
petition: *Come back to where you were. Do the old things again. Turn
back and pick up whatever it was you dropped.*

Recycle the old-time religion.

Come back to the Lord. Get right with God.

As the memories came back, I quickened my step, hurrying
down the quiet house-lined street. I was dreading the possibility
that Bob Fisher might drive by, offer me a lift, and invite me to the
Fudd revival meetings again.

He was my friend. He meant well. But when he approached me

after the ministerial with his invitation—"Hey Travis, come to the meetings. It'll be good for what ails you"—I could hear the message coming between the lines: *You need to come back to square one and do it all over again, just do it harder. You need to come back to the Lord.*

Come back to the Lord.

Come back to the Lord.

Just what did that mean, *really?* I chuckled. I could vow never to eat devil's food cake again, or deviled eggs, as Brother Fudd instructed us two years ago. I could think of all kinds of *things* to *do* to please God.

I whispered as I walked, "Lord, we *are* okay with each other, aren't we?"

There was no booming voice from heaven, nor was there any quickening in my soul. There was only the same silence I'd endured for months.

I kept walking, anger fueling my steps. Spiritual Band-Aids from friends, silence from heaven, and the same, unshakable sense of being on the *outside* of it all. The story of my life.

4

ON THURSDAY, Nancy Barrons sold a bumper crop of *Harvesters*, her biggest print run since the brush fire of '95, and the town became officially informed regarding the "Antioch Phenomenon." The story about Arnold Kowalski worked well because Nancy had a real Arnold to interview and photograph, as well as a doctor from Davenport to render his opinion about the arthritis mysteriously disappearing. I thought the accounts of the angelic sightings had a strange, groping tone, trying to be a story about something that might become news if it ever happened. No matter. News that might become news was still news enough. The photocopier at Prairie Real Estate got a lot of use that day, and single households were buying multiple copies of the paper. This news was definitely going to travel.

Their fervor renewed, Dee, Adrian, and Blanche returned to the church parking lot with a more favorable weather forecast—morning low clouds, but partial clearing in the afternoon. Blanche brought her camera and notebook to record whatever signs might appear, noting that they saw Jesus riding a white horse from 2:05 to 2:15, and then a big fist that could have been the hand of God. Dave White stopped by briefly to check the sky for himself, but he was the only person other than the three ladies to do so. This particular aspect of the Antioch Phenomenon hadn't made the paper yet.

Of course, the Phenomenon had no regard for Nancy's publishing schedule. Even as the *Harvester* was hitting the vending boxes around town and the checkout counters at Mack's Sooper Market, *it* happened again, to a person no one would have expected.

One look at Bonnie Adams and you just knew she couldn't have been born and raised in Antioch by parents who were born and raised in Antioch. It may have been Marc and Greg who first pointed her out to me and called her the "hippie woman." She was the one who lived on Birch Street with the "PEACE BEGINS WITH ME" bumper sticker on her car and the "KEEP OUT, NO TRESPASSING" sign on her fence. I was never sure how she made a living besides being an artist who created bizarre nudes and animals out of sheet metal and scrap aluminum. She had long, frizzy hair, granny glasses, loose clothing that had to have come either from India or Berkeley, and a particular scent about her, a strange combination of incense and burning hemp. The first time I met her, she was playing old Grateful Dead and Bob Dylan songs at a local jam for acoustic musicians. I did some lead fills on my banjo and we hit it off fine, but she turned a cold shoulder to any mention of the Lord. I quickly gathered she was into energy and vibrations, maybe a little karma, and that was about it. She was pragmatic, however, and that was why she showed up Thursday morning at Our Lady's with her daughter, Penny.

Penny was seventeen, had no memory of her father, and up until a year ago was constantly in trouble. Brett Henchle and his two cops had run Penny in several times for shoplifting, drug possession, and truancy, but her mother always seemed either helpless or indifferent, and Penny showed no signs of changing.

Until the accident.

Many folks were surprised the single-vehicle wreck hadn't happened sooner. Penny was out with two friends late at night, drinking and driving, when the car went off the road and rolled several times down an embankment. Penny was thrown from the vehicle and the open door landed on her right forearm, crushing it and mangling the nerves. The two friends recovered from their injuries, but Penny's hand was ruined and soon withered, curled back on itself like a broken bird foot.

After that, we didn't hear too much about her.

"Well," Jack McKinstry told me once, "she just can't be the thief she used to be." He ran Mack's Sooper Market, and Penny used to be a regular visitor who cost him a lot of money. Brett Henchle confided that things had indeed quieted down as far as Penny was concerned. "Maybe she's learned her lesson."

When Al Vendetti opened the church doors for the pilgrims, Bonnie was there with Penny in tow. Penny looked a lot like her mother, except that her frizzy hair had green streaks in it, her clothing was quite a bit tighter, and her face was pierced in far more places than Bonnie's. They took a seat in the second pew from the front, directly behind the young couple from Moses Lake. Bonnie had brought some granola bars and took her first bite as she gazed at the crucifix, waiting. Penny just slouched in the pew, bored and scowling.

After no more than five minutes, Penny snarled, "Can we go home?"

"No!" Bonnie answered.

"I need a cigarette."

"Shhh! You're going to disrupt the energy."

"There isn't any energy."

"There is. You just have to relax." Bonnie closed her eyes for a moment and took some deep breaths. "It's here. I can feel it. You just have to settle into it, let it flow." She opened her eyes again and looked around the room. "This could be big medicine. The Spokanes could have worshiped on this very spot."

The other pilgrims were giving them sideways glances.

"This isn't Indian," said Penny, "it's Catholic!"

"It's all the same, sweetheart."

Penny rolled her eyes. "It sure is."

"Shh," came a quiet suggestion from across the room.

"We're doing this for you, Penny."

"It's not going to work!"

Bonnie raised her voice. "If it worked before, it'll work again." Then she drew a deep breath, settled back in the pew, and tried to settle her nerves, relaxing, relaxing. With her eyes on the crucifix, she drew a deep breath and began to hum, "Ommmmmmmmmmm . . ."

Today Pete Morgan was the lay assistant keeping watch at the ladder. After another minute of Bonnie's humming he finally set down his psalm book and hurried off the platform to have a word with her. "Excuse me, I'm sorry, but I'll have to ask you to— "

Bonnie leaped to her feet and pushed him so hard he stumbled across the aisle and almost landed in a lady's lap. All around the room, there were gasps and ooohhhs.

"Way cool!" Penny exclaimed.

"Come on!" Bonnie hissed, yanking Penny by the arm.

Pete recovered just in time to see Bonnie racing for the platform, her full-cut clothing rustling behind her like natural, organic flags in a gale, pulling a running, off-balance Penny after her.

The couple from Moses Lake jumped up from their pew as the young lady gasped and pointed. "It's crying!"

Everyone stood, pointed, shouted. "Look at that!"

"It's crying, it's crying!"

"Saints be praised!"

Pete stared, aghast. Tears from both eyes now traced thin, meandering streaks down the wooden face of the image.

He took the arm of the young lady with leukemia. "Come on, I'll help you."

"But —" She pointed at Bonnie Adams, already grabbing a rung of the ladder and pulling at her unwilling daughter.

"Come on!" Pete insisted, and they hurried onto the platform, followed by an asthmatic man from Ritzville, a lady from Spokane with cancer and the friend who came with her, three elderly folks with arthritis, a Yakima man with a bad liver, and at least ten other people who were either sick or just plain curious.

"Get up there!" Bonnie yelled, pulling on Penny's arm. Penny tried to jerk away. "I'm scared!"

"Make way!" Pete shouted, bringing up the young lady. "Let us come through!"

"Only in your dreams, bub!" Bonnie started clambering up the ladder, stepping and tripping on her long, full pants legs.

The crowd stumbled and jostled around the altar and closed in around the ladder, pleading, praying, grabbing at the rungs in order to climb. Bonnie yelled back at them, stomping on any fingers that dared to climb after her. The two women from Spokane began to wail and weep. The man with the bad liver swore and said excuse me, swore and said excuse me. A forest of pleading hands reached toward the crucifix.

"Calm down now!" Pete hollered above the clamor. His back was against the ladder and some folks were trying to climb *him.* "I'm sure there will be tears enough for everyone! No shoving!"

Al Vendetti heard the noise from his office and came running into the sanctuary. *My God, they're going to break something!*

The young woman from Moses Lake began climbing the ladder. Bonnie Adams stepped on her hand, she fell back, and her husband caught her.

"Please!" Pete begged. "Let her come up the ladder! She has leukemia!"

Bonnie didn't hear him. Her full attention was on that wooden face. She brushed her fingers across the wet streaks, gathering the tears. A powerful tingle coursed through her hand and arm and she cried out, her hand trembling. Then she screamed, forgot her grip on the ladder, and fell, bowling over the two ladies from Spokane and the Ritzville man with asthma. "Penny!"

With help from Pete and her husband, the young woman from Moses Lake went up the ladder.

"Penny!"

Penny reached around the man with the bad liver and the three arthritics. "Mom, get up!"

Bonnie grabbed her daughter's withered hand, her wet fingers touching her daughter's skin firmly, purposefully. Penny began to tremble and scream, trying to pull her hand away, but Bonnie held on with all her strength, her eyes wild with excitement. "You feel it, Penny? Feel the energy? I knew it! I knew it!"

The young woman from Moses Lake reached for the face of the image, touched it, and found it dry. "Oh God, no . . ." She ran her fingers over the face imploringly, but there were no tears. "No . . . no, please, have mercy . . ."

The only tears now were her own.

Father Al worked his way into the crowd. "Please, let's calm down, everyone! Let's not endanger each other!"

Penny was the one doing most of the screaming, her body trembling, her eyes fixed on her right hand, now uncurling as it slipped steadily from her mother's grip. "I can feel it!" she gasped. The fingers wiggled. "I can wiggle my fingers! Mom, I can feel your hand!"

"It works!" Bonnie exclaimed, her wide eyes filled with awe. "This is a sacred place!"

Al reached Penny and took her shoulders to steady her. Bonnie let her hand go and Penny held it up in front of the priest's face, wiggling, twisting, and flexing it. "You see? You see?"

He took her hand and felt it alive and strong in his own. "Oh child . . ." Then he looked up at the crucifix and blessed himself.

WITHIN HALF AN HOUR, I heard about it from Sid Maher who heard about it from Paul Daley who heard about it from one of his parishioners who heard about it from Pete Morgan. Sid called Father Al to confirm it, and then he called me. Sid was a believer now, totally flabbergasted, unable to understand what it meant, how it worked, how he could explain it doctrinally. I had no answers for him; all I could do was thank him for calling, hang up, and get out of the house before Kyle took it upon himself to call me. The way I was feeling, I couldn't talk to him or anyone else.

By the time I even cared where I was going, I found myself near the cottonwoods on the little hill beside my house. I stopped, rested a hand against a gnarled trunk, and began to pray desperately, trying to think, trying to understand just what in the world I was supposed to do with all this. The thing that kept wrenching my insides was that I wanted to believe it was true, that God was indeed moving through our little town and, well, doing something, doing anything. But I'd already put in too many years of believing too many things too quickly. I felt cautionary red flags popping up everywhere. I had scoffed at the reports of people seeing angels, but I was now standing where something had appeared to me. The God I had known all my life didn't heal through tearful wooden images, and yet two witnesses—the biblical requirement—had confirmed the healings at Our Lady's. What must I accept next, that Jesus was really appearing in the clouds?

"Lord, please speak to me," I said aloud as I looked across the expansive farmland to the west. "Help me sort this out."

I quieted myself and remained still, scanning the smooth, gently rolling horizon as I waited for a clear answer to come to mind. I listened for sounds, and even stole a few glimpses of the clouds, just in case. I recalled and sang an old song we used to do at prayer meetings: "Speak my Lord, speak my Lord. Speak and I'll be quick to answer Thee. . . ."

I waited. I told myself I wouldn't wait long, but I waited.

Minutes passed. There was no remarkable vision, no voice. The only sound I noticed was the distant purring of a lawn mower in the neighborhood behind me.

Well, I thought, *I can spend the whole day up here doing and accomplishing nothing, or I can get on with my life.*

I turned and headed down the hill toward Myrtle Street, my prayers unanswered—again. I accepted that fact grudgingly even as I tried to remind myself, "Hey, time is one of God's primary tools for teaching wisdom." Time. And more time. And still more time. More praying, more asking, more weeks, months, or even years of anguish trying to pull it all together. This frustrating little session on the hill reminded me of something I'd learned over the years: God won't be hurried. *Or in this case*, I thought, *whatever he's doing, he isn't about to clue me in!*

I stepped out of the grass and around the wooden traffic barrier that marked the west end of Myrtle Street. The sound of the lawn mower was coming from John Billings's yard across the street from my place. Some guy was busily circling around the big yard on a little Snapper mower.

I checked my mailbox. Hm. More catalogs. Just what I need: a solid gold trailer hitch, a short-wave radio that fits on your wrist. . . .

The guy on the mower came whirring around the front of the yard. He was young, with long black hair bound in a ponytail, a beard, faded work jeans, a long-sleeved shirt, leather gloves. I couldn't recall John Billings ever hiring anyone else to do his lawn. Maybe he was a relative.

The young man looked at me, smiled, and turned the mower for another lap around the back.

I recognized him.

And I was stunned. Speechless. I stood there frozen, staring, my mouth dropping open so far I could feel the sun drying my tongue.

A landscape man?

My mysterious vision of Jesus on the hill was just a landscape man, a young guy with long hair and a beard? He must have been out for a walk, or maybe scoping out another mowing and trimming job. Maybe he was inspecting those trees for possible trimming or removal.

I felt silly and embarrassed. April Fool's. Just kidding. Gotcha! But after that, I felt wonderfully relieved! It was John Billings's landscape man. His landscape man! I burst out laughing.

I watched for him to come around the back of the house and toward the front of the yard again, trying not to have a silly grin on my face in case he should look my way. He appeared soon enough, circling around the back deck and weaving his way toward me through the fruit trees. It was him, all right. He spotted me right away, smiled that same pleasant smile, and this time he waved. I waved back. He seemed like a nice guy.

I looked down at the catalog in my hand so as not to stare at him. I was just debating whether to return indoors or walk over and say hello when I heard the mower stop in the front of John's yard.

"Hey Travis!" the man yelled. I looked up. "Got a minute?"

"Uh, sure." I set the mail in the mailbox and left the door open to remind me. Crossing the street, I kept looking at his face and probing my memory. He knew me by name, but had we met before? Had he ever been to the church while I was pastoring? Maybe he came into Judy's a few times, or attended one of the acoustic jams. I crossed the street, approaching the little lawn mower where he sat waiting. I did *not* remember this guy. He gave me a sympathetic smile. "You're really going through it, aren't you?"

I smiled to be pleasant. "Excuse me?"

"You'll be okay. It's just a little eye opener, that's all."

"Have we met before?"

"Never face to face." He offered his gloved hand. "Or hand to hand."

I took his hand to shake it and felt a weird tingling, like electricity. It didn't stop and I pulled my hand away. "Whoa!"

"What?"

"Got a little shock."

He chuckled. "Sorry. Must be the lawn mower." He rested his elbows on the mower's steering wheel and looked at me casually. "We've known each other for years, Travis, ever since you were eight years old." I was about to question him on that, but he didn't pause. "It's a lonely time for you, I know, especially when so many folks don't understand what you're going through. They've never been there. But you and I have." He chuckled, shook his head, then said in a mimicky voice, *"Travis, you need to come back to the Lord."* He told me sincerely, "They don't know your heart."

Just a landscape man? "Who are you?"

He gazed at me for just a moment, his head slightly cocked. "I've been with you all this time and you don't know me?"

Well . . . he could have been Jewish, from the Middle East. His skin was dark, his eyes a deep brown, his hair jet-black with a gentle curl at the ends. Then again, he could have been part Native American or perhaps Hispanic. He seemed to know a lot about me, even what I might be thinking, but I wasn't about to take the bait. "No. I guess I don't know you. But go ahead, I'm listening."

He drew a breath, sighed it out, and then said, "Travis, you've lived here for years. You know the people, you know the ministry. So tell me. I've sent some messengers on ahead to prepare people. How are people responding? What are they thinking?"

I was trying to remember what I had prayed for a few minutes ago. Whatever it was, I wasn't expecting *this* for an answer. "Oh, people are really buzzing about it. Yesterday the ministerial had its best attendance in years."

"They even let you in."

"I behaved myself. I didn't say much."

"What else?"

I thought a moment, then told him about Nancy's big write-up on the healing of Arnold Kowalski and the angelic visitations. "She sold a lot of papers this morning."

He smiled and nodded, obviously quite pleased.

"So, I'm to understand you're the cause of all this?"

"Well, I haven't appeared in the clouds. I haven't appeared to anyone except you. You know how it is. Some people receive the message and ponder it for what it is, and some take it like a hand-off and just run with it—usually out of bounds. It happens."

Wow. He knows football. But then I pulled out the old 1 John 4 test. "So let me ask you: Did Jesus come in the flesh?"

He held out his arm and pinched the flesh under his shirt. "What do you think this is?"

"But why all this show biz, all this angelic stuff and weeping images?"

He shrugged. "John the Baptist doesn't get out much these days."

In spite of myself, I laughed. "I can't believe I'm having this conversation."

"Give it time, Travis. I don't expect you to believe everything in one moment, not even one week. But I was kidding about John the Baptist. This all goes deeper than clouds and angels and images. You know that."

"This is a gag! Somebody sent you, right?"

"Actually, I came on my own."

I laughed at that as if it were another joke. "Yeah, right."

"I'm a little surprised you haven't asked me about Marian."

That was no gag. It was a sudden, very serious twist, and I could feel it. I studied him. He just raised an eyebrow and looked back at me, waiting.

So now we were going to talk about Marian? This man was a total stranger to me. My answer came with difficulty, but I hoped it would close the topic. "It would be a very big question."

He nodded as if he understood. "The answer's pretty big too." Then he added, "But she sends her regards."

If this was a joke, it was a sick one. I could feel my anger starting to rise—

A car pulled up beside us. "Hello?" a lady called from the passenger side.

I turned. "Yeah? Can I help you?"

Behind me, the mower started up. "We'll talk again, Travis!"

I jerked my head back to see him putting the mower in gear.

The lady in the car was saying something I couldn't hear over the mower. I turned to her again. "Excuse me?"

She repeated, "We're lost. Can you tell us how to get to the Catholic church?"

I approached the car so I could communicate better. I could hear the mower whirring toward the back of the yard. "You're looking for Our Lady of the Fields?"

"Yes, that's it!"

I noticed the car was full; four women and two men. It had an Oregon license plate. "Uh, well, you head down this street till you get to 7th—it's right where that red pickup is parked."

"Uh-huh."

"Turn left, go down the hill to Highway 2, that's the main drag through town."

The lady driving the car elbowed the older woman sitting next to her. "I told you we weren't supposed to turn!"

"Turn right, and it's down two blocks, on the left. Big stone church. You can't miss it."

"Do you think it's open today?"

I ventured a question. "Are you here to see the weeping crucifix?"

Every passenger in that car brightened up and leaned toward me. The passenger lady said, "We sure are! Have you seen it?"

"I haven't seen it cry, but I've seen it."

She nodded toward one of the gentlemen in back. "Barry has lung cancer. We've come clear from Oregon."

I noticed the gentleman had oxygen tubes attached to his nostrils. I didn't know what to say other than, "I think Father Vendetti is keeping the doors open all day."

She clapped, they giggled, the driver put the car in gear. "Thanks a lot! God bless!"

"God bless," I said, and they drove away.

I watched them until they turned left at the red pickup and drove out of sight, struck by what I had seen in that car, and so many times before: serious illness companioned with high hopes. I knew what that was like. I wondered how it would turn out.

But where did the Mower Man go? I no longer heard the mower running and I couldn't see it.

Hoping John wouldn't mind—and not really caring at the moment—I went into his yard, following the last mown path. As I rounded the back of the house, I found the mower parked by the patio, but no sign of its mysterious operator. I peered about the yard, over the fence, and through the back gate like a hound on a hunt, but there was no one around. I almost knocked on the door of the house, but finally put the brakes on and admitted that my emotions were getting the better of me. Whoever this man was or claimed to be, we had ended our conversation on a tedious subject that was best left closed for the time being. I took a moment to draw a long breath, then turned for home.

Between John Billings's yard and my mailbox I determined that John and I would talk about his lawn mower man. I would be in a cooler mood by the time John got home. I would quietly and politely find out who the man was, extend to him an opportunity to apologize for being so cruel and tasteless, and hopefully put this whole event to rest. Surely the Mower Man understood that the town was going through enough craziness right now and I was in enough pain. His witty masquerade would not help matters.

I would be civil. I would be Christian.

By the time I retrieved my mail from the mailbox, I'd dealt with my anger. I'd cooled down a bit.

But the pain was still there. The Mower Man had gotten to me. His words and actions, like slow venom, were still working, and by the time I reached my front door I felt nineteen again. Not young, just burdened with an old sorrow, a deep loneliness, a familiar despair.

Certain smells, like the odor of your grade school or even the scent of an old girlfriend, remain in your memory forever. An old song can bring back the feelings you had when you first fell in love. You may think you don't remember how the back door of your childhood home sounded when it swung shut, but if you could hear it again, you would know the sound.

As I sat on the couch and picked up my banjo, I knew this feeling. I knew when and where I'd felt it before. I was nineteen at the time, sitting alone on the bed in my room in Seattle. I still remembered the "new house" smell of that room, the texture of the Sears bedspread, the feel and color of the blue-green carpet on the floor, the exact position of my Glen Campbell poster on the wall. I had a banjo in my hands then too—a brown, fifty-dollar Harmony with a plastic resonator, and I could have been playing the same song I was playing now.

I was nineteen, alone, and there was absolutely nothing happening in my life.

It was a pivotal moment, I suppose, frozen in memory like a historic photo from the *LIFE* magazine archives, a passage out of childhood and a painful end to illusions. I'd been in love, but lost the girl; I'd been a prophet of God, but proven wrong; I'd prayed for the sick, but they didn't get well; God had called me to a faraway city, but hadn't met me there; my friends and I were going to change the world for God, but they had all scattered after graduation. I had been a young man of such hope and faith, but now my hope and faith were gone, slowly suffocated by disappointment and disillusionment. I felt desperately alone with no idea where to go next or why I should even want to go there.

Sitting on my couch at forty-five, banjo in hand, I could feel it all. The lawn mower man brought it all back. He was trying to be Jesus. He spoke of Marian. It made me realize how much I missed them both.

5

T HE *Harvester* didn't come out again until Tuesday, and
when it did, Penny Adams was on the front page, holding her
right hand high and wiggling it for the camera. It was a great picture and a great article, but oddly enough—and virtually unheard
of in our little town—a big, out-of-town paper actually "scooped"
Nancy Barrons on a local story. Someone—I'm guessing it was
Penny's mother, Bonnie—called the Spokane *Herald*, and they sent
a photographer and reporter to Antioch on Thursday afternoon.
The story ran in the "People" section of the *Herald* on Friday, with
a color picture of Penny and Arnold Kowalski standing on either
side of Father Al and the crucifix visible on the wall behind them.
But the outside news coverage didn't stop there.

Reporters and producers from three different Spokane stations
saw the Spokane *Herald* article on Friday morning and had their
crews out to Our Lady's before ten o'clock. Al, Penny, and Arnold
posed in front of the crucifix again and did their on-camera interviews with the crucifix specially lit by TV lights. Bonnie, being
Penny's mother and therefore worthy of quoting, elbowed her way
into the story and got her face on television. The camera operators
made sure to record the crowd of pilgrims sitting in the pews waiting for it to happen again, and also got sweeping shots of the

outside of the church. When I drove by about noon, I saw the news crews still walking up and down the highway, cameras aimed at the church, the highway through town, Mack's, Judy's, the street signs, and any people who might happen along. Our town—even our street signs and Maude Henley walking her three-legged toy poodle—had suddenly become interesting. But it didn't stop there.

Anything interesting enough to get the attention of the Spokane *Herald* is interesting enough to make the wire services. That same Friday morning, major newspapers and news broadcasters all over the country were reading the wire copy, perusing the wire photos of Penny, Father Al, Bonnie, and Arnold, and raising their eyebrows. They wanted more. The big newspapers called the *Herald*. The networks called their Spokane affiliates.

Of course, by this time the local reporters were after sidebars and spin-offs to the core story. Sally Fordyce made the Saturday editions and the weekend television news, her story corroborated by an anonymous, silhouetted member of the local Baptist congregation and the testimony of a police department spokesman who declined to appear on camera. By Sunday, the pilgrims coming to Our Lady's had doubled. That became a story in itself, which further increased the number of out-of-town reporters.

On Sunday, all the Christians and ministers in town were gathered at their respective churches, making them easy to locate and interview on camera as their services let out. Sid Maher expressed astonishment as the reporters interviewed him standing in front of his church, while Burton Eddy at least sneered civilly as he expressed skepticism in front of his. Bob Fisher had the Word of God to comfort him and that was enough. Morgan Elliott was indignant that such a private matter would become so public.

When a cameraman and reporter from Seattle came by Antioch Pentecostal Mission, Kyle didn't want to limit God but still called for caution.

Dee Baylor was waiting in the parking lot with a whole new spin-off. She had other witnesses camera-ready, Blanche had video and photographs, and Adrian had written records. By two in the afternoon, three stations from the west side of the state and two from the east side were aiming their cameras at the clouds while Dee provided the shape-by-shape commentary. That little twist on the story attracted more attention, which drew more pilgrims, which better filled the parking lot. All of which made it a better news story.

And people *did* start seeing things up there.

BY SUNDAY AFTERNOON, the Wheatland Motel had filled eight of its ten rooms, something Norman Dillard, the owner, hadn't seen in years. By the time a married couple and the man's brother-in-law arrived from Yakima to take the ninth room, Norman was beginning to reel off information like a tour guide.

"The weeping crucifix can be seen at Our Lady of the Fields Catholic church, up the highway and on the left, open twenty-four hours. Also, I understand they're seeing Jesus in the clouds at Antioch Pentecostal Mission, one block over and up the hill. Well, yes, I suppose you could stand anywhere, but Antioch Mission is the traditional place to gather, and facilitators are there to answer your questions. For angels—well, that could happen anywhere, any time. That's part of the thrill. Yes, cameras are allowed at all locations. Cloud watching will be pretty good for this afternoon, but the forecast is for decreasing clouds this evening and clear skies tomorrow, so keep that in mind as you make your plans."

Just outside, an older couple Norman had never seen before halted abruptly as the wife pointed at the hedge bordering the driveway. "I see him!"

The husband, somewhere near eighty and squinting through trifocals, studied the hedge. "Where?"

She was digging for her palm-sized camera. "Right there! Right there in those leaves!"

He muttered, "You're seeing things already?"

She yanked him by the arm. "You have to be standing here!"

He stood where she put him, studied the hedge, and never got the puzzled look off his face while she snapped pictures.

Norman signed in the new arrivals and gave them the key to Room Nine. Only one vacant room left, and that older couple was heading his way.

Hm. This religious stuff was good for business.

JACK MCKINSTRY noticed a lot of new faces coming through Mack's Sooper Market as well. The news crews stopped in for crackers, chips, and soft drinks. Out-of-towners were buying whole loads of groceries as well as film and batteries for their cameras. Others were stocking up on carry-along snacks for the vigils under the clouds or below the crucifix. He and his wife, Lindy, had little time to rest during checkouts at the cash registers.

"Hey," he called to Lindy, "what if we dress up our employees like angels? You know, little angel wings or something?"

He was at cash register two; she was at cash register three. She started speaking louder so she could concentrate—"Two at fifty, dollar twenty-nine, dollar forty, three ninety-nine . . ."—and then vetoed the idea with her eyes.

He chuckled as he counted cans of beans, sliding them along the counter with shuffleboard precision. Well, maybe that idea was a little too daring, but the way business was picking up lately, one couldn't be too quick to frown at new ideas.

Mack's was a family business, begun by Jack's father back when misspelling *Super* was still clever. It wasn't a large place, but Jack worked hard to keep pace with the big-town supermarkets while maintaining a neighborhood grocery attitude. The store had four checkout counters with one designated "Ten Items or Less," but the laser bar-code readers were still something he'd only read about. The automatic doors were still activated by pressure pads instead of motion detectors, but Jack saw no need to upgrade them as long as they worked and the customers didn't mind waiting a little. He kept a magazine rack at each checkout with a fresh rotation of *Cosmopolitan*, *People*, and *The National Enquirer*, but drew the line at any magazine that had to have its cover concealed. He'd finally put in a video rack, but only at Lindy's insistence. At heart, Jack was a grocery man, the kind of guy who did his own meat cutting, bought produce from local farmers, and always provided floor space for church bake sales.

"And that will be . . ." He scanned the register's display. "Fortynine eighty-two." He got the money, gave the customer the receipt, Ronny the box boy took over, and Jack was free for a moment. "Hey Nevin, the widow called. She's wondering where you are."

Nevin Sorrel, a gaunt-looking, blue-jeaned ranch worker in his thirties, had been waiting by the Rent-a-Vac carpet cleaners, fidgeting and fretting. He hurried forward and spoke in quick, low tones, "Jack, I can't find those groceries nowhere."

"Those four sacks you bought?"

"Yeah, they were the ones."

"Ronny took them out to your truck. I saw that much."

"But they ain't there!"

"I saw Ronny put 'em in."

It upset Nevin to have to repeat himself. "They ain't there!"

Jack stared at him a moment. "So . . . what am I supposed to do?"

"Have you seen 'em?"

Now Jack was getting impatient. "Yeah! I saw Ronny put 'em in the back of your truck and that was the last time I saw 'em. Mrs. Macon is wondering where you are. She sent you down here two hours ago and she wants her strawberries."

That was no comfort to Nevin whatsoever. He started reliving the past two hours. "I got in the truck, drove out toward the Macon place, I got sleepy . . ."

"Wait. You got sleepy?"

"Yeah. I pulled over and fell asleep, and when I woke up the groceries were gone."

Jack was amused even as he realized it was rude. "Well, there you are. You got ripped off." Nevin stared at him blankly, so Jack expounded. "Somebody stole the groceries while you were sawing logs."

Nevin had a hard time getting that to sink in. "What am I gonna tell Mrs. Macon?"

IT WAS BECOMING a fruitful day for sightings. As the number of pilgrims in town increased, so did the sightings of Jesus; and as more Catholics arrived, so did the Virgin Mary. It reminded me of a large scale, grown-up Easter-egg hunt. Everywhere you looked, folks were scouring the town—searching the sky, the potholes in the roads, the bark of trees, the water stains in ceiling tiles—hoping to see the Savior or his mother looking back. Both Jesus and his earthly mother appeared on the back of the highway sign denoting how many more miles it was to Coulee City and the junction with Highway 174. Mary did a solo appearance in the growth ring pattern where a tree trimmer sawed a rotting limb off the big willow tree next to Sawyer Memorial Playground. The pavement stones on the front steps of the library drew attention, but Catholics and Protestants were divided as to whether it was Jesus or Mary. The most unusual sighting I heard of was the face of Jesus beckoning from the mildew on the shower tiles in Room Five at the Wheatland Motel. Norman didn't know what to do about that one—whether to clean a dirty shower or desecrate a holy shrine.

As for me, I finally managed to catch John Billings at home. It turned out he had been gone most of the week installing a sprinkler system in Missoula, Montana.

"Hey, what happened to my lawn?" he asked me the moment I walked over to talk with him.

It seemed the Mower Man only mowed the lawn until he had his talk with me. Now John had a ring of mown grass around the outside of his yard and a wide border of shaggy lawn closest to his house.

"I saw a guy mowing your grass on Thursday," I said, eager to hear his reaction.

John was a tough old bird in his fifties who took great pride in his yard. He was a bit miffed. "Who?"

"Uh . . ." I almost answered, but then realized I didn't have an answer I could actually use. "I don't know. He didn't tell me who he was. But he was driving your Snapper around the yard, cutting the grass. I thought he was working for you."

"He wasn't working for me." He looked around his yard in disgust. "I wouldn't hire a guy who only does half a lawn. Did he think I was going to like this?" Then he jerked his head around to look at me as if something had finally sunk in. "He was driving my mower?"

I could see the Snapper from where we were standing and I pointed it out. "That one right there."

"On Thursday."

"Yeah."

"Ever seen him before? What did he look like?"

Well, *who* he looked like would have made a better question, but I proceeded to tell John what I saw, leaving out the details of the conversation we had. I was feeling an odd mix of triumph and mystification that I tried not to show: I *knew* that guy was some kind of phony . . . but if that was the case, who was he really?

BY THE TIME Nevin Sorrel got back to the widow Macon's ranch he was an hour late and carrying a whole new order of groceries, paid for out of his own pocket. Being late didn't worry him too much. Mrs. Macon would scold him about it, but she would tolerate it. Losing four sacks of groceries while sleeping was another matter. Mrs. Macon was wealthy, quirky, and very particular about her cash flow.

As he turned the golden brown pickup off the highway and through the ranch gate, he tried to concoct an explanation. A mechanical breakdown wouldn't work. This was the late Cephus Macon's truck, an immaculate Dodge with extended cab, custom running boards, and chrome-plated exhaust stacks, always kept in top condition by the widow out of respect for her husband's memory. He could say he met an old friend, got to talking, and lost track of time, but that would sound irresponsible. A flat tire? No, that would mean exchanging one of the good tires for the spare, and that was too much trouble.

He rehearsed some other excuses as he drove the mile-long driveway to the sprawling ranch house atop the rise, but none of them played out very well. By the time he eased the big rig into Mrs. Macon's four-car garage, he settled for no explanation at all. He was late, he was sorry, that was it. He'd bring in the groceries, apologize, and duck if he had to.

He grabbed two sacks from the back of the truck, knocked on the rear entry door, then cracked it open. "Mrs. Macon? I'm back."

Her voice came from the kitchen. "Where have you been?"

He hurried through the laundry room and into the kitchen, a gorgeous, expansive facility with a virtual warehouse of cupboard and counter space and a vast wall of windows offering a panorama of the Macon ranch lands. The moment he saw the widow sitting at the enormous breakfast table, the first excuse he rejected didn't seem so outlandish. "You'll never guess what happened! The alternator belt broke and I had one awful time—"

"You don't have to explain," she said gently. She was a small woman in her late sixties, with a trim figure and white hair tucked into a comb atop her head. She was sipping her afternoon drink of blended fruit juice—a blend that was supposed to include the strawberries she'd needed but he'd lost, bought all over again, and delivered late. He couldn't be sure, but the pink color of her drink sure looked like she'd found some strawberries. As she took another sip and looked out the windows, the expression on her face did not seem harsh, as he expected. It actually seemed peaceful. He began to breathe easier. "Uh, well, I got the groceries. I'll bring the rest in."

She gave him a puzzled look. "What did you do? Buy them again?"

It was tough trying to look innocent while feeling so cornered. "Uh . . . no, I got the groceries. I got 'em in the truck."

She set her glass down and looked at him with her head slightly tilted, her fingers drumming her chin. "They're already in the house."

His mind went blank. "Ma'am?"

"My strawberries, my oranges, my strawberry nonfat yogurt, the porkchops, the flour and my Knox for Nails, all of it. You got it all the first time."

"The first time?"

"Yes, before you decided to take a snooze by the side of the road, remember?" She went to the double-wide refrigerator and swung the door open. "Here are all the perishables, safe and sound, no thanks to you."

It took a few seconds for Nevin to conclude that whatever cover story he'd concocted had already failed. "I, uh, I didn't want to get into an accident, you know, go off the road in Mr. Macon's truck."

"You might try sleeping at night," she responded briskly. "Lucky for me, someone happened by and saw you sleeping in the truck with my perishables sitting in the back, out in the sun, about to go bad."

So he'd been caught. Worse than that: snitched on. "Who?"

She went to the windows and pointed. "My new hired hand."

What? Pain and jealousy twisted around inside him, and Nevin hurried to the window.

"He came to the front door with all four sacks in his arms and told me where he'd found you parked, snoring away while my yogurt sat in the sun. He's very sweet and conscientious."

Nevin saw the big John Deere tractor emerging from behind the horse barn, pulling a trailer of hay. "What's he doin' on my tractor?"

She cleared her throat. "On *my* tractor," she corrected. "He's transferring hay to the other barn."

"That was my job!"

"You were sleeping, Nevin!"

He looked at her with horror in his eyes and a wrenching pain in his stomach. "You're giving him my job?"

"Oh, we'll see." She cocked her head and gave him a motherly look. "*He* didn't lie to me."

"But I paid for 'em! I paid for the second load out of my own pocket!"

She waved her hand, not wanting to discuss it. "Give me time to think it over, Nevin. Take the day off. We'll just see how everything works out."

Before turning on his heels and getting out of there, Nevin took a long, careful look at the man he knew he would hate. The fellow was young, with black hair and a beard, dark skin, blue jeans, long-sleeved shirt, and gloves, now looking his way and giving him a friendly, gloating smile and a little wave.

LATER THAT AFTERNOON, with just a few hours of daylight left, Norman Dillard stepped out of his motel office and checked the sky. There were a few clouds up there still, drifting like small islands in a vast sea of blue and getting smaller and scarcer by the hour. The cloud watching at Antioch Mission might be ending soon. He removed his thick glasses and rubbed his eyes, resigning himself to the idea that he should get up to the church to see what was going on. He didn't want to. He was not a man of faith, and Praise the Lord types got on his nerves, especially women having Hallelujah conniptions. But he was supposed to be the knowledgeable guide who could answer questions and speak local facts, and that meant he had to see the sights for himself. It was business, pure and simple.

He drove the few short blocks and pulled into the church parking lot to find about two dozen people gathered there, necks craned skyward, cameras ready. *Hoo boy. Here we go.*

"Ooooh, it's Mr. Dillard!" a woman shouted. He winced. He could hear her shrill voice through his closed car windows.

Dee Baylor and Blanche Davis were right there to greet him as he stepped out of his car.

"Norman! Praise the Lord!" Dee gushed, giving him a bear hug he wasn't expecting and couldn't wait to get out of. "We were praying you'd come!"

"Just came to check things out," he said limply.

"Are you ready to see Jesus?" Blanche asked, pulling out some Polaroid snapshots. He tilted his head back so he could see the photos through his bifocals. "See here? He's looking toward the east."

"Uh, which way is east—I mean, in the picture?"

Blanche tilted the picture this way and that and finally decided, "This way. Now you can see his nose. Right there."

"Mm-hm." His agreement was less than enthusiastic.

"You can believe, Norman," Dee said reassuringly. "Just put your doubt aside and you'll be amazed at what you'll discover."

He shied away, turning his attention—and hopefully theirs—to one lonely cloud passing over. "So . . . you're the facilitators, right? Just how does one go about this? You know, what do you have to do?"

"Just yield to the Spirit," Dee told him. "Let God open your eyes and speak through his creation."

"The firmament showeth his handiwork," Blanche added.

Norman walked toward the front of the parking lot where people were standing about in couples and clusters, some singing softly, some praying, some counting rosary beads, all of them watching that one cloud approaching. He came upon the elderly couple who first discovered the face of the Lord in the hedge outside his office. They were sitting in folding lawn chairs with their heads resting back on inflatable neck pillows. She pointed. "Here comes another cloud, Melvin!" Her husband did not respond, but appeared to be praying. Then Norman heard a short little snore.

The married couple and the brother-in-law from Yakima quietly began to sing "How Great Thou Art," and others picked up the tune. Behind Norman, a rotund man with a Seahawks cap sang the words in a clear tenor voice, holding his small wife close to his side. To Norman's left, two couples he recognized as local residents added harmony as they sat on lawn chairs in the back of a pickup. To his right, a Hispanic family of parents, grandparents, and children huddled together on the church lawn, singing when they knew the words and humming when they didn't. Norman had to admit it sounded good, and as he stood in the middle of the music and watched the solitary cloud passing overhead, it even felt good. This was a nice place to be. It was sweet, peaceful, and enjoyable. It would be easy to send people up here who were inclined toward this sort of thing.

Definitely good for business.

Norman removed his glasses and rubbed his eyes. It had been a long day and he was getting tired.

He felt a hand on his shoulder. It was Dee Baylor. "How are your eyes, Norman?"

"Oh, about as bad as usual," he answered. He'd never been very happy about his poor eyesight and the thick glasses he had to wear.

"This is a place where God speaks through the eyes. I think he wants to heal you."

He rolled his eyes.

"Hey, come on, now. I really think he does."

"That would be quite a trick."

"Why don't you just take those glasses off and see?"

"See what?"

"Go on, take them off."

Well, it wouldn't be good business to have Dee and the others mad at him. He removed his glasses and gave his eyes a little rub out of habit.

"Now just look at the sky, Norman, and let God speak to your eyes."

He directed his gaze upward, but saw exactly what he expected: a vast, blue blur. If God was speaking, he was mumbling.

"What do you see?" Blanche asked.

"I see a blur."

"NO!" Dee corrected. "You have to speak your healing. Say you can see."

He looked at her. She looked better, he thought. "I beg your pardon?"

"Believe you can see, and you will."

He looked at the sky again because he didn't want to look at her. He was trying to think of a way out of this.

Blanche coached him, "Say you can see."

He was incredulous. "Say *what?*"

"Say, 'I can see'."

"I can see."

"Say it until you believe it," said Dee.

He laughed nervously. "Ladies, we could be here a long time."

"We have all night."

He fumbled, fumed, and finally put his glasses on. "Well, I'm sorry, I mean, I really do apologize, but I don't have all night. I have to get back to the motel and run my business."

"That's all right. Baby steps, Norman."

"One little step at a time," said Blanche.

He smiled at them and hurried to his car before he said something unkind. Once he got the door closed and drove away, he did say it. And he believed it too. He kept on saying it and believing it all the way back to the motel, gesturing wildly, wagging his head, addressing his reflection in the rear view mirror. Those people up there were crazy! They were an embarrassment! Fanatics! He was amazed they were allowed to roam freely about the town. People were traveling from far and wide for this?

Yes, Norman, and staying in your motel, he reminded himself. By the time he got back to his office, he'd taken some baby steps toward getting used to the whole idea.

MATT KILEY had no intention of getting used to it. Monday morning, when I stopped in at his hardware store for some molly screws, he was still fuming about a visit he'd had from some crucifix watchers.

"I told 'em to spend some money or get out of here," he said, propelling his wheelchair down the aisle where he stocked all his fasteners. He was still disgruntled. "If they can't cope with it, that's their problem. I cope with it because I have to and I'm not asking

for any favors. What are you hanging, anyway?" Matt was a decorated Vietnam vet. He was proud of that, and I was proud of him.
He still wore camouflage fatigues around the store when he felt
like it, flew a flag over his front entrance, and kept a POW–MIA
poster on the wall behind his cash register. I never found him
overly rude or obnoxious, but he was crusty, no doubt about that.
In his younger days he'd come out the winner in quite a few rib
and nose breakers down at Judy's—the other guy's ribs and nose,
not his. In Vietnam he'd dispatched his share of Vietcong and
taken more than his share of risks for his buddies before a sniper
put a bullet through his spine. Now, running his hardware store
from his chair, he wasn't bitter about the war or about his injury.
He just didn't like people fussing about it.

"Some more shelves in the bedroom," I told him. "A lot of
heavy stuff."

"Got a stud finder?"

"No, but you can sell me one."

"I'll do that. Anchor to all the studs you can find. And here,
these mollies'll do the trick through the drywall."

He pointed them out to me and I grabbed as many from the
little drawer as I thought I would need. Matt had four employees
to do most of the stocking and high reaching, but customers
helped by Matt were often responsible for reaching any items Matt
couldn't. We headed up the aisle.

"They were all hot to trot. 'Matt, you gotta come down to Our
Lady's so you can walk again!'" He abruptly turned left. "Stud
finder. Magnetic or fancy?"

"Depends on how much they cost."

He kept wheeling along, perfectly at home with every square
inch of this place. "Like all I have to do is look up at that crucifix
and believe, and that'll do it. Trav, you know what it's like. I've had
crackpots before try to get me to walk." He quickly added, "Well,
not all of 'em were crackpots. You know what I mean."

"Sure."

"There's just some people who can't leave it alone, that's all I'm saying."

"I know what you mean."

"Yeah, sure you do. You've been there." He grabbed a stud finder off the tool rack. "These are fun. You slide it along the wall and watch the little lights come on."

I checked the price. I figured I could swing it. "Great."

I followed him as he wheeled toward the front, executing snappy turns around corners and past merchandise. He rang up my purchase at a cash register built on a lower shelf just for his use. I paid him, he threw my goods into a sack, and then stopped to ponder. "Funny. I made some friends at the VA hospital, I've met some other folks in wheelchairs, and we got along fine. They never told me to go down and look at some crucifix or wash in some special kind of water or say some kind of magic prayer words. It's always the walkers who know what you need."

Our eyes met. We understood each other.

It's always the walkers who know what you need. Matt Kiley's words, his cynical wisdom born of experience, haunted me for the rest of the day. Yes, I understood. I had been there.

I just didn't want to go back again. . . .

6

I was seventeen the year my father took a hiatus from the ministry and relocated the family from Seattle to a small, almost nontown on an island in Puget Sound. Back in Seattle, we had a great church with great worship and a great youth program. I had a girlfriend. I was a junior at the high school my brother and sister and several uncles had attended and had school spirit that bordered on pathological. I had some friends at that school—it had taken me long enough to make them. Then we moved, and I began my senior year in a run-down, fund-hungry high school with caved-in lockers, sagging floors, and three hundred total strangers.

Like any plant torn up by the roots, I didn't take well to the transplant. I used to have the acceptance of my peers, and now I couldn't be sure I even had peers. I used to be part of something, but now I was an outsider. I was in pain. I was lost.

Lost, and absolutely certain that it couldn't be right, much less the will of God.

You see, I *knew* God back then. I knew exactly what he expected from me and what I could expect from him. I'd grown up attending the Allbright Gospel Tabernacle, a Pentecostal Mission church in Seattle's Rainier Valley, and when we gathered for worship, we always counted on God's tangible presence. We felt no qualms about calling out to him aloud, right from our pews, right when we felt the need or the unction. We heard from God regularly in prophetic utterances that usually began with "Oh my people" and admonitions that usually began with "I hear the Lord saying . . ." We prayed for the sick and expected they would get well.

Dad preached the Word of the Lord from the pulpit, and we worked it in at the altar afterward. Our sessions at the altar were usually noisy, often tearful, and altogether glorious. I couldn't tell you now how much of the commotion was due to the Holy Spirit and how much was simple Pentecostal fervor, but I know I did precious business with God in that place. I got saved in that church when I was eight years old. Being Pentecostal, I received the baptism in the Holy Spirit in that church when I was twelve, kneeling at that wooden rail with my head on my coat sleeve until the pattern was pressed into my face. Over the years, I dedicated and rededicated myself to the Lord's service, repented, praised, confessed, and petitioned, all from that little brick building in Rainier Valley. That was where I knew God.

But Dad was tired, Mom was unhappy, and the family needed a change, so Dad quit preaching and we moved.

The church we found on the island was . . . restful, you might say. Kind of like a stalled car. These folks didn't smile much, sang all possible verses of really slow hymns, and absolutely, positively, never, ever clapped. As far as I could discern, God was not expected to move, speak, or convict—he was expected to follow the printed order of service and keep quiet like everyone else. There was never an altar call after the service. Instead, people worked the sermon out of their memories over coffee, cookies, and idle chatter in the basement.

I was seventeen, living in a strange new place, enrolled in a school that felt foreign, and attending a church dedicated to deadness.

Which made me a prime target for the Kenyon–Bannister movement.

David Kenyon, a fellow senior I got to know in art class, pinned me down one day. "Hey, are you a Christian?"

"Sure!"

"Spirit-filled?"

"Yeah."

"Speak in tongues?"

"Yeah."

He extended his hand and we shook. "I knew it. I just knew it."

It had been a while since I'd met anyone excited about what God was doing, so while I worked on a sculpture and he worked on an oil painting, David talked and I listened.

"The Holy Spirit's moving," he said. "Just blows my mind what God's doing. I had a real confrontation with a demon yesterday. I think he knew we were moving into Satan's territory. We had a prophecy last week and God told us to get our act together, get off the acid and grass and get high on Jesus. He was talking *right* to some of the group and it really shook them up."

He started naming kids in school I'd known of but didn't know.

"Bernadette Jones—" Wow. She always impressed me as being tough and unapproachable. She had a crusty mouth when she could get away with it and never missed a chance for a smoke.

"Karla Dickens—" I knew of her from drama class. It seemed every skit she did had something to do with marijuana.

"Andy Smith—" Very musical. Had a rock band and was already working on a symphony.

"Clay Olson—" Uh, no. I couldn't think of a face to go with the name.

"Benny Taylor—" I didn't know him at all, except that he was one guy in school who had more pimples than me.

"Amber Carr—" A quiet girl from drama class. I always liked her long brown hair.

"Harold Martin—" What? Harold? The guy was a creative genius, but lived and breathed The Doors and always played knife-wielding psychotics in drama class.

He named about five more. They were all strangers to me, but that wouldn't be the case for long. During lunch period, David introduced me to every Christian he could find.

"Hey, guess who's a Spirit-filled Christian!"

Bernadette Jones looked up from her fruit salad. "You're kidding!"

"Hey Andy, guess who's a Spirit-filled Christian?"

Andy Smith looked up from a copy of *The Hobbit*. "Well, praise God!"

"Hey Amber! Guess who's a Spirit-filled Christian?"

Amber Carr pulled her long hair away from her face and smiled at me. "Wow. That's really nice."

Clay Olson was eighteen but seemed older, wiser, too cool to be in high school. He shook my hand. "Great to have you on board."

Benny Taylor not only had more pimples than me, he had more brains, at least as far as math was concerned. "God bless you."

Harold Martin, who looked like he'd spent the night in a ditch, stared up at me blankly for a second or two. "It's a heavy trip, isn't it?"

Karla Dickens, blonde, bespectacled, and jolly, shook my hand and giggled. "I sort of figured," she said.

I learned that this particular move of God centered around the Kenyon home on Wednesday nights, and the next Wednesday night, I was there to see it for myself. I wasn't disappointed. I could tell this was going to be good stuff, powerful stuff—the kind of thing I grew up with and needed more of. The cozy living room became even cozier as more than a dozen high schoolers filled the couches, the chairs, and several cushions on the floor. Mrs. Kenyon led the meeting, sitting in her big stuffed chair in the corner. She was a pleasant, conversational lady, short in stature and beyond rotund, wearing a loose, tentlike dress and slippers she didn't have to tie. Mr. Kenyon was quite "blessed" himself, sitting across the room with arms folded over his expansive paunch.

David, Karla, and Andy had guitars and we wasted no time launching into some praise songs, clapping—that's right, clapping—and getting into Jesus.

We sang songs like:

> Thank you, Thank you Jesus
> Thank you, Thank you Jesus

Thank you, Thank you Jesus in my heart.
Thank you, Thank you Jesus
Thank you, Thank you Jesus
Thank you, Thank you Jesus in my heart.

That song must have taken the composer months to write, but I learned it the first time through. The next one was a little tougher:

You gotta move when the Spirit says to move, Oh Lord
You gotta move when the Spirit says to move.
When the Spirit says move, you gotta move, Oh Lord
You gotta move when the Spirit says to move.

Then we replaced the word "move" with *dance, sing, pray, shout, preach, kneel,* and anything else that came to mind, and sang the whole thing again. This was an easy song to wear out.

After several songs, when things got cooking and the joy was just right, Mrs. Kenyon lifted her hands and started speaking in tongues, and that was everyone's cue. All around the room, hands went up like blooming plants and tongues started fluttering, making all nature of sounds with a commonality of rapid, repeated phrases, rolled r's, and stuttered t's and d's. David was the loudest and maybe the fastest, speaking phrases that sounded like a dirt bike downshifting. Harold stood with arms outstretched and eyes a little buggy, rolling his r's on a long string of rah-rahs. Amber wasn't saying much at all, just standing there with her palms upward, looking sweet. Benny Taylor could have been addressing invisible troops like Patton the way he was barking phrases and throwing in an occasional clap for emphasis.

I'll be honest: It was clamorous. This was not a convenient time to hear yourself think or compose a prayer of any substance. But that was okay. We didn't have to pray with understanding because we were praying in the Spirit, and I was right in the middle of it.

Then Mrs. Kenyon called out in a bold, loud voice, "My children," and we all fell quiet, our eyes closed prayerfully. I knew from my upbringing that an opening such as "My children," "My people,"

"Thus saith the Lord," or "I am here" meant the start of a prophecy. This was God talking.

Mrs. Kenyon continued, "Surely I have heard thy praises, and I receive them as a sweet smelling savor. Continue to praise me, and I will walk in your midst. Drink of my Spirit, and I shall grant you a mighty increase on this island . . ." She went on like that, delivering words of encouragement as we thanked God quietly but audibly and praised him for speaking to us.

Then Clay Olson gave a prophecy much like Mrs. Kenyon's, which really made my evening. I always thought this guy was so cool and sober about life, and now here he was, yielded and being used of God. Would wonders never cease?

By the time the meeting was over, we'd just about done it all. We had opened the Word, prayed for the sick, shared testimonies, even laid hands on some new kids so they could get the baptism like the rest of us. By the time I walked out of that house I was reeling with ecstasy and my emotions were in wondrous, healing reversal. Regret had turned to joy. Perplexity had turned to understanding. Loneliness had vanished. I was home. I belonged. "Hallelujah," I kept saying, hugging everybody. Hallelujah! For the first time, I was glad to be exactly where I was. God had a plan all along! He brought me here to find this bunch, to be a part of this mighty outpouring!

But I had to stretch my thinking a little. At the Allbright Gospel Tabernacle, being a Christian meant you didn't smoke. When we were kids we even equated condemning tobacco with preaching the gospel: "Mom, I witnessed to Robbie today. I told him we don't smoke." Well, not only did Bernadette, Harold, Karla, and Andy smoke; Mr. and Mrs. Kenyon smoked as well. In fact, the moment we said Amen to the closing prayer, she grabbed her pack and her lighter and started pulling down smoke like she was making up for lost time.

I think she noticed my discomfort. Between puffs, she let me know it was something she would be giving up in the Lord's time. The Lord had given her a vision about it. "I saw a huge garden full of weeds, and I saw the weeds being plucked out around the out-side of the garden, and then more weeds being pulled farther in toward the center, and in the very center of the garden was a big cigarette stuck in the ground, and the Lord said, 'This is the gar-den of your life. I'm going to start pulling weeds, working from the outside in, and after I take care of these other weeds in your life, I'll take care of this weed too.'" She laughed at the pun. "The Lord called it a weed. He really has a sense of humor." Then she added as she crushed out a spent cigarette and lit another, "But praise is the answer. God is perfecting things and all we have to do is praise. Every Wednesday night there's someone new at the door, and we just pray and praise them in."

And that's what we did, week after week, Wednesday after Wednesday, all through the fall and into the winter of my senior year. Every Sunday I sat in the quaint little quiet church, and I admit I got good preaching and teaching there, good meat and potatoes. But for spice, for energy, for a spoonful of Pentecost per week, I made it to the Kenyons' and hung together with my on-fire buddies at school. We witnessed around the school, got into reli-gious arguments with other students and sometimes our teachers. We won a few, lost a few. We developed a reputation, of course, but when people saw that Christianity was okay for guys like David, Benny, and Clay, they weren't so quick to say it was only okay for kooks like Andy and Harold. Things were going great.

Pretty much.

Harold became a puzzle to me. I vividly remember the cold Wednesday night in November when he and I stepped outside so he could have a cigarette and we could talk. It was a rule at the Kenyons': No smoking during the meetings, and only Mr. or Mrs. Kenyon could light up in the house afterward.

We stood out in the yard. It was dark and there was a cold drizzle. Harold hunched his shoulders and kept one hand jammed in his overcoat pocket as he used the other to hold his glowing cigarette. I could barely see him.

"Ever smoke pot?" he asked me.

"No."

"You ought to try it. I can get you some."

My answer came out halfhearted because he'd thrown me off-balance. "Well, no, I, uh, I don't need that stuff."

"Fair is fair. I came over to your side and gave the Holy Spirit a try. I got high your way. You need to see what marijuana's like. You'd be getting high my way, see what I mean?"

"Harold . . ." I really didn't want to become some kind of parent to this guy. "Smoking pot is wrong. It's against the law."

"Man's law. God gave us pot. It's a gift from him. You need to try it. If you love God, if you love me, you should try it. You can't say something's wrong if you haven't even tried it."

I couldn't think of what to say.

"Fair is fair, right?" he repeated.

I don't remember how the conversation ended. I only remember that it ended quickly and I went home to brood about it.

I'd seen Harold at almost every meeting, singing the songs, raising his hands, and doing his rah-rahs. I didn't get it.

But God was moving and he would perfect things. In time.

DAVID LOVED TO TALK about demons. No one else ever saw them, but David saw them all the time.

"Man, I had a scary experience with a demon yesterday."

"I saw a demon on Mr. Carno's desk."

"She has a demon. Sometimes I can see it looking out through her eyes."

"Last night a demon came right through the window and sat on my bedpost looking at me."

"There were two demons sitting up in that tree today. I think they're looking for somebody."

He'd point them out to me. He'd even draw them, and he was so casual about it. I would have been scared spitless, but he just gave us a daily update as calmly as reporting the weather. I was present at a meal when he told his folks about another incident, but they only listened, praised the Lord, and went on eating.

I finally figured it was his unique gift from the Lord, the discerning of spirits. I wasn't sure what good it was doing him or any of us, but I still had much to learn.

ANDY SMITH KEPT RUNNING HIS CAR on empty in full assurance and faith that the Lord would multiply his mileage. I had to bring him a can of gas a few times so he could get his car off the highway and to a gas station. I guess that made me the tool in God's hands to honor Andy's faith. Well, it worked. He got some gas out of the deal.

Karla converted about twenty kids in just one day. All they had to do, she told them, was say "Jesus" out loud, and they would be calling on the name of the Lord, and that meant they would be saved. What could be easier?

Mrs. Kenyon had a friend, Mrs. Bannister, who began to frequent our meetings and even take leadership. Mrs. Bannister was a normal-looking homemaker in tennis shoes, but she was also a prophetess, just like in the Book of Acts, and could tell you God's answer to most any question. Bernadette asked if she should continue going with some non-Christian guy named Barry, and Mrs. Bannister said it was the Lord's will, because Bernadette would win him to the Lord and they would further his kingdom together. Clay asked her if he would pass his U.S. Government final, and she said he would, and he did. One evening, Mrs. Bannister addressed the whole smoking issue by telling us about the vision she'd had regarding Mrs. Kenyon's cigarette habit, the vision of the garden full of weeds with the big cigarette growing in the middle. It made me wonder which lady actually had the vision, but I didn't push it. *Somebody* had the vision, and that was good enough for me. On another evening, Mrs. Bannister laid hands on Mr. Kenyon and appointed him bishop of the island. She didn't say what that was supposed to mean or what Mr. Kenyon was supposed to do, but okay. He was bishop of the island.

The Kenyons and Bannisters would often visit a large church in Seattle to pick up new ideas on prayer, praise, and gifts of the Spirit, but neither family was regularly committed to any church. They met with other adults on Sunday mornings, either in their home or over at the Bannisters' place, and the meetings were much the same as the ones on Wednesdays. It was a whole new concept for me.

Their way of dealing with problems was a new concept as well. Once a doctrinal conflict flared up at a Wednesday meeting—the old dispute between "once saved, always saved," and "stay holy or else." A newcomer from the "stay holy or else" camp started arguing that we'd better get holy or God would deal with us. I was from a strict Pentecostal background, so he made sense to me. Considering the smoking, crusty language, and romantic indulgences going on in the group, I was glad he'd brought it up.

We did not discuss the matter. Neither Mrs. Kenyon nor Mrs. Bannister would allow it. Instead, the two ladies broke into their heavenly languages, encouraged us to do the same, and filibustered in the Spirit until the problem went away—specifically, the new-comer let it go, held his peace, and never came back. I can't say he would have felt welcome if he did.

Praise was the answer. Moving in the Spirit. Praying in our heavenly languages. Through these things, God would perfect us.

God had a plan, and we were at the center of it. As for the rest of the churches on the island, they'd better get on board or fall behind.

But there was an enemy, lurking outside the walls of the Kenyon home, just beyond the safe cocoon of our joy. A Question kept occurring to me, but I dared not speak it, perhaps for fear that even Mrs. Bannister wouldn't have an answer. I know I turned away from it, blaming the very thought of it on the devil. God would perfect this too, I kept telling myself. God will speak, and move, and someone will come up with something. Until then, don't talk about it. Don't let it in.

But I could hear the Question rapping at the windows, scratching at the door, constantly whispering, "I'm still here."

It lived out in the everyday world where cars break down, children fall from their bicycles, and parents get into fights.

It hovered behind the big plastic jar on the checkout counter at the grocery store, the jar with the slot in top and all the small bills and change inside. Atop the jar was a small sign asking for help and a photo of a little girl with crutches and braces on her legs.

It leaped at me mockingly from between the lines as I heard about a school chum's mother: She had brain cancer and the doctors didn't expect her to live.

It rode on the wheelchair of Tim Ford, a young man at our church with multiple sclerosis. His parents had taken him to traveling healers and miracle evangelists, but still he could not walk. They requested prayer for his healing so often that their request should have earned a permanent slot in the printed order of the service. Tim was sixteen now and virtually helpless, and they could not rest, could not feel complete until God answered their prayers.

One Sunday morning, while the people sang the hymns, the pastor gave the announcements, and the church service plodded along at its customary cadence, I sat quietly in my pew, oblivious to it all, secretly laboring over the Question.

Must this be? What was still broken, still wrong with this world God had made? What were we leaving undone? How could this enemy, this pain and suffering and sickness still be hanging around when God was so powerful and his work so complete?

Maybe it was our fault. Christians today were spoiled from materialism and having it easy. We had no faith. If we truly had faith, we wouldn't be such helpless victims in an imperfect world. God could work through us to change things. We could be victorious.

Help me to have faith, I prayed. *Dear Lord, help my unbelief.*

A thought flashed through my mind.

Huh? What was that? Run that by me again.

The pastor's lips were moving, but I didn't hear his words. I was having a revelation. Of course God wanted to change things. It was God who was troubling my spirit right now, letting the Question nag at me. He was trying to get through to me, shake me up, and get me seeking his face for a resolution. He wanted me to do something about it.

Hope began to swell within me. Maybe this was God's plan all along. Maybe God was granting me a heart of compassion for the suffering so I could do something about it.

I looked down at my hands. *They shall lay hands on the sick, and they shall recover.*

I determined at that moment that I would begin a fast. I would pray, fast, and seek God.

I had just turned eighteen, and things can develop quickly when you're young. I began my fast on Sunday, and by Tuesday, I'd heard from God and could eat again. I had the gift of healing. I believed it, and that was all there was to it. *By his stripes we are healed. They shall lay hands on the sick and they shall recover. The prayer of faith will save the sick and the Lord will raise him up.* This was my world now. This was my life, my truth, my calling. When I passed by the plastic jar in the grocery store with the picture of the little girl in braces, I thought, *No more. It won't have to be this way.* I laid a hand on that jar and silently prayed for that child, allowing myself to think and believe nothing other than the child would be healed, right then and there.

I saw an older man out in the parking lot of the store, coughing violently as he tried to climb into his truck. *I could lay hands on him*, I thought. *I could heal him.* I was immediately timid and nervous. Instead, I prayed for him silently, remotely. God would hear my prayer.

I thought of the hospitals that would no longer be needed and the crutches that could be burned. I thought of the wondrous revival that would sweep the island and then the rest of the country because God was going to fix that one thing still wrong with the world.

It was such a wonderful hope, such a giddy elation. I was looking forward to Wednesday night.

At the Kenyons' on Wednesday night, we sang our songs, praised the Lord in a noisy, joyous circle, and then had our time of sharing.

Clay shared about a friend he'd been witnessing to who was still holding back, but God was working on him. The ferry dock hill was icy, but Clay prayed for his car while his friend watched, and then Clay made it up the hill. The skeptic friend tried it and his car came to a pitiful, wheel-spinning stop only halfway up. We laughed, cheered, and praised the Lord for such a direct demonstration of his power.

Amber had been witnessing to her friend Liz, and tonight Liz was there to observe. Mrs. Kenyon emphasized how getting high on Jesus was better than any drugs, and if there was any doubt in Liz's mind, she should just try it. "Instead of LSD, try some PTL," she said, and we all laughed.

I raised my hand, and then shared my journey of the past several days, how I'd been chased by the big, ugly Question until I finally confronted it in church on Sunday. I shared the illumination I received, the knowledge from the Spirit that God was speaking to me, shaking me up, giving me a heart for the sick and suffering. Then, feeling humbled by it all, and trembling a bit from nervousness, I said, "I think God has given me the gift of healing."

"Praise the Lord!" said Mrs. Kenyon as praises, sighs of joy, and claps went around the room. I could see in their faces that they had wondered about the Question also.

Andy spoke up. "I'd like healing. I've had diabetes since I was a little kid."

I sat there, not sure what to do. Clay exclaimed, "Step right up!" and put his chair out in the middle of the room as everyone cheered.

With anticipation, and maybe a little bit of sheepishness, Andy rose, went to the chair, and sat down. The others gathered around as I took my place directly in front of Andy.

This was it. I knew I had faith.

A doubt sneaked up on me.

No, go away. No doubt, no doubt. Only believe. God has spoken to me. I've hashed it all out with him, and he has called me to pray for the sick. *By his stripes we are healed. The effective, fervent prayer of a righteous man can avail much.*

The prayers, praises, and tongues began and I joined in, preparing myself, working out the doubt, working up the faith.

"And now," I said loudly, and all the prayer and praise fell to a low buzz of anticipation. I placed my hands on either side of Andy's head and spoke my prayer with authority, "we come against this diabetes in the name of Jesus. Andy, in the name of Jesus, be healed!"

And then I started to shake. I didn't know if it was I doing it or the Lord, but my arms were twitching and quivering as I held onto Andy's head. The kids around me were getting excited. Andy sat there with his eyes closed in prayer, his hands clasped in his lap. The praise raised in intensity. Hands went up. Tongues started rolling. Clay agreed with me aloud, not asking, but *demanding* healing in the name of Jesus. This went on, then it went on some more, and I just kept shaking. Finally, when we all felt we'd done enough, our prayers subsided, the noise died down, and we rested. I removed my hands and opened my eyes.

Andy sat there motionless, dazed, staring ahead. Nobody said a word.

"You okay, Andy?" Bernadette asked.

He didn't answer. He only got up slowly, shakily, and returned to his seat.

Everyone had a strong impression that something had happened. Bernadette put an arm around him. David patted him on the shoulder and said, "You're healed, buddy. You're going to be all right!"

"Let's thank the Lord," said Mrs. Kenyon, and we praised him again.

Karla spoke up. "I'd like prayer for my eyes. I'm nearsighted and I hate having to wear these stupid glasses."

"Get up there," said Amber, indicating the chair in the center of the room, the "hot seat."

I laid my hands on Karla's head and we did the whole thing again, shaking, praising, praying, demanding, and ordering that nearsightedness out of her. When we were finished, Karla took her place again, and removed her glasses. No one asked her how things looked. A song started and we all sang. I sat down, strangely glad it was over.

But I did hear Karla tell Amber that nothing had changed.

"Just give it time," said Amber. "God will accomplish it."

7

Round and round, round and round, water sloshing, suds swirling, a steady rhythm of *gush, hiss, gush, hiss, gush, hiss.* It wasn't that boring a show, Norman Dillard thought, especially if you placed bets on which garment would flop against the glass on the next tumble, the red shirt or the pair of jeans. Sitting here in the laundromat was actually a welcome break. The motel had been so busy over the weekend that he and Mona had to take turns sleeping and eating to handle the flow of guests and the calls from those still coming. Mona was running the motel's washing machines full time to handle the used linens from all—that's right, *all*—ten rooms.

So here Norman sat, enjoying a little escape on a Monday morning, watching his and Mona's clothes tumble round and round. As far back as he could remember, he'd never been squeezed out of his own washing machines. It was a nice problem to have.

And this time it'll be the jeans—come on, baby, come on, let's see those jeans—Yes! We have a winner!

He was thinking about the sightings, the pilgrims, the clouds, and the faces everywhere, all the craziness of it. It made him sigh and give his head a little wag. Why couldn't it have been UFOs and ETs, some *real* sightings, and *real* contacts? That would have been exciting—and believable too. Religious stuff was hard to get excited about when he didn't believe it.

Well, that doesn't matter, he reminded himself. *What matters is business.*

The motel needed a whole new paint job, some upgrades on the plumbing, some rewiring. The sign out front needed several bulbs replaced. The grounds needed grooming, planting, and fertilizing. The rooms—oh, those poor, pitiful rooms!—needed new wallpaper, carpets, fixtures, *everything.* All of this stuff was important if he was going to attract guests, but the bank saw no future for a motel in a town like Antioch, and there had never been enough guests to pay for the improvements so he could attract more guests.

But now things were different. People were coming to see Jesus in the clouds and in the hedges, and even in the mildew on the shower tiles.

Norman laughed, slapping his knee. As silly as it was, it was sweet, wonderful business. He'd waited a long time for this.

There went the jeans again, flopping past the glass, right past the face of Jesus.

Norman froze.

He couldn't really be seeing this. He leaned forward, staring at the glass porthole on the front of the machine. The clothes and suds inside were still tumbling over and over, but the face remained on the glass, looking at him. He could see dark hair parted down the middle and falling almost to the shoulders; a beard; a white tunic. He'd seen pictures. He knew the standard configuration.

Hypnotic suggestion, he thought. *All this talk around town is getting to me.*

He leaned to the left, watching his own countenance move to the left and then pass in front of the Jesus-face, obscuring it. It was a reflection of something behind him!

He jumped up quickly and nearly knocked over his chair.

A man stood there, leaning on a row of toploading washers, smiling back at him. With his hair, his beard, and that loose-fitting, long-sleeved, open-necked white shirt, he was a dead ringer for—

Norman got over his shock, and then he started laughing. "Ohhhh man! Oh man, that was good!"

The man laughed too, almost as loudly as Norman, showing a pearly white grin.

Norman felt he'd better explain. "You know what's been going on around here, right?"

"Oh yeah." The man nodded.

Norman pointed at the washing machine. "I was watching my laundry, and all of a sudden I see your face in the glass—" He burst out laughing again and could hardly finish the sentence. "And I thought, you know . . . hey, has anybody ever told you you look just like Jesus?"

"I've been told that."

"Oh man, you had me going. *You had me going!*" He wiped tears from his eyes. "Wait'll I tell Mona."

The man wiggled his index finger in Norman's direction. "Nice glasses."

"Huh?"

"The glasses. Nice glasses."

Norman sneered. "Yeah, for Boy Scouts starting fires. My eyes aren't very good."

"May I see them?"

Norman took them off and the world became a blur, the man by the washers a dark-topped smudge above a smudge of white. He extended the glasses, and saw the smudge reach out to take them. Their hands touched. There was a tingle.

Norman stumbled. "Oops!" He put out his hand to catch himself. He blinked.

His hand was perfectly clear, as was the chair he was leaning on. Had he put his glasses on? He looked up. He could make out every detail of the man's face, every hair of his beard, the depth of the dark brown eyes.

And the man who looked like Jesus was holding Norman's glasses. "Can you see okay?"

Norman looked, and saw, and replied with wonder, "Yeah."

"Good." The man folded Norman's glasses, set them on a washer, and turned for the door.

"Hey, wait. What did you do? How'd you do that?"

The man only looked back once, smiled, and gave Norman a little wave. Then he went out the door and was gone.

Norman blinked several times, then rubbed his eyes. What had happened? What was this? He looked up and could read the instructions on the washing machine. He could clearly make out the reverse-painted hours on the glass of the front door. What was the trick? He felt all over his face for some kind of device. Nothing.

He reached for his glasses, unfolded them, and put them on. The prescription was so strong and the image so distorted it made his eyes water. He took them off and the world was crystal clear again.

Jesus, he thought, not swearing. *Jesus*.

He'd read the paper. He knew what the "angels" had been saying. Had it really happened? Was this a sighting like the others?

No. It was more than that. A lot more. *If* it had really happened.

He looked every direction, gawking at what he could see with no lenses before his eyes. The prices on the wall, the selections in the candy machine, the pattern of the linoleum. Old Mrs. Tobin came in, her same crabby self, and found his stare offensive. "What are you gawking at?"

"You look beautiful!" he exclaimed.

"Yeah, well put your glasses on!"

He giggled with glee. "They *are* on! I mean, it's like they're on but they aren't! I can see you! I can see everything! It's a miracle, that's what it is!"

She put out her hand. "Stay away from me."

He ran to the door and burst out of the building. The whole, beautiful, clear-as-a-bell town of Antioch lay before him. He clasped his hands to the sides of his head, crazy with joy and amazement. He was staggering, stumbling, turning in every direction. He could read anything and everything. *VCRs repaired. Main Street, 200. In loving memory of John Nathan Anderson, husband, father, and friend. No parking within twenty feet. Kiley's Hardware.* Hey! His friend, Matt Kiley!

Matt had to see this! *What am I talking about Matt seeing this! I'm the one who can see! This is incredible!*

He ran across the street and burst through the door. "Matt! Matt, you won't believe it! I can see! I can *see!*"

MATT WAS STANDING behind the counter, his hands resting gently on the cash register to steady himself. He was trembling, gasping in shock and disbelief, his eyes darting everywhere. A few feet away, his wheelchair stood empty.

Bev Parsons, an employee, came out of aisle two with a question. "Matt, we don't have enough—" Her hand flew over her mouth.

Norman touched Matt's shoulder. "You—you're—" He stopped. "He was here, wasn't he? You saw him."

Matt just nodded. "Yeah. Yeah. A guy with long hair and a beard."

Norman squealed, his face red with excitement. "It was Jesus!"

"Jesus . . ." Bev whispered in shock.

Matt scowled. "You're crazy."

"You're *standing!* Get a clue!"

"I'm standing," Matt admitted.

"You're . . . standing." Now Bev's hand was over her heart.

"What'd he do, what'd he do?" Norman urged.

Matt lifted one hand from the counter. His legs were steady under him. He reached toward the shelves behind him, reenacting the event as he described it. "He came up here, and told me he wanted a screwdriver set—you know, these little jeweler's screwdrivers—"

"Yeah? Yeah?"

"I said, 'Go ahead and grab one and I'll ring you up,' and he said, 'Grab 'em yourself,' and then he poked me with his finger."

Norman slapped the counter.

"And I did," said Matt. "I wasn't thinking, you know . . ." He was recovering from his shock. His voice was getting strong. He was beginning to believe it. "I stood up. I got up out of the wheelchair and I grabbed the screwdrivers!" By now he shouted it. "I grabbed the screwdrivers! I grabbed 'em!"

Norman shook Matt by both shoulders. "Look at me, Matt! You see any glasses? You see any? No glasses, Matt! I can see! I can see everything!" His eyes fell on a pen on the counter. "Pilot Precise V7 Fine Rolling Ball! See that? I can read it right where it is!" Then it occurred to him. "Where'd he go?"

Matt looked around. "I don't know." He looked at Bev. She just shook her head, still staring.

Norman was desperate. "Where'd he go? Which way?"

Matt shrugged. "I don't know. He paid for the screwdrivers and he left."

"Come on, we gotta find him!"

Matt looked at the floor stretched out so far below him.

"Come on, you can walk!"

Matt put his hand on the counter and extended his right foot. It came to rest a short step away. Yeah. Sure. He remembered what this felt like. He'd done it before. He could do it.

He did it. First another step, then another, then two more, and then he was walking, around the counter, out into the store, past the rakes and line trimmers, past the stacks of lawn fertilizer. By now he was jumping a little, flexing his knees. He danced a little jig and Norman went crazy.

They bolted out of the store, Norman reading every sign he saw, Matt hopping, skipping, turning circles, the two of them laughing like idiots.

They encountered a stranger and his wife. Both had cameras.

"Have you seen Jesus around?" Norman pleaded.

Their eyes got wide. "No," said the man. "Have you seen him?"

Matt and Norman looked at each other. They started laughing and Matt started dancing. "Oooooh, *have* we!" said Norman.

AT THE FORDYCE HOME, Meg heard Sally answer the phone, gasp, squeal some unintelligible questions, gasp some more, and then run out the front door. It happened so suddenly and loudly that it scared Meg. She ran into the living room and found the receiver dangling off the table and the front door still open.

Something terrible must be happening, she thought. "Sally?" By the time she got to the front door, Sally was in the car and pulling out onto Highway 9, headed for Antioch. *"Sally!"*

A WILDFIRE HAD BEGUN in Antioch. The first spark ignited in the laundromat, then spread to Kiley's Hardware and from there into the street. First two visitors heard, then four more, then three customers at Anderson's Furniture and Appliance. Norman waved down a carload of visitors from Moses Lake and told them. Then the pilgrims at Our Lady's heard about it, followed by the cloud watchers who presently had no clouds to watch. Pagers began beeping, phones began ringing, and up and down the street, through the storefronts, and back into the neighborhoods, the fire spread: *He has been seen. Have you seen him? Where is he?*

Brett Henchle got the call he'd been wanting ever since this weird stuff began. Jesus had shown up at Kiley's Hardware, the caller said. *Yeah,* Brett thought. *It's him, the guy I'm looking for, my little angelic huckster.* He switched on his siren and flashers and got over there.

From where Brett parked, Matt's store looked like a stirred-up hornet's nest. People in tight little clusters were squeezing past each other as they came and went through the front door. More were arriving from across the street, up the highway in both directions, and from the quiet neighborhood behind. And just as many were leaving, eager to fan out in all directions and spread the news, whatever it was. They were agitated, talking excitedly, creating a constant buzz in front of the building.

Brett got out of the car, nervously checked his handcuffs, and felt for his gun. Then he crossed the street. Those on the fringes greeted him, "Have you heard? Have you heard?"

"Everybody take it easy," he cautioned, putting just enough edge in his voice to let them know there would be no unruliness today. "Excuse me, please," he said, and worked his way through the door and into the store.

He'd never seen so many people in Matt's store at one time, not even during the big Christmas Open House. The front of the store was packed, but no one was shopping. Some he knew, some were strangers. All were excited and chattering. Cameras were flashing, camcorders were blinking their little red lights. He could hear Sally Fordyce whining from somewhere in the crowd, "You don't understand! He's come here for *me!* We have an appointment!"

"He's come here for all of us," someone responded, and everyone wanted to know, *Where is he?*

"Let's get organized and start searching," one man suggested.

Finally, Brett could see Matt through the crowd, standing by the checkout counter, answering questions and looking wide-eyed.

Hold on. Matt was standing?

"Brett, have you heard?" said Don Anderson.

Brett was staring at Matt when he replied, "Tell me."

Jack McKinstry told him secondhand, then Norman told him almost secondhand, prefacing it with his firsthand account of what happened in the laundromat. When Brett finally made his way up to Matt Kiley, Matt saw him coming, stepped out from the counter, and did a little jig. The crowd went crazy.

Matt told Brett his story. He'd shared it countless times by now, but it hadn't gotten old and he hadn't gotten tired of it. Neither had the visitors pressing in close to hear it again.

As Brett listened, he almost felt foolish coming in here as a cop with handcuffs and a gun. Just moments ago, he was on a case, hoping for a lead in catching the hitchhiking con man. Now, as he heard Matt Kiley's account and saw him standing, even dancing, the hitchhiker's words took on a whole new meaning. Brett remembered them clearly, and now had to steady himself against the counter as he muttered, "My God. . . ."

"Yes, exactly!" several responded.

By now Sally was crying. "You don't understand . . . I need him. . . ."

JIM BAYLOR was an ex-marine in his forties with a crew cut he'd kept ever since boot camp and a low, growly voice befitting a former drill sergeant. He wasn't a tall man, but he was built like a solid, immovable rock and had a personality to match. Right now he was a surveyor, but he'd been several other things over the years: draftsman, carpenter, mechanic, plumber, electrician, painter, oil well worker. His garage workshop was worth visiting because he still had every tool he'd ever used in all those trades. He could build a house with the carpentry tools that hung on the wall. He could fix any vehicle with the automotive tools and specialized gizmos he kept on the workbench and in a big red metal cabinet on wheels—things like a wheel puller, a spring compressor, and a spark plug wire puller. In case anyone in Antioch needed an oil well fixed, he still had adjustable wrenches big enough to turn a tree. If nothing else, he could tell you how long, wide, tall, or deep something was because he always carried a twenty-five-foot Stanley tape measure clipped to his belt.

Jim was a hunter who stuffed his own trophies and had a room full of them. He was a storyteller who could share his marine, hunting, building, plumbing, and Alaskan oil adventures for hours, never raising his voice but keeping you enthralled from beginning to end. He enjoyed his friends, liked to get involved in projects that helped others, and wasn't much of a whiner. He was a reasonable, logical kind of guy.

And he was married to Dee Baylor.

As near as I can recall his account, he first met Dee when she was tending bar at a tavern near the marine base. She was as crusty and feisty as he was in those days and could hold her own in any stare-down or shouting match with any grunt or officer, she didn't care. She won Jim's heart by showing an interest in him to the exclusion of every other man who'd come through the place— something he took as a real compliment. He always liked her because, though he could scare most anyone else, he couldn't scare her. They were right for each other.

He insisted they still were. He loved her. But I could tell by the way he kept finding excuses to come over and talk—well, work on something and talk while we were at it—that he was troubled and perplexed.

Today the excuse was the shelves I wanted to hang in the bedroom. I needed more space for books, I had a small aquarium I wanted to put back into service, and I still had a portable CD player sitting on the floor. My landlord was going to deduct the cost from my rent, so I went for the idea. So did Jim. All I had to do was mention those shelves and he made plans to come over.

So we worked, finding studs, drilling holes, setting molly screws, and hanging shelves, and as we worked, we talked.

"Kinda glad the weather's cleared up," he said, sweeping my newly purchased stud finder along the wall. "At least now I get to see more of her." He looked at me suddenly, as if he'd said something amiss. "No offense, now, right, Travis?"

"No, no offense."

"I mean, Christianity's fine, I've got nothing against it. We've talked about that."

"Sure."

"And I didn't say anything when she started speaking in tongues over our dinner every night. I didn't want to get in her way if it meant so much to her." He found the stud and made a small pencil mark on the wall. "And when she started dancing and whirling around, I didn't say anything. She doesn't do it at home that much, so I don't have to worry about my floor joists. I, uh . . ." His voice trailed off and he drilled some holes.

"Yeah?" I prodded.

"I think maybe this cloud thing might be better for her. She might be getting—don't tell her I said this—she might be getting too old and too heavy to be falling down all the time. You ought to see the bruises she used to come home with." He added quickly, "Now I know it wasn't *you* knocking her down."

"No, it wasn't me." All I ever did was pray for her, usually during our Sunday morning service, often at midweek Bible study. She might have a cold, need some guidance from the Lord, or just need a refreshing in the Spirit. It didn't matter. Whenever I took her hand or rested my hand on her head to pray for her, I wouldn't get out more than one or two sentences before my hand would be touching thin air and she would be on her way to the floor, "slain in the Spirit." Sometimes a friend would be there to catch her and at least soften her landing. Sometimes she'd go over with nothing but the floor to stop her and you could hear her bones hitting the hardwood. Nothing could stop her. I once asked her not to fall down, but she went down anyway, unable to resist the power of God. The rest of the congregation had gotten fairly used to it—sometimes the ushers would just step over her when they had to collect the offering—but it often seemed a little weird to new visitors. Adrian Folsom fell occasionally, especially if Dee fell first; Blanche never did. Anyway, I knew better than to think it was from any great anointing on my part.

Jim threw up one hand in resignation. "She said it was God that knocked her over."

"That could be." It was a safe thing to say. I wasn't one to limit God, but right now I had a real *attitude* about the subject, so I had to be careful.

"But now she's watching the clouds and that's better. The worst she can get is a kink in her neck. Have you met that new pastor yet?"

"Kyle Sherman?"

"Yeah."

"We've met."

"What do you think of him?"

I had to skip over the first thoughts that came to mind and find some nicer ones. "He's young, but he's honest and means well. I think he'll be all right."

"Haven't met him yet, but I know I'm going to. One of these days he's going to be knocking on my door, trying to rope me in." We were ready to hang a shelf on the newly installed brackets. We each took one end and lifted it into place. Nice fit. "I've already got my wife leaving me little notes and Scripture verses on the fridge and the bathroom mirror. But if she thinks I'm going to start talking in Chinese and dancing around and falling on the floor, she's got another think coming."

"How about watching the clouds?"

He threatened me with his hammer, and we laughed.

"Did I ever tell you about Al Sutter's combine?" he asked.

"You were going to."

He launched into a tale about Al Sutter's nephew trying to run Al's thirty-year-old combine, and then we talked about a Cadillac he was thinking of restoring. The gospel came up again after that, with a few questions about Jesus and whether he ever went fishing, which got us on the subject of fishing, which led to the fish and game laws, which led to some political discussion, which got us back to religion again, somehow. This was Jim's way, like putting cream and sugar in a cup of coffee, and it worked for both of us. As long as we kept the serious subjects mixed in with easier ones and had some work to do, we felt comfortable and got along fine. By the time he left that afternoon, we both felt a little better and I had a beautiful new set of shelves.

And then the phone rang.

"Hello?"

The voice was familiar, but quiet, subtle. "I hope I'm not disturbing you. I waited until your guest left."

I could feel a tease in that last sentence, as if he wanted me to look around and wonder where he was. I didn't bite. "You didn't finish mowing John's lawn."

"Tell him to be patient. I'll get around to it next time."

I sat on the couch, taking only a quick sideways glance out the window. I didn't see him, but that didn't surprise me. "I suppose you know what's been going on in town these last few days."

"It's been exciting. I've enjoyed it."

"And I take it you're the one responsible."

He chuckled. "Hey, I'll take credit for some of it, but people seeing my face in the mildew of a shower or a hedge, that's absurd."

"What about the clouds?"

"No, no, that's passé. It's been done."

"Well, hasn't there been a weeping crucifix before?"

"Mm. Not that many. But it got their attention, didn't it?"

"Oh yeah. You made it on the evening news."

"So I got what I wanted. We've created a buzz, as they say." He seemed rather tickled with himself. "But what are you thinking, Travis? Are you getting the point?"

I fidgeted and shifted the receiver to my other ear. "I didn't know there was a point."

"People need results. They need to see something. You know how it was: 'Show us a sign so we can believe in you.' Give the people what they want and they'll show up."

I dug deep for some patience. "Doesn't it bother you that I have no idea who you are or why you're even calling me?"

He ignored me. "Be honest, Travis. Are you so much different from them? Haven't you ever felt the way they do? Haven't you ever wished I'd just do what you ask and not keep you guessing and waiting and wondering? Up until now you've never even seen me. I wonder if that's fair."

"You can quit the masquerade. You're not Jesus and you know it."

He paused just a moment, and then I could hear him stifling a little laugh, probably smiling. "Humor me, Travis, just for the sake of argument. You expected a lot from me when you were younger, remember? You thought I'd heal Andy and Karla. You thought I'd get you out of the shipyard. You thought I'd bring Amber back to you. You even thought I'd given you signs and prophecies, remember?"

If he was trying to scare me, he was succeeding. I had no words as I groped my memory for any clue about this man, any time or place I may have known him before.

"Travis, that's okay, don't worry about it. I'm only making a point. You expected a lot from me and I disappointed you. That's part of what you're dealing with, isn't it?"

"That was a long time ago. I was just a kid."

"So what happened to Andy?"

I didn't answer.

He goaded me. "Traaaavis . . . What happened?"

I snapped at him. "You're God. You tell me!"

"Remember the next day at school, Travis? Remember his hands shaking? Remember how scared he was?"

I could still see Andy and Karla together, confronting me in the lunchroom. Andy had skipped his insulin that morning, and now he was reacting. They were asking me what they should do. Karla was still wearing her glasses.

I told them, "Just believe. Believe and you'll be healed."

We prayed together, trusting God.

That afternoon, Karla took Andy home for some insulin. He made it through okay.

The voice sounded soothing, as if trying to comfort me. "So you can't blame people for getting excited. I'm *doing* things, Travis. I'm actually making things happen. I've changed."

I'd been holding back the question because I knew he wouldn't answer it, but now there was no other thought or question available. "I want to know who you are."

He didn't answer it. "I healed Norman Dillard and Matt Kiley today."

This could have been good news, but not the teasing way he said it. "You did what?"

"I *healed* them, Travis." He dragged out the word *healed* as if he enjoyed making me hear it. "Just like I'm supposed to do. Norman can see without his glasses and Matt can walk. It's all over town by now. People are going nuts."

I just wasn't going to fall for this. "I'm going to call Matt and ask him."

"He isn't home right now. I think he's walking around town showing off."

"I'm calling him."

"You'll have to talk to Kyle Sherman first. He's about to call you. Talk to you soon."

Click. He was gone.

I kept the receiver in my hand as I pressed the button to hang up my end. Before I could release it, the phone rang.

"Hello?"

"Travis!" It was Kyle Sherman. "Have you heard about Norman Dillard and Matt Kiley?"

I didn't want to hear about it from Kyle, but I *did* want to hear about it. I finally said, "Tell me."

He told me every detail. Apparently the town was still in an uproar and Matt really was taking a walk around the town to show off. "Norman and Matt say Jesus did it. They say he's in town, Travis. Remember what you said at the ministerial meeting? Well, it's happened."

I sat there, not a word coming to mind.

"What do you make of it?"

"Uh, I don't know, Kyle. I have to think about it." But what *could* I think about the man who mowed half of John Billings's lawn, called me after Jim Baylor had left, and knew all about Andy and Karla? "Did you see Matt yourself? Can he really walk?"

"Yes, Travis. He can really walk. He's healed. And Norman can read things far away without his glasses."

I just couldn't get into a conversation with Kyle Sherman. Not about this.

"This isn't Jesus, Travis! You know that!"

I kept silent.

"Hello?"

"I'm here. I'm thinking."

"What's to think about? We have to *do* something! We have to pray this thing into the open and come against it— "

"I said I have to think about it!"

Kyle heard the edge in my voice and backed off a little. "Okay. You think about it. I'm going to pray about it."

"Talk to you later." I hung up.

But the truth was, I didn't *want* to think about it. I didn't want to admit that somehow the man on the hill, on the mower, on the phone, had invaded my life and plundered my memories. *My* memories!

The same memories that had all come back so vividly, so hauntingly, in recent days, welcome or not. . . .

8

DID I HAVE FAITH when I prayed for Andy? I thought I did.
Andy got his insulin and pulled through okay. But he felt discouraged—not because he hadn't been healed, but because going
home and injecting himself seemed like a cop-out, a surrender to
doubt, a lack of trust in God. Somehow, he thought, it had to be
his fault that the healing had not happened.

I was upset as well, and for a short, awkward time, we tried to
do some spiritual troubleshooting.

If *I* had faith, maybe *Andy* didn't have enough faith when I
prayed. He was pretty sure he did, although he was feeling a little
uncomfortable at the time, and that might have jammed the signals somehow.

How about sin in our lives? That could mess things up for sure.
I kept confessing everything I could think of and then started
wondering if Andy was still hiding something. Nothing dramatic
happened, even with more fasting.

Did we still have ongoing faith for his healing, or were we
doubting? I was sure I had faith and did all I could to stay sure.
"We need to pray this through and believe," I said. "God is testing us, seeing if we really trust him. We have to hold onto the
promise!"

That didn't make it any easier for Andy. He was the one need-ing the insulin, risking death if he didn't get it, and feeling guilty every time he did. Besides that, his parents did not have the spiri-tual insight that we had, and told him he'd better stay on his insulin or they would kill him before his diabetes had a chance to.

Amber suggested we should just give God more time to complete the healing, and that concept, being open-ended, turned out to be the most comfortable. We fell into it easily, naturally, and went on praising, praying, and believing God. We were still counting on miracles, still hearing and believing prophecies, still expecting great things.

But I never again laid hands on anyone for healing at a Kenyon–Bannister meeting. No one ever said I shouldn't, and I never heard anyone say they didn't believe in my gift. We just didn't talk about it. Without a word or a spoken agreement, we let the whole mat-ter slip beneath the surface where it remained, right alongside the Question.

Karla still wears glasses to this day. Andy died from complica-tions related to his diabetes in 1985.

I DID NOT ENJOY such memories, but hey, I'd already been la-boring over them for months, bearing the pain in an honest effort to sort them out. I didn't ask for, nor did I need, old what's-his-name stirring up the pile.

He had certainly managed to stir up the town. Although he had made no further appearances since the big Matt-and-Norman incident, folks kept right on believing and hanging onto their excitement. For Antioch, just the fact that people were ex-cited was exciting. The media remained interested, but started dropping a few hints here and there: Competition for a slot on the evening news was fierce. Whoever this guy was, he would have to show up soon and do something worthy of television's attention or the story would die.

Norman Dillard didn't want that to happen. Neither did Matt

Kiley, or Gary Fisk, who ran the Sundowner Motel on the other end of town. Jack McKinstry was hoping the flow of business through his grocery store would keep flowing, and Don Anderson had just stocked more cameras and camcorders in his appliance store.

As for the ministers in town, I think they were mainly concerned with helping the Ship of Church maintain an even keel.

Bob Fisher, the Baptist, was busy with the Fudd Revival, and that occupied his mind until it was over. Afterward, Bob kept his Bible open, admonished his congregation to do the same, and warned everyone not to stray from that which was written.

Burton Eddy, the Presbyterian, made a veiled reference to the situation in a sermon entitled "What Hath God Wrought," in which he extolled God's lofty and unsearchable ways, whatever we might conceive them to be.

The crowds at Our Lady's spoke loudly enough for Father Vendetti. He had nothing to add, at least for the time being.

Sid Maher, the Lutheran, said absolutely nothing about it.

Morgan Elliott, the Methodist, stayed out of the discussion as well.

Paul Daley, Howard Munson, and Andy Barker could have been out of town for all the feedback we got from them.

Mostly, what Antioch got from its ministers was business as usual and apart from that, silence. I figured they were waiting to see what might develop before taking a position.

All except for Kyle, of course. He was still working on his position, but he kept nothing inside during the process: The sightings, the miracles, and the mysterious visitor were most likely the work of Satan, he said, and the folks in his church—the whole town, for that matter—needed to wake up.

As for me, I was hiding.

"TRAV, I like how the house looks, just in case you wondered."

Rene and I were in my kitchen. I was sitting in a chair with a sheet draped around my neck and shoulders, and she was behind me with her comb and scissors, attempting to make her brother look more presentable.

"Well, thank you," I replied, and let it go at that. But I was glad she had noticed. I'd been putting things away a little at a time for the last several days and I was finally getting ahead of the mess.

"How long are you going to keep screening your calls?"

Sharp gal, as always. "How did you know I was screening my calls?"

"Because I got through but Kyle didn't."

I started to turn my head but thought better of it. She had the scissors. "Don't tell me he called *you!*"

"Simmer down. I didn't mind."

"So what did he have to say?"

She kept on combing and snipping as she talked. "Just wanted to tell me what was happening at the church. *Hold still!* Some of the people are really getting obsessed with the stuff going on in town. Dee Baylor's got a regular cloud-watching detail organized, and they're using the telephone prayer chain to keep everyone informed in case 'Jesus' shows up again. It's kind of like a revival except it isn't."

"Rene, *I'm* not the pastor anymore. Is Kyle aware of that?"

She kept pushing it, and I kept still and listened. "Some of the people are cautious and wondering if it's for real, and the rest of them—Kyle says about half—are siding with him. They think it's demonic. So there's a nice split developing."

This time I did fidget. "I don't want to hear any more about it."

She sighed with frustration. "I know how you feel about all this, but just for the record, Kyle's scared. He didn't say he was, but I could tell."

My throat tightened up—the first sign that my old stress was returning. "So what do you expect me to do?"

"Actually, I expect you to keep on hiding."

I was about to defend myself when she added, "That's what I'd do."

My throat relaxed. It was comforting to hear her say that, and a little unexpected. "You would?"

"It's church stuff, isn't it?"

I sat still and let her continue cutting my hair. I had to think for a moment before remembering that, within days of her turning eighteen, she had moved out of the house and stayed away from church for years.

"Yeah," I said at last. "It's church stuff. You were never into that kind of thing very much, were you?"

"Sure I was, a long time ago. When I was little, growing up in church, I believed everything I heard, everything that happened."

"But not anymore."

Snip. Snip. "I don't have to."

She came around the front to look at her work. "Okay, you're done." But then she put her hand on my shoulder. "Do you know what I mean by 'stuff'?"

I nodded. "It's becoming increasingly clear to me."

She smiled. "That's all it ever was. You know I never turned away from the Lord. It was just . . ." She shrugged. "All the *stuff.*"

I nodded, then smiled as I realized how much I was finally beginning to understand her. "Kind of like having the same old conversation so many times you just don't feel like having it again."

She kissed my forehead and helped me get out of the sheet. I helped her sweep up.

WE USED TO HAVE plenty of dull moments in Antioch. They would pass through town in close succession like box cars at a railroad crossing, each one displaced by the next, but all of them alike, their steady, monotonous pace never changing. Anymore, such dull moments were hard to find, thanks to our newest Visitor. He had a knack for spacing things precisely, keeping us all guessing, waiting until we were just about to have a tiny dull moment before throwing another firecracker into the hen house.

I'm certain he chose the time, place, and people for such events. Wednesday afternoon, he chose Mack's Sooper Market, Jack McKinstry, and Dee Baylor.

Dee was grocery shopping, pushing her cart along, crossing items off her list, and considering what she would fix for dinner that night. These were routine tasks, but today she found them difficult. With every nerve energized with expectation and her eyes alert for any sign anywhere of *him*, it was hard to concentrate on calcium-enriched orange juice and coupons for a special on frozen peas.

When Dee rolled her cart up to Jack's checkout, she paid little attention to the man in line ahead of her. Just a long-haired, hippie-looking guy. Humming quietly to herself, she began pawing through her cart and double-checking her shopping list.

And then a haunting suspicion crept into her mind, and she looked again.

The man was young, with a beard and black hair tied back in a ponytail. He was wearing a white, long-sleeved shirt. He had a dark complexion—he could have been Jewish. She stared, studying his face.

He was just paying for his groceries, counting out bills into Jack's hand, when he glanced at her and smiled. "Hello, Dee."

She lost all awareness that she was holding a can of beans and dropped it with a clatter into her cart. For a moment, she forgot to breathe. "Are—" She gasped. "Are you *him?*" All he did was look at her, and she began to tremble. "It *is* you!"

Jack saw her shaking and looking pale and obviously thought it might be something medical. "Mrs. Baylor? Are you all right?"

She pointed a finger at the man. "That's, that's *him!* He healed Norman Dillard's eyes, and healed Matt Kiley so he could walk!"

Jack eyed the man curiously.

The man just looked back and said with a casual shrug. "It was their faith that healed them. I just happened to be there."

Dee let out a little shriek. "It *was* you!"

Now Jack's eyes widened. "Was it? Was it you?" The man gave a little half-nod as if confessing. "Who are you?"

"I work for Ethyl Macon. I'm her new caretaker, handyman, cook, whatever. It's a nice job."

Dee approached him fearfully, as if drawing near to a god. "But who are you? Please tell me who you are!"

He looked deep into her eyes. "Those with open hearts and seeing eyes will know who I am, just as you do." He gently touched her shoulder and she felt a tingle like electricity. "See that you tell no one."

KAWUMP! She hit the floor.

JACK SCURRIED from behind the counter. "Mrs. Baylor! Mrs. Baylor!"

"I'll call for help," said the man, hurrying toward a pay phone by the front door.

"Use the phone by the cash register!" Jack shouted.

The man didn't seem to hear him. No matter. Jack knelt by Dee and felt her pulse.

Other shoppers gathered. "Did you see that? All he did was touch her!" "Is she breathing?" "Get her a pillow, somebody!"

Someone handed Jack a bag of corn chips and he placed it under her head. The crackling of the chips seemed to bring her around. She began to mutter in another language.

Jack looked up, anxious.

There was no one at either telephone. The man was gone.

Jack grabbed the telephone by his cash register and dialed 911—not just for the EMTs, but for the police.

Mary Donovan happened into the store. She was Catholic, a good friend of Dee's, and intervened immediately, kneeling and cradling Dee's head in her hands. "It's all right, everyone. She's okay. She's just slain in the Spirit. It's a God thing."

By the time Brett Henchle and Deputy Rod Stanton came storming into the store with the paramedics, Dee was sitting up and muttering like someone just returning from the threshold of heaven. "I saw him. He touched me, and I could feel his power . . . oh, you have no idea. . . ."

The paramedic checked her pulse.

"She's okay," Mary assured him. "It's just a God thing."

Brett nodded. "There's a lot of that going around."

"It was that guy!" said Jack. "The guy that healed Norman and Matt."

That got Brett's undivided attention. "Did he look like . . . ?"

Jack and Dee exchanged a quick look of agreement. Jack answered, "Sort of."

Dee put her hand to her forehead. "Oh, it was him, it was him. Glory, glory, glory!"

"So everybody's okay?" Brett asked, looking from one person to the next.

With help from Mary and the paramedic, Dee got to her feet. Now her adrenaline was starting to rush. "He's here, and now we know *where!*"

"Where?" Brett demanded.

Jack answered, "He said he's the new caretaker up at the Macon place."

"The widow? Up there alone with that guy? Rod, get some statements. I'm going up to see the widow."

"I'm going with you!" said Dee.

"No you're not!" said Brett as he went out the door.

Dee and Mary looked at each other. "Oh yes we are!" they both said together.

MY ANSWERING MACHINE went through its "leave a message" routine and then I heard Kyle's voice. "Travis! If you're there, *please* pick up the phone!" He kept talking a mile a minute, telling me all about the Sooper Market encounter. I listened, debating whether to pick up the phone until he said, "I'm going to follow Brett Henchle up there and see who in the world—"

I picked up the phone. "Kyle!"

"Travis! They've just seen the false christ at Mack's—"

"I heard."

"Already?"

"No, I heard you on the answering machine. Kyle, don't go up there. Stay out of it."

"He's working for Mrs. Macon. Dee Baylor and Brett Henchle and some others are heading up there right now. I just saw Nancy Barrons drive by."

"Oh brother . . ."

"Somebody needs to be there to confront—"

"NO! Don't go up there." Somehow, I had to keep from saying, *Kyle, I'm afraid you're going to do something really stupid.* "Let Brett do his job and you stay out of it."

"But Brett isn't a Christian. He doesn't have any spiritual discernment—"

"Kyle! If you don't want my advice, why did you call me?" He finally put the brakes on. "It's going to be a circus up there and you don't want to be a part of whatever stupid thing happens. And you don't want to be part of a vigilante committee either."

I could tell he didn't like my terminology. "What do you mean, a vigilante committee?"

"A preacher and a cop, the church and state, on Mrs. Macon's front porch! How's that going to look, especially if Nancy puts a picture in the paper?"

"But we have to do something. We can't just let—"

"Kyle, listen to me. This guy knows what he's doing. That whole thing in the grocery store was planned. He knows who's going up there to see him and he's ready. It's his game. Trust me." Kyle hesitated, then asked curiously, "How do you know all that?"

All I told him was, "I've seen it before."

IT WAS LIKE A MINIPARADE on the open highway, a short little chain of cars moving together, up and down the gentle rises of prairie, never breaking formation. Brett was in the lead in his squad car, followed by Nancy Barrons in her Volvo. Behind Nancy was a Plymouth Voyager carrying Dee Baylor, Adrian Folsom, Blanche Davis, and Mary Donovan. A television crew from Spokane happened to be in town when the word got out, so they were bringing up the rear in their van with the big station logo on the side.

Nancy Barrons knew where the ranch was, but had never been there. Cephus Macon was a very private man when alive, and after his death his widow remained reclusive. The Macon money wasn't much of a secret, to Nancy or anyone else who had lived in

Antioch long enough. The town had been settled and built by generations of Macons, and most every renter and lessor in town knew how much of the town's real estate had been passed down to Mrs. Macon. Not a lot of people knew the widow personally, but everyone knew it was best to keep her happy. Nancy knew what Brett Henchle was thinking: This young whoever-he-was might be trying to keep the widow happy too, for all the wrong reasons.

Brett pulled to a stop at the big stone gate, parking his squad car so no other vehicle could get around him. Nancy pulled up behind him, got out of her car, and waited to see how he intended to control this situation. He stepped out, his eyes invisible behind his wire-framed sunglasses, and watched as the ladies in the Voyager and the crew in the TV van pulled over, jostled a little, waited for each other, and finally found parking spots on the highway shoulder. Dee and her friends launched themselves out of the Voyager and ran to him.

"Officer Henchle, we need to get up there!"

"You can't block us! It's our first amendment right!"

"Just sit tight," was all he said. Then he stood there ignoring the rest of their pleas as he waited for the others to gather.

A female reporter—dressed to appear on camera from the waist up, but wearing blue jeans came running from her car. "Officer, is it true?"

"Just wait."

"Is there a man claiming to be Jesus Christ living on this ranch?"

He just put up his hand and said, "Hang on."

Then Brett looked at Nancy and, unsmiling, gave her some welcome news. "Nancy, I talked to Mrs. Macon by cell phone. It's going to be you and me. That's it." The moans had already begun before he announced, "The rest of you have to stay off the property." A chorus of protests. "That's the way she wants it."

"What if *we* called her?" the reporter wondered aloud.

"That's up to you, and it's up to her." Then he said to Nancy, "She takes the paper. She knows you're the editor, so you're okay. Climb in."

"I need to get my camera." She started to reach into her car.

"No cameras," Brett advised. "The widow's orders."

Nancy didn't like that, but quickly adjusted and got into the squad car.

The reporter asked again, "*Is* there a man up there claiming to be Jesus Christ?"

"There's a man up there, and I don't know who he is. That's what I'm here to find out."

The reporter ran around to Nancy's window. "You'll share the information with us, won't you?"

Nancy was feeling a little smug. "We'll wait and see."

She heard the reporter let an unprofessional word slip out as the squad car started up the driveway.

The attractive, circular driveway in front of the house brought them right up to the front door. Brett stepped out and put on a casual windbreaker to cover his uniform. "We gotta make this look as nonthreatening as possible."

Mrs. Macon, dressed in denim shorts, spring blouse, and sun hat, answered the door. She was smiling, expecting them.

"Good afternoon, Mrs. Macon," said Brett. He introduced himself and Nancy.

The widow's eyes widened with delight. "Oh yes! Nancy Barrons! I read your paper all the time!"

"I'm flattered," said Nancy, shaking her hand.

"Won't you come in?"

They stepped through the big glass-paneled door and into the finest home anywhere near Antioch. Nancy guessed it had to be around six thousand square feet, all one story, with marble entryway, sunken living room, imposing stone fireplace, thick rugs, and exquisite décor, including Cephus Macon's many hunting trophies.

"Would either of you like a cup of tea?" the widow asked.

"Uh, thank you, no," said Brett. "We won't take up much of your time. I just need to ask you a few questions."

Mrs. Macon looked up at him with a motherly glint in her eye. "You want to know about the young man I hired."

"Yes, that's right, if you don't mind."

"Would you like to meet him?"

"I certainly would."

She led them through an arched hallway with huge vases in alcoves, then through an immense, immaculate kitchen. "He's a different kind of fellow, I have to warn you. Have you ever met a prophet of God before, Officer Henchle?"

Brett shot a glance at Nancy. "No, ma'am, I can't say that I have."

"Well, you have to make some allowances for them. They can seem a little abrupt and forward at times. But once you get to know Brandon you realize he has a heart of gold."

She led them through a French patio door and onto a covered patio. There they found a young, dark-haired man busily at work putting up some hanging baskets for flowers.

"Brandon? The officer is here to see you."

The young man turned, smiled, and offered his hand. "Hi. Brandon Nichols."

"Uh, Brandon, were you just down at Mack's Sooper Market in Antioch?"

He answered casually, without hesitation. "Sure was. How's Dee? Did she recover all right?"

"She's doing just fine as near as I can tell. Uh . . . would you happen to have any ID you can show me?"

Brandon pulled a wallet from his back pocket and produced a driver's license. Brett studied it as Brandon explained, "I just moved here from Missoula, Montana. I haven't had the license very long."

"So what brings you to Antioch?"

"I hired him," said Mrs. Macon proudly. "He used to work for some rancher friends of ours in Missoula and came highly recommended. He's a wonderful worker, he's knowledgeable, he's diligent, and besides that, he's a prophet of God, and those you don't find too often these days." She pointed to a small cottage built in the same style as the ranch house, facing them from the far side of the swimming pool. "I've put him up in our guest house. That's my prophet's chamber, just like in Second Kings."

Nancy could see suspicion in Brett's eyes and felt a good measure of it herself. The widow was lonely, rich, and eccentric. Brandon Nichols was young, handsome, maybe even charming. It was easy to see the glow in Mrs. Macon's face every time she looked Brandon's direction.

"So you're a prophet of God, huh?" Brett asked.

He seemed embarrassed. "That's what Mrs. Macon says."

"What do *you* say?"

"I *am* sent from God, but I let people draw their own conclusions."

"What were you doing down at Mack's?"

"Buying groceries for Mrs. Macon."

"That's right," the widow confirmed.

"How did Mrs. Baylor end up on the floor?"

Mrs. Macon answered, "Slain in the Spirit. It's a God thing."

"A God thing. Right."

Brandon volunteered, "I touched her in greeting, and I guess falling down was her religious response."

"Did you heal Norman Dillard's eyes?"

"Yes."

"And Matt Kiley?"

"Yes. Him too."

Brett appeared mystified. "Just like that?"

"Yes."

Brett looked at the driver's license again. Nancy ventured a glance over his shoulder. The photograph looked a little blurry, but it was the same guy, all right. Brett asked, "So you're from Missoula?"

"That's right."

"How come I never heard about you before this?"

"I've just begun my ministry."

"Oh."

Apparently Brett was out of questions. He gave a little shrug. "Well, Brandon, as far as I can tell you haven't broken any laws and you haven't hurt anyone." He allowed himself a quick little smile. "I guess the opposite is true. If none of these people has a complaint and Mrs. Macon is happy and willing to have you here, I've got nothing more to do."

He handed the license back. Brandon reached out to take it and their fingers touched.

Brett flinched as if he'd gotten a shock.

"Oh, excuse me," said Brandon.

Nancy could tell Brett was trying to maintain his tough cop image, but she also knew something strange had happened. The big officer's hand was shaking. He pressed it to his thigh to steady it. "Okay then . . ." His voice was trembling. He cleared his throat. "Guess that's it."

Suddenly he winced and grabbed his left leg just above the knee.

"Brett? What's wrong?" Nancy asked.

"Something's poking me."

He grabbed a pinch of his pant leg and shook it out. There was a faint, clinking sound as three jagged pieces of metal fell out onto the patio.

Mrs. Macon let out a little gasp. Nancy stared, her usual professional poise surrendering to gawking amazement.

Brandon stepped forward, stooped, and picked up the three pieces. "Vietnam, July 19, 1971. A grenade killed three of your friends—Franklin Torrence, Emilio Delgado, and Rich Trenner. It would have killed you too if Rich Trenner hadn't been standing in the way." He stood, holding the shrapnel in his open hand. "He took most of it. These three pieces are the only ones that hit you." Brett held out his hand and Brandon dropped the shards into his palm.

Mrs. Macon was beaming like a proud mother, wagging her head in wonder.

His face filled with fear and awe, Brett handed the metal shards to Nancy, and as she examined them, he pulled up his pant leg. Even the scar was gone.

So was Brett's tough cop image. He was visibly shaken, and could only gaze at the young man in stunned silence.

Suddenly there was a voice. "Yoo-hoo!"

Dee Baylor, her friends, and the television people came around the corner of the house.

"Well!" said Mrs. Macon.

Brandon Nichols cocked his head. "Now, now, I don't recall Mrs. Macon inviting you up here!"

Mrs. Macon grabbed his arm. "Brandon, let's invite them to have some tea! And the officer and Nancy too!"

He considered it, then playfully shook his finger at Dee and her friends. "No cameras! Let's just be neighbors today!"

Dee and her friends immediately looked at the reporter and her cameraman. The cameraman got his cue from the reporter and set the camera on the ground.

"Come on over!" said Mrs. Macon. She asked Brett and Nancy, "Would you like to stay a while?"

Nancy was intensely willing. "Oh yes! Absolutely!" She gave the shards back to Brett.

Brett dropped the shards into his shirt pocket. His hands were still shaking. "Uh, no, thanks . . . I gotta go." He started backing away, still unable to take his eyes off Brandon Nichols. "Thanks anyway, I—" He stumbled against a lawn chair and finally turned to see where he was going. "Uh, how do I . . ."

Mrs. Macon hurried over and directed him. "You can just follow the walkway around the house to your car."

"I'll ride back with . . ." Nancy looked at the reporter.

"Alice," the reporter replied.

"I'll ride back with Alice."

Nancy and Alice gave each other a thumbs-up. Now *this* was a story!

Brett stole one more look at the young man before turning on his heels and getting out of there.

"He even *looks* like him!" he muttered.

I DIDN'T HEAR MUCH about that meeting up at the ranch until Thursday. In the meantime, Matt Kiley took some time Thursday morning to walk the length of the highway through town, roughly a mile, allowing himself to be photographed, videoed, and interviewed by whatever pilgrim or reporter might happen along. For a man confined to a wheelchair for over a quarter of a century, his rate of recovery was remarkable. His legs, once thin and atrophied, seemed to be filling out by the hour.

Norman Dillard still relished every sign, book, and newspaper he could read. He even enjoyed trying to catch the license plates of passing cars as he worked in his motel office. He also learned of another benefit that came with perfect vision: One of the pilgrims passing by on the sidewalk happened to be a very attractive young lady. "Well, helloooo, what have we here?" She didn't know he was watching her and didn't hear him. It was a real kick.

THURSDAY was Brett Henchle's day off. He was out in the driveway shooting baskets with his two sons when his wife, Lori, brought him a cordless phone. "It's Kyle Sherman," she said.

He made a face, bounced the ball to his sons, and took the phone, sitting on the steps that led up to the house. Lori sat down next to him, listening while she watched the boys continue dribbling and shooting.

"Yeah, this is Brett." Brett listened for a moment, then repeated for Lori's sake, "Uh-huh. You want to know about the Jesus impersonator up at the Macon ranch. Right." Brett listened a while longer. "Pastor Sherman, he's not claiming to be Jesus. His name is Brandon Nichols and he's just a ranch worker from Missoula, Montana. Yeah, he really does have a name. He even has a driver's license. He's for real."

Lori could hear Kyle's voice squawking on and on as Brett rolled his eyes. She could tell he was anxious to get back to the game.

"Well, I'd say he's religious, yeah, but he hasn't done anything illegal. He's working for the widow, she's happy with his work, and that's that." More squawking, something about the people in church, the pilgrims visiting town, blah, blah, blah.

"Listen! People can believe whatever they want about this guy. If you think he's breaking the law, show me. Otherwise, this is none of my business. You're the minister. You work it out. Okay. Bye."

He clicked the phone off and handed it back to Lori. "That guy's a pain in the you-know-what."

"A little hard-nosed, is he?"

"You should have seen him at the ministerial meeting. 'It's demons!' It's none of our business, that's what it is! The guy's a pain!"

"Speaking of pain, how's your leg?" she asked.

The question changed his mood. He leaped to his feet, ran in place, then did some high kicks. "What pain? I feel great!" He hollered to his boys, "All right, let's get this game going!"

She marveled. She'd never seen him so alive. He seemed younger now than when she married him.

"WELL, THE PILGRIMS ARE GATHERING," said the smooth and soothing voice on the telephone.

"At least we know you're not Jesus—*Brandon,*" I replied.

"So you've heard from Kyle already."

"He's a very unhappy camper."

"Well, not to be critical, but he has a small mind. If anyone wants to consider me their Jesus, I allow them that. Kyle should do the same."

I had to laugh. "He's not wired up that way."

"So I gather. But how about you, Travis? I think you're ready to widen your world."

"I'm not about to believe a lie if I can help it."

He paused, I suppose to frame his question. "Why did you go to Minneapolis? Try to remember, Travis."

Brandon Nichols might not be Jesus, but he was supernatural. He knew all the right buttons to push, all the perfect thorn-in-the-side memories to dredge up. "What does that have to do with anything?"

"Fantasy, Travis. Like anyone else, you wanted a kinder reality, and I don't blame you."

"It didn't work."

"Well, that was then. The rules are about to change. My followers will be looking for a kinder reality, and they just might get it."

"Your followers?"

"Just don't blame them, Travis. You were there yourself, once. Oh, and Travis?"

"What?"

"Don't be like Kyle."

When the line went dead I stood there, unable to move, unable to think. Why *did* I go to Minneapolis, so many years ago?

My mind dredged up the only answer I had: *Because God called me.* Or had he?

9

Not long after I turned eighteen, God assigned me the holy work of discipling Amber Carr, the quiet girl from drama class who turned out every Wednesday for the Kenyon–Bannister meetings. She didn't smoke, and she seemed to maintain a quiet dignity while so many of the other kids were Spirit-filled Christians but still basically nuts. She came to me with her questions, I drew from the deep well of my experience for answers, and we hit it off. She came over to my house and we talked about the Lord. I went over to her house and we talked about the Lord. When we weren't talking about the Lord, we went to the movies or to an occasional concert. The rest of the time we just enjoyed how the Lord had brought us together.

It was a great time of year to help a pretty girl grow in the Lord. Spring was rolling around, the weather, though usually wet, was finally warming up, and there were plenty of days nice enough to get outside and walk on the beach. I found that the more time I spent with her, the greater the intensity of my calling, until it seemed God wanted me close to her, sharing my wisdom at every conceivable opportunity.

I remember the night I first kissed her. I did it in the name of Jesus and strictly for his glory. From that point, we continued to glorify the Lord in like manner whenever we got the chance, so often that my memory of it includes no specifics, only one murky continuum.

Oh, but the ecstasy of it, the lofty, dizzying heights of joy! The glory of the Kenyon–Bannister days had no glory like this glory. This was a calling from the throne of God strong enough to make me drive for miles when I had a car and walk for hours when I didn't, just to be with her. Nothing else was as important as getting to wherever she was to nurture her, protect her, instruct her, and participate in God's unfolding plan—which now included, I was certain, both of us, together, following his call.

The Lord began to confirm this to us separately. Amber had a dream about us and then, that very morning, the old song by Herman's Hermits came on the radio. It told her that, even though the young man she loved didn't know much about anything, if she loved him anyway, God would use us to make a wonderful world. God spoke to me in signs and prophecies, which I recorded in a journal. One day, while walking and praying, I saw a car go by with a license number the same as Amber's birthday, and then I got a prophecy: *This is my choice for you, the path I have chosen. Walk ye in it.* By the time we graduated, we knew we would be married as soon as the Lord made a way.

There were, however, some logistical details to work out. Amber was planning to start classes at the University of Washington in the fall, while I had virtually no plans except to minister the gospel, whatever that was supposed to mean. As the summer rolled by, she worked as a motel housekeeper to raise money for college. I spent most of my time playing my banjo. Her family threw their doubts right in her face. My family tried lovingly to express theirs. I prayed for them all. None of them—not even my dad, a man of God—realized what a powerful God we served, and how God could intervene miraculously for those who were totally sold out to him.

The clock kept ticking. Fall came around. In a few weeks, Amber would actually start classes at the university and live with her grandmother in the north part of Seattle. I had no job, no car, no savings, no plans, and no miracle. Of course, it was not unlike God to test our faith, to make us wait until the last possible moment before he opened our Red Sea and saw us through safely.

The Red Sea didn't open. Amber started her classes and started learning things I didn't know. After a summer of waiting on God and claiming the miraculous, she was going somewhere, while I wasn't. She even started to sound smarter than me.

Finally, bowing to pressure I was getting from all directions, I acknowledged that having a job while waiting on the Lord wouldn't be such a bad idea.

Thus began a darker time than I had ever known in my life.

COMPTON METAL FABRICATORS was a cavernous building on the ship canal in Seattle, a drafty, metal shell with glassless windows and gaping doors that let the cold wind through. Compton built crab boats, big metal hulls that filled the building, brown with rust, dirty all over, cold and dark inside. And the *noise!* Metal-bending machinery, air-powered grinders, rattling guns, hammers. The place smelled of sparks from grinders, arc welders, and cutting torches.

I got there at seven in the morning for my first day, a pristine and godly young man among rough-hewn, crusty shipbuilders who seemed obsessed with the obscene and knew only one adjective they applied to everything. Bill, the supervisor, a burly, hard-hatted guy with a lisp you didn't dare make fun of, handed me an air-powered grinder and set me to work grinding off the metal beads left behind by the welders. The thing weighed about ten pounds when I started in the morning. By ten o'clock it weighed twenty, and by noon it weighed forty. I climbed all over that rusty hull, up and down ladders and catwalks, inside and out, lugging that machine and pulling the air hose after me. My mission was simple: see the bead, grind the bead.

At four o'clock, nine hours and seventy years later, the big horn sounded and the place finally got quiet. I walked out to the parking lot with all the other guys in their dirty blue coveralls, got in Mom and Dad's Oldsmobile Cutlass and headed for home.

And the morning and the evening were the first day.

And the second day was like unto the first.

And the third day was like unto the first and second.

By the fourth day, I had become a man of prayer more than I had ever been before. Surely this was all a mistake. There must have been a clerical error in heaven. An angel had put God's plan for someone else in *my* file folder. I began crying out to God from below, above, and inside that boat, trying to bring the error to God's attention. I never heard back.

After about a week on the job, Bill asked me if I ever got claustrophobia. When I said no, he sent me down inside the double hull of the boat to rattle off the charred scabs of metal left by the welders and sweep out the watertight compartments. It was like working inside a metal coffin with just enough room to twist my body around and look for scabs with a work light.

Buried alive in the hull of that crab boat, I prayed. I needed to hear from God. I needed a sign, a prophecy, a word of knowledge, anything. God was in control and had a plan, I was sure of it. I wouldn't be there for long. God would get me out. I would marry Amber and we would go somewhere clean, quiet, and glorious, not dirty, noisy, and humiliating, and there we would serve the Lord happily ever after.

Every Sunday night, with Monday morning to look forward to, I prayed.

Every morning when the alarm clock rang, I prayed.

While perched on the high catwalks along the hull with my grinder, while crawling inside the hull with a work light and rattling gun, while sweeping out below deck while falling sparks from a torch burned holes in my shirt, I prayed.

I prayed for God to change things, to make a way for me to minister for him, to get me out of there. I was ready to hear him speak. I was ready for any thought, any impression, any hint of anything else *anywhere* else.

Finally, it happened. After two dirty, exhausting, deafening weeks at Compton, an answer began to dawn like a faint glimmer of light from heaven. I was at home with my folks, dead tired and about to go to bed when a Billy Graham crusade came on the television. Mom, Dad, my older brother Steve, and I all watched it, one wondrous and powerful hour of songs and gospel preaching. The bigness of it, the unique, unpretentious pageantry, and the crowds of people streaming forward at Reverend Graham's invitation struck a chord in my heart. I wanted to be a part of it. I didn't belong in a dirty shipyard among all those crusty, cussing shipbuilders. I belonged there, at that crusade, helping to spread the gospel.

I took the dream to bed with me and woke up with it in the morning. I thought about it all the way to work and sang "Just As I Am" as I picked up my grinder at the tool crib. I thought about preaching, teaching, prophesying, even playing my banjo for the Billy Graham Evangelistic Association. I could act in a Billy Graham movie. I could sing a song at a Billy Graham crusade. I could write songs, books, and Bible lessons. I could counsel.

The more I thought about it, the more excited I got and the more I prayed. This had to be it. God's calling. Of course! This short time in the shipyard was to humble and prepare me, that was all. It wasn't meant to last. My deliverance, the next step in God's masterful plan, was on the way.

The very next weekend, I visited Amber and told her I was hearing from God and carrying a burden to join up with Billy Graham. I told her how there could even be a connection between my playing bluegrass music and working for Billy Graham: both had the initials B.G. It had to be a sign.

She had never heard of Billy Graham so I had to explain it to her, telling her all about the crusades and the Evangelistic Association in Minneapolis and all the things I thought I could do there. After she heard it all, she smiled and told me about a vision she'd received from the Lord, a railroad boxcar with a big letter "I" on it. At the time she had no idea what it meant, but now we could interpret that vision in a better light: Perhaps this suggested my mode of travel to Minneapolis. We decided to write down anything the Lord might give us. Things were cooking and we had to keep a record of it. Someday it would make a great book.

Monday morning, seven o'clock, the big horn sounded. Armed with a broom and rattling gun, I headed for the hull. Bill sent me down into the double hull compartments again, this time to sweep, and to mark any cavities in the metal with white crayon so the welders could come through later and fill them in. Another helper had been there before me and had decided to favor future generations with some lurid artwork. I rubbed it out, and as I stood there, crayon in hand, God began to speak some new ideas to me.

This was a time of preparation. I wrote a P on the wall to represent that.

But soon there would come the call. I wrote a C on the wall.

I would go first, leading the way, blazing the trail. I wrote an L.

And then, having begun a wonderful ministry with Billy Graham, I would return—I wrote an R—and bring Amber with me. I wrote an A.

So there it was on the dark, rusty wall of a crab boat under construction: *PCLRA*. Where once a dirty picture had been, I had written an encoded prophecy in the same awesome vein as Daniel's *Mene Mene Tekel Upharsin*. The handwriting on the wall. It was God's plan for my life.

I called Amber that night and told her all about it. She was thrilled because she'd received another vision from God that day, this time of a huge banjo bridging Seattle and Minneapolis. The meaning was obvious and we were giddy with joy.

Now it was only a question of timing. Right now I was being prepared, but when would the call come? Perhaps we should set out a fleece as Gideon did in the Book of Judges, a way for God to indicate his will in a tangible way.

Well, the drumhead on my banjo needed replacing, but the size was nonstandard and the guy at the music store said he'd have to special order one. There it was, our fleece. Amber's vision of the huge banjo verified that. "Lord," I prayed, "when you want me to go to Minneapolis, have that drumhead come in."

I waited, and prayed, and worked at the shipyard another week.

And then the music store called. The banjo head I'd ordered had arrived.

The sign from God!

The next day, I went to Bill the supervisor and said, "I have to quit. God has called me to go to Minneapolis and work for Billy Graham."

He didn't seem very impressed. He just got me my paycheck and went back to work. I figured he'd never heard of Billy Graham either. I got out of that big, drafty building and walked into the sunshine. Even the weather was saying *Yes! This is God's will for you!*

The time had come to break the wondrous news to my folks. They were godly, Spirit-filled people. I knew they would be thrilled. As we sat at dinner that night, I made the announcement. "God has called me to work for Billy Graham. I'm going to Minneapolis."

They just sat there, looking back at me, chewing, not saying a thing.

Finally Mom asked, "What about your job?"

"I quit."

Dad asked, "Do they know you're coming? Have you written to them or called them?"

"No. I'm trusting God. It's all in his hands."

I told them how my last paycheck from the shipyard should be enough for a train ticket over there.

"Where will you stay?" Dad asked.

"Oh, God has that all figured out. I'm just supposed to obey and go."

I told them about the visions, and Mom got tears in her eyes. Apparently she was deeply moved by the miraculous touch of God upon my life.

"I'm ready to step out in faith," I said. "I'm ready to believe God and go to Minneapolis."

"Okay," Dad said. "Just be sure to buy a round-trip ticket."

I left Seattle on a Sunday afternoon. Before the train was to leave, I took the bus up to the north end of Seattle to say good-bye to Amber. It was a tearful good-bye, but a moment filled with holy expectation. We knelt together on the floor of her grandmother's living room, our hands clasped in prayer, and praised the Lord for this moment, this launching of a great mission. I paraphrased the Lord's words as I told her, "I go to prepare a place for you, and I will come again to receive you, that where I am, there you may be also."

"I'll wait for you," she replied, but her voice trembled a little. Was it hesitation? Doubt? No, it couldn't be. Just emotion, that was all. Anticipation of the great things God was about to do. Then we kissed in the name of Jesus. Her kiss was less fervent than usual, but I pushed the nagging thought out of my mind. This was God's will. I would go and find my place, I would send for her, and we would live together forever in service to the Lord.

With pack on my back, shipyard clothes on my body, and banjo and briefcase in my hands, I caught the bus heading south to the King Street Station. By four o'clock I was on a train bound for Minneapolis.

By now it was October. When the train arrived in Minneapolis on Monday, the leaves of Minnesota were in their fall brilliance and the wind was cold. As the train pulled into the station I looked across the railroad yard and there it was, just as I had expected: a big railroad boxcar with the letter "I" on it. God had spoken! He was with me! I was moving in the realm of the miraculous!

The city was big, busy, and totally alien to me. I had the address of the Billy Graham Evangelistic Association written on a piece of paper, so with directions from a porter at the train station, I set out walking, the very picture of a homeless vagabond.

I never got lost, not with the Lord guiding my every step, my every turn. Sometimes a cloud overhead would take on a shape to point the way. Once, a construction crane pointed left like a huge finger and I followed. I walked for hours and saw a lot of the city.

Then I came upon Hennepin Avenue and knew I was closing in on Canaan. God was faithful. Following the street numbers in descending order, I walked and walked, block by block, until I came to the front door of the Billy Graham Evangelistic Association.

This was the moment, and suddenly I felt nervous. How was

my faith? Did I still believe? I felt a little doubt, but refused to acknowledge it. A doubt just like this one may have kept Andy Smith from being healed, I reminded myself. There was no room for doubt in the service of the Lord, only belief.

Drawing upon the Lord for courage, I opened the door, and went inside.

The receptionist, a nice lady in a white silk blouse and navy skirt, looked up from her desk. I smiled at her the way Jesus must have smiled to those who were hurting. Perhaps the Lord was going to give me a word to share with her, a touch of healing, a message of hope.

"Would you like to talk to one of our counselors?" she asked.

Well, she must have been doing all right and didn't need a special touch from God today. I said, "Sure," and she placed a call.

A nice man dressed in a suit and tie came into the lobby, shook my hand, and directed me into a conference room. He had black, curly hair and a moustache and I'd never seen him on television. When he introduced himself, I didn't recognize his name. When I introduced myself, he didn't seem to recognize my name either, and he didn't seem to be expecting me. Somehow we got on the subject of happiness, and from there he began to ask me what my idea of happiness was. By the time he asked me how I thought I could obtain happiness, I figured he was getting ready to share the gospel with me.

"Oh, I'm already saved," I told him, and then figured it was time to enlighten him and get this meeting on the right track. I recounted the previous months of seeking and hearing from God—the signs and visions, the prophecies, the fleece. I knew he would be impressed.

Well . . . he didn't break down crying or anything. But he did invite me to pray with him as he asked the Lord to bless and guide me. Then he led me to the receptionist's desk and told her I would need an application.

The receptionist disappeared behind a set of double doors and came back with an application form several pages long. I took it and sat on the couch again.

And then I stared at it. An application? I had not seen this in any of my visions, nor heard about it in any of my prophecies. I began to try to fill it out, and it started badgering me about my education and experience. There were no blanks to fill in anywhere regarding my prophetic gifts, my preaching and teaching ability, or even my banjo playing.

At last I finished, saying all I could say about myself, which wasn't very much, then went back to the receptionist and handed the application to her. She thanked me for my interest, told me there were no openings at the present time, and pressed a buzzer to let me out.

That was it? My big calling from God? It was over?

Faith, I reminded myself. *You've got to have faith.* There had to be another door of opportunity somewhere. God wouldn't send me clear across the country just to fill out an application and be turned away.

I recalled seeing the offices of World Wide Pictures on the other side of the building, around the block. That had to be it. I wasn't supposed to work in Billy Graham's office anyway. I was an actor, an artist, a musician. I could serve God in the movies. I started walking.

The World Wide Pictures office turned out to be smaller than Billy Graham's office, and I quickly realized that they didn't make the movies there. But I pressed on, introduced myself to another lady receptionist, and got myself another meeting with another well-qualified and experienced man in a suit and tie. I repeated my story —the months of seeking and hearing from God, the visions and prophecies Amber and I had received, the vision of the banjo stretching across the country, the prophecy I scribbled on the wall just like God did in the Book of Daniel. All of it.

He told me he was happy about all the wonderful things God had done in my life, but he just didn't have any positions available.

I was in and out of there in less than fifteen minutes.

I spent the night at the Y, and when morning came, I was still a man of faith, trusting God to complete his purpose, but not having the slightest clue why I should remain in Minneapolis. I walked back across town to the train station and used the other half of my round-trip ticket. As the train rolled westward, the long, seemingly pointless journey began to make sense. God was testing me just as he tested Abraham, to see if I would obey. Of course. Sometimes God asks us to do things that don't make a lot of sense just to see how devoted and obedient we are. Well, I was sure I passed the test, and that meant God could trust me with the next step. I couldn't wait to get home and tell Amber.

In Seattle, I went straight from the train station and caught a bus to the north end of the city, where Amber lived with her grandmother. I didn't know if she would be home or in classes at the university, but I got right out there anyway, knowing it was all in God's hands.

Amber was home. My heart soared. I hugged her and kissed her and praised the Lord.

Her embrace was not so enthusiastic, and she quickly let it fall away as she asked, "Well? Tell me what happened."

I told her about my two brief visits in the offices on Hennepin Avenue and how they turned out. Then I added how God had set this whole thing up as a test of my faith. "I passed the test," I said, "and that can only mean that wonderful things are in store."

She nodded as if she knew all along what God would do. Then she scribbled a little note and handed it to me.

She was resigning.

Although I'd been through some very abrupt changes in the plan over the past few days, I still wasn't used to it. I had to ask her what she meant, and she had to tell me in several different ways. She didn't want to be my helpmate anymore. She no longer saw things my way. It would be foolish for us to get married. She wanted to pursue her education. There was no way our relationship would work out. We were through.

Standing in her grandmother's living room with that note in my hand was like standing in that lobby in Minneapolis. No position available. No reason to stay. Dead end. I did the same thing here as there. I responded in faith, seeing the miraculous hand of God even in this. I smiled, put the note in my shirt pocket, and spoke prophetically, "You'll come back, and I'll wait for you."

I HAD IT ALL PLANNED. I would give Amber some time to listen to the Lord and sort it all out, then go to see her on Christmas Eve, the ideal day for a heartwarming, tear-jerky reunion. I bought her a beautiful Bible. I found just the right spot in a nearby park where we could walk, talk, and embrace. I could see in my mind how she would run into my arms and kiss me, big fluffy snowflakes falling all around us.

On Christmas Eve, I fasted and prayed all day. Nothing had worked out from high school graduation up to this point, but *now* the time of testing was over, *now* would be the big turnaround. *Now* all my faith would be rewarded and the world would know that there was a God!

When I knocked on the door, her gift in my hand, she wasn't even there. Her grandmother told me she was over at her boyfriend's house and would be spending Christmas with him and his family. I left the Bible with the grandmother and walked back to the bus stop, taking a short side trip through the park where the tear-jerky reunion scene would never happen.

We didn't even get fluffy snow that day. It was raining.

In mid-January, I had my very last conversation with her by telephone. She thanked me for the Bible and said she planned to use it in her Bible as Literature class at the university. Apart from that, she had no other use for it. Christianity was fine for me, but not right for her. She and her boyfriend were now attending a Unitarian church and she felt far more comfortable with that.

How can I say it? Finally, my foot came off the throttle. The wind went out of my sails. My boiler blew a rivet.

It was a *moment*, that's all, a precise point in time when, at long last, a different kind of belief broke through to me. For the first time, I actually believed *her*.

She really was history. The love we had, transcendent and unassailable, a divine gift, a special miracle forged in the foundries of heaven, ended back in October, as quickly as her resignation. I had refused to accept it, but right now, with my hand still on the telephone, I finally let the truth in: our love was gone. It was over.

And then the dominoes began to fall.

That's the caveat that comes with being "led by the Spirit": if you dare to question one thing, you have to question everything. With Amber gone, what did that say about all those visions, signs, and prophecies that God supposedly gave us? What did the Minneapolis debacle tell me about my encoded prophecy scribbled on the wall of the crab boat? Could I finally admit that boxcars with a big letter "I" on them belonged to Intermountain Railways and were commonplace in most every major train yard in every major city in the country? Could I admit that a banjo head on special order was bound to arrive sooner or later, God or no God, fleece or no fleece? Could I face the fact that Billy Graham and bluegrass having the same initials carried about as much meaning as that license plate with Amber's birthday on it?

When I laid hands on Andy and Karla and prayed for their healing, God didn't heal them. It wasn't a matter of the healing taking time or them waiting until they had the right degree of faith, or any other explanation we came up with. *God didn't heal them.* I thought I had the gift of healing and didn't. I prayed for them to be healed and they weren't. And as for all the shaking I did, well that's exactly what it was: shaking *I* did.

As to the Kenyon–Bannister prayer meetings, the original fire had gone out for want of logs on the hearth. The Kenyons and Bannisters were still having their meetings and I suppose Mr. Kenyon was still the bishop of the island, but nothing more remained. David Kenyon had gone back east to college. Bernadette Jones had gotten pregnant—contrary to Mrs. Bannister's prophecy, Barry the boyfriend never became a Christian and they never furthered God's kingdom together. Karla Dickens was living in Seattle and pursuing a business degree, while Andy Smith had gotten his girlfriend pregnant, married her, and was currently trying to make a living as a composer and piano teacher. Harold Martin, who once tried to get me to smoke pot, was still smoking pot for all I knew, getting into yoga and eastern religion, and working as a flagman for the county road crew. Clay Olson had gone on to Bible college to pursue the ministry, and Benny Taylor, his pimples now fading, was racking up perfect grades at the University of Washington.

We used to be young, unstoppable soldiers of the cross, led by the Spirit, taking the world for Christ as we marched arm in arm. There was going to be a great revival, starting with us. We were on fire and those who were lukewarm would have to get on fire too or eat our dust.

But my fellow soldiers weren't there anymore. While I was chasing visions, signs, and prophecies all the way to Minneapolis, each of them caught a different train and left while I wasn't looking.

In mid-October, I was eighteen, in love, full of the Spirit, and on a train bound for Minneapolis. By mid-January, I was nineteen and a nobody with nowhere to go, sitting on the bed in my room at home, plunking absently on a brown, fifty-dollar banjo and feeling a new and frightening kind of loneliness. Jesus seemed far away, and strangely enough, I was content to leave him there. I didn't want to talk to him; I feared and distrusted anything he might say to me.

I was saved, sanctified, born-again, and Spirit-filled, but Jesus and I were strangers.

10

Brandon had warned Mrs. Macon that there would be phone calls and knocks at the door, and his prophetic gifts were right on the money. Ever since that Wednesday afternoon tea, visitors were coming up the long driveway to see the prophet, the Messiah, Jesus, the man claiming to be Jesus, the Avatar of Christ, or anything else people thought he was. On Thursday, just before Mrs. Macon and Brandon agreed that they should get Brandon's ministry—and access to the ranch—organized, scheduled, and restricted, the doorbell rang for the umpteenth time. Mrs. Macon steeled her nerves and opened the door.

A young man stood there, dressed in cut-off jeans and a white tunic, a shawl of some sort draped over his head and a long staff in his hand. He couldn't have been more than eighteen years old. His beard was immature and wispy, he was lanky, and his face was smooth and unwrinkled. When he spoke, it was in a forced, unnatural British accent. "Hello. My name is Michael. I am seeking the Messiah of Antioch."

The widow looked over her shoulder and beckoned Brandon with her eyes. He came to the door. "Yes?"

Young Michael immediately dropped to one knee, his head bowed low, his hand on his staff. "All hail." He looked up. "God has sent me to you. I am the voice of one crying in the wilderness, prepare ye the way of the Lord."

Mrs. Macon had seen a good measure of starry-eyed pilgrims and strange folks come by since yesterday, but this young man was taking strangeness to a new level. She looked at Brandon, wondering what he would do.

To her surprise, Brandon stepped forward, extended his hand, and rested it on the young man's head. "Michael, you are expected." He gently took the young man's arm and prompted him to rise to his feet. Then he looked at Mrs. Macon. "Michael will dine with us tonight. We have much to discuss."

THURSDAY EVENING, Jim Baylor was getting hungry and dinner was late. Not that it was ever on time. It happened when it happened. But tonight he came home from work and found little indication that it was going to happen.

The house was messy. It was never really neat, but it had an especially neglected look this evening, as if Darlene, their fifteen-year-old daughter, had passed through when there was no one there to yell at her.

Dee was sitting at the kitchen table talking on the phone, and that wasn't unusual either. But this evening she was *intensely* on the phone, so much that she gave Jim one quick little wave to acknowledge his presence and then went back to totally ignoring him.

"You have to meet him," she was saying. "Just one look in his eyes and you know you're in the presence of God! He has the anointing, absolutely!"

Jim came closer. "Who are you talking to?"

She waved him off and kept talking. "Get up here as soon as you can. I don't know if he really is Jesus, but . . . oh, you just have to see him, that's all. Once you see him, you'll know."

Jim surveyed the cluttered kitchen table. They were supposed to be eating off that table right now, but instead of dinner, Dee had a list of names in front of her with many checked off and many more yet to be checked off. "Dee, what are you doing? You gonna be on the phone all night?"

By now she'd shared all the information she had with the party on the other end, so she went back to go over every thought again. "Anyway, that's what we did, we went up to the ranch yesterday and had tea with him and Mrs. Macon—and that place was a palace! I *know*, some women have all the luck!"

Jim felt the sting of that and went into the living room of the crummy, inadequate house he'd provided. Maybe he could put away some of the things he'd sweated and toiled for so the room wouldn't be such a mess. At least he could clear some space on the couch he provided for his family so he could sit and read the paper, which he also paid for.

"You should have seen that cute outfit she was wearing! She looks great for her age!"

He sat and perused the headlines, tuning out her voice as he had unconsciously learned to do over the years. A door swung open and slammed shut down at the end of the hall. Darlene came into the room, her expression oblivious, her walk dazed and desultory like a week-old, half-filled helium balloon. "When's dinner?" she asked.

Jim looked over his shoulder at Dee in the kitchen, still on the phone. Well, he *might* be able to get a response from his daughter. He directed Darlene's attention to the socks, books, clothing, stuffed animals, and other debris that had somehow blown into the living room. "Darlene, pick all this stuff up and get it out of here."

"When's dinner?" she insisted.

"Get all your stuff out of here!" he repeated, and then went into the kitchen again. "Dee, you have a family, remember?"

She made a face at him but finally closed her conversation. "Okay. Love you too. Bye."

She pressed and released the little button on the phone, clearing it for another call. She consulted her list and started dialing.

Jim pressed the button on the phone and leaned in close. "You have a family."

She slapped his hand away from the telephone. "Don't you tell me what to do!"

He put his hand over it and kept it there. "How long have you been talking on the phone here? The house is a mess, there's no dinner —"

"You want dinner, get it yourself!" she snapped, and her voice could be like a trumpet when she was angry. "You think this isn't important? We're being visited—" She cut off her sentence.

"What?"

"You wouldn't understand."

The raucous sounds of MTV came blasting from the living room. Jim hollered at Darlene, "Didn't I tell you to put away your stuff? Now get at it!"

She wailed back, "When's dinner?"

Dee slammed the receiver down and came unglued. "I can't believe this family! You think my only purpose on earth is to wait on you two? You both have two hands!"

Having once been a marine drill sergeant, Jim was no stranger to yelling. "I've been working all day long with these two hands to put the food on this table that isn't on the table! What have you been doing all day with *your* hands? Have you even been home today?"

Then they got into it, and not even MTV could equal the racket. They yelled, raved, and waved their hands at each other. Jim slammed some pans on the stove and she slammed them back in the cupboards. She tried to tell him how unhappy she was while he tried to tell her how ungrateful she was while Darlene flopped into a curled position on the couch and withdrew from the fight, the family, the whole unkind world.

Only the slam of the front door could break through the noise and get Jim and Dee's attention.

"Oh, great, just great!" Jim fumed, storming into the living room. "Darlene!" He flung open the front door in time to see her running down the street. "Darlene, come back here!"

Dee yelled from behind him, loud enough for the neighbors to hear, "Don't yell! You want the neighbors to hear?"

He grabbed his coat out of the hall closet and the car keys off their hook by the door. "I hope you're satisfied."

"Yeah, blame *me!*"

Dee went back into the kitchen and picked up the telephone again, consulting her list.

Jim went out to the car and drove off in search of his daughter.

"AWAKE, PEOPLE OF ANTIOCH, and know for certain that the Lord has come to you! See and behold, his winnowing fork is in his hand to separate the wheat from the chaff! On which side will *you* fall?"

His voice was a bit shrill and his British accent had to be a put-on, but Antioch was no bustling city where street preachers could simply be ignored and pedestrians could hide behind anonymity. Michael, prayer shawl around his shoulders and staff in his hand, was demanding attention and getting it. It was Saturday, and he'd positioned himself on the highway between Kiley's Hardware and Anderson's Furniture and Appliance, the center of town. Weekend pilgrims with cameras stopped to take pictures. Newcomers stopped to ask directions. Natives like Pastor Howard Munson stopped to grill him.

"So who are *you* now?" Howard asked him.

"I am the voice of one crying in the wilderness, prepare ye the way of the Lord!" said Michael. "Make his paths straight! Every mountain and hill—"

"Yeah, yeah, I know the rest," Howard interrupted. "But who are you? What's your name?"

"Michael. It means, 'Who is like God?'"

"And what are you doing here?"

Michael lowered his voice to conversational level as others gathered around to listen. "I have come to guide people to the answer, to God himself! In a distant land, God spoke to me and told me to travel westward, but I knew not where—"

"A distant land? Where are you from?"

"Chicago."

"Mm."

"Then his clear word came to me. A newspaper carried news of a visitor come to your town, a man some thought to be the Messiah, the Son of God." His eyes widened in anticipation of a real zinger. "As I read more, I noticed the breakfast on my plate that morning included bacon. By God's divine plan, the very morning I learned of the Messiah I was eating a breakfast that rhymes with—" He held out his staff, the crooked tip pointing toward the widow's ranch. "*Macon!* My course was set, and just days ago, I found the object of my quest! The Messiah of Antioch, the Savior of this age!"

Howard shook his head. "Son, whoever that guy is, he isn't the Savior! *Jesus* is the Savior!"

Michael only raised his eyebrows with sweet, innocent insight. "This man *is* Jesus!"

That got the attention of a cluster of pilgrims. "Jesus? Where?"

Michael pointed his staff again. "He awaits you today, for the first time, at the Macon ranch, at two o'clock. Watch for the signs."

"The *signs?*" a man asked, his eyes darting heavenward.

"Cardboard signs that say 'Macon ranch.' I put them up this morning."

MICHAEL'S MESSAGE was vague, but his announcement of an open-to-the-public meeting was clear enough, and fell on eager ears. Judging from the stream of cars and RVs heading up to the Macon ranch that afternoon, the Messiah of Antioch was going to have a packed house.

Kyle Sherman wasn't about to miss it. Ever since the little tea party up at the ranch, his telephone had been ringing and his congregation buzzing about this Brandon Nichols character. Dee was plugging Nichols for all she was worth, wooing new followers from among the congregation and from other churches as well. Roger Folsom, Adrian's husband, was on the brink of buying in. Johnny Davis, Blanche's husband, wasn't about to buy in and was having one heck of a time with Blanche. Brother Norheim was convinced the Antichrist had arisen and was demanding to know what the church was going to do about it. Folks like the Whites and the Foresters were calling, asking him what he thought so they'd know what to think. The church was in confusion, and it was time for the shepherd to get the sheep back in line.

Kyle was going to address the whole matter on Sunday, so he planned to have a thorough knowledge of his subject. His was one of the first vehicles through the big stone gate. He had a microcassette recorder in his right jacket pocket and a palm-sized camera in his left. On the seat next to him was a spiral notebook for taking notes. If anyone in the church dared to tell him, "You shouldn't speak against this man without hearing him first," Kyle would be able to say, "I've heard him, seen him, taken notes on him, recorded him, and photographed him. I *know* whereof I speak!"

As he followed a van, a camper, and a huge motor home up the Macon driveway, he was already rehearsing his Sunday sermon, gripping the steering wheel as if gripping the edges of his pulpit. "Can't you people get a clue? Jesus warned us about this! 'False christs and false prophets will rise and show great signs and wonders to deceive, if possible, even the elect!'" Then he threw in a bitter, parenthetical gripe: "And a lot of help we're getting from the cops! Brett Henchle's been bought! He's been *bought!*"

The driveway came to the brow of the hill, and Kyle could see the big Macon ranch house for the first time. The van, camper, and motor home veered to the left, directed into a pasture by Michael the Prophet/John the Baptist/Voice in the Wilderness, now wearing a fluorescent orange vest and waving orange traffic batons. Kyle followed, parking alongside the motor home. The parade of vehicles poured in after him, parking in semi-neat rows on the grass.

He got out of his car and found it fascinating, if not frightening, to watch people arrive. Old pickups and vans were rolling in and parking beside zillion-dollar motor homes. Nice cars, beat-up cars, old Fords and new Mercedes all parked together. Kyle saw young, ragged folks with dogs in their cars, gray-headed retirees in garish summer shorts and white shoes, wheat farmers in jeans with big belt buckles, housewives carrying babies. Some carried cushions, some carried folding lawn chairs. The television folks were there, of course, the reporters well-dressed from the waist up and the crew people carrying cameras.

"Hey Kyle!"

Kyle turned to see Bob Fisher coming his way. He stuck out his hand and greeted the Baptist pastor. "Boy, am I glad to see you!"

"Come to check out the 'messiah'?"

"Exactly."

Bob looked around. "Will you look at this! We're talking a hundred people at least."

"Any other ministers here?"

"I saw Armond Harrison a moment ago."

Kyle winced. "I meant ministers of the gospel."

Bob laughed. "Just you and me so far."

They walked together toward the white paddock fence where the gate was open—and guarded by none other than Matt Kiley and Norman Dillard. Already some television camera people were coming back, turned away. A retired couple, cameras in their hands, walked back into the pasture and called to those still coming from their cars, "They won't let cameras in!"

"Hm," said Bob. "This guy has a thing about cameras."

Kyle said nothing about the camera he was carrying, and felt no moral qualms about it. The camera was going in with him, and that was all there was to it. This "messiah" had to be seen, known, and exposed. Kyle's only concern was how to get a picture without getting caught. He'd just have to pray for the chance.

They strolled nonchalantly through the gate, past Matt and Norman who waved them in with the mantra, "Come on in; no cameras please."

The ranch house was a beauty. The big doors of the four-car garage were open, beckoning to the gathering crowd. The widow's Town Car and her late husband's awesome truck were parked in the circular driveway in front of the house to make room in the garage for a sizable arrangement of folding chairs.

"There's Nancy Barrons," said Bob, nodding in her direction.

"Hey, and there's, uh, the Episcopal guy." Kyle waved.

"Paul Daley."

"What does he think of all this?"

"He says he's neutral, but boy, is he hooked. He really wants to know who this guy is."

"Just like us. Oh, there's the priest, uh, Vendetti."

Michael the Prophet stood out in front of the garage now, directing people inside. "Fill all the rows. Please move all the way down to the end to make room for those still coming. Thank you. Thank you. Right this way. Second row now, second row. That's it."

Kyle and Bob ended up in the middle of the third row. The chairs were arranged in a wide fan pattern facing the back wall of the garage. As far as Kyle could see, there was no pulpit or lectern, only the workbench with Mr. Macon's tools still neatly arranged on and above it. He spotted Sally Fordyce near the left end of the second row, and in the first row, dead center, were Bonnie Adams and her daughter, Penny. There were other familiar faces here as well, but also a preponderance of strangers from out-of-town, among them the motor home set bringing abundant riches from afar. The local business folks in the crowd had to be noticing that.

All this time, the widow Macon had been standing on the steps leading from the garage into the house, decked out in a blue denim western outfit with white fringe, silver buttons, and fancy white cowboy boots. Her arms remained folded and her face serene as she regarded each visitor taking a seat in her garage. As the last visitors still trickled in from the pasture, she crossed the garage and stood in front of the workbench, her hands clasped in front of her, and gave us all a greeting. "This is the day which the Lord hath made. Let us rejoice and be glad in it!"

Someone in the group let out a cowboy whoop.

She reminded everyone about the No Cameras rule, added a No Smoking rule, and then told the story of how Brandon Nichols first came to the ranch. It wasn't much of a story. He came to her door delivering four sacks of groceries and needing a job. She recognized a prophet of the Lord and hired him.

"But even now," she giggled, "it's not for me to say who he really is and where he is really from. I leave that up to you, just as he does. Brandon?"

The crowd broke into applause as the door to the house opened and a young man made his entrance, smiling, nodding at the crowd, shaking the hands that reached out. Kyle and Bob shot a glance at each other. This was their first sight of him. He was dressed in modern clothes—a white, long-sleeved shirt and white cotton trousers—but the resemblance to the traditional Jesus was striking. Kyle reached into his jacket and started the tiny tape recorder.

Nichols leaned against the workbench, looking relaxed, and scanned the crowd. Then he spoke clearly, informally. "I'd like to thank you all for coming and tell you from the outset that we tend to be a little unconventional up here. Jesus was unconventional for his times—or if you will, *I* was unconventional—" Several in the crowd laughed while several, including Kyle and Bob, cringed. "But whatever your religious background or belief system, don't worry, there's something here for each of you—"

He suddenly stopped, his eyes on a woman in the front row. "Pardon me, uh, Dorothy, is it? Your friends call you Dotty."

Dorothy was one of the well-to-do folks from the motor homes. She nodded while her husband and some friends looked her way, obviously impressed that Brandon Nichols knew her name.

Nichols reached out and took her hand. "No more arthritis, Dotty. You've had enough."

She lurched, cried out, shook a bit, and began flexing her hands, astounded and then ecstatic. She leaped to her feet, faced the crowd, opening and closing her hands rapidly for everyone to see.

Nichols had to raise his voice to be heard over the excited clamor. "If I *were* God, I'd do something about the pain in the world. I have the power, right? Why shouldn't I use it?"

He casually reached out and touched a long-haired young man who had come in a beat-up van. The young man immediately jumped up and screamed with joy and amazement, touching his ears.

"How's that?" Nichols asked.

"I can *hear!* I can hear everything!" His girlfriend jumped up and they embraced. The young man wept, then looked around the garage and outside as if seeing a whole new world. "I can hear the birds! I can hear the wind!"

Nichols had to shout now. The crowd was really stirring. "If God is truly visiting you, then he should be willing to prove it. I have no problem with that."

He gave his right hand a little twirl and suddenly, as if by sleight of hand, he produced a small loaf of bread and offered it to a little girl on the end of the second row. "Hungry?"

She took it and bit into it.

"What do you say?" asked her mother.

"Thank you."

He smiled at her as another loaf appeared in his hand, then another, then another. He tossed them into the crowd as hands went up to catch them. "Why do you worry about tomorrow, what you shall wear and what you shall eat, when you know that your God cares for you?"

"Let's see what's up your sleeves," a man wisecracked.

Nichols took it in stride. "Not today," he said, and then winked.

"Hm," said Kyle.

Nichols motioned for quiet and the crowd settled into their seats, wound up like springs.

"Don't forget me!" a woman in the back shouted.

"Alice!" said Nichols as if seeing an old friend after many years. "Bad hip, right? Don't worry, we'll get to it."

Kyle looked over his shoulder and saw Alice squeal, her hands over her mouth.

"This is incredible," said Bob.

"Really incredible," Kyle replied. He didn't know what to expect when he arrived, but it certainly wasn't anything as direct and intense as this.

"When Jesus came to earth the first time," said Nichols, "he went about doing good. Well, why not now? And I'm not just talking about myself. I'm talking about all of us. You may define me any way you wish. Maybe I'm Jesus. Maybe I'm the reincarnation of Jesus. Maybe I'm only a channel of his power.

"It doesn't matter. However I become Jesus for you, you have to be Jesus to others and the time to start is right now!"

"Oh praise the Lord!" a woman burst out. Kyle didn't have to look to know it was Dee Baylor, but when he did look, he saw not only Dee but her two friends, Adrian and Blanche. His hands were clenching into fists now and his stomach was in a tight knot.

Bob must have noticed. He leaned over and said, "Take it easy. Just pray."

"We have to come against this and bind it!" Kyle hissed.

"Let's get out of here alive first," Bob replied, and Kyle could see the fear in his eyes.

Bonnie Adams reached out to him and he touched her, apparently giving her the jolt she desired. She flopped back in her chair, trembling.

Paul Daley and Al Vendetti were sitting together toward the back, both wearing their black suit jackets and clerical collars, and both spellbound, their mouths agape, their eyes intense. Paul Daley had his hand over his heart. Al Vendetti was tightly clutching the jeweled cross hanging from his neck. Behind them, Armond Harrison was actually smiling and nodding in glad approval—until he saw Kyle. Then he gave Kyle a warning with his eyes: *Watch yourself, bub.*

Kyle couldn't alter the unkind facial expression he sent back. He was too upset, his heart pounding, his stomach churning, his hands shaking. "Antichrist," he whispered. "The spirit of Antichrist!"

"We can provide for those in need," said Nichols, producing several more loaves of bread out of thin air and tossing them to waiting hands. One flew Kyle's direction and he caught it for inspection. "Listen, God cares about your homes, your businesses, your health. He can bring new life to this community if you're willing to get on board. Wouldn't it be wonderful if people wanted to visit Antioch because here, more than any place else in the world, they could feel loved, welcome, and healed?"

Norman Dillard and Matt Kiley were grinning now, and Norman gave Nichols a thumbs-up.

Kyle examined the little loaf of bread. It was like a small sourdough roll. Nothing strange or unusual about it. He passed it along to someone else, not wanting to keep it, much less eat it.

Suddenly Nichols looked grim and pointed. "Sir, pardon me, no cameras."

Every eye turned toward a skinny, cowpokish fellow in jeans and work shirt standing in the back, a small camera to his eye.

"Nevin, really!" the widow scolded.

Nichols found a reason to look away as Nevin hurriedly snapped two pictures. Then Matt, Norman, and Michael grabbed him. He tried to get loose. They tried to grab his camera. It turned into a disturbing scuffle. The joy of the gathering chilled like a campfire doused with water.

"He's not Brandon Nichols!" Nevin yelled, trying to keep an iron grip on the camera while Matt and Norman almost carried him by the arms to remove him. "He's not!"

"Lean forward," Kyle whispered to Bob.

"Huh?"

"Scratch your head or something."

Bob saw the small camera in Kyle's hand and scratched his head. Kyle got a few shots of the distracted Brandon Nichols through the crook of Bob's arm. "Okay, that's it." He quickly slipped the camera back into his pocket.

The widow was trying to explain, "Shhh now, it's all right. Nevin used to work for me before I fired him. I'm sure you understand."

"Okay, okay," Nevin hollered in the distance, shaking the three men off. He turned to leave, but pointed at Brandon Nichols and shouted the last word as he went, "He's lying!"

Michael ran back to the garage and grabbed the staff he'd left leaning against a post. "Hear the Word of the Lord, my people!

Let not the siren song of deceit wrestle the blessings of God from you! The enemy roams about like a roaring lion, seeking whom he may devour! This man would rob you of your blessing!" He looked one more time as Nevin Sorrel disappeared over the brow of the hill, and gave a shrug. "He's crazy."

Brandon Nichols took charge again. "We've gained a valuable lesson, haven't we? Things haven't changed much since the first time I was here. There are still those who would judge and condemn and set themselves up as moral and spiritual lords over the rest of us." His eyes connected with Kyle's at that moment and then moved on. "But why let them? We can start again, start fresh right now. I'm willing to get you started. The rest is up to you. Are you going to try loving and accepting one another and enjoying your differences, or are you going to go on hating and killing for another two thousand years?"

Some applauded, others said Amen, some said Right On, and some were still bothered.

"Alice!" Nichols called. "Let's get that hip taken care of so you can get on with your life!"

He ran around and touched her. She leaped to her feet with a scream and started jumping and kicking. Nichols kept things rolling, restoring some eyesight, removing a cancer, producing more loaves of bread, healing more arthritis, and even causing a bald spot to fill in.

Kyle recorded it until his tape ran out and even managed to snap a few more pictures with Bob's help. He was over his initial shock by now, but feeling as comfortable as a soldier who suddenly finds himself in the very center of the enemy's camp.

"Adrian!" Nichols shouted, and Adrian Folsom leaped to her feet while Dee and Blanche squealed. Nichols approached her, extending his hand toward her face as he pronounced, "You will have a special place in God's plan for this town! Be listening, be watching, for you shall be a voice for God!" He touched her, and she collapsed into the cushioning arms of Dee and Blanche.

While Blanche fanned Adrian's face, Dee leaned in, expecting the very next touch. Nichols moved on without meeting her eye.

Ooh! Kyle thought. *That hurt.*

At three o'clock, just an hour after the meeting began, Mrs. Macon signaled Brandon and then pointed to her fancy jeweled wristwatch. He raised his hands in a gesture of blessing. "Our time is gone." People began to protest, but he didn't waver. "That's all for today. Spread the word to your friends and come again tomorrow, eleven o'clock in the morning."

Kyle and Bob both knew the significance of that time: It was when their own morning services began.

Nichols ran over to the door through which he first emerged as the crowd rose and applauded him. Then, with a Nixon-like farewell wave, he ducked through the door.

"Good-bye, everyone!" said the widow. "Thank you for coming."

A reporter shouted, "Can we have a moment with him?"

She shook her head. "He's not here to do interviews. He's here to minister."

Sally Fordyce hurried across the garage toward the widow, her eyes full of tears, her hands clasped under her trembling lip. "Mrs. Macon! I'm here! I've come to see him! I'm . . ." Her words became unintelligible as she wept.

Michael took his staff in hand and started herding the crowd. "Thank you for your presence with us today. Walk with God as you return to your vehicles! The Lord bless you and keep you! The Lord lift up his countenance upon you and give you peace! Watch your speed driving out."

"Mrs. Macon! I've, I've got to see him!" Sally cried.

Suddenly, Nichols appeared in the doorway again and aimed a warm and welcoming gaze at Sally Fordyce. "Sally!" he called, smiling and beckoning to her.

She crumpled to her knees, shaking with emotion. He took her hand, raised her up, and they disappeared through the door.

Kyle and Bob looked at each other.

"Sally Fordyce!" Kyle said. "The one who saw the angel!"

"He has plans for her." Bob shook his head.

"Oh God forbid!"

THE CROWD MOVED toward the pasture, almost every one of them wearing the same awestruck expression and talking about what they'd seen because they *had* to talk about it. Dorothy, who for years had had arthritis, was skipping, and showing off. Alice who once had a bad hip was prancing and square dancing with her husband. People were passing bits of bread around, sampling it and agreeing that it was the real thing. Matt and Norman manned the paddock gate again, nodding good-bye to everyone as they passed. They were beaming.

Now that they were in the pasture and away from the house, the television reporters took their microphones in hand and took full advantage of their cameras. They spoke excitedly, even frantically into the lenses. "We have seen incredible things today! A woman with a bad hip is now dancing! The legends of ancient times have become reality!" One reporter could hardly speak, his emotions choking his voice as he reported, "Brandon Nichols touched me, just in passing, and I felt a charge like electricity, and now, please look at my hand, can we get a close-up of this? The severed tendons are like new. . . ."

It wasn't at all difficult to grab someone for an eyewitness interview. Dorothy went on camera, and so did Alice. A man turned around so the camera could see new hair growing where his bald spot used to be.

Kyle and Bob moved with the crowd, speechless from horror and amazement, but also because any comment they could make would be dangerous to make here. Kyle kept doing visual three-sixties, trying to track down the other ministers. He caught a glimpse of Paul Daley and Al Vendetti already into the pasture, talking feverishly and visibly shaken. Armond Harrison was still back at the ranch house, apparently having a little conference with the widow. Sally Fordyce was out of sight, immediately part of Nichols's inner circle.

A reporter nabbed Paul and Al and shoved a microphone in their faces. As Kyle and Bob passed they could hear Paul stuttering a reply to a question. "W-we are in the presence of something immeasurable, unfath—unfatha—unfathomable . . . I'm sorry, I am really quite beside myself."

They hurried by, not wanting to be interviewed.

"We've got trouble right here in River City," Bob said finally, and very quietly.

"And some very serious preaching to do," Kyle replied.

Tomorrow, he determined, he would be ready. He would go home right now, get out his Bible, get on his knees, and arm himself for battle. His congregation and the town of Antioch wouldn't know what hit them.

If only he'd known how armed and ready his opponents were.

11

I DIDN'T ATTEND Antioch Pentecostal Mission on Sunday morning, but Kyle told me about it later, and I can imagine how it went. Attendance was good, the same kind of attendance you see at annual business meetings when there's a hot dispute in progress or a scandal has surfaced or the pastor is about to resign. Anticipation was in the air, to put it mildly. Kyle was so eager to preach he almost told the worship team to skip the music, but he thought better of it.

I know Bud Lundgren, the big-bellied, flannel-shirted guitar player, would have been difficult to disappoint. Once Bud had his day laid out, he was like a bulldozer without a driver, pushing relentlessly ahead and impossible to turn around. As for Bud's wife, Julie, playing her saxophone on Sunday morning was a matter of religious conviction, and not playing could amount to a desecration of the Sabbath. Linda, Kyle's trim little wife, saw the wisdom in going through with the worship service and encouraged Kyle to keep it in. The congregation and Kyle could use the uplift, she said.

So at five minutes to eleven, Linda sat down at the piano and got the preservice music started, a quick medley of worship choruses and hymns. She swept through the chords and fills in a Pentecostal style Kyle always admired. Bud wump-thumped a rhythm on his old electric guitar, and Julie made sure there could be no question anywhere in the building what the melody of the song was. Kyle was primed for preaching. His spirit was stirred and his adrenaline flowing. He was humming the songs as he took his chair on the platform, but when the little band came to "Victory in Jesus," he couldn't hold back any longer and started singing aloud. Some in the congregation joined in, some fumbled with the hymn books trying to find the words, and some just sat there not singing because that wasn't supposed to happen yet. Kyle didn't care. He sang anyway, his eyes closed, his heart touching heaven.

The song service went well. Katie Kelmer, a vivacious lady with blonde hair stacked high atop her head, led the singing in her flamboyant, hand-raised style. Halfway through, Brother Norheim started "Bless the Lord, O My Soul" and everyone joined in. That was a good sign. He usually did that in the evening service, but this morning he must have been feeling an evening kind of anointing.

Dee Baylor, along with the Folsoms and Davises, skipped the service. Brandon Nichols would be performing again that morning and they didn't want to miss it. In addition, they probably suspected what Kyle was going to say and didn't want to hear it.

But I have a good idea who was there: the Forester and White families, brand-new in the faith and growing in the Lord; three generations of Sissons; four generations of Bradleys; the Hansons, Parkses, Kelmers, Hiddles, and Lundgrens. I know they stood with him that morning. He heard their Amens.

In my mind I can see and hear how Kyle's sermon came across. I've heard Kyle preach, and when he's on a roll he's unstoppable. At times he can have a weakness for rabbit trails, and sometimes a particular illumination on the Scriptures will remain exciting to him but vague to his listeners, but overall, he gets from point A to point B, and persuasively. On this Sunday morning, by all accounts, he was on track, full of steam, and to the point. He'd heard and seen enough and it was time to get into the Word and settle the whole matter.

He launched his message from Matthew 24, repeating and expounding on warnings that came from Jesus himself: "Take heed that no one deceive you. For many will come in my name, saying 'I am the Christ,' and will deceive many," and "many false prophets will rise up and deceive many," and "if anyone says to you, 'Look, here is the Christ!' or 'There!' do not believe it. For false christs and false prophets will rise and show great signs and wonders to deceive, if possible, even the elect. See, I have told you beforehand. Therefore if they say to you, 'Look, he is in the desert!' do not go out; or, 'Look, he is in the inner rooms—' " At this point, Kyle felt it appropriate to add, "Or 'Look, he's up at the Macon ranch,'" and most of the folks nodded or even chuckled.

He was shouting with righteous energy by the time he read, "Do not believe it. For as the lightning comes from the east and flashes to the west, so also will the coming of the Son of Man be." He made a pretty strong point: Jesus coming to a crummy little wheat town in Eastern Washington didn't quite measure up to lightning coming from the east and flashing to the west. "Folks," he said, "the Messiah came once, was born in Bethlehem and grew up in Nazareth, not Missoula, Montana! I believe a false christ has come to Antioch, and I intend to use the Scriptures to make my case. Some are enthralled by signs and wonders, by a clever selling job, but I say we test this so-called christ by the Scriptures. As it says in Isaiah, 'To the law and the testimony! If they do not speak according to this word, it is because there is no light in them!'"

He got Amens to that. The people were with him.

Kyle took stern issue with Brandon Nichols's message, if there even was one. The "Jesus" up at the Macon ranch seemed happy to let people believe whatever they wanted about him or anything else. The Jesus of the Gospels claimed to be—and Kyle pounded this one in from several directions—*the* way, *the* truth, *the* life, and the only means of access to God. More than that, the Jesus of Colossians 2 was "the image of the invisible God, the firstborn of all creation, the creator of all things visible and invisible, before all things, the beginning, the firstborn from the dead, in whom all the fulness of deity dwelled." It was good stuff. Stern stuff. He pulled no punches. He got Amens and Praise the Lords and even some applause.

Then, for a big finish, he reminded everyone of the cross and the price Jesus paid for our salvation. Holding his arms out to re-enact the crucifixion, he spoke of the Roman spikes that pinned Jesus to the cross and then put out a challenge. "My Jesus died for my sins and washed me clean by his blood, and all creation will know this by the nail prints in his hands! If this man is the Christ, where are the scars?" He looked in the general direction of the Macon ranch and hollered, "Show me the scars that bought my salvation! Your tricks and healings and mind reading are impressive, but I need to be saved from my sins! Can you do that? Show me the nail scars!"

Amens! Applause! Agreement!

By the time Kyle said his closing prayer, his people were steeled in their convictions and the issue was settled. Kyle felt great.

He felt so great that he put all the main points of his sermon, including Scripture references, into a letter and mailed it to Nancy Barrons to print in the Antioch *Harvester*. That's how I first learned the content of his message. That's how the whole town heard about it.

And that's when the cow manure hit the combine blades.

ARE WE JEALOUS, *Reverend Sherman?*

I had not known Nancy Barrons to be quite so personal and direct in her editorials, but Kyle's letter, which she did print on the Op-Ed page, must have aroused more anger than her cool professionalism could contain.

> *When the word of a simple ranch hand draws more people in one weekend than your preaching has drawn for as long as you have been here, I see in this fact a message. Perhaps Jesus is more than just a white, middle-class, right-wing fundamentalist Republican. Perhaps he dwells outside the walls of our respective institutions and defies our*

petty descriptions of him. Perhaps he is more concerned with people than with opinion.

Everyone is free to see whatever he or she wants in this stranger at the Macon ranch. I saw a kindly doer of good who allowed everyone the dignity of their own convictions. He touched and healed but did not judge, he blessed and did not condemn. He dared to speak of the good in all of us and inspired us to do some good in this world. He was there for the people and not the other way around.

What a refreshing change: a Messiah who believes in us.

The town of Antioch could use such a message. Certain clergy of Antioch would do well to preach it.

As soon as I read Kyle's letter and Nancy's editorial I sank into my couch, raked my fingers through my hair, and cried out for deliverance, and not just for me. Kyle Sherman was more than an accident waiting to happen; he was a *disaster trying* to happen. I already knew which people were going to say what.

"HE COULD BE SUED for triple damages!" Burton Eddy squawked to Sid Maher. They'd happened upon each other in Mack's Sooper Market and short little Burton was red in the face. "Hasn't he considered how much money the widow's worth? She can hire a whole team of lawyers, believe me!"

Sid picked up a copy of the *Harvester* from Jack's news rack near the door, and Burton took it upon himself to point out the Op-Ed page. Sid read it and made a troubled face.

"Bravo for Nancy!" said Burton, tapping the page with the back of his knuckles. "Somebody needs to make it clear to the kid what the rules are around here!"

Sid made another troubled face. "Rules? Burt, Kyle has a right to his opinion."

Burton's voice grew a little cold. "Are you *siding* with him, Sid?"

Sid got flustered. "I didn't say that. I just said he has a right to his opinion. This is the opinion page, isn't it?"

Burton put a hand on his hip and shifted his weight to that leg. When his hips were crooked and his free hand was pointing, you knew he meant business. "This is a community, Sid, and we are professionals! We have a duty to this town to keep things running smoothly in a spirit of neighborliness. This kid is swimming against the current and he's making waves!"

Sid gave a weak nod. "His biblical arguments are sound."

Burton rolled his eyes. "Sid, people don't want to hear what this kid thinks the Bible says. That's the whole problem here."

"Well . . . the letter *is* divisive, that's clear."

"It's trouble, Sid, just like we had with Travis Jordan, and we don't need another round of that!"

Suddenly Jack McKinstry joined the conversation. "It's bad for business too. I mean, come on, what else does Antioch have going for it if people can't come here and see the Messiah?"

"BUT HE ISN'T JESUS," said Bob Fisher.

"I know that, I know that," Paul Daley replied. "But that isn't the point."

They'd met each other while picking up their mail at the post office. Neither wanted to get into this discussion, but each thought the other did, so they both did.

"Of course it's the point! It's the whole point of Kyle's letter!" Bob insisted.

"No, the point I'm trying to make is that Kyle's letter makes a point that brings out the point Nancy Barrons is trying to make: This Brandon fellow has a right to be wrong."

"She's saying it's right to be wrong?"

"No, no, no! She's saying even if you're wrong, that's your right."

"But what if you're deceiving others by being wrong? You think that's right?"

"He isn't deceiving others. He's letting them think whatever they want. That's the point."

"Well why is he even up there talking if people just think what they want anyway? What's the point of that?"

"There doesn't have to be a point. That's my point. Well actually, it's Nancy's point."

"So you're not making a point."

"No, I'm just trying to point out Nancy's point."

"And we're having a pointed conversation."

By now they were laughing.

"WELL, Kyle Sherman can come right in here and watch me run laps around the store," said Matt Kiley. "He's a talker just like all the others but he never made me walk!"

"He never fixed my eyes either," said Norman Dillard. They were standing in Matt's hardware store with the *Harvester* open on the counter between them. "Think *I'll* write a letter."

"Think I will too." Then he punched his palm with his fist. "Either that or show him my own version of righteous indignation."

"JUDGING, judging, judging!" said Armond Harrison, wagging his head. "It never ends! I thought we were finally going to get along in this town!" Don Anderson was trying to help Armond pick out a new propane space heater, but it seemed Armond had to talk out his frustrations first. "I should write a letter to the Pentecostal Mission headquarters and tell them to quit sending such arrogant bigots to our town! We were getting along fine without them!"

Don knew the Pentecostal Mission church had been in town long before Armond and his Apostolic Brethren ever showed up, but he didn't want to get into that. "Well, you and your people have always been good customers."

"We have, haven't we?"

"Sure."

"Always pay our bills, always come to you for our appliances."

"Sure." Of course, Armond never hesitated to buy in bulk from a discount supplier in Spokane, but he and his people often came in for smaller items.

"And we've never told you what to believe, have we?"

"Well . . ." Don shook his head, even though several of the Apostolic Brethren had been nagging him and his wife about coming to one of their meetings. They'd discovered real sexual freedom, they said, and suggested that without Armond's teaching, Don and Angela were most certainly stunted in their personal growth and development.

"I'm going to talk to the other ministers. I think this young upstart needs to write a letter of apology. And I'll have a talk with Nancy Barrons as well. There's no need to print such trash in her paper."

"Uh . . . how about this 20,000 BTU? I mean, if you're wanting to produce some heat. . . ."

"IT'S GONNA HURT my business!" said George Harding, the retired wheat farmer. Being retired, he didn't even have a business until the pilgrims came to town. He owned some nice shady land near a creek adjacent to the Macon ranch and was just in the process of putting in a campground for tents and recreational vehicles. He had customers too, lots of them.

"Yeah, and what about mine?" said Gary Fisk, owner of the Sundowner Motel, the only other motel in town. "The motel's full every weekend and most of the week. It's never been that way before this. If people like this Reverend Sherman can keep their mouths shut I just might be able to sell that place!"

They were sitting in a booth in Judy's, and Judy was standing there with her pad and pencil, waiting. "Well it's bad for my business too if you guys don't stop your yapping and order something!"

KYLE GOT PHONE CALLS, and they were nowhere near as enthusiastic as his congregation was Sunday morning. Dee Baylor called, of course, saying she was leaving the church and never coming back. Johnny Davis, Blanche's husband, wasn't angry but still thought Kyle should give Brandon Nichols a chance. Roger Folsom *was* angry and climbed all over Kyle's case for "picking a fight with such a nice guy." An anonymous caller said something about teaching Kyle love and tolerance with a cattle prod. When Sid Maher called, he was neither for nor against Kyle. He just wanted Kyle to know that some of the ministers—he wouldn't say which ones—were upset with him and hoping he would retract his unkind and judgmental words. "I understand you could be sued for triple damages," he said.

On an up note, Bob Fisher called to pray with him and tell him he did the right thing.

Then Melody Blair called. She was a girl in her late teens with a rough background who'd just started coming to church. Kyle and Linda had put in a lot of time and prayer getting her off drugs and into a steady job. "I'm not sure I should trust you anymore," she said in a troubled tone.

"Why? What's wrong?"

"Well, there was that letter you put in the paper, and then I just got a letter from Jesus."

"A letter from Jesus?" Kyle wanted to ask which Jesus, but chose a more general question. "Where'd you get that?"

"That nice lady Adrian Folsom. She said an angel spoke it to her and she wrote it down just for me."

"Adrian Folsom?" Oh no. Now *she* was getting into it. "What does it say?"

She read the note over the telephone. "'My dear child: Behold, I have a plan and a purpose for thee, shining clearer and clearer as the dawn of a new day. Do not let the words of your pastor trouble thee, for the light has not yet dawned upon his spirit. You must lead the way, for you are chosen. Hearken to my words and receive my love, and I will show thee a more excellent way, that you may show others.' It's signed, 'Jesus.'"

Linda told me later that in all their five years of marriage she'd never seen Kyle so upset. She had to keep telling him to wait a little while and pray before calling Adrian Folsom or driving up to the Macon ranch to have it out with Brandon Nichols. He didn't want to call me, which I could understand. I would have wrestled him to the floor and sat on him, and I think he knew it. He didn't want to call Bob Fisher, who would have been sympathetic, but would have advised him to keep calm. He didn't want to be calm. He just wanted to slug Satan and Adrian's angel and Brandon Nichols in their respective noses and go out in a flame of glory if need be.

He finally did call Adrian Folsom, but she refused to talk to him. He was in the flesh, she said, and could never understand anything as long as he was in that condition. He tried to talk about the note she gave Melody, but she told him no with a celestial tone in her voice and hung up.

BY WEDNESDAY EVENING, Antioch was not a very peaceful town. People were bickering from one end of town to the other, and strangely enough, the biggest issue wasn't Brandon Nichols but Kyle Sherman. Did he have the right, did he not have the right, was he judging, was he dividing, was he being truthful or hateful, was he nitpicking, and didn't he care about the town's best interests? Someone threw a rock through a church window. Kyle had to use his answering machine to screen his calls. Linda had to ask Michelle White to pick up some potting mix and garden gloves at Kiley's Hardware because Linda was afraid to face Matt Kiley.

By Thursday, Kyle decided it was time to break the pattern. His challenge about the nail scars was clear enough in his letter to the paper, but if words could only generate bickering and biting, perhaps it was time to make that same challenge face to face, in front of witnesses. People still had eyes even if they didn't bother to think.

Brandon Nichols had announced another meeting at the ranch that afternoon, and Kyle determined he would be there.

ACCORDING TO THE ANNOUNCEMENT going around town—
Michael the Prophet being the main source—the meeting was
scheduled to start at two. Kyle and Linda drove up the long driveway to the Macon ranch and found a spot among the large fleet of
vehicles already parked in the pasture—vehicles from Washington,
Idaho, Oregon, Montana, and a sizable contingent from California. Kyle parked next to a motor home from Nevada.

"What are you going to do?" Linda asked. She was there to
stand with him, but she was scared.

"Well, I'm not going to get into a big fight with him. But he has
to be confronted."

She drew a deep breath trying to calm herself and said in a quivering voice, "Well, please be careful."

"We'd better pray."

They clasped hands, said a prayer, then got out of the car.

Things had changed since Sunday. Mrs. Macon's humble ranch
hand was now holding meetings in a huge, blue-and-white striped
circus tent, and they could hear his voice inside, coming over a PA system. Six portable toilets stood in a neat row nearby. Ropes and flags
marked out the parking lot. He had obviously gained followers, both
local and out-of-state, and with those followers came money.

Gathering his resolve, Kyle started toward the tent, his gait
like that of a gunfighter, his eyes steady, his jaw set. Linda was
nervous and trembling, but stayed beside him, holding his arm.
They could hear Nichols talking rapidly, excitedly, saying something about Antioch becoming a wonderful town, better and
better, sweeter and sweeter. He was getting laughs and Amens
from the crowd.

Matt Kiley and two strangers were posted outside the tent,
wearing little plastic badges that said "Usher" but acting more like
Secret Service agents. The moment Matt spotted them approaching, he strode toward them and put up his hand like a traffic cop.
"What can we do for you, Reverend?"

Kyle tried to smile. "I've come to see Brandon Nichols."

It was surprising—shocking, actually—to see how cold and

mean Matt Kiley could be. "If you're thinking of causing any trouble you might as well turn around right now."

"I just want to ask a question."

The two strangers flanking Matt drew in closer as Matt replied, "No way."

Kyle looked directly and intensely into Matt's eyes. "Matt, do you even know who this man is? Do you *really* know?"

Matt thought only a moment. "Reverend, I don't much care. He's done all right by me and I like what he says."

"Even if he claims to be Jesus? Wouldn't that be lying?"

Matt only twirled his finger to indicate Kyle should turn around. "Better head back to your car."

Suddenly, Brandon Nichols stopped his preaching and called over the PA, "Matt, let Pastor Sherman in."

Kyle looked, but the tent walls blocked any view of Nichols, and any view Nichols might have of them.

Matt looked over his shoulder, scowling and ready to argue, but Nichols only said it again. "Let him in."

Before stepping out of the way, Matt poked Kyle's chest with his finger and warned, "I'm going to be watching you anyway, Reverend. You behave yourself."

The moment Kyle and Linda stepped inside, every eye in the place was on them, and there were a lot of eyes. At least a hundred people were there. For Antioch on a weekday, that was a good crowd. Kyle made it a point to meet their gaze and not shy away. His heart was pounding and his hands were starting to tremble. Linda was still holding onto his arm, but shying behind him. He could hear her praying in a whisper.

Brandon Nichols stood in front, a microphone in his hand, returning Kyle's gaze down the wide center aisle. Again, he was dressed in white. He smiled. "Pastor Sherman, I'm glad you came." He gestured and said, "Come on up. Don't be nervous."

Kyle, with Linda following, went halfway up the center aisle and decided that was far enough. He noticed Matt and his two fellow bouncers standing in the doorway behind them, ready to move at Nichols's bidding.

"Friends, this is Pastor Kyle Sherman. Most of you know him as the man who wrote the letter to the *Harvester*." That really turned heads and changed expressions in the crowd. "That's why I'm glad he's here. I've heard some pretty mean things said about him and I think we need to set things right. We're all neighbors, remember? We have to stick together if we're going to make this world work, isn't that what I've said?"

He looked at Kyle and spoke kindly, warmly. "Pastor Sherman, I'm sorry for all the trouble you've endured. I think you wrote that letter with the best intentions and I take no offense." He cast his gaze around the tent, meeting everyone's eyes. "Did you all hear me? I take no offense. The time for that is over. It's time to talk, to share, to get to know each other. Pastor Sherman wasn't trying to harm me. He simply had some honest questions. I don't despise his questions, and you shouldn't either. If we walk together long enough, and talk with each other long enough, we'll find we really can be neighbors with a lot in common. Isn't that right, Pastor Sherman?"

Kyle could feel everyone in the tent looking at him. He had to say something. He drew a breath and started carefully. "I want us to be friends and neighbors," he said finally. Nichols nodded deeply and affirmatively, as did his audience. "I guess I'm still having trouble with the introductions—you know, that very first part of getting to know someone when they tell you who they are. I—" They weren't going to like what he was about to say, but he had to say it. "I don't think you're being honest about who you are."

A woman in the audience piped up, "Well if you'd just *listen* for a change—"

"Alice," said Nichols. She halted. He smiled at Kyle. "You know me already. Most everyone in this room had a good idea who I was before they even got here."

"I'm sorry, but you are not Jesus Christ, the Son of God."

Many in the audience became visibly tense, but Nichols simply shrugged it off and gave a slight nod of concession. "To some, I am not. To some, I am. The same was true for the carpenter from Nazareth."

"No," Kyle objected. "I'm not talking about what others think. I'm talking about who you really are. If these people are seeking Jesus of Nazareth, they need to find the real one." He looked about, raising his voice so everyone would hear him. "The real Jesus bore your sins on a Roman cross two thousand years ago. The real one suffered nails driven through his hands." He looked directly at Brandon Nichols. "The real one set us free from the power of sin. Can you say that about yourself?"

Nichols hesitated.

Kyle hit him with another question. "Where are the nail scars? Everyone knows the real Jesus would have them."

Nichols remained silent and motionless. The people remained silent. The place was so silent Kyle could hear the breeze gently brushing the tent canvas.

Nichols sighed and dropped his gaze, a troubled look on his face, not a word on his lips.

Kyle relaxed and let out a sigh himself. He looked around at all the faces looking back. "I'm not here to hurt or embarrass anyone, and I'm not here to force my beliefs on you. I just wanted to make a point, that's all. If you're looking for Jesus, you need to know the real one—"

"Pastor Sherman."

Kyle—and everyone else in the room—looked at Brandon Nichols.

He was unbuttoning the cuffs of his long, white sleeves, the same troubled look on his face. "I . . ." He stopped, stole a glance heavenward, and sighed again as he looked at Kyle. "I didn't want to press the issue. I didn't want to force belief on anyone. That's all we've done for two thousand years, and somehow . . . I just thought we might do things differently."

He pulled his sleeves back and then extended his forearms at waist height, palms up. "Here they are."

Several gasps rose from the audience. People in the front rows half-stood, leaning, craning their necks to see.

"Come, Pastor Sherman. Come and see them. Place your hand on them. Touch them, and believe."

Kyle came closer. A woman from the front row began to whimper, falling at Nichols's feet. Other people were moving into the aisle, getting in line to have a look. Dee Baylor was among them, and met Kyle's eyes only long enough to give him a look of pity. A man in front touched Nichols's arms and then nodded a confirmation to all those behind him, his eyes filling with tears.

Kyle came face to face with Brandon Nichols and looked down at the scars just above the wrists. They were elongated, ragged. The scar tissue was a dull, off-white contrasting with his tanned skin. Kyle touched them. They were real.

"I was nailed through the forearms, not the hands," Nichols explained softly, as if sharing something just between the two of them. "It's the way they did crucifixions."

Kyle stared at the scars, then into the soft brown eyes, his mind confused but his heart dead certain. His words came in a strained whisper. "You are *not* Jesus Christ!"

Nichols gazed down at the woman weeping, hugging his feet, and at the crowd of followers staring at him in awe. In a chilling, hushed voice he replied, "I am now."

12

KYLE NEVER CALLED to tell me about his confrontation with Brandon Nichols.

Thursday evening, Brandon Nichols did.

"I'm sorry it had to happen this way, but what else could I do, Travis? He was trying to humiliate me in front of all those people."

I let my back come to rest against the kitchen wall and tried to recover from the news. "What did he do?"

"He turned around and left. I guess there was nothing more to say."

"So how *did* you get them?"

"What, the scars?"

I was strained and impatient and my voice betrayed it. "Yes, Brandon, the scars. How did you get them?"

He answered curtly, "They're nail scars, Travis. Do I have to spell it out for you?" He calmed and went on. "Anyway, I'm not mad at him. He actually did me a favor, the same as you did for Armond Harrison. Thanks to Kyle Sherman, I'm a victim, and that makes me the good guy."

That pill was bitter and I could still taste it. "You and Armond must have had the same teacher."

"And today I was Kyle's teacher. Hopefully he's a little wiser now, a little less sure of things. Just like you and me."

"Hey, don't lump me in with you."

He snickered. "Travis, come on, now. We're made of the same stuff. We've both been down the same road, and we have the same bruises. Kyle's just starting out, and today he got the same wake-up call we did."

"So what was your wake-up call?"

"Mm, not too different from yours. Remember that evening service at Christian Chapel? You kind of surprised yourself, didn't you? You didn't think you'd react the way you did. That's how it was with me. I just woke up one morning and realized, *Hey, I'm not so sure I buy into this.* It's nice to get a revelation like that, but it puts you on the outside in a hurry, doesn't it?"

The last thing I wanted to do was agree with him, but reluctantly, even angrily, I did. "Yeah. It does."

"At least Marian was on the outside with you. That part I envy."

The image came to my mind instantly, still vivid and clear. It was the first time we met. She was distraught, frantic, and angry, but at the same time, the most beautiful blue-eyed, long-tressed girl I'd ever seen. "It's a good thing she was there."

"I'm sorry I never met her."

"I guess I can't be too sorry about that."

"But it's tragic. Don't you see that?"

"See what?"

"*I* would have healed her."

The phone went dead. Once again, Brandon Nichols had done it—found an old doubt and thrown it in my face; ripped the scab from an old wound and left me to bleed.

And remember.

VERN. The one friend I had from earlier days in Seattle, a nice guy I grew up with. We were in youth group together back at the Allbright Gospel Tabernacle, and we were buddies in the Lord.

Both of us sang soprano in the youth choir until our voices changed—Vern moved to the tenor section first and I followed six months later. We got interested in girls about the same time and consulted regularly on the science of observing them from afar. He was better at shooting baskets and never missed an opportunity to remind me. I was better on the guitar and enjoyed proving it. My model airplanes looked better, but his flew better. When I prayed at the altar to get things right with God, he prayed with me, and I with him. He was a good friend.

I hadn't seen much of Vern since my family moved from Seattle to that little island, but with nothing else happening in my life, I decided to track him down again. He was twenty-one, working for a local trucking firm, rooming with two other guys, and starting to make a life for himself. I was twenty, playing in a bluegrass band in a sleazy waterfront bar in Seattle, still living at home, and spinning my wheels. He was going to an exciting new church and couldn't wait to get me interested. Despite my disillusionment, I was suffering from enough spiritual hunger to take him up on his invitation.

Christian Chapel in the south end of Seattle was exciting, all right. I used to think our little island church was dead and good old Allbright Gospel Tabernacle was on fire, but Allbright was old and stale compared to this place. When Vern first took me through the front door for a Friday night meeting, the sound of the worship washed over us like a tidal wave. The place was packed, and these people did nothing halfway. They were all standing, hands raised, swaying like trees in the wind as they sang the same joyous song over and over. The worship band was cooking, tambourines jingling. The song had no intelligible words, for each person in that congregation of hundreds was singing in tongues.

We found a place in a back pew. Vern set his Bible down and got right into the flow of things, raising his hands toward heaven and singing words to the song as the Spirit led him. I just stood there feeling overwhelmed and awkward—overwhelmed because it was overwhelming; awkward because all the guys had short, nicely

trimmed hair and I was in my wayward, wandering musician mode
with stubble on my face and hair down to my shoulders. They
were wearing nice shirts and slacks, and I was wearing an old shirt
and blue jeans. All the women were in dresses—long dresses. No
pants anywhere. I began to dread the moment when the song
would end and people would open their eyes and see me. They'd
probably think I wasn't saved.

The singing switched to English and stayed there for another
twenty minutes or so. That helped. I knew a lot of the songs, so now
I was on familiar ground and could sing with everybody else. By the
time the singing ended and we all sat down, I felt better. No one
seemed to be staring at me or my hair. As a matter of fact, a few
shorthaired guys with thick Thompson Chain-Reference Bibles and
thin black ties went out of their way to shake my hand in greeting.

I could have gotten used to that church. Pentecostal worship
was nothing new to me—this was more intense, but I could have
upgraded and it would have been fun. The personal testimonies
were encouraging. The Bible study led by the pastor was right on
the money and quite challenging. The people seemed friendly
enough.

Then the pastor decided to take some time to pray for the sick.
"I believe God wants to heal us tonight. If you have a sickness, an
infirmity, anything at all, I want you to come forward and receive
your healing in Jesus' name!"

About fifty people went forward and gathered around the pastor in a big huddle, laying hands on each other as the pastor laid
hands on the nearest of them. The pastor was invisible behind all
those bodies, but I could hear him praying and shouting into his
microphone, "Be healed! We come against this sickness and infirmity! Be healed!" as the congregation prayed along with him.

It was sweet and affirmative. There was nothing wrong with it.
I believed God could heal. I knew his Word promised it. I'd heard
people testify in the past that they had been healed miraculously and
I believed them. I grew up accustomed to expecting the miraculous.

But somehow, when Vern went forward with the others, it

brought everything a little too close. While he stood up there with his hands on the shoulders of the others and their hands on his, his eyes closed, his face uplifted, expecting God to heal his poor eyesight, I felt embarrassed for him. While people all around me shouted in tongues and wailed their petitions and Amens along with the pastor, I sat there, silent and cringing.

When the huddle broke up and Vern came back without his thick glasses, he was jubilant, convinced he wouldn't need them anymore. But I knew how it would turn out. Soon enough, probably before we drove home that night, he'd have to put those glasses on again.

I didn't ride home with Vern, however.

The healing idea really caught on. After the service, folks remained for prayer around the front of the church, and it seemed everyone and anyone was trying his or her hand at healing. A girl no older than sixteen was praying for an older woman, her hands clasped to either side of the poor lady's face and her arms shaking and quivering. It looked all too familiar, except she was adding a th-th-th-th with her tongue every time she drew a breath, and I hadn't thought of that one. Two of the shorthaired, thin-tied guys were hollering at a disease in a friend of theirs, embracing him as if they might squeeze the disease out. Folks were kneeling at the pews, bent over the altar, and sitting on the floor, all having very loud arguments with diseases.

I'd been here before, and didn't want to be here again. I watched from the sidelines, trying not to look sick and in need of prayer as I waited for Vern. He'd joined some friends who were sitting and kneeling around a young woman lying on the floor, and they were wailing, sing-songing, and shouting against a spirit of some kind. The girl on the floor did not look well, and the longer they carried on the worse she got.

There was something unsettling about this too. It scared me. I worked my way in closer, weaving around the kneeling and sitting clusters of praying people, hoping I could overhear something without being noticed.

"Spirit, come out of her this instant!" a young man with a crew cut shouted while holding the limp girl's hand.

A young woman kneeling by the girl's head kept kneading invisible bread dough as she did a sing-song kind of chant in tongues.

The girl on the floor looked pale and she was limp enough to be dead.

"We come against you, spirit of diabetes!" said a rotund young lady in a long, ruffled dress, waving her outstretched hand over the girl's body.

I took a long and careful look at the girl on the floor. "Uh . . . is she? I mean . . ." was about as much as I got out.

"Spirit, you are defeated! Come out!" the young man kept hollering, and the woman kneading the bread dough had to have the loudest, shrillest voice I've ever heard. I couldn't compete with the noise.

"Vern?" I said. His eyes were closed and he was praying feverishly.

Suddenly I heard one phrase come through the noise: "Diabetic coma!" I looked off to the side and saw a girl in a blue dress having a nose-to-nose discussion with an older man. She was upset; he was trying to calm her. I couldn't hear any more of what they were saying, but I did hear that one phrase, and it was enough.

I felt guilty and troubled as I stepped over and weaved through the people in prayer, but I was intent on getting out of there. Maybe I was quenching the Spirit, walking in disobedience, hearkening to the flesh, and deceived by the enemy, but I ran out of the sanctuary and into the foyer, hoping to find a telephone. Around a corner and down a hall I found a door standing open with a church office inside and a telephone on the desk. I ran straight to it and grabbed up the receiver.

"Excuse me, can I help you?" It was an older, sharply dressed lady, and I could tell this longhaired, blue-jeaned stranger barging in offended her.

"I need to use the phone."

She reached to take it from my hand. "This is the church office and this telephone is for church business only!"

I wouldn't give it to her. "There's a girl in there in a diabetic coma. I have to call for help."

She didn't like me and she didn't believe me. "What are you talking about?"

I'd already banged out 911. Someone answered right away. "Hello, I'm at Christian Chapel and there's a girl here—"

Footsteps running in the hall! The girl in the blue dress burst into the office and came straight at me. I thought she would claw the phone from my hands. "I need to use the phone! It's an emergency!"

"I've got 911 on the line right now."

"Tell them it's a diabetic coma."

"It's a diabetic coma," I said. "Christian Chapel . . ." I looked at the girl in the blue dress. "What's the address?"

"Two-three-three-zero South Walnut," said the Office Lady. She was starting to believe.

I repeated the address into the phone.

"They're going to kill her!" said the girl.

I got the word from the 911 operator and passed it on. "The paramedics are on the way."

She looked toward the hall, anxious and angry. "They'd better let them in!"

With that, she raced into the hall again. I followed, with the Office Lady behind me. We could hear the praying still going strong in the sanctuary. From all appearances, no one in there had a clue what we were doing.

When the ambulance arrived with its siren wailing and lights flashing, the girl and I led the two paramedics right up the center aisle to the front of the church. Vern and his friends were still confronting the spirit of diabetes and were quite startled when the paramedics pushed their way in. "Excuse us, please. Thank you."

Vern, bumped from his station by one of the paramedics, got to his feet and looked at me as if I'd betrayed the Lord himself. The young man in the crew cut tried to argue with them, "Sir, I'm telling you the truth, this is not a medical problem!" The rotund gal with the ruffled dress just kept on praying, kneeling as near as the aid crew would allow. As for the young woman with the shrill voice, she jumped to her feet, located the girl in the blue dress, and unleashed the full power of that voice at her. The rest of the people just kept on praying and wailing and praising, their eyes closed, their hands raised, oblivious to what was happening.

A paramedic tried to take the girl's blood pressure, his stethoscope on her vein. "Can we get these people to quiet down? I can't hear."

The pastor ran up, his face red. "What's happening?" One look and he figured it out. Then he angrily scanned the room. "Who called these people?" His eyes met mine and I knew we weren't going to be friends.

It was all backward. Vern and Crew Cut started yelling at the paramedics to leave the girl alone, Shrill Voice was begging the pastor to order the men to leave, and Rotund Ruffly started crying, "Begone, begone, you're ruining everything!"

Blue Dress bent down close to the paramedics. I heard her say, "She's my friend and she's a diabetic. Please help her."

Shrill Voice grabbed Blue Dress to pull her away. Crew Cut reached out to calm Shrill Voice down. Vern rummaged around the front pew until he found his glasses, then put them on so he could glare at me. The paramedic trying to take the girl's blood pressure shook his head and his partner yelled, "Could we please get all these people back? Give us some room and give us some quiet, *please!*"

The pastor finally went around calling for quiet and trying to calm people down. The EMTs wheeled in a stretcher, put the girl on it, raced her out to the ambulance, and sped away, lights flashing. It happened fast.

I remember standing out in front of the church with Blue Dress watching the aid car leave. We exchanged a look when we realized we had at least a hundred indignant people standing behind us.

"Maybe we should get out of here," I told her.

"I'm going to the hospital," she said.

I glanced over my shoulder. Vern was walking toward me, and I knew a sermon was coming. "Uh, can I catch a ride?"

"Travis!" Vern hissed, grabbing my arm. "Did you call the ambulance?" I was only starting to say yes when he opened up on me. "Do you have any idea what you just did? She could have been delivered tonight! She could have been free!"

"She could have been dead!" Blue Dress retorted.

"She was trusting God! It was her decision and you interfered!"

"Sharon's my friend and I saved her life."

Vern just rolled his eyes and shook his head. "You just—" He fumbled, shook his head again, threw his hands around in frustration. "You're a tool of the enemy, did you know that? You're playing right into his hands."

"And I see you're wearing your glasses again," I said.

That seemed to stun him. He quickly grabbed them off his face.

Blue Dress tapped my arm. "I can give you a ride."

I gave Vern a little wave to indicate our conversation—and the whole evening, for that matter—was over, and followed her out to the parking lot.

SHARON IVERSON was nineteen but still financially dependent on her parents. They used that fact to force her to move back home where they could keep an eye on her and, as parents will do, lay down some law. She'd been attending Christian Chapel's Bible Training Center, but that ended abruptly, as did her regular attendance at the services. I found out later that Shrill Voice, Crew Cut, and Rotund Ruffly—I'll call them Susan, Pete, and Monica— actually planned to kidnap her so they could finish her healing and deliverance. Fortunately, a lawyer friend talked them out of it and it never happened. Sharon went back on her insulin, remained under a doctor's care, and survived in spite of herself.

Most of this I learned from Vern after we got our own differences ironed out, which didn't take long. We'd been mad at each other plenty of times before this. It came with the friendship.

As for the girl in the blue dress, her name was Marian Chiardelli. She was eighteen, and turned out to be a deeply devoted Christian from a Baptist background. We spent several hours in the hospital waiting room, talking and comparing notes on religion, upbringing, and zealous friends like Sharon and Vern just to depressurize. She was just finishing high school and unsure of what she wanted to do. I told her I was a musician but I didn't say where or how.

She believed God could heal in answer to prayer and she wanted me to know that, but she was firmly convinced that tonight's prayer vigil crossed the line of good sense. I desperately needed to hear someone else say that, and I easily agreed with her, although it would have been too difficult to elaborate. I was still haunted by the sameness of it, troubled by the bizarre reenactment of my painful memories.

Around midnight, a physician told us Sharon was out of danger. Sharon's parents, Marian, and I went in to see her for a few minutes, restricting our conversation to safe topics.

By twelve-thirty in the morning, the crisis was over, and we were all tired. It was time to go home.

I shook Marian's hand. "It was nice to meet you," I said. "I enjoyed our talk very much."

"Same here," she said. "Thank you for all your help."

We would go our separate ways in a matter of seconds and suddenly that concerned me. "I . . . I'd like to talk again sometime."

She was picking up her handbag, slinging the strap over her shoulder. "I'm sure we will."

Sharon's parents were waiting to give me a ride to the ferry. They were standing by the front door, looking back at me. I could feel the gravitational pull of their bodies. If I didn't ask now, I may never get the chance again. "Say, uh, may I ask if it would be appropriate to ask if you might like to have dinner with me sometime?"

She smiled pleasantly. "I don't think I would recommend it. But I am flattered. Thank you."

I retreated quickly, backing away, rescued from total humiliation by the presence of Sharon's parents. "Hey, no problem. It was nice meeting you."

Well, it wasn't a rejection because I didn't really ask, so I took it well, sort of. Her warmth and graciousness made the letdown easy.

Sharon's parents gave me a lift to the ferry dock that night, and we had a nice visit on the way. They were thankful for what I had done and wanted to be sure I knew that. It made me feel a little better.

I was feeling better, anyway. As I sat in the ferry terminal waiting for the 2 A.M. ferry, I had time to reflect on matters Marian and I had been too busy talking for me to reflect on. It was encouraging to meet a girl so mature in the Lord already. After that whole thing with Amber, my thinking had been a little skewed regarding that possibility. I replayed our conversation in my mind, hoping I'd made it clear enough that I was saved, and worrying that perhaps I didn't look saved enough. I also reflected on that long brown hair held in place by a silver barrette, those sparkling blue eyes, and the freckles on her nose. Imagine. All that wisdom, all that sweetness, that inner glow—and she was beautiful besides.

No, I wasn't in love. After Amber, I'd learned my lesson. No more silly infatuations or crushes. No woman would have my heart again unless I really knew what I was getting into. I was going to go slowly and carefully into the next relationship, if there ever was one.

But boy, was I happy I'd met her!

WHEN I RESURFACED from the memory, I was seething, incredulous. The audacity! The calloused impudence!

Get a grip, Trav, I told myself. *Nichols has his reasons for saying what he does. Remember that.*

Yes. His reasons. What might they be?

I asked God why Brandon Nichols was doing this to me. He gave me only *part* of the answer in a small demonstration. When I hung up the phone with Nichols's words still turning my insides, I almost started brooding about it. *Almost.* I could have resorted to my old behavior. I could have sunk into the couch with my chin on my hand or gone for an agitated walk or just paced around the house, but suddenly it hit me: I'd been sinking into the couch and going for walks and pacing the house and brooding about virtually everything for months. Did I really want to do that again?

No. Seeing a future with more brooding in it, I put the brakes on. Having come to a full stop, I suddenly realized that the Messiah of Antioch *liked* me when I was broody. It made me a perfect pincushion for his little stabs. While he was finding just the right places to poke me, I was lying there like a lump and taking it—and then brooding about it.

Okay. That was part of the answer. As for the rest, that could be the key to the whole problem. I thought I should call Kyle.

The telephone rang again.

"Hello?"

"Travis, this is Linda Sherman. I'm sorry to bother you." She sounded very bothered herself.

"Is Kyle all right?" I asked.

She was on the edge of crying. "I don't know. He's up at the ranch."

"You don't mean the Macon ranch."

"Yes, the Macon ranch. He went up there to pray." She quickly added, "He said he wasn't going to go on the property. He just wanted to stand on the road. I couldn't talk him out of it." She must have heard my mournful sigh. Her voice took on a defensive tone. "Travis, I'd be up there with him except I have to watch the kids. But he hasn't come home and I'm worried about him."

"You want me to check on him?"

"And talk to him. He needs you, Travis. He respects you."

That was news, considering how well we'd been getting along. "He respects *me?*"

"Travis, every time we walk into that church and see all those people and how grounded they are in the Word and how much they love the Lord—and how much they love you—yes, we respect you. We can tell every place you've been."

Words wouldn't come. I didn't know what to do with what she'd just said.

"Travis, please go talk to him."

Linda wasn't the only one telling me to go. "Okay. I'll go right now."

I FOUND KYLE sitting on the hood of his car, on the opposite side of the road from the big stone gate, his wrists on his knees and his fingers interlocked, peering up that long driveway. As I got out of my car, I could see he'd taken a blow. He didn't leap to his feet or holler Praise God. He just gave me a tired little wave of greeting and looked up the driveway again. I walked over and sat beside him. The top of the ranch house was just visible beyond the distant rise, and to the left of it, the ridge of the big circus tent.

For a moment, we just sat there staring up the driveway. I'd never known Kyle to be so quiet.

Finally, I said, "I confronted Armond Harrison about his weird doctrines and sexual practices, and I raised the whole question about his belonging to the ministerial. I wrote a letter too—not to the newspaper, but to the other ministers, just asking if they had a problem with it. I guess I don't have to tell you what happened, or what people said, or how some of the ministers felt."

Kyle stared up the Macon driveway and said, "He isn't Jesus Christ!"

"No. Of course he isn't. But you have to remember, people like Brandon Nichols and Armond Harrison are always going to be around. If you use up all your energy trying to pull them down, you won't have enough left to do the Lord's business, building up the sheep and gaining new ones. You could crash and burn, and after you crash and burn, the bad guys will still be there. I guess you've noticed by now, there are people who like the bad guys. When you live in a world that likes bad guys, the bad guys don't go away."

"Dee Baylor's left the church and she's recruiting anyone she can find to follow this guy. Adrian and Roger have left, and now Adrian's passing around notes from Jesus that say people shouldn't listen to me."

I considered that for a moment, then nodded. "Hm. That sounds about right."

"It *isn't* right! It's deception! It's going to cost people their souls!"

I put up my hand. Truce. "You're right, you're right. Just trying to give you a perspective, that's all. Heresy loves company."

He pointed his finger in my face and spoke like a preacher. "He's a wolf in sheep's clothing and he's snatching my sheep! I'm not going to stand aside and let him do that."

"Kyle, as far as Dee and Adrian are concerned, if it hadn't been Nichols it would have been someone else. People like that don't stay in one church very long. They go where the goodies are."

"I won't stand for it."

"So what are you going to do?"

"Pray. That's the first thing. I'm going to be up here every day praying that God will defeat this man and his lies."

"But you're going to be wise, aren't you?"

He just about snapped at me, but I guess he got my point. He turned away, his pain showing.

I pressed it just a little, hoping he'd allow it. "Generally speaking, it's not wise to walk right into the enemy's cannon fire. A little caution, a little forethought, a little strategy never hurt anybody."

"I don't know how in the world he got those scars."

"He told me they were nail scars."

That turned his head. "He told you that?"

I nodded.

"When did you talk to him?"

"About an hour ago. He told me what happened between him and you. He sounded apologetic, if that helps."

Kyle's face seemed permanently twisted with amazement. "He talks to you?"

"Yeah. He calls and gives me regular updates."

Kyle's amazement twisted his face even more. "He *calls* you?"

"Yep."

"Why?"

I thought he'd never ask. "Heresy loves company. My hunch is, he's looking for some kind of sympathy, some kind of justification for what he's doing. He thinks I'll agree with him."

Kyle thought that over and then nodded with a hint of a smirk. "I guess that shouldn't surprise me."

"But that gives us a handle on him, doesn't it? He has a religious background he's not happy about and something he has to prove. He's after me because he thinks we have something in common. Well, if we have as much in common as he thinks we do, then I might know him better than I think."

"Are you saying you're going to help me?"

I remember thinking, *Now how in the world did it come down to this?* as I answered, "I guess that's what it comes down to."

I TOOK A SIDE TRIP along the river road just so the drive home would take longer. It was a nice day, I hadn't been down that road yet this spring, and I didn't feel like going home, not yet. I had the window rolled down, the smells of grass, wheat, and river water were rushing through the car, and I felt different. Not good, particularly—what I felt was a stirring in my heart I'd known before, a feeling that God was saying, *Okay, Travis, here's what I'd like you to do next.*

Kyle and I prayed together before we each headed for home. I prayed for him, he prayed for me, and we didn't pray *against* Brandon Nichols as much as *for* him. As mysterious and sinister as he was, I knew, and tried to tell Kyle, that he had an unknown side that needed to be reached. How that would happen there was just no saying, but—

Hold on! What was that in the river? I caught just a brief flicker of it through a break in the trees and brush.

I braked to a stop at the first gravel turnout and turned the car around. On any other day I might not have done that, but today—I don't know, I guess I was expecting something. I drove back, spotted it again, and pulled off on the opposite shoulder from the river.

Only weeks ago, the Spokane River had been running high from the spring snow melt, its banks nearly submerged, its water pea green from fine, suspended silt. Now it was dropping toward its summer level, changing from green to crystalline blue, and leaving muddy banks where river grass grew tall and sodden drift logs came to rest. I walked to the edge of the riverbank and found out I was right: I really *had* seen the rear end of an automobile just breaking the surface. It was brown with mud and silt, which relieved my concern that I'd come upon a recent accident. By all appearances, the spring current had pushed it along until it came to rest against a huge fallen log. I looked upriver. About thirty yards upstream was an embankment with access from the road. The embankment dropped like a cliff toward the water, but during the spring run-off the water would have been up to the top edge, making it a perfect spot to ditch a car—or have an accident. That thought now plagued me.

The fallen log provided a nice bridge out to the car and I took it, leaving my shoes, socks, and wallet in the grass. The current was brisk, rippling over the log, the car's trunk, and my ankles. The water was clear, however, and all I needed was an angle to avoid the glare of the sun off the water. Just above the rear bumper, I could see the license plate no more than a foot below the rushing surface.

It was muddy and obscured. Now I had to consider the temperature of the water, the quality of my clothes, and how far I would have to drive soaking wet.

I sat on the log and gasped as the cold water came up to my waist, then swept the mud away with my hand.

I could hardly breathe with the river chilling me, but I remained long enough to memorize the license number. Then, dripping and shivering, I hurried up the log and got out of there.

The effort may have been worth it. The car had a Montana license plate.

13

I GAVE BRETT HENCHLE a call and he came out to the river to have a look, putting on some waders and double-checking the license plate. I didn't say anything about the car being from Montana and what that could mean. I was hoping he'd make the connection himself. If he did make the connection, he didn't acknowledge it.

"Okay, I'll check into it." He threw his waders in the trunk of his squad car and drove off, leaving me standing alone on the riverbank, feeling let down. I wanted to think well of him. I wanted to believe he would be objective and do his job as a lawman, but . . . he had been healed by Brandon Nichols, hadn't he?

FRIDAY MORNING, halfway through my breakfast, I heard a lawn mower cutting laps around John Billings's place. I knew John wasn't home, so I had to wonder, *Now what?*

I stepped out on my front porch and looked across the street. This was something new: an older, chubby fellow in lemon yellow shorts riding a shiny red Honda mower. Did John hire this guy to do the job Brandon Nichols never finished? Was this the apostle Paul, or perhaps Abraham? Should I ask?

I tried to let it go and finish my breakfast, but two bites of Bran Flakes later, I couldn't stand not knowing. I put down my spoon, went out the door, and crossed the street. It didn't take long for the guy on the mower to come buzzing around again. I waved hello, hoping he'd stop.

He did.

"Hi, neighbor!" he said cheerfully. "Just finishing up the lawn here." He stuck out his hand. "Andy Parmenter."

"Travis Jordan. I don't think I've seen you before. Are you from around here?"

"Nope, Southern California. The wife and I are up here to visit Brandon Nichols for a while." He laughed as he said, "Guess that doesn't come as much of a surprise."

I smiled and wagged my head. "No, no."

"Brandon sent me down here to finish mowing Mr. Billings's grass. Heh. Looks to me like Mr. Billings already mowed it himself, but I guess it's the principle of the thing. Brandon doesn't like leaving things undone." Then he leaned forward over the mower's steering wheel and spoke intensely, "Have you ever met him?"

"Yes. On this very spot, as a matter of fact."

"He's a wonderful man, isn't he?"

"Is he?"

"Well just look at me. Retired executive, rich, successful—and miserable, until we came up here. Now here I am, sitting on a lawn mower mowing a stranger's lawn and feeling like a real human being for the first time! Brandon will do that for you!"

"Nice mower," I commented.

"My contribution to the cause. I've already mowed George Harding's RV park—that's where the wife and I have our motor home." He reflected, shook his head in wonder, and said, "You just can't believe the sense of community that's growing up at the ranch. People are helping, sharing, loving each other. In all my life I've never seen anything like it. I've never felt so glad to be alive." He looked around the neighborhood. "This town's a perfect place to start over and do things the right way. You're going to see some changes around here!"

THE CHANGES STARTED that very day, without announcement or warning. Norman Dillard didn't know what to think when six strangers showed up at the Wheatland Motel with ladders, brushes, and rollers, ready to give the old place a face-lift, free of charge. George Harding's dream of converting some of his land into an RV park flashed into reality as Andy Parmenter, his wife, and four other well-to-do Californians pitched in money and labor to get the place up to snuff. The Sundowner Motel, Gary Fisk's rundown enterprise, needed new plumbing and wiring; a plumber from Yakima and an electrician from Seattle showed up together to do something about it, compliments of Brandon Nichols.

Michael the Prophet became the energy, if not the brains, behind a project to repaint the white line down the center of the highway through town. A local artist joined that crew and painted colorful heads of wheat at each intersection and rain clouds to mark the location of the fire hydrants. "Soon the multitudes will come," Michael proclaimed as the rented line painter wheeled by, "and springs of water will burst forth upon the land!"

"NO, NO, my life isn't different, it's—it's like it's real, it's a life. It's like I've started living after being dead all my life. I just can't believe it!" a young girl with green, braided hair told a television reporter. She was operating a forklift, placing trees in big planters along the street. "My life used to be such a mess, and now it's, it's like it's just together, you know?"

"We were doin' drugs," said a big guy in a red tank top with blue-black tattoos on his arms. He looked at his two buddies installing the park bench near the new swing set in the newly mowed and weeded park with the new sign out front, CEPHUS MACON

MEMORIAL PARK. "Yeah, all of us, we were in the drug scene big time, but that was a dead end."

"And now you're disciples of Brandon Nichols, is that right?" asked the newspaper reporter.

The man nodded. "It clicked, that's all. Nichols knows."

His two friends liked the sound of that. "Yeah, Nichols knows!" they yelled.

Armond Harrison didn't look good in person and looked even worse on camera, but that didn't stop him from waxing verbose when given the chance. "We are now coordinating with the local businesses to carry out a major renovation of Antioch's historic district, hoping it will represent what we are as a people, a melting pot of different backgrounds, convictions, and ideals all living in harmony. This is, I believe, what Antioch stands for, and this is the ideal to which Brandon Nichols has lent his voice. At the core of our hearts, nothing is new here. But the time has come to bring our common vision into a tangible reality. We—" At this point, his lips kept moving but a reporter talked over him. Those who saw the news clip say his lips moved without sound at the beginning also, and the volume didn't come up until he got to "—this is the ideal to which Brandon Nichols has lent his voice."

Armond made it a point to get his people involved in the wave of goodness that swept over the town. Many of them were skilled craftspeople—masons, painters, dry-wallers, carpenters, concrete workers—and he wanted them seen as they turned out and pitched in, helping, joining, working hand in hand with the Nichols bunch. He never bothered to mention that he and his people were being paid for the work they did, meaning there was some hard practicality hidden behind all that benevolence. Few of his people asked probing questions, but all understood the money was coming from the direction of the Macon ranch.

Even Penny Adams, the girl with the healed hand, was moving into the realm of goodness. Out of the blue, she walked into Florence Tyler's little clothing boutique and offered to vacuum and dust. Florence didn't trust her, at least up until today, but things seemed so magically different in the town that she got caught up in it and gladly handed Penny a dust rag. Penny said nothing about what she expected to be paid. She just set to work, humming quietly to herself. Florence waited on customers, all of whom were buzzing about the changes happening in the town, and she marveled.

I WAS GLAD TO BE ON THE SIDELINES watching when the local ministers started to react to all this. Sid Maher was happy, neighborly, and neither for nor against it. Burton Eddy encouraged his congregation to join up, pitch in, and be a part of it, for this kind of unity, he said, was God's purpose for all of us on earth. Bob Fisher felt no hesitation in questioning Brandon Nichols's doctrine and intentions, but apart from that, he kept preaching according to the same format in the same order of service he'd always had at his church. His people, being warned, went ahead with a dessert auction and spaghetti social and hardly felt a bump. Father Vendetti encouraged his people to participate with anything that would be good for the town, but he reminded them that Our Lady also had its own charitable programs that should not be neglected.

Paul Daley was quite flustered when he talked to me about it. "I feel ambivalent," he said. "Nichols and his people are doing good works and that's good, but by joining him in doing good, we could be making his teachings and claims look good, which could be bad if Nichols himself proves to be bad, which means it could actually be bad for us to be doing all this good. But in not joining him to do good, we all look bad." He shook his head. "Whew! He has us over a barrel, doesn't he?"

AT THE END OF THE DAY, Florence Tyler was beginning to feel some ambivalence of her own. After Penny Adams had dusted, vacuumed, and left, Florence went to a dress rack to show a customer a cute flowery dress and discovered the dress was gone. She said nothing to the customer, but did take a look at the accessories rack, where she discovered a bracelet and necklace were also missing. The customer left without buying anything, and Florence, convinced she could have sold that flowery dress, began to imagine how right it would be for Penny's healed hand to be crippled again.

IN THE BACK of the Antioch *Harvester* and Office Supply, Nancy Barrons was bent low over her desk, carefully checking some contact prints with a magnifier. Kim Staples, her assistant, reporter, photographer, and lab tech, stood nearby to hear Nancy's verdict.

"I can't believe how everything's happening all at once," Nancy commented, her face only inches from the photo sheet.

"I ran my legs off today," Kim reported, "and I still didn't get it all. I just got word there's a roofing party going on over at Maude Henley's."

Nancy looked up from the prints. "You're kidding."

"I think it's the same people who fixed up the flower beds in the park."

"The Berkeley transplants?"

"Yeah." Kim pointed to a sheet of prints and Nancy took a close look with her magnifier.

"Heh. Yeah. Kim . . ."

"Yeah?"

"Is that really that guy's rear end sticking out?"

"Oh, did that get in the picture?"

"Man, with all this charity going around you'd think someone would give him a decent pair of pants. Oh brother."

"What?"

"There's Armond Harrison again."

"He was there. What can I say?"

Nancy straightened up to scan all the contact sheets before her. "He was at the sandblasting in the 'historical district,' the painting of the Wheatland Motel, the placing of the trees on Main Street. . . ."

Kim pointed, "And he was there for the refilling of the white line painter."

"How many Armond Harrisons are there?"

Kim gave a little shrug. "He likes to have his picture taken."

Nancy gave an irritated huff. "We ought to be charging him for all the free PR." She started circling her selections with a white marker. "Okay, let's run this one of the sandblasting, and this one of the tree planting. Is there a picture of the park without Armond in it?"

Kim tapped on one.

Nancy circled it. "And then maybe you can get a shot of the roofing job at Maude Henley's. But no Armonds and no rear ends!"

"You repeat yourself."

Nancy laughed. "I wasn't going to say it." The bell over the front door jingled. "Ah, a customer."

Kim took two steps into the store area and stopped dead in her tracks. "Oh . . ."

Nancy stood and looked around the room divider.

As soon as the customer walked closer and removed his baseball cap, she recognized Brandon Nichols.

"Hi," he said.

Anyone else could have come through that door and Nancy would have felt relaxed and neighborly. The sight of Brandon Nichols made her feel instantly . . . objective. "Hello. What can I do for you?"

"I was wondering if you might have a few minutes?"

Nancy looked down at her desk. "Um . . . I guess so." He approached her as if he would offer his hand. She nodded toward the chair. "Have a seat." He veered to the chair, his hat in his hands. She sat at her desk and put on a business smile. "Well, I never expected to see you come in here."

He smiled. "You look great."

"Thank you," she replied, taking it as flattery. She was wearing a loose knit blouse and jeans, something appropriate enough for the office, but not striking.

He leaned forward, resting his elbows on his knees. "The reason I came is, first of all, to thank you for your fair and understanding treatment of everything we've been trying to do. Obviously, it's easy to be misunderstood by the public at large and by the press, but I think your reporting on our efforts has been a credit to your paper and a good boost for the town."

"It's been interesting. Exciting. But do you mind if I ask you, where's the money coming from to pay for all this labor and material?"

"Donations. A lot of the folks who've come to the ranch had money but no purpose in life. Now they have a vision to embrace, something worthwhile to invest in."

"Which is?"

"Excuse me?"

"Why are you fixing up the town? What's the purpose?"

He smiled, a dreamy look in his eyes. "Maybe it's to get as close as we can to heaven on earth, a clean and lovely place for the spiritually seeking. And the work itself is a healing salve in people's lives. It gives them the ability to create change with their own hands and resources. In today's world that means a lot."

"I suppose a cleaner, brighter town would enhance *your* marketability."

"It would be good for *everyone*."

"Okay."

"But . . ." He nervously rubbed his hands together. "What I said about the spirit of the town . . . that's another reason I'm here. If I may, I'd like to speak up on Kyle Sherman's behalf." She made a curious face. "I know that he tends to be a little blunt—"

"A little?"

He chuckled and flipped his hands palms up. "Well, you know and I know . . ."

"We know."

"But I didn't come to Antioch to divide people. Mine is a mission of peace and brotherhood, and given time, I have hopes that Kyle Sherman and I can work things out."

"That's a lot of hope."

He gave a little shrug. "Well. We have to start somewhere. I'll go first."

"So you didn't care for my editorial?"

He slid his chair closer and lowered his voice a little. "It was brilliant, almost surgical in its precision. But it was cutting."

"No pun intended?"

He laughed, gazing at her. "Oh, perhaps intended."

She felt his eyes on her, but tried to quell the uncomfortable feelings that assaulted her. Of *course* he was looking at her. They were *talking*. "Um . . . I felt that Reverend Sherman was trying to bar you from the neighborhood on purely religious grounds, and from where I view history, that's something we've seen too much of already."

"Oh, I agree. It's people that matter, not what they believe."

"So are you Jesus Christ?"

He chuckled. "It depends on who you ask. People who wish to believe that may do so."

"And if they don't?"

"They just don't."

She leaned toward him. "I want to know who you are *really*."

"Brandon Nichols, ranch hand from Missoula."

"Who used to work at the Harmon ranch?"

There was the slightest pause before he answered, "That's right."

"I talked to the Harmons. They say you worked there for five years. Why'd you quit?"

"It was time to move on."

"They never saw you do any miracles, either. What changed? First you're in Missoula herding cattle and horses and the next thing anyone knows, you're in Antioch acting like Jesus."

He smiled knowingly. "At first, Jesus was a carpenter in Nazareth, and the next thing anyone knew, he was preaching in synagogues and turning water into wine."

"Got any family anywhere?"

He slid his chair closer. "I can see we have a lot to talk about. We should get together for lunch sometime, or perhaps dinner at the ranch. I'd feel freer to discuss such things"—he reached out his hand—"if there weren't other people around."

She had a pencil in her hand. She held it out to intercept his hand gently. "Could you do me a favor? I'd like you to refrain from touching me."

He withdrew his hand and leaned back in the chair. "Certainly."

"I've seen what happens when you touch people. Brett Henchle's never been the same."

He seemed pleased at her observation. "No, he certainly hasn't, nor have the hundred or so others I've touched. But what I've done for individuals I want to do for the whole town. This town needs a special touch and I hope to provide that over the weeks and months ahead."

"Where are you from originally?"

"You mean, before Missoula?"

"That's right. Where were you born? Where'd you grow up?"

"It'll cost you dinner with me."

He was smiling at her, waiting for an answer. Something in his eyes chilled her.

She called, "Kim?" Kim looked up. "Let's get a picture of Mr. Nichols to go with our story."

"Sure thing." Kim reached for her camera.

Nichols was on his feet. "Not today."

"C'mon," Nancy prodded, "it'll only take a second."

"The dinner invitation is still open. Call me at the ranch."

He turned and hurried through the store and out the door.

Kim stood with her camera, eyebrows high with surprise. "Wow."

"Like Superman and kryptonite," said Nancy.

"Was he . . . hitting on you?"

"Aw . . ." Nancy turned to her desk. "I could never prove it to anybody."

Kim stood there, waiting.

"Yes, he was," Nancy finally answered, and by now she was shuffling through papers and yellow post-it notes trying to find a phone number. Ah, there it was. Nevin Sorrel, Mrs. Macon's lanky, former hired hand, had said he had something very serious to tell her about Brandon Nichols. At the time he called, Nancy wasn't interested in gossipy stuff from a resentful semiliterate, but she was seeing things a little differently now.

AS FOR WHAT Morgan Elliott was thinking, I hadn't heard—that is, until she called and asked to see me, which was the last thing I expected. I'd mostly been friends with her late husband, Gabe, and apart from the ministerial meetings, hadn't seen much of Morgan after his death. Considering my reputation with the open-minded, liberal, and tolerant faction of the ministerial—and her apparent alignment with that camp—it seemed best to steer clear of her anyway.

Well, so much for that. What she wanted to see me about I had no idea, but I now had an official, three o'clock appointment with Pastor Elliott. I arrived promptly, parked in front of the Methodist church, and went through the big double doors. A lady in jeans was mopping the floor in the foyer and told me yes, the pastor was in her office, located at the front of the sanctuary, through a door just to the right of the chancel.

I'd forgotten how classy this old church was, and enjoyed my short walk down the center aisle. This was a building in the old tradition, dark stone on the outside, fancy woodwork and plaster on the inside, with a high, vaulted ceiling and stained glass windows. The pews were stout and hand-carved, the deep red cushions a later improvement. The original floorboards under the carpet had been squeaking in the same places for decades, and overhead were the black iron chandeliers that came by ship and rail from England in 1924—Gabe told me all about it.

The door to the pastor's office was open and I could see Reverend Morgan Elliott seated at her desk in a dark suit, white blouse, and dark blue scarf. Her long, curly hair was pinned back today and she was working intently, her round glasses perched on the end of her nose. Feeling some anxiety, I knocked gently on the doorjamb. She looked up and smiled, and then she stood, extending her hand. "Hi. Please come in."

I shook her hand and took the chair facing her desk. I had no idea how I should conduct myself: As a friend? A neighbor? A fellow professional? Maybe a condemned heretic. I'd just have to wait and see.

"So how in the world are you?" she asked, setting aside her work and then resting her chin on her fingers.

"Doing all right." It was a comfortable, generic kind of answer. "How about yourself?"

She didn't answer quickly, and her answer wasn't comfortable for either of us. "I have some things I need to talk with you about."

Uh-oh. I once had a vice principal who said exactly those words in exactly that tone of voice. Not knowing whether to expect a chat or a lecture, I ventured, "This is kind of unusual, you and I having a meeting."

She shrugged one shoulder. "I'm taking a chance that I've read you correctly. If I had this meeting with anyone else, I'd get a party line, predictable answer or no answer at all. But you seem to be in a different place right now."

"A different place?"

She cocked her head to one side and gave an apologetic smile. "You faced down Armond Harrison in front of the whole ministerial. You organized a picket protest outside the theater when they showed an X-rated movie. You led a March for Jesus down the highway through town. You were pastoring Antioch Pentecostal Mission long before Gabe and I got here, and we always knew what to expect from you."

I caught her point. "Things have changed a little."

"I'm guessing you're on the outside. Things have to look different from out there. Do they?"

I stared at her, off-balance.

"Do they?" she asked again.

I knew the answer, but I was dumbfounded to hear Morgan Elliott asking the question. "Yes. They do. Things look a lot different. Not always in focus, but definitely different."

"Then maybe we can compare notes. Things are starting to look different to me too, and I'm not sure what to do about it." She looked at the ceiling and squinted as if seeing something in the distance. "I have this picture in my mind. I'm eighteen, getting ready to leave home, and I'm standing out in the yard in front of my parents' house in San Jose. I've got clothes in a big duffel bag and a guitar in one of those cheap cardboard cases, and I'm leaving, heading out on my own. But I'm looking back toward the front door, and my folks and my brother and sister are standing there, calling to me, beckoning, telling me to come back inside. 'You don't belong out there, come back inside, you need to stay here.'" She stopped abruptly and asked, "Does any of this sound familiar?"

Maybe. "Is there more?"

She looked away, replaying the scene in her mind. "Part of me wants to go back. I mean, it was home. It was secure. I liked living with my folks. It's not like I was rebellious."

"Uh-huh."

"But somehow, I . . ." Abruptly, she reached for a yellow legal pad on her desk. "Maybe we can talk about that later." She nervously consulted a list she'd scribbled on the yellow pad. "I've been wracking my brain all morning—well, for several days, actually—and I've narrowed down the topics to three: My church and I aren't getting along; Brandon Nichols isn't Jesus . . ." That was two. I sat there waiting. She sighed, looked at the wall, built up her nerve, and gave me the third: "Michael the Prophet is my son."

I didn't react. I couldn't. I had to hear her say that again. "Excuse me?"

She looked directly at me. She even leaned into it. "Michael the Prophet—you know, that crazy guy with the shawl and the staff and the cut-off jeans—"

"And the phony British accent."

"That's the one. Michael is my son. Michael Elliott."

Slowly, jarringly, the memory dawned. "I remember you and Gabe talking about Michael. But I never met him."

"He didn't come to Antioch with us. He'd left home by then, and had started his, his wanderings. We got lots of letters and calls, but he never came home again. He had to be . . . *out there*. He took in about a year of college, then traveled to India to discover himself and got dysentery. On the way back, he had himself baptized in the Jordan River. He's, well, he's searching."

"And now he's found Brandon Nichols."

She gave a slow, painful nod. "He thinks Brandon Nichols is Jesus. He told me that to my face."

I didn't mean to smile. "And you have a problem with that?"

She huffed in frustration. "Isn't that the limit? I guess I'm upset because he's my son."

Now *that* was fascinating. "Huh."

"I know what you're thinking."

I hesitated to say it.

"Go on."

"Well, we have heard it said that love means you don't question or challenge another person's beliefs. But now we have a case in which, because you truly love someone, you don't want them to be deceived."

"Exactly."

"So it matters to you what they believe."

"And therefore I'm upset that Brandon Nichols is deceiving my son."

"How intolerant of you."

She nodded. "How *very* intolerant." She rested back in her chair, strong emotions just under the surface. "But I know—I *know*—that Brandon Nichols isn't Jesus, and if he isn't Jesus, then someone else must be, and I'm very sorry we never told Michael. Pardon me for baring my soul, but I'm haunted by the thought that he believes in Brandon Nichols because there was nothing for him to believe in at home."

"For what it's worth," I said, "Brandon Nichols isn't Jesus, and someone else is."

She said with a flourish, "*Thank you* for saying so."

We were eye to eye across that desk. "So things are looking different now?"

She drew a deep breath and stared into the past. "I *was* comfortable. I had my ministry, my little bag of pet beliefs and nonbeliefs, my own congregation of followers. But now I can't sit still. I can't rest. I'm like my son." She met my eyes again. "I want to know something for sure. Very radical idea, I know. And they—some of the people in my congregation; the old guard, the pillars, the heavy givers—don't want me to look. They're afraid of my asking. They like the old Morgan, the cheerful little lady who smiled and made them feel good and never ventured further than these four walls." She added with a bitter note, "The one who preached so much but said so little. *They* like Brandon Nichols. *They* don't see anything wrong with him—just like Michael!" She halted. Her eyes glistened with tears.

"So you're standing out in the yard again, and Mom and Dad are calling to you to come back."

"And I can't!" she said angrily, her voice cracking. She reached for a facial tissue and removed her glasses to dab her eyes. "Excuse me."

I rested back in my chair, stunned that I would have something in common with Morgan Elliott, of all people. "So you're on the outside too."

That touched just the right nerve deep inside her. The tears overflowed, and she chuckled with embarrassment. "I'm so sorry."

"It's okay."

She grabbed another tissue and blew her nose. "I'm forty-two, an ordained minister with a congregation—" She stopped, pulled in a deep breath, and spoke in a steadier voice. "And I don't know what I'm going to do with myself! I can't go back! I can't be what I was before, and the people are getting worried and I don't know what to tell them."

"And Brandon Nichols brought all this on?"

She shook her head. "I was working on it before this. He just pushed it ahead several spaces, that's all."

"He pressed the issue."

"Exactly."

"Well," I said with a hint of sarcasm, "I know your problem.

You just need to have a Quiet Time every day; you know, read your Bible and pray."

"I do!"

I scowled. "That's funny. It always works for everyone else."

She caught my drift. "So they tell me. Except I'm taking the Bible too literally."

"I've been told I'm backslidden."

"I've been told I'm starting to sound like a fundamentalist."

"I need to come back to the Lord."

"I need to quit sweating the details and just love everyone."

I started laughing. She started laughing. It was like having an inside joke between us, and I could hardly believe it. In that little cubicle in that staid old church in the center of that troubled town, two people who hadn't laughed in quite a while found something they could chuckle about together.

"So what can we do about Brandon Nichols?" she asked.

By now I couldn't help thinking that God had something brewing. "I guess we'll know when the time comes."

She smiled. "God is here with us, isn't he? Even on the outside."

We prayed, the Reverend Elliot and I. I think it worked. As I left the church, I asked the Lord just what he was doing, and as usual, he left me to figure it out.

At any rate, I was very glad she called. Glad I came. As she had said, God was with us, even on the outside.

I hadn't always felt that way. . . .

14

THERE ARE SMELLS you never forget. Every once in a while I'll sniff just the right combination of beer and cigarette smoke and immediately recall my short and failing career as a bluegrass musician. I was nineteen going on twenty, and still in a state of mind where what I wanted had to be what the Lord wanted. Consequently, it had to be God's will for me to be playing in dark taverns with black light posters on the walls and aging waitresses dressed in sequined, low-cut blouses. There had to be some kind of godly mission in playing my banjo until two in the morning while I absorbed cigarette smoke into my clothes.

Once an uncle asked me what I was doing, and I told him about my band. He asked me, "How many of them have you won to the Lord?"

I answered honestly, "As many as wanted to be," which was another way of saying, "None."

Our group, the Mountain Victrola, was about as stable as it was godly. The guitar player always had some weird chemical in his brain and a recent message from somewhere unseen. The bass player had a standing offer from another band that made better money, and he owned our PA system. The mandolin player owned the station wagon we used to haul ourselves around, but he was catching flak from his "old lady" and figured he'd have to quit. The dobro player was constantly depressed and kept talking about joining up with his brother in a fruit and produce business. We weren't very good and we weren't improving, and most of all, we were poor. Fifty bucks a night—for the whole band of five—was not what one would call a starlit stairway.

There's a psalm that tells us not to be like a wild donkey that needs to be bridled, and a proverb that says a wicked man will have his fill of his own ways. Mix those two ideas together and you have a good description of my spiritual state the last night I played with that band. We were taking a break, sitting in a booth in the Cedar Tavern in Seattle. It was after midnight, we still had two more forty-minute sets of music to play, and there were about five people there to listen to us. The place was dark and smoky. The jukebox was thumping. I could see my underwear glowing through my clothes under the black lights. My friends were smoking, griping about the money, and talking about what they could be doing instead of this. I was sipping from a Coke and pondering the same question.

Folks have asked me how and when God called me into the ministry, and I've never had a definite answer. The way God designed me, I would have ended up in the ministry eventually. I could have wandered around for a few more years pursuing all sorts of dreams and ambitions—music, acting, banjo making, ditch digging—but one overriding fact determined my destiny: I loved the Lord deeply and wanted to serve him. Given that, my being in the ministry was a foregone conclusion and only a matter of time.

All I had to do was make up my mind, choose the right road, and stay on it. That night at the Cedar Tavern, I did.

West Bethel College seemed the natural choice. It was strictly a "Bible Institute" when Dad went there, and there was only one, not an East in Wheaton, Illinois and a West near Portland, Oregon. It's where he met Mom, and I still have Dad's big exhaustive concordance with Mom's personal note in the front: "To Wayne Travis Jordan upon graduation, May 28, 1948, Bethel Bible Institute."

Three of my dad's brothers graduated from there, and a majority of my cousins. By the time my older brother, Steve, graduated from there in 1971, so many other Jordans had gone there over the years that the professors kept getting Steve's name mixed up with theirs.

In the fall of 1973, the profs had to learn the name of still another Jordan. I cut my hair, shaved my beard, bought a new Bible, and signed up. At twenty-one I was a little older than most of my classmates, but at least I'd worked some of the wild donkey out of my system. While my classmates were squirting shaving cream down each other's pants and putting detergent in the main entry fountain, I just wanted to study.

And pray. I'd been wandering long enough and I loved being home again, immersed in the Pentecostal culture I'd known since childhood. We called each other "brother" and "sister," said Praise God and Hallelujah whether things were going well or poorly, raised our hands toward heaven when we worshiped, and spoke in tongues when we prayed. God was free to move among us, and he did. I felt safe here. The presence of God in the chapel services was warm and familiar, and my faith became something I could *feel* again, something deeply human.

It was a protected environment. Pentecostal students from all over the country, and some from overseas, left their parents at home and came here to be parented by the college their parents paid for. We had a dress code and a hair code, strict rules governing dating, and required church attendance—you had to file a report every Monday morning. Going to a movie could get you expelled, and as for alcohol and tobacco, you didn't even want to have the *smell* on you. We didn't dance, gamble, swear, stay out late, or make out, and if anyone did, angels told the dean about it *every* time.

I didn't mind the rules. I didn't *agree* with all of them, but I didn't mind them. Shorter hair was easier to manage, I was a guy so it was okay to wear pants, and I liked the church I was attending without fail every Sunday.

As for romantic inclinations, the dean, the dorm parents, and the school administrators didn't have to worry about me. I still regarded my love life as something like electroshock therapy for smokers: Associate enough pain with it and you can kick the habit.

Then, much to my surprise, I saw an old acquaintance again. Halfway through the fall quarter, a girls' trio calling themselves The King's Carillons—back in Bible school, every music group was a King's this or a Master's that, besides all the different Maranathas going around—sang their debut number in morning chapel, and they had my undivided attention. For one thing, their style was really pushing the edge. One of the girls was actually patting out the rhythm on her leg, and I think I saw a few heads in the crowd bobbing with the beat. I was certain this song did not come out of our black, shaped-note hymnals.

But what threw me was the alto standing in the middle. It was Marian Chiardelli, the girl in the blue dress I encountered clear back at Christian Chapel! I wondered why I hadn't noticed her around campus before this, but taking a good look at her now, I could see she'd changed since our long talk in the hospital waiting room. Her hair was a little longer and had a gentle wave to it, and the silver barrette was gone. Her eyes seemed bigger, and today they were sparkling as the sunlight came through the chapel windows. Her figure was adequately shrouded in a purple dress that met college specs, but it did not escape my notice as being somewhat improved.

Marian Chiardelli! I couldn't believe it. I knew this girl . . . sort of. I mean, we had met once. I wondered if she would remember me.

C. R. Barnsworth, the college president, preached that morning. I don't remember much of that sermon—just him trying to get us all charged up and repeating the phrase, "fresh oil, fresh oil, fresh oil." I was too busy maintaining situational awareness as to Marian's location in the chapel—front row, right side, fourth from the right—and trying to figure out how I might intercept her on the way out, just to say hi.

C. R. finished, we stood to sing our closing song, Rick Parks, the student body president, said the closing prayer, and we were out of there.

I'd been sitting halfway back on the left side, in the middle of the pew. She left the chapel through the right front door. I maneuvered, dodged, and weaved through the body traffic, got to that door, and pushed my way outside.

She was with someone.

His name was Loren Bullard—a junior, a superjock, at least a foot taller than me and that much wider around the chest. A starter on the basketball and football teams. A weightlifter. He played classical piano with scale runs, rapid arpeggios and vast chord extensions. He drove a great car. And he was a nice guy, really. He was bold and confident, devoted to the Lord, and wanted to be a missionary.

I stood there a moment, watching them go down the brick walkway across the campus, talking and laughing, just the two of them. They were a charming couple. Marian had made a good choice, I had to admit.

Which didn't say much for me. My credentials—shipyard-working, bar-playing banjo picker—looked pretty dim next to the glimmer of Loren Bullard's.

Well, sometime I would say hi to her, just to say hi. Perhaps she would remember me.

A WEEK OR SO LATER, my roommate, Ben, and I were trying to play a few tunes in the Hub—that was what we called S. J. Marquardt Hall, the place where we bought snacks, got our mail, and socialized. Ben had learned to play guitar from a Peter, Paul, and Mary songbook and had no idea how to play a bluegrass rhythm. I wanted to play Foggy Mountain Breakdown, but for that song to work, the guitar has to be going *boom-chunk boom-chunk*. All I could get out of Ben was *sling-ading-adinga* and it sounded awful. I set the banjo aside, took the guitar again, showed him again, talked it through again. "Okay, bass string first, then brush down, then alternate bass string, then brush down—"

And then she came in. Not since the hospital had I seen her so close. She had her hair in a ponytail this time, and wore a colorful blouse with a denim skirt, kind of like a cowgirl. Our eyes met and, having no words come to mind, I smiled.

She stopped and looked at me, and I could see recognition working its way into her expression. "Have we met before?"

"Sharon Iverson," I said softly, knowing the delicacy of the subject matter. "Christian Chapel. The hospital."

She put her hand over her mouth and replied with wide eyes, "You look so different!"

"Well, so do you." And I meant every word.

She shook my hand. "What was your name?"

"Travis Jordan. This is Ben Springfield."

We exchanged introductions and majors: Ben and I were both Bible majors. I was heading for pastoral ministry, Ben felt called to missions. Marian was undecided as yet, but leaning toward a business major.

She noticed Ben's guitar still in my hands. "That's right! You said you were a musician! I *love* the guitar!"

Ben grinned at me.

"We were just, uh, playing some bluegrass," I said.

Her eyes brightened. "Bluegrass!"

And then *he* came in. The whole room seemed to sink under the weight of his glory, and he drew attention like a black hole sucking up all the light.

Marian jumped up and hurried toward him. "You're late!"

"Sorry," was all he said, moving toward the piano in the corner of the room.

Marian and the other two King's Carillons followed after him like baby quail after their mother, and gathered around the piano to work out a new song.

Loren Bullard took one look at the sheet music they placed before him and began to pound a veritable symphony out of that old upright—scales, arpeggios, minor sixths, thirteenths, dominant sevenths. The tall girl, Julie, started singing her lead part, then Marian and Chris joined in, and it sounded *better* than good. Conversation in the room stopped. Kids out at the mailboxes came into the room to see what record was playing.

I turned to Ben. He was watching and listening, his face—and his mind, I suppose—a blank.

I handed him his guitar and reminded him, "Boom-chunk, boom-chunk."

WINTER QUARTER, Marian Chiardelli and I finally landed in a class together, Old Testament Survey, and occasionally sat near enough to each other to exchange greetings and how-are-yous. The prof put us on a committee to create a huge banner of an Old Testament time line. She liked my cartoon renderings of Moses and Abraham, and I liked her lettering.

"So you play the banjo too?" she exclaimed when I finally told her. "You have to play it for us sometime!"

Loren Bullard accompanied me on that same upright piano in the Hub, and what he could do for the King's Carillons he did for Foggy Mountain Breakdown. That a guy with such musical ability would deign to boom-chunk for a banjo player really impressed me. He deserved Marian.

Thus Marian and I became friends, like a brother and sister in the Lord. We served on committees and tackled school projects together. She gave me advice on how better to socialize; I gave her advice on Loren. The King's Carillons even asked me to critique how they looked on stage—I used to be a professional musician, after all. It was a comfortable and mutually affirming relationship.

Even so, the better I got to know her, the more I could sense she had a hidden side. We could talk about Creation vs. Evolution, or whether we were Pre-, Mid-, or Post-Trib; we could discuss politics and how involved we should be; we could talk about my family and her family and how each of us was raised and how we'd want to raise our own kids whenever we had any with whomever we married.

But we couldn't talk about her. Not really. There was some kind of terrible wound deep inside her, and every time our conversation came too close, she'd shy away, change the subject, find something to laugh about. I knew she was hurting and I hurt for her, but I couldn't help.

The other two Carillons, Julie and Chris, had to be privy to whatever it was, because the three girls always made it to the altar after Saturday night chapel so Julie and Chris could pray for Marian. The way she would cry and her two friends wail and speak in tongues over her, I grieved to think what awful burden she had to be carrying. I determined I would pray for her as well. I couldn't pray for her in chapel because guys could only pray with guys and girls with girls, but I had a workable alternative.

Our church's missionaries always give out prayer cards to remind people to pray for them. Prayer cards are usually a photograph of the missionary or missionaries and their family, along with their name, the country in which they are serving, and whatever additional information will fit. You get a prayer card, take it home, post it somewhere, and it serves as a prayer request every time you see it. In the spirit of that tradition, I loaned Ben my camera so he could sneak some pictures of Marian. Her image measured less than an inch tall on the three-by-five prints, but I trimmed off the D. R. Smedley Residence Hall, the H. L. Boren Library, and four of the trees along the M. T. Herschieser Memorial Walkway and taped what was left to my desk. While studying, or while flossing my teeth before bed, I'd see that miniscule photo of Marian Chiardelli and I'd say a simple prayer for her: "Dear Lord, please take care of Marian. Take away the pain in her heart and grant her your grace and peace. Amen." Then I'd pray for Loren Bullard just to keep everything in balance.

THE HARVEST TIME SOCIAL at West Bethel College was, for all practical purposes, a Halloween party with all the evil elements expunged. Everyone else in the Western world was dressing up in costumes, bobbing for apples, and acting silly on October 31. The students at West Bethel wanted to do the same, but in a Christian context, and so it came to pass. Each year we decorated the B. R. Maguire Gymnasium with fall colors, autumn leaves, and dried cornstalks, then set up the hoop shoot, cakewalk, pie throwing booth, and dunk tank. The guys would bring dates, we'd have a talent show and costume contest, and we would go as nuts as kids at West Bethel College could go.

This year, the King's Carillons had their eyes on the costume contest and were determined to win it. The Christmas before, Julie's church in Anchorage had gone to great lengths to put on a gala Christmas musical with a singing Christmas tree and choreographed nativity scene. They'd constructed camel, sheep, and cow costumes for actors to wear and dance around in, and a special donkey Mary could ride. That donkey was the best part, something right out of Disneyland. The guy playing the front end could bob the donkey's head, make its mouth move, and even bat the donkey's eyelashes with a little lever. The guy playing the back end had the tougher job: he had to carry Mary on his back. When Julie returned from Anchorage in the fall, she brought that donkey with her, and she and Marian stashed it in their room, keeping it top secret until they could spring it on the rest of us.

Marian, Julie, and Chris signed up for the costume contest, putting down their names for the judges in case they couldn't be recognized—something worth extra points, by the way. They bought brown cloth and sewed in shifts, repairing rips and tears, adding row upon row of brown fringe, and tailoring the donkey's body to fit theirs. Since Chris was the smallest, they appointed her to ride. Since this was a Harvest Time Social and not a Christmas Social, they fashioned a beard and ragged robe for Chris and dubbed the donkey "Balaam's Ass."

The party was set for October 31.

October 30, Julie came down with the flu.

The day of the party, Marian pulled me aside and, with Julie and Chris's blessing, broke the code of silence.

I wanted to help, but . . . "You're sure you can't find someone else?"

She was begging me. "Lori's going as Lot's wife and Sue's going as Noah's Ark. I can't go asking all around because that'll spoil the surprise."

"Can't Chris be the rear end?"

"She's supposed to be Balaam!"

I thought it through. I couldn't be Balaam; I was too big. "Uh, what about you being the rear end?"

She was getting disgusted with me. "We tailored the front end to fit me, and besides, I can't carry Chris on my back, and besides *that*, the donkey in the Bible was a girl!"

"I have to carry Chris on my back?"

"Not all of her. You'll be holding my waist so I'll carry some of the weight."

Holding her waist. Wow. I may have been sinning, but boy, what a thought. It almost kept me from suggesting my final out: "What about Loren?"

She looked down and even blushed a bit. "*He's* the one we want to surprise!"

Oh, he was going to be surprised, all right.

We got into the costume behind a van in the gymnasium parking lot.

Chris kept repeating her lines as she put on her ragged robe and white beard. "Because you have abused me. I wish there were a sword in my hand, for now I would kill you!"

Marian was already wearing the donkey's front legs—baggy, fringie things with knobby knees and round black hooves, held up by thick suspenders. It was the first time I'd ever seen her in pants. She held the rear legs while I stepped into them. "What have I done to you, that you have struck me these three times?" she said, rehearsing the question Chris had already answered.

Chris and I lowered the donkey's neck and head over Marian and then I bent over and grabbed Marian's waist while Chris draped the donkey's body over me, and then a striped wool blanket for a biblical-looking saddle. Marian and I crouched, and Chris climbed on.

"Ohh," I said when Chris's weight settled. This was going to be a long night.

Chris whacked me with her stick, not meaning for it to hurt the way it did, I'm sure. "C'mon, you old donkey! Let's go!"

Marian led the way across the parking lot and I, with arms propped on her waist and Balaam on my back, followed. I could see the ground passing below me, then the steps up to the gymnasium, and finally the gymnasium floor. The party was already in full swing as we entered, and the reaction from all the partygoers was tremendously favorable. I could hear the gasps, applause, and cheers.

Whack! Balaam hit me again.

Marian wiggled the donkey's head around and said, "HawHEEE! What have I done to you, that you have struck me these three times?"

Chris hit me again, and I felt it, and she said, "Because you have abused me. I wish there were a sword in my hand, for now I would kill you!"

I could see the feet of the students gathering around to see the show. They caught on right away. "Balaam's Ass!"

"Try *donkey*," said someone else.

Marian kept walking around and I kept watching the gym floor passing under my feet: the center line, the three-point line, the foul shot line. She jerked that head around so much I thought we'd fall over. "Am I not your donkey on which you have ridden, and . . . you know, taken you places and stuff?" If Scripture memorization was good for points, we just lost some.

We made several circuits around the floor, repeating the same little scene as Balaam beat his donkey on the backside, and then someone finally helped Balaam get off and lead his donkey by the halter. I thanked the Lord.

We stayed inside that costume for another half-hour because Marian insisted we let the judges get the full effect. I could see drops of my sweat falling to the gym floor and I could smell my-self. Finally I heard the voice of T. N. Nelson, the dean of students, announcing that the judges had reached a decision. The place fell quiet. Balaam got on my back, gave me a whack, and we trotted to the front of the gym where a platform was set up. I could hear the tally sheet rattling in the hands of T. N. Nelson as he spoke. "Third place goes to . . ." Suspenseful pause. "Loren Bullard, as Samson!"

I could hear everyone applauding and I knew Loren was step-ping up on the platform. I'd heard that he borrowed a long hairpiece from one of the girls. The chest and arms he didn't have to borrow. No doubt he was scanning the crowd, wondering where his date was. Maybe we wouldn't win. Maybe we could just lose quietly and get out of there.

"Second place goes to . . ." Same pause. "Sue Dwightman, as Noah's Ark!"

The crowd hooted, cheered, and laughed. Sue was a real char-acter and a notable scale-tipper. I knew she'd be playing this for laughs.

"And . . ." This time he really milked the pauses. "First prize . . ." My back was aching. "The winner is . . ."

"Balaam's Ass," somebody whispered wishfully.

"Julie Ford, Marian Chiardelli, and Chris Anderson—" the crowd went nuts—"as Balaam's, uh, donkey!"

Marian squealed with delight while Chris bounced up and down on my back cheering.

"HaaHEEEE!!"

"C'mon, you old donkey!" *Whack!*

We went up the steps onto the platform, still one cohesive donkey and rider, as everyone clapped and cheered and brayed like donkeys.

As if being rescued from under a collapsed building, I felt the weight of the prophet lift from me, then the saddle blanket, then the donkey's back. The air in the gym wafted over my body, cool and refreshing. I stood, dripping wet, squinting in the light, stretching my spine.

From the expressions on the faces of all the biblical characters and objects standing below me, I quickly surmised they were expecting to see Julie Ford. Their eyes were wide. The guys were roaring. Some of the girls had their hands over their mouths. There were some red faces. I saw a few thumbs-up.

I looked at Marian, just taking off the donkey's head. She was drenched in sweat herself, her hair stuck to her forehead, but she was beaming. Loren just stood there grinning, shaking his head, applauding. She had surprised him, all right.

Victory!

Chris, Marian, and I took a bow and received our blue ribbon. It was a great moment.

But it wouldn't last.

I GUESS Chris didn't get in trouble because she remained above it all. Marian got in trouble because she headed up the team. I got in trouble because I was right in the middle of it.

"You had to be aware of how inappropriate it would be!" T. N. Nelson said, glaring at me across his desk.

I was standing in his office the morning after the Harvest Time Social, prepared to receive my blindfold and last request. Sister Dudley, the iron-jawed dean of women, sat to Brother Nelson's left. Brother Smith, the balding and tough-surfaced dean of men, sat to his right. All three looked grimmer than any Christian should ever look.

"Well?" Brother Nelson asked me in the arched manner of a holy inquisitor, weaving and wiggling a fountain pen through his fingers.

"Sir, my main concern was how much they wanted to win."

Sister Dudley mimicked Brother Nelson's expression, but with her tight lips and narrow eyes, she looked a lot scarier. "And what *else* were you thinking about?"

"How much my back ached."

She sniffed a derisive laugh and rolled her eyes. "You *enjoyed* it!"

I thought she was getting personal. "Ma'am, I could hardly enjoy sweating under a hot blanket with a girl on my back and— " I fell silent as the dual meaning of my protest washed over me. *Don't stop there, Jordan. Your grave's almost deep enough.*

Sister Dudley fell backward in her seat as if she'd been slapped. Brother Smith looked away so she wouldn't see him laughing.

"Uh, I don't think we need to pursue this any further," said Brother Nelson.

But Sister Dudley pursued it further. "You *did* enjoy it!"

Well, she pushed me. "Yes, ma'am, I did. I enjoy everything about Marian Chiardelli, whether I'm in the same room with her or in the same donkey."

Sister Dudley gasped. She even put her hand over her heart. It looked like bad acting. "Well I never!"

I had once heard Robert Mitchum use a line in an old western, and it had to have been stored in my memory for this very moment. "No, ma'am, I don't suppose you have."

Well, I didn't *have* to submit to their corrective action. I could have just left West Bethel forever. But to me, that would have been handing the administration a victory, another notch to carve in their big black Bibles. I was doing well at this school. I had good relationships with most of my teachers. My grades were excellent. I'd made some wonderful friends. Ben was getting to be a pretty good guitar player. Most of all, God had called me to this school and to the ministry that would follow, and I owed it to him to see it through.

So I stayed, and went on with my studies as usual, embracing my punishment. My sentence was harsh, thanks to my temper and Sister Dudley's indignity. They put me on probation and forbade me to be near Marian for the rest of the quarter. I couldn't talk to her, call her, or write to her. They put her on probation as well, and forbade her to have any contact with me. They allowed me to keep the prayer card I'd taped to my desk as long as I was *praying*, but I could only keep her head. The rest of her would have to go.

Now her image only measured an eighth of an inch.

This was to be a cooling off period, they said, a time to get focused on the Lord instead of each other. That was the most maddening thing about it. Marian was *Loren's* girl and they were picking on *me!* I heard no accusations of immorality over Loren's bare Samson chest. How many of the girls had enjoyed *that?*

I discovered a lot about myself the first few weeks of my probation. I discovered how much anger I was capable of, and how many different ways I could vent it without breaking anything. I discovered how close I could come to swearing without really doing it, and how limber my middle finger could be when separated from the others. I allowed myself to ponder whether Sister Dudley truly ever had, and wonder how holy and spiritual I had to be before I could reduce *my* first two names to initials.

All of which brought to mind the wild donkey needing to be bridled. It took at least two weeks for that question to work its way through, but I finally dealt with it: Was that really me? Was God trying to show me the waywardness that still remained in my heart? Was I really that rebellious and lustful?

My anger cooled. I adapted to the bridle. I prayed it through and repented of my rebellious attitude. I read my chapters and turned in my papers, I passed my quizzes and midterms. I plunked on my banjo, sitting alone on my bed.

I got over it. I even forgave Sister Dudley. After all, what was I losing anyway? Marian and I were just friends, just a brother and sister in the Lord making a donkey of ourselves. We would always be friends, and someday the whole incident would be funny.

A WEEK BEFORE THANKSGIVING, I heard what sounded like a mob outside my dorm window. My stomach turned. I ran to the window and looked, and sure enough, an old college ritual was underway. Some poor guy had gotten engaged and now his buddies and their buddies were carrying him up to the pond beside the chapel. I didn't even grab my coat, but ran down the hall, down the stairs, and out the door. By the time I got to the pond, they'd already thrown him in. He'd climbed out, someone had thrown a robe over him, and now he was wiping his head with a towel.

I waited as he bent and dried his scalp. Then he straightened up, laughing and waving at his well-wishing and mischievous friends.

I would live another day. It wasn't Loren Bullard.

BROTHER SMITH AND I had many conversations over that long fall quarter, and we got close. He was an honorable man and never violated the conditions of my probation. Nevertheless, he did pass information along as he acquired it.

"I heard today that Marian and the girls have named that donkey Travis. As I understand it, they feel they couldn't have won the contest without your help—inappropriate as it was."

"Yes sir."

"You appear to be doing all right."

"Oh, keeping busy."

"How did midterms go?"

"Better than I'd hoped."

"I understand Marian did well on her midterms, and it's also my understanding that she prays for you daily. What are you smiling about?"

"Oh, nothing, sir."

"But your smile does mean you're pleased at this moment."

I nodded.

"Just wanted to deepen my own understanding, of course, in case someone should ask me what I'm understanding these days."

"Of course."

Such conversations didn't happen every day, and they never seemed planned, at least by me. Brother Smith and I would pass each other on campus, a perfectly normal thing to do, and sometimes he just happened to be a trifle more chatty. Once we passed each other in the chapel foyer and he asked me my opinion of the shrubs by the front steps. "Think they ought to be pruned back?"

I looked through the window and saw shrubs, most of them bare this time of year. "Well, pruning never hurts."

"That reminds me: Loren Bullard has a friend thinking of getting a haircut. Loren thinks it would be a great idea, but the friend thought a second opinion might be helpful. Did I say something funny?"

I wiped the smile off my face, but it came right back. "They want *my* opinion?"

He shrugged and looked away as if totally uninterested. "The *friend* wants your opinion—but that's just my understanding."

I thought it over. "I think Loren should get used to his friend having longer hair."

He nodded. "I think the shrubs could be pruned back, though."

I looked at them again. "Sure. The shrubs could be."

ONE SATURDAY NIGHT in December, I came so close. Chapel had ended, and I was sitting near the back because Marian and her friends usually sat near the front. The altars were filled that night, but as the hour grew late, the crowd dwindled to two guys and one girl praying separately, and the trio praying in their usual spot on the right side. I watched and listened as Chris and Julie just kept hammering away in tongues, their hands on Marian's shoulders. It could have been an exact repeat of so many other occasions, except that this time, sooner than I expected, Julie and Chris called it quits, gave Marian a little hug, and left her there alone.

Then it was just two guys praying, me sitting near the back, and Marian weeping at the altar. Alone.

Sister Dudley had to be watching. I looked around the chapel and saw no one else, but those grim, narrow eyes had to be somewhere. If God wasn't watching, she was.

I sat glued to the pew as Marian wiped her eyes, stood up, and started for the door. I didn't wave to her or make a sound. I even slouched a little as if trying to hide.

Obedience. The word pounded in my mind. *To obey is better than sacrifice.*

Rebellion. I could feel the pang of guilt turning my insides. *Rebellion is as the sin of witchcraft.*

Submission.

Authority.

Sister Dudley.

I sat there until Marian was gone. Now it was just one guy praying and me sitting near the back, and Sister Dudley watching even if God wasn't.

And I bawled like a baby, my forehead resting on the back of the pew in front of me.

ON DECEMBER 22, at three forty-five in the afternoon, I held my pen high above my paper, began to hum the Hallelujah Chorus, and brought the pen down in slow-motion to place a period on the last sentence of my last final exam for the fall quarter. For me, the quarter was over. I had mail to pick up and some packing to do before going home for Christmas, but somewhere, sometime in the middle of all that, I absolutely had to see Brother Smith.

I hurried to the front of the classroom, set my exam on the prof's desk, told her Merry Christmas, and got out of there.

Brother Smith was waiting in the hall outside, still in his coat and scarf.

I hesitated. Was he really waiting there for me? I smiled, said hi, got into my coat, and just about walked on.

He wiggled his finger at me, beckoning.

My pulse quickened though I tried to act cool and collected. "Yes sir?"

He gave me a gentle shove on the shoulder, leading me toward the door. "The quarter's over, son. Now listen, things are happening quickly and we're going to be cutting it close. Did you hear about Loren and Marian?"

Oh no. I braced myself. "No sir."

We pushed our way out the door and into the cold December afternoon.

"Their relationship is a thing of the past. It was over a long time ago." He had to nudge me. "Keep walking."

"It's over? You mean they broke up?"

He sneered and rolled his eyes. "There was no enduring relationship in the first place. The appearance was there, but listen, I've watched students match up for years and I knew they were heading opposite directions." He snickered. "And him losing the contest to you and Marian didn't help."

"Well why didn't you tell me?"

"I couldn't burden you with it. You would have violated probation and you know it."

Suddenly I felt scared. "Oh brother. Now what do I do?"

"You listen real careful, that's what you do." We hurried down the brick walkway from the chapel, watching for ice, the bare, black branches of the maples overshadowing us. It seemed so still and deserted now. At least half the student body had finished the quarter already and evacuated the place. "Marian's out of the trio too. They asked her to quit."

"What?"

"Sister Dudley wouldn't divulge the details—"

"Sister Dudley!"

"—but it's my understanding that there's something amiss in Marian's life, something she refuses to deal with. Julie and Chris felt it best to let her go."

"You didn't tell me that either!"

"Same reason. But I've got one more item for you."

I cringed as I said, "Okay."

"She's leaving West Bethel. She won't be back."

"She won't— "

He nudged me again. "Can't you think and walk at the same time?"

"What happened?"

"I don't know, but I'm not sure she's making the right decision.

She's hurt, fed up, devastated, whatever. That's why you need to talk to her, and that's why I came and got you."

"Where is she?"

"I saw her packing her car in the parking lot out in front of the women's dorm."

I was getting nervous. My hands were shaking. "Man . . . I haven't talked to her in months."

We were coming to the women's dorm at that very moment. The parking lot was just on the other side. "Well, take my advice: Skip talking about the weather."

"Brother Smith." I stopped walking again. This time he stopped instead of nudging me. "Do you think she loves me?"

He pointed toward the parking lot. "The quarter's over. Why don't you ask her?"

He remained where he was. I ran down the walkway and around the D. R. Smedley Residence Hall. There were a few cars left in the parking lot and I immediately recognized Marian's blue VW fastback. The back was open, there were suitcases and clothing inside. I planted myself by that car and waited.

When she came out, she was dressed in a blue ski jacket, a crocheted blue stocking cap . . . and a pair of jeans. She was carrying only a small, overnight case, her last item. I was hoping she would be glad to see me, but the smile she gave me was brief, and strangely guarded. As she walked to her car, her eyes seldom left the pavement.

"Hi." She tossed the small case into the back of the car and closed the rear door. Then she shook my hand. "Long time no see."

"Up close, anyway."

She looked down again. "Yeah."

"I heard you were leaving. I mean, leaving for good."

There it was again, that strange, evasive fidgeting. She looked around, looked back at the dorm, anywhere but at me, and said, "Things haven't worked out."

"I'm real sorry."

She looked at me again, probably thinking the subject had closed.

"So am I. I guess I'll go home for a while, get a job, just wait and see what the Lord wants me to do."

Now *I* started to fidget. "Think we could take a walk?" She hesitated. "Just a short one?" She still wouldn't answer. "Hey, after this, it's good-bye, you know? We may not get another chance."

She thought for a moment, and then joined me. We headed for the lower end of the campus where the big maples formed a majestic canopy over the groomed lawn and park benches. The wooden benches were cold and deserted. Red leaves that had fallen after the caretaker's last raking lay scattered on the grass.

"So, I hear you and Loren have parted company," I said, afraid as I spoke each word.

"We're still friends."

"That's good."

Then we walked in silence. It became clear that I would have to carry this conversation. "Listen, for whatever it's worth . . ." Brother. Was there no subject I could start easily? "I know you've been having some kind of difficulty. I mean, I heard you were asked to leave the trio, and I saw the three of you praying after chapel . . ." She just looked away. "But I want you to know, that means nothing to me. I don't care. I mean, I still love you and I accept you and you're still my friend, okay?"

She sniffed a little chuckle. "Chris and Julie told me the same thing."

What was I to say to that? I groped for words. I sighed. I got frustrated. Finally I came up with, "Well I'm not them."

She didn't seem overjoyed, but at least she looked at me. "Travis, you don't know anything about it."

"I don't have to." We came to a bench. It was dry enough. "Could we just sit down a moment?"

She sat. I couldn't. I was too nervous. "Marian, I just, uh, I just want to give you something to take with you when you go, I mean, for whatever it's worth. I mean, this is it, the last time we'll see each other, and, well, I just . . ." She was looking at the ground and only occasionally looking at me. "I just want to say that, I've had some time to really think about things, and I've decided—I mean, *I know* what's important to me, more than anything else." I had to push myself to get it out. I counted the items, all two of them, on my fingers, my hands only inches from her nose. "Serving the Lord wherever he might send me . . ." I couldn't get to the second one. I was choking up. My voice was quaking as I finished. "And having you with me. Always."

Her lip quivered. She broke down. "Please don't."

"No, I mean it."

She shook her head. "Please don't say any more."

"I have to. I'll hate myself forever if I don't."

"I can't . . ."

Well, I was going down in flames anyway. "Then just let me say it so I'll get it said. You can say no, you can walk away, you can go back home and find God's will for you, whatever it is, but at least I gave it a shot. Okay?" She didn't answer. I didn't wait for an answer. I fell to one knee, right there by the bench, right next to that beautiful blue-jeaned girl, and took her hand. It was trembling and one of her tears fell on my thumb. "Marian, I love you." Now my voice fell all apart again. I kept going. "I love you and I believe God brought us together. Ever since that time we first met you've been my girl, my dream, the only one I've ever wanted." I took a breath, but I did it quickly. "Marian, if you'll have me, I'd like for you to be my wife." I was still holding her hand. She didn't say anything. "I, I know we haven't talked about it before this, but—"

Her hand squeezed mine. Her eyes were streaming with tears. "I'd like to."

I felt she might give a reason why she couldn't. I was ready for anything: she wasn't a virgin, she couldn't have kids, she already *had* kids, she was wanted for murder in six states. *I didn't care.*

"Travis, I can't be the kind of wife you need. I'm just not right with God."

But I knew the love I had for her was from the very heart of God in the first place. It was so overwhelming, so rich and sweet. I could love this woman as God loved, without qualification, without requirement. I spoke gently, imploringly. "Tell me."

She whimpered, shook her head, and finally confessed, "I can't speak in tongues!" And then she let go all her pain, sobbing, her hands over her face. "I don't know what it is. Maybe I wasn't being honest with Loren. I thought I loved him, but I was always thinking of you! I didn't mean it! I love the Lord and I never wanted to grieve him. . . ."

I went slightly limp. After all the buildup, all the suspense, this was the problem? "Is . . . is that it? Is that what's wrong?"

She didn't want to look at me. "Sister Dudley prayed for me, and Julie and Chris and all the girls in the dorm, and I just can't get prayed for anymore. I just can't go through that again."

I pulled a handkerchief from my pocket. Thank God, it was brand-new, never used. I gently dabbed her eyes and cheeks and even wiped the tears from our clenched hands.

Then I kissed her, right on the lips.

And she kissed me back! A wishful kiss, laden with sorrow that there could never be another.

I cradled her face in both my hands and looked in her tear-filled eyes. "Marry me. I want *you*, Marian. I want *you* to be my wife!"

SPLASH! Ben told me it was coming and when. We rented a wetsuit and I wore it under my clothes. I pretended to be none the wiser as I walked out of the dorm and into the middle of a laughing, roaring mob. I never thought I'd feel so glad to be carried by all those arms. I never thought I'd rejoice to be thrown into the pond in the middle of January.

But when I came up out of that water and heard the cheers of my friends from the banks all around me, I felt I'd been baptized all over again. I could look up and see heaven, and God was smiling.

15

MRS. MACON wasn't at all happy to see her former hired hand at her door. It was Monday morning, she was tired and cranky, and Nevin Sorrel could only mean trouble. "What do you want?"

He held his hat in his hands and looked altogether contrite. "I don't want no trouble at all, Mrs. Macon, no trouble at all. I was just thinking that maybe, you know, since things are bustling so much around here, you could use an extra hand."

She began to close the door. "We're fine."

He leaned forward in earnest. "How about Brandon—I mean, Mr. Nichols? There's work going on everywhere around town. There must be something I could do—and by the way, I apologize for any trouble I've caused. It won't happen again."

Then a voice came from inside the house. "Mrs. Macon, would that be Nevin Sorrel?"

Nevin hollered through the open door, "Yes it is, Mr. Nichols! I'm here to offer my services!"

Brandon Nichols appeared, looking freshly showered. He studied the lanky cowboy a moment, then asked, "Who's the boss around here, Nevin?"

"You are, sir. No question about it."

"You know how to run a backhoe?"

Nevin grinned and nodded. "Been running that very machine for years."

"We're developing a spring up in the willow draw. I have plans drawn up but I need someone to do the excavation, lay the pipe, haul the gravel. . . ."

"I've done all of that!"

"It'll pay twelve bucks an hour."

"I'll take it!"

"And you live here on the place."

Mrs. Macon balked at that. "What?"

Nichols told her, "He can have that trailer the Pearsons donated. We'll park it out back of my place." Then he told Nevin, "I want you around where I can keep an eye on you. No more goofing off."

"No sir, not one bit."

"No hanging out at the tavern and getting into fights."

"No."

"You're the kid now, and I'm your old man. Got that?"

"I'll try to be worthy of your trust, Mr. Nichols."

Brandon Nichols looked him up and down and reached a decision. "Okay. Start today. Make me proud of you."

I PULLED UP in front of the little brick police station on the main highway. Brett Henchle's squad car was still parked in front so I figured I'd find him inside. I rattled off the days in my mind as I pushed through the front door: Thursday I found the car . . . Friday, Saturday, Sunday . . . well, maybe he had time to do some checking on Friday or this morning.

He was seated at his desk behind the counter, going over some paperwork. A cup of coffee sat on his desk, steaming and looking desirable. "Hey Travis, how's it going?"

"Oh, fine. How's the leg?"

The question seemed to embarrass him. "It's okay."

"Any information on that car in the river?"

He shook his head. "A dead end. We'll probably just impound it and scrap it."

I could tell he didn't want to get into it. That didn't matter to me. I did. "You didn't find out *anything?* Even with a license number, a make, a model?"

"The car was probably stolen and ditched in the river. We can't find the owner, we can't find the suspect. End of story."

"So who is this owner you can't find?"

Now he was irritated. He reached for a file folder on the corner of his desk and opened it. "Somebody named Herb Johnson. He used to work for a wrecking yard in Missoula but he quit. He used to live in an apartment in Missoula but he moved. There's no forwarding address."

He closed the folder and tossed it on the corner of his desk again, his way of saying he'd answered all my questions.

"May I see it?" I said, indicating the folder.

He wrinkled his brow at me. "Travis, just what are you fishing for?"

"I'm—"

"Just what do you think you're going to do that I haven't?"

I didn't want to offend him. "Just curious, that's all."

"Well the case is still pending so it's confidential."

"I thought the case was closed and you were going to scrap the car."

He leaned back and clasped his hands behind his head. "That's right. Soon as we pull it out of the river I'll button up the case and you can read to your heart's delight." I was looking at him funny. "What?"

"The car's gone."

That was obviously news to him. "What do you mean, it's gone?"

"Somebody already pulled it out. I thought it was you."

He thought a moment. "Somebody pulled it out? You sure?"

"Drove by there just this morning. Saw the tire tracks, deep ruts, and no car."

He looked puzzled, but then he shrugged and went back to his paperwork. "I'll look into it."

Well, I thought, *so will I.*

I NEVER WANTED to resist the Lord if I sensed he was nudging me. When Brandon Nichols took an intrusive interest in me, that was probably a nudge, but okay, I didn't catch on. Kyle getting broadsided made the nudge more noticeable, however, and Morgan Elliott's distress over her son cinched it. I now considered myself officially nudged.

I went from the police station directly to Mike's Towing, only two blocks away. Mike Downing had run his little tow truck business from the same cubicle of a garage for at least ten years, and had a contract with the local police and state patrol. Any time a vehicle broke down or was abandoned on the highway or somewhere in town, the authorities called Mike. If he didn't pull that car from the river, he might know who did.

I didn't drive into the yard surrounding Mike's garage. I valued my tires too much, so I parked out on the street. Mike hauled hulks for scrap, and over the years he'd gleaned from every hulk whatever he took a shine to: a fender here, a bumper there, a headlight, a window, an engine block, you name it. He had no specific place for anything, so every piece lay where it first fell, filling the yard from fence to fence. If you wanted to visit Mike's Towing, you definitely kept your eyes on the ground, and you didn't even consider driving in there.

I found the lower half of Mike's son Larry in the garage. The upper half was under the hood of a '57 Chevy and didn't know I was there until I hollered hello.

"Yeah?" He was dirty but happy. "Oh, Pastor Jordan, how are you?" Pastor Jordan? It *had* been a while since we'd seen each other.

"Just fine. I came to see Mike."

Larry broke into his grin with one tooth missing, then hollered, "Hey Dad! Pastor Jordan's—"

"I heard him," came a rude reply from the back room. Mike

appeared, yawning and rubbing his messed-up hair. His lip was puffy, his left eye was nearly swollen shut, and he had a sizable white patch on his forehead. He could see the look on my face and explained without my asking, "I got in a fight."

"So I see. How's the other guy?"

He went to a coffeepot sitting on a hot plate on the workbench. "Oh, Matt looks about the same, maybe a little better. Want some coffee?"

"No thanks." It felt so strange to be asking, "Matt *Kiley?*"

"Yeah, good ol' Matt. Can't blame him. I borrowed a set of wrenches from his store three years ago and never did pay him. He was in a wheelchair so it kind of slipped my mind, you know?"

I was still incredulous. "And he came after you?"

"Well . . . I got in a few good licks myself, but he got the price of those wrenches, let me tell you. The tavern's lost a chair and a window, but they're still open. You lookin' for some tires?"

"No."

"I got some that'll fit your rig. Studded snow tires, real cheap."

"Let me think about it."

"What else you want?"

"I was wondering if you pulled a car from the Spokane River."

That widened his good eye. "From the river? Who went into the river?"

"I'm not sure. But I found a car in the river Thursday, and now it's gone."

"Did you tell the cops about it?"

"Brett Henchle knows about the car, but he didn't know somebody pulled it from the river."

Now he looked perturbed. "Henchle never told *me* about it. The cops want a car pulled, they're supposed to call *me.*"

"But you didn't pull any car out of the river since last Thursday?"

"No. And I'm sure gonna find out why."

"WELL," said Morgan Elliott over my speakerphone, "Brett Henchle isn't the only cop on the planet."

Kyle and I looked at each other across my kitchen table, the telephone between us. She had a point there.

It was the first hush-hush meeting of the Jordan–Sherman–Elliott underground resistance movement. Kyle even parked around the block and came through my back yard to keep from being seen, which seemed a little excessive to me.

"You know another one?" I asked.

"Gabe used to go hunting with a guy who's a cop in Sandpoint, Idaho. I'm still good friends with him and his wife."

"So, you're saying a cop in Idaho can do a check on a car from Montana that's found in Washington?"

"Law enforcement people are all linked together by computer these days. Any cop can find out who owns any car anywhere, it doesn't matter."

"Well okay."

"What kind of a car was it?" Kyle asked.

"Ford LTD, probably early '70s. It was red where it wasn't covered with silt."

"Okay," said Morgan, "I'll pass that along. What about the pictures?"

Kyle answered as he leafed through the snapshots he'd just gotten back from the drugstore. "I got some good shots of Nichols's face. I'll get some extra prints made up."

Morgan asked, "So what if the car doesn't belong to Brandon Nichols?"

"That won't surprise me," I answered, "But that car went into the river during the spring run-off, and that's the same time Nichols showed up in town. That and the Montana license plate are enough to make me curious."

"Plus Brett Henchle's silence about it," said Kyle.

"You think Nichols bought him by healing his leg?" Morgan asked.

I hesitated a little, but Kyle didn't. "Absolutely. We're not going to get one bit of help from him."

"So, okay. I'll get back to you as soon as I find out something."

"Before you hang up, let's pray," I said. "I'd really like the Lord to shield us a bit. I, uh, I don't want Brandon Nichols to know what we're doing."

"TWO-TWO-ONE-ONE-TWO South Maurice . . ." Kyle flipped and folded and gathered an unruly map of Missoula as we drove on the outskirts of the town, looking for numbers, signs, anything. "I don't know. I don't think anybody actually *lives* around here."

The drive through Idaho and into Montana had been beautiful, weaving through mountains and along rivers. Missoula itself was nestled in a wide, flat valley, surrounded by green hills and timbered mountains. This *part* of Missoula could be pleasing to the eye as well, depending on how excited you got about metal buildings and cyclone-fenced yards filled with big things: tractors, trucks, farm machinery, concrete sewer and drainpipe, roof trusses. We passed a John Deere dealer with a whole fleet of green tractors lined up along the street, and then a masonry supply company with neat stacks of concrete block, decorative stone, and a zillion different colors of brick. This was definitely the *guy* part of town.

"Hey, wait, wait," I said, releasing my foot from the gas pedal. "'Abe's.' The car owner's name is Abe, right? Abe Carlson?"

Kyle looked up and saw it too: a sheet of plywood painted white with big blue letters: Abe's Auto Wrecking. It was hanging crookedly next to an opening in still another cyclone fence, this one festooned with automobile wheels painted red, white, and blue. "That's it," he said, reading the numbers under the name. "Two-two-one-one-two South Maurice."

I turned left and pulled up to the opening, but took a moment to survey the place before driving in. We were looking at an acre of dead cars in long rows, their carcasses dented, hollow, and vacant, picked clean of chrome, glass, mirrors, wheels, and anything else a living car might need in the world beyond the fence. In the center of it all, like an old barge floating on a multicolored sea of metal, stood Abe's big shack wearing hubcaps like sequins.

"Maybe we should have called first," Kyle suggested.

I eased the car down the long, jagged aisle toward the big blue shack.

Two pit bulls came charging out of a yawning garage door. A grisly looking character in gray coveralls came quickstepping after them, hollering their names so loudly it sounded like "KAP! FREET! GEBACKERE!!"

"Kap" and "Freet" didn't hear him. They had a mauling to attend to, circling the car, barking, growling, and waiting for either of us to stick a leg out.

"HAH! GEDOUTHERE!" This guy had to be Abe. A face and bark like his made me wonder why he needed dogs. He shooed them away, yelling and banging on the nearest hulk with a tire iron. They both scampered into a dog pen alongside the building and remained there while he slammed the gate on them. I was impressed.

He returned to our car and may have smiled, at least around the eyes. I rolled down my window. "That's Casper and Frito. They just ate a Jehovah's Witness. Whatcha after?"

"Uh, are you Abe Carlson?"

"Yeah. Who are you?"

"Uh, may I get out?"

He backed away from my door and I got out. Kyle got out too and walked around to join me. We introduced ourselves and told him where we were from.

The moment I mentioned the town of Antioch, he scowled at us. "You cops?"

"Uh, no. Kyle here's a pastor and I teach the sixth grade."

"Got a call from a cop in Antioch. Is this about that car?"

"We—yeah. If we could—"

"I got nothing more to say about it." He turned and started walking away.

I turned to Kyle. "Get the photos." He reached inside the car while I hollered after Abe, "Could you just look at a picture for us?"

He turned. "What?"

Kyle handed me the photos. I said, "Look at a picture? These pictures right here?"

He glanced thoughtfully at Casper and Frito, then walked back. I guess I got him curious.

I held up the best photo we had of Brandon Nichols, a nice shot of him preaching in Mrs. Macon's garage. "Do you recognize this man?"

He took one look and his expression turned so dark I almost backed away.

"You know him?"

He nodded. "That's Herb Johnson. Where'd you get this?"

I exchanged a glance with Kyle. "Herb Johnson?"

"He used to work for me."

Kyle asked with surprise in his voice. "He worked *here?*"

"Yeah, worked here for a year or so."

"We thought he worked on a ranch somewhere."

"I don't know what he did before Hattie brought him over."

"Who's Hattie?" I asked.

"My girlfriend. Herb was one of her tenants and he needed a job." He paused to spit on the ground. "Worst mistake I ever made."

"Your girlfriend owns some apartments or something?"

"She manages a building over on Myers Way. She gets some flaky characters in there. I about gave Herb that car just so he'd leave."

Bingo. I tried not to look too excited. "The, the, uh, Ford LTD?"

"Yeah."

"So, did he buy it from you, or . . ."

"I sold it to him cheap. He wanted to move on and I wanted to help him."

"But the car was still in your name."

"I've already been through all this with that cop." He started looking elsewhere.

I didn't want him getting away. "Uh, Kyle took this picture on a ranch near Antioch." Abe stood still. "Herb's working there, only he's using another name. He's calling himself Brandon Nichols."

Abe cursed. He looked scared. "I don't need to hear no more."

"But . . . did the cop tell you the car was ditched in the river? I mean, it looks like somebody tried to hide it."

Abe waved me off, shook his head, backed away. "I don't want to hear no more. Now that's it. We're through talking and you guys can just get out of here."

Kyle pleaded, "We're afraid Herb might be up to something and we were hoping you could—"

"GETOUTTAHERE!"

Casper and Frito went crazy, leaping against the fence of their pen. He headed their way with an obvious intention. I got back in the car and Kyle followed my lead. We got out of there.

I DROVE BACK into Missoula while Kyle flipped and folded and rattled the map. "Myers Way, Myers Way . . ." he mumbled, trying to find it.

"So let me think: Brett said he couldn't find the owner or the thief. But he talked to Abe . . ."

"But Abe isn't the owner. He doesn't *want* to be the owner."

"Right, he wants to be *through* with Herb and the car."

"So it's *Herb* Brett can't find."

"Because Herb's *Brandon*."

"And the car was never stolen because Abe sold it to Herb."

"Unless someone stole it from Herb."

"But Herb Johnson never reported it stolen."

"No, he just ditched it in the river." I got a hunch. "Which could make sense if Herb is trying to break all ties with his past and become somebody else. Remember when I said it wouldn't surprise me if *Brandon* wasn't the owner?"

Kyle looked up from his map to exclaim, "It sure scared Abe when you told him Herb had a different name."

"Yeah, like Herb Johnson might not be Herb Johnson."

"Which also means Brandon Nichols might not be Brandon Nichols."

"So . . . Myers Way . . ."

Kyle went back to the map. "Okay, turn right. We need to double back."

WE FOUND MYERS WAY, a residential street lined with well-used cars and low-cost fixer-uppers. The yards were small, many were unmowed, many populated by mongrel dogs and rusting tricycles. Aging McDonald's cups and hamburger wrappers lay fading along the street curb, and graffiti marred the sidewalks. We found four apartment buildings occupying the four corners of an intersection. We could see more multi-units farther down the street. This could be a long day.

Kyle knocked on the first manager's door. He'd never heard of anyone named Hattie.

I went across the street and knocked on another door. A young mother with an infant in her arms and a toddler in tow sent me two doors down. The manager of this building didn't know a Hattie.

By now Kyle had checked the third apartment building. No Hattie.

I went to the fourth.

"Hattie Phelps?" said the manager, a young bachelor with a cluttered computer desk in his living room.

"I don't have a last name, but she's the girlfriend of Abe Carlson."

"Yeah, sure, I know her. She manages the Crestview Apartments." He stepped outside to direct me. "Two blocks down, on the left."

The Crestview Apartments were not high-rent property. The building was a sagging, wood-frame structure that instantly made you wonder how close the nearest fire station was. From the street I could count ten apartments, six below and four above. The wooden stairway leading to the second floor was a lawsuit waiting to happen. A leaky hose bib was feeding a permanent puddle in the small courtyard. Kyle and I went to Hattie's door together, fully expecting another pit bull to answer our knock.

It turned out Hattie was a very pleasant woman, a plump little lady in a loud flowered dress who owned a cat but no dog. All we had to do was mention Abe Carlson's name and she started talking right there on her landing.

"Abe's a nice man, he really is. You just have to get to know him."

"Well, he can sure control Casper and Frito."

She laughed a loud, cackly laugh. "So you met the dogs! Oh, my word!" She then proceeded to tell us how many people had been frightened by Casper and Frito and where Abe got the dogs and how they didn't seem to mind when she came around but she would never take her cat over there. We let her talk, we laughed at her wisecracks, we told her whatever we could about ourselves when we got the chance. She could have carried on most of the conversation without our even being there.

"Well anyway, what brings you two gentlemen clear over here?"

I tried to ease gently into the subject. "We've just had someone move to Antioch that we thought you might know." I handed her the photograph and we watched her face closely.

Her eyes grew large and her hand went over her heart. She drew a little gasp and then looked up at us. "He's in your town now?"

"Yes. He's living on a ranch and preaching under a big circus tent. You may have read about it in the papers."

She was puzzled. "No, not Herb . . ." She figured it out. "He's *preaching?*"

"People think he's Jesus," said Kyle, "and he's letting them believe that."

She gasped again. "I did read about that! That's Herb?"

I pointed to the photo. "If Herb is the man in this photograph, then it's Herb."

"There was never a picture in the paper and I think the name wasn't the same."

"He's going by a different name now."

She was afraid. The hand holding the photo was trembling and her other hand was still over her heart. But she looked up at us and said pleadingly, "He's a wonderful man. You have to believe that."

"Well . . ." Kyle had to swallow before he spoke. "There are many people who are impressed with what he's doing."

"He's a good man! I would never do anything to harm him in any way. He knows that."

I asked her, "Does the name Brandon Nichols mean anything to you?"

She gawked at me, still plainly terrified.

"Did Herb ever mention that name?"

"No . . ." Her eyes seemed so vacant, as if looking into another world. "Herb's a wonderful man, very sweet."

Kyle asked, "Did he ever work at a ranch around here?"

"He was a good worker. Abe loved having him around."

"Well, yes, but did he ever work on a ranch?"

"I don't know. I only know that he worked for Abe for a while."

"So—"

"He rode horses. He went somewhere once to ride horses."

"A ranch around here, I suppose?"

"He was quiet, and clean, and never missed a rent payment, and he was courteous."

I asked, "Did he impress you as being a spiritual man?"

That got her going. "Oh, yes! Very religious! You knew that just being around him! He wouldn't hurt anyone, and I know he won't hurt me!"

"Did he—"

"Because I'm on his side. He doesn't have to hurt me, I'm his friend, I'm his neighbor. I'm Hattie. He knows me."

"Where's he from originally? Any idea?"

"California. He talked about Southern California once in a while, but always fondly. He liked it here too, and we liked him, didn't we? Of course we did."

I was getting a very creepy feeling. She wasn't looking at us, but beyond us. Kyle shot a quick glance over his shoulder just to be safe.

"Hattie?" I asked, trying to get her to meet my eyes. "Are you all right?"

She pushed the photograph back at me. "Please leave him be. I'm his friend and he knows that. He's the most wonderful man in the world. I loved having him for a tenant!"

Kyle spoke gently. "Hattie, do you need us to pray for you?" He lightly touched her shoulder.

She jumped as if he'd given her a shock. "NO! No! I don't need any praying, not by you!" She looked past us as if seeing wolves lurking in the neighborhood. "I haven't really talked to you, have I? I haven't told you anything."

"Don't be afraid," said Kyle. "It's all right."

She gave a little yelp and ducked inside her door, slamming it after her. We could hear her whimpering behind the door, "Go away! Just go away!"

Kyle squeezed his eyes shut and extended his hands toward her door. "Lord God, we bind the enemy in Jesus' name!"

I pulled him by the arm. "And we leave Hattie in peace. Amen."

Neither of us said much on the drive back to Antioch. In the silence, my mind began to move through a series of inexplicable connections. Brandon Nichols . . . Herb Johnson . . . Abe and Hattie . . . and then further back, into the past, to places I thought I'd never go again. . . .

16

T<small>RAV</small>," said Marian, her arm tightly around me—it was a new and wonderful sensation. "Let's go ice-skating."

It sounded cold, and I'd just gotten warm after my dip in the West Bethel pond. "Ice-skating?"

"It's how I'd like to celebrate!" she said.

I'd never been ice-skating before and the very thought, well, *chilled* me. I'd done plenty of roller-skating with my old youth group, and Marian insisted it wasn't that much different. I suppose she had visions of us skating in tandem like those Olympic figure skating duos, arm in arm, one leg stretched out straight behind us and our smiling faces turned directly into a sixty-mile-an-hour wind while stirring orchestra music came out of the sky. I had serious doubts that vision would ever come true, but, hey, I'd gotten her father's blessing, my folks were ecstatic, she was wearing the ring, I'd been thrown in the pond—what else was there? We went skating.

We did skate arm in arm our first time out, mostly to keep me from falling and making a fool of myself in front of all those little kids on the rink who could skate circles around me. The first half-hour or so, I tried to enjoy it. Marian was having the time of her life. After an hour, I really did begin to have fun, and my progress earned me a kiss once we were safely stopped and gripping the side rail. After another hour and a cup of cider in the café, I stepped up to Marian, bowed with a flourish, and said, "May I have this lap?" She graciously accepted, extending her hand, and we managed to work our way around the rink several times, my arm around her waist and my other hand in hers—kind of like dancing, but it was skating, and that's different. The music over the sound system was rock-'n'-roll and not very stirring. We weren't sticking one leg out straight behind, and I wouldn't say we were graceful.

But I remember the moment it connected for me: We were coming around the turn near the café for the zillionth time. Her face was so young, so close. I was holding her hand. The café was passing behind her in a soft blur. There was a light in her eyes and a special smile that told me, *I'm yours. It's going to be us now, you and me, and I couldn't be happier.*

When we stepped off the ice to sit down and rest, she thought I had something in my eye and I was too embarrassed to tell her I'd gotten all emotional out there. That *look!* I could actually feel the depth of her joy, the laughter in her heart. Our love became *real* in that moment. I could finally believe it. Ever since that night in the hospital waiting room, I never believed that such a lady as this would so gladly accept my love and love me in return. I just didn't feel that lucky or that blessed, and I still thought I had to be dreaming when I saw that ring on her hand. But that moment, when she gave me that one special look, I knew. I finally knew.

She would give me that one special look the day of our wedding. I would receive it across the breakfast table almost every morning and from the front pew every time I preached, year after year. I would look for it and find it each night as she rested on her pillow and reached to turn off the lamp. I would always catch a glimpse of it when I took one hand from the steering wheel to grasp hers for just a moment. It spoke volumes without a word. It was life to me. To the end, it never faltered, and before she slipped away, she summoned it once again, for one, fleeting instant, grasping my hand.

But this was the first time I saw it, and I can see it even now.

MARIAN AND I WAITED two years to get married. It gave us time to test the relationship and decide if we could really stick together for the long haul. It gave us time to finish our schooling—mine at West Bethel and hers at a business college. It encouraged discipline and diligence in our lives.

It almost drove us crazy.

It was a good policy, however, especially for me. Having been bowled over and burned by love before, I was able to think just a shade more clearly even while I climbed the walls.

Sister Dudley kept her eye on us, so we found times and places where God could watch but she couldn't. Brother Smith didn't seem to worry, and we gave him nothing to worry about.

She graduated in 1976 and worked until I graduated in June of 1977. A week later, we were married in the Baptist church Marian's family attended, the daughter of a Baptist marrying a flaming Pentecostal. She was giddy with excitement and I wasn't even nervous. Marian's sister, Lisa, was her maid of honor. My brother, Steve, was my best man. By now, Dad was back in the ministry, and he performed the ceremony. With obvious pride, he pointed out to everyone that I was graduating, marrying, and taking my first pastoring position all in the same year, just as he did over thirty years before.

As we stood in the reception line greeting our guests, it was like having my whole life pass before me. Two old friends from the Mountain Victrola showed up. The mandolin player was pumping concrete for a living and had a baby daughter. The dobro player was now a partner with his brother in the fruit and produce business.

My old friend Vern had married Susan—the gal with the shrill voice—and they were still attending Christian Chapel. She was expecting and his hair was getting thin.

Mrs. Kenyon was still beyond plump but had finally quit smoking and was attending a Charismatic Episcopal church in Seattle. Her son, David, who first introduced me to the Kenyon–Bannister praise meetings, was pastoring a small church in Chehalis, Washington, married, and raising two kids.

Karla Dickens, still wearing glasses, was married to an accountant and had a daughter.

Andy Smith, the diabetic, was divorced and teaching at an avant-garde music school in Seattle.

Clay Olson was about to leave for the mission field in Kenya.

Benny Taylor was still a long, tall, nerdy-looking fellow, still brilliant, and hoping to get a job with a little garage-sized company called Microsoft.

Harold Martin, our born-again purveyor of pot, wasn't there, and I couldn't find anyone who knew where he was.

Brother Smith kissed the bride, shook my hand, and said, "I'm at least as happy as you are."

Sister Dudley gave Marian a gushing, loving hug. I expected she would just shake my hand and move on, but she grabbed my shoulders, pulled me into a hug, and gave me a peck on the cheek. Then she told me, "You're gonna *love* it," and winked.

She was right. We loved it. We took our honeymoon in two shifts, first in Ben's parents' cabin on Camano Island in Puget Sound, and then in Victoria, B.C. After that, we moved into a little apartment on a busy artery in Seattle. On the first Sunday in July, we dressed up nice, walked into a struggling Pentecostal Mission church in Seattle, and began our ministry.

The year that followed was a greater education than the previous four. We learned things they never taught us in Bible school, probably because no one ever lived to come back and tell us about it.

Did I say it was a struggling church? That's incorrect. The *pastor* was struggling. The *church* was content.

The pastor was Olin Marvin, an old Bible school chum of Dad's who contacted me only a month before graduation. "Hey, come aboard," he told me. "We need fresh blood, someone with vision, someone with the old Jordan fire." Marian and I figured this was the hand of God. The only other offer I'd had was from a church in Pocatello, Idaho, and that seemed so far away from our friends and family that we hesitated. When Pastor Marvin offered us a position with a good salary and an apartment right in our own neck of the woods, that sounded right. I would take charge of the youth program, he said. I would preach on Sunday nights, and he and I would be like partners in ministry. Marian wouldn't have to work, so she could be as involved in the church as she desired.

In the intense days before graduation and the wedding, Marian and I talked about our upcoming ministry as if it were a done deal, a plan set in stone, the will of God. We would be married, we'd settle down in Seattle, and then be part of a marvelous move of God. Almost every night I lay in bed imagining what it would be like to preach to a whole roomful of young people. I envisioned hundreds coming forward to receive Christ while Marian played the piano and everyone sang an invitational song, something like "Just As I Am." I could hear myself holding forth on Sunday nights, see myself helping Pastor Marvin lead his church into revival, awakening, and explosive growth. I had ideas, ideas, ideas, and couldn't wait to implement them. We were going to take the city for Christ.

On the first Sunday in July, there was no revival or explosion, but there *was* an awakening.

Northwest Pentecostal Mission was a generally unheard of little chapel nestled in the center of a closely packed Seattle neighborhood. Without detailed directions through that complicated grid of streets you'd never find it, and I suppose there were many folks who never did. Pastor Marvin met us at the door, informed us there would be a board meeting immediately after the morning service, and then hurried away. It was Sunday morning, and he was understandably busy.

The sanctuary was pretty standard: dark, gluelam beams forming a sharp A-line roof, red carpet running up the center aisle and down the sides, a soaring chancel with a big cross hanging over the baptistry. The pews could hold about two hundred. The Sunday school rooms were in the basement, the undersized parking lot was on one side.

When the Sunday school hour began, everyone—adults, teens, and little kids—gathered in the sanctuary for opening exercises, singing songs like:

> Deep and Wide
> Deep and Wide
> There's a fountain flowing deep and wide.
> Deep and Wide
> Deep and Wide
> There's a fountain flowing deep and wide.
>
> (hmmm) and (hmmm)
> (hmmm) and (hmmm)
> There's a fountain flowing (hmmm) and (hmmm).
> (hmmm) and (hmmm)
> (hmmm) and (hmmm)
> There's a fountain flowing (hmmm) and (hmmm).

Marian had attended Baptist Sunday school, and I had gone to Pentecostal Mission Sunday school, but we both knew that song and had friends from other denominations who also knew it. Our parents probably sang it in Sunday school opening exercises just like we did. Now we were beholding the next generation of Deep and Widers singing the song and doing the "Deep and Wide" hand motions. It boggled my mind to think that kids all over North America—maybe even the entire Western Hemisphere— were *hmmm* and *hmmming* this very moment, or according to their respective time zones.

It also occurred to me that adults and teenagers all over North America were sitting in opening exercises with the little kids, do- ing that song for the zillionth time and feeling silly.

We were sitting in the back. I scanned the pews for the young people. The best place to look was either in the very back or as far as anyone could sit to the side. I counted about twelve, including two silly girls, two stoics, and three Outsiders—cool guys making a statement by slouching together as far away from the proceedings as possible.

We sang a few more standards—"Stop and Let Me Tell You What the Lord Has Done for Me," and "Climb, Climb Up Sunshine Mountain." Then the lady in charge brought out the big plywood figure of Barney Barrel. Barney, a wooden barrel, had long, skinny arms that formed a tipping scale with a coffee can hanging from each hand, and it was his job to collect the missionary offering. Today it would be the girls against the boys. Sister Marvin, the pastor's wife, played the piano, we all marched around the room, the girls put their offering in the pink can and the boys put their offering in the blue. Today the girls won—I saw which one put in the roll of pennies. Clever kid.

Finally we dismissed to our classes. Pastor Marvin would be teaching the adult class in the sanctuary, but Marian and I wanted to check out the teenagers in their classroom in the basement. We followed the Outsiders downstairs and into a small, windowless, echoing room with folding chairs, a low table, and a chalkboard. The rest of the kids straggled in, talking and giggling among themselves, but obviously a little quieter since two strangers were in the room. Not one of them said hello or asked us who we were. I wasn't about to let them get away with that.

"Hi," I said, jutting out my hand. "Praise God, I'm Travis, and this is Marian!"

The first kid shook my hand and said hi back, looking immediately at the floor.

"What's your name?"

I heard him mumble something like "Bernn."

I leaned closer. I knew I was invading his comfort zone, but that was the idea. "Say again?"

He spoke up a little. "Brian."

We went after the Outsiders. "Hallelujah! Who are you?"

Donny and Steve barely got their names out, but Trevor spoke right up with his. Trevor seemed to be the leader. As soon as he opened up, the other two did. I found out what grade they were in, and what some of their interests were. In the meantime, Marian had struck up conversations with the girls. It was going well when the teacher finally arrived.

She was a young, curly headed gal. She took one look at us and said, "Hi. Who are you?"

'Praise the Lord," I said, reaching over some chairs and kids' shoulders to shake her hand. "Travis and Marian Jordan."

"I'm Lucy Moore. It's nice to have you visiting with us today." Then she said with a chuckle, "Are you sure you're in the right class?"

"You bet," I said. "I'm the new youth pastor."

She looked at me blankly for a second, then smiled and shook her head. "No, you're not."

Then she dove into the lesson like a windup toy with the spring too tight and never made eye contact with us again. Marian and I sat there quietly, hesitant to say another word. I shot a glance at Trevor. He just gave me a shrug.

And there was the strangest smell in that room, like someone left a dirty diaper under a chair. I saw a few noses wrinkle, but nobody said anything, and I wasn't about to.

IT WAS ACTUALLY A RELIEF when Pastor Marvin had us stand during the morning service so he could introduce us. "I'd like you all to meet Travis and Mary Jordan, our new assistant pastor. He'll be helping us out with the youth program and whatever else his hand finds to do, so make him welcome." He got Marian's name wrong, but at least we knew we were in the right church.

"WHAT'S HE DOING HERE?" a board member asked before Pastor Marvin even got his office door closed.

Pastor Marvin sat down at his desk and answered like a cornered witness, "Well, we did discuss this, Bill."

Bill, a wiry, curly haired man in his fifties, had veins that stuck out on his forehead, and I think his eyes may have been sticking out a bit too. "You didn't discuss it with me!"

"I didn't know he was coming *today*," said a shorter, thinner, younger man.

Bill glared at the younger man. "So he told you about it?"

"He said we might try someone out. That's all I heard."

"Well, I should have told you he was coming today," said Pastor Marvin. "It's my fault."

"You shouldn't even have invited him without consulting with the board!"

"Bill," said an older man with a lower lip that stuck out, "we *have* talked about it."

"We've talked about it; we have not *approved* it!"

Pastor Marvin broke in, "Gentlemen, before we start the meeting I should introduce Travis and Mary to you."

"Marian," I corrected.

"Oh. I am sorry. This is Travis and *Marian* Jordan. Travis recently graduated from West Bethel." Then Pastor Marvin formally introduced us to Bill Braun, the angry one; Ted Neubaur, the younger, thin one; and Wally Barker, the older one with the lip. "Uh, where's Rod?"

Ted answered, "He and Marcy had to go right home. Trevor messed in his pants again."

Bill rolled his eyes. "Oh great!"

Wally explained to us, "Trevor's a weird kid. He messes in his pants."

"He doesn't need to know that!"

"Well, he does if he's taking the youth."

"Well, what about Lucy? Has she been told about this?"

No, I thought.

Ted answered, "She was pretty upset when I talked to her. She said he came into her class and tried to take over."

"What?" I said.

"We did no such thing!" Marian objected.

Ted continued, "*She's* the one in charge of the youth right now. Nobody told her these two were coming."

"Nobody told anybody anything!" Bill snapped. "See? Now you've hurt Lucy!"

"Well," said Pastor Marvin, "why don't we open in a word of prayer? Dear Lord—"

Let us live, I prayed silently, clutching Marian's hand.

The moment Pastor Marvin said Amen, Bill spoke the first words of the formal meeting. "And you announced his appointment from the pulpit! Before we've even met him or got to know him!"

"I knew your dad," Wally told me with a smile. "How's he doing, anyway?"

"Does he have another job?" Bill asked.

"We'll get to that," said the pastor.

"This was something we talked about, remember? Wally, you're the accountant. Tell him. *Again*."

Wally's face turned sad as he told the pastor, "We can't swing a full-time salary, especially since we've lost the Cravens and the Johnsons."

"We told you that!"

Pastor Marvin defended himself. "I think we can do it."

"If he has another job," Bill reiterated, and then he looked at me and cocked his eyebrows, expecting an answer.

Now they were all looking at me.

"I . . . I understood that *this* was going to be my job."

"What skills do you have besides Bible college?"

The question stung, not only because it was mean-spirited, but because of how I had to answer. "I don't have any."

"Get some."

"Now Bill . . ." the pastor tried to admonish.

Bill came right back, "I'm being honest. He can't work in a church this size and expect a big church salary package. That's the truth of it."

"Who's paying for the apartment?" Ted asked.

Bill's voice approached a squawk. "*What* apartment?"

"We discussed that as part of the package," said Pastor Marvin.

"He has an *apartment?*"

It went on and on, with Marian and I cowering in our chairs

while the pastor and the board argued right in front of us. I've never had such an experience before or since then, watching my hopes dashed to pieces while almost laughing at the absurdity of it. Finally, I suggested, "Why don't Marian and I leave so you can discuss this freely among yourselves?"

"Yeah, fine," said Bill.

"Okay," said the pastor.

We got up to leave.

Bill didn't even watch us go. "If he can get another job then maybe we can work something out."

MY SHIFT BEGAN at 9 P.M., as soon as the mall closed. My first task every night was to scrub and shine all the public restrooms. The toilets came first, then the sinks, then the stalls, walls, and floors. My supervisor said each rest room shouldn't take more than an hour, but after a week on the job I had yet to cut my time down to less than two. I was working four nights a week and making five bucks an hour.

The toughest toilets to clean were the ones that got clogged sometime during the day but patrons kept using them anyway until the bowl was full. Then the only way to clean them was to ladle the stuff into a bucket, get the toilet unclogged, and ladle it back in again, flushing it down in smaller loads. When I finished, I headed outside to get some air, laughing at the sign on the back of the rest room door: *Employees Must Wash Hands Before Returning to Work.*

This toilet in the north men's room was the worst I'd seen all week.

I flushed the last load and grabbed the toilet brush out of my tool cart. Under my meticulous care, the porcelain bowl would soon be white again.

With her business degree, Marian had landed a good job as accountant and office manager for a small firm that manufactured hydraulic valves and couplings. Suffice it to say, she was making better money than I was and providing the bulk of our living, including the apartment the church decided it couldn't afford.

What skills do you have besides Bible college?

I wanted to slug that guy. Did he think four years of college counted for nothing?

Well, apparently it qualified me to scrub toilets and sinks, re-fill soap containers and towel dispensers, and mop the floors.

C'mon, let's go, let's go, let's get it down to an hour.

I moved to the next stall. Ah. The last patron's mother had taught him well. This wouldn't take long.

My emotions and thoughts kept shifting back and forth from minute to minute. First, I felt okay about it. As weird, disappointing, and even maddening as it seemed, I accepted this as God's calling. He was using this time to humble me. I needed to accept and embrace it. I needed to stay put and see it through.

Then I thought of Minneapolis and the well-dressed man with the curly hair and the lady in the white silk blouse and navy skirt. After so many years, the image still made my stomach hurt. I felt like I was standing in that office again, unqualified, unfit, inadequate, a loser.

What skills do you have besides Bible college?

The answer was the toilet brush in my hand.

C'mon, Trav, two more stalls to go.

God was in control. He knew what he was doing, and he knew what I needed.

Then my heart sank and my arms went limp. I'd failed again. I'd married the most beautiful woman in the world, given her high hopes, and let her down. She was the one supporting us, not me. I thought I was going to take the city for Christ, and now here I was, alone and scrubbing toilets in the middle of the night.

My "position" at Northwest Pentecostal Mission remained undefined by the pastor or the board. I wasn't associate pastor or youth pastor, I didn't preach on Sunday nights, and Lucy Moore still had charge of the youth Sunday school class. I did whatever was left to do—it was up to me to think of what that was—and I got paid fifty dollars a month plus a gas allowance to do it. I think Pastor Marvin tried to apologize once, but his expression of regret quickly shifted into a short homily about the Lord using all this to show me the importance of sacrifice. It seemed rather convenient for him to find a lofty, inscrutable purpose of God in *his* foul-up, but I held my peace.

The church in Pocatello, Idaho, had found someone else for that position. I checked.

17

IT WAS MARIAN, God bless her, who helped me turn it around—or rather, turn *myself* around. I still remember the evening I lay on the couch with my head in her lap. I had tears in my eyes, but she just stroked my hair and told me, "Travis, you're a man of God and this is your calling. Don't worry about me having to work. Just be faithful. Whatever your hand finds to do, do it with all your might. God will do the rest." She tilted my head toward her and I looked up into her eyes. "And I will always love you, T. J. You're my man, and don't you forget it."

I called Lucy Moore and apologized for all the misunderstanding. I didn't want to take over, I told her. I just wanted to help. Could I? She said sure.

At work that night I finished up each rest room in less than an hour.

Wednesday evening, one of my nights off, Marian and I showed up to help Lucy with the youth meeting. I played guitar and helped lead the singing. We goaded and challenged the kids during discussion times. We did anything we could to help while letting Lucy be the boss. It clicked. Before long we were all team teaching the Sunday school class. We worked together planning a camping trip to Corral Pass, and it came off without a hitch.

After I'd been on the job two months, the boss let me try my hand at the big mall sweeper. Now that was fun, driving that thing up and down the vast floor, buzzing past all the store windows and around the big central pillars, singing praise songs only the Lord could hear. How many shoppers ever got a chance to visit the mall as I did?

For the first month I took care of mowing the church lawn, and then Lucy, Marian, and I organized a work day for the youth group to mow, weed, and fix up the church grounds. The kids did a great job, and we were proud of them. I rewarded them by taking them all swimming.

Sister Marvin heard that some of the girls wore two-piece swimsuits and walked right by the groomed lawn to give me a stern rebuke. It was the first feedback I'd gotten from her.

THE SUNDAY SCHOOL CLASS was perking up. We got into heavy discussions about morality, sex, authority, respect for others, honesty, and what the Scriptures had to say about it all. The kids opened up about school, friends, parents, hopes and fears, what was cool and what wasn't. We talked about Bible prophecy and how it could apply to happenings in the Middle East. Even Trevor and the Outsiders got wrapped up in it. They talked about inviting their friends.

When they didn't invite their friends, I asked them why not.

They said they didn't want their friends to have to sing "Deep and Wide" and "Climb, Climb Up Sunshine Mountain" and march up front to put money in Barney Barrel.

Well, that seemed an easy enough problem to overcome. I told Lucy, "Hey, why don't we just have them come straight to class and not sit through the opening exercises? They never get anything out of them anyway."

Lucy balked. "Um, we'll have to talk to Sister Dwight. She's the Sunday school superintendent."

Sister Dwight didn't jump at the idea either. "You'll have to bring it up at the next Sunday school teachers' meeting."

The meeting was after church the first Sunday of the month. We were there and we brought it up.

And that's how I got to know Sister Rogenbeck.

She was an ancient lady who taught the primary class, and by the look on her face you'd think we suggested denying the virgin birth and the resurrection. She scolded me as she answered, "The children are to be together for the morning exercises!"

Being young and inexperienced, I tried to reason with her. "Well, that's okay for the little kids, but the teenagers don't have any interest in that stuff."

"Then they can learn to have interest."

"You think kids who listen to the Rolling Stones and Led Zeppelin are going to want to come here to sing 'Deep and Wide'?"

She crossed her arms and looked toward the front of the sanctuary. "They belong in the morning exercises with everyone else!"

From her body language I gathered she thought the discussion was over.

It wasn't.

"Do you agree with her?" I asked Sister Dwight.

Sister Dwight gave me a deep, slow nod as if the Word of the Lord had come down from Mt. Sinai.

"But aren't you the Sunday School superintendent?"

She was mildly offended. "Of course I am."

I turned to Sister Rogenbeck. "So what are *you?*"

She didn't answer but just kept looking forward, her arms crossed.

"Look at me." Marian tugged at my arm but I ignored it and demanded, "Look at me!"

Sister Dwight became indignant. "Travis, I don't think this is appropriate!"

Sister Rogenbeck's head and eyes turned toward me only as much as necessary.

"Are you the Sunday school superintendent?" I asked her.

Sister Marvin's indignity surpassed that of Sister Dwight. "Travis Jordan, that will be quite enough!"

"Are you?"

"No."

"Do you hold any elected office whatsoever in this church?"

"No."

"Then who are you to sit there and dictate policy to the rest of us?"

"Trav . . ." Marian whispered, tugging at me.

"My question was addressed to the Sunday school superintendent, and I expect the decision to rest with her." I looked straight at Sister Dwight. "It *is* your decision, isn't it?"

"Well—"

Sister Rogenbeck huffed rather loudly, "They belong in the morning exercises!"

"I was asking Sister *Dwight*," I said.

But Sister *Marvin* answered, "Travis, that's the way we do things!"

I stayed on that merry-go-round for another twenty minutes, going round and round, hearing the same tune over and over and getting madder and madder. In the end, I accomplished nothing more than getting everyone upset, including myself. I was permanently angry with Sister Rogenbeck and permanently in the gunsights of Sister Marvin. I never did get an answer from Sister Dwight.

And our Sunday school class continued to sit through "Deep and Wide" and march to put money in Barney Barrel. It was, after all, the way we did things.

But the Wednesday night youth meeting held great promise. The time was all ours. We could lay out our own format. We painted posters, made announcements, and got the kids making announcements. I visited the junior high and high school as often as I could just to make contact with the kids. Marian and I attended the games, the concerts, the plays—anything that would get us close to them.

The meetings began to grow. We were singing, worshiping, getting excited about Jesus. The fellowship hall began to fill up and we ran out of chairs. The kids brought pillows and sat on the floor.

Shy Brian turned out to be a pretty good guitar player and I got him up front to help me lead worship. Then a kid named Robbie joined us on electric bass. As soon as they were clicking, I switched to doing fills on my banjo, which I plugged in for volume. We got into the Word and the kids started praying.

And then Sister Marvin called a meeting.

"I think you can find instruments more appropriate for worship!" she said archly.

We were sitting in Pastor Marvin's office, just the Marvins and me. I could tell she'd already had a pre-meeting with her husband to get him in line.

"There's nothing wrong with our instruments," I said. "The kids are into it. I've even got two of them playing up front."

"Playing rock-'n'- roll in church!"

"It isn't rock-'n'-roll. It's contemporary worship."

She rolled her eyes in disgust. "Well I don't believe that! I saw the electric guitar!"

"That's a bass."

"We could hear you clear upstairs."

Pastor Marvin ventured, "At least they were singing." It was very bold of him.

She stared a few daggers at him and then conceded, "Well, I might be able to put up with the guitar, but the *banjo!*" Then she rolled her eyes again, sending a loud and clear message of disdain that I took personally.

Pastor Marvin offered, "Why can't Marian play the piano?"

"We don't have one down there," I answered. "The only piano this church has is in the sanctuary."

"Then maybe you should just join the adults upstairs," said Sister Marvin.

I thought of all those kids finally coming around, finally getting excited because something new was happening, something just for them. I thought of them having to listen to Sister Marvin play the organ and sit through one of Pastor Marvin's sermons. "That's not going to happen."

Bull's-eye. I hit her primer and the powder exploded. "*Excuse me?*"

I was angry enough—and just plain *right* enough—to face her down. "That's not going to happen." I turned to the pastor and said, "Our youth group has grown from a dozen to over forty and I expect it to grow even more if we can just be left alone to do what we're doing. If that's agreeable with you, then I'd like your approval."

"We don't approve," Sister Marvin answered. "Not at all!"

I leaned over Pastor Marvin's desk, looking him right in the eye and effectively blocking out the participation of his wife. "I would like *your* approval, sir."

He looked at her, and I could read her signals in his face. "Well, you're doing a good job, but you need to be careful, Travis." He glanced at his wife. No doubt he would have to say more if he wanted dinner tonight. "We'll have to talk about it. We'll work something out."

The banjo stayed, as did the guitar and the electric bass. Pastor Marvin declined to confront us, and the youth group grew to over sixty on a Wednesday night. Sister Marvin derived no joy from that fact. Sister Rogenbeck wouldn't look at me even if I was standing right in front of her. Bill Braun, the board member, demanded I turn in every gas receipt directly to him, and then he grilled me for any and all details.

TWO GIRLS, Cindy and Clarice, along with shy Brian and Robbie the bass player, had formed a nice quartet and volunteered to sing a special number for the Sunday evening service. Because they were there, about twelve of their friends were there as well, so we had sixteen teenagers willingly turning out for church on Sunday night. I was sure Sister Marvin would be pleased.

When their turn came, Cindy, Clarice, Brian, and Robbie took their places in the front of the sanctuary, nervous but excited. The two boys started an introduction on their guitars, and—

Amos Rogenbeck, Sister Rogenbeck's husband, growled at

them from his reserved, exclusive, usable-only-by-a-Rogenbeck place in the pew, "Young people, I'll thank you not to stand in front of the altar!"

The musical introduction stopped cold. The kids didn't know what to do. They looked at each other. They looked at me. I got up from my seat on the platform and showed the kids a better place to stand, over in front of the piano.

Shy Brian whispered, "What'd we do wrong?"

"Nothing," I whispered back. "Just sing for Jesus."

I'd heard them sing before and they were great. This night, thanks to Amos Rogenbeck, their song fell apart and they sat down humiliated. The incident was not wasted on their friends. After the service, I scrambled to talk to as many kids as I could before they all left bitter and disillusioned. Some got away, and I knew it would take weeks to repair the damage.

But Brother Rogenbeck didn't get away. That would have happened over my dead body. I pulled him aside for a discreet, private confrontation. "Brother Rogenbeck, you embarrassed and hurt those kids tonight—"

"They should show respect for the altar!"

"They meant no harm by it. They were nervous, they just wanted to sing for the Lord and minister—"

"Young brats don't have any respect! You should be teaching them that!"

I grabbed his arm and got right in his face. "Now you listen to me! These kids mean the world to me and they just want to glorify Jesus. If you embarrass them again—are you listening to me?—*I'm* going to embarrass *you*. We're having a private meeting now, but next time it'll be in front of everyone, you understand?"

"You need to show respect!"

I would have had a more fruitful conversation with a grapefruit.

WE WERE PUSHING SIXTY in attendance, almost filling the fellowship hall. The worship music was great. Cindy, Clarice, Brian, and

Robbie finally got a chance to sing their number and do it right. The kids spoke right up during our sharing time, telling the others what the Lord had done in their lives over the past week. We had some new kids attending. Everything was going great—until the night we discovered a mouse behind the door.

The fellowship hall had rest rooms and a stairway at one end, a kitchen at the other, and doors to the Sunday school rooms on the sides. As I stood up to speak, I thought I heard a noise from the room directly behind me and glanced at it. That door, like all the others, was closed. I went on teaching, telling illustrative stories, cracking jokes, getting laughs.

And then I heard the noise again. A squeak. Some rustling.

Two girls sitting in the front row started chittering to each other, pointing toward the door and apparently seeing movement under it. Pretty soon, five in the front row were looking. Finally, one of them squealed, "There's a mouse in there!"

Announce the presence of a mouse to thirty teenage girls sitting on the floor and thirty teenage guys who would love to catch it, and you will have a roomful of kids who aren't interested in the triumphal entry. I went to the door.

"Don't open it!" a girl shrieked.

"All *right!*" said the guys.

I jerked the door open and everybody screamed.

It was Sister Marvin, sitting just inside the door with a notepad in her lap. There was no other way into that room except through the fellowship hall, so she had to have been sitting there for over an hour. Her face was so red I thought she'd pop a capillary.

"Oh," I said, "I'm sorry. We thought you were a mouse."

And then I closed the door again.

It took a little while to get the kids calmed down. Some gave no thought to the pastor's wife lurking behind the door taking notes. Some thought it was perfectly, classically funny and couldn't stop laughing. I just went on with the Bible study and finished up the meeting. The kids went home, and Lucy, Marian, and I cleaned up. I don't know exactly when Sister Marvin finally came out of that room, but it was after we were gone. I left the hall light on so she could see her way out.

AFTER SIX MONTHS, the board voted to raise my salary to a hundred dollars a month. Brother Bill Braun was adamantly against it, but the other board members voted against him, and that sealed Brother Braun's opinion of me.

I confess I didn't help matters. I failed to wear a tie one Sunday night, which got me into trouble with the Rogenbecks, Peeleys, and Schmidts. These formed a cadre of big givers in the church, a group you wouldn't want disgruntled. Pastor Marvin offered to buy me a tie, but I took the hint and never came to church again without one.

My hair got a little too long for their liking as well, but I let it grow longer just to stretch them a bit. They didn't stretch.

About eight months into the ministry, Marian was sitting in a pew, praying quietly while I prayed with some of the kids up front. Sister Peeley and Sister Schmidt sat down on either side of her and asked if she had any needs they could pray about.

"Well," she said, "you can pray for those kids up there. Isaac is from a broken home, and Diane is coming out of a Satanist group."

"Anything else?" probed Sister Peeley.

"I'm witnessing to a girl at work and I hope you'll pray for her. Her name is Susan."

"But what about yourself?" they asked. "Is there anything we can pray for?"

Marian already knew what they were after. Lucy had attended the women's ministry meeting at which Sister Marvin shared her concerns about Marian. Marian seemed overly occupied with a career instead of her husband, she'd said. Marian seemed a little hesitant to let the Spirit flow in her life. And, Sister Marvin asked, has anyone ever heard Marian speak in tongues? The women compared notes and were a bit stunned to find that none of them had. Isn't she from a Baptist background? someone asked. Lucy said it wasn't right to be talking about Marian this way, but Sister Marvin replied, "We have a problem and we need to discuss it."

Now Sister Peeley and Sister Schmidt wanted Marian to remain while they laid hands on her. Marian and I already had an understanding. She scratched her nose, I got her signal and stepped in.

"Pardon me," I told all three. "Marian, I think Lucy needs some help praying for Diane."

Marian rose with her usual grace. "Please excuse me," she said, and went to pray with Lucy and Diane.

Sister Peeley and Sister Schmidt opted to pray between themselves, but they didn't stay long.

Marian was teasingly jubilant as we drove home. "Well, now *I* have a reputation too!" she announced, patting my hand. "Why should you be the one who gets all the attention?"

MY MINISTRY POSITION at Northwest Pentecostal Mission lasted one year and five months, growing and dying at the same time. I got along grandly with the youth, and by the end of our stay we had about eighty coming out on Wednesday nights. The death of our ministry was something that built over time, grievance by grievance, misstep by misstep, and finished with a loud bang.

At the 1978 Christmas banquet, I threw the scales so out of balance that no amount of devoted ministry would right them again.

The church had rented a banquet room at a local hotel and decorated it to the hilt. The adults were decked out in their finest and sat at formally decorated tables for a candlelight dinner. Lucy, Marian, and I brought a youth choir made up of twenty-four kids, the girls in long dresses, the guys in white shirts and ties. Marian played a rented piano, Shy Brian and Robbie played guitar and bass, I directed, and those kids sang some terrific arrangements of traditional carols as well as some fun, upbeat songs. The evening was going great—up to a point.

We'd just finished a comical rendition of "Children Go Where

I Send Thee," with costumed kids portraying Four for the four that stood at the door, Three for the Hebrew children, Two for Paul and Silas, and One for the little bitty baby born, born, born in Bethlehem, when Brother Rogenbeck decided it was time for a loud, growling admonition: "You'd better change your direction, young people! We're not here to listen to this nonsense! We're here to worship the Lord!"

I was facing the choir with my back to the room, but I knew who it was. I had my hands up, ready to start the next song, but my arms wilted and I could feel my temperature rising. There were moans all over the room. I could see the hurt in the kids' faces, the embarrassment and fear. Cindy and Clarice had been through this before and weren't hurt but angry. As for Shy Brian and Robbie—

"Why don't you just shut up?" Brian cried.

I turned. I could see Sister Marvin about to step in.

"No!" I said, looking at her and then all the others. "No, he's absolutely right. These kids have worked hard and done it prayerfully, and they don't deserve this kind of treatment."

There were Amens and expressions of agreement from some corners of the room. The rest just stared at me, aghast. I caught a quick glimpse of Marian at the piano, expecting her to give me her usual cautionary expression. Not this time. She was on her feet, her eyes on fire, and on the very brink of saying something if I didn't.

"Brother Rogenbeck," I said, "the last time you pulled a stunt like this I told you if you did it again, I'd correct you in front of everybody. Well, here we are."

He just glared back at me through his thick glasses, his jaw set and his face like stone.

I stepped closer to him, demanding his attention—what there was of it. "Apparently, in all your seventy-some-odd years of life, no one ever taught you as simple a thing as common courtesy. Well, sir, *I'm* going to teach you, so you listen carefully. When these kids are up front doing anything for the congregation—and I don't care what it is—you are to sit quietly and keep your mouth shut. *That's* the courteous thing to do. You may think it's holy and righteous to spout off and hurt my kids' feelings, but you're not being holy, you're being a jerk." I could see Sister Marvin seething out of the corner of my eye, but I also saw Pastor Marvin nodding in agreement. I felt vaguely aware that I was about to torpedo my ministry at this church, but by now, after so much of this stuff, one thought washed like a tidal wave over all the others: To *heck* with it! I took another step toward Brother Rogenbeck. "You keep quiet, Brother Rogenbeck—you hear me? Because the *next* time you open your mouth and hurt my kids, before God and this congregation, I promise I'll personally knock you right on your Stay-Dries. Is that understood?"

My kids applauded and cheered.

There were gasps of horror all over the room—and a few cheers.

But apparently three out of the four board members weren't cheering. Wally Barker was the only one who thought I should stay.

The banquet took place on a Friday night. Pastor Marvin and Wally Barker came by to give me my last paycheck on Saturday. The board had trouble deciding whether I should be paid for my participation at the banquet, but Wally finally prevailed and they agreed to prorate my December check for the first two weeks. I got fifty dollars. Pastor Marvin told me in several ways that he wasn't unhappy with me, and then he asked me not to show up at the church again. It would only stir up the hornet's nest, he said. I never went back.

Lucy kept the youth group going, but finally married and moved away. The youth ministry dissolved, and the older folks got their church back just the way they liked it.

I've never forgotten that year and five months, nor have I ever been able to settle in my mind how I could have done better. I could have been less feisty. I could have submitted more to the leadership over me. I could have kowtowed to Sisters Marvin, Rogenbeck, Peeley, and Schmidt. Maybe rebuking Brother Rogenbeck *did* set a bad example in front of the kids. I *was* young and headstrong back then, I admit.

But still . . . there was so much good that happened during those days, so many things that I know will last. Some of those kids came from home situations that never would have gotten them saved, to put it mildly, but they're still serving the Lord today. Somehow, Trevor Neilson got the kinks out of his mind and quit messing in his pants. His mother sent me a thank-you card.

And there were good-bye and thank-you cards from the kids, too. . . .

"HEY TRAVIS, you okay?"

Kyle was driving us back from Missoula. I guess I'd gotten a little too quiet.

"I'm—" I didn't expect my throat to be so tight. I swallowed. "I'm okay. I was just thinking about things. Thinking about . . ."

"Yeah?"

"My wife used to say something to me that you might benefit from hearing," I said at last. "Kyle, you're a man of God and this is your calling, so don't worry. Just be faithful. Whatever your hand finds to do, do it with all your might. God will do the rest." Then I added, "And Kyle, don't let anybody put out your fire, you hear me?"

Kyle hadn't been inside my mind or privy to my memories for the last hundred miles, so he looked a little quizzical. "Okay. Thanks for that."

The highway blurred in front of me. I rubbed the tears out of my eyes so I could see the mountains and the blue sky over Idaho.

18

At our lady of the Fields, Arnold Kowalski, his hat in his hands, moved slowly down the center aisle, passing through the squares of sunlight on the floor and looking up at the crucifix on the wall. He was the only one there, the only one who still believed. The pilgrims were gone, along with the reporters and their cameras. The fame had moved to the Macon ranch.

But Arnold's faith was here because the crucifix was here. The stranger at the ranch he didn't know, but this image had been a part of his life for years. He'd dusted it, polished it, straightened it, respected it. It had touched his pain and taken it away. His faith was here.

He looked around to be sure he was alone, then walked slowly toward the platform, his head bowed in humility and reverence, counting twelve steps between each genuflection. Every step hurt just a little. His joints were complaining again, but it wouldn't be for long. He still believed. He was wearing a tie today. He'd combed his hair before leaving home and once more after removing his hat. He'd blessed himself with holy water before entering the sanctuary. He'd recited twelve Hail Marys and twelve Our Fathers.

Father Vendetti had mentioned taking the ladder down and

putting it away, but Arnold had put off doing it, knowing he would need it as soon as he had prayed enough to be worthy. He stepped on the first rung, feeling the pain, then climbed slowly, his eyes on the carved face crowned with thorns.

When he had climbed to the same level as the wooden Christ, he reached into his pocket and pulled out the small crucifix that had hung on his bedroom wall for decades, a gift from his mother. With great care and reverence, he had drilled a small hole in the top and threaded a neck chain through it.

"See?" he said, holding it before the wooden eyes. "I have you at home too."

He extended the crucifix until it touched the one on the wall. Nothing happened. Everything was safe so far. He pressed the smaller cross flat against the larger, then rubbed it up and down as a child would rub a nail across a magnet, reciting the Lord's Prayer and another Hail Mary. Then he said, "I know there's plenty of blessing in there. I know you won't mind."

Satisfied after a few final strokes, he hung the little image around his neck and blessed himself before the image on the wall. "Thank you."

He descended the ladder, then put it away as Father Vendetti had asked. The blessing was close to him now, and would go with him everywhere, every moment. There would be no more pain.

I COULDN'T BELIEVE Brett Henchle was actually pulling us over. I was the kind of driver who obeyed the law out of my love for the Lord and not for fear of punishment, and therefore I never went over the speed limit even if there were no cops around. Well, that little policy didn't work this time. As soon as we passed Judy's Eat-a-long and Tavern, Brett was behind me, his lights flashing.

"What'd you do?" Kyle asked.

I felt rather snide. "Went to Missoula to trace that car."

Kyle glanced backward. "You think so?"

"We'll see."

I rolled the window down as Brett walked up alongside, noting how he kept his billy club in his hand until he was right outside my window. "Hi, Travis," he said, slipping the club into the loop on his belt. "In a little hurry, aren't you?"

I spoke politely. "I was going less than twenty-five miles per hour, and twenty-five is the posted speed limit."

He leaned against the car, his hands on the window sill. "My radar told me otherwise."

I glanced at Kyle. "I have a witness."

He stooped in close, his eyes invisible behind his gold-rimmed sunglasses. "Okay, I'll come right to the point. I know where you've been and I know what you've been doing. I shouldn't have to re-mind you that's my job and none of your business."

I thought I might reason with him. "Brett, come on, we've known each other for years—"

He put his finger in my face. "This isn't a discussion, Travis. This is a heads-up for both of you. I'm watching. You make things difficult for this town, I'll make things really difficult for you. Those are the rules."

"Don't we have to break the law first?"

He almost smiled. "That'll be my call, won't it? Now let's have your license and registration. I clocked you going forty."

WE MET in Morgan Elliott's office. Both Kyle and I had qualms about it, but she insisted. "Michael is my son," she said. "This Brandon or Herb or whoever he is already knows he has to deal with me." We told her about our trip and what we had learned. We also told her about our encounter with Brett Henchle on the way into town.

She cocked an eyebrow at Kyle. "Looks like you were right."

"Nichols is out to make friends," Kyle observed. "People with power, people with money."

"Like Mrs. Macon," I added.

"And the business folks like Norman and Matt," said Morgan. "And as many of the local clergy as he can muster to his side."

"Armond Harrison, for one."

"Absolutely, and as many of the other ministers Armond can guilt-trip into joining. Burton Eddy is almost a confederate by now. Sid Maher and Paul Daley don't like Nichols/Johnson, but they aren't going to say a word against him." She sneered. "They don't wish to seem intolerant."

"So where do you stand?" Kyle asked her.

I almost objected to his forwardness, but Morgan answered directly, "That man is not Jesus."

Kyle was not rude in tone, but he was still being Kyle. "What about the real Jesus? Have you met him personally?"

She paused to consider the question, and then answered, "No." Then she added, "But that can change—"

"We can pray right now—"

"At the proper time." She shifted her focus toward me. "So what now?"

"I think it's time I had a little talk with Brandon Nichols," I said.

"I'll go along," said Kyle.

"Uh, no. Let me do it. He and I have talked before, and it's always been just the two of us."

"Are you sure, after what Abe and Hattie told us? I don't know. . . ."

Even Morgan seemed uneasy. "I'd be careful not to be alone with him."

"He came to me first, as if he wants me in his confidence," I told them. "I think we could talk freely. There might be a way to get through to him, maybe unravel whatever his problem is."

"I haven't told you yet," said Morgan. "Nevin Sorrel is dead."

Kyle took the news badly, but I was only vaguely familiar with the name. "Who is that?"

"Remember the guy I told you about?" asked Kyle. "He was there at the meeting in the garage. He's the other guy who tried to take pictures of Nichols."

Now *I* started taking the news badly. "You're kidding."

"He used to work for Mrs. Macon before Nichols came along," Morgan explained. "From what Michael tells me, Mrs. Macon fired him and hired Nichols, and Nevin was not happy about it."

"He broke up the meeting." Then Kyle added with dramatic force, "And he said Brandon Nichols was *not* Brandon Nichols! He said Nichols was lying!"

"He was right."

"What happened to him?" I asked.

"Nichols hired him back," said Morgan. "Michael told me he was working with Nichols on a water project, developing a spring up in the hills somewhere. Apparently, Nevin was riding his horse back from the project when he fell off and hit his head. His foot was caught in the stirrup, so the horse dragged him all the way back to the corral. At least, that's the story. Nobody actually saw it happen."

"He was working with Nichols?" I wanted to verify.

"According to Michael."

"Nichols *hired* him?" Kyle asked. "After that scene in the garage, he still *hired* him?"

"Michael says Mrs. Macon was against it, but Nichols wanted Nevin to live on the place and work for him. You can draw some nasty conclusions."

Kyle shook his head at me. "I wouldn't go up there alone."

He and Morgan waited for my answer.

I thought it over and said, "You two just pray for me. I'll be all right."

SATURDAY, at least three hundred people from almost as many faraway places filled the folding chairs under the blue-and-white striped big top, and Brandon Nichols/Herb Johnson held forth in a glorious manner. It was the first of his meetings I'd ever attended, and I could quickly see why Kyle got so upset and wrote that letter to the paper. This guy could sell snow to an Eskimo. The healings were dramatic to say the least, and all the wonderful talk—of love, brotherhood, peace, safety, a new world—just went on and on, and the people ate it up. I recognized several familiar faces: Matt Kiley was in the back, apparently an usher; Michael Elliott was helping direct traffic and bring prophetic comfort wherever needed; Dee Baylor and Adrian Folsom were present, but not sitting near each other, which was a little unusual. Don Anderson the appliance dealer actually went forward with the other petitioners, wanting a special blessing for his business.

Before Nichols preached, several went to the podium to give testimonies. All I had to do was mentally substitute a few key names and words—"Brandon" for Jesus, for example, or "follower" for Christian—and the testimonies could have come right out of a Sunday night church meeting.

"My life used to be a mess," said a young professional from Colorado. "I had a great job running a resort in Vail and I was making plenty of money, but it just didn't satisfy. Something was missing. Then I found Brandon, and that's made all the difference!"

"I became a follower two weeks ago," said a young woman from Redding, California, "and my life has never been the same. I used to be on drugs, but now that's over. Brandon—" Then she giggled and said, "I like to think of him by his *real* name," and everyone chuckled at what she was implying. "Brandon has brought real meaning to my life and I love him dearly."

Then Andy Parmenter, the retired executive from Southern California, stood behind the podium and said, "Brandon has dramatically affirmed what I have always believed, that whatever it is, I can do it. There's no mountain too tall to block your path if you just believe in yourself. I think this little town is going to become a world-renowned showplace for exactly that principle! We are here, we are strong, we have what it takes to build a better world. So don't miss out. Get on board. Let Brandon touch your life and believe!"

He sat down to whoops and applause.

Nichols sat on the platform listening to all this and obviously enjoying it. Sitting to his immediate right was, of all people, Sally Fordyce. One look told me she was a total, 100 percent follower—and maybe more. She was wearing a long white dress that matched his white tunic, and the shawl and sandals made her look like a biblical character. There was an obvious affection between them.

They touched and held hands frequently. Their eyes met as they shared the laughter. When someone praised him, she would stroke his shoulder. My guess was that she no longer went home to Charlie and Meg at night.

Sitting to Nichols's immediate left was Mary Donovan, the Catholic friend of Dee Baylor. I didn't know her very well, only that she tagged around a lot with Dee. She was wearing a long, blue dress and a shawl over her head, like every statue of the Virgin Mary, and she seemed to be acting very . . . shall we say, *icon*-like?

Nichols gave her a kindly, playful nudge, and she giggled with embarrassment. The audience picked up the idea. "Mom!" they called. "God bless you, Mom!"

She rose slowly, gathering her shawl about her head and taking small steps with a fluid, dancer-like gracefulness. She approached the podium and then, both hands extended, said airily, "Blessings to you all!"

"Blessings," they echoed back.

"Today the Lord has done great things, and holy is his name! He has touched the weak and made them strong. He has brought wealth to the needy and courage to the fainthearted. Be thankful, one and all. Be thankful!"

"Thank you," rippled through the audience, and Nichols nodded back.

"From the earth comes water, from the water comes new life. Be thankful, one and all!"

"Thank you," they repeated.

And Nichols smiled and nodded again.

They have a regular liturgy going here, I thought.

But just who is Mary Donovan supposed to be? They're calling her Mom. *The* Mom? I had to wonder what Dee, Mary's former mentor, must be feeling about all this. *Mary* was getting the attention now.

This was too much.

I noticed Nancy Barrons standing in a doorway of the tent with

Mrs. Macon. The two were talking quietly, but Nancy didn't appear to be acting as a reporter today. If I learned Nancy had become a follower I knew I would scream.

The moment Nichols rose to speak, he told the crowd, "Turn to someone and say, 'This world needs someone like you.' Go ahead."

Someone turned to me and said it, but I didn't even turn. I had made up my mind long ago I'd never turn to anyone and say anything ever again, but mostly, I was stunned. Where'd *Nichols* pick up that little routine?

"Folks, I'll have you know, we are now officially county-approved!" Everyone cheered. "The spring is developed, the water system is upgraded, the storage tank is in, and we have our permit for the new headquarters! The porta-potties will soon be a thing of the past!"

More cheers.

"But wait, I see something," said Nichols, closing his eyes, seeing spiritually. "I see a spirit of doubt in this place, clinging to minds, spreading a poison of fear and anxiety. Do you feel that today? Do you?"

Several muttered affirmatively.

"BEGONE!"

His shout made me jump, as it did others. There was a wail from the crowd as, supposedly, the spirit of doubt departed.

More cheers and applause.

I had to do some praying. This whole thing was bigger and moving faster than I had imagined. What in the world was I doing here? Would Nichols even have time to talk to me?

TWO HOURS LATER, Brandon Nichols and I were walking along the white fence that bordered a large horse paddock. As it turned out, he saw me in the audience as soon as the meeting began and couldn't wait to take this walk with me. We weren't necessarily alone. We could talk privately, but Matt Kiley and two other men stood across the paddock to keep an eye on things.

He was giddy with excitement. "Things are moving right along, Travis, faster than I'd hoped!"

"So I see," I replied with a lack of enthusiasm. "I was surprised. I really was."

"Give the people what they want, they'll come."

"It's quite a show."

He paused and leaned on the fence. "It always is. Everywhere, every Sunday." He looked directly at me. "Am I right?"

I saw no need to get into that. "We need to talk about Herb Johnson."

He only smiled. "Maybe we should talk about that speeding ticket you got from Brett Henchle."

I took a breath and made a decision not to get angry. "I'll contest it in court and probably get it thrown out. I wasn't speeding, I have a perfect driving record and a witness, I know the judge, and the judge knows me. There, we've talked about it." I waited, then I prodded, "Herb Johnson."

"Herb is a plant you grind up and put in soup. Call me Brandon."

"I talked to—"

"To Abe. And Hattie. I know. They have terrible memories if they can't even remember what my name is."

"So you do remember them. Well they remember you, and Abe remembers the car."

Now he got impatient with me—what did I expect? "Travis, you are way behind and way off! You sat through the whole meeting. Didn't you learn anything? People are people and they always will be people, and people don't care what I am or who I am, they care about what I provide. Give them what they want and they'll *think* what they want. You can go to Missoula, you can go to L.A., you can dig up whatever you want, but it'll only make *you* the bad guy, not me."

I frowned. "What's in L.A.?"

He looked away and laughed. "Travis, please tell me you're not a hypocrite."

"Are you going to answer any of my questions?"

"I'll do better than that." He turned toward me, his elbow on the fence. "I'll tell you my intentions."

I was skeptical and made no effort to hide it. "Knock me over."

He gave a sly smile. "I intend to take this town for Christ."

I knew what he really meant. It felt like a hot needle going through my heart but I tried not to flinch. "I can't believe the gall you have."

"Travis, come on, now. You've tried the same thing, be honest. Outreaches and bus ministries and youth evangelism, anything to bring the people in. It's all a big game, Travis. It's called building a kingdom, having followers, changing the order of things, and I'm better at it. You got some, but I got more. It took you fifteen years. It took me a few weeks. Argue with that."

"It's a big *lie*, Brandon!"

He slapped the fence and rolled his eyes in a circle that could be seen for miles. "Travis, Travis, how many times do we have to go over that? It doesn't matter! I produce! I provide results! I get things done! While your God is stalling and hem-hawing and forcing you to make excuses for *him*, I'm right here, right now. You can't compete with that." He got close and pointed his finger at my heart. "And you can't stop it, either. People will let you define their beliefs, did you know that? Give them a homey feeling, give them security, and they'll give you their minds and hearts. That's how I'm going to control this town, Travis. First the adults, and then their children." He leaned back against the fence and stretched his neck. "It's scary how easy it is." He snickered. "'I see a spirit of doubt!' As soon as I saw it, so did they."

"And you're saying you didn't?"

He gave me a comical shrug. "Maybe I did, maybe I didn't, but how's anybody going to know?" Then he pointed at my chest again and said with wild eyes, "Turn to somebody and say, 'I do everything he tells me!' Go ahead!"

I turned away, disgusted.

"Travis! Travis! Don't go hypocritical on me now! You've had the same doubts about this whole racket that I have! Or are you sitting alone in your house on Sundays because you still buy all this stuff?"

"Stuff," I muttered. The word had a private meaning for me— at least until now.

"Stuff," he agreed. "The game." He gripped the fence tightly as anger filled his eyes. "Herd them in, herd them out, brand them, shear them . . . *butcher* them!" He hit the fence with the heel of his hand, a snarl on his lips. He recovered, calming himself. "Travis, I hope you realize we're both angry at the same things. We've been in the same places, felt the same pain."

"We're different, Brandon. Way different."

He wagged his head. "No, we're not. Not at the core. You're mad and I'm mad." He thought a moment, then suggested, "If there's any difference between us, Travis Jordan, it's that I'm doing something about it while you're still trying to make up your mind. So let me be as friendly as I can: Make up your mind and do it soon. I'm going to own the people of this town—their wills, their money, their children. They are going to give themselves to me because I'm a better Messiah and I play a better game. Now I've let you into my circle of confidence because I know you really do see things as I do. I know we could work together. But the opportunity won't last."

"I can't let you do it."

"I *am* doing it." With his hand, he signaled across the paddock. "You know Matt Kiley, of course. Now that his legs are working so well, he can help you find your way out of here."

I DROVE TO THE BOTTOM of the driveway and through the big stone gate. Kyle was sitting on the ground across the road, his back against a fence post, waiting. I parked the car, got out, and sat beside him.

"How'd it go?" he asked, but I could tell his face was already mirroring mine—quite unhappy.

"We need to pray for this guy."

We sat there together on the bank beside the road, a pasture at our backs and the Macon ranch on the wide, gradual hill before us, and prayed. My emotions were a swirling mixture. I loathed the man's evil and cunning, but felt so deeply sorry for him. It angered me to hear him suggest we were so much alike, but I knew he was dredging soil from my soul that he recognized in his own, and as much as I knew my own heart, I knew his.

And knowing his heart, I feared for those who followed him.

DON ANDERSON WAS A GADGET GUY. He sold appliances, CD players, VCRs, remote controls, stereo headsets, radio-controlled models, radio-controlled doors and light switches, key chains that chirped, bedside environmental sound machines and ultrasonic pest repellers—just to name a few—because he loved that stuff. A sign hung in the front window of his Pepto-Bismol pink appliance store: "Better Life Through Creative Technology." The store was his own little world where he could surround himself with myriad little plastic boxes that beeped, blurped, lit up, entertained, informed, and did zillions of other amazing things. It was a wonderful kingdom to rule, when he could.

But sometimes his subjects would get the better of him. Once a customer brought in a VCR that ate tapes. He fixed it, the customer took it home, and that very night, the thing ate her collector's edition copy of *Gone with the Wind*. Once a remote control for a customer's television wouldn't switch the channels but would open the garage door. He knew how to lick that: He just switched the frequencies around. This time when the customer tried to change channels, the lights in the house dimmed, and the FM radio started searching for another station.

Right now he was having to deal with a CD player that wouldn't go around. There was no other problem with it. It just wouldn't go around. He couldn't make it go around, and that vexed him severely. A radio scanner that wouldn't scan also vexed him, and if he couldn't get a decent solenoid for Mrs. Bigby's washing machine he'd have to refund her money.

Don's sovereignty over his little kingdom was far from complete. Even the gadgets in his home could be wayward and noncompliant, and his wife, Angela, never missed an opportunity to remind him about it. Just as a plumber's wife will complain about her clogged sink and running toilet that never get fixed, so Angela often reminded him of the stereo that only played on the left side, the hair dryer that didn't turn on at all, and the television that kept blinking in and out.

Don had trouble remembering the stereo or the hair dryer, but the television got his attention almost every evening, and especially *this* evening. There was a prizefight coming in live over the satellite dish, a fight he'd paid forty dollars in advance to view. Now, as he sat there with his dinner on a TV tray and his wife looking for something to read, the tube blinked out.

"NO!" he wailed, almost knocking his dinner over.

"Too bad," Angela said with a curt little smile, thumbing through her *House and Garden*.

He set aside the TV tray and approached the big television with the massive oak cabinet, forty-four-inch screen, and surround sound. He stood before it, he spoke to it, he gestured. It only hissed and threw a snowy picture at him.

"Gotcha stumped?" Angela asked.

"No!" he growled. It was just that problems like this took precious time to figure out, and he didn't have time. The fight was going to start in a few minutes—and knowing the champ's record, it would only *last* a few minutes. "C'mon, c'mon . . ." He banged the television on the side. That didn't work.

"You have tools, don't you?"

No time, no time. Too much trouble.

He could feel Angela on the couch behind him, enjoying her magazine and trying to pretend she wasn't really enjoying this.

Nuts! He'd been up to that Brandon Nichols character and received some kind of magical touch from him, something to help his business. Angela didn't think much of that either, and maybe she was right. Nichols gave him a touch on the forehead, he felt a tingle, he went home, his television didn't work. End of story.

So it was mere impulse, and perhaps a little sarcasm, that caused him to reach out and touch the television in the same histrionic, Brandon Nichols fashion.

He felt the tingle again, and the picture tube came on with a flash. The champ was winning thirty seconds into the first round. "Yes!"

Angela looked up. "What'd you do?"

He ducked behind his TV tray, his eyes glued to the screen. "Uh, just tweaked it, you know, adjusted the do-jiggy."

She went back to her magazine.

He saw the rest of the fight—all four rounds—and then stole into the bathroom for a little appointment with Angela's hair dryer. *This is nuts*, he kept telling himself, but he pulled it out of the drawer by the sink, plugged it in, and gave it a little touch. He felt the tingle again. The dryer came to life.

All right, all right, one more time now, just to be sure. He walked—if he hurried, Angela might notice—into the den, strolled nonchalantly by the stereo, and gave it a tingly tap. Without his having to touch the on button, it came to life and played beautifully out of both sides.

Don looked at his trembling hand. "This is . . . this is incredible!" He looked around the room, counting all the gadgets. The implications were staggering.

"I can't lose!" he said. People were coming from miles around to have Brandon Nichols touch their bodies. Would they do the same for their gadgets and appliances? This could be the dawning of a new day for Anderson's Furniture and Appliance!

Angela came into the room, pleasantly surprised at the full stereo sound. She even had to speak loudly. "You fixed it! You genius, you!"

"Yeah," he said, awestruck at his new ability. "Pretty impressive, huh?"

King of the gadgets, that was Don Anderson.

ADRIAN FOLSOM closed her eyes and listened for the voice of the angel Elkezar, her pen poised over a sheet of stationery. Sally

Fordyce sat nearby, unconsciously wringing her hands in nervous anticipation, waiting to hear a word from the Lord. Suddenly, Adrian smiled as if listening to a voice on a telephone, and began to write. "Mm-hm. Mm-hm. Uh, what was that again? Mm-hm. Okay."

Sally was in Adrian's home with Brandon's permission. "Let Adrian tell you," he said. "Let her bear witness."

Adrian finished writing, and turned toward Sally, the letter in her hand. "You'll like this."

Sally leaned forward, still nervous.

Adrian, her reading glasses on her nose, began to read. "'This is a mystery of my true church, that all God's children should be one, with no sense of other. As my servant is in unity with the Christ, so you are in unity with him, and the oneness that you are in spirit, you portray in your bodies. Fear not to submit to him and let your body be his, for this is higher than flesh. This is spirit, and all that is spirit is one.'" Then Adrian grinned, anticipating what she would read next. "'Just as my servant is in unity with the Christ and you are in unity with him, so your friend Mary Donovan is in unity with the Virgin Mother, Michael Elliott is in unity with John the Baptizer, and you . . .'" Adrian smiled teasingly at Sally. "'. . . are in unity with Mary Magdalene, whom the Christ loves as his own flesh!'"

Sally was not so thrilled, and made a face. "Mary Magdalene?"

Adrian glowed. "Isn't that incredible?"

Sally only looked at the floor, her head quivering little nos. "That's not incredible. It's crazy. I'm not Mary Magdalene."

Adrian tried to explain. "Well, remember how Jesus said that John the Baptist was Elijah? This is the same kind of thing."

"Brandon yelled at me last night. That doesn't sound like Jesus loving Mary Magdalene."

Adrian puzzled over that one a moment. "That's possible. Even God got angry with Moses."

Sally didn't buy that either. "I was too tired to have sex, Adrian. Brandon got all mad over a stupid thing like that. That doesn't sound like God or somebody at unity with the Christ or whatever he's supposed to be."

Adrian gasped. "Oh my . . ."

"What?"

"It's Elkezar. He's speaking again." She turned to her table and started writing. "Oh my. Oh my oh my."

Sally looked over her shoulder. "What? What's he saying?"

She could read Elkezar's words as Adrian wrote them: "Remember the fate of Korah and Miriam."

"Who's Korah?" she asked.

Adrian's voice was hushed with fear. "Korah led a rebellion against Moses in the wilderness. The earth opened and swallowed him up, him and his followers." Sally was about to back away, but Adrian grabbed her arm. "Miriam stood against Moses and the Lord struck her with leprosy!"

Sally sank to her knees, weak with fear. "I thought he loved me!"

"*Brandon* loves you! This threat is from *God.*"

Sally thought it over. It didn't take long. "I'd better get back."

"Brandon will receive you. You'll be safe there."

Sally kissed Adrian on the cheek and hurried out the door.

Adrian stared at the paper before her with its cryptic message. "Elkezar. I've never known you to be so harsh."

She felt an icy breath of wind at her back, though the curtains at the window did not stir and the houseplants did not waver. She felt it again. Her skin crawled as she turned and saw nothing, but *felt* something there. "Is that you?"

There was no answer.

"Elkezar? Is that you?"

He had never hidden from her before, never lurked like a prowler, but now she could feel him watching her, just out of sight.

"I gave her your message. She's going back to the Christ right now. You saw her go, didn't you?" She felt as if cold, heavy lead was filling her stomach. She began to tremble. "Elkezar? Please, don't tease me now."

It was the eerie stillness that scared her, the deadness in the air, the chilling cold. The waiting.

He stood there—somewhere—his presence like a poison, the pendulum on the wall clock swinging away the seconds, Adrian's short, frightened little breaths the only sound.

At last, without a word, he turned away. She could feel him retreating slowly, taking his own time, letting the effect linger as hideous terror seeped out of the rooms and hallways in small, agonizing degrees.

Several minutes later, only when she was sure it was safe to do so, she stirred, turning once again to the paper on her desk.

Now it read, "So also for Adrian."

JACK MCKINSTRY was having doubts, but neither he nor his wife Lindy dared say anything for fear of jinxing business. The Sooper Market was doing well. Mack's was still the prime location where the denizens of the Macon ranch got their groceries, and Michael the Prophet came through almost every day to post flyers and announcements of coming meetings. Brandon Nichols and his followers always plugged the store to the pilgrims coming through, just as they talked up the other businesses in town. It was best not to tamper with a good relationship, but just keep sacking up those groceries and filling the tills.

But how were they supposed to handle a visit from the Virgin Mary?

Sure, they knew who Mary Donovan was. She'd been a regular customer and they knew her by name. She was a friend of Dee Baylor. Since she was a young divorcée, it was safe to assume she wasn't a virgin. But here she was, decked out in a robe, shawl, and sandals, pushing a cart up and down the aisles, grocery shopping for Mrs. Macon and . . . her son.

"Oh, he used to love this when he was little!" she exclaimed, taking a box of Cap'n Crunch off the shelf. Then she'd stroll past the bread and bakery shelves recalling, "Oh, these are just like the ones he multiplied on the shores of Galilee! I was so proud!" She picked up a jar of tartar sauce. "My son will provide the fish!"

Jack had a good guess that, if she *had* a grocery list, she wasn't following it. Mrs. Macon wasn't going to be happy about this. He hurried to join Mary near the frozen vegetables. "How you doin', uh, Mary?"

"My soul doth magnify the Lord," she replied. "And behold, these peas are on sale!"

He opened the freezer door to grab some. "Yeah, they sure are. How many packages do you need?"

She giggled. "Jesus can start with just one and take it from there."

He put one package in her cart and then craned his neck to see her grocery list. "You finding everything okay?"

"He leadeth me beside the still shelves and restoreth my memory."

He could see the list—and the contents of the cart. "Uh, you sure you need all these olives?"

She looked at the dozen cans strewn in the cart and mused, "Blessed is he whose quiver is full of them, for we lack oil and our lamps have gone out."

"Well, yeah, your list says olive *oil*. That's on aisle twelve."

"Oh, thank you. I will turn aside and see this great sight." She stopped when she saw bags of popcorn. "Jesus was such a creative child! He could pop popcorn by the breath of his nostrils!" She threw four bags into the cart. "He'll be so excited!"

Jack hurried back to the checkout counter. Ringing up groceries he could deal with. Mary as Virgin Mary was a little out of his realm.

"Should we call Mrs. Macon?" Lindy asked from her cash register.

He thought only a half-second and then shook his head.

Don't meddle, he thought. *Don't mess things up.*

JIM BAYLOR was in his basement sharpening the lawn mower blades when he heard the front door slam and the heavy footsteps of his wife thumping and creaking over the floor joists. She had been to another meeting up at the Macon ranch. She was getting to be a regular Nichols junkie, always going back for more spiritual happy pills. Yep, she was laughing again. She laughed from the front door to the kitchen, and then from the kitchen to the bathroom. After the toilet flush rushed through the black pipes over his head, he could still hear her laughing in their bedroom and then back in the kitchen again.

He hated when she was like this.

Now he heard smaller thumps leaving the living room and going into the kitchen. That would be their daughter, Darlene, roused from her place in front of the television.

"Wuzzofunne?" came Darlene's voice. Coming through the floor, "What's so funny?" was a bit muffled.

Jim figured out that Dee said, "The Spirit's trickling through me, and it tickles!" She started laughing again. A chair squawked over the floor and *thump!* Dee sat down.

Well, is she gonna cook this time? Jim wondered. He figured he'd better make sure, much as he longed to keep his life as simple as sharpening a lawn mower blade.

When he got to the kitchen, Dee was doubled over the table, red in the face, eyes full of tears, laughing herself silly.

"What's so funny?" he asked.

She couldn't answer, not then, not ten minutes later. It was much worse this time. She'd been giddy before, tittering and giggling, praising the Lord and seeing something humorous in everything, but tonight she was out of control, maybe out of her mind. He couldn't handle it, so he returned to the basement. Mower blades he could handle.

He could hear her moving around up in the kitchen, still laughing, but calming down to intermittent giggles. She was opening cupboards and drawers. Good. She'd come down from her spiritual high long enough to fix dinner.

Then the joists started creaking overhead and he could hear her feet shuffling about as she sang. She was dancing up there, shuffling in circles.

The door at the top of the stairs opened and Darlene hollered down the stairs, "Dad, would you make Mom stop?"

"Is she cooking dinner?"

"I don't know."

"Well, see what you can do to help her."

He could hear Darlene walk into the kitchen. The shuffling stopped, although he still heard some giggles. Then he heard water running.

And Darlene screaming.

He bolted up the stairs and ran for the kitchen, passing Darlene coming the other way, drenched. He got into the kitchen in time to see Dee dancing in circles, waving the sink sprayer over her head and drenching everything including herself.

"Thou hast turned my mourning into dancing for me," she was singing. "Thou hast put off my sackcloth!"

"Dee!" He grabbed the hand holding the sprayer and got a good dousing before he wrested it from her. "Are you crazy?"

She calmed. "Oh, I'm sorry, honey."

He put the sprayer back in its place. "Look at this mess!" He grabbed a towel from the rack by the sink and started wiping.

"Gonna get the French fries now," she tittered and sang, dance-stepping to the refrigerator. She opened the freezer side, took out a bag of frozen French fries, zipped it open, and dumped the French fries all over the kitchen table. "Dinner's on!" She thought that was funny, and collapsed into a chair, hysterical with laughter.

Darlene stood in the kitchen doorway, her wet hair matted to her forehead, her expression pathetic. "You want me to order out again?"

Jim was standing in a puddle of water and the towel in his hands could hold no more. Dee was still laughing, starting up again each time she looked at the French fries strewn on the table. "Yeah, I guess so."

"What do we want? Pizza?"

"How about Chinese? The Wah Hing ought to be open."

Dee looked at him. "*Chinese!*" she cackled, then exploded with more giggling.

Jim envisioned chow mein, rice, sweet-and-sour ribs, and fortune cookies all over the floor. "Make it a pizza. Something plain and simple."

"MATT KILEY, if you ever show your ugly face around here again I'll rearrange your nose and mash it into the highway myself!"

Judy Holliday could take quite a bit of irritation before she got riled, but now she was threatening and cussing a blue streak, and had a frying pan in her hand to back up every word. She was standing over Matt Kiley, and he was lying in the front doorway, half-inside and half-out.

"And don't you get none of your blood on my carpet!"

Judy's granddaughter Gildy brought a towel for Matt to dab his face and head. "I think you'd better leave."

Judy turned on Irv the trucker, the winner in this particular brawl even though he didn't look like it. "Go on, go in the washroom and wipe that blood off before you drip on something. Greg, go with him, and Linda, there's some iodine and bandages above the freezer. Go on, all of you!" She turned back to Matt, still lying at her feet in the doorway. "I don't see you moving!"

He tried to move and got as far off the floor as his knees before he teetered forward again. At least now he was a few feet farther outside.

"He's out far enough," Judy observed. "Gildy, get my towel back."

She knelt gently and took the towel from Matt's swelling face. "Sorry."

"Mmph," he said with swollen lips. He rolled and managed to sit up, looking up at Judy standing in the doorway. "Why's Irv get to stay?"

"'Cause you're the ornery cuss that started this whole fight and you know it!" she answered. "Dumb cluck! You knew how Irv feels about that truck of his and you called it names anyway!"

"He had it coming! Used to call me little four-wheels, and I couldn't do a thing about it!"

"Well, my late husband's got more brains than both of you, and he's been dead twenty years! Now git!"

Matt struggled to his feet, his face still smarting as if Irv's big fist were still buried in it. This hadn't turned out the way he planned.

He should have been able to whup Irv, whup him good. It should
have been Irv staggering out of Judy's and not him.

His legs felt weak and he had trouble standing, but it wasn't just
because Irv had made a milkshake out of his brains. He'd been
wondering about himself even when he went into Judy's. He just
didn't feel the old strength. He expected a good fight would bring
it out.

Well, he expected wrong. It used to be there, but not tonight.
The power had faded when he wasn't watching.

He stumbled and almost fell.

My legs, he thought. *My legs.*

What happens when all the guys I've whupped find out?

I gotta see Nichols and get this fixed.

KYLE AND I SPOKE OFTEN by telephone or in person over the
next few days, and prayed for the people who came to mind: Don,
Adrian, Mary, Dee, and Matt being among them. We also discussed
a hunch that kept nagging me but seemed terribly farfetched. He
thought I should check it out, but I kept stalling. It would be hard
enough just for me to make the phone call—I really did not want to
talk to those people again. Once I got someone on the line, what in
the world would I say? How could they have any idea if Nichols/
Johnson had ever been there?

Still, I couldn't shake the notion that our local messiah *wanted*
me to make that call. He had mentioned L.A. and gave me the
"turn to somebody and say" routine. He was too subtle, too cunning, for that to be a blunder. "We're both angry at the same
things," he said. "We've been in the same places, felt the same pain.
Herd them in, herd them out." He was dropping clues.

He had to know I'd been down there—just like him.

On Thursday, nearly a week after my conversation with
Nichols/Johnson, I got the number from information and placed
a call to Los Angeles.

"Hello," said a cheerful female voice. "Thank you for calling The Cathedral of Life. Our Sunday morning services start at seven, eight-thirty, ten o'clock, and eleven-thirty; our evening service starts at 6 P.M. Our Wednesday evening service begins at 7 P.M. Childcare is available for all services. If you know your party's extension, you may enter it now. For a ministry menu, press 9."

I pressed 9.

"For nursery and Sunday school, press 1. For youth ministry, press 2. For college and career, press 3. For young marrieds, press 4. For family ministries, press 5. For seniors, press 6. For singles, press 7. For weddings and funerals, press 8. For more options, press 9."

I could feel my throat tightening up. I often had that problem when Marian and I lived down there. I pressed 9.

"For men's ministry, press 1. For women's ministry, press 2. For children's ministry, press 3. For counseling, press 4."

A counselor may have known him. I pressed 4.

"For marriage counseling, press 1. For addictions, press 2. For financial counseling, press 3. For other counseling, press 4. To learn how you can begin a new life in Jesus Christ, press 5."

I banged 4.

A lady's voice came on the line. "Norm Corrigan's office."

"Hello, my name is Travis Jordan and I'm calling from Antioch, Washington."

"And are you calling for counseling?"

"No, I'm—"

"Well this is the counseling department. Did you dial the right extension?"

"It's all right. I wanted the counseling department. I'd like to speak to one of the pastors or counselors."

"Are you currently attending The Cathedral of Life?"

I stifled a witty comeback and answered her question. "No, I'm living in Antioch, Washington."

"Are you attending a church there?"

"Uh . . . listen, I'd like to speak to a pastor."

"Are you currently receiving counseling from a minister at your own church?"

"I am *not* calling for counseling. I need to speak to a pastor, somebody in charge, please."

"Well, you've called counseling."

"Then how about connecting me with Dale Harris's office?"

"Thank you."

Praise music came over the line as I waited. "*Great and mighty is he, Great and mighty is he, Great and mighty, Great and mighty, Great and mighty is he . . .*"

"Pastor Harris's office."

"Hello. This is Travis Jordan. I'm calling from Antioch, Washington and I'd like to speak to Pastor Harris."

"Is he expecting your call?"

"No."

"Pastor Harris is unavailable. I can connect you with someone on the pastoral staff."

"Okay. Sure."

"*Great and mighty in the morning, Great and mighty at noon, Great and mighty in the evening, Great and mighty all the day through . . .*"

"Norm Corrigan's office."

"Hello. This is Travis Jordan from Antioch, Washington. I'd like to speak to, uh—" The name escaped me. "The pastor."

"Well, this is Norm Corrigan's office. Did you wish to speak to him?"

"Is he someone in charge?"

"Oh, yes."

"Then I'll speak to him."

"He's out of the office right now. Would you like to leave a message on his voice mail?"

I don't know why I fell into it. "All right."

"Hello. This is Pastor Norm Corrigan. I'm away from my desk right now or on another line. You can leave me a voice mail message after the beep, or dial one-two-two-zero to speak to my assistant, Joanne Billings. God bless you and have a great day."

I decided to try for Joanne Billings. "One-two-two-zero!" I muttered as I pounded out the numbers.

"Hello, you've reached Joanne Billings, Pastor Norm Corrigan's assistant. I'm away from my desk right now or on another line. You can leave a voice mail message after the beep, or dial pound-star-nine-nine for an operator to assist you."

"Pound . . . star . . . nine . . . nine . . . "

"The Cathedral of Life. How may I direct your call?"

I sighed and actually groped with my hands as I tried to think of what to say next. "Can I talk to someone in charge, uh, preferably a pastor?"

"I can connect you with our counseling department."

"No, no, I was just there. How about . . . is there a pastor I might talk to?"

"Great and mighty is he, Great and mighty is he . . . "

"Hello. This is Pastor Norm Corrigan. I'm away from my desk right now or on another line. You can—"

I slammed the phone down and sat there quaking with an old, familiar anger. Things hadn't changed much at The Cathedral of Life. If anything, they'd gotten worse.

I'd have to go down there.

But I didn't want to. Didn't want to set foot in the place ever again. The very idea dredged up painful memories for me, memories I'd rather just forget. . . .

19

M Y FIRST CRACK at the ministry, and I'd blown it. After we were cast out of Northwest Pentecostal Mission on our ears, I spent at least a month wallowing in self-doubt, self-pity, and self-flagellation. I never heard a peep from anyone, but still I imagined the talk circulating through the denominational district: "Look out for Travis Jordan. He's a hothead. He's cantankerous, disrespectful, and big-mouthed." I would have agreed.

Well, I asked myself, *what can I learn from this? What's the Lord trying to teach me?*

I supposed the Lord was trying to teach me to be more cool-headed and cooperative, more respectful. I had some repenting and changing to do, most of which took place on my knees—scrubbing toilets. No more of this young ruler conquering the world for Christ stuff. Next time—if there was a next time—I'd be thinking more in terms of what it meant to be a servant, in submission to the authority God placed over me. After all, God loves a servant's heart.

Fortunately, Marian stood with me. "Travis, you don't think I knew what I was marrying? I don't have any misgivings. A few bruises, sure, but I got them by standing with you." I remember her resting her arms on my shoulders and looking at me with admiration—and maybe a little mischief—in her eyes. "When you stood up to Brother Rogenbeck—" She drew in a breath and let out a deep sigh. "A little more patience might have been a good thing for both of us," she admitted, "but that didn't mean Sister Marvin wasn't an old busybody. As for Brother Rogenbeck, the only reason his head is wrinkled is because it's low on air."

Thankfully, our loss of the ministry position did not have a significant impact on our monthly income. Marian still had her job at the hydraulic valve and coupling company, and I still had my janitorial job at the mall. Even so, we were restless.

"We'll try again," she said. "We'll trust God, and we'll try again."

"If God will have me," I retorted.

"I'm not worried," she said. "He knows you."

It's typical of the Lord to close one door only to open another. A month after Northwest Mission threw us out, Marian's company offered her a higher paying position with the parent company in Los Angeles.

"Hey," she said, "you could go to school down there and get your teaching degree."

That seemed prudent. I'd always felt that, were I not a pastor, I would just as soon be a teacher, and I minored in education at West Bethel. With the credits I had earned so far, I was within easy reach of a teaching degree—a safety net should I get booted out of the ministry again, or be unable to re-enter the ministry at all.

We saved our money, applied for some grants, filled out some paperwork, and went through that open door in the spring of 1979. We found a small apartment, I enrolled at UCLA, and we settled in for a two-year stint.

That's how we started attending The Cathedral of Life. According to the Christian grapevine, it was the place to be. Pastor Dale Harris was reputed to be an incredible teacher. Anybody who was anybody went there—actors, recording artists, Spirit-filled billionaires who flew Lear jets. I don't know what I was thinking when I decided we should go there. I guess I expected I would learn something from such a godly man. Perhaps I would gain new wisdom and insight into the ministry. Maybe I'd get my spiritual cobwebs cleared out just by being shepherded, nurtured, and pastored by someone so highly respected. I was ready to submit to good leadership. I was ready to do it right. While getting my degree and widening my skills, I could submit to mature, godly leadership and deepen my spiritual walk.

Looking back, I think I did learn things I never would have known otherwise. It just didn't happen the way we expected.

When we showed up at the Cathedral for our first Sunday, we discovered church as we'd never experienced church before. We were accustomed to arriving for church, greeting our friends, shaking hands and jawing with the pastor, casually finding our way inside, and sitting down. We had never worried about finding a place to park, never seen "FULL" signs on the first, second, and third parking areas, never been directed down side streets by parking attendants in fluorescent orange vests with walkie-talkies. We'd never been to a church where the congregation worshiped in shifts and you had to be early for your shift or wait for the next one. We'd never had the church door closed in our faces and locked by a polite usher who placed a sign in front of the door: "SERVICE FULL. NEXT SERVICE AT NOON. DOORS WILL OPEN 11:45."

There were four Sunday morning services. We arrived entirely too late for the seven o'clock and eight-thirty services, but on time for the ten o'clock, which was still too late. Enough people had already gathered on the front steps and down the sidewalks to fill the sanctuary before we could get through the front doors. We ended up standing on the front steps of the church under the midmorning sun with a few hundred other people we didn't know, not yet aware that none of these people knew anyone else either. Little introductory conversations started up throughout the crowd. Marian and I met the people immediately around us. "Hi, I'm Travis, this is Marian." They were Bob and Joan, Mike and Carol, James, Ronny, and Andre. Marian told them how she worked for a company that manufactured hydraulic connectors and valves. I told them I was going to UCLA, working on my teaching degree. They told us how they sold real estate, custom-painted expensive cars, managed a Taco Bell, went to school. After that morning, we saw one or two of them from a distance, but never met or talked with them again.

At 11:45, the rear doors opened. The third shift flooded out onto the streets, sidewalks, and parking lots, combining their numbers with the fourth shift still arriving and throwing the main avenue and surrounding neighborhood into gridlock.

As for those of us already waiting at the front door, we poured like floodwater into the sanctuary, moving down the aisles and filling the pews to the music of piano, organ, worship leader, and three-voice worship team. Folks all around us knew the drill; they were taking up the song even as they moved along the pews to sit down: "Making melody in your heart, unto the King of kings . . ." They were raising their hands, getting into the worship. The place was already cooking.

Marian and I joined in. She wasn't a tongues-speaker, but she was a God-lover and a hand-raiser. We knew the songs and we were enjoying it.

The good things we'd heard about this church were true. The worship was robust, joyous, and heartfelt. Emotion was natural and flowing, without excess. The song leader at the pulpit was a handsome, articulate man who sang with gusto and displayed his joy with dignity. The worship team standing to one side, two women and a man, were polished and well dressed, each with a color-coded microphone. The pianist and organist were polished and coordinated—they even had an intercom between them.

This church seemed to cater to the educated. Anyone who spoke from the platform spoke well, using words like "problematic," "specificity," "pedagogical," "well-orbed" and even college-brewed hybrids like "distantiate." You never heard a double negative, and I never caught anyone using "where" and "at" in the same sentence. There had to be teachers in the congregation. Cool.

Pastor Dale Harris lived up to our expectations and then some. A man of medium height and broad build, he was animated, personable, and articulate, and he loved to work the audience. "The psalmist says that praise is comely for the upright, which you can take to mean that praise and worship lift the countenance. When you praise more, you look better. Turn to somebody and say, 'You look like you've been praising the Lord.' Go ahead."

Marian and I turned to the people on either side of us and said at the same time they did, "You look like you've been praising the Lord," and then we all had a pleasant, social laugh about it.

Pastor Harris taught out of Ephesians that morning and we hung on his every word. It was great stuff, insightful and eloquently presented. When he was finished he gave an altar call, and even that had a nice touch of no-nonsense sophistication: "We offer you two questions. The first is, Do you know Jesus? The second question is simple and direct: Would you like to? If you'd like to know Jesus, after the closing prayer just slip through this door to my left and our pastoral staff will meet with you, pray with you, and show you how to find him. We're not set up here to argue or debate. You know the answers to the questions I've offered. You know what to do."

We sang the closing song and I saw six or seven people go to that door. Souls finding Jesus! What a feeling!

At the close of the service I decided I'd like to go to the front and greet Pastor Harris, just let him know who we were, where we were from, and how happy we were to be in the service. We stepped into the aisle and had to swim against the current—everyone else was heading the opposite direction. I looked around all the heads, returning smiles as I tried to see up front. I couldn't see him anywhere.

"I think he's gone," said Marian, holding my hand so we wouldn't get separated.

I kept going anyway. I'd never been to a church like this and I didn't know any better.

We broke into the clear near the front of the sanctuary and found one man standing near a door to the right of the platform. He was either an associate pastor or an usher. He had that man-in-charge look about him. "Good morning," he said.

"Good afternoon," I said, aware of the time. I shook his hand and introduced us.

"Miles Newberry," he said. "Associate pastor."

"We just moved down from Seattle. I'm going to UCLA, working on my teaching degree, and Marian's working for . . ." I went on. I thought it would be okay to be conversational.

An usher came up. "Miles, did you check with Ron about the alternate scheduling? I don't think we're reading off the same page."

Miles said to me, "It's good to have you with us this morning. Have you filled out a visitor card?"

"Oh." We had. I dug it out of my jacket pocket. "Yeah, here you go."

But Miles was talking to the usher. "The page is right. Ron is wrong and I told him that." He saw the visitor card in my hand. "No, don't give it to me. It's supposed to go in the offering plate. Were you here for the offering?"

Suddenly I felt a little stupid. "Uh, yeah, sure. We just didn't have it filled out in time."

He shook my hand again. "Well, next time just drop it in the offering plate. It's nice to have you here." Then he turned to the usher. "Henry and Al have it squared away. Let them handle it."

Marian tugged at my hand.

I thought I was still having a conversation with Miles Newberry. "I'd like to say hello to Pastor Harris."

Miles Newberry smiled. "I'll tell him you said hello." He went back to the usher. "We're implementing it this Sunday but locking it in next Sunday. That's the mix-up."

Marian got the hint long before I did and tugged at my hand again. I finally followed.

"Elvis has left the building," she said.

I looked again toward the empty platform and toward every door where people hurried to join the gridlock. No Pastor Harris. As a matter of fact, no pastor at all. This wasn't the chatty, leisurely after-service leaving we were used to—this was an evacuation.

"Please keep moving toward the doors," said another usher, his hands extended to press upon our backs if need be. "We need to clear the building."

Well, I thought, *this is how they do things in L.A. I have a lot to learn.*

Because we were the last shift, we could go out any door we wanted. Marian and I chose the front door again, and walked several blocks back to our car.

"Pretty neat service," I commented.

"They move you through there quick, don't they?" she replied.

"Yeah." At the moment I wasn't sure whether that was good or bad.

"He snubbed us."

"Huh? Who?"

"That Miles Blueberry or whatever his name was."

"Well, I don't think he meant it. He was busy."

"The usher was more important than we were, didn't you notice?"

"Well . . ." I did notice, but I didn't want to fuel any negative feelings by saying so. "It's a big church; they have to keep things running smoothly."

"Then the *church* is more important than us."

I wanted to try the church for a while. This was Southern California, I told her. People down here are used to standing in line two hours for a three-minute ride at Disneyland. They did hours of business by cell phone just waiting for a chance to pull onto Ventura Boulevard. Everywhere they went was far and through traffic, so they described distances not in miles but in minutes. There was more to do than time to do it. Churches could get so big that the pastor couldn't possibly stick around to greet everyone. We could learn to live with that. We could get used to it. It was a different world down here.

I gradually talked her over to my side. That was in the days when I prided myself on my logical, empirical way of viewing things and figured she responded too much from emotion.

Actually, she had already seen the end from the beginning.

We made The Cathedral of Life our church home, and just as I was raised, we never missed a service. We were there Sunday morning for whatever service could fit us in; we turned out Sunday evenings and always got in, even if we had to watch the service on closed-circuit television in an overflow room; we were there every Wednesday night without fail. We planned our day in order to make it to the Young Marrieds Sunday school class, one couple among fifty other couples. When there was a business meeting, we were there, on time, thoroughly studied, and ready to vote.

This was a deeply religious matter for me. It was time for me to humble myself and submit to God-appointed authority. If the man of God was sharing the Word, it was our duty to be there.

So we were always there, humble and submitted. For ten straight months we waited on the front steps for the ushers to unlock the doors, entered praising the Lord, and got out fast so the ushers could lock them again. In every service, we stood when told to stand, sat when told to sit, raised our hands, clapped our hands, said Amen, and turned to greet those around us the moment we were told to do so. Every Sunday the pastor told us to turn to someone and say to them whatever catchy phrase he wanted us to say, and we always turned and said it, laughing a social laugh at the cuteness of it. If Pastor Harris warned us against being prideful and self-willed, we repented and prayed that the Lord would help us be more childlike and submissive. When he said he saw an ugly spirit of pride attaching itself to members of the body to make them rebellious, we believed him. When he spoke about laughter being good for the soul, we all broke out laughing.

We even did what we were told when sitting in the overflow room watching Pastor Harris on television. The image on the screen would tell us to stand, clap, greet one another, say something to somebody, repent of this or that, and say Amen if we agreed, and we did it. It was a little bizarre at first, responding and talking to a television image that didn't see or hear us.

It seemed odd to turn to a total stranger at Pastor Harris's prompting and bare our souls—what we were feeling, what we were hearing from God, what we wanted to change in our lives, what temptations were still a snare to us. But we did it, and we got used to it.

WE WERE NEW to the Young Marrieds Sunday school class: fifty couples wearing nametags and setting their own trend in polyester. During the brief coffee and fellowship time, we tried mingling. I stepped up to meet two young urban professionals, nose to nose in a theological discussion over Styrofoam cups of coffee.

"Don't you think the Pauline approach is epistemological, at least in part?" said one.

"Well, only if you bring epistemology to bear on the order of the list," said the other.

"But I'm not talking about the specificity of the order."

"You can't force the specificity."

"Oh no, not at all."

"I think Paul intended a general, well-orbed presentation. Otherwise the whole list becomes problematic. We're distantiating election and free will."

"But there *should* be a distantiation, that's what I'm saying!"

Should I say hello? Would that be interrupting? Should I wait for them to notice me standing there? Should I stick my nametag on my forehead?

They never noticed me standing there and never paused long enough for me to enter in. They just went on with their discussion, talking like Pastor Harris and oblivious to my presence.

Perhaps I needed to learn the vocabulary. Perhaps I needed to comb my hair straight back and get a pair of white shoes and a white belt.

Marian tried to join a conversation between three mothers.

"Well, *sometimes* I spank her on her bare bottom," said one, "but you're talking heavy logistics!"

The second shook her head shamingly. "But you have to *deal* with that spirit of rebellion! The correction has to be felt."

"I tried the Gerber peaches but they gave Jamie the runs," said the third. "I'm going through more diapers. . . ."

"Try the peas," said the first. "Buddy loves the peas."

"But Jamie hates peas."

The second lady leaped on that one. "Ah-ah-ah! Rebellion! Deal with it!"

Marian decided it wouldn't be courteous to introduce herself. Kids were the subject here, not hydraulic valves and couplers. No one asked her who she was anyway.

We met back at the refreshment counter and picked up a cookie for each of us.

"Well," said one gal to her friend, "I can't tell you the details or I'll speak it into existence."

"It depends on how you phrase it, I think."

We headed for our seats.

"How often do you make love?" Miles Newberry asked another couple as we walked by—he could have been a doctor asking about their frequency of bowel movement.

Conversations in that class were a little hard to get into.

BUT YOU *could* get into a program. The Cathedral of Life had programs, conceived and administered from the top down, and no program, event, or activity ever materialized without a logo. The morning service had a logo: the sun rising with little Y-shaped people praising the Lord in front of it. Wednesday night's logo was a long, winding trail with a glowing mountain in the middle and on each end. The Young Marrieds class had a Y-shaped father and Y-shaped mother with little Y-shaped kids. Every class, every activity, every age group, had a logo.

Our Young Marrieds class was a program with its own program, Young Marrieds Fellowship Night. Once a month, someone at the top would sort through the roster cards and assign each couple to a group of four couples. That group would then go out together and fellowship—go to dinner, play miniature golf, whatever the group coordinator decided. We all wore tee shirts with a classy looking YMFN logo on the front and a scripture, "Endeavoring to keep the Unity of the Spirit in the Bond of Peace—Ephesians 4:3," on the back. The next month, someone would shuffle the cards so we never went out with the same people twice. To hear Miles Newberry tell it, this was to ensure a "well-orbed" relationship with the rest of the body of Christ. We went along with it, tapping colored golf balls through windmills and past waterfalls and carrying on superficial conversations, all the while stifling suggestions from Satan that the church was picking our friends for us.

I REALLY HAD A HARD TIME getting it through my head that The Cathedral of Life did not need nor desire my help. Every church I had ever been a part of always needed help with something, whether it was teachers for the Sunday school or volunteers to clean the building once a month or just greeters to stand inside the doorway and pass out bulletins to people arriving. I was ready to be a servant, to do things the right way, to humble myself and be useful somewhere, somehow.

"We already have a trained staff," said the youth pastor. "Thanks anyway."

"The banjo?" said the music minister with a half-smile. "Why?"

The chief usher shook his head. "I've got all the greeters I need. You'd have to complete a greeter program anyway, and that would require a year's membership."

"We'll talk about it, brother," said Miles Newberry, and we never did.

They did everything and had no procedure for dealing with two unknown faces emerging from the multitude and wanting to do something.

So month after month we continued to show up, hurry in, praise the Lord, hear the Word, and hurry out with the thousands. We put our tithe check into the offering plate and supported those highly trained, handpicked folks who ran all those programs with all those logos. Surely we could get used to feeling unknown and unneeded every Sunday. Someday we would conquer the cynicism we felt every time we turned to greet those around us, knowing the likelihood of ever seeing them again.

After all, this was our role as members.

THE ROLE OF THE PASTORAL STAFF, apparently, was to create and maintain the proper image.

Pastor Dale Harris took full advantage of video, which seemed reasonable, given the size his task would have been without it. The drawback for us was the subtle awareness that crept in as we sat with hundreds in an overflow room watching his image: To all the thousands, whether in the sanctuary or in the overflow room, an *image* was all he was and ever would be.

When we joined the church as members, we gathered in the overflow room with about thirty others for a new members' orientation and welcome meeting. Pastor Harris came in to greet us; and I'd never seen him so close. I'd never heard his voice unamplified. I'd never seen the natural color of his face or the blemishes on his jaw. He said a few words of introduction, and then we watched a video recording of him speaking to us about the duties and obligations of church membership.

"Unity, unity, unity," he said. "As God has brought us together to be stones in his temple, so we must be set in place by his Spirit and mortared to one another by love. We are a worshiping church," he said, "and in our meetings we strive to touch the throne room of God in our praise of him."

"Oh dear," he said. "Pardon me, but if this is not your heart, if you do not wish to enter the presence of God with us in this way, please don't join the church.

"We are to be of one mind," he said, "an army marching together."

These were fair and honest words, and on their face they were agreeable enough. It was only in the months that would follow that we realized the prerequisite for such unity: the abandonment of our wills and judgment to the organic will of the thousands, which, in turn, was controlled every Sunday by the man at the top.

The man we did not know.

When the video ended and the screen went to snow, he returned to extend to us the right hand of fellowship and welcome us into the congregation. I can still see the face of one young man weeping, embracing Pastor Dale Harris. He was home now, part of the family. He'd found a shepherd.

Months later, I would reflect on that moment and wonder, *Did that young man know that this was the only time he would ever embrace his pastor? Did he consider that his pastor would never again touch or look him in the eye?* This pastor would never turn aside to greet him by name or return his smile from the platform. After this evening, his face, his name, his very existence would drop from the pastor's memory and the pastor would retreat once again behind his phalanx of associates who spoke his jargon and kept the machinery running from behind those dark cherry office doors.

After this evening, Pastor Dale Harris would once again be a face, a voice, a two-dimensional, unknowable, untouchable image, and all of us would become unseen, unknown, nameless faces in the sea of thousands, all marching in step.

I don't suppose that young man thought of such things at the time.

When I embraced the pastor, I wasn't thinking of such things either.

But I think Marian knew it all along.

IT TOOK MY SISTER, Rene, to hit us over the head with it. She'd been hitting me over the head with her big sister wisdom ever since we were kids, so she had no qualms or hesitations. She came to visit us in the spring when we'd been at the Cathedral for ten months and been members for six. When we took her to church with us on Sunday morning, it was the first time she'd ever been there.

We got to the sidewalk at our usual time, but for some reason the main sanctuary filled up before we could get in. The ushers, standing in a long, tight line like traffic cones, directed us downstairs into the overflow room where the television was set up. We and three hundred other people went through the Sunday routine in front of that tube, worshiping, greeting one another, saying things to each other, asking the stranger on either side a personal question about their spirituality, hearing the message, and then getting out of there, walking along another line of living traffic cones. Rene wasn't much of a participant that morning. She just sat quietly, listening, observing, and being a courteous guest.

Sunday evening, she didn't become difficult, but she did ask with wonder, "You're going back there *again?*"

I knew Rene wasn't an avid churchgoer. Our strict, church-first upbringing seemed to have had the opposite effect on her. "Well," I said, "it's how we do things. It's part of our covenant with the Lord and with our local church body. If the man of God is sharing the Word, it's our duty to be there."

She looked horrified, but said nothing.

She came with us to the Sunday night meeting, and this time we got into the main sanctuary but had to sit up in the balcony. I was a little nervous because she was new and hadn't had a chance to learn the balcony rules.

"Make sure you keep your purse tucked under your seat," I instructed her, talking close to her ear so she could hear me over the worship music. "We have to keep the aisle in front of us clear."

We managed to find some seats at the very front of the balcony. Uh-oh. There were a *lot* of rules here.

"Uh, make sure you keep your Bible beside you, not on the railing." She moved down the pew ahead of me toward the wall.

"No, don't sit there, you'll block the television lights. And don't touch the brass railing; the fingerprints dull the shine."

She sat down slowly, looking at me and giving me time to stop her in case that was a wrong thing to do. I nodded to her that it was okay.

An usher hurried up. "Pardon me, we're trying to keep this row clear." There were already thirty people moving down the row behind us. He called to them, "We have to keep this row clear, folks. Sorry."

We backed all the way out and found the next row up. It was a thirty-foot pew and there were enough bottoms to far exceed that capacity. Rene sat across the aisle from us and got out her pen to jot something down. I tried to warn her, but—

Too late. An usher tapped her on the shoulder. "Excuse me. We can't allow fountain pens in the balcony."

She put her pen down, stroked her forehead a moment, and then looked up at the usher. The worship singing was full and spirited, but I imagine half the balcony could hear her question. "Is there anything *else* I'm not supposed to do? Do you have a *list* I can read? Is there a *class* I can take? Is there *any* way I can save you the trouble of harassing me!?"

I had seen people get booted out of the balcony before. I started to cross the aisle.

A second usher stopped me, his hand on my chest. "Sir, please sit down. You're disturbing the service."

I sat down. My sister was going nose to nose with an usher and about to be removed, and I sat down. Marian gaped at me. "What are we *doing?* Rene's in trouble!"

Rene was gathering her things. "Travis, I'm leaving!" She stood and waved to the people in the balcony. "Good-bye, everyone! Happy churching!"

Marian and I got up.

An usher held up his hand at chest level in front of us. "Please sit down—"

Marian maintained a mature dignity and poise. "Stand aside," she told him, "or I will scratch your eyes out."

He stood aside. Marian followed Rene and I followed Marian, cringing to think how grieved the Holy Spirit must be.

We tried to keep up with Rene as she stormed down the sidewalk, heading for our car in parking area two. Knowing Rene, I was aware she'd been patient to the point of sainthood, but now her time had come. She'd seen it all, heard it all, digested it all, and she was ready to comment. "Why, oh *why* do you subject yourselves to this?"

"Well, it's a big church in a big city—" I started to say.

"That is religious, God-tripping, cockamamie—" I won't complete her full description of my excuse. "Have you lost your mind? That's not a church, it's a Christian factory!"

"They have to control— "

She stopped and looked back at the building, pointing. "Do they even know who you are?"

"Well, it's—"

"*Do* they? Does anyone at that church know who you are?"

Marian answered, her own pain showing, "Not really!"

"You say it's your church home. Does it know when you're home? Does it even care?"

I tried to shrug it off. "You get used to it."

"NO!" She grabbed my arm, on the verge of tears. "Don't get used to it, Travis! Don't you ever get used to it! Don't let them do this to you!"

We went back to our little apartment, had soup and sandwiches, and talked until close to midnight. To summarize the whole evening, we were hit soundly over the head by an outsider who still had eyes to see. We broke down and wept, finally getting in touch with the pain we'd been trying to suppress for ten months. We concluded that the Cathedral did not attract people like Rene, and accepted the truth that the Cathedral could never hold much attraction for us either.

We never went back.

But more than a year later, we continued to receive a monthly calendar and letter from Pastor Dale Harris, telling us how much we were loved and how he appreciated our continuing participation and support.

WE FOUND ANOTHER CHURCH, also well spoken of, and were astounded and relieved to find that there was nothing seriously wrong with *us*—we weren't in the wrong; we were just in the wrong *church*. We met the pastor the first Sunday and he remembered our names the next Sunday. We could easily join conversations with people just like us and made friends immediately. We got to know the pastoral staff the way people get to know people, and we didn't even need nametags!

And we could serve! When the pastor announced they needed help carrying in folding chairs, we leaped at the chance and just about cried from the joy. Next we handed out bulletins at the door and welcomed people coming in. I got out my banjo and helped with the worship at our Wednesday night home group meeting. Three months later, I was leading a home group myself.

So we grew in the Lord. We learned, we matured, and when we finally left Southern California, we had made friends for life. After the Cathedral, it was surprising how easy it was.

I DON'T CONSIDER MYSELF SCARRED or wounded by the Cathedral of Life experience, but I admit I picked up a few quirks. I never believe anything just because a big-named Christian leader says it. I never do anything I don't want to do just because a pastor, presuming to be the voice of God, tries to coerce me with guilt or threats. I no longer respond to visions God gives to others about what I should or should not do, think, or be.

And since the Cathedral I have never, and will never again, turn to someone and say something the pastor tells me to say. Never.

20

When I told them about my telephone encounter with The Cathedral of Life, Morgan and Kyle laughed, then apologized for laughing and offered to help me out with airfare to L.A. So with teeth gritted, I called the Cathedral one more time, got bounced all around the premises by secretaries and answering machines, and finally—miracles still happen!—got an appointment to see Associate Pastor Norm Corrigan on Tuesday, June 9, at ten in the morning, for one hour.

Tuesday, June 9, at nine-thirty in the morning, I was there, dressed in suit and tie and ready to go nose to nose.

The new building was spectacular. Stone, brick, and acres and acres of tinted glass. Fountains, walkways, trees, shrubs, and tons of beauty bark and lava rock. Inside, miles of rich carpet and fine woodwork. Sitting areas the size of major hotel lobbies. Fine furniture, high ceilings, and massive chandeliers. A huge brass plaque bearing the names of all those who gave ten thousand dollars or more to the building project.

The receptionist in the front lobby sat inside a circular reception desk the size of a ten-person hot tub. She pulled out a map and traced a route for me to follow to the administrative offices. I thanked her, and holding the map before me, set out.

I took a brief side trip to peek through one of the ten rear sanctuary doors. The sanctuary reminded me of some of the finer performing arts centers around the country. It was capacious, high-tech, and very, very nice.

I moved on, guided by the map, walking down one hallway, then making a right turn into another, fascinated by the mixture of emotions and attitudes churning within me. On the one hand, I felt dazzled and excited. What a success story! On the other hand, I still had a chip on my shoulder: If anybody tried to play the bureaucrat or hassle me I wasn't going to take it. Was anyone going to recognize me? My eyes darted about, looking for familiar faces or pictures on the wall to tell me who was still there. How about the usher who harassed my sister, Rene? Hopefully he'd let me read the list of *don'ts* for this building before asking me to leave. I wondered if Miles Newberry was still there, still teaching the Young Marrieds Sunday school class. It would be the Middle-Aged Marrieds by now. I envisioned the logo: the letters MAM resting in an empty nest.

And what if I actually bumped into the pastor of this place? What would I do? What would I say?

The answers that came to mind betrayed my attitude: *You'll never bump into him because he gets in and out of here through a secret tunnel. Even if you did see him, he'd be flanked by at least two associates and on his way somewhere important.*

I rebuked myself, asked the Lord's forgiveness, and pressed on.

I could see a wall of glass at the end of this hallway, with two glass double doors and an office space beyond. As I approached, I could make out the bold gold letters on the glass: "The Offices."

I went through the doors. Beyond the reception desk were six office cubicles and six secretaries, and beyond the cubicles was a hallway with lots of dark cherry doors on either side. I told the receptionist who I was and with whom I had an appointment, and she directed me to a long, overstuffed couch where I could wait.

From where I sat, I could see down the hallway with the dark cherry doors and make out some of the brass nameplates. The names I could read I didn't recognize. It had been almost twenty years. As for those big, double, paneled doors at the end of the hall with their own secretary sitting at a desk nearby, they could only belong to the man who was unavailable for telephone calls and would take three months to see if I made an appointment: Pastor Dale Harris.

I held a black leather valise in my lap. It contained every scrap of information I possessed about Brandon Nichols, alias Herb Johnson, alias . . . whoever he claimed to be when he had been here. *If* he had been here. That was still a strong hunch, but not a certainty. This whole visit could turn something up, or it could end up a waste of dwindling time and scarce cash.

I still had fifteen minutes until my appointment—fifteen minutes and another hunch that might expedite my visit. There was a water fountain between the hallway and me. I rose casually from the couch, helped myself to some water, and then walked casually down that hall past all the closed cherry doors. Most of the names were new. Richard Drake. Ben Montesque. A few others. Ah, here was Norm Corrigan's. I kept walking. Miles Newberry! He was still around!

Then I stood before the desk of Pastor Harris's pleasant, middle-aged secretary. She looked up.

"Can I help you?"

"Hi. I'm Travis Jordan from Antioch, Washington. I have an appointment with Norm Corrigan in fifteen minutes."

She indicated the couch I'd just come from. "If you'd like to take a seat, Pastor Corrigan will be right with you."

"Oh, I've already checked in." I opened my valise. "I thought while I was waiting I might see if you could help me out." I read the name plate on her desk. "Uh, Mrs.—or is it Ms.?"

She smiled. "It's Mrs."

"Mrs. Fontinelli, a man has come to our town who, in certain ways, is claiming to be Jesus Christ." That raised her eyebrows and, I hoped, piqued her interest. "We're trying to find out who he really is, and by certain hints he's dropped we think he may have attended this church at one time. Have you been here at the Cathedral for very long?"

"Ten years or so."

I handed her a photograph of Nichols/Johnson. "Have you ever seen this man?"

This gal would never win at poker. Her reaction was so strong you could read it a mile away. "Um . . . my word." She looked down at her desk and would not look up at me. This was one of those silent, awkward moments, but it gave me time to consider: If Pastor Harris's secretary instantly recognized one face out of thousands and had such a strong reaction, that said a lot.

"I take it you've encountered this man before?"

"Yes." She volunteered nothing beyond that.

"Have you been Pastor Harris's secretary for very long?"

She seemed glad I asked her a question she could easily answer. "Oh, um, five years."

"And was it during that time that you encountered this man?"

She tried to compose herself. "Um, who was it you were here to see?"

"Norm Corrigan."

She tapped the photo lying on her desk. "Were you seeing him about this?"

"I sure was."

She made a little *o* with her mouth and nodded to herself. Then she picked up her telephone. "Could you . . . excuse me? Please, have a seat on the couch?"

"Sure thing."

I took back the photograph and walked slowly, hoping, even praying, I'd be able to overhear what she said into the telephone. All I could make out was "Tammy . . . talk to Norm . . . we need Miles . . ."

I sat down on the couch and watched the little stir my photograph and questions caused. One of the six secretaries at this end—her name card said Tammy Orenfeldt—was stealing little sidelong glances at me as she and Mrs. Fontinelli spoke in hushed tones. "Yes," I heard Tammy say, "for ten o'clock. All right, I'll ask him." Both secretaries hung up at the same time. Tammy punched in another number and said, "I need to interrupt you." Mrs. Fontinelli made a quick call herself and then ducked into Miles Newberry's office while Tammy hurried down the hall and ducked into Norm Corrigan's.

I knew Brandon Nichols was the kind of man who would not allow himself to be lost in the crowd. One way or another, he would make himself known, especially to the leadership—especially to the pastor he could describe so well and seemed so bitter against.

Now a man who had to be Norm Corrigan came out of his office and crossed to Miles Newberry's as Tammy came back to her desk acting like she wasn't watching me. There was a three-person conference going on in Newberry's office. I checked my watch. My appointment with Corrigan was coming up. I wondered what their line would be.

The door opened. Norm Corrigan hurried back to his office, Mrs. Fontinelli hurried back to her desk, and Miles Newberry came strolling down the hall toward me. He was graying nicely and had put on a little more weight. He looked good for being twenty years older. I knew he wouldn't notice whether I looked different.

"Hi," he said, extending his hand. "Miles Newberry. And you are . . . ?"

I stood, shaking his hand. "Travis Jordan. I have an appointment with Norm Corrigan—" I looked at my watch. "Right now."

"Norm's had something come up. May *we* talk?"

It felt funny to be standing eye to eye with this man, having his undivided attention. Twenty years ago, he promised we'd do this. "Okay."

We went into his office and he closed the door. Rather than sit behind his desk, he sat in one chair facing me as I sat in another. It didn't exactly make me feel more comfortable, but I appreciated the protocol.

"Now, what can we do for you?" he asked.

"I imagine you've heard from Mrs. Fontinelli," I said. "I'm here trying to find out anything you can tell me about this man." I gave him the same explanation I gave Mrs. Fontinelli and showed him the same photograph.

He was not at all happy to see it. He scowled, drew a deep breath, sighed it out, then asked me, "What do you intend to do with this?"

"I need to know who he is, who he *really* is, and how I can deal with him. I need to know his background and what would motivate him to get into this false christ routine. If you can tell me anything you know about him, I'd greatly appreciate it."

He ignored my question. "What makes you think he was here at this church?"

"He talks like he was here, and he's very bitter." Oops. That sounded unkind, but then again, it was true.

Miles Newberry chuckled—to shed my unintentional stab, I thought. "Well, this is a big church and we get all kinds. Not everyone who comes through here is going to be happy with us."

I wanted an answer to my first line of questions. "Do you know this man?"

"Not personally, no."

I noticed his body language. We were in *his* office, but he was the one acting cornered. "But you know who he is?"

I could sense reluctance in his answer. "Yes. We know who he is."

"So he did attend this church for a time?"

"I already told you that."

"Actually, no. You didn't."

"Well, he did."

"And when was that?"

He looked at the ceiling. He took another breath. He was clearly not comfortable. "I would guess two or three years ago."

"Did he have a name?" He looked at me curiously. I explained, "He's used two different names that I know of and I'm suspecting a third."

He whistled his amazement, but said nothing further.

This guy was not a bubbling spring of information. "Is there a problem here? I feel like you don't want to talk about this."

"You have to understand that we do a lot of counseling here and that we hold a lot of information in confidence."

"Even his name?"

"Well . . . please don't take offense, but we don't know who you are. We don't know what you're going to do with the information. We have relationships and confidences we have to protect. I'm sure you understand."

"Perhaps I should tell you what this man is doing to our town." I recapped Nichols/Johnson's career, showing Miles Newberry some news articles from the local paper as well as from the bigger papers in Seattle and Spokane. "I can understand your wanting to protect whomever he may have hurt, but given the circumstances, I'm not so sure you'd be wise to protect *him*."

Newberry studied the articles. "So now he's healing people?"

"I've seen him do it."

His pain was showing as he handed back the articles. "When he was here, he went by the name Justin Cantwell." Then he conceded, "And he was trouble." I waited for him to elaborate, but he didn't.

"What kind of trouble?"

"I can't go into that."

"Justin Cantwell." I wrote it down. "Any idea where he was from? Any background?"

He sighed. "I need to talk to some people before I can give out any more information. Will you be around tomorrow?"

This was a major frustration and I didn't try to hide it. "I have to fly back tonight. It's one of those round-trip discount things."

"Well, leave us a number and we'll call you."

Now where had I heard *that* line before? "What about Pastor Harris? Does he know anything about Cantwell?"

"I'll have to ask him."

"Let's ask him now."

"He's unavailable right now."

"Is he here on the premises?"

"He's unavailable."

I tried to control the emotion in my voice. "He's always unavailable. What about Norm Corrigan?"

Miles Newberry shrugged. "He wouldn't know anything about this."

"He's new on staff?"

"That's right."

"But Mrs. Fontinelli's run into this guy. The photograph really upset her."

He nodded. "She was here then."

"So it makes sense that Pastor Harris knew him."

He got tense. "Are you digging for something?"

"Only because it's buried. Please don't take offense, but I have a very dangerous man deceiving my town according to an agenda, my friends and I spent a good deal of money getting me down here, and when you stonewall on behalf of Pastor Harris, I get uncomfortable. If you know about Cantwell and Mrs. Fontinelli knows about Cantwell, it's inconceivable that this hasn't somehow touched Pastor Harris. I'd like to talk with him."

His eyes narrowed. "Before we go any further, I need to warn you about something."

I was listening.

"This church has been appointed by God as a light in this city. It has his blessing and his mandate to spread the gospel and make disciples." He indicated my valise. "If you try to cause this church any harm with this information, you'll be opposing God, and that's never advisable."

I stopped. Twenty years ago, his warning would have scared me. Today, I felt vindicated. "Reverend Newberry, when I attended this church, I always sensed that kind of attitude trickling down from the leadership. I never thought I'd hear anyone verbalize it." He gave me a curious look. He was about to ask me, so I told him, "Yeah, my wife and I attended this church about twenty years ago. I don't expect you to remember me because you never knew me in the first place, and it's obvious you don't know me now, or you wouldn't have said what you just said to me. But I thank you for your candor, and I'm sure I can count on your help."

I leaned toward him, eye to eye. He was going to regret not

sitting behind his desk. "I need to hear from anyone who has had direct dealings with Justin Cantwell, and if that includes Pastor Harris, I need to hear from him, not you on behalf of him. No more running interference, okay? No more putting me off. The devil's at work in Antioch and we don't have time for that."

He returned my gaze for a moment, and then nodded as if in agreement. "Leave me your number."

BRANDON NICHOLS chuckled and lovingly petted Matt Kiley on his bowed head. "Get up, Matt. No need to grovel."

Matt Kiley was on his knees in the straw before the Messiah of Antioch, ready to plead, bargain, cajole, do anything to get his strength back. The moment the Boss touched him, he felt it coursing through him. His arms, his back, his legs were strong again, maybe even stronger. He leaped quickly to his feet, flexing and stretching.

"All there again?" the Boss asked, holding Matt at arm's length and inspecting him.

Matt was about to answer, but his throat choked with emotion. He nodded instead. They were standing in the barn at the Macon ranch. The Boss was supervising as two new followers unloaded a truckload of oats, stacking the sacks on a pallet.

The Boss nodded toward the feed sacks. "Let's try those arms out."

Matt put up his dukes and gave the sacks a few solid punches. His legs felt like powerful springs under him. He danced, bobbed, weaved like a boxer. *WHAM! WHAM!* He pounded dents in the sacks. It felt great.

"Yeah!" he hollered, then threw his arms around the Boss. He'd never been a hugger before this.

The Boss was pleased. "All right, then. You have your strength. But remember, Matt: Your strength comes from *me*. It's mine, for my use. No more wasting it in foolish brawling!"

"Okay. You got it. Oh!" He remembered something, and reached into his pocket. "The other merchants asked me to give you these gift cards. You can use them to get discounts on lodging, meals, just about anything in town. Pass them out to the pilgrims. It's our way of saying thanks."

"Tell them thanks for me."

"My Lord!" called Michael the Prophet, hurrying into the barn. "Armond Harrison is here!"

Nichols's eyes brightened as he turned to see Armond Harrison and a lovely young lady walking in with Michael. "Hello and welcome!"

Harrison shook hands with Antioch's Messiah, then introduced the young lady. "This is Gail, the one we talked about." The Messiah was delighted. Gail was in awe. Harrison told her, "He'll take good care of you, and trust me: You'll be a different woman when you leave here."

"Michael, take her to her room in the guest house. I'll be along shortly."

Michael gave a little bow and then led Gail along with a touch of his hand.

"Her husband's gone," Armond explained. "In the navy. She's had some real problems with that."

Nichols gave a wise and understanding nod. "She needs comfort. Fulfillment." He smiled. "Don't worry."

Armond smiled. "I won't."

"Cindy, the young woman I spoke to you about, is a gentle sort and reasonably well-adjusted. But I've told her she could benefit from the communal environment you have with your group—and, of course, your wisdom regarding . . ."

"Of course."

As they left the barn, chatting enthusiastically about their ministry relationship, Matt only sighed with envy. The Boss always got what he wanted.

DON ANDERSON was turning around repair jobs so quickly people were starting to comment on his speedy service. He was careful never to let visitors see him using his special gift, and often he'd tinker away with his tools just for show. But in the week that followed that special touch from Brandon Nichols, he had cleared almost every item to be repaired from the shelves of his workroom. Now he was actually getting a little bored, and started tinkering just for the fun of it.

Some more repair jobs came in today. The Steens' VCR wouldn't rewind—until he touched it. He made out a bill for how much time it *would* have taken him to fix it.

It would have taken him three hours . . . well, more like four . . . to fix Lonny Thompson's tape deck that wouldn't go around. With one touch that took less than a second, he made it go around. Lonny was still going to be billed for four hours.

An electric mixer came to life again, as did a wireless doorbell. Don spent most of his man hours just writing up the bills.

Then there was the Boresons' CD player—a nice one with a rotating deck that held five CDs at once. The rotating deck didn't rotate. He hit the open button and it slid open. Hm. Kenny Boreson left a heavy metal CD in this thing. No wonder the deck was malfunctioning.

Then the craziest notion came over Don, and he ran his finger in a circle around the face of the CD as if he could actually read the digital recording through his fingertip. It was just a silly whim, but still he wondered—

Somewhere in his head he could hear some raging, wailing, wildfire guitar work, every blasting, distorted note like a toothache set to music. It was giving him a toothache.

He removed his finger. The sound stopped.

He looked at his fingertip. *Nawww*, he thought. *Don, now you're leaping a little too high.*

Well . . . there were other CDs in the store. A little experiment would settle any doubts. He found one of Mozart and no sooner picked it up than he heard the opening strains of Symphony No. 40 in G Minor. He shifted his gentle hold on the CD so that his fingers rested in another spot. Symphony No. 39 in E-flat.

Man oh man, he thought, *what else can I do?*

WHEN JIM BAYLOR came home from work, the house was quiet. In this household, such quiet was seldom a normal or good thing, and it made him uncomfortable.

"Dee?"

No answer. His first thought was that she was up at the ranch again, lingering after the afternoon meeting, all gaga over Mr. Messiah and forgetting her starving family at home. But this was Wednesday and Mr. Messiah wasn't holding any meetings on Wednesdays.

He went into the kitchen, then the living room. "Dee?"

"What?" Her voice came from the bedroom, low and muffled, and she certainly wasn't laughing.

He hurried down the hall and to the bedroom door.

She was curled up in a near fetal position on the bed, hugging a pillow to her head, her expression just this side of death.

"Dee? What's wrong?"

She muttered into the pillow. He could hardly hear her. "What do you care?"

Jim hated it when something would happen to Dee that he just couldn't understand and didn't know how to fix. He suspected this might be one of those times. "What's bothering you?"

"Nothing."

He approached the bed and sat on the edge.

She rolled over, turning her back to him. "Just leave me alone. You always do anyway. You don't care about me. Nobody does."

"Sure I care about you. I love you. You're my wife."

"If I died you'd all be a lot happier."

Jim tried to tell her that wasn't true and Dee kept talking about how worthless she was and how no one loved her and how she wanted to die, and the conversation went around and around on the same merry-go-round for several minutes. Finally, Jim got impatient enough to ask, "What happened, did Brandon Nichols hurt your feelings?"

That raised her temperature a little. "What do you care?"

"You know what Jack McKinstry told me? He said Mary Donovan thinks she's Mary—you know, the Virgin Mary."

"Yeah, so what?"

"And I hear Adrian's talking to an angel. Did you hear about that?"

She curled up tighter. "Will you just get out of here?"

"Dee, maybe you're just bugged because they've got this stuff happening to them and none of it's happening to you."

She flipped over like a fish on a rock. "You don't know *anything*, Jim Baylor! How could you? You don't know the Lord, you don't care, and you don't know diddly squat about spiritual things or what God's doing on the earth, so don't try to tell me—"

He matched her volume, and by now it was getting high. "You don't think I know anything? Hey, I'm not laying on the bed like some kind of beached whale—"

Her strength was returning. "What did you call me?"

"—wanting to die."

More strength, more voice. "*What did you call me?*"

"I'm not the one who spilled frozen French fries all over the table and cha-chaed for Jesus while my family went hungry!"

"That was the joy of the Lord!"

"We could squirt each other and then dance a bit! Maybe look at the clouds. It'll be a blast!"

She nearly screamed, "That was the joy of the Lord!"

"*What* joy of the Lord? You're lying here wanting to die! What kind of joy is that?"

"You wouldn't understand!"

"I understand you lying on the bed feeling sorry for yourself! What's *that*, the *pits* of the Lord?"

She let out a war cry and threw the pillow at him.

"Yeah, that's it, that's it!" He backed out the door, angrily pointing his finger at her. "Go ahead and stew! We'll see if Brandy boy comes to cheer you up again!"

"Aaaaaghhh!" She reached for the lamp to throw, but he slammed the bedroom door and stomped down the hall.

He got out of the house. He'd eat at Judy's tonight. Maybe he'd get good and drunk too.

"I'LL BET you never imagined you were so enlightened."

I'd no sooner come in the door than the phone rang. It was Brandon Nichols alias Herb Johnson alias Justin Cantwell. I half-expected this call. "Hello, Justin."

He betrayed no reaction to my use of his third name. "Did you talk with Pastor Dale?"

I sat on the couch, smiling at his question. "Pastor Dale was unavailable."

"Oh *really?*"

"I talked to Miles Newberry."

He laughed. "Ah, good old Miles. A man you can talk to for hours and never really meet."

I had to laugh. "That *was* the feeling I got." I quickly added, "But he says you were trouble, Justin."

"I was. They all came within a fraction of an inch of being embarrassed. As the saying goes, I wish I'd had a camera. But did you notice, Travis? There's something different about you. You've grown. The old game hasn't changed, but you have."

I suppressed a little chuckle. He was right. "I used to buy everything that guy said."

"And you did what he told you to do."

"Oh yes."

"And you felt guilty whenever he said so."

"Oh yeah."

"And any misgivings were your fault, every time."

"Yep."

"And this time he tried to scare you . . . but you didn't scare. Why is that?"

"I've been trying to figure out why."

"You weren't born yesterday, that's why. Time's gone by, water's flowed under the bridge. Their game only works on certain people and you don't fit the profile anymore."

"I *think* that's a good thing."

"Oh, it's good, Travis."

"Sometimes it can feel pretty miserable."

"I'm not worried. Day by day I can see you coming around. The more you try to find out about me, the more you discover about yourself. It's just like I've always told you, we're very much the same. Of course, you didn't find out much, did you—about me, that is?"

"Miles gave me another name for you. That's number three now."

"But you don't know if that's the right one, either. How much time are you willing to waste tracking it down?"

"I don't know. I think it would help greatly if you'd stop the charade and just tell me who you are."

"Stop the charade?" He laughed a spiteful laugh. "And be the first man of God on the face of the earth to do so?"

"Hey, c'mon now, you know that's not fair."

"No malice intended, Travis. That's just the way it is. Ministers are supposed to have their lives together and be an example. They're supposed to have all the answers. Well, they don't, so they pretend because they have to."

"Some of them get sick of pretending."

"And I commend you." His voice turned bitter. "But some of them *love* pretending. It gives them a rush to think of all the people they're fooling." Suddenly he mimicked the tone of a fiery, southern preacher. "You are a sinnuh, saved by grice! Come to Geee-sus and you shall be clean—then follow *me*, 'cause *I* make the rules!"

"Salvation by grace. Christianity by performance."

"You *have* been there! Travis. Move on. Let it go. You've grown since the Cathedral. You can keep growing. I still have a place for you."

"Hm. Get out of one charade so I can join the biggest charade of all? I'll have to think about that one."

"I'm not worried."

"And I'm sure you have nothing more to say to me about yourself."

"Not today."

"Good-bye, then."

NANCY BARRONS sat at her desk in the back of the Antioch *Harvester* and Office Supply, listening to hold music on her telephone. It was usually this way whenever she called the county Health Department.

Finally, "This is Pete Jameson."

"Hi, Pete. This is Nancy Barrons."

"Oh, hi, Nancy. What's up?"

"I've got some questions about that water project up at the Macon ranch. You inspected that, didn't you?"

"Uh, yeah. Let's see, that was an upgrade, wasn't it? A new storage tank and three pressure tanks."

"What about the water source?"

"Uh, that was a private well."

"And?"

"What do you mean, *and?*"

"I was talking to Mrs. Macon the other day and she told me they had to develop a spring two miles behind the house."

"Not for me, they didn't."

"You didn't require an alternative water source?"

He laughed at the silliness of it. "No. Cephus Macon upgraded that well for commercial use just before he died. I required a new well head and some weatherizing of the well house, but that was it."

"You didn't require them to develop that spring?"

"No. I didn't require or inspect development of any spring."

"Okay. Thanks."

"Let's have dinner sometime."

"Check your calendar and call me."

"You got it!"

Nancy hung up and turned to Kim. "I was right."

21

WHILE JUSTIN CANTWELL was working his magic at the Macon ranch, Brett Henchle was doing his best not to think about it. It was Deputy Rod Stanton's shift, his turn to serve and protect the town, so tonight Brett sat at home with his wife, Lori, and their two boys, Dan and Howie, enjoying a rented movie on video. They were watching, of all things, a cop movie. The obligatory car chase was just starting.

"Okay, watch now," said Brett, taking popcorn from the big bowl he was sharing with Lori. "They're gonna turn into that alley and hit some garbage cans."

The bad guys' big Lincoln screeched and fish-tailed into a narrow alley, bashing aside some garbage cans, sending them flying.

"Now they're gonna splash through some water."

The bad guys' car, followed by the cops' car, hit a big puddle in the alley, sending up sheets of spray while the long telephoto shot made the cars appear right on top of each other.

"Dad," Howie whined, "you're ruining it."

"Next they're gonna crash through some construction barriers."

"Dad!"

The bad guys were cornered. They screeched through a tight

turn and into a construction site, splintering several construction barriers.

"There's gotta be a flip coming up somewhere..." Brett mused.

The bad guys roared up a street, swerved to avoid an oncoming truck, hit the back end of a parked truck—

And sailed into the air, twisting upside down. Their car came down in slow motion on top of some other cars, then flipped again, landing in the street.

"Cool!" said Dan.

"So much for those guys," said Lori.

"They'll live," said Brett.

The bad guys climbed out of the inverted car and ran, shooting at the good guys.

"Have you seen this before?" Lori asked.

"Didn't have to," Brett replied. "It's the same every—" He winced, grabbing his leg.

"What is it?"

HISSSSS. The television screen went snowy.

"Hey!" said the boys. "Right at the good part!"

Brett rubbed his leg. "It's that shrapnel wound. It's really poking me."

"But—" Lori looked at the little jar on the mantel. The shrapnel that had fallen out at Brandon Nichols's touch was still there. "The shrapnel isn't in there anymore."

Brett recovered a little. "Eh, it hurts anyway. I don't know why."

"Why'd this thing stop?" Dan fussed, reaching above the television to tinker with the VCR.

"GET BACK!" Brett shouted, leaping to his feet, almost spilling the popcorn.

Dan leaped back, his hands quivering, startled and scared. Howie sat on the floor wide-eyed and frozen.

"Brett..."

"Now just take it easy," Brett said to ... whom? He was looking toward the corner of the room near the television. "Lori, take the boys into the kitchen."

"Why?"

"Do it now!"

"Come on, boys. Howie! Come on, get up!"

"What are you looking at?" Dan asked.

"Go with your mother."

Lori looked in the same direction as Brett and saw nothing. But she *felt* something. "Boys, get into the kitchen and stay there!"

"What do you see, Dad?" Dan was getting scared now.

"Go!" Lori herded the boys behind her as she backed toward the kitchen, watching her husband talk to the wall.

"Listen," Brett was saying, "I don't know what you want, but you made a big mistake coming in here." His right hand was behind his back. He was snapping his fingers. A signal. "I can't hear you. Speak up."

She ran into the kitchen, yanked a locked box from the cupboard above the refrigerator, and opened it with a key hidden behind the flour jar. Inside was a 9 mm pistol. She grabbed a loaded clip from a drawer, slammed it into the pistol, and returned to the living room.

She stopped at the edge of the living room. She peered intensely in the direction her husband was looking but there was no one there.

Snap! Snap! Snap! He wanted the gun.

She saw nothing, but felt a jittery sensation, like standing on the edge of a cliff. Her pulse was hammering. Behind her the boys were starting to cry. Was her husband hallucinating? Dared she give him a loaded firearm?

He grabbed it from her forcefully, pushing her behind him, taking a shooting stance. "Freeze! Turn around slowly, put your hands on the wall!"

Whatever it was, it was beginning to move. He followed with his aim, the muzzle of the gun sweeping across the room toward the hallway. She could feel something getting closer.

"Stop or I'll shoot!"

It didn't stop.

"Stop!"

Her skin was tingling, like a static charge. She backed away. She may have seen a shadow that didn't belong—

BANG!

The boys screamed. She jumped, her trembling hands went to her ears, her eyes searched and searched.

Brett aimed down the hall.

BANG!

The bullet slammed into the back door. Brett ran down the hall. "Hold it!"

She dashed into the kitchen, crouching, shielding the boys in a corner with her body as they screamed and cried. She heard the back door open, felt cold air crawling around her ankles. Her ears were humming from the shots.

The telephone rang, startling her like another gunshot. She was protecting the boys. She didn't even think of answering it.

Brett slammed the back door and scrambled up the hall through a blue haze of smoke, limping and cursing.

The telephone rang again.

"He's gone."

The cop movie came back on the television. *Shooting, yelling, sirens.*

The telephone rang. She turned but did not rise.

In anger Brett grabbed the phone off the kitchen wall. "Henchle!" Then, "Rod, get your butt over here, I've had a suspect right here in the house! The hitchhiker! That guy I told you about! He was right here in the house! What?" He listened, then cursed again. "Did you put her in custody?" His hand went to his leg and he bent a little, wincing in pain. "No, you did the right thing. I think it's already hit the fan. Get Mark on the radio and get the two squad cars over here, one on Maple, one on Elm. I want the neighborhood combed for this guy." He listened to another question. "Leave her there. We'll sort that out later."

He hung up, hurried into the living room to pause the VCR, then returned to the kitchen and his wife. He noticed the gun in his hand. He quickly removed the clip and set it aside. He touched her. "Lori, it's okay. Boys, it's okay, it's all over."

"What was it?" Dan cried. Howie was speechless with fear.

"It was a man I picked up on the highway some weeks ago. He sneaked in somehow. He's gone now. You're okay."

Lori stood. The boys just held onto her legs and remained there as she asked, "The hitchhiker?"

"Yeah, the blond guy who told me Jesus was coming? That was him. I don't know what he wanted, but—" He lowered his voice for the sake of the boys. "He was up to no good. We'll have to lock the place up tight tonight. If you want I can take you to your mother's."

"The hitchhiker?" she asked again.

He nodded. He held her. "Yeah. I knew that guy was trouble the moment he pulled that stunt in the car."

"Honey . . ." She was afraid to say it. "I didn't see him."

"It's okay."

She pushed him back just enough to look in his eyes. "No, really. I didn't see him. I didn't see anyone there."

He returned her gaze with a blank look. "He was right there, right by the TV cabinet. He must have been hiding behind it."

She began to feel another fear—a fear for her husband's sanity. "Sweetheart, that cabinet's right up against the wall! You can't hide back there!"

He backed away. "You didn't see him? He was standing right there!"

She could only shake her head no.

"Didn't you see him run down the hall?"

She switched subjects. "What did Rod say?"

Brett stood in the middle of the kitchen looking disoriented. "He arrested Penny Adams tonight."

"Oh no."

"She'd been shoplifting from Florence Lynch's store. He and Florence went over to Bonnie Adams's place and found a closet full of stolen merchandise."

"And she just got her hand back."

Brett winced again, his hand on his leg. "Yeah, just like I got my leg fixed."

She didn't understand. "What?"

He picked up the gun again and slammed in the clip. "It'll be okay. I'll get it straightened out."

He went into the hall and grabbed his coat from the closet.

"You're not *leaving!*" Lori pleaded.

"The town's falling apart. I can't just sit here."

He kissed her and limped out the door, leaving her alone, bewildered and afraid. Dan and Howie would not let go of her.

MONA DILLARD didn't know how to feel: happy or troubled, encouraged or frustrated. The Wheatland Motel was seeing all kinds of changes and enjoying a steady flow of business. Norman had a great brainstorm—a costly one, but it worked out: They converted two of their units to kitchenettes, and the moment they were ready they were rented—by the *month*—by some of Brandon Nichols's followers. A steady stream of pilgrims took up the rest of the rooms, and now Norman was thinking of buying the old auto shop next store, razing it to the ground, and putting in a whole new wing. Things were going great—for the business.

Things were not going so great between Mona and Norman. Oh, things seemed okay on the surface, but in her mind she was plagued by misgivings, by the nagging questions that can bother a woman when her man seems . . . uninterested. He'd been busy and preoccupied, of course, but it was more than that. It was . . .

Well, it had to be another woman. It was unthinkable, but that's what she thought. She had no direct knowledge, but she was sure of it. He was looking elsewhere.

But it was worse than that. It was hard to describe, harder to believe, but she could sense a shifting, leering menace in his eyes that had never been there before, as if a different mind had moved in behind them, lustfully gazing everywhere else while looking toward her with disdain. She and Norman weren't talking much. She couldn't look at him. He showed no desire to look at her.

Today, she was trying to bury her worries by concentrating on linen inventory: what they had, what they needed, and how much of each. She was rummaging through the supply room, counting sheets and towels shelf by shelf, trying to figure out Norman's rotation system. Managing the supply room was usually his job, but he'd been busy with the kitchenettes, so the task had fallen to her.

When she pulled a stack of folded sheets from a top shelf, a magazine slid out and fell on the floor.

It was not necessary to pick it up or even look closer to know what kind of publication it was. The glossy photo on the cover told her all she would ever need to know. She backed away, clutching the folded sheets as if they would soften the pain now spiking through her heart.

Was this the other woman? No doubt she was not the only one.

Mona threw the sheets aside and reached up on the shelf, just above eye level, to feel for more. There were more. She pulled one out, saw it, dropped it, then pulled out another.

She dropped it as if it were a poisonous snake baring its fangs, then backed away, clutching the sheets to her breast. Time froze, and so did she, her arms wrapped around the stack of folded sheets, gawking at the images on the floor. Every pain she had ever felt—and thought she could avoid by working in this room—tumbled back upon her.

She'd buried herself in this task to forget her troubles with Norman, but now . . .

AS SOON AS I returned from Southern California, I thought it important to discuss with Morgan and Kyle what I'd discovered, as little as it was, and to plan our next course of action. Kyle had church commitments that evening, but said Morgan and I should meet anyway. I called her and suggested we meet over dinner.

"Uh, where can we do that?" she asked.

It was a valid question. She was a minister, and it wouldn't look right for her to have a man in her home. I wasn't a minister anymore, but I was still concerned about appearances, and we both knew it wouldn't be appropriate for her to be in my home either. If we met at Judy's it would look like we were meeting socially, and the town was too small with too active a grapevine for something like that.

"Why don't we get out of town?" I suggested. "Maybe some place in Spokane."

"That would be more prudent," she said.

"Where would you like to go?"

"Oh, why don't you pick a place and let me know?"

"All right."

That, too, was an overwhelming question. This was going to be a meeting with a professional lady of distinction. We couldn't go to McDonald's or Burger King. It would have to be a place with some class, some atmosphere, but not too much because this wasn't a date. What did she *like?* I knew of a nice Italian place with great salads, but you usually had to sit and wait for a table. There was a Japanese, juggle-the-knives restaurant, but it wouldn't be a good place for a serious discussion. I liked Mexican, but the salsa would have me blowing my nose all evening. We could try Mongolian barbecue, but building your own meal from raw meat and vegetables seemed too informal. There was a nice steakhouse overlooking the Spokane River. The falls would be spectacular this time of year, but that might seem presumptuous.

"wow!" she said. "Look at those falls!"

We had a table right next to the windows. White tablecloth, cloth napkins, an oil candle in the middle, two forks. She was wearing a dark purple dress with long, sheer sleeves and delicate silver earrings that dangled almost to her shoulders. I'd settled for a sport jacket and tie, but wore a cream-colored shirt, less formal than a white one.

We started looking over the menu, talking about what we were in the mood for.

"You ever done any singing?" I asked offhandedly, not looking up.

She replied offhandedly, "Star Cloud Marmalade."

I couldn't find it on the menu. "What's that?"

"The rock group I sang with. We did two albums and once warmed up for Led Zeppelin."

I dropped my menu. "You really did sing in a rock group?"

She nodded. "I probably scarred my vocal cords. But we were quite good if I may say so, and I *emulated* Janis Joplin."

"Vocally," I tried to qualify.

"Gabe rescued me from the drug scene before I ended up like her."

"'There, but for the grace of God . . .'"

"'. . . would have gone I.'"

"How did you meet Gabe?"

"He was a youth minister at a Methodist church and a friend introduced us. I liked him the first time we met, and we ended up falling in love. I'd done a lot to mess up the world. Gabe and I did what we could to put it back together again, at least our little corner of it. We were together fourteen years."

"I liked him."

"I liked Marian."

The waitress came and took our order. I went for a steak. Morgan decided on a spinach something-or-other.

I told her about my visit to The Cathedral of Life. She listened raptly, her fingers on her chin, often chuckling at my account. Our dinners came and we gave them half our attention.

"You really said that to Miles Newberry?"

"I wouldn't have been so bold twenty years ago."

"Justin Cantwell," she mused. "I wonder if we'll find another name beyond this one."

"Our local messiah isn't telling."

"But he still talks to you. He still tries to pull you in. That really interests me."

"He's looking for someone to share his bitterness and disillusionment."

"No doubt." She smiled and cocked her head. "So do you?"

The thought chilled me. "I don't want to end up like him."

"So how did he end up the way he is?"

"The same way I got where I am, to hear him tell it."

"That's spooky."

The waitress checked back. "Everything okay here? Can I get you anything?" The food was great and we were fine. She made her exit.

"So how are things with you?" I asked.

"Better." She smiled a whimsical smile. "Remember that list of three items from our first meeting?"

I probed my memory. "You and your congregation aren't getting along, Brandon Nichols isn't Jesus . . . and Michael the Prophet is your son."

"The third one is still a problem, but the first two . . ." For a moment she looked at the falls outside the window. "I'm moving into an irreversible situation. Jesus has become an issue for me, and some—not all—in the congregation don't want me going there." She smiled. "Still, like it or not, I'm there. I'm starting to address him by name, starting to view my faith as a relationship. I'm sure you know what I mean."

I tried not to fully express my joy lest I embarrass her in public. "I know what you mean."

"Travis, I've been to seminary. I've been an ordained minister for ten years, and I was married to an ordained minister for fourteen. Gabe and I did all we could to bring out the best in people, but—it's one of those things you only see looking back—there was always an evasive, missing element: relationship. Jesus was a religious abstraction, a historical figure we discussed and debated but didn't *know.*" She looked around the room. "Some of my parishioners would make an issue of my having dinner with an evangelical, fundamentalist, Pentecostal whatever-you-are, but they'd be missing the point. It's not my church or your church or which tradition is right or how many candles we light—it's knowing Jesus for who he is."

Oh, I was enjoying this. "Preach on, sister."

She preached on, leaning so low toward me that her earrings almost went in her spinach. "And I think that's Justin Cantwell's problem. Plenty of church, but no relationship." She settled back in her chair and thought a moment, the white, cascading falls reflected in her glasses. "Maybe Michael's problem too."

"But . . ." I really wanted to ease her pain. "There could be a new beginning here, a new twist to the story."

She gave a weak smile. "Let's hope so. Who knows? Maybe if Michael's mother knows the real Christ, she can somehow wean him from a false one."

I smiled at her. "I'll concur with that."

She abruptly switched subjects. "So how long did you pastor in Antioch?"

"About fifteen years."

She leaned back as if for a better view and said, "Tell me about it."

"Oh, there's not much to tell. . . ."

"How'd you wind up in Antioch in the first place?"

I closed my eyes and could see the memory playing through my mind like an old home movie. Some memories just never fade. . . .

IT WAS A CALLING that made no practical sense. Marian was working at her company in Los Angeles and doing well. I had my teaching degree and some great prospects for employment in elementary education. Our budget was finally starting to look healthy. We'd moved to a bigger apartment and bought new furniture. We even had a second car.

And then Dad called. Some folks wanted to start a Pentecostal Mission church in a little eastern Washington town called Antioch. He just thought I might like to pray about that. No pressure; he was just letting me know. I said I'd pray about it, and I did—"Dear Lord, I hope they find somebody"—and immediately put the subject aside. It came back. Sitting in our living room and hearing the police helicopter circling the neighborhood for the fifth straight night got me thinking about living in a quiet place and being a pastor again. Then I thought of Northwest Mission. *No way*, I thought. *Never again.*

I mentioned Dad's call to Marian. "They're dreaming," I said.

"Maybe not," she answered, but said nothing more.

A week later, a voice from my past called: Brother Smith, the dean of men when I was in Bible college. He now held a position with the Northwest District of the Pentecostal Mission, and noticed how I'd taken pains to maintain my credentials. Perhaps I'd be interested in taking a new church in Antioch, Washington.

"Well who's running it now?" I asked. I didn't want another territorial battle with somebody already there.

"Nobody," he said. "You'll have to run the whole show, start it from the ground up. It'll be your church, Travis. It'll be your vision." Brother Smith was no stranger to my nature, or my illustrious ministry career thus far. He knew I'd find the opportunity tantalizing.

And I did. My own church! No religious machinery already in place. No customs or traditions to fight against, no one to say, "Well that's the way we do things here!" No Sister Marvins, no Brother Rogenbecks. Just Marian and me.

I tried to talk myself out of it, reminding myself that for the first time in our marriage we had some stability, some hope for a normal life. But the more I talked to the Lord and myself—aloud, pacing about the apartment—the more stirred up I got and I couldn't sit still. "It'll never work," I told the mirror. "*Would* it work?" I asked the Lord.

What about Marian? She had a good job with a great salary and chance for advancement. I couldn't ask her to move to Antioch, Washington! I looked for Antioch on a map. It was marked with the tiniest little circle available. She'd never go for it.

Brother Smith gave me some phone numbers in Antioch. I made some calls and got some details.

I knelt by our bed and prayed some more. After I rose from my knees, I started preaching to the empty apartment. I already had a great idea for my first sermon. I'd talk about relationships, I thought. We didn't have a big city church, but we had each other, and that was what mattered!

Oh brother. What's Marian going to think?

"Lord, if this is your will, then speak to Marian's heart. Give her a peace. No, not peace. Make *her* excited! Make *her* want to do it!"

I was excited. The more I thought about it, the more excited I got. I couldn't wait for Marian to get home.

I was out of school and still waiting on a steady job, so I was pulling my weight by fixing dinner every night. Marian would scribble out instructions each morning and I'd give it my best shot. That night, when she got home, I served up pork roast and stir-fried vegetables over rice, and brought up the subject of Antioch.

"How many are in the church now?" she asked.

"Well, I talked to a guy named Avery Sisson. Right now there's him and his wife and their four kids."

She held her fork in midair. "And?"

"That's it. Right now there's no Pentecostal Mission church in that town."

"Why should there be?" She wasn't trying to be difficult. It was a fair question.

My answer was just as fair, I think. "I don't know. According to Avery, there isn't another Spirit-filled church in Antioch, and according to Brother Smith, the district thinks it's time to get a church started there. Avery's looked at a church building. It used to be an old Congregational church, but now the guy next-door owns it. He says we can rent it or buy it from him."

"And what would we do for a living?"

"Avery says I can work for his brother in construction until I get a teaching job. Antioch has a grade school and a high school."

She took another bite of stir-fried vegetables, chewed a while, thought a while, and then said, "What are you feeling, T. J.? What's in your heart?"

I looked down at my plate, a little reticent. "I think maybe I'd like to find out more . . . you know, think about it."

She reached over—we always sat close together—and tapped on my heart. "What's in here?"

I took a moment to search out the answer. "I just . . . I just want to do, you know, what Jesus did: I want to go about doing good.

Win some souls, change some hearts, bring some light into this world. I want to tell people about Jesus because he's a wonderful Savior and Friend."

"You think God put that in there?"

I actually got choked up. "Since I was a kid."

She gave me that smile that always made me feel like a conqueror, and then she rose and hugged me from behind. "Then we'd better check it out."

MR. FRAMER owned the building, and met us there. "It needs a little fixing up. It hasn't been used for a church in fifteen years."

Standing there on Elm Street with Avery Sisson, his wife, Joan, and Marian, I saw only future potential, not present condition. The plywood over the windows, the paint peeling off the lap siding, the wrinkled, moss-covered roofing didn't discourage me at all. This was an adventure, a vision to be fulfilled.

"How's the roof?" Marian asked.

"It leaks," said Framer.

"What about plumbing?" I asked.

"Just a sink in the basement and no toilet. There's an outhouse out back."

"Any pews?"

"Burned 'em. There's nothing in there but a bunch of lockers."

The old chapel sat forlornly in the middle of an unmowed field, looking as discarded and neglected as the rusting harrower, burned-out van, and immovable old bulldozer that sat in the grass alongside it.

Mr. Framer led us through the grass and weeds to the front steps. "That bulldozer belongs to my son. He can come and move it if you want. I don't know where that harrower came from."

"What happened to the van?"

"Kids set it on fire. I was hoping to sell it, but now . . ."

The front door sounded like it hadn't been opened in a while. Inside, Mr. Framer turned on the lights—the building *did* have electricity and four simple chandeliers hanging from the vaulted ceiling. It was cold in there. It smelled musty. The floor was old tongue-and-groove planking painted gray.

All we could see was lockers. Stacks of them. Rows of them. Ugly, green battered lockers.

"My son got these lockers when they tore down the old high school. I don't know what he was planning on doing with 'em, but they've been sitting in here for eight years and I'll be happy to get rid of 'em."

I squeezed through the lockers to the front and found the platform and the square footprint of unpainted planking where the pulpit used to stand. I stood on that spot and looked back at my congregation—three people and maybe Mr. Framer, standing among the lockers. I could see pews in that room and a hundred people filling them. I could see sunlight coming through the windows, feel the warmth of the oil stove, and hear the sound of singing. I could see people kneeling at the front pews and at the foot of the platform. There were Bibles and hymnals in every row, and boxes of Kleenex up front.

And the bell! "Does the bell work?"

Mr. Framer walked to the back of the room and unlooped the rope from its hook on the wall. He gave the bell three gentle yanks to get it rocking, and then we heard it ringing from the steeple outside, *clang, clang, clang,* like a sound out of history, a sweet, old-timey voice of hope reawakening in a new generation. Marian broke into a wide grin and clapped.

"Praise God," I said, and beckoned to Marian. She joined me on the platform and looked out over all those lockers in the yellow light of the chandeliers. "What do you see, Marian?"

"We could put the piano over there. And maybe we could get some carpet to run up the middle and sides. We need a cross, a big cross to go on that wall. What about classrooms?"

Mr. Framer looked at us funny. "It's got a basement with a sink, that's all."

We went down the steep, narrow stairs. The basement wasn't

much more than a crawlspace barely high enough to stand in. It was dark and tomblike, smelled of earth and dead mice, and the floor timbers hung low above our heads, festooned with spider webs.

"We could divide this into four, maybe five classrooms," I envisioned.

"Where are we going to put the bathrooms?"

"There's an outhouse out back," Mr. Framer reminded us.

I tried the sink. The water came out a rusty brown. "We could fit a kitchen in here, I suppose."

"It's going to be a lot of work!"

"All in good time. A building does not a church make. We could meet in our home while we're fixing this place up."

"As soon as we get a home."

We could read each other's eyes. This was it. We had to be here. This was where God wanted us.

"We'll take it."

"WELL, it needs a lot of fixing up, but if you want to put the work into it, I'll count that as rent."

To this day I'm not sure what it was, a storage shed or an old bunkhouse or perhaps a shop. It sat out behind Mrs. Whitfield's place between her barn and her chicken coop, roughly ten feet deep and forty feet long, with a sagging shed roof, three doors, eight four-paned windows in the front and four in the back. It had shiplap siding on the outside, and on the inside, bare studs and the backside of the shiplap. It was divided into three rooms, all cluttered with farm machinery, engine parts, old lumber, poultry feeders and brooders, and broken bales of straw. The middle room had a toilet and sink. The wiring was exposed and very basic: a bare light bulb in each room and maybe an outlet or two nailed to the bare studs.

The roof was good. Mrs. Whitfield had it redone just a few years ago. The floor was good—as much as I could see under all the junk.

"What do you think?" I asked Marian.

She cringed, and then she gave the place her best try. "That could be the living room. This could be the kitchen, and maybe we could put a wall in here to make this the bathroom. We could make a bedroom out of that last room, but we'll have to put in a closet."

"Dad'll help us. If it's church, he's in."

"My dad'll help too. He loves doing things for his kids."

Avery nodded confidently. "One month and you won't know the place."

I turned to Mrs. Whitfield. "We'll take it!"

WE WERE STAYING with the Sissons, sleeping on a borrowed hide-a-bed in their garage and sharing two bathrooms with Avery, Joan, and their four kids. Our small, apartment-sized collection of furniture and almost everything else we owned was locked in a rented storage space in Spokane. We would be living in a renovated shack between a barn and a chicken coop, and pastoring a church without a usable building for who-knew-how-long. Neither one of us had gainful employment and we had only three to four months of savings.

But we were the happiest we'd been in five years of marriage.

22

MARIAN AND I pastored in Antioch for fifteen years. We lived in five different houses, worked at ten different jobs. I didn't draw a full-time salary from Antioch Pentecostal Mission until we'd been there ten years.

Antioch Mission began with Avery and Pete Sisson and their families, and we met in Avery and Joan's living room. Within the year, we moved into the old church building we rented from Mr. Framer, and three years after that we finally got an indoor toilet. We bought that building from Mr. Framer in 1987, the same year Marian and I got burned out of our home. We started our new building in 1990, were approved for occupancy in 1995, and moved in Easter Sunday.

On my last Sunday in November of 1997, the church was well established in its new building on the west side of town, on a quaint knoll just above the highway. There were one hundred and fifty in the congregation, a bank account in the black, a big yellow bus that ran well, a good youth program, and the church's name on a fancy, sandblasted sign out front.

Fifteen years. A journey that felt so long and was over so soon, in a little town few people ever heard of. Fifteen years. Ninety-three souls saved. Twenty-three weddings. Fourteen funerals. A small retirement account, no real estate, a little savings.

When I left the ministry, I was alone, and wondering what in the world I thought I'd been doing all that time.

MORGAN AND I declined a dessert but asked for coffee.

And then she just looked at me, studying me. I regretted sounding so depressed at the end of my recap. My stories tended to end on a blue note these days.

"Give me some names," she said.

"Beg your pardon?"

She gave a half-shrug and picked up her coffee cup. "Just some names. People you remember from those fifteen years. Tell me some stories."

JOE KELMER. He was in his fifties, a rancher with five hundred acres south of town. I was working with Pete Sisson's crew, preparing to pour a slab for a new stable out on his place. Pete, Johnny Herreros, Tinker Moore, and I were knee-deep in a ditch, digging footings and hurling dirt like a chain gang when Joe came out to see how we were doing, his hands in his jeans pockets, his face a little glum. It wasn't like him. Usually he'd come over to check on our progress and talk so much he'd hinder it.

"How's it going?" We told him fine, and Pete said we were hoping to get the steel in and pour by the day after tomorrow.

"So how's Joe today?" Pete asked.

"Oh, not too good," he replied, sitting on an overturned five gallon bucket. "My bowels ain't worth the poop that goes through 'em."

"What's the problem?" I expected one of Joe's typical complaints about the water, his wife's cooking, or his advancing age.

"Cancer," he said. "Just found out this morning." We stopped digging. "Doc says they'll probably have to take the whole thing out."

We all stood in the ditch, our shovels in our hands, trying to adjust to the news and wondering what we could say.

"We'll have to pray for you," said Pete. "Get old Travis here to lay hands on you and get the Lord to chase that cancer out of there!"

Oh, thanks a lot, Pete! Set me up, why don't you?

But Joe just got up like a tired old man and said, "You'd better keep working. I'd like to see this barn while I'm still around." Then he left.

I first met Joe and Emily Kelmer on another project the year before, and immediately returned, more appropriately dressed, for a pastoral call. It turned out they considered themselves Catholics, meaning that was their background, but they never attended mass and had never been inside Our Lady of the Fields. They didn't have much use for my ministerial side, but they did appreciate my skill with hammer and saw and shovel and said so.

After Joe gave us the news, I did pray for him. I led the guys in prayer right there in the ditch that day, and Marian and I remembered him in our prayers every evening. I trusted God. There was no way in the world I could predict what the Lord would do, but I trusted him.

Well, God is never short on surprises. Joe told me he hadn't been inside a church since the day he and Emily were married, but the very next Sunday, he and Emily came into our little church on Elm Street arm in arm. We'd been meeting in that building for close to three years. The lockers were finally gone. Avery and Pete had recently completed a labor of love: a pulpit, a communion table, and a matching cross for the back wall. For now, we were using any chairs folks could bring from home—folding chairs, lawn chairs, plastic chairs, and dining chairs. Joe and Emily went right to the front row and sat in two green, plastic patio chairs.

I was leading some opening worship choruses, playing my guitar while Marian played the piano, but I let the others keep singing while I ducked aside and greeted Joe and Emily.

"Okay, Travis. I'm here," he said. "You can go ahead and pray for me."

I went back to leading the singing, my mind half on what I was doing and half on what I would have to do in a few minutes. It's easy to pray for colds and flu, final exams, and unsaved loved ones. Most of those things work themselves out in God's own good time. Colon cancer doesn't do that. The worship was sweet. Mine was intense.

"Folks," I finally said, "a lot of you know Joe and Emily." Those who did said hi, and Joe and Emily said hi back. "Joe's here because he needs prayer."

Joe stood and faced the thirty or so people who had gathered. "I'm not a religious man. Haven't had much time for God most of my life. But that doesn't mean he isn't there and can't hear me if I want to talk to him, you know what I mean?"

"Amen," some said. "Praise God."

"And I'm hoping he won't mind if I decide to come to him now after waiting so long."

He paused, perhaps to gather his resolve, perhaps to corral his emotions. "I have colon cancer. You know how it is, you get sick and you think you'll get over it and before long you've waited too long. The doctor says—" He stopped. Crying was something Joe Kelmer didn't believe in. He took a breath. "He says they'll have to take the whole thing out, put me on chemotherapy, pump me full of drugs and whatever. Won't be able to take a crap like most people—excuse me, I didn't mean to say it that way."

He turned and faced me. "Anyway, I made God a deal. If he takes this cancer from my body, then I'll give him my attention, first thing, above everything, the rest of my life. If he'll give me my life, I'll give it back to him. And that's about it."

I absolutely did not know how this was going to turn out. Joe was either going to have a great reason to serve God or a great reason not to, at least in his thinking, and it was hard to be comfortable about it.

And then, when he came forward and stood facing me, ready to be prayed for, I couldn't banish old memories from my mind. I could just see myself standing in front of Andy Smith and Karla Dickens back in the old Kenyon–Bannister days. I could remember the episode with Sharon Iverson, the girl with diabetes who almost died at Christian Chapel.

Well, Lord, I prayed, *you know all about that. You know I don't want to get into any kind of pretensions or showiness. I didn't ask for this. You brought it about, and now, here we are, that's all I know. Here we are.*

Joe was waiting.

I took my little vial of olive oil from the back of the pulpit and put a drop on Joe's forehead. "This oil is a symbol of the Holy Spirit," I told him. "In the Book of James it tells us to anoint the sick with oil and pray, and the Lord will restore the sick. Do you believe that, Joe?"

He shrugged. "Sure, why not?"

"Let's pray for Joe," I said, beckoning to the Sisson brothers and Bruce Hiddle, my elders, to join me. We laid hands on Joe, and then I prayed. I don't remember much of my prayer. I said something about Joe wanting a touch from God, and humbling himself in meek petition, and I know I requested that God would just glorify himself in Joe's body, in the name of Jesus.

And just like that, it was over. "Thanks for coming, Joe."

"Thank you, Travis," was all he said as he sat down.

They stayed for the rest of the service, received love and greetings from all of us, and then left.

Monday morning we were framing up the walls of the new stable and wondering how Joe was doing. He never came out of the house and we didn't hear a thing from Emily or anyone else. We remembered him in prayer at lunch time.

Tuesday, it was the same thing. We watched the house to see if any cars were gone, and one was. Maybe Joe was in the hospital. Maybe he was in for tests, chemotherapy, or even surgery to have his colon removed. We couldn't find out.

Wednesday morning, after we'd put in about an hour, Joe came out to see us, his hands in his jeans pockets, his cowboy hat set firmly on his head.

"Hey Joe," I said, "how's it going?"

He looked straight at me, that old Joe Kelmer half-smile on his face, and said, "Guess who doesn't have cancer anymore?"

The silence that fell over us was just as long and awkward as when we first heard the *bad* news.

I was being cautious, I guess. I actually said, "Who?"

Joe gave his chest two little taps with his thumb.

We were amazed. That's all there was to it. "You're kidding!" "Praise God!" "Are you sure?" "What'd the doctor say?"

"Went in on Monday." He laughed. "I told the doc something was feeling different all of a sudden and he got me right in like it was an emergency. They about took me apart trying to find something wrong. They spent two days at it and—" He gave his hands a quick wave like an umpire signaling *safe*. "It's gone. I'm clean! They can't figure it out. But I know."

We couldn't believe it. We looked at each other.

He almost touched noses with me. "Jesus healed me. He answered your prayer, and he answered mine." He backed off and addressed all of us. "So you boys might want to knock off for a while. Emily's got some coffee on and we can microwave some cinnamon rolls. We're gonna give our lives to Jesus. You just tell us what to do."

When the apostle Paul told the Philippian jailer "Believe on the Lord Jesus Christ and you shall be saved, you and your whole household," his words could have applied perfectly to Joe and his family. On Wednesday, Joe and Emily knelt in their living room with me, Pete, Johnny, and Tinker, and received Jesus Christ as their Lord and Savior. On Friday, Joe and Emily's daughter, Claudia, and her husband, Nate, knelt in the same living room and turned their lives over to Jesus.

On Sunday, Joe and Emily sat in the same green, plastic chairs, and Claudia and Nate sat right next to them. Their son, Larry, and his wife, Shirley, had come from Oregon to fill out the row, and they dedicated their lives to Christ that morning.

Joe was not a shy man, and if you bought a horse from him or sold him feed or asked him directions or called to sell him a magazine subscription or just pumped some gas for his truck, you heard about Jesus and what Jesus had done for him. He wasn't one to debate or hard sell, but it was hard to argue with his testimony. Norm Barrett, the diesel mechanic, along with his wife and three kids, came to the Lord because of Joe Kelmer. Bud Lundgren, our permanent guitar player, got saved while he and Joe were out bass fishing, and Bud's wife, Julie, our permanent saxophone player, got saved while shopping with Emily. The Barretts and the Lundgrens shared Jesus with other friends, some of them got saved and shared with *their* friends, and for a while we had ourselves a nice little revival rippling through town.

And it all started with Joe Kelmer.

BRUCE HIDDLE. He was a good-looking guy in his thirties, an electrical engineer for Washington Water Power. He had a sweet wife named Annie and two cute kids, Jamie and Josh. In May of 1990 he displayed a quiet peace and faith in the Lord that became an example to the rest of us.

Bruce and his family were returning from a visit with Annie's folks in Electric City, driving a long, monotonous two-lane late at night. Bruce was at the wheel, Annie was on the passenger side, the kids were secured in child seats in the back.

The last thing Bruce remembers was the oncoming headlights of a large vehicle, most likely a truck. There was nothing amiss. The truck was in its own lane. They passed each other, going opposite directions.

And then Bruce woke up in a daze, in the dark, his body numb, slumped against his shoulder restraint. The kids in the back seat were screaming. Blood was streaming from his forehead and dripping off his chin. Beads of shattered windshield lay like gravel on the seats, in his lap, on top of the dashboard. The car was leaning precariously, apparently in a gully beside the highway. He reached for Annie, but felt rough wood. A twelve-inch log had come through the windshield and now lay where Annie's head and shoulders should have been. He twisted around, trying to see the kids. They were spattered with blood, flesh, and Annie's blonde hair.

A logging truck had lost part of its load just as the two vehicles passed. A log, perfectly timed and aimed, went through the windshield of Bruce's car, missing Bruce and killing his wife. The truck driver pulled over and became incoherent when he saw what his lost load had done. Another motorist saw the wreck and went in search of a telephone.

I was working as dispatcher for the volunteer fire department that night and took the emergency call. I sent out the dispatch, telling the volunteers there'd been a fatality accident, but I had no idea the accident involved a family from my church. When the aid crew arrived and radioed back, I got the news. By that time, Bruce and the kids had been trapped in their car for over an hour. Numb with shock, I remained at my post, coordinating communications and crews until Pete Sisson burst into the station and bumped me from my chair. "I'll handle it. Get going."

Bruce and the kids were airlifted to a hospital in Spokane, and that was where I found them. Bruce had broken ribs and facial lacerations. The kids had minor injuries from flying glass and seat restraints. He was coherent, but we didn't talk. There were no words, only shock and an insurmountable disbelief.

Annie was gone. Instantly. Before any of us could fathom that we had lost anything, she simply wasn't there. We could not believe it that night. We could scarcely believe it the next morning. Shock did not give way to grief until well into the next day.

And then the questions came: With miles and miles of open road, why *that* truck, *that* car, together at *that* time in *that* place? Why was the accident so ruthlessly, savagely perfect?

Like everyone else, I drew upon my faith for comfort and tried to share that comfort as best I could. But inside, I was asking the same questions as everyone else, knowing there would never be answers.

There was no funeral, only a memorial service once Bruce had healed enough to attend. All who knew and loved Annie were there, and took turns sharing their thoughts and remembrances. I spoke briefly about the need to trust God in all circumstances, for

his ways are unsearchable. I reminded everyone that Annie, knowing Jesus, was in a better place and just fine, but I could feel my
insides quaking and I teetered on the brink of tears with every sentence. After we sang our last song, I stole quietly into a back room,
sat down with my face in my hands, and lost it completely. *Oh dear
Lord, why? Why Annie? What's Bruce going to do now? What about
Josh and Jamie?*

I didn't hear anyone come in. I just felt a hand on my shoulder
and heard a quiet whisper, "It's okay . . . it's okay."

I reached up and touched the hand touching me, then looked
into the scarred, black-and-blue face of Bruce Hiddle. He sat down,
put his arm around my shoulders and let me cry, not saying another
word. I was supposed to be the minister bringing comfort to the
grieving, but I was drained of comfort. Bruce, a quiet serenity showing through his scars and his tears, was ready to share what he had.

In the months that followed, Bruce often got tearful, at any
time, in any place, usually without warning, but he didn't seem
self-conscious about it. "It's for Annie," he would tell people.
"Don't worry, it's just something I have to do." The rest of the
time, he was the friend, daddy, and brother we all cherished, with
a glow about him that the scars and the stitches could not extinguish. The scars eventually faded. The glow still remains.

"It's Jesus," he always explained. "He knows the answers. He'll
work it out."

Two years later, the Lord brought Libby McLane into Bruce's
life, and in the summer of 1992, they were wed in our little church
on Elm Street. Josh and Jamie stood with their dad and their new
mom as I performed the ceremony, and once again, I teetered on
the brink of tears with every sentence.

"It's okay," Bruce whispered to me as he held his bride's hand.
"It's okay."

MR. FRAMER. He said he'd been to church already and didn't
need any more of it. Well, we saw no need to argue with that, but
church wasn't the question, Jesus was.

But although Mr. Framer didn't need any more religion, he did need a haircut. Marian volunteered and gave him a trim every two weeks. Having accepted her help, he was ready to accept mine, and so I helped him put a new roof on his house over several weekends. The next thing we knew, he was mowing the church grass every week without anyone asking him. When we started running a bus ministry around town, he was the guy who provided the bus and kept it running.

Four years after we started renting the church building, he finally came to a Sunday morning service, slipping in behind a group of folks to escape notice. I saw him come in but didn't make a big deal out of it. I just winked at him. We played that little game for the next few months, long enough for him to discover he could talk to just about anyone in that church without something spooky or "religious" happening to him.

Only when I was sure it was safe did I ask him about Mrs. Framer, and why she was not attending church with him. He didn't give me a clear answer that Sunday, but the following Wednesday he gave me a strong enough hint.

He brought over a portable, battery-powered chemical toilet for us to install under the basement stairway. That way, he said, the ladies wouldn't have to trek out to the outhouse during a service, but could fulfill their natural obligations with some comfort and delicacy. I could tell he thought very highly of his gesture, so I didn't refuse it. We put the toilet under the stairs and nailed up a plywood wall and a thin little door with a springed hinge.

A chemical toilet is a box-shaped contraption with a toilet seat on top that doesn't flush to an outside sewer or septic system. It has two tanks inside it, one for fresh water and chemicals, the other to hold all the flushed waste. When you're finished and you press a little button, the electric pump kicks on, the blue water and chemical mix swirls around the bowl, and the toilet tucks away your contribution in its holding tank.

The toilet Mr. Framer gave us was comfortable. I know that from personal experience, and others would agree. As for delicate, well, that toilet just couldn't keep a secret. The electric pump was *loud*, and it would grind on *forever*, announcing to the entire congregation seated upstairs that a modest user had just finished and would be rejoining the service directly. If that wasn't announcement enough, the slam of that plywood door was.

And then there was the smell. Though intended for the ladies and their need for comfort and privacy, it's just a fact of life that one good toilet among forty churchgoers is going to get used by *everyone*. Our little camping toilet wasn't meant to handle a load that size, and it didn't.

No matter. As soon as that toilet was in, Mrs. Framer came to church. The Framers heard the gospel every Sunday for two more years, and finally came forward to receive Christ one Sunday night. Nothing tragic had occurred in their lives. There was no crisis or desperate material need to make them turn to God. They were just ready, that was all. It was time.

But I do credit the Framers with our board's unanimous decision to do "whatever was necessary" to get a septic system approved and a real flushing toilet installed. That motion was seconded and carried within a month of the chemical toilet's arrival, and when we installed men's and women's flush toilet restrooms in the basement, the Framers were there to cut the ribbon.

RICH WATKINS. A former biker, now a trucker, with long, black hair in a ponytail and eagles, skulls, snakes, and naked women tattooed all over his huge arms. When we marched for Jesus down the main highway through town with signs and placards proclaiming his name, Rich happened to be in the tavern and stepped outside to watch us go by. Some of his drinking buddies laughed at us, but Rich just read our signs and listened to us sing. I saw the look on his face and thought, *Dear Lord, protect us. That guy looks like trouble.*

He pulled up in front of our church on his Harley Sunday morning, sat quietly through the whole service, and then said to me afterward, "So this where you find Jesus?"

"It sure is," I said.

"Well, I've decided I gotta square up with my old lady, but I'd better get right with God first, know what I mean?"

I prayed with him, led him to Christ, and eventually met his wife, Clarice, and their four children. Now this guy was one *monumental* discipling job. He'd never been to Sunday school or had any kind of Christian upbringing, so Marian and I and our church family had to do it all. We had to teach him the subtleties of doctrine, concepts such as, *You don't usually lead a person to repentance by breaking a beer bottle over his head,* and such fine points as, *Turning the other cheek doesn't mean you walk up and moon somebody you don't like.*

He's still growing in the Lord, and recently took a big step we were all proud of: He volunteered to go into the public schools and give the kids a no-holds-barred lecture about staying off drugs. The kids love his presentations. The parents and teachers do too, especially since we finally broke him of the habit of referring to Satan as "that dirty SOB the devil."

If I ever needed a mental image of the early Simon Peter, I just imagined Rich Watkins and I had it.

GUY FORBES. He ran the local movie theater. When he showed an X-rated movie, I got some of the other pastors and their churches to join us in picketing the theater both nights. I thought he'd be mad at us—many of the folks going into the theater were—but he called me that week and apologized for showing the movie. We got together for lunch after that, got to know and trust each other, and later started up our own, impromptu movie rating committee between the two of us. He didn't always go along with the other half of the committee, but we reached more agreements than disagreements, and our town enjoyed a little more peace because of it. He has yet to get saved, but we have a strong, mutual respect.

BOB FISHER, Paul Daley, the Sisson brothers, Jake Helgeson, Rudie Whaler, Tinker Moore, and twenty other guys and gals who showed up the night our house caught fire. You never appreciate your neighbors quite so much as when you're in trouble, and that night, when Marian turned away from some French fries to answer the phone and a grease fire broke out, we owed those folks everything. The fire took out most of the kitchen and blackened the rest of the house, but thanks to the faithful folks of the volunteer fire department, most of our belongings made it through. After the fire, the town almost buried us in clothing, food, dishes, and utensils to replace what we had lost. I'd done a lot of visitation around town, knocking on doors to get acquainted with people, but I don't know that I ever met as many folks as when we were in need and they came by to help out.

Antioch's a great town, it really is.

THAT FARMHAND—I never learned his name. Tom something. He was working for George Harding during harvest and got his foot caught in a combine auger. I was driving the truck and heard him screaming. By the time we shut the machine down and got him out, his ankle had made at least two full rotations.

"Pray for me, preacher!" he kept screaming.

I touched his ankle—very gently—and prayed, "Lord, please heal this leg, please restore it in Jesus' name."

He was back at work the next day, climbing all over that machine as if nothing had happened.

He moved on after harvest. I don't know if he ever got saved.

LANCE MONTGOMERY; Tiger, Cecily, and Moira Bradley; Ron and Vicki Hanson and their sons, Ned and Tom; the rest of the youth group and a fair share of the town. One of the kids got an old 8mm home movie camera, and I got an idea. I wrote a script and our youth group made a movie, a fifty-five minute epic shot on location in and around the town of Antioch. The whole production cost us five hundred dollars and took a year to film. We staged a big car wreck, burned down a barn painted to look like a house, kept our characters in constant peril until they got saved, and pulled in as many people as we could to be extras and walk-ons. By the time the movie premiered in the high school auditorium, at least a hundred folks came to see it because they were in it. The film was grainy and jerky. Sometimes our actors sounded like munchkins and sometimes they sounded like dopey giants talking through molasses. Sometimes the movie camera picked up the local radio station and we got music and news along with dialogue, but our show was a hit and we broke even. I don't think the showing of the film won any souls to the Lord, but the making of it helped us get to know a lot of folks around town, and they all heard the gospel in the process.

The youth are grown up now and starting families of their own, but they fondly remember their brief and meaningful stint in the gospel movie biz, and I can't think of any who are not serving the Lord today.

LORRAINE BRADLEY, Mrs. Framer, Libby Hiddle, Emily Kelmer, and all the wonderful ladies in the church who brought dinner over while Marian was sick. They had it all scheduled out, every day of the week. They cooked, they cleaned, they did our laundry, they helped me get Marian in and out of the car, they helped me get her to and from the hospital. . . .

MY COFFEE CUP was cold and empty. I was staring at it, wishing I could hide in it.

"You can stop," said Morgan.

I had been enjoying the stories up to this point. "Okay."

She touched the back of my hand. "Thank you."

I shrugged. "You asked. I hope I delivered."

"I loved it."

I looked at my watch. "Man, is it that late?"

"Time flies."

I pushed away from the table. "It's been a great evening."

"It's been absolutely wonderful. Thank you." She rose from her chair and I held her coat as she slipped into it.

"So anyway, I might be hearing from the Cathedral—that is, if they remember to call me—"

She held up her hand to stop me. "I don't think that's what this evening was about, do you?"

Maybe I was unwilling to explore it. "I'm not sure what you mean."

She buttoned her coat as she looked up at me over her glasses. "All those people, Travis. They're still with you, right in here." She tapped on my heart. "When you go home tonight, don't think about old what's-his-name up at the Macon ranch. Think about *them*. They're what the last fifteen years were all about. They're what *Jesus* is all about. Old what's-his-name can't touch that."

We came to the restaurant in separate cars and left the same way. All the way home I reflected on the evening, warmed and healed by Morgan Elliott's discerning spirit, soothed by the acceptance I saw in her eyes. I had to wipe some tears away as I drove. I hadn't felt this kind of kinship with anyone since Marian went home. Maybe we could have dinner again sometime. Maybe we wouldn't need a particular reason.

Perhaps we could even go in the same car.

23

"WHERE HAVE YOU BEEN?" Florence Lynch had been cranky to begin with, but after waiting until past her bed time for a cop, any cop, to show up, she was *beyond* cranky and not to be trifled with.

Brett Henchle stepped through her front door and into her living room, nervous and agitated. "We had another incident across town—"

"Well what about *my* incident? You keep me waiting here all night . . ." Florence went to her dining room table and grabbed up the list she'd compiled. "I have it all right here. Two dresses, three hair combs, two bracelets, four blouses, and a pair of shoes." She handed it to him and he looked it over with a certain detachment. "I caught her red-handed, in the very act. Did Rod tell you?"

"Uh, no . . ."

"She was trying to sneak out of my store with the Stoendegger— that's the purple dress—" she pointed to the list in his hand—"this one right here. A hundred and twelve dollars retail. She was wearing it under her own dress, but I saw the hem sticking out. Rod and I went over to Penny's house and—" She snuffed and rolled her eyes. "Have you ever smelled that place? The carpet's woven marijuana!

Has to be! And the clothes Bonnie Adams wears! No wonder Penny was stealing from my shop."

"So that's where you found the rest of this stuff?"

"In Penny's closet and right on top of her dresser! Oh, Bonnie Adams had a fit, just screaming at Penny and slapping her around. But you know what? All Penny did was sit there and shrug and flip her hair out of her eyes. I don't think she's a bit sorry."

"Well, I'm sure she is."

"You're sure she—*what?* You've got to be kidding! You've hauled her in before, several times! Rod told me!"

"Yes, but that was—"

"That's why he jailed her. She can't be trusted."

"I'd still like to talk to her. Penny's not a bad girl at heart. If she spends some time in the jail this evening and gets a good talking to, we may not have any more trouble from her."

She gawked at him. "You're dreaming, right?"

"No, I'm—"

"Well, wake up. I'm pressing charges!"

It was easy to tell he didn't like that news. "You're asking for a lot of trouble, a lot of time, a hearing, a trial—"

Perhaps he was hard of hearing. She said it slower and louder. "I'm pressing charges! You're a police officer! Now see to it!"

He grabbed his leg and winced. "Did . . . did Rod get your statement?"

"Yes, he did. And he told me to write up this list of the stolen merchandise, so now you have it."

He turned toward the door, and yes, he was definitely limping. "Well, I'll get back to you in the morning." He pulled a card from his pocket and scribbled a phone number on the back. "If you decide to change your mind you can call me at home." He handed the card to her.

"That's highly unlikely!" By now she was angry with him. "Penny Adams is a thief, she's always been a thief, and this town needs to be rid of her once and for all."

He answered with an edge in his voice, "Yes, ma'am," and went out the door.

DON ANDERSON awoke from a restful sleep, disturbed by a strange, low hum he'd never heard in the house before. He raised his head from his pillow and listened. It sounded like a sixty-cycle hum, the same noise sometimes picked up by amplifiers and sound systems. Had he left something on?

He got out of bed, careful not to wake Angela, and went into the living room to check the stereo. It was off. The television was off. The fluorescent lights in the kitchen were off. The furnace wasn't running.

He listened to the refrigerator. Wow! He could hear everything that compressor was doing: the whir of the motor, the high-pitched rushing of the Freon through the condenser. There was a sixty-cycle hum down in the middle of all that noise, but it wasn't the hum he was after.

Where was it coming from?

He walked down the hallway toward the bedroom again, still hearing the hum like a steady note in his head. The bathroom light was on. He reached for the light switch on the wall and clicked it off.

The humming stopped.

Oh. The wall switch. He clicked it on again.

There was that hum. He bent close to the switch and listened. Well . . . it wasn't just in the switch.

He straightened slowly, his ear close to the wall. Then he moved a foot or two down the hall, still listening. Then he backed up again. He raised as high as his tiptoes, then squatted. He shook his head in amazement.

He could hear the wire in the wall—or more exactly, the electric current flowing through it. He could hear where the wire was, which way it went up the wall, where it turned. Incredible!

He chuckled with delight. Like his other new abilities, this could be useful. Imagine being able to find wires in walls, maybe cables underground, maybe hear bad connections or short circuits!

He clicked off the light—the humming stopped—and headed for the bedroom, grinning to himself in the dark. This was going to be great.

Back in bed, he listened again for the hum of the wires. Not too many things were turned on right now. The house was dark and quiet. Good enough.

But what would it sound like during the waking hours, when things got turned on and power was flowing through the wires? Well, he'd worry about that in the morning. He rolled over and closed his eyes.

What was that? It sounded like an ant doing a tap dance on his night stand. *Tick, ticka tick tick tick, ticka tick tick tick.*

He rolled over and looked. Too dark. He clicked on his bedside lamp. The wires in the wall hummed.

Angela woke up and groaned, "What're you doing?"

"Checking out a noise." He reached for his digital watch. The moment he touched it, the little tap dance came through loud and clear, *TICK, TICKA TICK TICK TICK, TICKA TICK TICK TICK.* He put the watch down.

"What noise?" Angela asked.

"Oh, it was just my watch."

"Your *watch?*"

He clicked off the lamp. The humming stopped.

Angela went back to sleep. Don lay there, eyes open, wondering whether he should be worried as the sound of his watch kept tap dancing in his ears, *tick, ticka tick tick tick. . . .*

FLORENCE LYNCH lay in her bed, troubled and tossing, dreaming of a deranged and bug-eyed Penny Adams reaching out and grabbing things. Penny was ghostly, transparent around the edges, drifting and floating through Florence's house with long, sticky fingers clutching after everything in sight, and Florence kept chasing her, never keeping up, trying to stop her, screaming at her. Penny just laughed a witchy laugh and kept grabbing, grabbing, grabbing, taking dishes out of the cupboard, knickknacks off the shelf, a scarf from around Florence's neck. *Stop that, put that back, put it back, that's not yours!* More witchy laughing, green, fuzzy teeth, the touch of long, cold fingers—

Florence awoke with a jerk, her heart pounding, her face slick with sweat, the darkness like a mask over her eyes.

Terrified. A nightmare. She tried to calm down. She couldn't. *It was a nightmare!* she told herself. *It's over now.*

It wasn't over. Her terror would not subside. With a death grip around fistfuls of down comforter, she covered her face up to her eyes and searched the deep, endless darkness of the bedroom.

A man was standing in the corner.

The terror felt like a hammer blow to her heart. Her throat constricted, her hands trembled.

His gaze emerged from the blackness like dim, yellow headlights emerging through thick smoke. There was something vaguely recognizable in their expression, a glint she'd known for years and hadn't seen in ten.

"Louis!" she gasped. "Louis?"

The form of her dead husband inched toward her, the darkness receding like tidewater from the old gray shirt and jeans, the pale, veined skin of the face. Except for the unbroken glare of those eyes, he looked the same as the moment he died. The pale, blue lips were moving but there was no sound.

She managed to breathe again, in short, shallow gasps. "Louis. What is it?"

He raised his finger and shook it at her, his eyes angry and scolding, his lips forming the word *no. No, no, no!*

She no more than *felt* the question forming in her mind before she had the answer. She knew what he was trying to tell her.

PENNY ADAMS was not asleep, but she was comfortable, lying on a cot under clean, warm blankets. Compared to some of the other jails she'd occupied, this cell wasn't bad.

Even so, she felt disappointed. Her new hand was supposed to be something magical, something shielded from hassles. She'd been in and out of Anderson's and Kiley's with all kinds of great stuff and they never noticed. Florence Lynch never noticed either—until today. That's what Penny couldn't figure out. Where did she slip up? What killed the magic?

People could be so weird, getting all shook up over a few dresses, a few blouses, a few watches and CDs. She liked them, she wanted them, Don Anderson and Matt Kiley and Florence Lynch never even missed them, so what was the big deal? They had plenty of stuff and she didn't, and that wasn't fair. What good was having a new hand if you couldn't use it?

She heard the front door open and footsteps moving across the front office floor. She sat up in time to see Brett Henchle come through the cellblock door, the keys to the cells in his hand. He was wearing civilian clothes and hadn't combed his hair. He must have gotten out of bed to come down here.

"Well," he said, "you're still awake."

She shrugged and flipped a lock of hair out of her eyes.

He paused outside her door. "You don't know how lucky you are. I just got a call from Florence Lynch. She says to let you go, to forget about the whole thing."

Way cool, she thought, but said nothing.

"So I'm going to let you out of here, but I want you to do us all a favor. You listening?"

She looked up at him. "Sure."

"You got a new hand, maybe from God, and I know he wouldn't do that just so you can go on stealing. So try to do something else with it. This town doesn't need the trouble, and neither do I, and neither do you. You got it?"

She knew how to answer. "Okay."

He unlocked the cell door. "Get your coat. I'll take you home."

She followed him out of the station and to the squad car, feeling relieved and giddy. Maybe the magic *was* still there. Officer Henchle was in a good mood, going easy on her.

She also noticed he wasn't limping like before.

WHEN MY TELEPHONE RANG Friday morning, it could have been Kyle Sherman calling for an update, or maybe Jim Baylor calling to talk about Dee. Bob Fisher still called once in a while just to call; Bruce Hiddle or Joe Kelmer called occasionally to make sure I was still breathing. My sister, Rene, called whenever there was family news; it could have been Morgan Elliott following up on last night's dinner meeting (I would have liked that). I was *half* expecting a call from the Cathedral, probably from Miles Newberry or some other well-screened and thoroughly instructed Cathedral associate, but I still considered that too much to hope for.

There was no way in the world I could have expected *this* caller.

"Travis Jordan?"

"Speaking."

"Mr. Jordan, my name is Elise Brenner. My maiden name is Harris. Dale Harris is my father."

I sank onto the couch, more than a little intrigued. "*The* Dale Harris? Pastor of The Cathedral of Life?

"One and the same. Have I caught you at a bad time?"

"No, no, no, I'm free, I'm okay."

"I understand you visited my dad's church a little while ago."

"That's right."

"Did you talk with my father?"

I broke into a grin and hoped she didn't hear me chuckle. "No. He was unavailable."

"But you did talk to Miles Newberry."

"Uh, yeah, that's, that's right. I, uh, talked to Miles—uh, Pastor Newberry."

"About a mutual acquaintance? Justin Cantwell?"

I leaned forward, pressing the receiver to my ear. "That's right. He, uh, he was going to get back to me."

"He won't. None of them will. Mr. Jordan, it's only by a fluke that I heard about your meeting with Miles. They weren't about to tell me. They don't like this sort of thing getting out."

"Why are *you* calling me?"

"Because I know Justin Cantwell and I can tell you about him, which means I *have* to tell you about him. It would be wrong not to. The others—my father included—don't want anyone to know about him because it would be too embarrassing."

I grabbed a notepad I kept by the phone and flipped to a clean page. "So . . . you understand who I am and what my needs are?"

"Mrs. Fontinelli told me. You remember her, my dad's secretary?"

"Oh yes, Mrs. Fontinelli. She seemed like a nice lady."

"One of the nicest. She's like a second mom. She told me about your visit and how the staff handled it. She's a professional and she does her job, but she's a friend too. She wasn't going to tell me unless I asked her, but I asked her, so she told me."

"Okay."

"This conversation is going to be confidential, all right?"

"All right."

She took an audible breath. "I'm married to one of the associate pastors at the Cathedral, Tom Brenner. I used to be the head of the music department at the church. I directed the choir, ran the worship team, organized the Christmas and Easter pageants, all that sort of thing. Three years ago, Justin Cantwell auditioned for the choir and we put him in the tenor section. That's how I got to know him. To make a long story short, we ended up having an affair."

I tried to keep my voice from betraying my wide-eyed facial expression. "I see."

"Now, you have to consider who my father was. He had a monstrous church with three services on Sunday morning, a book deal with a major publisher, a television ministry, a tape ministry. He was a district presbyter for our denomination and serving on the board of Horizon Bible College. He had a professional, big time booking agency to line up his outside speaking engagements and another company managing annual vacations to the Holy Land with his name in the logo. He had a well-trained professional pastoral staff and we had ourselves an efficient, smooth-running church with a multimillion dollar annual budget. Mr. Jordan, I guess I've made it clear, my dad was successful in . . . well, the popular word is, the *ministry*."

"Oh yes. Anybody can see that."

"So, next thing you know, his daughter, married, with three kids, has an affair with a stranger from the teeming masses of that congregation. The, uh, powers-that-be—the board, the pastors, and my father—feared it would mar the image of the church and the pastor. They thought it could snarl the ministry's momentum—let the church roll on, as the song goes. I was ashamed and felt foolish. My husband's ministry was going to be in jeopardy as well. So we got together, prayed about it, and then, to put it simply, we covered it up. The church kept me on staff through Christmas— hey, it was the big Christmas pageant, they couldn't let anything jeopardize that—and then they let me take an indefinite leave of absence in January. My husband went right on serving as an associate pastor, doing all he could to act normal, to keep the College and Career department rolling while we worked things out. The official word was that I'd worked very hard and needed a rest and time to be with my family—which was true. It just wasn't the whole truth."

"What happened to Justin Cantwell?"

"He vanished like he was never there. I've read a few things in the paper about Jesus showing up in Antioch, but I didn't have a clue it was him, not until you came down here asking questions."

"So how are you and your husband doing?"

"We're still working it out. It hasn't been easy."

"Does he . . . does he know you're talking to me about all this?"

"I told him I was going to call you today."

"And what was his response?"

"He had to leave. The College and Career department has a meeting this morning. But that's . . ."

"Yes?"

"I don't know if you'll be able to understand this, but it's part of the story so I'll tell you. I almost couldn't help being drawn to Justin Cantwell. He was the first man in my life I could really talk to. He understood me, he understood my pain, he took the time to talk with me and, you know, just share his feelings about things." She took a breath to clear her mind. "I did not know my father. I can't say that I know him now. We never really talked, never spent time together— unless it was in church. Hey, as long as I played the piano or led the choir or worked in the church office, we had a relationship. It was mostly professional, but at least we had *something*."

I could feel my insides twisting a little. "I, uh, I think I do understand."

"That's what people don't realize: On the surface, it's a wonderful church and we have a happy, Christ-filled family. Dad likes to brag about his kids in public, but my sister, Judy, is divorced and bulimic and my brother, Sam, is an alcoholic. My oldest brother, Dale Jr., turned out pretty well, but that's because he's just like Dad. He's in the ministry, pastoring a church in Oklahoma. As for me and my husband, Tom . . ." She dropped off in midsentence.

"Did Tom go to Horizon Bible College?"

"Yes." She sounded surprised.

"And he talks and thinks like your dad."

Now her voice carried her amazement. "Have you met him?"

"No. But he's on the pastoral staff, isn't he?"

She laughed. "So you've been to our church."

"I've seen how it works."

"Dad handpicks every associate. I love Tom. But he's Dad's kind of man. All church. They fuel each other. It's all they talk about. I should have seen it coming. It's as if you can't love and serve the Lord by being with your family, you have to be doing church stuff."

Ah yes, the *stuff*. "I'm sorry." I really was.

"Again, I don't expect you to understand, but in our home, you had to be involved in the church to feel like part of the family. Dale and I could play the game, Sam and Judy couldn't." She gave a bitter chuckle. "I was always at the church, so Dad used to talk to Sam and Judy through me. He'd say things like, 'Tell Sam I like that paint job on the house,' or 'Tell Judy she should sell that car and get an automatic.' Sam used to brag about being a pagan just to send a message. Dad never picked up on it. Maybe the affair was my way of sending a message to Tom. Sometimes I think he may have received it, but sometimes not."

"What about your mother?"

"The same rule applied. So they'd fight a lot. Then she'd run into the bedroom to cry and he'd go out and cut the grass. Nothing ever changed that I could see. She threatened to leave him once, but then she felt so guilty about it that she ended up asking *him* to forgive *her*. I wanted to scream."

"And . . ." Pieces were coming together in my head even as I formed the question. "Justin Cantwell knew all about this, didn't he?"

"Yes."

"He could tell you all about it, just like he'd been there."

"Just like he'd been there. So, we just clicked, you know what I mean? Our hearts touched and he showed compassion and love and warmth—and it didn't have to be church related!" Then she asked, "Is he doing the same thing to someone up there?"

I was too blown away to answer. I had to think.

"Mr. Jordan?"

"Oh yes. Definitely."

"You have to warn whoever it is. Don't let him do it. Listen, he'll come on at first like he's—well, like he's Jesus himself."

"Right."

"But he's not a healer, Mr. Jordan—I don't care how it looks. He knew about my hurt, but he didn't heal it, he just brought it out and made it worse. I think he looks for people to share *his* anger and *his* hurt and then he brings out the worst in them. He *uses* them."

"Do you know anything about his background, where he's from, who his family are?"

"Once I saw a letter he got from Nechville, Texas, just the envelope. He told me it was from his mother."

"Nechville . . ." I asked her to spell it and wrote it down. "Did you catch his mother's name?"

"Lois Cantwell. He wouldn't talk about her, or any of his family, for that matter. He's bitter, and having known him and the way he knew me, I can guess where the bitterness came from. He knows the Christian language. When he joined our choir, he already knew the worship songs. He could raise his hands and praise the Lord. He could pray and quote from the Bible. He talked about Jesus and used Jesus' name just like a real Christian. He's been there."

"But it didn't go well for him."

"That would be an understatement. But Mr. Jordan, think twice before you pity him. He's not just a wounded soul. He's a destroyer, with a destroyer driving *him*. He never did miracles while he was here. A little prophetic insight, maybe, just enough to carry out his agenda. But if what I've read is true, that demon is still growing, and now it's in your town. Better be prayed up."

24

Nancy Barrons stared at the image on her computer monitor, then sighed, dropping her gaze. She wagged her head, her face despondent.

Kim Staples didn't notice. She was busy at her own computer, tapping keys and moving her mouse, pasting and assembling Tuesday's paper. "Uh-oh, I've got a problem."

"We've all got a problem," Nancy replied.

Kim turned from her monitor, hoping Nancy would look her way. "See here? Kiley Hardware's full-page ad landed right opposite Anderson Furniture's full-page ad at the center spread. You think that's too much ad all in one place? Nancy?"

Nancy rested her forehead on her fingertips, and gave her screen a less-than-enthusiastic glance. "I can't run this story."

Kim pushed with her feet, propelling her wheeled chair across to Nancy's desk. "But it's news."

Nancy waved her off, a little angry. "No, no, no, I don't want to hear that excuse anymore. We've been using it for weeks." On her monitor was the headline, A BETTER HOME FOR THE MESSIAH. Underneath was a full-color photo of the new public restrooms and showers under construction at the Macon ranch. "What in the world are we doing? This isn't a news story. It's another full-page ad!"

Kim shrugged. "He's employing local workers, buying materials from local businesses, drawing pilgrims from all over the country who spend money here. That's news for this town. People want to know about it."

"But we're helping him. Knowing what we know, we're still helping him!"

Kim nodded forlornly. "When I was up there to take the picture, Nichols's people told me they wanted five hundred copies when the story ran."

"Yeah, free publicity. More clippings to put in their PR package. An endorsement, if you ask me! He's using us just like he's using everyone else in this town!"

"What if we toned down the headline and didn't call him the Messiah?"

Nancy leaned back, folding her arms. "I notice we've never run a story on Mary Donovan."

Kim snickered. "Or Michael Elliott."

"Our own Virgin Mary and John the Baptist. Kind of like meeting Mickey Mouse and Goofy at Disneyland."

"So why haven't we? The big papers have."

"Because . . ." An animated, geometric screen-saver started up on Nancy's computer. She let it run. "We live here and we don't want to hurt our friends—not to mention we're covering our own rear ends. If we ever did an honest story about any of this, we'd be right alongside the big papers in showing how ludicrous it all is." For the first time, Nancy looked at Kim. "But it's going to blow up. Adrian Folsom's talking to an angel, but have you seen how paranoid she's gotten? And the other night, Rod Stanton and Mark spent a couple of hours looking for a ghost Brett says appeared in his living room: that hitchhiker he picked up months ago."

"You're kidding!"

"We've got all these people and all this money coming into town. There's building going on. Businesses are expanding and sticking their necks out, and for what? For this supposedly upgraded version of Jesus Christ who performs miracles but has a thing for women, is probably a crook, and—" It was a difficult realization. "And have you noticed how nobody's *really* better off? Business is better, sure, but Matt Kiley's nothing more than a thug, Norman Dillard looks at you everywhere but in the eye, Penny Adams is stealing again, Adrian's paranoid, Brett's, I don't know, seeing things, and Don Anderson—"

"Him too?"

"Well . . . he's not entirely there when you talk to him."

"Maybe he's been playing with his toys too much."

"It's going to blow up, and when it does, where's this town going to be? We should've gotten a clue when we first talked to Nevin Sorrel—who's now dead, of course."

"Definitely not better off. But what can we prove?"

"No, take it to the next step. Say we *can* prove something. This late in the game, how's the town going to react? We're talking wallets and purses here, a mighty big balloon to pop, and we helped, Kim. That's the sad thing. We beat the drum for this guy. We contributed to the problem."

Kim nodded. "I think I'm feeling scared."

"You and me both."

"So what now?"

"We're backing away. This guy's a leaking gasoline truck, and when everything blows we don't want to be in league with him. We can cover the story afterwards, and then who can blame us?" With a few quick keystrokes and moves of the mouse, Nancy erased the headline from the front page of Tuesday's issue.

"Are you going to tell Travis Jordan what we know?"

"I'm sure it would be of interest to him, but—" Nancy stopped short, her brow crinkling.

"What?"

"The Harmons in Missoula . . ."

"Yeah?"

"Have they ever seen a picture of Brandon Nichols?"

SATURDAY MORNING, when I dialed the Macon ranch, Mrs. Macon didn't answer her own telephone. A machine did.

"Hello, you've reached the Ranch of the New Dawn. If you know your party's extension, you may dial it now. Otherwise, remain on the line and an operator will assist you. Another gathering of the human family will begin at 2 P.M. today, Saturday. See you there."

I remained on the line and got the operator. "Hello, Ranch of the New Dawn."

"Hello. This is Travis Jordan and I'd like to speak with Mrs. Macon." I didn't really have anything to say to her. I just wanted to find out if she could talk on her own telephone.

"Mrs. Macon is unavailable. Would you like to talk to her assistant?"

Mrs. Macon has an *assistant?* "Okay. Sure."

Hold music started playing. I about fell over.

"Hello, this is Gildy. How can I help you?"

"Gildy? Gildy Holliday?" Judy Holliday's granddaughter who used to wait on me at Judy's!

"Oh, is this Travis?"

"What are you doing up there?"

"Taking care of Mrs. Macon. You know, cooking, cleaning, answering the phone, helping her get around."

"Since when?"

"Two weeks ago. I'm lovin' it. It's a nice house to work in and the money's good."

"So how is the widow?"

She sighed. "Not very good. Sometimes she's there and sometimes she isn't—if you know what I mean."

That answer I was not expecting. "Are we talking about *Ethyl* Macon?"

"Yes."

"Who used to be married to Cephus Macon?"

"Sure."

"The lady who owns the ranch?"

"Well, the corporation owns it now, but she still lives here. It's a good thing because the stroke really put her down."

Was I on the right planet? "*What* stroke?"

"Haven't you heard? She had a stroke two weeks ago."

I had to recover from that blow before I could ask the next question. "What corporation?"

"Well, New Dawn. Brandon Nichols and the widow signed a deal before her stroke."

I was stunned. "Things happen fast up there."

She laughed. "You ought to see it."

"I'm planning on coming to the gathering this afternoon."

"Just pardon the mess. We're building, you know."

"HEY, KYLE. Want to go to a meeting?"

"You read my mind."

I picked him up and we headed for the ranch. "You don't have to say or do anything," I told him. "I just need you praying. This one's going to be tense."

THEY WERE BUILDING, all right, although at this point the new rest room and shower facility was still more mud and mess than building. The concrete slab was poured, the rough-in plumbing sticking up through it. Open ditches for sewer lines and drainage were all around it—barricaded for safety. A sign posted in front showed the architect's drawing of what it would look like. It was going to be nice, the envy of any national park.

Just in time too. We'd driven by George Harding's place on the way and quickly estimated a minimum of a hundred trailers and RVs parked in his still-developing RV park. As we came up the hill to the ranch and into the parking area, we estimated another hundred up there, not counting all the cars.

And now there were two circus tents side by side, joined like Siamese twins with the middle wall removed and the stage centered between them. Brandon Nichols—for that was his name for these folks—would now be performing in the round for a crowd approaching six hundred. Ushers with red shirts and walkie-talkies directed the flow of people coming in. A six-piece band—two guitars, bass, drums, keyboard, and a female vocalist—were performing feel-good songs like "Everything Is Beautiful," "Don't Worry, Be Happy," and "What a Wonderful World." Matt Kiley was serving as head usher now. We avoided him, finding two seats halfway back and in the middle. From there, we could see a roped-off corridor from the stage to a tent door that led to Mrs. Macon's house. That had to be where Elvis—excuse me, Nichols—would make his big entrance. By two o'clock, almost all the folding and plastic chairs were taken and the two tents were filled with the excited, preshow murmuring of the crowd.

I also heard babies and kids, lots of them, and noted that a good number were loose, running up and down the aisles, chasing and hollering, falling and crying. Apparently, the New Dawn Corporation hadn't yet thought about childcare, and many parents had chosen not to be responsible for their children. I smiled. I couldn't help it.

It was two o'clock and folks were still trickling in, still talking among themselves as they looked for seats. I kept on smiling.

The drummer in the band let out a drum roll.

"And now, ladies and gentlemen, brothers and sisters," announced the pretty, female vocalist, "please welcome our Messenger of the New Dawn, Brandon Nichols!"

The band started a peppy tune, the crowd rose to its feet applauding and cheering, and in came Nichols, decked out in white tunic and glittering gold jewelry, and sporting a brand-new wavy permanent. He waved and smiled as he ascended the stage, then held both hands high over his head like a fighter entering the ring. The applause went on for a good, long minute.

"So where's Sally Fordyce?" Kyle asked me.

Nichols was onstage alone, without Sally Fordyce in a biblical robe, or the Virgin Mary Donovan. The size of the crowd could have explained why we didn't see Dee Baylor or Adrian Folsom, but perhaps they weren't here, either. I recognized some of Armond Harrison's women sitting toward the front, but apart from them, this was a crowd of strangers.

Nichols sighted us in the crowd and his smile faded for an instant. He forced it back, flashing some teeth in our direction as he said to the crowd, "We've come far, haven't we?" The crowd cheered again.

We didn't cheer, but I did flash a smile back at him, and he must have caught the meaning in it. He had trouble getting started.

"Well, anyway, here we are, and, uh, we've got, we've got things to do today, yes sir, it's, uh . . . how are you all doing?"

After a few false starts he finally got his talk rolling, telling some stories, getting some laughs, and encouraging everyone about how wonderful they were. I didn't catch most of what he said. I was more interested in the edge in his voice, the tenseness in his walk, the way he kept drumming his fingers against his thigh. I looked around the tent. Was anyone else noticing the same thing? Possibly. A man leaned and whispered an observation to his wife and she nodded, watching Nichols intently.

I looked around. The kids were still loose. There were gaggles of latecomers still wandering around and chatting in the back.

Kyle's eyes were open, but his lips were moving vaguely. He was praying. Good. I did some praying myself, but never took my eyes off Nichols.

"And that's why we where with—why were whennit—" One more try. "That's why-we-were-where-we-were when . . ." He was flustered but kept going, his voice tense and his good humor strained. He was trying to promise us a better world, trying to convince us how such a dream was in our hands. He lost his train of thought and stopped cold. He backed up, picked it up again, hurriedly mumbled some point about how we could achieve heights our parents never dreamed of—

"I WANT IT *QUIET* IN HERE!" It was a sudden, alarming flash of temper. The people sitting near me reacted as if they'd been slapped. He pointed to some kids running up the aisle in front of him. "Whose children are these?" He didn't wait for an answer. "I want them out of here! NOW!"

A burly usher grabbed the arm of a little boy running by, whip-cracking him and hauling him in. The kid screamed bloody murder, kicking and punching as the usher carried him toward an exit. His mother popped up out of the vast, seated crowd and started hollering for him, tripping over chairs and feet trying to get out of her row.

"Take him out!" said Nichols, and then he pointed to some other children still running loose. "And those too! That girl, and that girl, and those two boys, and that one running back there! Get them out of my sight!"

Now there was a murmur in the crowd. People were looking at each other, whispering, concerned. *This isn't like Jesus,* I could imagine them saying. Kyle and I drank it all in. I caught myself smiling again and put my hand over my mouth.

Parents were popping up all over the crowd, working their way into the aisles, hollering, clapping, and finger-snapping at their kids. Some returned to their seats with their fussing children in tow. Many headed for the exits, indignant. For several minutes, two couples had to chase their kids around the tent and actually catch them before hauling them out, kicking and screaming.

Nichols pointed an accusing finger and sighted down it at some latecomers meandering around in the back. "And you people! You're late! Do you have any idea what message that sends to the rest of us, or to me? Now find your seats and *please stop your talking!*"

Now *this* was quite a show. Brandon Nichols stood there like iron, scanning the crowd with a seething expression, waiting for his orders to be fulfilled. When it was quiet—nervously, tensely quiet—he said, "I hope today will set a precedent in your minds. We may be under a tent, but this is not a circus, nor is it a playground, and I am not here to compete with unruly children and gabby latecomers!" He drew a breath. "Now. Where was I?"

He went on for a while, trying to throw in some jokes about the kid and latecomer problem but getting half-laughs for his trouble.

His talk came to an anticlimactic ending, and I sensed that all of us—including Nichols—were just as happy to have it over.

He moved on to the spectacle he was known for: going to people in the audience, apparently with no prior knowledge of who they were or what their problem was, and touching them. He ventured into the audience and started healing bad eyes, bad knees, bad lungs . . .

A short but very fat woman came running down the aisle, reaching out toward him. Matt Kiley and two other toughs waylaid her and started walking—and almost dragging—her back to her seat. "You haven't helped me!" she screamed at Nichols. "Look at me! Just look at me!"

He'd been trying to ignore her, but finally pointed at her and growled into the wireless microphone, "It's not my fault you're fat! You're fat because you lie around eating Big Macs and bonbons all day! Now sit down in however many chairs you have back there and be quiet. I've already touched you twice!"

He did his best to recover his momentum, working his way around the two big tents, naming and healing sicknesses and sometimes granting favors. I watched in fascination. This used to be easy for him, but not tonight. People were getting out of their seats, clogging the aisles, shooting out their hands to touch him. "Back in your seats, people! Get back in your seats!" He had to repeat the same order, and then his head swiveled and his hair flew out sideways as he angrily searched the room. "Where are my ushers?"

Matt and his heavies could only hold so many back before others broke through the line. They were wrestling with four or five petitioners when a young, trench-coated man broke through and almost tackled Nichols. Nichols spun around and gave the man a shove that floored him. "Don't touch me! Just keep your hands off, all right?" He beat away another hand reaching toward him. "Get away! I told you before, I don't heal procrastination! And you! If you want a million dollars, try working! What do you think I am, a genie?"

A man behind me quipped, "Welcome to earth, God!"

Kyle and I cracked up, careful to do it quietly.

WHEN MATT KILEY bumped up against me with an invitation to meet with Nichols, he made it sound as if I had no choice. I followed him into Mrs. Macon's living room to find Antioch's Messiah pacing and cursing, his brand-new perm getting a little frizzy. "Get out of here, Matt! If I need you I'll call you."

Matt didn't take kindly to being barked at, but he left us alone.

Justin Cantwell—that's what I now called him—went to Mrs. Macon's mini-bar and poured himself a drink. He did it so hurriedly I thought he'd spill it. "Travis, you are wasting your time, as always. There is nothing to discover in Nechville, nothing that you don't already know. You've already been there, believe me!"

"I have to follow it up. You ought to know that."

I thought he'd throw his drink at me, but he contained himself. "LIES! All you will hear is lies! Travis, they've done the same thing to you as to me: It's all *your* fault! *You're* the one who's out of step, out of God's will, full of sin, destined for hell! *You're* the one who has to give up his questions and fall in line! *You're* the one who has his whole life shredded to pieces—" He spread his arms and drawled like a southern preacher. "All, uh, in the nime of raaghteousness!"

"What are you so afraid of?"

He gulped from his drink and leered at me. "You think you can analyze me? There's no fear here, Travis! Not of you, not of the kid preacher you dragged along. Why'd you bring him, anyway? For backup?"

"Of course."

He just rolled his eyes at me. "Oh, I'm petrified!" Then he took another swallow. "I *am* upset, that's obvious. I'm upset at you and your refusal to let the slightest clue penetrate that skull of yours. I'm upset at all those people out there and all their crap!" He paced in tight little circles, his hand messing up his permed hair. "The people in George Harding's RV park think they should have equal time parking up here like the others, the people parking up here want lifetime spaces and special rest room privileges. They bring all their kids but nobody wants to take charge of them. Some don't like the music. Some want more music. The chairs are too hard. It's too hot in the tent. It's too cold. I've got a bunch of old people who won't sit anywhere but clear in the back and then complain because they can't hear. I've got another bunch who are always late—always!—and have a different excuse every time! I've got four different factions in a big fight over what to do with our Web site—and we don't even *have* a Web site!"

I smiled gleefully. I couldn't help it. "Having a little trouble there, Justin?"

"Why are you smiling? You did no better!"

I gave a little shrug. "I lasted longer. Hey, Justin, fifteen years in this town. You haven't even gotten to year one."

"I've got six hundred followers. Top that!"

"And no one to run the nursery."

He refilled his glass and paced toward the fireplace. "I'm *not* worried about it. It's only a wrinkle in the process. We'll iron it out." He rested his arm on the mantle and took another gulp. "But if you had *these* people in your church! They're asking for fancy cars now, and houses, and bags of money! Can you believe that? That same guy was back today, wanting me to heal him of procrastination. *Procrastination*, as if it's my fault he can't get his act together!"

"I thought you said you give them what they want."

"But they never stop *wanting!* I healed a guy's thyroid. He came back the next week wanting me to heal his baldness, and then he came back wanting me to help him play piano better, and this week he came back with three friends who want to be more sexually attractive! There's that other woman who wants me to make her thin but she won't stop eating, and this other jerk who wants to be rich but never worked a day in his life."

I could only shrug. "What did you expect?"

"They could grow up a little."

I feigned wide-eyed surprise. "They have to grow up? Really?"

He threw back his drink, drained it, and slammed down the glass. "You may as well stop gloating, Travis! They are *going* to fall in line! It's *going* to happen, believe me, and I hope you'll be around!" He went to the couch, sat down, then got right up again. His hands wouldn't stop moving, his fingers drumming. "Elise. One of the Cathedral's finest. Did she bother telling you how I reached out to her, tried to comfort her, tried to bring some minuscule token of human warmth into her life?"

"She did."

That answer seemed to mollify him, if only slightly. "I was trying to prevent another casualty."

I nodded. "I understand."

"Then why are you going to Nechville?"

I'd never seen that crazed look in his eyes before. It made me take note of how I could avoid the furniture and how far it was to the door. "Easy, Justin, easy. I'm here to talk to you first. You can save me the trip."

"You will *not* corner me!"

I threw up my hands, palms forward. "Okay, okay. Just be mindful of who's forcing whose hand here."

He leaned against the hearth again, glaring at the flames, silent and brooding. After a long, uncomfortable moment, he faced me directly, his lip drooping into a sneer. "So, *go* to Nechville! You'll recognize it. It's where we started, you and me." He looked away as if viewing it in his mind's eye. "Meet my daddy. Talk to my mom. Hear what a lie really sounds like. Maybe you'll finally wake up." Finally, he looked at me. "When you come back, we'll talk about it, have a drink, compare notes. I'll enjoy seeing your conversion." He pointed his finger at me. "Just be sure you find out *everything!*"

"Have you got your mom's phone number?"

He turned away. "It's your voyage."

I FOUND MY OWN WAY OUT to the front porch where Kyle was waiting. We moved toward the parking lot. Most of the cars were gone by now. The RV people were milling around their big vehicles, apparently discussing the meeting—their faces weren't this glum the last time I was here.

"What do you think?" Kyle asked.

"He's heading for rough water," I replied. "And you and I are part of the storm."

"*I* think we're being followed."

I had no reason not to look back. The moment I did, a hooded figure walked faster, moving toward us, looking down, face concealed.

We were near my car. "Let's get the doors open."

Kyle opened a rear door as an invitation, then got in the front passenger seat. I got behind the wheel and then beckoned to the hooded stranger to hurry and get in.

The figure slipped quickly into the back seat and closed the door. "Thank you. Please get me out of here."

I started the engine and got moving. "Better lie down."

She slumped over, the hood of her coat over her face.

It was Sally Fordyce. We knew her voice, and saw part of her face as she climbed in. It was bruised yellow, green, and black. One eye was swollen shut.

I reached over and locked all the doors with the autolock.

"Lie still," Kyle cautioned her without looking back. "We'll get you out of here."

"Please hurry."

"Just keep calm," I said. "We aren't going to stop, not for anybody."

We drove past the parking lot attendants in their bright orange vests. One eyed us suspiciously, his walkie-talkie close to his jaw. I couldn't be sure if he knew. I kept driving, not looking his way in case he tried to signal me. I turned down the driveway and added some speed. In a few minutes, we were out on the highway. I hit the accelerator.

Kyle turned. "Have you seen a doctor?"

She sat up but kept her hood around her face, embarrassed. "No. Brandon wouldn't allow it."

I could see her face in the rearview mirror. "You'd better see a doctor. I'm not kidding."

"I want to go home first."

Kyle was visibly angry. "Did he do this to you?"

She broke down weeping as she nodded. "He's going crazy."

"What about Mary Donovan?" I asked.

"She's okay." She could see us both giving her a second look and added, "She's not one of his lovers."

Kyle flopped back in his seat. "Lord, help us . . ."

"Oh, great!" I said.

"What?"

I was watching the rear window past Sally's battered face and saw blue lights flashing.

Kyle twisted around and looked back. "It's Henchle!"

Sally wailed, "NO! Don't stop!"

"Take it easy," I said, watching the image in my mirror.

She was desperate, frantic. "He's working for Brandon, can't you see that? He's trying to take me back."

"She's probably right," said Kyle.

I wanted more. "Sally, listen to me. That's a police officer back there. I have to stop."

"NO!"

"Then I need a good reason not to."

She dropped the hood from her face. I could see Kyle's face twist with horror and disgust.

"Trav, she's been bleeding."

I saw enough in the rearview mirror to turn my stomach.

"You think Brandon would want people to see this?" she asked.

Kyle took her side. "Brandon's the one who beat up Sally, so why's Henchle chasing *us?*"

Did I trust Brett Henchle? Not anymore. "Okay, okay, we won't stop. But I want witnesses." I grabbed up the cell phone lying next to the gear shift and handed it to Kyle. "Sally, what's your home phone number?"

She said her number and Kyle tapped it in.

"Tell Meg and Charlie we're taking Sally to the clinic and to meet us there. Tell them to bring some friends. And then call 911 and tell them we're transporting a beating victim to the clinic—

and you can tell them we're being escorted by Officer Brett Henchle." Then I prayed out loud, "And Lord, please help us."

I caught Sally's eye in the mirror. "Don't worry, Sally. I'm not stopping, not for anybody."

25

B RETT TURNED ON his siren. My heart was pounding and I
felt guilty—hey, I was disobeying an officer—but I kept going, driving under the speed limit. Sally whimpered and cowered
in the back seat, her hood over her face.

"Lord God, send your angels to help us!" Kyle prayed aloud,
and then said into the cell phone, "Hello, Mrs. Fordyce?" He was
too excited to talk slowly. He had to keep repeating himself.
"We're on our way now. We're on our way into town. No, we're
on the highway *west* of town, going *into* town. No, Sally's in the car
with us. She's in *our* car. We're going to the clinic. No, the *clinic*."

I could see Henchle through his windshield, talking on his radio. I rolled down my window and signaled with my arm for him
to come alongside. He gunned his big engine and pulled up beside
us, rolling his window down.

"Pull the car over, Travis!" he hollered, jabbing the air with his
finger.

"We're transporting an injury victim to the clinic!"

"*Pull the car over!*"

In my right ear, Kyle was talking to the 911 dispatcher. "We're
inbound on the highway west of town. Yeah, that's right. Officer
Henchle is—well, he's right beside us at the moment."

Henchle shouted over the roar of our engines, our tires, and the wind, "Stop and we'll transfer the victim to my vehicle!"

"She can't be moved!" Well, it was going to be the truth as far as I could help it.

"Pull over—" And then he swore, hitting his brakes, ducking his car behind us just in time to avoid an oncoming semi.

"This could get hazardous," I said, slowing down to thirty. We were approaching the edge of town.

"Now the *dispatcher's* telling us to stop," Kyle reported. Then he told the dispatcher, "Why don't we just all meet at the clinic? Huh? Well, could you call Officer Henchle and explain our situation? And tell him he doesn't need to be sounding that stupid siren. What?" He listened, then told me, "Henchle's called for a backup. Rod Stanton's going to block the road into town."

"I see him," I replied.

Rod's squad car was parked along the highway at the western edge of town, but something was a little odd. Cars were slowing in our lane, brake lights shining, and there were people standing in the street and gathering on either side. I gathered we weren't the only show in town. I slowed.

"Oh no," I said.

"Oh no," Kyle echoed.

"What?" said Sally, leaning forward between the front seats.

There was another Jesus standing in the middle of the highway, a long-haired, bearded man in white robe and sandals. He was blond, and I could imagine him being a yoga-humming, yogurt-eating surfer in California before coming to Antioch to try the messiah game. He appeared to have a whip in his hand and he was flailing each car as it passed, hollering and preach-pointing with his free hand. The first car passed him by, and then the next. The third stopped to listen and I could see the passengers snapping pictures through the closed windows. I was coming up behind them.

Stuck between False Christ Number Two and a cop! I couldn't stop with Henchle after me, but the right lane wasn't moving. A car came by us in the opposing lane, and then I pulled around, hoping to get by.

This latest Jesus put out his hand and stood right in front of me, ranting and raving about something.

"What's he saying?" Sally asked.

I rolled down my window. Brett Henchle was pulling up right behind me, his siren still blaring.

"Can we get through here, please?" I shouted, and I didn't sound nice. By now I had a real gripe against false christs messing up my life.

This one approached my window, whip in hand. "No motor vehicles, sir! Thou shalt not pollute the air, a gift from the Father's own hand!"

"We have to get to the clinic!"

"It is written, my town shall be a house of prayer for all nations, but you have turned it into a garbage dump!"

"This isn't your town, bub!"

"I'll get him to move," said Kyle, opening his door.

"What?" I said, but it was too late to stop him.

"Extinguish your engine, my beloved," said the christ, "and partake of the clean air God has—"

"Excuse me!" said Kyle, coming around the front of my car.

The phony Jesus brandished his whip as if defending himself. "Touch me not!"

Brett Henchle cut his siren and got out of his car.

Kyle held out a dollar. "See this here?"

"You would bribe the holy one of Israel?"

Some pilgrims were moving closer, cameras ready. A woman in pink shorts and a plastic sunhat touched him, stood there a moment, then turned to walk back to her friends. "I didn't feel anything," she reported.

Kyle held the dollar out, coaxing the christ toward the left side of the road. "Whose face is this, and whose inscription?"

The christ took the dollar and looked at it. "George Washington."

"You're standing in George's road, did you know that?"

The christ looked down at George's pavement.

"Render unto George the things that are George's . . ."

"Can I keep this dollar?" the christ asked.

"Okay, hold it," said Brett Henchle, striding from his car, pushing through the pilgrims, his club ready.

But a woman in a biblical outfit got there first, embracing the christ. "Son! My beloved son!"

The christ looked baffled. "Who are you?"

She stepped back and gave him the classic *mother* look, her hands on her hips. "I happen to be your mother!"

Wow. Another one.

Brett was getting close.

"You'd better go," Kyle told me.

I knew Kyle was sacrificing himself. I gave him a nod of thanks and eased forward through the gathering bodies.

"Travis! Don't you leave!" Brett warned, pointing his night stick at me.

I hollered out my window, "Just meet me at the clinic!" and kept going.

In my mirror I saw a four-way spat going between Brett Henchle, Kyle, the christ, and his long-lost mother. Then Rod joined up and they had a five-way going. Antioch was definitely an exciting place to visit.

I reached the clinic in two minutes. Charlie and Meg Fordyce were already there and took Sally inside. They'd gotten the word around. Morgan Elliott was also there, along with Jim Baylor, Joe and Emily Kelmer, and Bruce Hiddle. They all saw Sally's condition before her parents hurried her through the door, and now they gathered around me.

"Don't worry about a thing, Travis," said Joe.

Morgan put one arm around me, gave me a quick hug, and let go.

"We'll see whose side old Henchle's on," said Jim.

Brett Henchle screeched to a halt right beside my car and almost fell out, he was so upset. "Travis—" Then he regarded the others standing around me and balked a little. "Now folks, I wouldn't recommend getting involved in this."

"Come into the clinic and have a look at Sally," I said.

"First I'm taking you in!"

"No you're not," said Joe. "He was transporting an injury victim. It was an emergency."

"I'll be the judge of that!"

Rod Stanton drove into the parking lot of the clinic with Kyle sitting in the back of his squad car.

Brett nodded toward his backup and said, "It's over, folks. Now unless you all want to be arrested, you'll stand aside and let me do my duty."

"I think you'd better take a look at *Sally* and do your duty!" Jim demanded.

"Let's do it," said Rod.

Brett jerked his head around and glared at his deputy. "*I'm* giving the orders here, deputy!" Then he noticed Kyle wasn't handcuffed. "Where are his cuffs?"

"He's not under arrest." It wasn't just a statement of fact. It was an act of defiance, and I could tell Rod knew it. "He hasn't done anything wrong, and besides that, he helped me quell that second Jesus situation."

"Nobody's getting arrested here today," said Joe.

"Unless it's Mr. Brandon, the home wrecker and lover beater!" said Jim, jabbing his finger toward the ranch.

"Brett," I said, "I'm hoping your loyalty is still to the law and to this community. If so, I'm sure you can understand my not stopping—"

"You resisted an officer, Travis! You resisted an officer, fled an officer, disobeyed an officer, acted like a jerk, made an officer *look* like a jerk . . ."

"Don't give us that 'officer' business!" said Kyle. "You're not an officer of the law—you're an officer for Brandon Nichols and you know it!"

Brett turned deliberately and put his hand on his gun. "You want to say that again?"

Bruce interceded. "Officer, I think Kyle is asking you to clarify where your loyalties lie: with the law, and justice, and the good of this community, or with Brandon Nichols. Just who's calling the shots here?"

Brett just stood there, stuck.

Rod tapped Brett's arm with the back of his fingers. "C'mon. Let's talk to Sally and take it from there."

For an agonizing moment, the only sound was Brett's labored, angry breathing.

Finally, abruptly, Brett started toward the door of the clinic, but not without barking a few "last word" orders. "I want this parking lot cleared! If you've no business here, then clear out! Now!"

I tagged Kyle and Morgan. "Let's get to a phone."

I HELD THE RECEIVER to my ear and dialed the number I got from information. "Come on, now, time's getting tight."

I was sitting in Morgan's office at the Methodist church. Morgan and Kyle were sitting in the church office behind the foyer, listening in on a speakerphone, its microphone muted. We all listened as the telephone rang at the other end once, twice, three times, four times—

"Hello?" The voice sounded grumpy, gravelly, and a little slurred.

"Hello, is this the Cantwell residence?"

"Yeah, who's this?" The man could have been drunk. It was hard to understand him.

"Hello, I'm Travis Jordan. I live in Antioch, Washington. I suppose you've read about us in the papers—"

"No."

"Oh. Well, I'm calling to speak to Lois Cantwell."

"She's not home right now." This guy could never get a job telephone soliciting, that was for sure. He could get a job *discouraging* solicitors.

"Well then, is this Reverend Ernest Cantwell?"

"Yeah, who's this?"

I told him who I was again. "I think we might have a mutual acquaintance. Would you by any chance have a son named Justin?"

There was silence at the other end, but I could hear a labored breathing.

"Are you there?"

"I don't have a son named Justin, no."

"Any relation at all named Justin?"

"No."

"Do you have a son?"

"No!" The tone of his voice told me otherwise.

"Well . . . I happen to know a Justin Cantwell who hails from Nechville, Texas, and has a mother named Lois."

"I don't know any Lois, either."

Oh? "Uh, excuse me, sir, but you just told me Lois wasn't home right now. I'm calling a number listed under both your names, Ernest and Lois Cantwell."

"Don't call this number again!"

Click.

I hung up and sat back to wait for Kyle and Morgan to journey through the church sanctuary and join me. As they entered the office, I looked up at them for their reaction.

Morgan shrugged a little. "I guess I'm not surprised."

Kyle patted his pockets symbolically. "Anybody got change for airfare?"

"I could sell my mother's old watch," Morgan quipped.

"GILDY!"

The scream rattled the house and made Gildy Holliday jump in her seat. She was already nervous and frightened. She'd been working at the quaint desk just off the kitchen, writing checks to pay the help and compiling a grocery list, when she heard the crashes, tinkles, and rips coming from the guest room. That was Nichols's room now.

He'd decided the main house was more to his liking than the guest cottage, the big kitchen more practical for his parties, the larger, more elegant guest bedroom more conducive to his romantic flings.

But the arrangement also put him under the same roof as Gildy with no walls or bars between them. She didn't answer him, but clicked off her computer, threw the corporate checkbook into a drawer, and grabbed her coat. It was time to get out of there.

Brandon Nichols was moving through the house like a man possessed, his footsteps quick and pounding, his breath chugging. She headed for the back door—

He was there, his eyes like those of a stalking panther, his hair dangling like black lightning bolts across his brow. He moved toward her.

She ran behind her desk to keep it between them.

"Call Brett Henchle!" The voice was low and sinister. "My room's been vandalized!"

She picked up the telephone receiver on her desk but hesitated to dial, staring at him.

His eyes were darting about the room as if watching a swarm of tiny, invisible demons. "Torn up! Broken! Everything a disaster, a *disaster!*" He noticed she hadn't dialed. "Well, *call them!* Somebody's been here! It's a senseless, despicable act of hatred! We have enemies, Gildy! They're trying to destroy us!" He stopped in the middle of the room, wiping drool from his mouth with the back of his hand. "Trying to destroy us. Hate. It's everywhere, all around. Notify the staff! We're going to heighten security tonight! No one comes or goes. We're locking the place down."

"I'll tell them," she said weakly, still holding the receiver but not calling.

Now he seemed dazed by his own anger, scanning the room, slowly turning as if searching. "That bedroom is swimming with evil. It's crawling. It's alive. I can't sleep there anymore."

"You can sleep in the third bedroom. No one's using that room right now."

He nodded, his eyes still crazy. "Good. Don't call the cops." She put the telephone down. "They don't need to know. Nobody needs to know. Nobody." He moved toward the hall as she stood behind her desk watching his every move. "You can't trust them anyway. You can't trust cops. They stand by and let horrible things happen to you, did you know that? They stand by . . . just stand by . . ."

"I need to check on Mrs. Macon."

He nodded. "Go ahead. Go." Then he laughed, apparently at himself. "Don't mind me. I'm just a child of the devil."

He headed down the hall to his room and closed the door behind him. She heard him roar like a madman. There was another crash. A piece of furniture hit the door. The house quivered. A window broke.

Gildy buttoned up her coat, went straight to Mrs. Macon's room, knocked lightly, then went in. In a matter of minutes, she emerged again, carrying Mrs. Macon, now wearing a robe and wrapped in a blanket. The widow's eyes were open, but she seemed oblivious to the fact that she was being carried hurriedly down the hall and through the kitchen. Gildy went out the back door, put the widow in her car, and drove away.

KYLE, MORGAN, AND I put our heads together, pooled our bank accounts, and called the travel agent. She could get me into Dallas/Fort Worth where I could rent a car to drive to Nechville, and fit it into our waning budget *if* I flew out of Spokane that night and out of Seattle at one in the morning. I had to brace myself before agreeing, and then it was settled. Kyle left for home. I remained with Morgan in her office.

"What is it?" she asked.

After months of playing Justin Cantwell's strange game, things were becoming clear. "I know what I'm going to find in Nechville."

She nodded.

"You know what Marian said when we found out she had lung cancer?" I was still sitting at Morgan's desk. She sat down across from me and listened as she always did. "I didn't know what to say.

I didn't know what to tell her or what to do, and she just said, 'Travis, take me ice-skating.'" The vision flashed across my mind: We were kids in our twenties, I had my arm around her waist and her hand in mine, and the world was rushing by us—we were in our forties, on the ice again, and she was giving me that one, special look.

A wave of emotion hit me and I could hardly speak my confession. "I could barely remember how. It'd been so long. . . ."

Morgan heaved a troubled sigh. "I should have gone fishing with Gabe. He asked me so many times, but always ended up going with his buddies. I had to stay here, studying, fulfilling some counseling appointments I could have scheduled for another time. Hey, it was ministry. I was doing it for God. And now I've never been able to understand why I never got it through my head: I was his first choice for a fishing buddy. His first choice, and I never went!"

I found a smile somewhere, passed it on to her, and wiped the corners of my eyes. "I think Marian and I enjoyed ministering together. We lived it, we talked about it, we spent our days and nights immersed in it. But now I'm afraid . . ."

"Mm-hm."

"I'm afraid that, that maybe it was the *ministry* that defined us, that somehow it was *church* that summarized what we were. We were the program, the preaching, the Sunday school, the youth choir, the bus, the building, but were we ever *us?* When Marian died, it hit me so hard and so cruel: all the church stuff was still there—the service schedule, the song sheets, the visitation committee, it was all still there. But Marian was gone. The church stuff would always be there in one form or another, always needing, always demanding—but there was only one Marian, only one chance to know her, and that was over.

"You know, we prayed around the clock for Marian's healing. The whole church fasted and we had people assigned to twenty-four one-hour shifts. Dee and her friends tried to speak a healing into existence. I got a note from somebody who said they had a dream: If I'd dip Marian seven times in the baptistry she'd be healed." My little laugh was sad. "I almost tried that.

"I took her to some faith healing meetings. You know the kind: You go in there and some loud, flamboyant evangelist with big hair starts laying hands on people and they start falling over while the organ player runs his finger down the keyboard. It was strange, I guess, kind of hokey. But when you're grasping . . .

"I believe God could have healed Marian. I still believe the Lord heals—I mean, look at Joe Kelmer. *Bang!* Healed, just like that.

"But can you figure God out? All the things we tried, all the faith and the methods . . . and the shadows on her x-rays just kept getting bigger, kept spreading. They took out her left lung and the shadow spread to her right, and then the cancer started popping up other places.

"I think she knew—I mean, clear back when she wanted to go ice-skating again. She always had a special intimacy with God, an inside line or something. I think she knew. But she stuck by me: She hoped right along with me, and we fought together against the whole idea of her dying, and we both tried to faith our way out of it. But we, uh, we finally got a clue—or *I* got a clue. God has his ways. He just plain has his ways. By the time she died it was almost a nonevent, we were so ready for it.

"She was holding my hand, and I could feel the moment she slipped away. It was June 12, 1997, just five months after we saw those first x-rays." I drew a deep breath and sighed it out, bringing my recollections to a close. "God will do what God will do."

Morgan studied me a moment, then asked, "Do you still trust him?"

I had no trouble nodding yes.

"Then you're one up on Justin Cantwell."

That came as a revelation, and it made me chuckle. "When did *that* happen?"

She had a playful delight in her eyes. "Sometime after Justin got here. As you said, God has his ways. Maybe it took a bitter man *not* having to show you what you *did* have—and to show me." She reached across the desk and took my hand as tears filled her eyes. "Jesus was hiding, that's all. Hiding in the memories—all the places you've been, all the people you've known, all the paths he's walked with you, whether you understood it all or not." She paused to reflect, then told me, "What Justin Cantwell wouldn't give for just one good memory."

I PACKED A SMALL BAG with enough clothes and necessities for an overnight in Texas, and drove to Spokane to catch an eleven o'clock flight to Seattle. The flight from Seattle to Dallas/Fort Worth would arrive around six-thirty in the morning, Dallas time. The drive to Nechville would take about three hours, which meant I'd be arriving in that little town just in time for Sunday morning services. Needless to say, I wouldn't be sleeping much.

ARMOND HARRISON finally left Anderson's Furniture and Appliance after bickering over the price of a television and whether or not the stand should be included or be extra. Now Don Anderson was alone in his big glittery store, surrounded by washers, dryers, televisions, CD players, VCRs, DVD players, all shapes and sizes of radios, telephones, toys, CDs, cassettes . . .

And he *had* to get a handle on his new ability. He had to control it, channel it, rein it in, and use it in some orderly, controlled fashion. If he didn't . . .

He could hear the lights overhead humming at him like a swarm of bees, so loud it was hard to hear someone talking to him from across the store. Well, okay, he could always stand closer to someone talking.

When he started up a kerosene heater to demonstrate for a customer, it roared like a toilet refilling after a flush. He had to ask the customer to repeat himself a few times. Well, it only made that noise when it was running. He could always turn it off—and hope he'd never need the heat.

But the CDs—oh, the *CDs!* All he had to do now was touch the plastic cases and they would start playing in his head, right through the shrink-wrap! He put one of the girls in charge of stocking the CD rack and left it to her to sell them as well.

And now there were the radios! He could hear them all over the room, wailing and thumping the rock stations, crooning the easy listening stuff, or garbling out the news and sports, no less than fifty of them at once—and they were all turned *off!* Maybe he could tune them all to the same station, something sweet and relaxing. He went to the first radio, a portable CD/Cassette/AM-FM Virtual Surround Sound unit. All he did was touch the tuning knob and he could hear the station as if he were wearing headphones.

He twirled the knob until he heard the kind of music they play in elevators. Ah. He could live with that. He went to the next unit, another portable stereo, but this one bigger, with more bells and whistles. He set the station.

Hey, this was going to work!

See there, Don? One step at a time! We'll get a handle on this—I hope, I hope!

Then it occurred to him. Sure, there were no less than fifty radios on display in the store. He could get to them easily. But there were at least a hundred more in unopened boxes stacked under the shelves and in the back room, and he could hear them too!

Oh, man. This was going to be a long night.

As he headed for the counter for a carton knife, he passed by the washing machines. Oh no, now what? It sounded like a squadron of B-17s flying overhead. He leaned on a washer—

The *rumble* made him jump. He could feel it all through his body.

"NO!" He faced the washing machine, staring it right in the control knob, and pleaded with it, "You're not running! You're not turned on! You're not even plugged in!"

It rumbled at him. Its companion dryer rumbled too. The whole row of washers and dryers rumbled like circus lions in a cage.

He backed away. The rumbling quieted a little. They seemed

to be consulting one another, rumbling and mumbling. Could he live with this too?

"You don't scare me," he muttered.

They RUMBLED at him.

It scared him to death.

MATT KILEY burst through the door of his hardware store, startling Bev Parsons, his soft-spoken right-hand gal. "How's it going?"

She was checking out a customer, and held her peace until the customer stepped out the door. Then she showed a sour side he'd never seen before. "If you expect me to run this store all by myself, I expect to be paid accordingly."

He brushed past her. "You're not running it all by yourself!"

She was never one to be forward, but today she was angry enough. She followed directly behind him, down the aisle past the lawn sprinklers and garden sprayers, talking to his back, but getting it said. "I've kept track of the hours I've been here running this whole operation while you've been up at the ranch, and let me tell you, I might as well own this place!"

He stopped and turned so fast she ran into him. "You think you're the only one who has problems? If anything happens to Brandon Nichols, we could all be out of work!" He continued toward the back of the store.

She followed him. "What do you mean?"

"I mean he has enemies! Somebody came right into the house and trashed his room!" He reached the gun counter. "Barney!"

"Yeah?" Barney Myers replied from the automotive section.

"Let's have the key to the gun cabinets!" He turned to Bev. "Happens every time. Somebody starts doing the right thing and somebody else decides they have to harass him. Well nobody's gonna harass Brandon Nichols, not if I've got anything to say about it!"

Barney brought the key, and Matt opened the gun display case. He reached for a semiautomatic pistol, ripped off the price tag, and slipped it in his coat pocket. "Get me two cases of 9 mm rounds, those hollow points, and two boxes—no, make that four boxes of 12-gauge shells, 00 buckshot." Barney selected the ammo cartons while Matt took a shotgun from the rack behind the counter.

Bev's voice quavered with fear. "But you can't just shoot somebody!"

Matt took the boxes of shells from Barney. "Well they don't have to break into Brandon's house either, now do they? Thanks, Barney." He hurried around the counter and up the aisle again. "They don't have to get near him, they don't have to come on the property, they don't have to come nose to nose with me. It's all up to them. Close up tonight, same as usual. I'll be back sometime tomorrow."

26

I WAS DRIVING across Texas in the early morning, covering miles and miles under a golden dawn, and feeling continually deceived by the crumpled, wrongly folded road map on the seat beside me. Maps of Texas still have to fit in your car, so they make Texas look smaller than you first assume. Twice I was sure I'd missed a town or a turn, only to find it thirty or forty more miles down the road. Nechville looked like a quick trip, but it was three hours at legal speeds, as promised.

The lady who rented me my car told me I would probably smell Nechville before I saw it, and she was right. At first, I thought something in my car was overheating or shorting out, but I soon discovered it was just the wind coming through my vents after blowing through Nechville's stockyards and oil rigs. It smelled like a herd of cattle tarring a roof, the scent of manure and ammonia interlaced with the stench of black crude. Undoubtedly the people of Nechville had long ago learned to live with it, since the town wouldn't be there at all without it.

I drove by the stockyards, the ground trampled and fertilized to a thick, gamy black under hundreds of hooves, and saw the oil wells on the right and the left nodding slowly, emphatically, yes, yes, yes. Slowing to twenty-five miles per hour, I passed the city limit sign—

NECHVILLE, population 2,125. It was not a bad little town at first glance, almost a Texas version of Antioch. They had a feed store, a tractor and implement dealer, a True Value Hardware, even a local appliance store—only it wasn't Pepto-Bismol pink.

So here I was, a stranger in a strange town in the middle of the vast state of Texas and feeling like it. Now what?

I pulled over at a service station to top off the tank and check the yellow pages of a phone book. As I flipped the phone book open, I was praying for help and guidance. I could feel butterflies in my stomach.

Churches, churches . . .

I would know it when I saw it. It wouldn't be Catholic, Methodist, Lutheran, or Baptist. I was guessing it would be—how shall I say it?—hyper-Pentecostal. Judging from Justin Cantwell's bitterness and the reception I got from the Reverend Ernest Cantwell, it would be stridently, strictly, inflexibly, legalistically, pharisaically Pentecostal. There would be a long list of complex, tangled, sometimes contradictory, often hypocritical, but absolutely essential requirements and taboos defining what it meant to be a Christian. I was familiar with that kind of church and glad I never had to attend one. I was guessing that Justin Cantwell did.

My finger stopped on a promising possibility: The Nechville Church of the True Gospel.

"Good morning and praise God," said the cheerful male voice. "True Gospel."

"Hi. What time is your service this morning?"

"Sunday school's at nine forty-five and morning worship's at eleven."

"Is Pastor Cantwell preaching?"

"Oh, absolutely. You can't hold him back. Think you can join us?"

"I'll be there."

"Well you're gonna hear the truth. That's what we're all about. And your name is?"

I said "Thanks a lot" cheerfully and hung up. They'd picked the right guy to answer the phone. If I were them, I sure wouldn't want the pastor doing it.

I checked my watch. It was just before ten, so I had an hour. I asked the man at the cash register how I might find the church and he drew me a map. Then I returned to my car and drove through town in no particular hurry. I didn't want to attend Sunday school because I'd be sitting in the adult Sunday school class where I'd have to introduce myself to everyone else, and most likely Reverend Cantwell would be teaching. I wanted a chance to get a feel for the place first. Now *I'd* be the timid visitor sitting in the back.

What happened next had to be the gentle, guiding hand of God. I was driving by a quaint, wide-porched home on Main Street and spotted a sign in the yard: H. K. Sullivan, M.D. I got a hunch, I felt in my spirit that I should stop, and so I did.

Parked across the street, I took a moment to rethink it. I didn't know how many doctors were in this town, probably not many. Whenever and however Justin Cantwell got those scars on his arms, this doctor might know about it, or perhaps know the doctor who did. There was a car in the driveway. I thought I saw someone in the backyard. It couldn't hurt to knock on the door and ask.

DR. HOWARD SULLIVAN was in his seventies, dressed in work jeans and a tee shirt advertising Imodium A–D. He sat beside Mrs. Sullivan on their couch while I sat opposite them, waiting for the doctor's verdict on the photographs I'd handed him.

"So now he's claiming to be Jesus," he muttered.

"He's allowing people to believe and say that about him," I qualified.

The doctor laid the photos out side by side on the coffee table, studying them. His wife held his arm, her eyes troubled.

"There's a whole lot I could tell you about him, but I can't."

I closed my eyes and sighed in disappointment and frustration. *Don't be rude*, I reprimanded myself. "You do understand my situation?"

He nodded. "I sure do. More than you think. And I want to help you, but I can't tell you anything without the Cantwells' consent. That's just the way I do things."

"Is his name Justin Cantwell?"

The doctor nodded. "I can tell you that. Yes."

"Was he ever a patient of yours?"

The doctor nodded again but said nothing.

"Did you treat the wounds in his forearms?"

I didn't get a response. Mrs. Sullivan pulled her husband's arm and said, "I don't think you'd better go any further."

"I did," said the doctor.

"Honey, now that's all!" she warned him, and then she told me, "This is a small, close-knit little town and we watch out for our neighbors. If we violated any trust, we wouldn't survive here."

"Talk to the Cantwells," said the doctor, picking up the photos and handing them to me. "Please. I *want* to help you. I *want* to bring this whole sad story to a close."

"They'll be in church pretty soon," said Mrs. Sullivan, looking at the mantel clock. "That would be a good place to meet them."

"He'd have to behave himself in front of his congregation."

She jabbed him. "Honey!" Then she told me, "You may not get far with Pastor Cantwell, but I think Mrs. Cantwell will be sympathetic. Work on her if you can."

"All I need is their consent. I need to hear from them that I can talk to you."

"It's the Church of the True Gospel, is that right?"

"Over on Dunbar Street, two blocks down, turn left, three blocks on the right."

IT WAS AN OLD BRICK BUILDING with thick concrete steps and a blue neon "JESUS SAVES" sign bolted to the top of the facade. Worshipers were gathering, moving from the gravel parking lot, approaching from either direction on the sidewalk, dressed in their Sunday best, toting their Bibles. It might mean different things to different folks in different parts of the country, but, for these people in *this* part of the country, they looked very religious.

I was parked across the street. I checked my tie in the rearview mirror—it was black; very safe. I ran a comb through my hair—recently cut, with ears and collar uncovered. I'd already given my face a once-over with a small travel razor. I had a suit coat ready on a hanger and a good-sized Bible on the seat. Hopefully, I would look righteous enough not to disturb anyone.

I stepped out of my car, slipped into my suit coat, straightened and adjusted everything, and crossed the street, returning whatever smile or greeting came my way. The piano and organ were already playing the prelude. I followed the other folks up the front steps. Passing through the door, I noticed a yardstick tacked to the doorpost for measuring the height of hemlines. I'd heard about that practice, but this was the first time I had actually seen it.

Being a Pentecostal, I gravitate toward the livelier kind of worship. I'm not a dancer, jumper, or roller, but I like a good tune, a catchy rhythm, and lyrics that express how I feel about my Savior. This church had them. The worship was great—a little protracted and repetitious for my taste, but nobody else seemed to mind, so neither did I. The young fellow leading worship did plenty of jumping, and when he spoke I recognized the cheerful voice I'd heard on the telephone.

But I wasn't prepared for the pastor, the haggard, graying wraith sitting in a wheelchair on the platform. He clutched a huge Bible in blue-veined, seemingly palsied hands and glared at everyone. Sure, he smiled frequently, raised his hands in praise, sang the songs, and shouted Hallelujah, but his eyes never lost that steely glare and he never lost that weird hunch either, like a buzzard perched in a dead snag waiting for his next meal to die. This was Reverend Ernest Cantwell? This was Justin's daddy? I had food for thought already.

They went through announcements and some testimonies, and then it was the reverend's turn to preach. When he raised his arms to grip and propel his chair wheels, I saw that big buzzard again, ruffling his wings, ready to fly. He wheeled up to a specially made, lowered pulpit, set his big Bible on it, and then gaffed our attention with those eyes.

"I would that you were either cold or hot," he began, and I rec-ognized the voice I heard on the telephone, a coarse, ragged, booming voice you didn't trifle with, slurring the words. "But since you are lukewarm, and neither cold nor hot, I will spew you out of my mouth!"

"Amen," they said. "That's right."

"The axe is already laid to the roots, and every plant that does not bear fruit will be cut down and thrown into the fire!"

"Save us, Lord! Amen."

"I looked throughout the nation for a righteous man, and I found none! There was none righteous, no, not one, and my an-ger was kindled against my people and it repented me that I had made them and set them on a hill, but woe to them, for now that hill will be brought low!"

"Amen!"

"So come out, my people! Come out from among them and be ye separate, for great is their destruction, and their destruction is nigh at hand, and the smoke of their destruction shall go up like the smoke of a furnace forever and ever!"

The locomotive started rolling, leaving the station, gaining speed . . .

"Our nation is ripe for judgment!"

"Amen!"

"Our towns and our cities are ripe for judgment!"

"Amen!"

"The church is ripe for judgment!"

"Yes!"

"And *you* are ripe for judgment!"

"Amen! That's right!"

"Did you hear me? I said *you* are ripe for judgment!"

"Lord save us!"

"*You* are ripe for judgment!"

"Amen!"

"I said *YOU* are ripe for judgment!"

With a steady, pounding cadence he went down the universal

list of vices, added a few of his own—sports on Sunday and cable TV—and condemned them all. He warned the President, he warned Congress, he warned Hollywood, and he warned the game shows and soap operas. He dealt in depth with the horrible things God had planned for sinners like us and told us he'd learned how hot hell was—at least ten times the heat of a nuclear blast, the difference being, it lasts and lasts. With help from the song leader he took off his suit coat and then wiped the sweat from his brow. He kept going, hot and heavy, wheeling from one side of the platform to the other, his weak and faulty arms swatting invisible bees, his voice bouncing off the walls.

For forty minutes he scared the bejeebers out of us, and when our terror of God and judgment had reached just the right level, he brought Jesus into it, rolling along at such a clip that "Jesus" was "Jesus-uh" and "judgment" was "judgment-uh." The place was rocking with the rhythm of his words: He'd say it, we'd answer; he gave it, we took it; he shouted, we praised; back and forth, back and forth, yea and Amen. Finally, he gave the invitation and folks began moving to the altar to pray as Sister Cantwell, white-haired and serene, softly played "Almost Persuaded" on the organ.

So this was Sister Lois Cantwell. I had to wonder about her. She seemed so gentle, so small, such a contrast to the fiery, rough-hewn reverend. She was dark-skinned too, probably of Hispanic or Native American descent. Recalling Mrs. Sullivan's advice, I thought I might approach her first.

I got my chance as the service ended and the refreshed and rededicated saints filed out. "Sister Cantwell?"

She was still seated at the organ, just saying good-bye to a sister in the Lord. She extended her hand. "Hello. And you are?"

"Travis Jordan. I was wondering if I might have a word with you and your husband?" I dropped a hint. "I'm from Antioch, Washington."

That didn't faze her. "My, you're far from home, aren't you?"

"Yes, ma'am."

"So what brings you here?"

I braced myself, lowered my voice, and said, "Justin Cantwell."

That did faze her. She placed her hand over her heart and I thought she'd stopped breathing. "Who are you?"

"I'm Travis Jordan," I repeated. "I'm a schoolteacher from Antioch, Washington. I was also a minister in the Pentecostal Mission church for over fifteen years."

"Have you seen my son?" she nearly whispered.

"Yes, I have. He's in Antioch. We've visited on many occasions."

She was obviously starving for news, any news. "Is he all right? What's he doing?"

"Hello!" With a booming, gravelly, slurred voice, the reverend rolled up. "Ernest Cantwell!" He offered his bent, half-limp hand. "And who might you be?"

"Travis Jordan," I said, knowing his toothy smile was going to vanish the moment I said more.

Sister Cantwell said it first. "He knows our son." The reverend seemed perplexed. She further clarified, "Justin."

The smile vanished and that glare intensified. "So what are you doing here?"

With my eyes I indicated that other people were still around. "Is there someplace we could talk privately?"

"What about?"

"About Justin," his wife whispered with a plea in her voice.

"Conway!" the reverend hollered, and a man near the door immediately turned our way. He was big and had those cold, animal eyes required of any good tavern bouncer. *Oh brother*, I thought, *I'm going to get thrown out of here.*

"Ernest . . ." Sister Cantwell pleaded.

Reverend Cantwell spun his chair around and started wheeling toward the center aisle, zigzagging between folks visiting and praying. "Conway, open up the office. We have to meet with this, this, whatever he is."

I stood there. Sister Cantwell gave me a gentle touch on the arm, prodding me. "Please."

I weaved past the petitioning saints and down the center aisle with Sister Cantwell right behind me and Conway the bouncer dead ahead. He had opened a door on the left side of the foyer and now stood there while the reverend wheeled inside. I followed the reverend, and the reverend's wife followed me.

We were in the pastor's office. He wheeled himself behind his desk and hollered to Conway from there, "You want to hang around, Conway? I might need you."

Conway nodded a slow, insider's kind of smile, and closed the office door as a sheriff would close a jail cell.

"Have a seat," said Cantwell.

His wife already occupied one of the two available chairs. I planted myself in the other, my Bible and valise in my lap.

The reverend glared at me a moment, then at his wife, then snapped at me with a flicker of his hand, "So, speak!"

I reached into my valise and pulled out the photos and news clippings again. This was getting to be a routine. I passed the photos to Mrs. Cantwell, explaining who I was, where I was from, and what was going on up there—and how a young man had come to town acting like some kind of new, improved messiah. At first sight of the photos, Mrs. Cantwell gasped, her hand over her mouth. Tears filled her eyes.

"Conway!" the reverend yelled, and the door burst open. Conway looked ready to pummel me. "I want to see these pictures!"

Conway walked right in front of me, grabbed the pictures from Mrs. Cantwell, and handed them over to the reverend.

"Stick around," the reverend ordered, and Conway took his place against the door like an obedient, 280-pound Doberman. Cantwell studied the photos one at a time, his hands inept and fumbling. Then he threw them spitefully on his desk. "So what?"

My eyes drifted to a picture on the bookshelf: Reverend and Mrs. Cantwell in their earlier years. Reverend Cantwell was standing.

Cantwell didn't appreciate my looking at it. He reached over and tried to grab it, fumbling the picture frame so that it fell face down with a loud smack. The cuff of his shirt sleeve was unbuttoned. I saw a jagged scar on his forearm, but looked away before he knew it. Conway stepped in and positioned the picture safely on the shelf, face down.

"Is this man your son?" I asked, indicating the photos.

"Our son is dead."

Mrs. Cantwell groaned in anguish. "Ernest, don't say that!"

He only reaffirmed it. "Justin is dead as far as I'm concerned. He's dead to this house, dead to this church, dead to this town. We don't want to see him again." He used both hands to gather up the pictures. "And we don't appreciate your bringing him back!" He handed the photos to Conway, who handed them back to me.

"Sir, I'm not so sure I want him in *my* town either. I'm not here to defend him or meddle with the past—"

"Then don't!"

Mrs. Cantwell pleaded, "Ernest—"

He pointed a jagged finger at her. "And you be still! I've said all I'm going to say about this. Conway, show this man to the door!"

Conway opened the office door and, valuing my life, I took my cue. I packed up my photos and clippings and got out of there. I could hear Mrs. Cantwell sobbing as I left, and her husband barking at her, "Stop that! Just stop that right now! He's dead! *He's dead!*"

Conway not only showed me to the door, he accompanied me clear across the street to my car. I scanned the surrounding street and sidewalks. Some people were still around, meaning there would be witnesses if this guy clobbered me. Unfortunately, they seemed to be making it a point not to look in our direction. We reached the car and I pulled the keys from my coat pocket.

"Uh, listen, Conway, I'm not trying to stir up trouble. I *have* trouble and I'm trying to get some help. If you know anything—"

"Let me give you some advice." These were the first words I'd heard Conway speak. "Go home and take care of your own problems, and don't bring 'em back here again." He lowered his voice but didn't sound any kinder. "Justin Cantwell is pure poison. That's all you need to know. I ran him in several times and I never saw anybody come closer to being the devil than that kid."

"You ran him in?"

"I'm the cop around here."

"Oh." That did not make me feel safer.

"He's probably told you some really juicy tales about us, but he's a liar. He'll lie to you like you wouldn't believe. Everything he says is a lie."

I thought of the scars on Cantwell's arms and asked, "How did Pastor Cantwell end up in a wheelchair?"

"Car wreck, six years ago." He jerked his thumb toward my car door. I unlocked the door and climbed in. Conway held the door open so he could deliver his final message. "Get out of town, Mr. Jordan. Get out fast, and don't come back, you got it?"

I nodded and started my engine. "Got it."

So ended my visit to the Nechville Church of the True Gospel.

BUT MY VISIT to the *town* of Nechville was not about to end so abruptly. Morgan, Kyle, and I had assumed I would actually be able to talk with someone and would need the time, so we included one night's stay at a motel in the budget. I'd flown all night and driven all morning and I was tired. I was going to spend that money. I found a little motel at the far end of town and got a room. It was cheap but it was clean, and the bed was more than adequate for a man whose eyes were burning for sleep and whose heart was pained with frustration.

I lay there on top of the bedspread, my wrist on my forehead, my eyes closed. The glaring expression and harsh voice of Reverend Cantwell kept replaying in my mind, as well as the tears and timid pleadings of Justin Cantwell's mother. If "Justin Cantwell" was the question, the answer was sealed behind her tears and her husband's defiance. I saw in her a mother mourning for a wayward son; I saw in him a dog growling, barking, and lathering from inside a parked car.

"Precious Lord," I prayed, "there's got to be a way."

After fifteen minutes of stewing and praying, I opened my eyes. I was in Justin Cantwell's hometown. Until Cantwell himself had an overwhelming change of heart—something on the order of getting *saved*—I would never be closer to the truth than I was right now. I was nearly exhausted but could not sleep because *I had to know.*

And I would know. God help me, before I left this town, I would know.

I knelt by the bed and, in prayer, grabbed the hem of Jesus' garment. "Dear Lord, You've brought me this far. Please open the door."

"HI. I'm sorry to disturb you again, but if we could just talk—"

The doctor's wife didn't wait for me to finish pleading. The moment she saw me, she swung the door open and invited me inside.

Dr. Sullivan was sitting in a comfortable chair across from the sofa, still wearing his work jeans and tee shirt. He acknowledged me with his eyes and a warm smile but didn't say anything. I gathered he was waiting to get a reaction from me.

Sister Lois Cantwell was sitting on their couch, clutching a crumpled, wet handkerchief in her hands and weeping. The moment our eyes met, her sobs broke forth again and she covered her face. "Oh, praise God, praise God!"

"I would say so," said Dr. Sullivan. He extended his hand toward another chair. "Have a seat. It's good to see you again."

"*Really* good," his wife agreed.

I sat across from Sister Cantwell. Mrs. Sullivan sat beside her, her hand on Sister Cantwell's, and softly explained, "Lois told us about your visit at the church this morning."

I had to ask, "So where is Reverend Cantwell?"

"He's home taking a nap," Lois answered. "I told him I was going to go see Laurie for a while."

"I'm Laurie," Mrs. Sullivan explained.

"And now here *you* are," said the doctor. "We thought you'd left town."

I was stunned and afraid to presume what would happen next.

"How is my son?" Lois asked.

Now, *that* was a tough question. I tried to consider how I would answer, and it took time. "He's . . . he's all right physically, as far as I can tell."

"And what is he doing? Tell me again."

I took it slow, but didn't try to soften it. "He's allowing himself to be regarded as a new, improved version of Jesus. He's performing miracles, healing the sick, the lame, and the blind. He's preaching a new, superpotent religion that helps people have faith in themselves and what they can do. He's set up headquarters at a ranch near town, and pilgrims are coming to Antioch from all over the country. The local economy is booming and people are excited."

It was interesting how news that *sounded* so good could produce such horrified reactions.

"My God," said the doctor.

Lois silently shook her head in horror, then said in a barely audible, trembling voice, "I'm so sorry."

I added, "I believe he's out to prove he can be a better Jesus because he's quite unhappy with the real one—or at least his idea of the real one."

Lois absorbed that for a moment and then replied, "How could he feel otherwise?"

Dr. Sullivan leaned forward and asked her, "Are we going to tell him?"

She nodded emphatically, without hesitation.

The doctor was at a loss. "Where do I start?"

Lois started, straightening a little, looking directly at me. "Justin is my son, but I have to tell you, his miracles are from the devil. All his power comes from Satan. If he has touched or healed anyone, those people are in desperate trouble. *Desperate* trouble!" She looked at Dr. Sullivan as if needing his help.

Dr. Sullivan began, "The, uh, the accident—"

Lois jumped in again. "He was . . . he was just so angry at our church, at everything we were doing. He hated going, he hated our religion. He went the other way. *Clear* the other way. He . . ." She looked at the doctor again.

"He's a ticking time bomb," he said, "and when he explodes, there are terrible results." He kept looking at Lois as if to get her okay to proceed. "I don't know what I believe about the devil, but *something* is driving him. There's more there than just an angry young man. A severe psychosis, perhaps, or—"

"He *prayed* to the devil. He told me that."

"Or indeed, something diabolical, something more than human, more than evil."

"We had to send him away. He couldn't be around his father anymore."

"The *accident*. Let's get that out."

Lois fell silent, her eyes closed in pain, her fist holding the wadded handkerchief over her mouth.

Dr. Sullivan directed all his attention toward me. "You met Ernest Cantwell?"

"Yes."

"So you understand he was severely injured some time ago. He has only partial use of his lower body and impaired use of his hands. His speech is affected, as well as some of his memory. Now—" he met the eyes of the others—"the rest of the town has been told he was in a car wreck, and that's been the popular belief for over six years." He looked at me again. "But there was no car wreck. No one has ever seen a wrecked car. The local police never looked into it, never investigated, never reported anything—"

"Excuse me. Would that be Conway?"

They all nodded knowingly.

Dr. Sullivan said, "I understand you met him as well. Conway Gallipo is our chief of police and he's also head deacon at the church." He looked at Lois as he told me, "I guess we could say he's Ernest Cantwell's right-hand man." Lois nodded in agreement. "His muscles, his bodyguard." Lois nodded again. The doctor looked at me. "Anyway, he was helpful in spreading the myth that Ernest was in a car wreck. The Cantwells—mostly Ernest—didn't want anyone to know that it was actually . . . that it was Justin."

I vividly recalled the pitiful wreck of a man in a wheelchair. "What are you saying?"

"It's, uh, it's the time bomb I told you about. Justin and his father did not get along—"

"We had to send Justin up to Illinois to live with my sister," Lois blurted. "We told people it was just so he could get to know the rest of the family."

"I don't think that story worked very well," said Laurie.

"No," said Lois. "People weren't blind."

"Well, let's not get things all confused," the doctor cautioned. He turned back to me, "Justin was fifteen when they sent him to Illinois."

"It was to save him from his father," Lois blurted out, "and maybe, just maybe help him get away from all the anger and the hate." Then she added, "And it was also to protect my husband's ministry. I knew he couldn't continue the Lord's work with such a terrible problem at home." She dabbed her eyes and continued. "Justin stayed with my sister until he was eighteen, and then we brought him back. Everything seemed all right for three years. He acted different, like he'd met the Lord at my sister's church, like he really wanted to serve the Lord. He got active in our church, he sang in the choir, he led us in prayer and prophesied. People thought he'd changed. Somehow, he got along with Ernest."

She stopped. I could see the pain of the memory flashing through her eyes. "But he was waiting, just waiting for the right time, the right moment. He bought a gym and set it up in the basement—he was still living with us—and he kept working out, getting strong, really developing his body. And then, it wasn't too long after his birthday—he'd just turned twenty-two—he found that moment."

Laurie interjected, "But weren't there some woman problems in all this?"

Lois nodded, obviously sad to be reminded. "He was sleeping around. One of the girls was the daughter of a deacon. And that's what set it off. Ernest found out about it and came after him, and—" She stopped abruptly, her face and hands quivering. "Justin was at home, waiting for him. I just thank God I wasn't there to see it. I was at a women's meeting. I think that was part of Justin's plan too, to even the score with his father when I wouldn't be there to see it."

Dr. Sullivan picked up the narrative. "I don't think there were any witnesses to the actual beating, but when Lois came home . . ." Lois broke down again, sobbing as Laurie put an arm around her. The doctor took a ragged breath and continued, "Ernest was in the back yard. He'd been . . ." Now *he* was having trouble telling it. "He'd been beaten repeatedly with a baseball bat. Nine of his ribs were broken. His skull was fractured. He was bleeding from head wounds and unconscious. And . . ." He held out an arm and indicated the forearm just above the wrist. "He was nailed—literally nailed, like a crucifixion—to the apple tree in the back yard with spikes about—" he held his index fingers apart about eight inches—"that long. The spikes were still in his arms when the ambulance brought him into the clinic. I had to remove them surgically.

"Some of the tendons were severed. He had several operations, but never fully recovered the use of his hands. There were spinal injuries that partially paralyzed him from the waist down. It's a wonder he's alive at all, hanging from his arms with broken ribs. He would have suffocated if Lois hadn't found him."

I was horrified and incredulous. "And people think this was a *car wreck?*"

The doctor allowed himself a slight, cynical smile. "That's what you'll hear on the street. But there are police and paramedics and medical personnel—and this doctor right here—who know otherwise. Up to this point, none of us has said anything. Ernest came to this town first and he still holds the high ground. He can make things difficult for anyone who invites trouble."

"He has that kind of power?"

The doctor cocked an eyebrow. "The power over heaven and hell and who goes where, to put it simply."

He looked at Lois, but she declined to look back.

"He's still my husband," she said in a whisper.

"Religion misused," the doctor continued. "It's not uncommon. He has the personality—and the followers, the chief of police being among them." With an arched eyebrow he added, "Chief Gallipo has his own nasty part in this."

"So . . . what happened to Justin?"

"He vanished. We never saw him again. Lois did get some letters occasionally."

Her voice was still trembling when she said, "I didn't get my first letter for two years."

"But he went free. The whole matter was buried. Ernest Cantwell had his ministry to think about—I'm sorry, Lois."

"No," she said, dabbing her eyes. "That's all right. It's true."

"The letters," I said. "Did he have an address in Southern California?"

"Yes. But that was all. He moved two years ago and I never heard from him since."

"So he was in the Los Angeles area for two years."

"Yes, I think that's right. I don't know where he was before that."

"I believe he went to Missoula, Montana, after L.A., and from there he came to our town, just this spring. He's using an assumed name, posing as someone else."

"He's still running," the doctor suggested.

"And he's still angry."

"And still very dangerous. Do you have any idea, any plans at all, to stop him before you have an incident like we had here?"

"I'm not sure it hasn't happened already."

"What about the police?"

"He healed the war wound of our police chief." They all groaned. "But more than the wound has changed."

The doctor shook his head in wonder. "He hates and emulates his father all at the same time."

"Well, he and his father are made of the same stuff. We *all* are. But I'm finally getting a clear picture: He's going to self-destruct."

They were silent, perhaps a little surprised, but I could see Lois nodding.

"How?" the doctor asked.

"Have you ever tried to be Jesus? Believe me, only the *real* one can manage that."

"Amen," Lois managed.

"But that brings me to the scars on *Justin's* arms. Doctor, you said you treated those wounds."

Dr. Sullivan looked at Lois and she gave him a barely visible, affirmative nod. "I believe we mentioned how Justin was sent to Illinois to live with his sister when he was fifteen. Again, the real reason was hidden from the public, especially from the church."

"*Especially,*" Lois emphasized, then lowered her head and shook it mournfully. "Justin was like a wild horse with no way to corral him. Ernest was determined to have it otherwise. And things got out of hand."

"What was it you said?" I asked Lois. "Something about Justin wanting to even the score with his father?"

"You can blame me," the doctor interjected. "I treated the wounds in Justin's arms, but I did nothing about the wounds to his soul. There was nothing to be done in this town, but I could have gone beyond this town for help. I could have done more." He took a moment to compose himself. "But Justin was quickly sent off to his aunt's in Illinois, so we thought that would be the end of it. He was several states away from his father, no one in town saw what happened, and the rest of us went on with our lives, keeping the matter quiet."

Lois raised her eyes and looked into mine. "I found him in the back yard, and I . . . I held him in my arms. I prayed for him. I sang to him. But the Justin we once knew was gone. He never came back." With frightened eyes she peered into the past. "And we had no idea what kind of . . . creature . . . had taken his place."

The doctor drew another deep breath. "Seven years later, Justin nearly killed his father."

Now I realized why Justin Cantwell had warned me, *Just be sure you find out everything.* I shifted my weight forward and said, "Tell me what happened in the back yard."

I CLOSED THE MOTEL ROOM DOOR behind me, rested against it, and let the tears come. I cried and cried, quaking against that door, wanting to slap myself, feeling so foolish, so blind.

Forgive me, Lord. Forgive me.

No, Justin Cantwell and I were not that much alike. Sure, our church worlds were similar. Both our dads were preachers. We read from the same Bible, learned the same doctrines, sang the same songs, followed many of the same rules.

But I had *never* been in such a place as Nechville—and I know I'd never been in such a place as Justin's back yard.

I only thought I had, and I was acting like it—until Justin came to my town and I went to his.

Now I was sorry. Desperately sorry.

27

MONDAY MORNING, Michael Elliott felt called to go for a short, very spiritual walk across the rolling pastureland of the ranch. He took his staff in his hand, wore his prophetic mantel over his head and shoulders, and set out on his journey knowing not where it would take him—God would lead. As he walked along the white paddock fence, past horses lazily grazing, he looked frequently toward heaven, praising God and listening, always listening, for the next prophetic message, the next inkling of what God was about to do. He knew he must obey every word. He must watch for every sign. The Messiah had come, Antioch was the New Jerusalem, and he, Michael, blessed among men, was to be the Messiah's messenger.

"I will obey, my Lord," he said. "But speak the word, and I will obey. I am your servant."

His heart soared. He felt filled with God, in tune with the divine, cosmic mind.

And greater works than these shall ye do. The promise coursed through his soul like marching orders from on high. *Greater works.* These would require greater faith, greater obedience, but the world would behold and tremble, and then it would change. It would grow. A new thing would occur upon the earth, the news of which would make all ears tingle.

Michael raised his staff toward the heavens and sang forth in joy, turning the heads of some steers who grazed beyond a wire fence with bright plastic numbers on their ears.

He came to the pond, an acre of quiet water reflecting the deep blue of the sky and the June green of the gentle hills. Mr. Macon had built a fishing dock there, and his old skiff lay on a split rail rack by the shore. Across the water, four ducks paddled in formation, dipping their heads, rustling their wings, and conversing in duck-ese.

This was one of Michael's favorite spots for reflection. He often took the skiff out just to float quietly, lie on his back, and watch the sky. The mud along the shore became his canvas, and his most recent etching—the word *ALLELUIA* in Gothic lettering—was still intact, though some ducks had waddled through it.

Standing at the end of the dock, he sniffed the natural, living odor of the pond, the scent of mud, algae, ducks and catfish. He received the kiss of the breeze upon his cheek and heard the song of the earth the breeze carried—the rustle of the spear grass, the lowing of the cattle, the murmur of the ducks.

Walk upon the water.

Below him, the pond was a sheet of glass, and his reflection nearly perfect.

Walk upon the water.

The voice was the same, the one he had always heeded and obeyed. It brought him to Brandon Nichols. It had led him through the streets of Antioch. It had opened his understanding to the mighty move of God.

Walk upon the water.

This was the Messiah's pond. He was the Messiah's messenger. All things were the Messiah's—all works, all miracles, all things.

Greater works than these shall ye do.

As God tested Abraham, Gideon, Joshua, and even the first Christ in the wilderness, so now he, Michael, was being tested.

It is mine to obey, he responded in his spirit. *Far be it from me to turn away from the voice of God.*

He obeyed. He stepped off the dock.

IT WAS COLD THIS TIME OF YEAR! Deep too. He thought he would drown before he finally grabbed hold of the dock and worked his way toward the shore hand-over-hand. Dripping and shivering, he clambered out of the water, shocked by the cold and by the very fact that he was wet.

Looking back, he saw his staff floating on the water, far beyond reach without a boat—or another swim. As for his prophet's mantle, by now it was somewhere on the bottom.

FATHER AL VENDETTI was rather surprised to see a sizable crowd once again sitting in the sanctuary of Our Lady's, visiting quietly, eyes rarely wandering from the crucifix that hung on the wall. Some he'd seen before, in those few days between the first miracle and the advent of Antioch's messiah. Penny Adams was there, apparently unhappy with her hand, though it looked all right. The young woman from Moses Lake who had leukemia was back without her husband, looking well physically, but strangely ill in her demeanor.

Others were new to this place, but Father Al had been told a little about their stories: the exceedingly fat lady who still wanted a miraculous reduction in her size; the young man who couldn't get a million dollars out of Brandon Nichols and still hadn't thought of working; the man who had important things to do but had to put them off so he could be healed of procrastination; the man wanting to be more sexually attractive, along with his three friends.

But Father Al wasn't quite as familiar with the common motivation these and the hundred others freely acknowledged among themselves: They couldn't get it at the ranch, so they were going to get it here.

He moved among them, greeting them, asking if there might be anything he could do to meet their spiritual needs. Might he pray with them, or hear their confession? He would be happy to conduct a special mass just for them.

"I'm not Catholic."

"Not now."

"Uh, you're standing in the way."

"How often does it cry?"

"Is this going to cost us?"

"What is this, a commercial?"

Their message was clear: He was intruding.

An intruder in his own church!

He retired to his office and closed the door, weighing a new fear he hoped was ill-founded. He wanted to believe these pilgrims were the same as they were before: pious, penitent, humbly petitioning. This was Monday morning, he told himself, that time of rude awakening that can bring out the bad side of people. Surely he had only *imagined* their tense expressions, edgy voices, and scavenger eyes.

Even so, an ominous possibility made him shudder: *Suppose the crucifix doesn't cry?*

IN THE VACANT LOT beside Mumford's Machine Shop, Dee Baylor sat alone on the hood of her car, watching the sky. There were no clouds overhead and only a few near the horizon, but this was where the Lord had spoken, and this was where the joy had been. Now Adrian had her angel and Mary had become the Virgin Mary. Blanche had long since pooh-poohed the whole thing and gone back to church. Brandon Nichols wasn't seeing anyone today.

But the sky was still here, right where Dee had left it, and if it took all day to see one little cloud bearing a word of hope to her soul, she would remain here.

A car drove into the parking lot and two couples climbed out, one older, one younger. They had cameras and binoculars and ran up to her eagerly.

"Is this where you see the Virgin in the Clouds?" the older man asked.

Dee felt her heart soar. The Lord had brought these seekers to her. The miracle would return and she would guide them. "This is the place. If you have faith and a willing heart, God will speak to you."

The young man checked the sky and smirked. "There aren't any clouds."

"There will be."

"We don't have time for this!" said the older lady.

"What about the trees in the park?" asked the young lady. "Somebody saw Jesus and Mary there yesterday."

"Let's go!" said the older man.

Dee called after them, "But this is the place!"

"You can have it!" the young man mocked.

And just that quick, they were gone.

Dee's heart sank, but she remained there, sitting on the hood of her car. The clouds would return. She had faith.

"HOW MUCH do we really know about this guy?" asked Richard, the real estate broker from Wisconsin.

"Everything we need to know," replied Andy Parmenter, the retired California executive. "He's a messenger of God—"

"No, no, now come on, that's a cop-out and you know it!" said Weaver, the CPA from Chicago.

"There's something he's not *telling!*" warned Richard.

"Like *everything*, maybe?" said Weaver.

They were gathered around the front of Andy Parmenter's big motor home, all three of them in sour moods they'd been working on for days.

"It hit me this morning," said Real Estate Richard. "Here we are in this RV park with—what?—three hundred other people?"

"Four hundred, I think," Weaver the CPA offered.

"I'm *still* waiting to have my water turned on, I'm smelling the sewage from sixty other vehicles in my row that isn't going anywhere, it's just sitting in the sewer lines—"

"The whole system's backed up."

"And we've got kids crying and couples fighting and radios blaring while I'm trying to sleep—"

"And who's that loud-mouthed prophet lady over in Row Four?"

"Which one, Moses' sister, Miriam, or Isaac's wife, Rebecca?"

"She doesn't know when to shut up, does she? Who's listening to her?"

"Your *point*, Richard!" Andy demanded. "Get to your *point*!"

Richard leaned forward and gestured like an angry Italian. "My point is, this morning it hit me: I am not better off than I was back in Wisconsin. Back there I had a house and a job and people who looked up to me. I didn't *like* it, it didn't feel like it was *about* anything, but—" He looked around the RV park hastily laid out on George Harding's property. "What's so great about this? I may as well be back in Wisconsin!"

Andy shook his head impatiently. "Richard, you have to be willing to sacrifice."

"*What sacrifice?* I didn't come here to sacrifice! I came here because you told me Nichols could produce."

"He can't produce!" said Weaver.

"Wait a minute, Weaver!" said Andy. "He healed your bald spot, didn't he?"

"My bald spot? My *bald spot*? Winnie and I came all the way out here and she still has her hay fever and she still bugs the heck out of me and now my motor home's in mud up to the axles! And you want me to be happy about a freakin' *bald spot?*"

"*So leave!*" Andy snapped.

"Uh-uh!" said Richard. "I'm coming to my point here: *You're* the one who talked us into this!"

"I sold my house, remember?" said Weaver, who started poking Andy in the chest. "You told me to sell my house, so now I'm sitting in the mud with that stupid motor home in a wheat field with a wife I can't stand who has hay fever!"

Andy grabbed the poking finger and pushed it away. "Don't touch me again, Weaver!"

"Why? You gonna do something about it?" This time Weaver shoved him.

Andy outweighed him. His shove put Weaver on his back in the stubble. Richard got into the fight, then Weaver again. Andy's neighbor sided with Andy and threw his weight into it. Weaver resorted to straw and mud, Richard to lots of high kicking, Andy to more shoving and a little biting.

A bigger crowd would have gathered to watch, but theirs was not the only fight worth watching. Over on Row Four, Dorothy who once had arthritis and Alice who once had a bad hip were in the middle of a face-scratching, hair-pulling catfight over whose grandkid broke out a window, and Row Two had two fights involving six people and plenty of black, sticky mud to make it interesting.

"AND WHERE HAVE YOU BEEN?" Brandon Nichols growled as Michael came in the back door to the house dripping wet. Nichols was standing on a chair while Melody Blair worked hurriedly, pinning the hem of his new white robe.

"I'm afraid I've taken a swim."

Nichols's fiery eyes glared at him through his disheveled hair. "You went swimming when I need you?" He snapped at Melody, "Are you through?"

"Just a few more pins and—"

"The people need some enlightenment! They need their eyes opened! Who put their bodies together? Who put bread in their stomachs and hope in their hearts? TELL ME!"

Michael jumped a little at Nichols's outburst but answered loyally, "You did, my Lord! You and only you!"

Nichols gave a slight nod of approval though the anger did not leave his face. "Then we'll have to go over it again for the sake of those who've forgotten! Did you hear there's another messiah in town? There's somebody else telling people he's the christ! In my town!"

Michael was quite dismayed. "How can this be, when you are the Christ?"

Nichols glared at nothing, half in a world of his own. "Sally Fordyce is a poison to us. She's lying. We'll have to take care of that. And Mrs. Macon . . ." He cursed. "I fault myself for hiring

Gildy Holliday." Nervously, he swept his hair from his face with his fingers. "We've got a lot to do and not a lot of time. Michael, who is the Christ?"

"You are, my Lord."

"Who, Michael? Who is the Christ?"

"You and only you."

Nichols leaned, pointing his finger, his eyes like cold, white marbles. "WHO IS THE CHRIST, MICHAEL?"

Michael shouted back, "You are!"

Nichols nodded approvingly. "Simple. It's as plain as anything can be. We just need to tell them, Michael, and keep telling them until they get it. We're going into town today. We're going to make it abundantly clear!"

"You—you're going into Antioch?"

Nichols screamed toward the hall. "Mary!"

The voice of the Virgin Mary Donovan came from a distant room in the house. "Yea, my son?"

"Be ready in ten minutes!" Then he glared at Michael. "Put on some dry clothes and then go out and help Matt prepare the truck. You're my prophet, Michael. You're going to prophesy." He reached down and swatted Melody on the head. She cowered, fearing another blow. "Hurry it up!"

AT OUR LADY'S, Arnold Kowalski brought in the ladder. The pilgrims wanted it in place, ready for the next miracle. His feet hurt, his hands hurt, and carrying that ladder up the platform steps was no easy task, but no one in the crowd offered to help. This was his penance, he figured, the price to pay for a refreshing of his own private blessing.

His personal crucifix was still around his neck, and judging from the recurrence of his pain, it must need recharging. He didn't think anyone would get upset if he went up the ladder to, uh, dust off the crucifix. He was, after all, the church maintenance man. He'd brought the ladder, hadn't he? For all his trouble and pain he deserved access to the wonderful wooden image.

Setting the ladder carefully in place, he started climbing, one painful step at a time. He could hear the people beginning to stir behind him. He looked over his shoulder and produced his dust rag. "Church maintenance. Just gonna dust things off."

They didn't seem too sure about that.

He reached the top of the ladder, face to face with the image, and began to feign dusting as he carefully, stealthily pulled his crucifix from under his shirt. Leaning awkwardly—he still had the chain around his neck—he managed to touch the big crucifix with his own.

"Hey!" a man yelled. "What are you doing?"

"Uh . . . just dusting."

"Whatcha got in your hand?"

And then it started. "What's in his hand? What is he doing?" People got out of their seats, ran for a better viewing angle. "He's trying to steal the blessing! Look! He's got another crucifix!"

People were running onto the platform for a better look—and they were mad!

"Get down from there!"

"You think I came all this way—"

"How dare you!"

The ladder started shaking.

"Oh no, no, please!" Arnold cried. A hand grabbed his ankle. "OHH!"

The ladder shook again. Another hand grabbed Arnold's other ankle. "Get down from there!"

"Well if he's gonna get some, I'm gonna get some!"

"You'll have to wait your turn!"

The lady who once had leukemia slapped the fat lady, who slapped her back, the procrastinator shoved them both, and Penny squirmed through the opening in the crowd trying to get to the ladder. A mob was forming on the platform and the ladder was beginning to teeter away from the wall.

Arnold was sure he was going to die.

There was a crash. A candle stand had fallen over.

"Now look what you did!"

"Look what I *got!*"

"Give me that!"

Slaps. Punches. Screams.

Arnold tried to climb down. Hands yanked him and he fell into the crowd. Now there was a free-for-all for the ladder. *OOF!* They were walking right on his back!

Father Vendetti came racing in, yelled something, waved his hands, yelled again. Nobody listened.

A burly character who'd been sitting in the front row reached the top of the ladder and grabbed the crucifix with both hands, making it wiggle on its wall mountings.

"Is it loose?" someone asked.

"Loose enough."

"Yeah," said the fat lady, "why does it have to be up there where we can't reach it?"

A riotous yell went up from the crowd and the burly man started heaving and yanking.

Father Vendetti ran for his office and the telephone.

"GUESS WE'RE GONNA have ourselves a little parade," said Matt Kiley, strapping down some loudspeakers in the back of the ranch's big flatbed. "The Boss likes attention, ever notice that?"

Michael was yanking the starter rope of a small Honda gas generator anchored between some hay bales. It wouldn't start.

"Choke it."

"Where's that?"

Matt flipped the choke up. "Try it."

Michael yanked again, and the generator came to life.

Matt opened the choke and then switched on the PA. He spoke into the wireless microphone. "Hello, testing, testing." His voice boomed out of the speakers, echoing off the ranch house and barn. "Brandon Nichols, you are ready to greet your public!" He handed the microphone to Michael. "Go on, get out in front and try it out."

Michael took the microphone and hopped down from the

flatbed. For the first time since he'd knocked on the door of the Macon ranch house, he felt a little foolish.

"Come on," said Matt, "let's hear something prophetic!"

"Hello . . . testing . . ."

"Come on, come on! We're driving through town, remember?"

"Let the, uh, ears of the multitudes be opened before the, the, uh, coming of the Lord!"

"Go out a little farther," Matt directed. "We're getting some feedback."

This is dumb, Michael thought. He'd never spoken a test prophecy before. He walked several yards out in front of the truck, talking as he went. "Let those who have seen no mercy now see mercy! Let those who are hungry come and dine! Let the blind see the light of the Messiah come to this place!"

The back door of the ranch house opened and Brandon Nichols walked out from under the patio roof and into the sunlight, his image reflected in the swimming pool.

His hair was neatly combed, parted in the middle, and cascading to his shoulders. His beard was shaped and trimmed. He was wearing a white robe and mantle, and biblical leather sandals. The full sleeves of his robe were just short enough to reveal the scars on his arms. He looked like a piece of religious artwork, and he was ready. Mary Donovan followed him, her robe and shawl perfectly in place, her eyes full of wonder.

"Let's go," he said.

MONA DILLARD knew she would lose her mind. As if she wasn't sickened and frightened enough over dirty-eyed Norman, now it turned out that the couple who'd rented Number Eight weren't really a couple. They were two halves of two other couples, and one of the other halves, a semimaniacal black belt, was kicking on the door, trying to smash it in, yelling and swearing.

"Now, now you stop that!" Mona pleaded from a safe distance across the parking lot. Where, oh where, was Norman?

The brute just kept kicking. "Sutter, you're gonna pay for this!"

Another kick. A woman inside screamed. A man inside screamed something about being sorry and making a mistake and why don't we talk about this.

The door caved in. The brute ran in. A woman ran out, hands over her head, screaming, while all hell broke loose inside. A lamp went through the window and landed in several pieces on the concrete. Then a suitcase.

Then Sutter.

Mona ran to the office to call the police.

ADRIAN FOLSOM opened the bottom drawer of her dresser and pulled out the remaining stationery she'd purchased for her special ministry. She wouldn't be needing it anymore.

"Is that all of it?" asked her husband, Roger.

"This is it. I wrote . . ." She consulted a list she kept in the box, counting all the names. "I wrote fifteen letters from Elkezar to all these people."

Roger was dismayed. "Fifteen!"

"I thought he was—" Adrian winced with shame and embarrassment. "I thought he was an angel of God. I really did."

"Where is he now?"

"Oh, I don't know! He's a spirit, Roger! You can't just go out and find him."

"Well he'd better take his business elsewhere, that's all I've got to say." He shouted to the air, "You hear that, Amazar?"

Adrian whispered, "You'll scare Melissa! And his name's Elkezar."

"He knows who I mean."

She looked at the list of names in her stationery box. "I'll have to write back to every one of them and tell them to throw the letters away."

Roger nodded with a smile. "I'm feeling better already."

Just then, they heard the voice of their granddaughter Melissa, playing in the living room. "Hi! What's your name?"

Roger and Adrian exchanged a look, then ran.

Five-year-old Melissa and Jillie, the schnauzer, had been playing fetch with Jillie's ball, but now they stood in the middle of the room looking up at . . . nothing. Melissa was making a face. "That's a funny name. I'm Melissa." Seemingly in answer to a question, she looked at Jillie and said, "This is Jillie. She won't bite you."

Adrian and Roger stood frozen in the hallway.

"Melissa," Adrian said, her voice trembling with fear she tried not to show, "would you come here please?"

Melissa looked their way but didn't move. She was still talking to someone. "This is my gramma and grampa." She told Adrian and Roger, "This is Alka-Seltzer. That's his name; I'm not making it up."

"Melissa! I want you to come here this instant!"

Melissa shrugged and came toward them. Adrian stepped forward, reached, and yanked Melissa to her side. Then she scanned the room, her eyes darting wildly for any stirring, any shadow or sign.

Jillie was the best sign. She was still looking up at something no one else could see.

Melissa got fussy. "He wants to play with me!"

"Alkanar . . ." said Roger.

"Elkezar," Adrian corrected.

"Elkezar, get out of the house. Right now. You're not welcome here!" Even his voice was shaky.

Jillie watched something move through the room, then followed it past the kitchen and toward the back door, her eyes locked on it, panting, trotting, and leaping playfully, but not barking.

The back door opened by itself and Jillie dashed into the back yard.

"Jillie!" Adrian cried, running after her. "Jillie, come back here!"

"Adrian!" Roger ran after her with Melissa at his heels.

Jillie snarled and then yelped. Adrian flung the back door open and stepped onto the walkway.

She screamed, stepping backward, turning her face away, covering her eyes.

Roger grabbed Melissa, but too late. She saw it too, and shrieked, burying her face in his leg.

Jillie lay twisted and dead on the grass, eyes vacant, legs crookedly skyward, her innards strewn about the yard in torn lengths and pieces.

JIM BAYLOR didn't even get through the police station door before he bumped chests with Deputy Mark Peterson coming out. "Hey, whoa there!"

"In a hurry, Jim!"

Jim followed, almost running alongside, as Mark strode toward his truck—the town had three officers and two squad cars, and it was his day to be the odd man. "What's the deal on Sally Fordyce? You gonna do anything?"

"We've got it on the list, Jim. That's all I can tell you."

"On the list? What's the matter with you, didn't you see what that creep did to her?"

Mark was wound up tight and not feeling kind. "Jim, our phones are ringing themselves off the desks. We've got fights, we've got riots, we've got destruction of property—Brett's out on a call, Rod's out, I'm heading out, and we're still not going to get to everybody. Sally's okay, she'll live, she has time to press charges and go through the process. We can't mess with her case today." He opened the door to his pickup and climbed in.

"You're supposed to be doing your job!"

Mark's hand was on the door handle, ready to close it. "I *am* doing my job, or don't you have eyes?"

"I don't believe this!"

"Jim!" Mark took a breath, a moment to calm himself. He let go of the door handle. "If you'd like to help, you can corral that wife of yours before she kills somebody. Brett just saw her driving through town like a nut case. He would have pulled her over if he wasn't trying to calm a riot at the Catholic church."

Jim was shocked. "You talking about Dee?"

"How many wives do you have?" Mark grabbed the door handle again. "Take away her car keys and we'll get to Sally Fordyce quicker, okay?"

He slammed the door shut and drove off, emergency lights flashing.

I'd better get home, Jim thought.

I WAS TIRED AND EMOTIONALLY SPENT as I pulled into Antioch. All the way from Nechville to Dallas, then to Seattle, then to Spokane, then all the way home to Antioch . . . I wanted my couch, if not my bed. Nothing, I thought, would dissuade me from my course. Not the mobs scurrying around the streets of Antioch with their cameras and recorders. Not the people running from the Catholic church with—was that a wooden foot in that lady's hand, and were those two guys fighting over a wooden arm? Not the—oh brother, was this another Jesus?

He was standing on the sidewalk near the Laundromat signing autographs and having his picture taken with smiling visitors. He had the traditional long hair and beard, but he could have put some more thought into his outfit: a tan bathrobe with tee shirt and jeans underneath, and a circle of plastic, dime-store ivy for a crown of thorns. I rolled my window down and caught his southern accent: "Well, verily, verily, I say to y'all . . ."

No, not even him. Not even—oh no. There was a fight going on in the park. It looked like some of Justin Cantwell's followers were having it out with some of Armond Harrison's. They'd been working together on that park, and now they were fighting in it.

I just wanted all the more to get home, close my door. . . .

Kyle had left a note on the door and a message on my answering machine. I'm sure if I'd turned on my computer I would have found an e-mail from him too.

I called him, he said he'd call the others, and I doubled right back to the Methodist church. By now it was late afternoon. The meeting was bigger this time. Not only were Kyle and Morgan there waiting for me, we also had some guests: Nancy Barrons and Gildy Holliday.

"It's time we laid all our cards on the table," said Nancy. "This town's in trouble."

"I'm ready," I said.

We sat down in Morgan's office and Morgan closed the door.

ON THE WEST END OF TOWN, near the vacant lot next to Mumford's Machine Shop, Matt Kiley brought the big flatbed hay truck to a halt. Justin Cantwell, robed and ready, climbed out of the cab and took his place on the flatbed. Michael the Prophet, wireless microphone in hand, walked out ahead. The Virgin Mary Donovan took her place behind, and a gaggle of about thirty Macon ranch hangers-on, arriving in cars and RVs, gathered behind her. Andy Parmenter and his wife were there—Andy looked a little bruised, but they were still believing. George Harding came along hoping to improve his business. Melody Blair had brought extra pins along, in case Brandon's robe needed adjusting. She just wanted to keep the Messiah happy.

From where he now stood, Cantwell could look south and see the little hill with the cottonwoods near my place where he first came eye to eye with that pitiful, burned-out former minister. Looking ahead and to the left, he could see the church that minister no longer pastored sitting on the knoll above the highway.

"Let's take this town!" he hollered, pointing ahead like a general commanding a charge.

The band and the female vocalist had quit. Matt had a cassette player on the front seat. He hit the play button and an old *Reader's Digest* collection of inspirational favorites started broadcasting from the speakers: "When you walk through a storm, hold your head up high . . ."

Michael stood there a moment, looking bewildered. Matt tooted his horn at him and he jerked to life. "Uh, behold he comes forth, his power in his hand, to touch this land and bring forth new life!"

The procession began, and already, heads of wandering pilgrims were turning.

WE HUDDLED in Morgan's office, and although we were alone, we still spoke quietly as if an enemy could be listening. I shared my Nechville experience with everyone, and if they felt concern before that, I doubled it.

"Just got a call from Adrian Folsom," Kyle reported. "If Elkezar left, it was on a bad note." He told us about Elkezar, Melissa, and the horrible death of Jillie. "I'm going to get over there and get that whole problem prayed through."

"She's back in the fold, I take it?"

Kyle nodded, but seemed sorrowful. "I'm just sorry it had to happen this way."

"I need to have a good long talk with Sally," said Morgan. "She's afraid to be left alone, afraid her 'angel' might show up again."

"Well, all of these people need to come clean with God and rebuke these things in the name of Jesus," said Kyle. "That's what Bob Fisher told that member of his congregation to do, and the thing hasn't been back."

"Brett's still looking for the hitchhiker," said Nancy. "He's convinced the man, the thing, whatever, was in his house." Then she said something to Kyle that surprised me. "Looks like your little theory about demons was right." She caught us all staring at her. "Well they aren't *angels*—just take a look outside!"

MICHAEL KEPT WALKING ahead of the truck, staying right on the white line he helped paint down the middle of the street. "He is, uh . . . he's . . ." Suddenly Michael wasn't sure. He forced the words out. "Come to him, all ye who are weary and are heavy-leaded—uh, heavy-laden—and he will give you best! His yoke is in his hand to separate the cows from the goats and the wheat from the flakes, and his words are a mighty wind to quake the hay stalks of confusion that roll through the oceans of grief and pain and . . . you know, other messy stuff . . ." His British accent was failing him.

Now Matt was playing a gospel album by Elvis with the Jordanaires: "Then sings my soul . . ."

And Justin Cantwell, the Messiah of Antioch, waved to the crowds, blew them kisses, made sure they could see the scars on his arms, and tossed them loaves of bread he produced out of thin air. "I am he," he cried. "I am he and there is no other!"

It was working. Cameras were flashing, camcorders were blinking. Young and old scrambled after the loaves. People were running up to the truck, reaching for a touch and getting one.

"Come to *me!* I will hear your cries! I will give you blessing!" The tone in his voice and the steely glare in his eyes would have made his daddy proud.

Mary Donovan followed behind the truck, blessing the crowds, waving to them, spouting any Magnificat that came to mind. "Magnify the Lord! Let his joy dwell in your hearts for his time has come! He is our hope, he is our joy!"

The Macon Ranch hangers-on brought up the rear, waving, shaking hands, shouting greetings, passing out flyers, pointing at Cantwell. Two women sang and rattled tambourines.

"Now just a minute, young lady!"

Mary jerked her head around and saw another woman in robe, shawl, and sandals coming toward her, a nasty expression on her face. "Uh, blessings and peace to you!"

The woman aimed an angry, shaking finger at her. "I'll blessings and peace you, you little snip! My boy was here first!"

Mary looked toward the real estate office and gasped. There was another Jesus standing there—or some young character in jeans and a bathrobe trying to *look* like him. Whoever he was, he was frightfully indignant. There had been a crowd around him with cameras and autograph books, but now they were all moving toward Cantwell and reaching out to catch the loaves he was tossing.

The mean, old Mary stood directly in the Virgin Donovan's path. "Now you can just turn around and take your big show elsewhere! This is our street!" She turned and chased the flatbed, banging on the boards to get Cantwell's attention. "Hey, creep! Yeah, you! Get this rig out of here!"

That finally spiked Mary's ire. "Don't you talk to my son that way!" She ran after the older Mary and grabbed her by her shawl. The mean Mary quickly showed how mean she could be.

"I am he!" Cantwell shouted at the other christ, who extended a finger at him and bellowed in a southern accent, "Well y'all just come down off that truck and we'll see about that!"

From the sidewalks, it was the most bizarre show in town: Two christs yelling and giving each other obscene gestures while their two mothers scratched, tore, and screamed at each other in the middle of the street. Crowds on the sidewalks took pictures and home movies.

"Glory, glory hallelujah!" sang Elvis.

"YOU AREN'T GOING TO BELIEVE THIS!" said Gildy. "Everybody thought Mrs. Macon had a stroke, right? This morning she got out of bed and came down for breakfast all by herself. They *drugged* her! The last thing she remembers is the first shot they gave her." Then she added with a note of dread, "And let me tell you, she's hopping mad!"

"The Macon estate owns half the property in this little square mile," I observed. "If the corporation's legit and Cantwell's the main stockholder, he could control most of the town."

"Not from jail, he won't," said Nancy. "Did you know about the Harmons in Missoula?"

We all looked at her blankly. "Speak on," I said.

"I've sat on this information long enough. Remember Nevin Sorrel?"

"He was killed," said Morgan.

"He was working for me, in a way." said Nancy. "After Cantwell wowed Mrs. Macon and took his job, he came to me wanting to give me some inside stuff on him. I didn't listen at first. I thought it was just gossip and mud-slinging, but once I met Cantwell face to face, I thought better of it. It turns out Nevin Sorrel and the real Brandon Nichols used to be ranch hands together on the Harmon ranch rear Missoula. That's how Nevin knew that our Brandon Nichols wasn't really Brandon Nichols."

"Whoa," I said. "You mean, we're talking about *another* Brandon Nichols, as in, a real one?"

"A *real* one," Nancy replied. "Buck and Cindy Harmon are good friends with Mrs. Macon. They knew Cephus, of course, and they did business with each other. Nevin came from the Harmons to work for the Macons, and then, so did Cantwell, posing as Brandon Nichols, with a good reference from the Harmons."

"How in the world did he do that?" Morgan wondered.

Nancy opened her valise and pulled out a photograph, a snapshot of some ranch hands leaning on a fence. "The Harmons sent this to me. Check out the two guys in the middle." We all leaned in to study the picture. Nevin Sorrel was easy to pick out. Next to him was a young man with long, black hair and dark skin, apparently of Hispanic or Native American descent. "Meet the real Brandon Nichols."

"Kyle," I said, "remember Hattie in Missoula? She said Herb Johnson used to ride horses on a ranch around there."

"Herb Johnson?" Nancy asked.

"Justin Cantwell," I explained, "before he became Brandon Nichols."

"Oh great." Nancy shook her head in dismay. "Another name." She continued, "Anyway, piecing it together from what Nevin told me, Justin Cantwell—alias Herb Johnson—visited the ranch a few times to ride horses, and met the real Brandon Nichols. They even joked about how they could be mistaken for each other."

We looked at the photograph again. It was possible.

"If Cantwell wanted to call himself Brandon Nichols and get a Washington State driver's license, it's conceivable he could have done it. So Cantwell came to Antioch, posed as Brandon Nichols, introduced himself to the widow, and he had a job. Mrs. Macon called the Harmons for a reference and they gave her a glowing report of what a great worker Brandon was—and the description was the same: dark-skinned, long black hair, medium build." Nancy smiled whimsically. "The Harmons were a little amazed to learn their former ranch hand was such a spiritual man and miracle worker. They'd never seen him do anything of the kind."

"No cameras," Kyle mused. "Cantwell never allowed cameras on the ranch."

"The Harmons had never met Cantwell and the widow had never met Nichols. It was a perfect switch." Nancy shrugged. "But I sneaked a camera onto the ranch and got a shot of Cantwell, just as you did. I sent it to the Harmons and they confirmed: Cantwell isn't Nichols. No way."

"Which raises a dark question," I said. "What happened to the *real* Brandon Nichols?"

"Brandon Nichols was unknown, with no family, and had no address other than the Harmon ranch where he worked. He was transient, and moved from place to place, job to job. If someone wanted to slip into his shoes and carry on his life in his place . . ."

"And use his driver's license and social security number," added Morgan.

"You're saying Cantwell killed Brandon Nichols?"

Nancy returned my gaze. "From what you've told us about Cantwell, he may have done more than that."

28

BRETT HENCHLE stood on the front steps of Our Lady of the Fields, notepad in hand, trying to find out what made so many people go so wild. The way Arnold Kowalski was carrying on, you'd think the mob had murdered his mother.

"It's all my fault . . ." Arnold wept, sitting on the steps with his face in his hands.

Father Vendetti sat beside him, his arm around his faithful old maintenance man. "Arnold, no, not with this bunch. They were different, they were . . ." Words failed him.

"Can you name any of them?" Brett asked, notepad ready. He'd managed to nab five people carrying various pieces of what used to be Our Lady's crucifix, but the rest of the mob and the rest of the pieces were quickly scattering.

Al Vendetti only shook his head. "We want no vengeance here. What's done is done."

Brett wasn't ready to accept that. "Father, they destroyed church property. They made a mess of your sanctuary."

"And they chopped up the Savior!" Arnold lamented. "What will we do without him?"

"Arnold." Al patted his shoulder with his free hand. "They were the same as you: They thought they could take a little bit of Jesus with them."

"Well, he's gone now!"

"No, Arnold. We can always buy another one."

The handheld radio clipped to Brett's belt squawked: "Car One, Car One, Brett, you there?"

Brett tweaked the talk button and spoke into the mike clipped to his shoulder. "Yeah, go ahead."

"Mrs. Fisk called. There's some unknown character lurking around the Sundowner Motel. Might be a peeping Tom."

Brett winced. "Brother. What more do we need?" Then it hit him. "The hitchhiker!" He hit the talk button. "Rod, let's get over there. It might be our man from the other night!"

Rod came back, "I'm trying to break up a fight right now."

Brett was already heading for his car. "Rod, I want this guy!"

"Okay, I'm rolling!"

JIM BAYLOR burst through his front door. "Dee?" No answer. "Dee?" The other car was in the driveway. She had to be here. He ran into the kitchen. Her purse was on the table. She was home, all right. "Dee?"

"I'm in the bedroom," she finally replied. Her voice sounded low and strange.

He hurried down the hall. "You okay? Mark Peterson says he saw you ripping through town—"

She was sitting on the end of the bed with his .357 Magnum revolver in her hand.

He froze in the doorway. He tried to smile. "Hey, Dee. What's, what's up?"

"Ichabod," she said, her eyes cold and brooding. "My life is Ichabod, our house is Ichabod, and it's all your fault!"

"Ichabod. Who's that?"

"The clouds never came and the blessing is gone—and it's because you drove them away! You and your spirit of unbelief!"

"Uh, Dee? Why don't you just put that gun down—"

"If thine right eye offend thee, pluck it out!" She pointed the gun his direction and—

He was already on the floor when it fired and a slug punctured the wall behind him. "DEE!"

She jumped to her feet, clasping the gun in both hands. "Purge out the old leaven and let there be a new lump!"

Should he wrestle her, try to take the gun?

She was aiming it again. He scurried, half crawling, out of the doorway as the gun fired and another slug hit the wall.

BANG! She was in the hall now and the bullet went right over his head.

He ran.

NANCY LEANED TOWARD US, her voice hushed and intense. "I talked to Pete Jameson, the county health inspector. He never required an additional source of water for Cantwell's building project, so Cantwell never had to develop that spring up in the willow draw. But he had Nevin dig a huge hole up there, bigger than was needed. Nevin thought there had to be something else going on besides a water development—but then he had that 'riding accident' and came back dead."

I turned to Kyle the same time he turned to me. "The car," I said.

"The car!" he echoed.

"What car?" Nancy asked.

"The car that might be buried in that big hole!" I answered.

"Let's go!" said Kyle, jumping to his feet.

"Let's plan," I said, and he sat down again.

ROD TOOK THE HIGHWAY. Brett took the back road behind the grain elevators. No sirens, no lights. They were hoping they could surprise—

"Got him!" Rod hollered into his radio. "He's behind the building right now!"

He screeched and fish-tailed off the highway, rolling and bouncing through a yard and a flower bed and finally into the overgrown field behind the Sundowner Motel. Brett came the other way, hitting his brakes on the gravel road and sending up a cloud of dust.

The Sundowner Motel was a long, one-story building with ten units and plain, evenly spaced, rear windows. Their man, wearing sunglasses and a low hat, was standing just outside the ninth window when they converged on the scene. Now he took off running.

Rod and Brett were out of their cars in an instant, Brett closest to the suspect, about to head him off. But Brett was limping on that leg of his. The suspect got by him and headed up the road toward the grain elevators.

"Don't lose him!" Rod hollered, then got back in his car and rolled like a tank through the field and onto the gravel road. He turned left, heading around the block, hoping to block the suspect's route of escape.

DON ANDERSON crouched behind the counter like a soldier under siege, eyes darting about, fists clenched, looking for his next move, his way of escape.

The washing machines were rumbling like Patton's tanks, mobilizing, marching, forming a blockade to trap him. The CD players were screaming and cheering and the televisions, with their big, gray eyes, were watching his every move and giving away his location.

Of course, the customers in the store had no idea what Don was so agitated about. Was he just kidding around or what?

"No, no way!" Don whispered. "Not today!"

The CDs on the rack were scraping and scratching like little flat rats, trying to dig and gnaw their way out of their shrink-wrapped boxes. They wanted him. He was their jailer!

The radios were blaring like an angry mob, hopping, rocking, and rattling on their shelves as their ringleader, a Sony Surround Stereo, bellowed in a deep, slow-speed voice, "When Don Anderson screams his last, hear it first on K-I-L-L! You want Death? *We've got it!*"

"We're bad, we're bad, we're bad, we're bad!" sang the others. "Radio Kay Eye Double Ell!!"

Don feared it would come to this. He had brought a baseball bat to the store just in case. Now he intended to use it.

A million angry bees swarmed through every wire in the place, fighting to get out, to get to *him*.

The radio control race cars were spinning their wheels, wearing their way out of their boxes, wanting to run over him.

The metal detector on the wall was beeping, probing, bending and weaving like the head of a cobra, trying to send a signal that would fry his fillings.

The microwaves were inviting him in.

The flashlights were looking for him.

The international power converters were trying to step down his nervous system.

The remote controls were jamming his brain.

And the washers and dryers kept marching, marching, rumbling and rocking, getting closer and closer, closer and closer—

"YAAAAAAHHHH!!!" He leaped over the counter with his baseball bat and pulverized a radio control car.

Crunch! Smash! Radio after radio went flying from the shelves.

Rattle, crack, crinkle! The CDs flew like Frisbees and fluttered like snowflakes.

"YAAAAA!!"

The customers cleared out as Don started discounting all the washing machines. Off went a lid, off went a door, a stacked washer and dryer toppled like a crumbling tower. He smashed away a shelf, then a row of TVs, and then his bat went through the gas line feeding the store's furnace. He smelled the stench of leaking gas.

"Try to poison me, will you?" he screamed, and dispatched a row of clock radios.

MICHAEL KEPT MARCHING along that white line, prophesying to the point of pitiful fabrication. "Though an army of evil rises against him, still the good of his hands and the fire of his mouth will be felt and seen, beginning here, and spreading there, and waking people up from their slumber of unbelief and making them, uh, pay attention to what's going on, for he is come to . . . to, uh, do good works in the earth . . ." *Brother, what am I saying? What am I doing?*

Suddenly, he heard a vicious, villainous laugh from somewhere behind him, so wicked that he spun around, looking for danger.

It was the Messiah. He was leaning over the side rail of the flatbed, pointing and laughing, his teeth bared in a snarling grin.

The mean old Mary had come out second best to Virgin Mary Donovan. With her shawl in tatters, her face scratched and her nose bleeding, she lay on the sidewalk as her son in the bathrobe comforted her and the tourists took more pictures.

"I am he!" the Messiah bellowed tauntingly, his eyes crazy, his hair flying. "Hey, Cracker!" he hollered to the cowering christ in the bathrobe. "You're next! Any time, Cracker, any time!" Then he materialized some more loaves and tossed them to the crowds. "Come and get it, my children! Come to me!"

Matt kept driving as another Reader's Digest inspirational favorite played over the loudspeakers, "Who made the mountains, who made the trees . . .?"

Uninvited, maybe even unseen by Cantwell, big, blustery Armond Harrison got a leg-up from some of his men and climbed onto the flatbed. As his followers cheered and the crowd snapped pictures, he smiled, waved back, then held up the Messiah's hand like a referee announcing the winner of a boxing match. "We're standing with you, Brandon! All of us!" Harrison's people let out one big, organic whoop.

Justin Cantwell smiled, waved, and eased Harrison toward the edge of the flatbed.

Then Cantwell shoved him off, right on top of Harrison's followers who collapsed like a house of cards under his weight.

"I am he," Cantwell reminded him, "and there is no other!" He returned his attention to the crowds. "Come to me! Whatever you need, I will give it! I am the one and only Messiah in your future!"

Matt stuck his head out the truck window. "Michael! I don't hear any prophesying out there!"

Michael turned his eyes forward again. He kept walking, but not a word would come to his lips.

Here came a vendor selling picture postcards of Jesus in the clouds and bumper stickers that read, *I SAW Him IN ANTIOCH, WASHINGTON,* or *I SAW Her IN ANTIOCH, WASHINGTON.*

They passed a booth where a man sold Antioch billed caps and tee-shirts that boasted, "I saw Jesus in Antioch, Washington." You had your choice: a picture of a farmer Jesus driving a combine or a jazzy, comic art face of Jesus between two sheaves. The Virgin got a tee shirt too, a more reverent pose of her standing on the curve of the earth, arms outstretched over the wheat fields of Antioch.

A barbecue-on-wheels had come to town, selling ribs and hot dogs, and right next to that was an out-of-nowhere artsy booth featuring little crosses, bookends, napkin holders, jewelry, and even Bible covers made from . . . *used lumber from Antioch, Washington?*

Sirens and screams broke through the din. People started running out of the way and Michael stopped dead in his tracks. Matt jammed on the brakes. Here came Rod Stanton in his squad car, blowing his siren, flashing his lights, easing from a side street onto the main highway as the crowds scurried aside. He stopped in the middle of the street, jumped out of his car, searched through the crowd, then got back in and kept going.

And now, here came another christ, a blond one carrying a whip and yelling something about pollution, filth, and greed. He tried to overturn the barbecue-on-wheels in righteous rage, but it was too hot to handle and too heavy to upend. The owner scurried around and slapped him a few times, this way and that, and he moved on, dragging his whip. He had a mother too, who followed him, sharing bites of pocket bread filled with sprouts.

A skinny pilgrim in a straw hat stepped up to Michael, munching on a hot dog and grinning as if something were funny. "Michael! I'm confused! Which christ is the real one? Do you have a word on that?"

Michael had no word. No word at all.

Then a gunshot rang out, and Jim Baylor ran onto the highway from a side street, scrambling in circles, screaming something about his crazy wife.

Behind him came Dee, waving a gun in the air and prophesying—"Thou art a robber and a jerk, and thy time has come!" People scattered like frightened rats as she fired the gun and ran by, but then they laughed and took pictures. The sight was so ridiculous it had to be a show!

But wait. A young girl had fallen to the street, her shoulder bleeding. There were screams. This was no show.

The Messiah was laughing again.

AMID SCREAMS, RUNNING, AND RUCKUS, Don Anderson came swinging and shattering his way out the front door of his store, yelling like a warrior, swinging and battling unseen enemies on every side. A teenager wearing a walkman happened to be nearby, and Don went after the walkman. "Take that!" He shattered the walkman, breaking the kid's pelvis. "Don't let them get you! Take them out! It's every man for himself!" The kid's father tried to grab the bat away and Don opened his skull. A lady in a sunhat got it next, collapsing to the street, her camera and the wrist that held it shattered.

The front door of Don's store was broken and hanging open. Penny Adams saw that as an invitation and stepped inside to help herself. Her life ended three seconds later.

Some say she did something to cause a spark. Some say it was Dee Baylor's last bullet that missed Jim and went through the store's front window. The explosion and fireball incinerated any way of knowing for sure, blowing out the store's front windows. Flame and shards shot out, killing fourteen people on that side of the street, setting four parked cars on fire, and breaking the windows out of a plumber's supply and beauty shop directly opposite.

The Messiah looked behind him to see the conflagration, the

burning cars, the screaming people, and flaming bodies. He raised his hands heavenward and rejoiced.

Don Anderson, now a block away, saw his own store go up in a fireball and shouted "YES!" Then he saw a hair dryer in the front window of the pharmacy and promptly broke the glass. "Roast me, will you?"

"Let me handle it!" said an RV lady from the Macon ranch, who quickly helped herself to the hair dryer.

"Partake, my people!" the Messiah cried, his wounded arms outstretched. "The bounty of the earth is yours! Partake!"

Even as the appliance store and the adjacent structures went up in flames, windows began to break all over town—some with stones, some with boots, some with tire irons. The people began to partake.

HER EYES BLINDED AND STINGING from smoke, her hair singed by heat, Dee fled from the inferno, stumbling, bumping into other frantic bodies, trying to run, trying to see. She bowled headlong into another woman and they both went sprawling. A stolen box of hot curlers broke open, the rollers tumbling and scurrying along the gutter. "Now look what you've done!" the woman yelled.

At that moment Dee realized she no longer had the gun in her hand.

Across the street, another window shattered. Folks started helping themselves to paper, pens, and office supplies from the Antioch *Harvester* office while Kim Staples, shrieking in anger and terror, tried to fend them off with reams of paper and boxes of pens.

The souvenirs, art, and trinkets fashioned from used lumber from Antioch went next, and there was nothing the poor wood carver could do about it.

The ribs and hot dogs were too hot to steal and the vendor too tough.

The blond christ with the whip had encountered the southern

christ in the bathrobe, and now they were duking it out, rolling, kicking, and biting in the street.

The Messiah's prophet was cringing and tongue-tied, and the Virgin Mother was clinging to the back bumper of the truck, cowering like a frightened child. Unflustered, even ecstatic, Justin Cantwell threw out some more loaves. "Come and partake!" He began singing along with the recorded music, "Walk on through the wind, walk on through the rain . . ."

The loaves landed on the pavement, ignored. His sheep weren't interested in bread anymore. They wanted toys.

No matter. The flatbed kept rolling, the music kept blaring, and Justin Cantwell kept right on singing as the town came apart all around him.

ROD FLOORED THE GAS PEDAL. After losing his man between houses and trees, he spotted the suspect again and shouted into his radio, "He's heading up Maple, the three hundred block!"

The suspect ducked down an alley and through a yard.

Rod drove down the alley. "He's running through the Wimbleys' yard! Should come out right in front. I'm going on foot." He stopped his car, leaped out, and started running through the yard as a German shepherd chased and snapped at him and a cat in his path panicked and ran up a tree. The suspect ran into the street. Rod bolted into the street to cut him off.

SCREEECH!

A hard, steel bumper clipped Rod at the knees, flipping him onto the hood of Squad Car One. He tumbled against the windshield and then rolled off onto the pavement, dazed and bruised, with one knee snapped sideways.

Brett jumped out of Car One and limped after the suspect. "Halt! Halt or I'll shoot!"

The suspect ran.

Brett grabbed his leg, then crumpled to the sidewalk. He pulled his gun, aimed. The suspect was looking back . . .

Mark Peterson darted out of an alley and collided with the man, tackling him to the ground. With a knee in the man's back, he slapped on the cuffs.

Brett hobbled up the sidewalk, gun in hand. "Mark! What timing!"

"Heard the radio," he answered, yanking off the suspect's hat and sunglasses.

Then he backed one step away, surprise all over his face.

The suspect was Norman Dillard.

OUR HUSHED, CLOSED-DOOR MEETING broke up the moment we heard the gas explosion. We ran out on the front steps of the church to see what had happened. Several blocks up the street, flames were billowing out of the appliance store, making black silhouettes of the scurrying mobs. The town looked like an anthill set on fire.

"It's Armageddon!" said Kyle.

Nancy was down the steps in an instant, obviously concerned for her newspaper office and store.

The siren atop the volunteer fire department began to wail. Five volunteers were already rolling out the fire trucks.

"Oh Lord," Morgan groaned. "Oh precious Lord, that's Michael!"

We all spotted him, walking out in front of the big flatbed truck. There was no question who the character riding on the flatbed was.

"What are we going to do?" Kyle asked.

"Same plan, everybody," I said. "Kyle, meet me at my place." I turned to Morgan, "You have to go to that engagement dinner. Try to act normal. We'll call your cell phone." Then I dashed to my Trooper.

I drove right up the center line of the highway and then slowed to a careful, deliberate crawl, weaving my way through the looters with my windows rolled up and my doors locked. I had an appointment with that flatbed, that ludicrous one-vehicle parade with

Justin Cantwell waving to the crowds and the voice of Elvis singing about believing that "for every drop of rain that falls a flower grows." Michael Elliott was walking in front of the truck, a microphone in his dangling hand, and I could tell from his face and posture that he was having the same, woeful awakening I once had. It was time to grab that kid.

I pushed forward, braking as a lady ran by with a lamp and two kids ran by with computer games still in the boxes. Broken glass littered the street and crunched under my tires. The whole town was cast in a flickering, orange glow.

When I was within two blocks of the flatbed, Justin Cantwell's eyes locked on me with radar precision and remained there. I stared right back and kept rolling, not straying from the center line. After one block for each of us, his truck and my Trooper came bumper to bumper in the middle of the street, and Cantwell's parade came to a halt.

Matt Kiley leaned on the horn. I put my gearshift in park. I had the Messiah of Antioch's undivided attention and I was going to seize the moment. I wanted him to read in my eyes that he no longer had advantage. I'd been to Texas, and now I knew him the same as he knew me.

I understood those scars he was trying to show off. I could clearly imagine the fence in his back yard on that blistering day in Texas. I could see how the galvanized spikes went through those arms and into the fence rail, and how they tore his flesh as he struggled. I could imagine the pain, the terror, the horrible bewilderment of a fifteen-year-old accused of being "full of the devil," an embarrassment that needed to be corralled.

I understood, and I wanted him to know.

He knew, all right. He turned away quickly, but I caught it in those crazed eyes, in that sweating, wild-haired visage backlit by orange fire. I had breached his mystique, and by doing so, deflected his power. That could make me his closest confidant—or his most dangerous enemy.

Enough. I turned my eyes away and searched for Michael. He was standing beside my rig, staring as if he couldn't believe what was happening. I lowered the power window on his side. "Michael, hop in."

He came closer, looking at me puzzled.

"I'm Travis Jordan. I know your mom."

That turned a light on. "Oh."

"Climb in."

He climbed in.

A loaf of bread landed on my hood. I saw other loaves flying through the air, bounding off the big truck, bouncing off my rig. The loaf on my hood had been bitten into, and now green worms were crawling out of the bite.

So, Justin's product quality had gone south and people were finding out. I knew that would be the script from now on. It was time to get out of there.

I slammed the Trooper into reverse and left Cantwell with his public. At the first cross street, I got off the highway just as Brett Henchle and Mark Peterson came on the scene in Antioch's two squad cars, sirens wailing and lights flashing. Was that Norman Dillard in the back of Car One?

In my mirror, I could see Antioch's two fire trucks arriving on the scene, and two volunteer firemen raced by me in their private vehicles. Crossing Elm Street, I stopped to let an ambulance roll by with its lights flashing. I found out later it was carrying Rod Stanton.

The folks along Myrtle Street were out in their yards, clustering with their neighbors, looking up at the black plume of smoke rising only blocks away. I kept driving toward my place, glad it was as far away from the war zone as a home in Antioch could be.

I noticed Michael was fighting back tears. When he lost it completely, I put a hand on his shoulder.

"Michael, let me tell you about the time I took a trip to Minneapolis."

JIM BAYLOR peeked out from the alley near Florence Lynch's boutique. The fire trucks were getting water on the blaze. Brett

Henchle and one of his deputies were fanning out, night sticks in hand and whistles in their mouths. Loot thudded, crashed, plopped, and tinkled to the street as the looters emptied their hands and ran for cover. The two scrapping christs suddenly found they had something in common—their fear of cops—and slunk off in different directions. Jim tried to see Dee through all the smoke, steam, and confusion, and finally spotted her.

No, no, no! She was joining up with that crowd of Nichols Nuts around Brandon Nichols's big truck! They were clambering onto the truck as Nichols and anyone else already aboard reached down to pull them up. They were clearing out, and Dee was going with them!

Jim ran out of hiding. "DEE!"

She didn't hear him. Maybe she was ignoring him.

"DEE!!"

A gray-haired executive in lemon yellow shorts offered his hand and pulled her up.

Jim broke into a run. He couldn't let her go with this bunch. "DEE! Wait a minute! Stop!"

Nichols banged on the roof of the truck cab and Matt Kiley got rolling, turning off at the closest cross street and roaring away from the trouble.

Jim almost tripped over his gun lying on the sidewalk. He checked which way the cops were looking, timed his move carefully, and recovered it. It was empty now, but he could remedy that. He tucked the gun in his belt, draped his shirttail over it, and got out of there.

MICHAEL CALLED HIS MOTHER from my place to tell her he was okay and with me, and then we sat at my kitchen table eating microwave pizza. I recounted my story about Minneapolis and then, for good measure, told him about my Nechville trip. Hearing my accounts brought him as much enjoyment as a stomach cramp, but it was medicine he needed at the time, and he hung on every word. I threw in some sweetener as often as I could, telling him in dozens of ways that there really was a Savior—he just wasn't

Justin Cantwell. For one thing, Justin Cantwell was too small. The real Jesus was greater than the best show any man could put on. He was greater than any building you could put him in or any tradition you could wrap around him or any expectations you could impose on him. Throughout my life, in a variety of ways, I'd tried to do all four of those things, but now I was learning—again—that it's only when you're willing to know him on his terms, for who he is, that you really start to know him at all.

I could see some light bulbs coming on in his head. They were dim, but they were coming on. I was thankful just to have him in my house, quiet and sitting still, so I could work him through all this. When the daylight began to fade, I checked the clock on the wall. Kyle was due at any time, and we still needed a map. "Michael, I need to ask you a favor."

By now he was ready to tackle the job as a moral duty. "Here's the ranch house," he explained as he drew, "and the main driveway. But you can't go in that way if you don't want to be discovered. The spring development is in the willow draw, way up in back. . . ."

IT TOOK BOTH COPS to contain Don Anderson's one-man war against the great technology takeover. He thought the handcuffs held a personal grudge against him. The squad car *meant* to slam his leg in the door. The speed radar was aiming at *him*—he could feel it homogenizing his brain.

Mark found one fleeting moment when either Don's head, arm, or leg wasn't protruding and got the door shut. "Whew! What's gotten into him, anyway?"

Brett was somber, staring as the crazed appliance dealer screamed and pounded against the car window. "He has a bad case of Brandon Nichols—just like the whole town."

Mark surveyed the damaged storefronts and littered streets. They wouldn't know the extent of the fire damage until the flames were out and the smoke cleared. "Guess the honeymoon's over." Then he had to ask, "But what about your leg? I mean . . ."

"I'm taking it back." Brett felt his leg, then flexed his knee. "It's just about normal—I mean, the way it was before Nichols messed with it—and it can stay that way." Don was still hollering, something about the squad car having indigestion in its fuel line. "You'd better get Don to the clinic. He needs a shot or something. I'll lock up the window peeper—and then I'm gonna call the county sheriff and get us some help."

MICHAEL SKETCHED EVERYTHING OUT, showing me how the "willow draw" was a small valley between rows of hills two miles north of the ranch house. The hills could be seen from the house, he said, but not the valley between them. Cantwell could have been doing most anything up there without being discovered.

Hopefully, Kyle and I would have the same advantage.

The disadvantage was the ranch's backhoe. Michael couldn't be sure where it was.

"The last time I saw it, it was in the low red barn, but the tractor might not have the backhoe attachment on it. They don't have that hooked up when they're stacking hay."

"Oh brother."

"But here's the other way to get in . . ."

He went to the opposite edge of the paper. "Figure on about six miles across here—" He drew the north highway, then a road entering the ranch from the north side. "There's a gate, but you can just open it. Make sure you close it behind you, or the cattle will get out. Then you follow this road . . ."

The road penetrated vast rangeland, then forked: The north fork led into the hills and the willow draw between them. The south fork led back to the house.

"What are the chances of navigating that road in the dark?"

Michael seemed hesitant to answer. "Physically speaking?"

I knew more was coming. "Right."

"There's nothing out there to bump into, except maybe a cow. There, uh, there might be another problem, though."

"Go ahead."

It embarrassed Michael to be afraid, but his fear was real, and it showed. "When you're up at the ranch, you can feel it." He struggled for words, got flustered, then tried, "Have you ever had somebody sneak up on you from behind, and something told you they were there right before they jumped you? That's the way it always feels up at the ranch, like somebody's there, just out of your field of vision. You can turn your head but you still won't see them. They don't jump out and scare you or anything, but they're around. And that's why . . . Cantwell . . . always seems to know everything. He has other eyes working for him. I used to think they were angels . . ." He stared into space—and maybe some terrifying memories. "I wouldn't go up there in the dark."

A knock at the door made me jump. The door cracked open. "Hello?"

"Yeah, Kyle, come on in. Michael, have you met Kyle?"

Kyle strode directly to the kitchen table and gave Michael his best pastor's handshake. "Praise God! It's great to see you free of that mess up there!"

Michael didn't know how to reply to that, but I just indicated the map he was drawing. "He didn't actually see them dig the spring, but he knows where it is."

"I've got two shovels in my car."

Grave robbers, I thought grimly. "Uh . . . okay. But what we really need is a backhoe. We aren't going to have all night."

Another knock at the door. "Travis?"

Jim Baylor! This was no casual visit. Jim was breathing hard, sweating, and agitated, and he was wearing a sidearm. I didn't even have to guess the source of the trouble before he said it. "He's got Dee."

He told us his story and we told him ours.

"Hey, I've got a backhoe!" he said.

"I know," I replied, nodding a strong hint at him.

By the look in his eye, you'd think I'd invited him to help us sneak under a farmer's fence to steal some corn.

Michael did not look so gleeful.

"Let's have a word of prayer here," I suggested, "and then we'll get started."

We gripped hands in a circle and yes, we *all* prayed.

I GOT MY CELL PHONE and called Morgan. She was still at the engagement dinner, but would be heading home soon. "Be very careful," she said. "I want to see you again."

"Talk to you soon." I put the cell phone in my coat pocket.

BY THE TIME KYLE AND I reached the north gate to the Macon ranch, there was barely enough light to see it. The sun had set, and only a thin band of pink remained on the horizon. Overhead, the sky was shifting from indigo to black and the stars were coming out. Jim Baylor got there five minutes after we did, chugging up the shallow rise in his big dump truck, headlights blazing, his backhoe on a trailer. Michael said he'd rather wait at my place, so it would be the three of us. He was right about the gate, though. All we had to do was swing it open. We moved quickly and got inside the fence before any other traffic came by.

I felt like I was doing an Isuzu Trooper commercial, taking my trusty rig into the rugged outback over rough roads and uneven terrain and doing it in the dark, no less. Kyle kept studying Michael's map with a penlight and peering out through the windshield, trying to find the landmarks Michael had noted. The dirt road, still rutted and soft in places, weaved and wound, rose and fell, went on and on. We often passed small, idle bunchings of the Macon herd, resting by the road, grazing in the fields, paying us little mind. Jim stayed right with us, his headlights bright in my mirrors. After five miles I could make out the soft, roundish lines of the hills that sheltered the willow draw.

We came to the grade, climbed, bumped, and wound our way upward, then dropped into a valley on the other side.

I saw a distant, vague form in my headlights. "I think I see the dead tree."

"Uh . . ." Kyle checked the map. "It should have a feeder on the south side."

I slowed and swerved the Trooper that direction. The headlights finally caught a white planked cattle feeder with a dozen head of cattle dozing or munching.

"Okay," said Kyle, "straight on for another mile, then left where you see the willow grove."

A mile later, we found the grove and turned left. There had been some work here. The road was wider. It had been scraped and spread with coarse gravel. We came to a wide, flat area.

"Here's the turnaround," said Kyle.

"And there's the fence," I said.

Michael had come through.

I drove into the turnaround and circled to where I'd be out of Jim's way. He rolled in, found a good spot, and shut down his engine. When his headlights winked out, the darkness moved in like a presence on every side, heavy and close, almost a liquid we could feel between our fingers. Our flashlight beams seemed pitifully weak in opposing it, like three tiny fireflies in a vast cavern. While Jim set about unchaining his backhoe, Kyle and I went to scout out the gully on the other side of the fence.

There wasn't much to see. Apparently, this used to be a boggy area filled with weeds and willow saplings. Now it was cleaned and carved out, filled with washed rock, and dammed with pressure treated timbers. A pipe ran out under the dam, with a large gate valve to control flow. It was neat and simple.

Clean too.

"What are we looking for?" Kyle asked.

"A car."

"Well, I mean . . . you know, how do we—"

I was shaking my head. "I don't know."

All we could see in our roving cones of light were the wide, graveled turnaround, the post and wire fence to keep cattle out of the gully, a little bit of bare, brown soil where the gully had been scraped out, and a thin, green mantel of grass just coming up wherever the original soil had been disturbed. One fresh, car-sized hole, recently dug and then covered over, would have been nice.

Beyond our little circle of light, coyotes yowled and yapped somewhere in the same valley, and shadows, only shadows, provided cover and hiding for any kind of beast or spirit to come close. Was it just *Michael's* paranoia creeping into me? No, I had some of my own. I'd dealt with Justin Cantwell myself. I knew what it was to be watched by eyes that were . . . somewhere . . . but not really *there*.

CLANG! I jumped.

It was Jim, dropping a come-along on the deck of his backhoe trailer. He was working efficiently, but for me it wasn't fast enough.

I kept my light moving, both to search and to cut through the shadows to make sure they were empty. I could hear Kyle muttering little Pentecostal prayers. It wasn't paranoia. He was feeling it too.

Jim started up the backhoe, and its headlights and floodlights chased the shadows from a sizable piece of ground, a precious piece of illumined real estate we could stand and defend. While the engine warmed up and the lights consoled us, he walked along the fence line, eyeing the ground, digging in his heel here and there.

"What do you think, Jim?" The sound of my own voice startled me.

He leaned over the fence at the lower end of the turnaround and pointed his floodlight into the gully. "This here's fill dirt, fill gravel." He came to where we stood and studied the dam and catch basin. "Eh, they didn't work those banks much, just filled in between 'em with the rock. But lower down . . . they put some dirt in there." He went to his truck and grabbed a shovel from the cab. "Somebody hold my light."

I held his flashlight while he went along the fence, stomping the shovel in and spooning up the soil every few feet. "Eh, yeah, you see that? This stuff here is new, it's fill." Kyle and I looked at him like two disciples of digging awaiting wisdom from the master. "This shoulder's new. It's all fill. Let's give it a scratch."

He climbed into his backhoe and backed up to the lower corner of the turnaround overlooking the gully, his floodlights illuminating the work area. He lowered the first outrigger, a big hydraulic foot to stabilize the machine for digging. The backhoe tilted as the outrigger contacted the ground. He lowered the opposite outrigger. It contacted the ground—

And kept sinking, breaking through. We heard something crinkle.

Jim cut the throttle on the backhoe and hopped out. We ran up, our lights searching the broken ground around the foot of the outrigger.

There was broken glass down there, and beyond that, a dark cavity.

Kyle had Jim's shovel. He reached into the hole and scraped out some dirt and gravel. I recognized the chrome around the doorpost and the vinyl roof.

"That's it!" My voice squeaked a little, but I hardly noticed.

Jim said nothing. He just climbed into the cab again, repositioned the machine, gunned the throttle, and started digging. Kyle and I stood as close as safety allowed, our lights and eyes following every scoop of dirt he took from atop and around that car. In no more than ten minutes he'd cleaned out a ditch along the car's right side.

Kyle and I jumped in with our shovels to do the delicate unearthing in the wash of his floodlights. Jim's outrigger had shattered and broken a hole through the front passenger window. We cleared away the dirt and then broke out the rest of the window so we could search the car's interior with our lights. We saw nothing but the rundown interior—the seats, steering wheel, dashboard, and ashtrays—still coated with brown slime and river mud. It still smelled like the river . . .

And maybe something dead.

We crawled out of the hole and I hollered up to Jim, "Let's get into the trunk."

He jogged the backhoe a few feet sideways and started scooping again, lifting the dirt and gravel out of the hole like big scoops of flour.

The car was sitting level and upright, the roof no more than a foot below the graveled surface of the turnaround. Jim moved his big bucket deftly over the rear end of the car, pulling loads of dirt from the trunk lid. The bucket's teeth creased the metal a few times, but we didn't care. We figured the trunk lid was going to receive far worse as soon as the dirt was gone. As soon as Jim took out his last scoop, Kyle and I hopped into the hole to finish the job, scraping and hurling the wet clay. We got the trunk clear, and just to take a crack at it, pried on the trunk lid with our shovel blades. It was jammed tight. I couldn't see Jim behind those bright floodlights, but I knew he was watching. We got out of the hole so he could take his turn.

He drove around to the side of the hole so he could get the bucket teeth up under the lid from behind. Kyle and I stood opposite, light beams fixed on that seam.

Jim curled the bucket and the trunk popped open.

There was something in there.

Jim swung the boom aside and set the bucket on the ground. He reduced his throttle to idle and centered the floodlights. Kyle and I stepped into the hole again, the soft, wet clay sloughing and sliding under our feet, our flashlights aimed at the object in the trunk as if they were protective weapons.

Now we didn't just *smell* something. The stench, the thick, nauseating *atmosphere* came at us like a wave, worse than a dead rat in the attic, or a cat's corpse under a back porch, or a run-over possum in the road ditch. I turned away for some fresh air. Kyle was ahead of me. We hadn't even seen what it was.

I breathed a moment, then tried again, my mouth and nose buried in the crook of my arm.

"What is it?" Jim called.

We had only told him about possibly finding a buried car. We hadn't told him what might be inside.

Every surface in the trunk was brown with river silt. I discerned the shape of a blanket, silty brown, with something underneath. With my free arm I extended my shovel, dipped the blade under the blanket, and lifted it aside.

"Aaaaww!" I know Kyle didn't mean to holler. It just happened. Jim found words, but I can't repeat them.

The remains of a face glistened wet and brown in the floodlights, the eyelids crinkled and sunken into the sockets, the decaying lips shrunk back from crooked teeth. Shoulder-length hair lay matted on the trunk floor, patches of black showing through the brown. Under the mud coating, we could recognize jeans, a denim jacket, and cowboy boots. The throat was sliced open.

Kyle had already cleared the hole and was gasping for fresh air topside. I followed, coughing, clawing with my hands, acid rising in my throat. I slipped in the wet clay and fell against the side of the excavation.

The cell phone in my coat pocket shrieked and stopped my heart. I rolled onto my back, the rotting corpse before my eyes.

It bleeped again. *Answer me! Answer me!*

I pulled it out, could barely get my shaking fingers around the antenna to extend it, and flipped it open. "Yeah," I gasped, "Morgan?"

"Surprise!"

Terror knotted my stomach, and I fought for air. The eyes were here. By reflex I searched for them, trying to see into the darkness beyond that pit. Finding nothing, my gaze could only return to that rotting, muddy mask grinning in the floodlights.

Cantwell spoke for the corpse, his voice low and taunting. "Looks like you founnnnd me."

I couldn't speak. I could only stare.

He became himself. "C'mon, Travis, say something. Tell me how it feels to know so much."

I tried to form a word. It wouldn't come.

"Maybe you should climb out of there and get some air—"

The word came. "Better! It feels better!"

He laughed at me.

"I'm, I'm looking at your bottom line, Justin! I'm looking at what you produce! I've got my answer!"

His voice went cold. "You've got nothing! I am he, and I hold the keys of life and of death—"

"Oh no! You're, you're dreaming, Justin! But it's over. This is the end of the dream, right here."

"We are not finished with our discussion, Travis!"

"We're *not?* What could you possibly have to say after this?"

"You mean you *STILL* DON'T GET IT?" His voice was so loud it distorted in the phone. "What's it going to take to get through to you? Life and death are in *my* hands now, and it's *my* call! I'm not nailed to the fence anymore, Travis, or haven't you noticed?"

"Justin. It's *over.*"

"No. We're not finished. Take a good look in front of you, Travis! I give life and I take it away. That means I can bargain with it. So it's *not* over. I'm not alone up here, remember?"

That twisted my stomach another turn. "Justin . . . don't make things worse for yourself—"

"That would be impossible!"

"Don't, don't make it worse. Please. Those people trust you—"

"I trusted *God!* Now give me another reason!"

I struggled, stammered. "Justin, you don't have any options. If you try to hold out you'll only get yourself killed."

"I won't be the first one to go. Make sure everyone knows that. And while you're at it . . ." He trailed off. Silence.

"What?"

"Tell them I have Morgan."

29

I FOLDED THE CELL PHONE shut and fumbled to get it back in my pocket as I clambered, stumbling and slipping, out of the hole. Kyle and Jim grabbed my hands and yanked me to the top.

"That was Cantwell," I said. "He's got Morgan!"

"Oh Jesus," Kyle prayed. "Oh Jesus, help us!"

"He's got Morgan?" said Jim. "What's he doing, taking hostages?"

"C'mon!" I urged them toward my Trooper. "There's somebody watching us and I don't know if it's spirits or—"

"We rebuke them in Jesus' name!" said Kyle.

Jim drew his gun. "What about Dee? He must have her too!"

"He'll have *us* if we don't move."

"My machine . . ."

"I don't think they'll shoot your backhoe. It's *us* I'm worried about!"

Jim scanned the darkness and saw my point. He ran with us.

We jumped in my Trooper and I threw gravel getting out of there. The road dipped, jolted, shook us this way and that. I tried to steer around the bigger holes and ruts, but I didn't take my time—I didn't have any.

I tossed my cell phone to Kyle. "Call 911. Tell them about Brandon Nichols in the trunk of that car, tell them about Morgan and Dee."

Kyle's finger hesitated over the 9 button. "They're going to give this to Brett Henchle."

"Tell them it's a, a *cult* thing, it's *big*. We need the county sheriff, the state police, *lots* of help. Cantwell's at the ranch right now with hostages, and he's a *killer*. We've all seen that!"

"Why's he holed up at the ranch?" Jim wondered. "If I was him I'd *run*."

Kyle pressed in the number and put the phone to his ear. He pulled it away. I could hear the crackle and static from where I sat. "No reception here," he said.

I hit the gas.

WELL, thought County Sheriff John Parker, *I knew it would come to this sooner or later. We should have had a betting pool on when I'd get the call.*

He was no stranger to the religious movement in Antioch. He and his deputies drove through Antioch regularly. They'd seen the pilgrims, noise, and hubbub. They'd watched it building for months. They didn't interfere. This was Brett Henchle's jurisdiction, his turf, his problem.

But now Parker was driving his own squad car behind Brett Henchle's, rumbling slowly up the Macon driveway in the dark. Henchle said he needed at least two cars to show up at the ranch to make the arrest. He needed a strong presence, he said, so Brandon Nichols would know they meant business. No lights or sirens, just *presence*.

Okay, Parker could do that. He'd already sent four deputies into Antioch to help the town's one remaining cop restore order. If things got stickier, Parker was ready to bring in still more backup, even the state patrol, if he had to. This cult stuff could get complicated very quickly. Weird too. Henchle had said, "Don't let him touch you, whatever you do." It would be interesting to see how Henchle planned to arrest this guy without touching him.

They came over a rise and Parker saw the ranch house. There were some exterior lights on in front and a few lamps in the windows, but other than that the place was dark. To the left of the house, dimly lit by some yard lights, were two huge circus tents joined together, and in front of them a small block building—it could have been rest rooms—under construction. To his left was a ramshackle community of recreational vehicles, campers, and tents, gas lanterns burning, some campfires flickering. By the looks of it, this messiah could be booked on health code violations if the other charges didn't stick.

Parker smiled sardonically. Yeah, getting the charges to stick, that was the rub. Domestic violence, assault and battery, inciting a riot, malicious mischief, holding a parade without a permit, and—this was the best part—littering. The other charges were more serious, but the littering charge had the better story behind it. Henchle said Nichols had tossed hundreds of loaves of wormy bread all over the street in Antioch and just left them there. And where did he get the loaves? Great story. *Great* story.

Henchle followed the paved, circular driveway to the front of the house, and Parker followed Henchle. Some curtains moved, shadows hurrying behind them, and Parker quit smiling. With a glance, he checked the shotgun mounted against the dash. This wasn't a high crime district. They weren't busting this guy for weapons violations, crack cocaine, or bank robbery. Even so, Nichols had plenty of friends up here, it was dark, and as yet Parker hadn't seen a face, friendly or otherwise. If these people were armed—

Without warning, the rear window of his car shattered. He saw the flash of a muzzle from a living room window. He flopped down for cover, his hand wrapping around the shotgun.

Another shot. Breaking glass. That had to have been Henchle's car.

Parker stole a look. There was a shadow in the window, the outline of someone's head.

He saw a flash, and heard three shots. The right side of Parker's windshield shattered. Another shot pinged off his fender.

The situation: an armed assailant in the house in front, a whole community of hostile campers behind. Not workable. "Henchle, let's get out of here!"

Henchle's engine roared and his tires squealed. Parker jammed his own car into gear, his head just high enough to follow Henchle in a tight one-eighty away from the house and down the driveway.

Two more shots just missed as he went over the rise.

His radio squawked, and the dispatcher came on. Something about a body being found on the Macon ranch . . .

I WAS BACK ON THE HIGHWAY, racing toward town and just coming by the main entrance to the ranch when I saw the lights of two vehicles speeding down the driveway. When they reached the highway they spun around, halted, and lit up all the lights they had. I slowed. Cops. Just what we needed.

Kyle got reception. He was talking to the 911 operator. "Yeah, Macon ranch. He has followers up there and—"

"Looks like Henchle," I said. "And the sheriff."

I pulled up and stopped. Sheriff Parker ran up to my window. "Get outta here! You're in a crime scene!"

"We're at the entrance now," Kyle said into the phone.

"The caller is at the entrance now," said Parker's radio.

"We're the ones who called in!" I said.

"My wife is up there!" Jim yelled.

Parker turned from us and replied to his shoulder mike, "Say again."

"I think we're talking to the sheriff now," said Kyle.

"The caller says he's talking to a sheriff right now," said Parker's radio.

Parker's smirk showed the extent of his amusement. "Okay, I got 'em. They're right here in front of me. How's that backup?"

"En route."

He turned to us. "All right, what've you got?"

Both Parker and Henchle were ready to listen. We tumbled out of the Trooper and then stumbled over each other's sentences trying to tell our story: Morgan/Dee/hostages/buried car/dead Brandon/cult situation/dangerous.

Henchle sniffed a bitter chuckle. "We came up here to arrest him for assault. The Sally Fordyce thing."

"He's got Morgan," I repeated.

"And he's got Dee," Jim hollered.

"So we've got problems," said Parker. "We need to contain the area. Where's that other road onto the ranch?"

Kyle pulled out Michael's map of the ranch and Parker studied it with his flashlight, speaking into his shoulder mike. "North 102, mile marker 20. Look for a gate." He asked us, "How far does this road penetrate before it splits?"

"About three miles," I replied.

"How far to the ranch house from there?"

I had to admit I didn't know. Michael didn't tell us.

Brett Henchle had a cell phone of his own. He was flipping through his notepad. "I've got the ranch's number here somewhere . . ."

I saw flashing lights come around the distant corner to the south and more coming over the horizon to the north. Parker was getting his backup.

"Kyle." I reached for my phone, still in Kyle's hand. I punched in my home number. "I'll get Michael on the phone. Maybe he can tell us some of the distances on that map."

Brett Henchle got through. "Hello? This is Henchle, Antioch police. Who am I speaking to? Matt?"

We looked at each other. *Matt Kiley!*

"Matt, this Brett Henchle. Somebody just shot at us." Brett crinkled his forehead. He was hearing a *bad* response. "Now just calm down. You don't have to shoot anybody, nobody's going to do anything that stupid. We're going to talk about it, that's all."

I wasn't getting an answer at home. I ended the call. "Is Morgan up there?"

"What about Dee?" asked Jim.

"Put your sidearm in your vehicle and leave it there," Parker warned.

"Is Morgan Elliott up there with you?" Brett asked. "Travis Jordan wants to know." He heard an answer, then handed me the phone. "He wants to talk to you."

"Hello, Matt?"

Matt's voice was agitated, his words rapid, as if he were back in the foxholes of Vietnam. "They aren't coming anywhere near Brandon, Travis! If they come up here I'll shoot 'em!"

"Okay, okay. Listen, nobody's moving right now, we're just sitting down here trying to figure out what to do. . . ."

"They're not going to arrest him! That man gave me my legs!"

"Okay. Message received. Matt, can I, can I talk to, uh, Brandon? Can you get him for me?"

"He's here. He's here in the house."

"Well can I talk to him?"

"He's on the other line."

"What other line?"

"You know, the other line, line two. We've got two lines up here."

Who in the world could he be talking to?

"What's he saying?" Brett Henchle wanted to know.

I waved to Brett and the others to stand by. "Uh, Matt, have you seen Morgan? Is she all right?"

"Dee!" Jim whispered at me.

"How should I know?" Matt came back.

"Well is she there?"

"DEE!" Jim hissed.

"No. She's not here. *Dee's* here."

"She's there," I told Jim.

Jim tried to grab the phone, yelling at it, "She'd better be all right, you hear me? You touch her and I'll kill you, so help me God!"

With Kyle's gentle help I got the phone back. "Sorry, Matt. You've got some folks really upset down here."

"Dee's okay," said Matt. "Tell Jim she's okay."

"She's okay," I told him.

"But I'm gonna do what I gotta do, Trav. I mean, I lost my legs once trying to fix the world, and I can do it again."

"I understand."

Brett took the phone back. "Yeah, Matt? This is Henchle. Listen, we've got no gripe with you. But Nichols has some really terrible things to answer for, some things you don't know about. No, I'm not lying. Matt, come on, you don't want to be an accessory. All you have to do is put your gun down and walk out of there. . . ."

"Why aren't we talking to Nichols?" Parker asked.

"He's on another line," I said. "The ranch has two lines."

"Well let's get the number!" He started signaling Brett.

Other cars were arriving, lining the highway shoulder with lights flashing. State police and sheriff's deputies were blocking off the highway, working the airwaves, scrambling for containment.

I got my own phone out, praying that Morgan would be at home.

"How many hostages are up there?" a patrolman asked me.

"Well . . ." I had to turn my phone off in the middle of Morgan's number. "It's a religious group. There are hostages and there are followers. I don't know how many of each, how many are being held there and how many *want* to be there."

"Oh great."

"There could be as many as a hundred *followers*. There's a whole RV park up there."

"Jonestown all over again."

"Maybe."

The patrolman moved on, barking orders to subordinates. I'd never seen so many cops appear so suddenly in the middle of the prairie. I punched in Morgan's number again.

"TRAVIS?"

I almost collapsed from relief. "Morgan! Are you all right?"

"I'm fine. I just came in the door."

"How are you? *Where* are you?" *That conniving liar,* I thought. Sheriff Parker butted in. "Where's the guy who drew the map?"

"Hang on, Morgan." To Parker, "Uh, I've got his mother on the phone right now."

"Does he know the layout of the house and grounds? If he does, we need to get him up here. We'll send a squad car if he needs a ride."

"All right. Morgan?"

"Yes, Travis." She sounded impatient.

"I'm at the ranch—well, down on the highway in front of it." More sheriff's deputies arrived, then some formidable police vans. I could see police officers in flak vests and helmets hustling up the hill in the dark, fanning out to contain the house and the RV village. "The place is swarming with cops."

"Are you all right?"

"I'm okay. I'm shaking a bit, but I'm okay."

MORGAN DROPPED INTO THE CHAIR nearest the door, not bothering to take off her coat, a flurry of dark possibilities at the threshold of her imagination. "Tell me what happened."

She heard a quick recap of our excavation, what we found, and how all hell was breaking loose at the ranch even as we spoke. She didn't hear about Cantwell's boast regarding her.

"Travis, can you leave? I want you to come home—I mean, go home—I just want you out of there and safe."

"I'm safe, Morgan."

"I want to *see* you safe."

"We need Michael."

"Travis, we are not talking about Michael, we are talking about you and where you are and how I feel about where you are!"

"The police need to know the layout of the house—you know, rooms, hallways, how to get in and out. Michael would know that, and he's good at drawing maps."

Take a breath, Morgan, take a breath. "I'm not sure where he is."

"What do you mean?"

"I called your house but he didn't answer."

"Oh brother. I tried calling him too. No answer."

She was trying not to worry. She was failing. "I'm going over there. He might be asleep. He's a sound sleeper."

"Hey, that's what we can do: Swing by there and get him and then both of you come up here."

"You can't be serious!"

PARKER WAS STANDING right by me, waiting.

"Morgan . . ." I still had Cantwell's vicious boast in my mind. "I'd feel better if you were here. I mean, I'm surrounded by police, and right now I'd rather you and Michael were too."

"You got him?" Parker wanted to know.

"Morgan?"

She gave in reluctantly. "The Macon ranch?"

"Just head out the highway. You'll see the cop cars, believe me. And listen—" I told Parker, "Uh, Sheriff, I'd count it a great favor if you could send somebody down to my place to make sure everybody's okay, that they get here all right."

"Where do you live?" Parker didn't wait for an answer but hollered around, "Anybody know where this man lives?"

"Hello, Morgan?"

"I'm listening, Travis. I'm *still* listening."

"Uh, hold on . . ."

Brett Henchle hurried forward, got a quick briefing, and volunteered.

"Uh, it'll be Morgan Elliott—you know, the minister lady—and her son—he used to be that radical prophet."

"Don't worry." Then he touched my shoulder. "By the way: You were right." He ran to his car.

"Morgan, Brett Henchle's going to meet you at my place to make sure you get up here okay, so just wait for him, all right?"

"BRETT HENCHLE? Travis, were you present when we discussed him?"

"He's snapped out of it. He's talked to Sally Fordyce, he's had to quell a riot, he's had to clean up wormy loaves of bread—and now he has a homicide on his hands. He's with us now, really."

Everything was happening very fast and not at all sensibly. She put on the brakes, took a deep breath, and regrouped. Like it or not, it was time to rise to the occasion and take charge of her part in it. "All right, Travis. I'll get Michael and wait for Brett Henchle, and we will meet you up at the Macon ranch."

"Love ya."

"Good-bye."

She ended the call—then replayed the last few lines in her mind. "Ohh!" Now she wanted to kick herself. Love ya! *Love ya*, and all she said was *good-bye?*

Travis, how could you do this to me!?

She turned on her heel and went out the door. She didn't mean to slam it—at least, that's what she told herself.

"WHAT DO YOU KNOW about this Matt character?" Parker asked me.

"He's a decorated Vietnam vet. He's intensely loyal. He held off the Vietcong by himself so his buddies could make it out in a chopper."

Parker looked toward the ranch with regret in his eyes.

"Don't . . . don't hurt him. Please."

Parker didn't get a chance to reply. Another deputy was handing him a cell phone. "Sheriff, we got him on the line."

"Nichols?"

"It's him."

Parker pushed the phone at me. "I understand you know him better than anyone. Talk to him. Calm him down." I hesitated. "Just get him talking, get things on an even keel."

I took the phone and gingerly held it to my ear. "Hello. This is Travis."

"My, my, my, what a gathering!"

"Yeah, they're throwing quite a party down here."

"Parker isn't smiling."

I glanced at Parker. "No, he sure isn't. Not too many of them are. So how are you doing?"

"Oh, well enough. I have my own little family up here, ready to stand with me and go out in a flame of glory. This is the New Jerusalem. We can't let it fall to the infidels."

"Do they *all* feel that way?"

"Well, just the ones that matter: Matt, Mary, Melody—"

"What about Morgan?"

He laughed. "Rest easy, my friend. She's not here."

"Who else, Justin? Who's in there with you?"

He only sighed. "Why don't you go home, Travis? You can't do any good up here."

"I'm supposed to be the negotiator. You and I are supposed to talk things out."

"Oh, right. I give you a list of my demands, they say they'll think about it, they cut off our water and power and blast us with loud music for a few days, and then they storm in and shoot all of us. That *is* what we're talking about, isn't it?"

"Hey, it's your call, right? I told you not to make things worse for yourself."

"Go home, Travis."

"What about our discussion?"

"It's hard to speak freely and openly when there are a million cops around."

"We may not get another chance."

"Oh, we will, you can count on that. Hey, gotta go."

"I met your father, Justin. Boy, now there's something we can talk about."

"TRAVIS! Go. Home."

He hung up. I let Parker know. Parker signaled the men standing by him. "Okay, let's cut the power and water. Have those floodlights arrived?"

"On their way," said a cop with "POLICE" emblazoned on the back of his jacket.

"Let's get a better phone system going here, something we can monitor." He addressed me. "Can you get him on the line again?"

I shrugged. "I can always ring the number. I don't know if he'll answer."

A deputy with a handheld radio had gotten the word. "The RV village is secure." He listened further. "There's no resistance and a lot of them want to leave."

Parker sniffed a sneering chuckle. "Loyal followers!" He ordered, "Okay, search and screen each vehicle and roll it out of there, the whole village, one by one. We'll eliminate the hiding places and tighten the perimeter."

MORGAN HAD NEVER BEEN INSIDE THE HOUSE but she knew where it was, and thankfully, she didn't have to navigate the main street through town to get there. The local fire department was out, lights flashing. The ambulance was deployed, lights flashing. Antioch's second squad car was blocking access to the damage zone, lights flashing, and some county sheriff's vehicles were on the scene as well, lights flashing. The center of town had become a major wreck on the highway.

Myrtle Street, on the other hand, had quieted down. The porch lights were on up and down the block, and an occasional TV screen glowed blue through a front window. She drove as far as the highway barrier at the west border of the town, and there, on the right, was my little bungalow. The porch light was on there too, and lights were on inside. The shades were drawn

She went through the front gate, up the short walk, and onto the porch. The front door was unlocked. She knocked, cracked it open, and called, "Michael? Michael, it's Mom."

No answer. She looked over her shoulder for the approach of Brett Henchle, but realized she had to be well ahead of him. The ranch was several miles out of town, and he'd have to drive through some of that chaos on the main street before he could turn off to get here.

She went inside to wait, and immediately, unintentionally began to acquaint herself with how Travis Jordan lived and kept house. The living room wasn't too bad. A model airplane, still in progress, lay on a table on the back porch. The kitchen was a mess with empty root beer bottles on the table, and two pieces of cold Canadian bacon pizza on a plate.

The bedroom was just off the dining room and the door was open. She debated for just a moment and then stole quietly in to have just a quick look. The bed was made, and that pleased her. The stuffed lion and lamb posed against the pillows made her smile. Books were neatly perched on the shelves, and an aquarium, home to four tropical fish and one tiny frog, gurgled peacefully.

She heard a noise and turned. Nothing there but the messy kitchen and two pieces of cold pizza.

The bedroom closet was along the wall to her immediate right, closed off with bifold doors. She was tempted to take a peek in there as well, but drew the line right where she stood. Privacy was privacy. Besides, there was a smell in here, like body odor. *He has some dirty tee shirts hiding somewhere*, she thought, *and I don't want to find them.*

Then she saw the picture beside the bed, and paused. It was Marian, looking the best she'd ever looked in one of those perfect hair, hand-to-chin studio poses. She walked quietly, even respectfully, around the bed and to the nightstand to take a closer look. This was Marian in her prime, before the cancer and chemotherapy. Morgan couldn't resist. She had to touch it, then pick it up, charmed by Marian's smile, saddened by the loss. She could identify. She had a picture of Gabe by her bed.

She looked over her shoulder.

Nothing there but shelves, a banjo, and the door to the kitchen. Sometimes light reflected off the inside of her glasses and made her think she was seeing something. That must have been what it was.

Plus the fact that she was nervous and still hadn't found her son.

And afraid, maybe. Just a little afraid. Not that there was any reason to feel fear, not in this place, not in Travis Jordan's house.

She turned her back to the wall and looked all around the

bedroom. The only sound was the gurgling of the aquarium. Everything looked fine. It didn't *smell* fine, but—

She didn't know what was in that closet, did she? She hadn't looked in there.

Well, she hadn't looked under the bed, either.

Every child's silly fear. Monsters in the closet and a bogeyman under the bed. Fear for no reason. *Enough!*

"Michael?"

No answer. He simply wasn't here.

She walked out of the bedroom—FRONTDOOROPENED! She jolted.

"Hello? Reverend Elliott?" It was Brett Henchle.

She wilted.

She found some air, drew it in deeply, and sighed it out, her hand over her heart. "Officer Henchle, you scared me to death."

He smiled, embarrassed. "Whoa, sorry. Do you know why I'm here?"

She managed a smile although she was still trembling. "I think we're both here to get Michael, only he isn't here."

He immediately turned grim. "Where is he?"

"I, I don't know. He's been gone a while, I think. Travis and I have both called him but there's been no answer . . ." Her legs felt wobbly. She shook her head, trying to clear it.

"You okay?"

She pulled a chair from the kitchen table, sat down, and didn't answer until her head was between her knees. "A little over-wrought, I guess. Too much excitement . . ."

"I'll get you a glass of water."

She didn't trust him enough not to raise her head and watch him go to the sink. He no longer stood between her and the front door. She thought of running.

Control, Morgan! Come on!

NANCY BARRONS and Kim Staples made it to the ranch after news hounding and shooting several rolls of film in town. With a word to the police from Kyle and me, they were permitted under the yellow barrier tape and into the thick of the action. The main attraction right now was the slow, relentless parade of campers and motor homes coming down the driveway, each one bearing a red tag indicating it had been searched.

"The end of Cantwell's heyday," Nancy commented.

"We don't know how many are still with him in the house," I replied. "But he's keeping hostages."

"Kyle?"

"Yeah?"

"I'll be writing another editorial, something I hope will bring some balance to the first one. Sorry for the trouble."

Kyle smiled. "Well, praise God."

"Kyle!" someone shouted from beyond the yellow tape. "Travis!"

It was Bob Fisher, the Baptist minister. He was standing out there with Howard Munson the independent Pentecostal, Sid Maher the Lutheran, and Paul Daley the Episcopalian. We hurried down to the tape and ducked under to their side. They were full of questions and concern. Could they help? Was there anything they could do?

"Pray," said Kyle. "Just pray that no one gets hurt, that somehow the Lord will open the eyes of Cantwell's followers and bring freedom to the hostages."

"Cantwell?" Paul Daley asked. "Who's Cantwell?"

Explaining the new name meant telling a lot of the story. While Kyle began the account, I stepped aside to watch the police setting up floodlights and loudspeakers along the brow of the hill. No doubt they were setting up speakers and lights all around the house.

"He's not going to like being surrounded," I said.

"What was that?" Nancy asked.

"I'm not too sure how he's going to respond to being surrounded by all the . . . authority figures. It might be too much like the fence . . ."

Nancy moaned, "I think you're right."

"If he feels corralled . . ."

"FEELING BETTER?" Brett asked.

Morgan had downed most of the glass of water he'd brought her and was sitting upright. She nodded. "I'm with you. Just needed some time to steel my nerves." Her heart was still racing.

"We'd better find Michael."

"He probably decided to walk home—to my place. You may have noticed, he likes to walk." She saw my telephone next to the couch in the living room, and crossed over to it. "I'll see if I can reach—"

"HOLD IT! HOLD IT RIGHT THERE!"

She jumped and then she froze, hands half-raised and trembling. She turned her head.

Brett Henchle wasn't talking to her. He was looking into the bedroom, sighting down the barrel of his gun. He motioned to her, *get back*. "TURN AROUND SLOWLY AND PUT YOUR HANDS AGAINST THE WALL!"

She ducked behind the far end of the couch, her heart pounding. She managed a prayer, only three or four words, then concentrated on breathing.

Brett advanced on the bedroom, gun extended. He disappeared through the door. "AGAINST THE WALL! SPREAD 'EM!" Something jingled: *His handcuffs*, she thought.

Morgan heard sounds of scuffling and blows. Books thudded and crashed to the floor. A body hit the wall. She half rose from her hiding place, longing to help.

A shot went off. She dropped behind the couch again.

A sound like tearing cloth, the impact of a punch. Brett cried out in pain. More scuffling.

Quiet. Then feet stumbling, dragging.

A hand came through the door, grabbing the doorpost, streaking the paint with blood.

Brett's face appeared, twisted, shaken, pale. He stared at her, trying to form words. He gagged and drooled red. She jumped up to help him. He had prevailed, but he was hurt. He—

His body lurched forward, and his torso slipped from around a bloodied blade that remained poised in the air, the handle invisible within the doorway. He collapsed, coming down on his knees, then buckling forward, his head thumping on the vinyl flooring.

The knife entered the room, followed by the hand that held it. The bloodied hand of Justin Cantwell.

30

Dressed in white but bloody as raw meat, Cantwell leaned against the doorpost and gazed at her, eyes crazed, knife ready.

Morgan ran for the door.

A man stood there, Near Eastern in appearance—olive skin, black curly hair, a wicked gaze. He reached for her. She spun away.

The Hitchhiker was right behind her, looking pale and dead, his blond hair hanging limply to his shoulders. He didn't grab for her. He just stood in her path, smiling a toothy grin.

She went for his face with the heel of her hand—he wasn't there. She fell forward, off-balance.

Justin Cantwell caught her, clamping his bloodied hands around her wrists. His hands were cold like steel, their grip unbreakable. He reeked of sweat—the smell from the bedroom—and blood. She struggled and kicked, twisted, but he got behind her and twisted her arm behind her back. His knife went to her throat.

"Uncle?" His tone was mocking and patronizing.

The Hitchhiker was back, right in front of her. Near Eastern approached from the front door, taking his time, his eyes menacing. She squirmed and pulled, and the tip of the knife poked her neck like a hot needle. She cried out.

"Uncle?"

She held still, gasping, whimpering. The knife had to be cutting her. She was going to die.

"I can't hear you."

She formed the word several times before she could finally utter it in a quaking whisper. "Uncle."

The tip receded. "That's better."

A third figure appeared from nowhere, dressed in white and looking like an angel. The three came close, lining up like a wall before her.

"You saw what I did to Officer Henchle?"

Father, receive my spirit . . . She swallowed, then nodded.

"And you see my friends?"

She couldn't believe it even as she nodded again.

"So you know your options are limited. As a matter of fact, you don't have any."

"Oh, Jesus . . ."

The knife jabbed her neck. "Say that name again and I will surgically remove it."

His "friends" were a vision she could not blink away. "Who are they?"

"They came to my rescue when God didn't. We've been a team ever since."

"Are they . . . ?"

He snickered. "Who do you want them to be?"

Near Eastern suddenly gained weight, turned pale and gray, and stared at her through the sunken eyes of an old man: Louis Lynch, Florence's dead husband.

The man in white suddenly wore a dark suit and turtleneck, the same as . . .

His face changed, shifted, became . . .

Gabe Elliott. He smiled and nodded to her.

No greater pain could have gone through her heart. "NOOOO!!"

THE POLICE WERE STILL WAITING for a van from the phone company that would provide extra phones and monitoring equipment. I had to use their cell phone to call the ranch's second line one more time.

"Hello?" It was Cantwell.

"Justin, this is Travis."

"I thought I told you to go home!"

"I have to know—"

Click.

CANTWELL TOSSED HIS CELL PHONE on the kitchen table so he could finish duct taping Morgan to a chair. "The miracle of call forwarding," he explained. "But he's going to figure it out. We'll have to be ready when he does."

"You could have escaped." Morgan said it in a very quiet voice. She had agreed to his offer: If she kept her voice quiet, he wouldn't tape her mouth shut. If she cried out he would slit her throat. It was a solid offer. The body of Brett Henchle lying in a pool of blood at her feet convinced her.

"My loyal followers think I did. They're buying me precious time."

"Then why don't you?"

He cinched down the last strip of tape around her wrists and stood back to admire her helplessness. "I still have to settle my dispute with your boyfriend—if he ever gets here! I was waiting for *him*, not you and Henchle!"

"What about my son?"

She thought he would strike her. "Your son! The traitor? The turncoat? The coward?"

"Where is he?"

His anger cost him some strength. His face paled and he dropped into another chair. "Don't worry about him. It won't do him any good."

I CALLED THE RANCH'S FIRST LINE.

Matt answered, "Yeah?"

"Matt, can you tell me how many are in the house with you?"

"About twenty."

I got ready to write. "I need to know their names."

"I don't know all their names."

I could feel Sheriff Parker's eyes on me. "Matt, the police need to know who's up there. You have to give them a good reason not to come storming in there right now."

"Mary Donovan."

I wrote her name down. "All right. Who else?"

"Dee Baylor."

"All right." He went silent. "Who else, Matt?"

"Brandon's here."

"Yeah."

"And there are twenty others."

I heard a commotion behind me and turned. A motor home had come to a stop at the bottom of the driveway, and the door was opening. Jim Baylor stood right below that door, and let out a whoop when his wife, Dee, appeared, hopping out and embracing him. They started kissing, explaining, apologizing. The scene should have had music.

"Um, Matt, Jim Baylor would like very much to talk with his wife. Would that be possible?"

"No. She's with the others. We have 'em all confined."

Jim waved at me as he led his wife away. She was crying, clinging to him. I told Matt, "Okay. Then how about some more names?"

"I told you, I don't know their names."

"Then how about getting Brandon on the phone?"

"You have to call the other line. That's what he says."

"Well he can't be that far—" I felt a turn in the gut.

"Just call him on the other line."

"Well . . ." I didn't want Matt to know my own thoughts were running me over so I forced myself to say, "Okay. I'll call on the other line."

I ended the call. Parker was muttering something but I didn't hear it.

Cantwell had eyes. He didn't need to be here to know what the cops were doing or whether Sheriff Parker was smiling.

Parker asked me, "Well?"

"Matt won't, uh . . . I'll give it another whirl."

No. Cantwell wouldn't want to be surrounded or fenced in. Fences were a big issue in his life. So he wouldn't hole up at the ranch, would he?

"Are you going to dial that thing?" Parker demanded.

I dialed the ranch's second line. It rang repeatedly without an answer, and then a recording came on: "The cellular phone you called is not answering. Please try your call again later."

"No answer?" Parker asked.

"I have to talk to Dee," I said, handing him the cell phone. "JIM! Hold up!"

Jim and Dee waited near the front gate. The loudspeakers on the hill were playing Jimi Hendrix and the floodlights made it look like a night baseball game was in progress. Television reporters were standing just on the other side of the yellow tape, talking into their microphones and looking back at their cameras. The whole landscape was flickering with white, blue, red, and amber sweeps from the police vehicles.

We hadn't finished our discussion, he said, but we would. I could count on it.

Go home, Travis. Go home.

"Dee," I asked, ducking under the yellow tape to get to them. "Is Brandon Nichols up there?"

She was still wiping tears from her eyes. "I don't want to see him. Not anymore. I feel like a fool."

"But *did* you see him?"

"No. He wouldn't even come out of his room to talk to me. He wouldn't talk to anybody. People are leaving. He's just . . . I just want to go home!"

Jim gave her a squeeze and led her along. "C'mon, hon. We'll get you home. Thanks, Travis. Thanks for everything."

"You too, Jim."

I took out my own cell phone and punched in Morgan's number. "The cell phone you have called is not answering. Please try again later."

I punched in my home phone number. My hand was shaking so much that I got it wrong. I punched it in again. I felt sick.

The telephone rang, and then—

"Okay, we are ready to talk," said Justin Cantwell. Before I had time to think it, he added, "Don't look around, Travis. Don't say anything, don't signal anyone. I have someone here who'd like to speak with you."

"Travis?" It was Morgan's voice, trembling with emotion, her little rasp unmistakable. "Travis. I love you too." The end of her sentence broke apart as she started to cry.

"So I wasn't lying the first time," said Cantwell. "I was just a little early. Do we have an understanding?"

Not far from me, Kyle and the other ministers continued to pray in a circle. I knew I had help.

"We still have to have our discussion," I said.

"So come home, Travis. *Alone.*"

"I'll be right there."

I came up with some lame excuse I can hardly remember, something about being sick, tired, or incompetent. I don't know. But I told Parker I was leaving for a while and ran to my Trooper.

I climbed in, closed the door, started the engine, then bowed my head to pray, gripping the steering wheel tightly enough to reshape it. I intended to burst into desperate prayer. I was going to tackle, wrestle, and grapple with God, crying out in earnest supplication for Morgan's life and my own and for the tattered soul of Justin Cantwell. I was going to bind and rebuke the powers of darkness and cast them out. I would be waging holy warfare in the heavenlies. It was going to be a struggle—

Before you pray . . . said the Lord.

I looked up. It was quiet inside the Trooper, and suddenly, strangely quiet in my heart. It threw me. What happened? One moment I was ready to leap into the fires of hell and whip-in-the-spirit whatever evil forces might come my way, and the next moment—well, I felt as if I were sitting in heaven. I saw nothing unusual—no visions, no angels, no lightning bolts or faces in the sky. The same cruel, crazy world was in full swing outside my windshield: The lights were still flashing, the cops were still running around, and the floodlights were still there, along with the TV cameras.

But I felt as if I were somewhere else.

How can I describe it? Jesus was in the Trooper with me. I would never presume to put words in his mouth, but I felt him saying, *Could we take a moment to review?*

I let go of the steering wheel and listened.

MORGAN SAT QUIETLY, praying only in her mind, her wrists anchored to the arms of the chair, her ankles taped together and immobile between the chair legs. Cantwell was sitting at the table, leaning on his left elbow, breathing hard, the knife dangling in his right hand. Though he looked fatigued, the vicious, animal expression never left his eyes. He had made no effort to clean any of the blood off himself. If anything, there seemed to be more blood than before. A pool of red was gathering in his chair and he was sitting in it.

"So you're one of them, aren't you?" he asked.

"One of . . . whom?"

He leaned forward and held the knife under her chin. "You're a church lady, aren't you? One of the 'reverends.' Did Travis tell you what I did to a 'reverend'?"

His raging eyes were only a foot away. She could smell his breath, his sweat, the blood, now spoiling like meat left out too long. Near Eastern, the Angel, and the Hitchhiker were hovering, lingering, present in the room, sometimes visible, always felt. The house had become an outpost of hell.

It made the peace she felt all the stranger to understand. She never would have expected this enveloping sensation of rest, as if she were somehow separated by a holy capsule from all that was occurring around her. It settled over her the moment her struggle was over and her options gone—the moment Cantwell's last strip of tape went around her wrist and there was nothing more she could do but trust.

Her voice was steady and gentle as she replied, "He mostly told me what the 'reverend' in your life did to you."

He leaned back, letting the knife rest in his lap. "Maybe he *did* find out everything." He looked down at Henchle's body. "Did he tell you who else was there?"

Morgan thanked God as she recalled the name. "Uh, I think the name was Gallipo."

Cantwell looked pleased. "Conway Gallipo, Nechville's permanent chief of police! Very good."

"Travis pieced it together, the part about Gallipo. He figured it would take two people: one to hold your arms, the other to drive the nails."

He waved his knife in her face as he lectured, "That should tell you a lot about me and why we're sitting here right now." Victoriously, he placed his foot on Henchle's back. "This little act of God was for Gallipo's sake." He saw her grimace. "Hey, come on. You didn't trust Henchle either—"

He straightened and looked around the room like a guard dog alerted by a noise.

Morgan felt a stirring in the room, a cold flutter in the air, a sense of alarm—on *their* part.

Then she heard the slam of a car door.

THE BUNGALOW LOOKED COZY and inviting. The porch light was on, and warm lamplight created a glow behind the drapes.

But it *felt* cold and sinister, and I knew the devils were inside. I stood by the gate for just a moment, gathering my thoughts and reviewing what the Lord and I had discussed all the way down here, that he and history were on my side. There was never a moment or aspect of my life God didn't have his hand on, and this little adventure was no exception. All I had to do was walk into the house and let him take it from there.

I knew Kyle and the others were still praying. I said a last prayer of my own and stepped through the gate.

I had never regarded myself as a man of keen spiritual discernment. Sure, I could usually get an inkling that something or someone wasn't quite right, but it was Marian who could sense the presence of a demon and be correct every time. I used to wonder and even ask her how she did it and what it felt like. Tonight I didn't have to wonder. I could feel a presence in my house as directly, as pungently, as any man could feel a hateful stare or a poisonous taunt. I gazed at the drawn drapes as if the spirits might be looking back at me from behind them. I glanced into the tops of the trees, a little surprised not to see some shadowy creature perched in the limbs.

They were watching me, waiting for me, expecting to play the game by their rules. *Come on in*, they dared me.

I continued down the walkway and stepped onto the porch.

I heard some movement inside. The scraping of a chair. Morgan gasping. A muttered threat.

I called through the door, "Justin. It's Travis. I'm coming in."

There was no reply, although I did feel a painful twist in my gut as if I were stepping off a cliff. I took hold of the doorknob.

We're ready, they seemed to say. *Come on in.*

Well I'm ready too, I thought, *and* we're *coming in*.

I turned the knob and opened the door slowly.

The first thing I saw was Justin Cantwell in my dining room, streaked and stained with red, gripping Morgan by the hair and holding a knife to her throat. The second thing I saw was the tape that bound her to the chair. The third thing was Brett Henchle, dead on the floor. I was sickened but not shocked. I remained still. Cantwell was breathing hard, shaking—and desperate.

"Hi there." I thought my voice would crack or quiver, but it didn't. "It's me."

"Close the door!" he hissed.

I closed the door.

"You weren't here for the first part of our meeting!" he said, nodding at Henchle's body. "But you can see who's in charge!"

I raised my hands so he could see them, then went slowly to the chair by the door and sat down. "I'm all ears."

The ceiling felt low, as if the joists were supporting a mountain. Breathable air seemed scarce. Though I had just come through the front door, I felt it would not open again. The house, with only three living people in it, felt suffocatingly crowded.

Cantwell released his grip on Morgan's hair and she shook the kink out of her neck. By leaning shakily on the back of her chair, he made it to the table. By steadying himself against the table, he worked his way back to his own chair and sat down.

"Justin," I said, "you're hurt."

He ignored me. "You see, Travis?" His voice was weak. "I've played a better game. I've healed more sick, fed more hungry, brought hope to more hopeless, and now I even decide who lives and who dies. People are afraid of me!" He slumped forward, his elbow on his knee, his head drooping. "And that makes me God!"

I shrugged. "If you can't trust him, *be* him. Is that how it works?"

"It works."

"So I see. I can also see you need a doctor."

He raised his head and grinned at me. "I got what I wanted ever since my back yard."

"What was that, Justin?"

His head sank again and he spoke to the floor. "Not to be nailed to the fence anymore."

I hurt for him, even in the midst of the terror. "I hear you."

"You've been there. You know what I'm talking about."

I had to set the record straight. "Justin, I haven't been hurt nearly as much as you have. I was discouraged, I was fed up—"

"But you know what I'm talking about!"

"Yeah. I do."

"So where do you stand?"

"Justin," I said, staring at his abdomen, "you're bleeding."

He leaned toward Morgan, brandishing the knife. "Don't change the subject, Travis!"

"Okay. Easy." He relaxed and I continued. "Listen, we were both angry. We were both fed up. We both had wounds and questions. But Justin, my problem was with the church, with all the church stuff. Your problem is with God. There's a difference."

His eyes bored into me as he displayed the scars on his arms. "I'm perfectly willing to blame them both."

I pressed it, hoping I wouldn't set him off. "But your father wasn't speaking for God, and Jesus didn't nail you to that fence."

He grimaced as if feeling the pain again, then wagged his head. "The point is past arguing!"

I argued anyway. "Remember when your mother came home and got the hammer and pulled the nails out? Remember when she held you and sang to you? That was Jesus. He took the nails. He doesn't drive them."

For the briefest moment, his face softened as if he were recalling the moment.

"I met your mom. I can see Jesus in her."

The hardness and loathing flowed into his face again. "She's the one who got beaten, torn down, and pushed around every day of her life."

"It wasn't Jesus who—"

"It was Jesus who let it happen. Don't tell me you can't see that. You've had forty years to see it."

I wasn't going to lie. "Justin, after forty years of knowing Jesus and just a few months watching you, I've decided I can trust him."

He absorbed the blow, then snickered and shook his head. "You're just like Mom. You love losing."

"No. I love winning. It just takes longer."

He jolted, his eyes darting about the room as if watching a frightful vision. I figured his invisible henchmen weren't too happy by now. When his gaze finally returned to me, he was weaker.

"Well, I love winning too. Daddy found that out." He waved his knife at the body on the floor. "And . . . and Gallipo. He found out. And God's finding out!" He stared at me a long moment, his body swaying like a drunkard. "And you're going to find out too, Travis! Just you wait!"

"Oh, I'm waiting, all right. After forty years of serving the Lord, you learn to do that." I relaxed and slouched in my chair. "But if we wait much longer, it'll be too late to help you. Let me call the paramedics." I didn't get out of my chair. I only leaned toward the telephone.

He held the knife out, showing it to me, sending me a message. Blood was dripping steadily from his chair to the floor. "You should have joined up with me when you could." I could barely hear him. "You could've beaten God, just like me." His hand went to his abdomen and he winced in pain as fresh blood oozed through his fingers. "I am he. I'm the one."

He pitched forward suddenly, sooner than I expected, one hand on his stomach and the other still holding the knife. For a long moment he lingered there, head close to his knees.

"Justin . . ." I got up.

With a groan, and before I could catch him, he slid off the chair and flopped over Henchle's body, his head hanging loosely above the floor. He still held the knife.

Morgan cautioned, "Wait, Travis."

I stopped a few feet short of Cantwell's dying body. Morgan was looking at something—or someone—across the table from her and directly in front of me. There was no fear in her eyes. "Do you see them?"

I looked around the dining room and kitchen. I saw nothing but the walls and cabinets, but I could feel my skin crawling. "Who are they?"

Morgan looked from one to the other as she named them off. "The Hitchhiker, and Sally's angel, and I suppose this one here is Elkezar, the one who appeared to Adrian Folsom." Now she appeared angry. "They're laughing at him."

Just as they've been doing all along, I thought. "The party's over," I said. "Get out of here."

It felt like a puff of wind, but it wasn't. Morgan gave a little gasp and I could sense what she was seeing.

Evil was leaving the house like a receding tide. The weight I felt, the suffocating closeness of the room, lifted from me. Pain, bitterness, hatred, arrogance—they'd all had their season, but now it was over.

It was time.

I reached for the light switch and flipped the living room light off and on again, twice. We heard shouts and footsteps at both the front and the back door, and then Mark Peterson and four sheriff's deputies stormed in like commandos, guns drawn, fanning out, hollering to intimidate, positioning, crouching, covering Cantwell from every angle.

The swarming and clatter became a silent tableau.

"Oh my God . . ." said Mark, sinking to his knees beside his fallen boss. "No. No, no . . ."

I knelt by the Messiah of Antioch. His eyes were half-open, half-alive, but not watching me. They were looking into the distance, filled with dismay and the pain of betrayal. I knew he was watching the retreat of his minions, the evaporation of his power. I took the bloodied blade of the knife between my index finger and thumb, and lifted it from his hand. By the time I stood to my feet, the eyes bore no expression at all.

Two deputies moved in, checking both bodies for any sign of life. One deputy stood up, said simply, "That's it," and it was over. He spoke into his radio, "Sheriff, this is Jones. We have Cantwell. Repeat, we have Cantwell. He's dead from a gunshot wound. Officer Henchle is also dead."

"Michael!" Morgan cried as I cut her loose with my pocket knife. "We have to find Michael!"

"He's outside," said Mark. "We picked him up. He was walking to your place to find you!"

"Mom?" came his voice. "Mom, you okay?"

Morgan ran out the door. "Michael!"

"Hey," Jones said, "don't leave! You're a witness!"

"Don't worry," I assured him, stepping around all the officers and getting out the door.

Mother and son were embracing just outside the front gate. She was a small woman and he towered over her, but she was still his mother and acting like it. "You had me scared to death. I thought something terrible had happened to you. Why didn't you call before you left? Are you sure you're all right?"

"I went over to your place," he tried to explain. "I guess we missed each other."

I glanced back into my house. Mark Peterson and the others were just beginning to clean up what Michael had barely avoided. It made me think of Kyle Sherman and the other ministers praying in a circle. When I looked back, Morgan was finally convinced of her son's safety enough to let go of him.

She looked at me. I could read in her eyes what I knew in my heart, but there was no way either of us could say it. We just ran for each other. She put her arms around me and clung to me tighter than would normally be considered a sisterly hug. I returned her embrace, and I wouldn't say I was careful or socially self-conscious, either.

We just had to hold each other, that's all.

EPILOGUE

THE "SIEGE" at the Macon ranch didn't last long enough even to justify the name. The motor home crowds wanted no trouble and most of them had already cleared out. The wanderers and seekers in pickups and old cars had already taken their kids and dogs and hit the highway again, looking elsewhere. The reformed and visionary work crews who spruced up the town had long since lost their vision when they ran out of money, and moved on. When the police finally entered the Macon house, they encountered no resistance and found only two people inside. Matt Kiley was lying by the telephone in the living room, crestfallen to hear of Cantwell's death and unable to move his legs. Mary Donovan was in her room, still convinced she was the Blessed Virgin and praying for deliverance. They later found Melody Blair hiding in the barn.

BY THE FOLLOWING SUMMER, Antioch was a different town. Don Anderson had a new furniture and appliance store, and this one wasn't pink. Kiley's Hardware was now a True Value under new ownership. Nancy Barrons had sold the Antioch *Harvester* and married the columnist in Spokane. Our Lady of the Fields got a whole new set of pews, a new altar, and a new crucifix.

Some remnants of the previous summer remained. The white line Michael Elliott helped paint down the center of the street was still there, along with the heads of wheat to mark the intersections and the rain clouds to mark the fire hydrants. The trees planted along the street were growing quite well, and the townsfolk had pitched in to add some more.

But there had been no further sightings of Jesus or Mary in the clouds, in the highway signs, in the hedges, or even in the mildew on the shower tiles, and none were expected. The townspeople had undergone a notable change of mind: They were looking forward now, and saw no need to dredge up and relive the past.

I never thought I'd say that about Antioch.

By the following summer, I was a different man too. I didn't fully realize it until I set foot inside Antioch Pentecostal Mission for the first time in over a year. The place was packed, and I was deluged by the same smells, sounds, and sights that had been a regular part of my fifteen years of pastoring. I was a little worried that the old symptoms would return: the upset stomach, the scrambled thoughts, the swelling tongue, the fear of being trapped.

But none of that happened. It was actually good—no, I'll say it was *wondrous*—to be in that building again, standing before all those friends and family. When my time came to enter from the right and stand on my little "X" of masking tape, I could have remained in that spot for hours, as long as it took to read back from each face a portion of my life.

The mandolin player from my band. My old buddy Vern, with his second wife. Al and Rose Chiardelli, my "other parents," who would always love me and consider me as their son. Some of the old youth group from Northwest Mission, with their wives and husbands and children, so grown and changed that I hardly recognized them. Joe and Emily Kelmer—Joe still healthy, and his family all saved. Bruce and Libby Hiddle, the only ones who could truly understand our shared tragedy, and our shared joy. Jim, Dee, and Darlene Baylor, sitting together as a family.

To my left stood my brother, Steve, living proof that a man

doesn't have to enter the ministry to honor God in every aspect of his life. Behind me stood Dad, decked out in his tuxedo. Tradition did not dictate that he wear one, and he never did for the hundreds of other weddings he had performed. But when he married his own kids, he put it on. That was *his* tradition.

From the front pew, my sister, Rene, winked at me, and I winked back. I used to wonder what in the world her "problem" was, but now I knew what she knew: It was never a *problem*, but a *passage*.

We had come far, these friends and family and I. Most of the journey we'd made separately, but today we journeyed together.

As a sweet lady who once sang in a rock band told me, *we* were what Jesus was all about. Over the years we'd dispersed ourselves among many churches, denominations, traditions, and little things held sacred, but today none of that mattered. *Jesus* mattered. *We* mattered.

And *she* mattered. Everyone rose to their feet as she entered the room. Morgan's widowed father came all the way from Michigan to escort her down the aisle. Her son, Michael, had a front-row seat, and her sister from Florida was her matron of honor. Both our former congregations were there to honor her.

As she came down the aisle in a gown of pastel blue, her eyes shining and never leaving mine, I could hear the same voice in my heart I'd been hearing since I was in kindergarten: *I carried you, Travis, just as a father carries his son, in all the way that you went, until you came to this place.*

He was still the same old God, ordering my life and doing all things well.

MONSTER

To Barbara Jean, my true love,
and my best friend through it all.

One

The Hunter, rifle in his hands, dug in a heel and came to a sudden halt on the game trail, motionless, nearly invisible in a thicket of serviceberry and crowded pines. He heard something.

The first rays of the sun flamed over the ridge to the east, knifing through the pine boughs and morning haze in translucent wedges, backlighting tiny galaxies of swirling bugs. Soon the warming air would float up the draw and the pines would whisper like distant surf, but in the lull between the cool of night and the warmth of day, the air was still, the sounds distinct. The Hunter heard his own pulse. The scraping of branches against his camouflage sleeves was crisp and brilliant, the snapping of twigs under his boots almost startling.

And the eerie howl was clear enough to reach him from miles away, audible under the sound of the jays and between the chatterings of a squirrel.

He waited, not breathing, until he heard it again: long, mournful, rising in pitch, and then holding that anguished note to the point of agony before trailing off.

The Hunter's brow crinkled under the bill of his cap. The howl was too deep and guttural for a wolf. A cougar never made a sound like that. A bear? Not to his knowledge. If it was his quarry, it was upset about something.

And far ahead of him.

He moved again, quickstepping, ducking branches, eyes darting about, dealing with the distance.

Before he had worked his way through the forest another mile, he saw a breach in the forest canopy and an open patch of daylight through the trees. He was coming to a clearing.

He slowed, cautious, found a hiding place behind a massive fallen fir, and peered ahead.

Just a few yards beyond him, the forest had been shorn open by a logging operation, a wide swath of open ground littered with forest debris and freshly sawn tree stumps. A dirt road cut through it all, a house-sized pile of limbs and slash awaited burning, and on the far side of the clearing, a hulking, yellow bulldozer sat cold and silent, its tracks caked with fresh earth. A huge pile of logs lay neatly stacked near the road, ready for the logging trucks.

He saw no movement, and the only sound was the quiet rumble of a battered pickup truck idling near the center of the clearing.

He waited, crouching, eyes level with the top of the fallen tree, scanning the clearing, searching for the human beings who had to be there. But no one appeared and the truck just kept idling.

His gaze flitted from the truck to the bulldozer, then to the huge pile of logs, and then to the truck again where something protruding from behind the truck's front wheels caught his eye.

He grabbed a compact pair of binoculars from a pocket and took a closer look.

The protrusion was a man's arm, motionless and streaked with red.

Looking about, the Hunter waited just a few more seconds and then, satisfied that no one else was there, he climbed over the log and stole into the clearing, stepping carefully from rock to stump to patch of grass, trying to avoid any soil that would register his footprints. The truck was parked in nothing but loose soil, freshly chewed by the bulldozer, but he would have to deal with that problem later. He was planning his moves as he went along.

He reached the truck, slowed with caution, and then eased around it, neck craning, in no mood for gruesome surprises.

What he found on the other side was no surprise, but it was gruesome, and definitely a complication. Cursing, he leaned against the truck's hood, warily scanned the tree line and the logging road, and started weighing his options.

The crumpled body on the ground was obviously one of the logging crew, most likely the foreman who'd lingered alone too long on the site the previous evening, judging from the stiff condition of his body. He lay on his belly in the dirt, his body crushed, dried blood streaked from his nose and mouth, his head twisted grotesquely on a broken neck. His hard hat lay top down several feet away, and the ground around the truck was littered with metal shreds of what used to be a lunch box and scattered, chewed-up plastic wrappings that used to hold a lunch.

I don't have time for this!

The Hunter quickly stifled his rage. He needed to calculate, foresee, plan.

His gaze shifted to the pile of logs. That might be an option. He could make it look like an accident that would explain the bent, torn, rag-doll condition of the dead man.

Were the keys in the bulldozer?

Leaving his rifle by the truck, the Hunter ran to the bull-dozer, clambered up on the big steel track, and stepped into the cab. He sank into the worn and torn driver's seat and searched the panel for the keys. Then he sniffed a chuckle of realization: Of course. This wasn't in town, where idle punks drifted about look-ing to steal anything not locked up or bolted down, and this machine was no car for joyriding. The key was in the ignition.

It had been a while since his college summers with the con-struction crew, but if this thing was anything like that track hoe he used to operate . . .

He clicked the key over to *Preheat*, waited, then turned the key to *Start*.

The dozer cranked to life with a puff of black smoke.

His mind was racing, still planning, as he put the mountain-ous machine into gear and got it moving. Reverse came easily enough. Forward was easier. With careful manipulation of the brakes and levers, he brought the dozer to the back of the log pile, then left it there, still running.

Hauling the dead man across the ground would be messy, but it was the only option. The Hunter grabbed the man's wrists—the right arm was intact, but the left arm had been snapped above the elbow and flexed like a rubber hose—and started pulling. He tugged and dragged the body over limbs, grass, rocks, and debris. The man's head dangled from a wrung neck and scraped on the ground. When the Hunter reached the front of the log pile, he let go of the arms. The stiffened body flopped into the dust.

Seated once again in the dozer, he edged the machine for-ward, reaching under the logs with the bucket. With a calculat-ing, steady pull of the lever, he raised the bucket, lifting the logs, lifting, lifting, until . . .

The pile upset. The logs rolled and rumbled down, bouncing,

tumbling one over the other, drumming the ground, kicking up dust.

The dead man's body disappeared beneath a jackstraw pile of logs.

No time, no time! The Hunter eased the dozer back to its resting place, switched it off, and leaped to the ground. He ran back to the idling truck and pocketed every metal scrap, every torn plastic wrapper he could find. Then, slinging his rifle over his shoulder, he spotted and grabbed a broken-off evergreen bough and went to work, retracing his every step, brushing and erasing each footprint with rapid side-sweeps as he backed out of the clearing.

As expected, he heard the slowly rising sound of a vehicle coming up the logging road, climbing switchbacks, lurching through gears, rattling over potholes, and growling over gravel.

He crouched and headed for the trees, tossing away the branch. Just as he slipped into the forest, a truck pulled into the clearing on the other side. He stole through the crowded timber, planting every footstep silently in the soft, pine-needled ground. Truck doors slammed. Voices lifted, followed by cries of alarm. Those loggers were going to have quite a morning.

"So we stay on the Cave Lake Trail for 3.4 miles, and then we come to this fork where the Lost Creek Trail branches off to the right—Beck? Are you following this?"

Rebecca Shelton, twenty-eight, looked up from her compact, unhappy with her clumpy mascara but resigned to leaving it as it was. "W-which trail?"

Her husband, Reed, a six-foot hunk and very aware of it, was trying to be patient, she could tell. She'd seen that understanding but slightly testy expression many times over their six years of marriage. He pointed once again to the map he'd spread out on the hood of their Ford SUV, their route boldly marked with orange highlighter. "This one. Cave Lake. Then this one. Lost Creek."

"Mm. Got it."

She'd been trying to pay attention and even scare up a little enthusiasm all during their long drive, or as Reed called it, "Insertion into the Survival Zone." They'd had a nice picnic lunch—"Preexcursion Rations"—on a log, and even now—at "The Final Briefing" on the hood of their car—she was doing her best to match Reed's excitement, but it was hard to be interested in how many miles they would hike, the hours it would take to get there, the trail grades they would encounter, and their available physical energy. This whole adventure was never *their* idea in the first place, but *his*. He was so *into* this stuff. He'd picked out all the gear, the boots, the backpacks, the maps, the freeze-dried apricots and trail mix, everything. He let her choose which *color* of backpack she wanted—blue—but *he* chose which *kind*.

"If we average four miles an hour, we can be there in . . . three hours," he was saying. There he went again. Beck sighed, and Reed stole a sideways glance at her. "Uh, but considering the rough terrain and the two-thousand-foot climb, I've allowed for six hours, which will still get us there before dark. Got your canteen?"

"Chh-ch-check." Well, *check* was supposed to sound cool, but the word made her stutter flare up, especially now, when she was upset.

"Potable water only, remember. Treat any water you collect before you drink it."

"B-beaver fever."

"Exactly."

Beaver fever. According to Reed, beavers pooped and peed in the creeks, so they weren't supposed to drink the water or they'd catch whatever contagion the beavers were passing, something she wouldn't even try to pronounce.

"Beaver fever," she repeated, just for the satisfaction of saying it clearly. *B*'s didn't bother her much, especially when she was alone with Reed. *W*'s and *s*'s were the toughest, especially around people or when she was on edge. *R*'s and hard *c*'s made her nervous; that was why her name had shrunk to Beck—she didn't have to say an *R*, and once she got the *c* out, the task was over.

"Now, you're going to need a minimum of two or three quarts of water a day," Reed said, "and that's if you aren't exerting yourself, so don't push it too hard on the way up there. And pay attention to your urine output. You want at least a quart in a twenty-four hour period."

"R-r-reed!" She was incredulous.

"Hey, you're looking out for dehydration. If enough water's going out, then you know enough's going in."

"Sss-so are there any b-bathrooms up there?"

Reed smiled playfully. "Honey, what do you think your camp shovel's for?"

Oh, right. Those little collapsible shovels hanging on their packs. Wonderful.

"You did bring toilet paper, right?"

She couldn't help rolling her eyes. "Yes. I've got s-some in my pack and some in my pocket." It was the first thing she packed, and she brought extra. It was the last vestige of the decent, civilized, sensible life she was being ripped away from—besides a folding hairbrush and a small makeup bag.

"Ah, good. Leaves and grass can get a little itchy."

She'd worked up the perfect angry wife look over the years, and now she gave him a good dose of it.

But it didn't faze him. He laughed and gave her a playful rub on her shoulder. Her tension eased. "Don't worry, sweetheart. Once you get up in those mountains and start learning how to survive, you'll wonder why we never did this before."

"I'm w-w-wondering why we're doing it *now*."

Reed studied her face a moment. "Because it'll be good for us." She was about to counter, but he headed her off. "No, now, it's something we need to do. We need a week away from the grind, away from TV and cell phones and the little holes we've dug ourselves into."

"You and Cap maybe."

"Sing's coming too."

"It's a guy thing. You and Cap. Admit it."

"No, come on, *you* admit it. You need to stretch a little. Comfort can be a dangerous thing. You stick around home all the time where it's safe and nothing ever changes, and before you know it, you get set in your ways and you quit learning, you quit changing, you don't grow anymore." He gestured toward the mountains before them, vast, towering, fading from sharp green to soft blue in the immense distance, with snow still visible on the rocky crags. "This will keep you growing. There are things out there you've never seen, never felt, things you need to experience. It'll be worth the trouble." He gave her a knowing glance. "Sometimes even the *trouble's* worth the trouble."

"Are you talking down to me?"

Now he was openly miffed. "I'm talking about *all* of us."

"Right. All of us." She gazed at the mountains, then down at her hiking outfit—rugged boots with high socks, khaki shorts with pockets for just about everything, and on her back a very slick and efficient backpack with a million zippers, cinches, and Velcro flaps, a sleeping bag, and a tiny, rolled-up tent that really did unroll and become big enough for two people to sleep in. Reed had already seen to it that they'd taken three—not one or two—short, "shake-down hikes" to test all this stuff: the fit of the clothes, the weight of the packs, the effectiveness of the hiking shoes, how fast they could set up the tent, *everything.* "Well, I'm not home and I'm not c-comfortable, so I think you can b-be satisfied."

Reed looked pleased. "It's a good start."

She wanted to hit him.

He turned to the map again, and she tried to follow along. "So, all right. We take the Cave Lake Trail from here to the Lost Creek turnoff, then take that trail for another 8.6 miles, and we should have no trouble reaching the hunter's cabin before night-fall. It's right here, right on the creek. Randy Thompson'll be there waiting for us."

"With dinner?"

"If I know Randy, he'll show us how to build the fire our-selves, without matches, and how to cook our own dinner from what we can find in the woods."

"That'll take forever."

Reed cocked an eyebrow. "Randy can whip up a pine needle tea in under two minutes—and after this week, we'll be able to do the same thing."

Beck made a face. "Pine needle tea?"

Reed shrugged, undaunted, undimmed. "I understand it's not too bad. We might even like it."

"He's not going to make us eat b-bugs and worms, is he?"

Reed wouldn't give up that playful smile. "Mm, you might like those too."

She drew a breath to make a snide comment—

"We'd better get going." He folded up the map and tucked it away in one of his backpack's many zippered compartments, then hefted the pack to his shoulders and put his arms through the straps.

She followed his cue, and Reed held the pack aloft as she

wrestled and squirmed her way into the straps. The thing wasn't as heavy as it looked—and then again, maybe it was.

Reed led the way across the gravel parking lot to the trailhead. Beck followed, looking back once to be sure she hadn't left anything behind, besides her sanity. The SUV sat there all by itself, like a faithful dog sitting in the driveway watching his masters leave.

"You're gonna roast in that jacket," Reed observed.

Beck regarded her fringed buckskin jacket, a gift from her father—he was an outdoors nut too. She never wore it, but for this outing, it seemed appropriate. "S-so I want to be Daniel B-boone, all right?"

"You'll be carrying it."

"Just look out for yourself, Mr. Know-It-All."

Reed kept walking, a spring in his step despite the load on his back. He was so pleased Beck was sure he had a screw loose. "Yeah, this is just what we need."

What I *need, you mean!* Part of her could have, peradventure, at a better time, admitted he was right, but right now she wasn't in the mood to admit anything.

The moment came. Feeling like a Neil Armstrong, Beck followed her adventurous husband and took that One Small Step out of the parking lot and onto the trail. Other steps came after that, and she looked back twice before the deepening forest hid the familiar world from view.

Then, looking back no more, she pressed on, leaving one world for another.

Road 228 was "maintained" in the summer, which was Idaho's way of saying it would be filled back in if it washed out, and you could still drive it if you didn't mind the washboard rattle under your wheels, the blinding dust, the constant growl of the gravel, and the rude bumping of the rocks.

Dr. Michael Capella, a stocky, dark-haired college professor in his thirties, was driving 228 in a Toyota 4Runner, climbing, ever climbing into the mountains, his eyes intent on every curve, every bump, every rut as he maintained a speed just a notch short of dangerous. His wife, Sing, a lovely Coeur d'Alene Native American, sat next to him, her face clouded by a list of concerns, not the least of which was his driving.

"Incredible mountains," she said, admiring their beauty.

Cap nodded, gripping the wheel.

"Cap, there really is some great scenery out there."

"And your point is?"

"It's just a little after four. We'll make it to the resort with time to spare, so relax. Kick back a little. Isn't that what this trip's all about?"

He eased off the accelerator. Sing said nothing, but a faint smile traced her lips.

Cap allowed himself a quick look to the right, where the edge of the road dropped off sharply to the St. Marie's River below and a lone osprey circled above a fathomless, forested valley. He drew a breath and loosened his grip on the steering. "It's hard to let go of things."

She smiled. "You may as well. They aren't there anymore."

He pondered that a moment, but shook his head, still unable to grasp it. "No, *I'm* the one who's not there anymore. And I keep thinking I should be, because they *are*."

She chuckled. "You and that confidentiality agreement! It makes you talk in riddles—ever notice that?"

"Sorry. I know it must seem rude."

She touched his hand. "You don't have to say anything, and you don't have to prove anything, especially to me. I know the man I married."

He nodded a deep nod just to avoid the debate. They'd had this conversation before, and she'd been right, but he'd had trouble buying it. He still did. "Well, call it a sabbatical, then. Call it a break."

"It's a sabbatical. It's a break. And Reed had a good idea." Then she added, "I think."

Cap shifted his thoughts to the coming week. "Well, Reed says Randy Thompson's the best. He's a Native, by the way."

"Well, there *are* some of us still around."

"Randy's up there right now, getting the cabin ready, laying in supplies. He does these survival courses all the time, winter or summer, it doesn't matter. Reed says you can drop that guy anywhere in the world and he'd know what to do to stay alive."

Sing gave a barely audible sigh and looked out the window a moment. "So what do you do while you're living? Staying alive is nice, but you can't do that forever. It's *how* you live the life you have while you have it."

Cap smirked just a little. "I should stick that on the refrigerator."

"I'll write it down for you." She turned her body to face him and put her hand on his shoulder. "Cap, you did the right thing. I'm proud of you."

"At least the house is paid for." He forced a smile. "It's where we go from here that bothers me."

She smiled. He felt her acceptance, as he was. Without changing him. "We go into the mountains, we learn to survive, and we hear from God. That's enough for now."

He drove quietly for a moment, noticing mountain peaks and waterfalls for the first time, and then placed his hand on hers and gave it a squeeze.

Thirty miles of grinding, growling, gravel road later, they reached Abney, a once-booming mining town that had long since withered and now had trouble remembering why it was there.

"Well, it has ambience," said Cap as they eased down the main road past sagging storefronts, well-used vehicles, and mangy stray dogs.

"Rustic," Sing observed politely, kind to choose even that word.

They drove by a forlorn clapboard tavern with one corner sinking into the ground, an auto garage with dismembered cars and trucks scattered about and a snow cat up on blocks, a combination hardware store and mining museum—noteworthy because this building actually had a new front porch—and a post office not much bigger than a phone booth. They had yet to see a human being.

"Can't wait to see the *resort*," Sing quipped.

"I hear it's the real thing, right out of the rich, historical heritage of Idaho."

They drove to the end of town—not far from the beginning—and found a large log cabin to which someone had added another story, to which someone added another wing and a dormer, to which someone added another bedroom, to which someone added four more bedrooms like a motel and then tied the whole thing together with one continuous wraparound porch that bumped up and down to line up with all the doors to all those additions. A sign strung on a chain over the driveway read, "Tall Pine Resort." On the rail fence was a weathered VACANCY sign with an empty nail for hanging a NO in case that should ever be the case. Judging from the scarcity of vehicles in the parking area, the Tall Pine was not seeing a booming business at the moment.

Cap pulled in next to two pickups rigged with high sides for hauling firewood and a station wagon with a sad old dog—he must have been the sire of all the others in town—staring at them through the back window.

"Hm," Cap mused. "Reed said this place is really hopping this time of year."

The lobby was a cubbyhole wedged between the café and the souvenir shop, with trophies of moose, deer, elk, and bear crowding the walls, and one huge chandelier made of antlers that hung over the front desk.

The white-haired, leathery proprietor broke into a silvery grin from behind the front desk. "So you must be the, uh, the Campanellas . . . ?"

"Capella. This is my wife, Sing."

Sing shook his hand. He had gnarled fingers that had hewn many a log and tanned many a deer hide.

"Sing," the old man said quizzically. "It's gotta be short for something."

"Sings in the Morning," she answered. "My parents like the old traditions." Not that she didn't; her and Cap's home boasted some of the finest Salish artwork, and she often wore her long black hair in traditional braids as she did today.

The silvery teeth showed again. "It suits you." He extended his hand to Cap.

Cap gripped it firmly. "I'm Michael, but my friends call me Cap."

"Arlen Peak, pleased to meet you. Now we're friends and I can call you Cap."

"Got that room?"

Peak slid a room registration card toward Cap to fill out. "One-oh-four, just right for you and the missus."

Cap started scribbling, a hint of a smile on his face, his first since they'd left Spokane.

"So . . ." Peak said, watching Cap scribble, "Randy says you're planning on a week up there."

"Yep. Our friends ought to be getting there right about now. We're going to hike up and join them tomorrow morning. We're a day late, but we'll catch up."

"Had to wait to get off work, I suppose."

"Sing did."

Sing shot him a loving but scolding glance, then she broke the silence with a question. "So what's this cabin like?"

Peak chuckled apologetically. "It's not the Hilton, but it's in good shape. We gave it a once-over a little while ago, me and some hunter friends. Put in a new floor, patched the roof, got it all up to snuff again. You understand it's just a shelter for hunters. It's got a few cots, some shelves, and some hooks for hanging things, but that's about it. Randy prefers it that way. Helps people get into the wilderness frame of mind."

"We're ready for it," said Cap, sliding the completed card back across the desk.

"Yeah, well, Randy headed up there this morning, so he's ready for you." Peak thought for a moment. "But you'll wanna be careful. Keep your eyes and ears open, and don't, uh, don't hang around if . . . you know, if you think better of it."

Cap and Sing looked at him, waiting for more.

Peak met their eyes. "Kind of late to be telling you, I know."

Cap sensed something in Arlen Peak, a warning they should heed. "Is there a problem?"

The old man's face became grim. "Well, Mr. Capella . . . Cap . . . we've never had any trouble around here. Randy knows that, and that's what he tells all his clients, but like I tried to tell him, something's not right. Wish he would've been here a few hours ago and seen that whole herd of elk come through, right in broad daylight, all going someplace in a hurry. That's not like them. It's too early in the year for them to be down this low."

"What are you saying?" Cap asked. Both he and Sing were motionless, their eyes on the old man.

He seemed hesitant to answer. "I've lived here a long time, Cap, right here in this lodge, and when you live in a place a long time, you get to know how things are supposed to happen." He leaned over the counter for a better view out the front windows. He pointed as he spoke. "I know when the elk are supposed to migrate to the lower ground, and I know what time each day the deer are going to cross that road to get to the river. I know when the bears are going to run out of forage and start coming down here to raid the apple trees. I know when things are all right." Then he looked at them again and added, "And I can tell when they aren't." He gave his hands a little toss up. "But you have to live here awhile to understand what I'm saying."

Cap drummed one finger on the counter. "Is there a *specific* danger we should be aware of?"

Peak thought it over, came to some kind of agreement with himself, and answered, "You may have noticed there aren't a lot of folks around. Not that I don't want their business, I surely do, but what I know, I tell 'em, 'cause I know what I know, and nobody's gonna tell me I don't." Then he nodded toward a yellowing poster tacked to the wall.

Cap thought he'd seen this picture before, a blurry blowup of a massive, apelike creature. It strode on two legs across a logstrewn riverbed. Suddenly his uneasiness melted away.

"*Bigfoot?*" Sing said. Cap could tell she was holding back a smile.

"Don't laugh."

"No, no, I'm not laughing."

Peak's eyes were intense as he listened to something only he could hear, an old memory playing in his mind. "I heard one howl once, maybe eight, nine years ago. It wasn't like anything I ever heard before. Chilled my blood."

Sing leaned forward, obviously intrigued by the old man's earnestness. "What did it sound like?" she said.

He wrinkled the bridge of his nose, listening some more.

"Something between the howl of a wolf and the roar of a lion. Real long, and echoing. Scary."

Cap wasn't doing much to control his smile. "But that was nine years ago?"

Peak locked eyes with Cap, not smiling at all. "That was the first one. But I was meaning to say, I've heard it again the last few nights. Sounds like more than one, and they're upset about something."

Cap had read such nonsense before on grocery-store tabloids. He leaned back and crossed his arms over his chest, allowing his eyes to wander toward the cluttered shelves behind the old man.

"Nine years without making a sound," Peak insisted, "and now they're making all this noise? Cap, they don't howl for nothing. Something's wrong."

Cap met his gaze again, indulgingly. "It could be a wolf. I understand they've been reintroduced up north."

The innkeeper raised his hands in a brief sign of surrender. "All right, believe what you want, but just do me one favor—be careful."

Cap nodded. "We'll be careful."

Sing was looking at a glass display cabinet immediately below the poster. Inside were yellowed news clippings, photos of footprints, and in the middle of it all, a plaster cast of a huge footprint. "Huh. Look at this."

Cap leaned against the counter, detached and happy to remain that way. "Guess you're quite the Bigfoot enthusiast."

"Not by choice," Peak answered.

"Ever seen one?"

"Nope. Ever seen a wolverine?"

Cap thought the question a little strange. "No."

"Very few people have, but it's out there, isn't it?"

While Sing perused the contents of the cabinet, Peak pointed at the plaster cast. "Got that from a Sasquatch researcher just a year ago. He found that footprint right around here, right up in these mountains."

"And you paid good money for it, I suppose," said Cap.

"Well, that's between him and me."

Sing leaned for a closer look at the cast.

Cap had to grill Peak a touch longer. "But how many people have lived in this county all their lives and never seen a thing?"

"These creatures are smart, and they don't *want* to be seen. Did you ever think of that?"

"That still doesn't mean—" Cap didn't like the look on Sing's face or what it told him she might be thinking. "I'd say someone did a real good job carving that out." Sing unfolded her glasses and put them on. She began tracing a line on the cast, eyeing it over her finger. "A *very* good job."

The hike was going well—physically. Beck always ran two miles before breakfast, so she was up to the arduous trek, and Reed, being a sheriff's deputy, prided himself on his physical condition. They maintained a brisk pace, Reed bounding along the trail, fully demonstrating the strength and efficiency of his muscles and cardiovascular system, and Beck keeping up just fine, not about to be one-upped. The day was getting warmer, and okay, Reed was right about her buckskin jacket: she'd shed it only a few minutes into the hike, and now it was draped on the frame of her backpack.

Uphill, uphill, uphill had been the rule of the day. They'd just climbed along a steep, forested slope, half a mile one way, then around a switchback and another half a mile the other way, then back again, the steep mountain drop-off on their right, then their left, then their right, and so it went.

It was when they finished that climb and descended a north-facing slope into old-growth forest that the hike turned from a physical competition to something almost . . . profound. This wasn't common, everyday forest with trees the size of telephone poles all close together and stickery bushes between them. No, this was something out of a Tolkien or Lewis fantasy, a wondrous, otherworldly place where the earth was soft and deep with moss and peat; where tiny white wildflowers twinkled in the green carpet, iridescent bugs with fairy wings flickered in the sunbeams, and every footstep was muffled in the pulverized red bark of a million trees that lived there before. Now, *this* caught Beck's fancy. She'd read about this place, even written her own whimsical stories about it when she was a girl. This was where hobbits and elves, fairies and princesses, knights and ogres had their adventures and intrigues, and where all nature of mischievous creatures lived among the snaking, claw-foot roots. This was where—

"You can eat cattails, did you know that?" Reed still had not run out of things he knew and just had to share. "You can eat the stalk; you can eat the pollen; you can even eat the roots. Of course, they grow in swamps and wetlands, and we're up a little high for that." He sounded like a forest ranger on a nature hike, and he was past getting on her nerves.

She held her peace and concentrated on the coarse, furrowed sides of the huge trees. How old must they be by now? How many centuries had they seen? How many—

"Hey, a slug. Did you know those are edible? 'Course, they're supposed to be better if you cook 'em, but you can eat them either way."

Enough. "R-reed. You c-can barbecue one and s-serve it with A1 Sauce and I will never eat it. Change the s-subject."

"How about grass? Remember that meadow back there? We

could have cooked up a kettle of grass stew, maybe even made some tea."

"If I recall c-correctly, we have p-pine needles for tea."

"*Now* you're learning. Hey, you know how to find north and south without a compass?"

"D-do you ever stop talking?"

"Beck, we're supposed to learn all this stuff."

"Reed, I am happy with my life, I really am! I have a novel to work on, two paintings, and a stack of research. I could be doing all of that right now and enjoying my life, but *nooo*, I have to be hoofing out in the middle of nowhere, listening to my back-to-earth husband talk about eating slugs."

"One of these days, Beck, you're gonna wish you knew this stuff."

She fully intended to learn it, but she wasn't about to tell him. She did sneak a look at the slug as she passed by. Ooookay. That settled that.

Reed held back, which gave her precious time to mellow and enjoy things—well, more than just enjoy. She already understood what Reed had been trying to tell her. There were sights out here she'd never seen, and there were feelings that could only be felt by being here: the solitude, the wonder. The unique song of the woods could only be heard in nature's kind of *quiet*. She wanted to capture it, but what camera was capable of conveying the depth of such an image? What words could evoke the emotion? God spoke through His creation, and the message went past the mind, straight to the heart. It was all so—

"Uh-oh." Reed stopped, and in her reverie Beck almost ran into him.

"What?"

"Is that the cabin?"

Ahead, the trail meandered downward into a quiet, tree-shaded ravine where an ancient fallen log formed a bridge across a creek. On the other side, the remains of a man-made structure huddled against the slope in what could have been—should have been—a quaint setting. Once it had been a crude but effective shelter built from hand-hewn logs and split shakes, perched on footings of river rock. Once it had a sheltered front porch, a front door, and a window on each side. Once it had been just as Randy Thompson's survival brochure had described it—"a wilderness retreat well worth the hike."

They kept an eye on it as they silently worked their way down the trail, the cabin peeking and hiding, peeking and hiding through the trees. With each new view came more woeful news: The porch roof had collapsed, its support posts snapped in two; just visible under the sagging porch roof, the front door hung crookedly from only one of the two strap hinges; on the shallow creek bank below, the remains of a cot lay ripped and crumpled, the frame splintered like matchsticks.

At the log bridge, the cabin was in plain sight. Reed rechecked the map and Randy Thompson's detailed instructions. "This is it. This is the cabin."

One window was shattered; the other was torn out, frame and all. Through the window, and on the porch, and on the ground around the cabin lay gutted food containers, shredded wrappers, crumpled cans, spilled flour.

"Someone's been here," said Reed. "Maybe a bear."

Beck called, "M-Mr. Thompson! Mr. Thompson!"

The only answer was the mournful sound of Lost Creek moving under the bridge.

TWO

Reed didn't like not knowing. He started toward the cabin. "Guess we'd better check it out."

"I-I'm n-n-not going i-innnn there!" Beck protested, staying right where she was on the log bridge.

"Okay, fine." Reed slipped his backpack off. "Stay here and watch the stuff."

He grabbed his digital camera from a side pocket of his pack, snapped some wide shots from the bridge, and then went across to the other side.

The cop in him was coming out. He stepped carefully, not wanting to contaminate the site with his own disturbances, moving over the rocks, avoiding the softer areas that might reveal footprints. He snapped some more pictures of the litter, the cabin, the torn-out window, the collapsing front porch, the broken cot on the creek bank.

He ducked under the sagging roof, pushed the broken door out of the way, and took a look inside. The other cot was still here, but splintered like the one outside. Shelves along the back wall were smashed, and the shredded, depleted remnants of the food supplies spilled all over the floor, along with a rusty shovel, most likely the cabin's "toilet." A sack of pancake mix had been ruptured, dusting the floor and shelves with a translucent layer of white. At his feet lay an empty bread wrapper, a can of Spam torn open and licked clean, a crinkled and empty package of jerky, a canteen still full of water.

Beck called, "Is anybody in there?"

"Yeah. Me."

"Very funny!"

He ducked back outside.

Beck had ventured close enough to pick up and examine an empty can of beans, its torn edges jagged as if it had been bitten or clawed open.

"There's more of that inside," he told her. "Had to have been a bear. That's what happens when you leave food around. That's why you never leave food in your camp. You store it up high, out of reach, away from your campsite."

For once she was listening, with no comeback or protest—not with that torn can in her hand.

"But that makes me think somebody's been here recently," Reed said. "The food around here was all fresh stuff, like somebody just brought it."

Maybe he shouldn't have told her that. She sighed, threw up her hands and brought them down with a slap against her legs, twirled in place, scanned the forest all around. "Oh, that's just g-great! So w-where is he now?"

"Beck."

"Looks like your b-b-big vacation plan just went s-south—"

"*Beck!* Come on, now. We're adults. We're professional people. We work the problem!"

Good. That seemed to hit home. Beck breathed a moment, brushed a lock of her reddish-brown hair from her face, and asked him, "So w-what do we do?"

"We get a grip—"

"I've got a grip! What do we do?"

Well, this was his moment. He was the stud here, the man with the plan. He drew a breath to buy a little time. "We think things through. Now, we've only got an hour of daylight left. We'd better get our camp set up."

She cocked her head and looked at him with unbelieving eyes. "Y-y-you—"

"Yes. We're going to camp here. We don't have time to hike back down."

"S-s-s-so w-what if the b-bear comes-comes back?"

"We've got our shovels and there's a shovel in the cabin. We can bury all this garbage so he doesn't return, and then we'll camp somewhere else and hang our food up in a tree far away from where we're sleeping. No problem. That's the way campers do it all the time."

"S-s-s—" Beck sputtered and spit through her fumbling lips in frustration. "So w-where's Mr. Thompson—that's what I want to kn-n-n—"

"Beck, we're in the wilderness. The rules are different out here. If we don't keep ourselves alive, Mr. Thompson isn't going to matter one way or the other."

Beck finally sighed, "Ooo-kay."

He led, she followed, and they found a suitable spot farther up the creek, high, dry, and mostly level, encircled by hefty firs and pines. It provided a good view of the cabin below, but was hard to see from below—Beck liked that part. Reed got out a length of rope, and between the two of them, with some shin-nying and climbing, they were able to suspend their food containers on a clothesline between two trees a suitable distance from their camp. Other than the food, they didn't unpack much. Reed spread out a ground cloth, and they unrolled their sleeping bags on it.

In the ebbing light, Beck changed into jeans and a warmer shirt. Now the cool air moving down the ravine made her glad she'd brought that buckskin jacket. She gladly put it back on.

Their camp prepared, they sat on their sleeping bags in the deepening dark and munched on cold sandwiches.

"We'll stow our sandwich boxes and wrappers up in the Remote Storage Apparatus along with the other rations," Reed said.

Beck's sandwich was cold and soggy. "So much for hot pine needle tea."

"Maybe tomorrow." He snapped a few pictures of her.

She smiled, a shade of smirk on her lips despite the wad of sandwich still in her cheek. "So I wonder what happened to Mr. Thompson?"

"The bear wouldn't have raided the cabin if he'd been here. I'm guessing he went back down to Abney to bring up more supplies."

"Well, Mr. Survival wasn't too smart to leave all that food in the cabin in the first place, am I right?"

Reed nodded, conceding the point even as it puzzled him. "It sure didn't work out, did it?"

Beck swallowed her bite of sandwich before she spoke again. "Maybe he's planning on coming up with Sing and Cap in the morning."

"That's why we need to sit tight. Stick with the plan."

Beck chewed and thought it over. It did make sense. Sometime in the midmorning, Randy Thompson would come up the trail from Abney. Cap and Sing would be right there with him carrying in more supplies. Everything would fall together, and they would all make the best of it. She allowed herself to breathe a little easier. Reed seemed to have a handle on things. Maybe she'd trust him. Maybe.

She lay back on her sleeping bag, finishing up the last bite of her sandwich. The treetops converged around the circle of darkening sky. The first stars were visible. She had to admit, this part of it was pretty nice.

It couldn't have been more than a half hour since they crawled into their sleeping bags that Beck sat up, blinked, stared straight ahead, and saw nothing. She turned her head, felt her eyes moving in their sockets, blinked to be sure her eyes were open.

Where was she? The darkness was so total, so enveloping, that she had to tell herself she was in the woods, somewhere along Lost Creek, above a torn-up little cabin.

She couldn't see the cabin. She couldn't see the creek or the trail.

She groped for her flashlight and found it just inside her sleeping bag. *Come on, come on, where's that button?*

It clicked on and almost blinded her.

Okay. Squinting in the sudden light, she could see the trees encircling their camping spot. She could see a few bushes, ferns, roots, and rocks, stark in the flashlight beam with nothing but bottomless black behind them.

What happened to that wondrous place she'd seen by day, that enchanting forest where the elves and princesses and heroes had their adventures and intrigues and little bugs with fairy wings floated in the sunbeams?

Obviously, that was *then*, and this was *night*. Suddenly she felt lost. What were the rules *now?*

"What are you doing?" Reed's voice made her jump.

She settled, breathed, her hand over her heart. "Y-you—" She stopped without saying, *scared me.* "N-nothing. Just looking around."

"Go to sleep."

She clicked off the flashlight. Now the darkness was darker than before and she saw nothing but afterimages floating on her retinas.

Go to sleep, girl, she told herself. *This is night. It happens every day. No, every night. Every—what?—sixteen hours or so? No, more like eight hours that start after sixteen hours of daytime. Anyway, it only lasts so long.*

She lay back and closed her eyes.

Snap.

She froze, her eyes wide but unseeing. "Did you hear that?"

Reed didn't answer. She wanted to nudge him but didn't.

There it was again, only more of it: a twig snapping, a bush swishing. *Crack!* Definitely a stick on the ground breaking.

Now she did nudge him.

"What?"

"There's s-something out there."

Reed propped himself up on an elbow with a sigh of exasperation and listened for at least half a minute. All was silent. He turned as if to chide her, but then—*Snap!*

Reed's stomach wrenched inside him. *Brother, now she's got me worked up.* But he couldn't deny it. He heard it too: something was moving in the deep blackness beyond, somewhere down in the ravine.

A rustling. *Thump!* Something heavy and wooden tipped over.

It's wildlife, he told himself. "It's wildlife," he whispered. "You know, deer, elk, something like that."

"A b-b-bear?"

"Well, it could be the bear. Animals do a lot of foraging at night. There's nothing weird about it."

She insisted, "W-w-what if it's the b-bear?"

"He's after food, remember? If he goes anywhere, it'll be to the cabin to clean up whatever's left. He doesn't even know we're up here."

There was a breathless moment of silence.

"Oh, shoot," Reed whispered.

"What?"

"I forgot to hang up the sandwich containers. We still have them here."

"M-m-maybe he won't s-smell anything."

"Air moves downhill at night. We're upwind."

But then it was quiet, and stayed quiet.

Reed spoke first. "Guess it's over." He lay back down.

Beck sat up for another moment, then eased back and pulled the sleeping bag up to her chin. She lay on her back, then one side, then the other side.

Finally, she whispered, "Arrre y-you asleep?"

"No," he answered out loud.

"How you doing?"

"I'm okay."

"M-me too."

"You sound nervous."

"I'm not." Silence. "Well, aren't y-you?"

"Nope. Not me."

"You're not asleep."

He sighed and rustled around. "You woke me up."

He was getting to her again. "I'm r-reeeally not afraid. I can handle this just as w-well as you can."

Well, *he* wasn't afraid, no way. "Beck, you know what? The

only creatures out here afraid of the dark are us. All the other animals are out there stomping around in the dark like it's nothing, and here we are, scared to death—"

"Oh, *w-we're* scared to death?"

"I'm talking in *group* talk here. We're a team, we're—"

"Oh, w-we're a team? Well just-just tell me this: Which t-team has the advantage here? I mean, just *who* is on *whose* turf?"

"The animals don't mind. They're just doing what animals do—"

More noise. Something moving.

"I th-th-think it's near the c-cabin," Beck whispered.

"The cabin's *that* way."

"W-what way?"

"That way."

"I can't see where you're pointing."

"Well, just sit tight and—"

The sound was nothing like they had ever heard before, and it wasn't quiet. It was so clear, so loud, that even though Reed knew it was somewhere down in the ravine, it seemed as if it was *right there* next to them.

It was like a woman wailing in grief and anguish, weeping over the corpse of a loved one, her cry rising, wavering, holding, then falling off into a hissing sob, then . . . gone. Silence.

Snap! Crunch. Whatever it was, it was coming up the ravine.

The woman wept again, her voice quaking, the note rising to a nerve-rending peak and then trailing off.

Beck saw nothing with her eyes, but her imagination was providing the most horrible images of dismembered witches, transparent banshees, rotting corpses walking about seeking revenge—

Oh, stop it! she scolded herself.

Reed fumbled for his flashlight.

"D-d-don't-don't turn that on! She'll see where we are!"

Reed's voice was shaking. "Nothing's gonna sneak up on me—I mean, I just, I just wanna get a fix on it."

Then came a quieter whimper, as if through clenched teeth.

Reed found the button. Suddenly, shockingly, the beam of his flashlight cut through the darkness, reached as far as the immediate trees, then stretched itself into oblivion in the tangled forest, bringing back only dim images of leaves, dead branches, dancing shadows. Beck didn't look—she was afraid of what she might see.

"What if it really is somebody out there?" Reed whispered. "What if they're in trouble?"

"Th-th-then w-why don't they say s-so?"

Reed hollered, "Hello? Is anybody out there?"

No answer.

Beck thought, *Well, if* he's *going to holler* . . . "Hello? Ar-rrr-re you okay?"

Nothing.

They waited. They listened. Was that thing *hiding*?

"I don't think it w-was a woman," Beck whispered.

Now Reed was whispering. "It sounded like one."

"N-no, no it didn't."

"I think we made it go away."

A growl and a short snuff. It was low, quiet, from the other side of the ravine, somewhere high up the slope. Beck envisioned something big, with lots of teeth and a bad attitude as it crouched in the bushes, feeling intruded upon—

There it was again, more insistent this time, edged with anger. It was moving. The direction was hard to tell, but it could have been away from them, which was great, and so far, it was *out there* and not . . .

A chuckle sniffed out Reed's nose.

Beck thought that was quite out of place. "W-what are you laughing at?"

"It's a joke."

Somehow she wasn't ready to accept that.

"It's a joke," he insisted. "Cap and Randy Thompson are try-ing to scare us."

"W-what makes you so s-sure?"

"Well, it's obvious. Everybody knew we'd be coming up here one day before Cap and Sing, and then Thompson just happens to not show up, and then we start hearing stupid noises out in the woods. It's a big put-on."

Beck sat there, her frightened face indirectly lit by Reed's flashlight beam. She longed for him to be right.

He kept trying. "Don't you remember when we were going to United Christian and we went to that party for the young couples' group?"

"Sure."

"We all went for that hayride in the back of George Johnson's truck—"

"A-a-and the truck b-broke down, and a bear came out of the w-woods." Her nerves calmed. "And it was just what's-his-name—"

"Mr. Farmer wearing that bear rug." Reed snickered. "But you sure were scared."

"I was young! And so were *you!*"

They sat still and listened.

"S-so you think that's what it is?" Beck asked.

Reed hollered, "Okay, you can come out now! Very funny! Ha-ha!"

"Very funny, Cap!" Beck shouted. "Cap?"

No answer.

Then they heard, of all things, a strange, hissing kind of whistle, like a teapot at a boil, but bigger, louder, warbling a little. It sounded like it was far up the opposite bank of the ravine. It could have been moving . . .

Another whistle answered the first one. This one was much closer, on this side of the ravine, off to their right. Between the pounding of her heart, Beck heard something leaving heavy, munching footfalls on the dead needles and twigs.

"What if it isn't a joke?" she asked.

"Hey—"

"N-no, no, what if it *is* Cap and Mr. Thompson, but they're testing us, trying to demonstrate something, t-trying to show us w-what the mind can do in the dark, in the woods, late at night?"

Reed thought about that. "Like a simulation?"

"Y-yeah. To show us how e-e-easy it is to panic and d-do the wrong things."

Reed nodded. "I've done those before in the department's training sessions. Crime scenes and hostage situations . . ."

"Yeah."

"That could be it!"

"So . . . how do we handle this?"

"Well, if it's supposed to be a bear, then we should holler and make a bunch of noise and chase it away."

She looked at him; he looked at her. They got to their feet, shouting, hollering, shooing. "Yaaa! Go on! Get out of here!"

The woman outscreamed them in length, in volume, and definitely in terror effect, her cry searing up the ravine like black fire as she thrashed in the brush.

A wooden creak, a splintering snap, cloth tearing.

That broken cot in front of the cabin. She was that close.

A very loud, throaty growl shattered the air and rippled through the trees. Whatever had made that first whistle was bursting out in anger or fear or—whatever it was, it wasn't good. They heard footfalls moving quickly, pounding and thrashing up the bank.

The woman screamed in reply, splashing in the creek, then moving up the bank as if in pursuit.

Reed and Beck shied back in the dark. Beck clicked on her flashlight to match Reed's. They swept the perimeter. Trees. Brush. Bony, dead limbs. Blackness beyond.

"Th-th-th-three of them," Beck said, her voice broken with terror.

"*Think*," Reed said, to her *and* to himself. "Don't panic, just think."

Beck thought out loud, "B-big, hungry beasts, two t-t-tender, chewable people—"

"You're letting your imagination run away with you."

"It's *my* imagination!"

She exhaled, trying to steady herself.

It was quiet out there.

"I'm think-th-thinking something," she said.

"I'm listening."

"Cap and Sing w-wouldn't do this. They'd never b-betray our trust. George Johnson, yeah, but not Cap, and not Sing."

Reed mulled that over for a precious second. "You're right." In a moment, he came back with, "But if something out there was hunting us, it wouldn't be making all this noise. It would've sneaked up on us."

More listening. More silence. Then some rustling and movement up the bank. Whatever the creatures were, they were still there.

"I s-say we get out of here," she said.

Snap! Thud.

"Don't panic. If we panic, we're sunk." He tried to steady his voice as he quickly added, "If we stick with the plan, Mr. Thompson and Cap and Sing will know where to find us. If they get here tomorrow and we're not here—"

A howl up in the woods. Something—and it was no small coyote or wolf—was very upset.

"They might be going away. Don't panic," Reed pleaded.

"You're s-s-scared too; come on."

"I'm not scared."

"Come on, your voice is shaking!"

"I'm cold."

"W-w-well I'm wearing a jacket, s-so there!"

Reed started scrambling around the campsite.

"What are you doing now?"

"I'm getting rid of these sandwich containers."

"You, youuu can't hang those up in the trees now!"

"I'm gonna *throw* 'em, just get 'em away from us!"

"Yeah, and leave me here?"

"What's the matter, you scared?"

She didn't answer. He turned, his arms full, and left.

She stood there, alone in the dark, her flashlight shining into a black infinity. The quiet out there was not comforting. At least when those unknowns were making noise, she knew where they were.

Uh-oh, there was that growl again, somewhere up the bank across the ravine. Now it sounded alarmed. But no response from the wailing woman. Where was she?

A whistle! Long, loud, like escaping steam, warbling—and close.

Beck swept the woods that direction with her flashlight. Tree trunks. Dead limbs. A broken snag. Nothing beyond.

What on earth . . . ? Now she smelled something. She sniffed, first one direction, then another. It was terrible, like the worst body odor, like something rotten.

"R-r-reed? D-do youuu smell that?"

No answer.

"Reed?"

Something rustled behind her, and then came that whistle

again, this time low and hissing. She spun, her hands shaking, and shined her light up the hill, across a row of tree trunks, past a black chasm of nothing, over some more trunks—

Something glimmered in that black chasm. She returned to the darkness between the trees.

She knew what it was. Anytime Jonah, their dog, looked back at a flashlight beam, anytime a cat would look into their car's headlights, the eyes always reflected the light back like . . . like what she was seeing right now.

Two huge eyes, like silvery green headlights floating slowly in the dark. They blinked at her, then vanished as if blocked by a hand or arm. *Heavy footfalls, snapping, crunching!*

Beck plunged into the trees, looking for Reed. She may have been screaming; she only knew she was running, dodging tree trunks as they leaped from left and right into her light. "R-r-r-r-r—" His name just wouldn't form. She abandoned consonants and let any sound leap out that would.

"Here—"

This time a scream came out easily, without forethought or construction, mainly because she ran right into him.

"Whoa, whoa, easy!"

She screamed and stuttered and spit something about seeing the eyes and the smell and how close it was and how high off the ground those eyes were and the noise it made and how—

Screams! Savage screeches! Howls! The rage and thunder of demons, banshees, black minions of hell, roared, echoed, crackled down the hillside, reverberating off the trees, quaking and bouncing through the ravine, rippling up the creek. The beasts were close, so close, the thump of their footfalls like subwoofers in the ground.

Reed and Beck found the same tree in the quaking, sweeping beams of their flashlights, a tangled, half-dead cedar. Both had the same thought: *Climb! Climb and never come down, never ever—*

He got one hand under her foot to give her a boost. The first limb she grabbed wore a shirt and gave way the moment she touched it. A bloody, broken arm dropped out of the tree. She didn't scream this time. No sound would come. She only fell away, numbed by the sight, as she dropped for a slow-motion eternity before landing in a tangle of bushes.

A wide-eyed, crazed-faced man dropped into the beam of their lights. He was upside down, swinging, flopping, limp and purple with death, his legs snarled in the branches, his long braid dangling like a black viper below his head.

The man's head was barely attached.

They ran, through tree trunks that flashed and flickered across their light beams, over uneven, leg-grabbing tangles of growth, into endless night and darkness, oblivious, reckless, mad with fear.

Their backpacks were nearly an afterthought, but a shred of wisdom still remained, and they grabbed them up as they passed by. They didn't know where the trail was, only that it was below them in the ravine, so down they went, over the bank, grabbing roots, plants, tree trunks, anything to keep from tumbling head-long as they dropped down, gripping, heeling in, slipping, grabbing, dropping again.

The beasts, the demons, the spirits of the forest were still screaming as if in the throes of battle. Their voices were everywhere, so loud that Beck had to scream to be heard. She sputtered something about seeing the trail.

One more leap and they were on the path, running up the trail out of the ravine, hoping and praying it was the right one, the one that would get them out of this hellish place and down to Abney, a town they'd only heard about.

They ran as fast as they could see to run, adrenaline rushing, the trail, the trees, the turns quaking in their light beams. They climbed, cut around switchbacks, clambered over rocks, dodged around windfalls, getting distance, getting away, getting distance.

But another enemy was stalking them, overcoming them like a slow, creeping death: fatigue. The steep grade, the altitude, and their heavy packs pulled them down, stole their breath, consumed their muscles.

Beck was in the lead, groping up a steep, precarious portion of trail on all fours, gasping for breath, whimpering. She looked over her shoulder. Tears streaked her face. "W-w-where . . . ?"

"I don't know." Reed stopped, trying to stop panting long enough to hear if they'd outrun it.

There was a moment when they couldn't hear anything. But only a moment.

The woman was still out there. She wailed again and wouldn't stop screaming while another beast howled, its voice rumbling and fluttering from a deep, slimy throat.

"Behind us," Reed finally answered.

They kept going, inch by agonizing inch.

They made it up out of the ravine, and the trail finally began to head downward. They stumbled along, feet like lead, legs screaming in pain, lungs laboring for air.

Beck's legs collapsed. She went down and stayed there. The ground felt good. Not moving felt like life itself.

Reed crumpled just behind her, gasping, slick with sweat, wiping salty perspiration from his eyes.

They listened, eyes darting.

The screaming and wailing had stopped. Maybe it was over. Maybe they'd outrun the danger. Maybe the rest on the ground and a few precious molecules of oxygen were bringing the inkling of hope now rising in their hearts, the vague and dreamlike notion that they just might get out of this alive.

Reed pulled the map from his pocket and unfolded it, the crinkling, creased pages rattling loudly in the dark.

"Oh, quiet, quiet!" Beck pleaded.

"Got to see where we are, where we're going."

He shined his light on the map, turned it right side up, searched up and down the page for something familiar. "The trail's going . . . southeast, I guess."

"Sounds right."

Wump! Thump! The ground quivered.

"Oh, dear Lord, no!" Beck cried in a whisper.

Reed clicked off his light, then tapped Beck, who did the same. They stifled their breathing and heard it plainly: heavy footfalls and snapping twigs, something moving above them, moving fast, moving . . .

It stopped. Not a sound. They waited, longing for air but hardly breathing, probing the darkness with inadequate eyes.

"If we keep quiet," Reed whispered in Beck's ear, "maybe it'll give up and leave."

But Beck touched his nose and sniffed, a signal. Reed sniffed quietly. They'd both been running, panting, sweating like crazy, but nothing coming from them could match this stench. Beck pointed up the hill, and he understood. Night air moved downhill. That thing was above them somewhere.

Then came the whistle, long and steady, with a little warble at the end. It was closer than they'd thought.

Sitting still wasn't going to work. They eased back onto the trail and started to run again, but their legs were feeble and teetering, their bodies exhausted, and they had no choice but to use their lights.

The whistle sounded again, keeping pace.

Faster, faster!

The footfalls and thrashing in the brush did not fade back but only came closer, louder, closing the distance. They were being hunted. That thing was running them down, keeping up with no problem, and *it* could see.

Beck heard the rush of a waterfall. Abruptly, the trail cut through a streambed, snaking through and over slick, sharp-edged rocks. Reed stopped, stumbling on the rocks, his legs wobbly. He bent as if searching for rocks to throw, a stick he might use as a club, *anything*.

Beck just wanted to get across, get on smooth trail again. The waterfall was loud, close, just to her right—

The rocks broke away under her foot. She tumbled sideways, then fell headlong over the precipice, flipping end over end—

Her backpack absorbed some of the impact with the rocks, but she was still tumbling, her flashlight flipping in midair.

Her head hit. A blinding flash exploded in her brain.

Reed heard her go down, and he searched with his light.

"Beck!" There she was, flailed like a rag doll on the rocks about ten feet below the trail, her leg dangling in the flowing water, a streak of blood reaching down her face. He found a way down, a slow but sure course through brush, limbs, and saplings. "Beck!"

He grabbed the first limb and swung himself down, then another limb, then a fistful of brush. Lower, lower!

"Beck! Say something! Talk to me!"

There was a commotion across the stream. *Oh dear Lord, don't let it be—*

The beam caught the silvery-green glimmer of two retinas suspended within a massive black shadow that swallowed up his light. He screamed, half out of his own terror, half to cause terror. Would nothing chase this thing away?

The shadow moved so fast he lost it. He searched, waved his

light about. It caught one fleeting image of his wife's body swept up like a toy, arms limp, long brown hair flying.

The shadow enfolded her like a blanket. There were heavy, bass-note footfalls up the bank, and then . . .

Nothing.

THREE

Reed dashed across the stream, frantic, shining his light in every direction but seeing only thick, tangled forest. The stream and waterfall made so much noise he couldn't hear anything else. He got out of there, clambering up the other side, only guessing which way that thing went.

"Beck!" he called.

No answer.

But she wasn't dead. No. He would not allow himself to think that. She was alive and breathing, and any moment she was going to hear his call and answer. If she screamed for help, he would hear her.

Think, he told himself. *Don't panic. You can't see much at all, but can you hear anything? Can you smell anything?*

There! He heard limbs snapping farther up the slope. He raced along the trail, probing with his flashlight. A broken tree limb! Then another! He slipped out of his pack and dove into the trees, probing, climbing, looking for signs, listening, then calling.

From deep in his mind came a warning: *You have no gun. No weapon. You need to find something—*

Another rustling sound grabbed his attention and spurred him upward. He found a game trail where the ground was disturbed by hoofprints of elk and deer. Among these prints he found a deep, half-round impression, perhaps a heel print. With new strength he climbed, and then traversed the slope, then zigzagged as he lost, then found, then lost the game trail. With the trail gone, he followed sounds, any sound.

"Beck!" The forest swallowed his voice.

He hurried, he struggled, he climbed, he doubled back, he climbed again, then descended, then climbed, until fear and desperation gave way to exhaustion and he began to realize that he was like a mite in a carpet. As loud as he might call, this wilderness stretched farther than his voice could reach. The light from his flashlight had dimmed to a dull orange glow, but the mountains had darkness to spare, plenty to swallow up any light.

The seconds had stacked up and become minutes; the minutes had stretched into hours. Steps had become yards, and yards had become miles, but the forest had not shrunk. It was still bigger than he could ever be, with more obstacles, tangles, confusion, and dark, dark, dark!

When he broke into a meadow where the stars were visible and a waning moon was finally rising, he collapsed to the ground with a quiet whimper, limp and totally spent, head hanging, conflicting thoughts bantering in his head.

She's gone.

No, no, she isn't. Just have to find her, that's all.

Where? Where could you even start looking?

Well, some daylight would sure help.

She'll be somebody's dinner by then.

No. God won't let that happen.

Look at what He's already let happen! Remember where you are! There are different rules out here!

Reed's hands went to his head as if he could corral his thoughts. His aimless thrashing around in the woods for hours had accomplished nothing; a mad and frenzied mind would accomplish even less. He forced himself to lie still, breathing for breathing's sake until he could construct a coherent thought.

First coherent thought: He hadn't found his wife.

Second coherent thought: In all his mad scrambling and searching, he could have wandered farther from her, not closer.

Third coherent thought: He'd become part of the problem. He was lost, without provisions, without a weapon.

He still had his map and compass. If the sun ever came up again sometime in his life, he could take a look around and hopefully get his bearings. For now, he was too tired and emotionally spent to work it out, and any more wandering would only make things worse. Until he got some rest and some real light, he would be no help to Beck or himself.

The dying orange beam of his flashlight found an old fallen snag just a few feeble steps up the hill, with a hollow in the ground beneath it. His heart screamed against the decision, but his mind made it stick.

He would shelter himself under the snag to maintain his body heat, and rest until daylight.

"Beck . . . Beck . . . Beck!"

Beck was dreaming, far from fear in the dark, merely puzzled by her husband's anguished voice as he screamed her name.

Beyond her dream was a faraway pain, a dull throbbing, a dizzy world tipping and turning, a body aching, but she didn't wake up from the dream. She didn't want to. Waking would hurt; the dream didn't. In the dream she was floating as if in a stream, gliding past limbs and trees and leaves that went *swish*, with the ground so far below.

She was warm, as if cuddled in a furry blanket, but it was dark, like being in her bedroom at night.

Can't wake up, won't wake up, eyes won't open, staying in the dream, moving fast, can feel the breeze . . .

Monsters, snorting, drooling, stomping, invisible in the dark. All around, closer, closer. Beck! Beck! His legs wouldn't move—

"Reed! Beck!"

Reed awoke with a start.

"Reed!" That sounded like Cap.

He stirred, unclear as to where he was, but willing his legs and arms to move, to pull, push, and claw his way into the open, through tangled exposed roots and crumbled rocks into eye-stinging daylight.

The distant call came again: "Reed! Beck!"

Reed rolled out into the grass, the dew soaking through his clothes. Everything looked so different. "Hello!" he cried.

He heard Sing's voice call, "Reed! Where are you?"

"Up here!" he called.

He leaped to his feet, but his head emptied of blood and he fell, reminded of how weak and shaken he was. They shouted again, he answered again, and that was all he was good for until his friends reached him, snapping and rustling their way through the thick undergrowth until they emerged into the clearing.

They looked prepared for a week in the wilderness, with packs on their backs, hats, boots, jackets. Reed figured he must look pretty horrible, judging from their expressions.

"Reed! We found your pack down by the creek. What happened?" Cap asked.

"Where's Beck?"

By that afternoon, the Tall Pine Resort began to see more activity than it had all season. Two squad cars from the Whitcomb County Sheriff's Department were angled in against the meandering, up-and-down porch. On either side of them were the pickup trucks, SUVs, cars, and motorcycles that had brought the Search and Rescue volunteers. The volunteers, more than a dozen strong, wasted no time unloading and filling backpacks with needed gear, testing portable radios, and organizing survival equipment and medical supplies. Some of the guys prepared high-powered rifles and stowed cases of ammunition. A van arrived and lurched into a space at the far end of the parking lot, an eager German shepherd barking and whining in the back. Across the parking lot, hooked to an RV power outlet, was the Search and Rescue command vehicle, a converted school bus now crammed with equipment, supplies, a computer, and radios. Close to the main door was a sharp-looking King Cab pickup with an Idaho Department of Fish and Game insignia on the side.

Deputy Sheriff Dave Saunders, in green field jacket and billed cap, walked briskly out the main door, reporting into a handheld radio, "Yeah, Jimmy Clark's here debriefing the witness. We'll all get rolling when he's done. It's a probable bear attack, so we're lining up some hunters—"

Sheriff Patrick Mills signaled a halt right in front of Dave's mouth and whispered sharply, "Dave, let's not say it so loud, shall we?"

The deputy followed the sheriff's glance to where Reed Shelton sat on a wooden bench farther up the meandering porch, just outside Room 105. He was haggard, dazed, and dirty, apparently trying to make sense to Jimmy Clark, the conservation officer who asked him questions.

"Oh, man, sorry," the deputy said.

Sheriff Mills, a tall man weathered by experience and sporting a graying mustache, went back to a conversation he'd been having with Cap and Sing on the slapped-together porch near the main door. He was dressed for wilderness work, in the standard-issue green jacket with *SHERIFF* in large yellow letters on the back, but instead of a policeman's hat, he wore a cowboy hat with a county sheriff insignia on its front.

"Sorry," the sheriff said to Cap. "Now, you were saying?"

Cap stood nervously, taking deep breaths, shifting his weight, grasping the porch post as if to steady himself. The college professor's words raced and his voice seemed weak. "We found—it was on the rocks below the waterfall."

"Blood," Mills refreshed him.

"Yeah. We checked all around the creek area, both sides of the trail, up and down the slope . . ."

"How wide a radius?"

Cap shrugged. "I don't know, maybe forty feet, maybe fifty . . ." He looked at Sing, passing her the question.

She was sitting on a hand-hewn bench against the old log wall, her face troubled as she studied the LCD of Reed Shelton's camera. She was reviewing the digital photographs Reed had taken of the splintered cabin and the shots of Beck sitting in their campsite, her cheeks plump with a mouthful of sandwich. Sing and Cap's backpacks rested against the wall next to her, packed to bulging but never opened. Leaves and needles clung to her clothing and her braids. "I would say a hundred-foot radius. But it was difficult. The brush is thick in that area."

Mills looked over Sing's shoulder at the small camera screen. "Did he get any shots of Thompson's body?"

Sing came to the end of the pictures in the camera's memory. "No. Apparently Reed was in no picture-taking mood when he and Beck were running for their lives."

"And you never got back to the cabin to check it out?"

Cap was obviously on edge, tiring of the questions. He wagged his head. "We only wanted to find Beck, that was all."

"So you didn't see whether or not there was a body up there?"

"No!" Cap lowered his voice. "Reed said Randy was dead, and that was good enough for us. Beck was the one we were concerned about."

Sing stroked her forehead. "We weren't getting anywhere. Reed didn't want to leave, but we had to get back here; we had to get some help."

Mills regarded the folks gathering in the parking lot, well trained, some specialized, all there to find Beck Shelton no matter what. "You made the right decision. Sing, you've been our forensics specialist for five years now. You've teamed up with some of these people before. You know they're good at what they do."

Sing nodded and gave a wave to the dog handler, who was sharing a piece of breakfast toast with Caesar, the German shepherd. "I never thought I'd be part of the case we're working on."

Sheriff Mills looked past Cap and Sing to where Reed was still being questioned by Jimmy Clark. "So how clear do you think Reed's head is right now?"

Cap stole a glance. "I don't know. He's in some sort of shock, like he's having waking nightmares. If he tells Jimmy what he told us . . ."

Sing shivered, putting the camera in its case. "Reed was right about the cabin. If we find Randy Thompson thrown up in a tree, we might have to believe the rest of his story."

"Being in the dark, in the woods, can make things seem a lot worse than they are," the sheriff suggested.

"Maybe finding Randy's body was the thing that shocked him," Cap offered, "and after that, well, then, Beck gets grabbed . . . I don't know, I'd probably be seeing some pretty horrible things by then."

"Reed's a deputy sheriff!" Sing's voice was edgy. "Let's not underestimate him!"

Awkward silence followed.

"Duly noted," Mills finally said. "Sing, take Reed's camera over to Marsha in the command vehicle. See if she can download those shots of Beck and print 'em up."

Sing got to her feet, as if eager to do something, anything. "And then can we please get up there?"

Mills looked at his watch. "Pete said he'd be about ten minutes."

Cap started to say, "We don't *have* ten—" when tires growled on the gravel.

An older brown pickup with a rumbling muffler pulled in and nosed up against the building four vehicles down. The fellow who got out looked as though he'd already been in the woods most of his life and would be out of place anywhere else. He was dressed in tired jeans, a frayed leather coat, and a drooping, wide-brimmed hat with a rattlesnake skin for a hatband. He may have had a haircut three or four months ago but obviously hadn't thought much about it since then.

"Ah," said Mills, "there he is."

Pete Henderson, search manager and tracker, was already sizing up the situation when Mills met him in the center of the parking lot. "Huh. Jimmy's here," Pete said, "so it was a bear. You're here, so somebody's dead. You've got me and my searchers here, so you can't find whoever it is."

"Come on." As they crossed the parking lot, Mills gave Pete an abridged version of Reed's account.

"You are kidding me—Reed said that?"

"Let's hope his head starts to clear up."

They walked quietly, unobtrusively, up to where Jimmy was finishing up with Reed. The conservation officer sat on the edge of the porch, pen and notepad in his hands, questioning, almost grilling Reed in his eagerness to get the information and get going. His conservation officer's uniform spoke well of his manner, meant for the wilderness, not the town or city; no creased trousers with a stripe, but tough, forest-green Levi's; no spit-polished shoes, but oiled boots for slogging through rough and often muddy terrain; his gray shirt had a shoulder insignia, but it was rugged enough for the wilderness and had obviously been there. His billed cap with the Idaho Department of Fish and Game insignia rested on the porch nearby.

Reed was sitting on the bench against the building, seemingly immovable as if he were a fungus that had grown there. His hair was matted from sweat; his face and clothes were those of a desperate man who'd lost his wife and spent the night under a fallen tree. Reed's voice was barely audible as he said, "It had to be Randy. He had a long black braid, I saw that clearly."

Jimmy looked up at Sheriff Mills and Pete. They knew that described Randy Thompson.

When Reed lifted his face, a tiny hint of hope came to his eyes. "Hey, Pete!"

"We're here for you, partner," Pete said.

"We're almost finished," said Jimmy. He prodded, "How did he look to you, Reed? Was there anything about his condition that would indicate an attack by a—"

"He was thrown up in the tree!" Reed insisted as if he'd said it before. "His head was practically torn off!"

"But he could have been climbing the tree, trying to get away from a bear, right?"

Reed thought a moment, then nodded. "Yeah. That makes sense, if that's what you want to think."

Jimmy looked around, apparently for the right words. "Reed, I'm hating this. You know that."

Reed's head sank. Tears filled his eyes. "If we hadn't camped there that night, if we'd only buried that garbage, if I hadn't forgotten to hang up those stupid sandwich containers . . .!"

"Was Beck having her period?"

"No."

"Did she bring any makeup along?"

Reed looked at him blankly.

Jimmy explained, "To a bear, the smell means food."

"I didn't see a bear," Reed emphasized as if for the hundredth time.

Jimmy just looked at his notes. "There could have been any number of factors, Reed. You don't need to blame yourself."

"Are we through?"

Jimmy nodded. "Yeah, Reed. We're through. We're gonna get on this, right now."

Reed bolted to his feet. "I've got to get my gear ready." He ducked into Room 105 and slammed the door, not looking back.

Jimmy rose from the porch and drew in close to Sheriff Mills and Pete.

"Pete."

"Hi."

Jimmy reviewed his notes and spoke in secretive tones. "Guess you've heard the story by now."

"Has it changed any?" Mills asked.

Jimmy stole a furtive glance at Reed's door. "Don't think so, so I can't tell you what happened up there besides the obvious. Reed's so shook up right now he's hallucinating, talking about a woman screaming and big monsters fighting in the dark. He insists something really big and foul-smelling chased him and Beck along the trail and then grabbed her." Jimmy's expression said, *Need I say more?*

Mills asked, "Did he say anything about Beck falling over a waterfall?"

"Yeah, right before the attack. If it really happened, I'd guess that's where the Abney Trail cuts across Scatter Creek."

"Cap and Sing can show us the spot. They just came from there."

Jimmy consulted his notes again. "Reed drew a map to show where he and Beck found Randy's body. It's up the creek a little, on a knoll above the cabin."

Mills spoke to Pete, "Looks like we'll need two teams, one to work the cabin site and one to work the creek."

"We'll most likely be picking up the pieces," Pete muttered, bitterness in his tone as he peered over his shoulder toward the volunteers.

Jimmy leaned close to Mills. "Sheriff Mills, I can't let Reed go on this hunt."

"Good luck holding him back."

"He's gonna be a liability."

"*If* he's crazy," said Pete.

"Guys, I can't allow it, even if he is my friend," Jimmy insisted.

"I'll talk to him," said Mills, "and we'll take it from there."

Jimmy's glare was unmistakable. "Sheriff. This is a bear attack. It's my jurisdiction."

Mills didn't get ruffled. He'd been sheriff—and known Jimmy Clark—too long for that. "Jimmy. We don't know what it is, not yet. Let's see if we can be a team until we get it sorted out."

"There's nothing to sort out!"

"Okay, try this: Anything having to do with the bear, that's your jurisdiction. Anything having to do with bodies, living or dead, that's mine. Can you work with that?"

Jimmy sighed through his nose, his face still defiant. "I'll work with it. For now."

"That's right. You will." Mills let that settle the matter and moved on. "So tell me where you want to start hunting your bear."

"The cabin's the most likely center of the bear's foraging range right now. I'll start there."

"Okay, Dave and I'll go with you. Pete, I'd like two or three searchers."

Pete was counting noses. "I've got 'em."

"And we're gonna need weapons on both teams," said Jimmy.

"My regular guys are here, and . . ." He scanned the crowd some more. "Looks like we've got a few more I haven't met yet."

Mills instructed Pete, "Your team'll be looking for Beck, starting at the Scatter Creek waterfall. Take the search dog. Jimmy, I want Sing to have a good look around that cabin area before anybody contaminates it."

Jimmy smirked in Sing's direction and did not succeed in keeping his voice down. "So now you're trying to make this a crime scene?"

"I get the bodies, remember?"

Jimmy waved it off. "Whatever." To Pete, "Just hurry up with the dog."

"Don't worry," said Pete. "Are we about ready?"

"Pete, one more thing," said the sheriff, detaining the search manager a moment. "Forget any tales or theories you've heard thus far. You find whatever you find and let it speak for itself, you got it?"

Pete gave a nod and adjusted his hat. "I'll get the volunteers assigned."

The sheriff and Jimmy Clark watched Pete head into the parking lot, his volunteers gathering to him like Israelites to Moses.

"He's right about one thing," said Jimmy. "There won't be much left to find."

"We'll know when we know," said Mills.

They went to join him.

Pete craned his neck, hands on hips, and looked over the small and willing crowd. They were his neighbors: a carpenter, a housewife, two firemen, a schoolteacher, a machinist, a dental assistant, a heavy equipment operator, and several others, all away from their jobs, geared up and ready to trek into the wilderness, even sleep there if necessary, for no pay. They'd been together many times before, in every season, in every kind of weather, because someone was lost or in trouble. If anyone were to ask them why, they'd just say it was the thing to do.

Pete spoke out, "Okay, everybody, listen up. You all know the situation. We've got a three-way problem: a possible bear attack with two possible victims who need to be found. Anybody working the bear issue, you're gonna be following Jimmy Clark's lead. Anybody searching for the victims, you get your orders from me. If you can't stand me or Jimmy, you can grouse to Sheriff Mills here. We all take our orders from him. Now, Sing—where are you, Sing?"

Sing and Cap were just stepping out of the command vehicle, fresh computer-generated fact sheets in hand. Sing waved the papers in the air for all to see.

"Okay, Sing's gonna hand out photographs and detailed descriptions of the missing persons. Give these papers a good looking over."

The listeners stood quiet and grim, receiving the quickly compiled information sheets from Sing's hand. Most of them already knew Randy or Beck or both.

Jimmy took his turn, his voice trumpeting over the crowd, "We're going to be working two teams from two locations in the Lost Creek drainage. We need people who are capable in tracking, hunting, and—don't miss this, now—recovering human remains. This is a bear attack. It's serious business." That caused a stir. "Pete knows what your skills are, so he'll select the teams. Pete, go ahead."

Pete Henderson addressed the crowd again. "You medical folks stick around, and let's see, how many marksmen do we have? Okay, the two of you go with Jimmy; you two come with me. Don, you'll work with me at flank. Tyler, you here? Okay, Tyler, you be the other flanker."

Cap stood on the edge of the crowd, hanging on every word.

"Hi there."

Cap winced at the greeting. This was not the time for idle chat. He turned only half his attention to a buzz-cut man somewhere in his thirties, dressed in camouflage like a hunter—or a marine. He was carrying a rifle, obviously one of the marksmen.

"Hi," Cap said.

"Steve Thorne. I understand you found one of the victims?"

Cap shook his hand. "Michael Capella. Yeah. We're friends of Reed and Beck Shelton. This is my wife, Sing."

The man whispered a greeting to her. She returned it with a quick smile, trying to listen to Pete's organizing.

"I'm really sorry," said Thorne.

Cap said, "Thanks," his eyes on Pete.

Thorne didn't go away but pressed with another question. "So what was it your friend saw?"

What kind of a question was that? Cap gave the man a long look, then, deciding he was trying to be helpful, said, "I don't know what he saw. We're trying to find that out."

"I suppose it had to be a bear. Is that what he said it was?"

"I don't know. The whole thing happened in the pitch black, and . . . I don't know. It was a horrible experience, and he's still very shook up about it."

Now Pete was calling, "The rest of you folks, talk to Marsha. She'll get you working support and communications here at the command post."

"So he didn't see anything," the guy pressed.

Cap was trying not to be abrupt. "Not that he's been able to say for sure."

Thorne gave him a gentle pat on the back. "Thanks. Just wondering."

Cap turned his full attention back to Pete Henderson, who caught his look. "Cap—is that what they call you?"

"Cap'll do."

"Nice to meet you. Which team you want to go with?"

"I want the waterfall," he answered.

"Who was that guy?" Sing asked.

Cap shrugged, impatient. "One of the hunters. Some thrill seeker, if you ask me."

Reed had yanked off his dirty clothes and pulled a fresh shirt and jeans from his backpack—and then put on the dirty jeans with the clean shirt. He took off the shirt. No, it was the clean one. He put it back on and tried to take off the pants—he forgot he'd put on his boots. He unlaced them and pulled them off. Now, where were the clean pants? He'd thrown them into the pile of dirty clothes. He fished them out and put them on. Now if he could find his belt—

There was a knock at the door. "Reed?" It was Sheriff Mills.

"Yeah, come in."

Mills stepped inside and closed the door quietly behind him. "How you doing?"

Reed didn't answer because he didn't want to lie. He only hurried to pull on a boot as he sat in one of the room's two chairs.

Mills grabbed the other chair and set it down directly opposite Reed, almost in his way as he tried to pull on the other boot. "I said, how you doing?"

It felt like an interrogation. Mills pressed into Reed's space big time, and Reed didn't like it. He met Mills's gaze deliberately, angrily. "With all due respect, sir, that's a stupid question."

"I need a firm answer, Reed—"

"Are we heading out?"

"—or you don't go."

"Arrest me!" Reed said.

Mills whacked Reed on the side of the head. Reed froze in disbelief, staring into the eyes of his superior officer, who still held that hand close to his face, forbidding Reed's eyes to stray.

"You can thank me later," said Mills. "In the meantime, you'd better listen. There are more than a dozen trained volunteers out there who just might be risking their lives on your behalf, so before I let you out that door, you'd better decide what role you're playing. We need men on this job, not victims. Not basket cases. If you need time to work this through and pull yourself together, I'll grant you that, no questions, no shame, but I need to know."

Reed gave some thought to his attitude and tried to ease down. "Sure didn't turn out right."

Mills was listening.

"It was supposed to be good for her, supposed to get her out of the house, get her out where she could just, just live a little without having to talk to anybody. Out in those woods, there aren't any social rules, you know? No expectations." He looked Mills squarely in the eye. "She would have aced it. She would have done great. I knew she had it in her. I don't think people give her credit."

Mills nodded. "She would have aced it. You're right."

Reed's eyes teared up again. He looked away to clear them, to clear his mind. "I just didn't want her to be afraid anymore."

"Reed, look at me."

Reed met his eyes. The gaze coming from under that hat brim was kind but would not be trifled with.

"You and Beck signed up for a challenge. Well, now you've got one, only there's no teacher and there's no pretend, no trial run. There's just a truckload of real trouble, and Beck doesn't need you fumbling around and getting in the way because you're wallowing in what should have been. She needs you to get your mind cleared up and on the problem. She needs you to do your job. We all do." He rose and went for the door. "We're pulling out of here in about five minutes. Let me know what you decide."

Mills stepped out onto the porch, caught a breath, then signaled for Sing's attention. She joined him near the main door.

"Don't imagine you have any of your gear with you?" he asked.

"I was on vacation!"

"Got your camera, though."

"Yes. And my notepad. I was supposed to be taking survival training this week."

"I want you to come along with Deputy Saunders and me to the cabin area. We'll treat it like a crime scene, document everything so we can figure out what happened up there—and what didn't." He saw the question in her eyes. "Reed's got a wild story, one that people won't want to believe, and that means they'll start believing other things. Let's get that door closed right away, first thing."

Reed emerged from Room 105 correctly dressed, his backpack slung over one shoulder, but walking like a drunk man, his face reddened with emotion, his hand against the wall to steady himself.

Jimmy was finishing the briefing in the parking lot. His voice carried well enough for Reed to hear the gist of it: ". . . the bear could still be around guarding its kill, so, hunters, be sure to take point position and secure the area. Prepare for the worst, and by the way . . ." He lowered his voice, but Reed still heard him admonish, "Let's be careful what we say. Reed's a little crazy right now, and I would be too."

Several folks noticed Reed and nodded a greeting or even gave a little wave. Some were jerking their heads, pointing, shifting their gaze, trying to let Jimmy know of Reed's presence, but Jimmy, with his back toward the resort, just kept going. "Bears usually go for the soft organs, but any fresh meat will do; they'll eat arms and legs too. Let's be sure to bring several body bags, because she may not be in one piece."

Reed's feet wouldn't move. All he could do was stare at Jimmy's back and wonder why he couldn't find the strength to deck the guy. Jimmy finally got a clue from his listeners and looked over his shoulder. Jimmy's face flamed with embarrassment. Too late. Reed felt worse.

Reed ducked inside the lobby, clumsily closing the door behind him. The floor reeled as if he were on a ship in a storm. He staggered to the counter, stomach churning, as the pack fell forgotten and unnoticed to the floor. With elbows on the countertop and his face in his hands, he tried one more time to pull himself together, to be the man Beck needed, to do his job.

Now even the countertop seemed to be moving, but at least the room was empty, and he was so thankful for that. He drank in the silence, waiting one moment, one breath at a time for his mind to settle on some workable scheme of reality, just one simple pathway to sorting this whole thing out.

Maybe I am *crazy.*

A simple conclusion of insanity was pretty tempting right now. It would be so much easier. It would explain away everything, and he could dismiss his nightmarish memories like any other outlandish dream.

But he found no comfort in such thoughts. Even if his mind was creating nightmarish memories of hellish things that never happened, it was probably to replace worse memories of even more hellish things.

Either way, here he was with only the counter to keep him from collapsing to the floor, an official basket case. Wasn't that what Sheriff Mills said they didn't need?

He breathed a moment. He prayed, and his mind cleared just enough for him to realize he was too messed up to be safe out there. He could never survive or be any help to the search teams or to Beck when he couldn't trust his own senses.

So, looks like I won't be going, he thought.

He rubbed his face, partly because it expressed his pain and confusion, mostly because his face was a tangible reality he could be sure of. It was still there. He could feel it. He guessed he still had elbows too; they were holding him up.

What else was real around here? He let his eyes drift around the lobby, taking in the trophies—the moose head, the elk head, the deer head, the big bearskin, the many sets of antlers. So it seemed *somebody* knew his way around out there and had come back the winner, somebody way out of Reed's league.

His eyes drifted down the wall and almost passed over a yellowing poster—

His gaze returned and parked there. The dark, two-legged creature striding along a log-strewn riverbed was blurry and grainy, but it was looking his way. A shiver coursed through Reed's limbs. He saw no silvery-green retinas glowing in the dark, but something about that image brought back the same nerve-jangling, hand-trembling terror.

His eyes went to a glass case below the poster and focused on a plaster cast of a huge footprint. As he leaned close to the glass, the sound a foot like that could make in the soft earth of the forest came back to him. Suddenly the speed and mobility of the shadow he'd seen did not seem impossible.

His heartbeat quickened. His hands trembled. He looked around the lobby, through the windows at the people gearing up for the search after Jimmy's lecture on how to handle dismembered bodies and fear-crazed, delusional family members. Hadn't any of these people seen this stuff in the glass case or that picture on the wall? Had it never occurred to them that it might not be a bear, that it might be—

Caution took hold, and Reed didn't run anywhere to yell anything.

Of course they'd seen it. They'd heard his story too. He tried to understand why their minds would only go one direction, locked on only one explanation, and he could settle on only one answer: they weren't there last night.

He looked at the poster again, trying to imagine that thing in the dark—

"I don't know if you ought to be looking at that."

Arlen Peak, the owner of the place, had come into the lobby from the souvenir shop. Worry in his eyes, he stood beneath the huge, clawed bearskin, watching Reed.

Reed looked toward the glass case. "I never saw one before."

"It's hard to find anybody who has, and anybody who has usually won't talk about it."

"Have you ever seen one?"

The old man shook his head, almost sadly. "No."

Reed knew it would be safe to tell this man. "I think I have."

Peak approached and spoke gently. "Son, you need to be sure about that. I don't want anybody thinking I've put ideas in your head."

Reed gazed at the big footprint. "Do they . . . make a crying sound like a woman? Not screaming, but, you know, wailing and crying?"

The innkeeper half-smiled and shook his head.

"How do you know?"

"Let's just say nobody's ever heard one do that."

"Do they smell bad, like the worst armpit in the world?"

Peak hesitated just a moment, then answered, "Only when they're frightened or upset. It's what a lot of apes do. It's a defense mechanism."

"Do they howl and scream like, well, like apes?"

The old man's silver fillings twinkled in the windows' light. "Now, *that* I've heard."

"Do they whistle?" Reed tried to mimic what he'd heard, the long, soaring whistle with the little warbles in it.

Now Peak actually straightened, staring at him.

Outside, the teams were ready to trek into the woods. Jimmy Clark and Sheriff Mills, rifles slung on their backs, exchanged a look with Pete Henderson, then glanced toward the front door.

"You saw him, didn't you?" Jimmy asked. "He was so wiped out he looked like he was *on* something."

Sheriff Mills waited only a moment, looked at the folks gathered for the search, then sighed through his mustache. "Let's do it." He shouted, "Okay, everybody, let's go!"

The front door opened. Everyone froze on the same cue.

Reed stepped out, a little pale, just a little wobbly, but standing tall, his pack on his back, his deputy sheriff's cap on his head. He was ready with an answer and spoke in strained tones to Sheriff Mills, "Ready when you are, sir."

Beck heard a long, soaring whistle with little warbles in it. Then a deep-throated, disgusting grunt, like a gigantic old sow in the mud. Another low grunt. Another soaring whistle.

And then Beck was aware of gook in her mouth—clumpy like gooey raisins and tart like wild berries—and someone wearing big leathery gloves shoving more gook into her mouth.

She gagged, then coughed, then spit it all out—

And the whole world shook.

Beck opened her eyes. They were still slimy from a long sleep, and her vision was blurred. Nothing was real, not yet.

Someone was holding her, cradling her in a smelly brown blanket.

Rescue! I've been rescued!

There came that whistle again, like a boiling teakettle.

Shmoosh! More gooky berries in her mouth, and she could feel some of them smeared on her face. She jerked her head away, spit them out, blinked to clear her vision.

The world came into focus, and she gathered she wasn't home. All she could see were tangled branches and green leaves. The cool breeze told her she was still outside, somewhere in the mountains, somewhere in the shelter of thick bushes. Bushes with berries. Huckleberries?

She looked up—

NO!

Her lungs pulled in a long, quaking gasp and held it there as her mouth hung open and her jaw began to quiver. Though her hands began to shake on their own, she dared not move or utter a sound. She could only lie there, stiff with terror, and gape at the deep, monstrous eyes looking back at her.

The eyes were dark amber, with muddy brown around the iris instead of the usual white. They were intense and probing—studying her as if she were a specimen under a microscope—deep set under a prominent brow. The face was reddish brown, leathery like an old saddle, bordered by thick, straggly hair.

Beck felt hot breath passing by her face in sour little puffs. The bulging lips tightened against a row of white teeth and the thing whistled at her.

The same whistle Beck heard in the dark when glowing eyes bored into her and a dead man dangled from a tree.

FOUR

Unthinking, her mind paralyzed by fear, Beck responded as she was taught to respond to hornets, bees, rattlesnakes, and assorted monsters of childhood: she froze—except for the trembling in her hands, which she couldn't help.

The thing shoved more berries into her mouth with fingers the size of sausages. Beck forgot her mouth was already open, and now suddenly it was full again. She closed her mouth, an unconscious reflex, and the berries remained inside, an unchewed mass. The beastly eyes locked on her, waiting, the face stern under a heavy, furrowed brow. The thing grunted again, then tapped on Beck's mouth with thick, berry-stained fingers.

Somehow, it occurred to Beck to chew. The berries burst in her mouth, filling it with juice, half-sweet, half-tart. The wizened face waited and watched, huge volumes of air rushing in and out through the broad, flat nose.

Still chewing, and just now remembering to breathe herself, Beck let her eyes drop enough to see another huge hand with dirty black fingernails curled around her, pressing her against a mountain of dark, reddish-brown hair. The hair was coarse and oily, the body beneath it warm and moist, with a familiar—and unpleasant—sweaty smell. She could feel the rib cage expanding, pressing against her, then easing away as the mountain breathed. She'd never been this close to anything with lungs this big.

Oh, please, don't kill me . . .

Could she run? Where? As near as she could tell, she was in the woods somewhere. Beyond the tangle of the huckleberry bushes, she could see the thick forest, and through its canopy, a blue sky.

A powerful, hairy arm reached up and grabbed another cluster of berries from a branch.

When the hand that was bigger than her whole head descended to deliver the berries, Beck didn't dare argue. She opened up, let the berries tumble in, and started chewing.

With the taste of the berries and her ability to chew them came a conscious realization that she was still alive—quite notable, given the circumstances. How long she would remain that way she had no idea and no encouraging thoughts.

She turned her head just enough to study her situation. She was being held by what appeared to be a huge ape, similar to a gorilla, but not quite a gorilla. The crown of its head extended to a narrow crest like a gorilla's, and it had a prominent brow ridge over the eyes, but the jaws didn't protrude as much and the lips were more flexible and expressive. As near as Beck could tell, the creature's legs were folded beneath it, but one large, hairy foot jutted out, with a wrinkled, hairless sole and all five toes aligned in a row. By its ample, fur-covered bosom, Beck concluded it was a female. They were now sitting in a cavity created when a tree upended, pulling the root ball out of the ground. Thick bushes, most of them huckleberries, had since moved in and now provided a blind that hid them from the outside world. The female held Beck inescapably in her lap with her left arm while feeding Beck with her right.

Another load of berries was on the way. Beck couldn't take much more of this, but unless she wanted more berries smeared all over her face . . .

She opened up and let the beast dump them in. She chewed but did not move, did not stir, did not make a sound. Her hands were still trembling.

Suddenly the big arm loosened and the creature let her go. She slid down that big hairy body to the ground.

Run! her instincts screamed at her. It didn't matter which direction. *Run for the trees!*

All it took was the slightest weight on her right ankle. "Oww!" With a shriek of agony, she fell in the tangled limbs and stalks, grabbing her ankle, grimacing. She checked for a break, for—"Awww!" The pain flashed up her entire leg, red-hot and lingering. She settled backward on a bush, bending and crumpling branches, gasping. She thought of crawling, pulling herself out of the woods with two hands and one good leg.

Not good enough. The beast lunged forward faster than Beck could pull to get away. It overshadowed Beck like a rust-red thundercloud, nudging her, poking her with a big finger, nearly flipping her body over. Terror in combination with her stutter took away Beck's ability to speak, even to scream. The creature backed off, resting on all fours, and gave her some space.

Daring to move, Beck felt her ankle again under the creature's sentrylike stare. The ankle wasn't broken as near as she could tell, but she did have a cruel souvenir from her tumble over the falls— a bad sprain. She wouldn't be walking, much less running, anytime soon.

Beck lifted her eyes to the creature. Was it possible to make peace with this beast? A cluster of berries was within reach. This beast seemed to want Beck to eat them. If it would make it happy . . .

Daringly, her hand still quaking, Beck reached halfway to the berries, hoping such personal initiative would not seem threatening.

There was no violent reaction. The thing didn't growl or bite her.

Slowly, inch by trembling inch, she reached the rest of the way and grabbed them. The ape-thing let her, making strange, guttural rumblings and a clicking sound like wood hitting bamboo: *Tok! Tok! Tok!*

Beck placed the berries in her mouth and reached for more, eating them slowly. The beast's expression softened. She eased back onto her haunches and watched. From this slight distance Beck got a first full look at her. She was very much like a gorilla, but with a body like a barrel and a neck so broad it blended with her shoulders. Her legs, thick as tree trunks and covered with hair, were longer than one would expect in an ape, but the arms were definitely ape arms, long enough to reach Beck's neck and wring the life out of her.

As Beck lay still, chewing berries, the pain in her ankle subsided enough for her to notice a dull ache in her head. She touched the side of her forehead, felt a bump—Ouch! *Another* spot that hurt!—then found dark, flaking blood on her fingers.

Ohhh . . . dear Lord, what happened? She remembered falling, but after that, nothing. If she was this beat up, what had happened to Reed? Was he lying somewhere in worse shape than she was? Her backpack was missing. Maybe this monster tried to raid their backpacks for food and Reed had tried to resist, tried to save Beck, gotten the brunt of this monster's rage—

She dared not think it.

But then came more bad news. A further inventory revealed a large smear of blood on her leather jacket where she'd been pressed against the creature's side. She looked and found a corresponding dark stain on the big ape's shoulder and left flank.

If her fear had ebbed even slightly, now it returned. She met the creature's eyes and thought, *What have you done?*

The monster stiffened, suddenly alert and alarmed. The lips pulled back slightly, revealing the edges of the teeth—sharp, white incisors between an imposing set of canines.

Beck cowered. *Oh no, I've made it angry.*

But the big female wasn't angry. It wasn't even looking at her. It was listening. The look on its face, the piercing stare of its eyes, its motionless body reminded Beck of their dog, Jonah, and how he reacted whenever he heard a distant coyote or the UPS truck approaching a half mile away. And there was that foul smell again, a new, sickening wave of it.

It happened so fast Beck didn't have time to object or resist. Before she could even scream, the big hands enfolded her and snatched her from the ground, shaking her insides and nearly giving her whiplash. Limbs, leaves, and berries blurred past her eyes and whipped her head and shoulders. She covered her face.

There was a burst of acceleration so fast that the wind swept her hair from her face. She lifted her eyes.

She was flying, lunging through the forest at an altitude of six feet, her body held fast against that abundant bosom by two muscular arms. Tree limbs blurred by like fence posts on a freeway. She curled her legs up as her hands grabbed fistfuls of red hair in a death grip. Beneath her, the creature's big feet pounded the ground as she leaped over logs and dodged thickets and brush with incredible agility, slowed by nothing.

With a little whine, Caesar the German shepherd balked only a few yards into the trees, turned back, looked down the hill at Agnes, his handler, tried again, whined again, and finally, at a timid trot, ran to his master and cowered behind her legs. Agnes, whose dogs had served the county sheriff's department, the state patrol, and local police departments for the past twelve years, looked puzzled to say the least as she stroked the shy dog's neck. "Caesar, what is it? What's the matter, boy?"

Reed did not find the dog's behavior one bit surprising. He felt that way himself—he just wasn't going to whine about it.

Pete Henderson and his team of searchers looked as mystified as Agnes, gawking up into the woods from a small clearing on the mountainside. Scatter Creek ran through this clearing, cutting across the trail just below them and cascading over a ten-foot waterfall. Agnes had taken Caesar to the base of the waterfall, the spot search teams call the "LKP," the Last Known Place Beck had been, and let him go. He'd hesitated, whined, followed a scent up to the trail, spun in circles, followed it across the trail and up the clearing, turned back at the trees, and then, with some goading from Agnes, continued into the trees. A few yards in, he'd had enough.

Pete's radio squawked. "Team 1 in position at the campsite."

Pete spoke into the handheld, "Team 2 above the waterfall at the LKP." He gazed curiously at the dog. "We're, uh, working the K-9 right now. Good hunting."

He clipped the handheld to his belt and looked down toward the trail where Reed and the others waited for further orders.

Reed tried to keep his impatience in check. He knew all these people were as eager and on edge as he was: the two Search and Rescue volunteers, one the dental assistant and the other the heavy equipment operator, both tracking apprentices; the two marksmen, one of them a newcomer named Thorne who looked like a marine; two medical technicians with emergency kits and a stretcher; Don Nelson and Tyler Jones, experienced trackers, who would form the three-man tracking team with Pete; Agnes Hastings, the K-9 handler; and Cap Capella, there because he was a friend. All were dressed for the job and grim with the business at hand, but any hasty move at this point could destroy important signs and evidence. Pete had to make the calls.

Pete was obviously troubled over the dog. He asked the handler, "Has he ever done this before?"

She was still petting Caesar, who refused to budge from her side. "No. Never."

"But he has tracked bears before?"

"Nine times in the past two years."

Pete gestured toward the trees from which Caesar had fled. "Well, he found something. It turned him back, but it's something." He reached for a set of short aluminum poles that hung on his tracker's vest and began to screw them together into one five-foot length. This was his tracking stick, a rod marked in one-inch increments, with movable rubber O-rings for marking on the stick the size of prints and the stride length between them. "Don and Tyler, I'll take point; you flank. We'll start where Caesar's afraid to go. Reed and Cap, you follow the flank men. You step where they step and don't disturb anything. Agnes, I know Jimmy's real eager to have Caesar help out at the other location. Want to head up there?"

The dog handler gave a resigned shrug, put Caesar's leash on him, and led him up the trail toward the cabin. Caesar was more than happy to go.

Pete took a moment to focus on Reed. "Reed, buddy, you ready?"

Reed knew he didn't know what he was saying, but he answered, "I'm ready."

Pete told Cap, "You stay close to him." He directed his attention downhill. "Joanie and Chris, stand by. When we find the trail, we'll need you to cross-track. And you guys with the guns, guard our flanks. Everybody keep quiet. That bear could still be around. Medics, stand by on the radios."

Pete led the way up the hill. The flank men took positions just behind him, one on his left and one on his right, forming a triangle with Pete at the "point." Reed fell in behind the man on the left, Cap behind the man on the right. The marksmen, guns ready, eyes and ears alert, followed wide to the sides. When Pete moved, they all moved as one body.

Pete led the train slowly, eyes scanning back and forth as they all moved into the trees, his tracking stick ready in his hand. Only a few steps in, he used the stick to point out bent grass and crushed twigs where an animal—or a human—had passed through. "Had a lot of traffic through here this morning," he said in a quiet, stealthy voice, "so the trick is gonna be telling the difference between everybody else's sign and the sign we're looking for."

Reed and Cap exchanged a look. Yes, they and Sing had spent quite a while thrashing through these trees and thickets, leaving their own disturbances everywhere and possibly obliterating everything Pete needed to find now. Reed didn't know whether to feel sheepish at the blunder or just plain aggravated at life's unfairness.

"Boot print on the right," said the right flank man, pointing with his own stick.

Pete saw it. "It's coming your way, Tyler."

The flanker to the left inched forward, carefully checking for more prints. "Okay. Got it." He pointed out a depression in the pine needles at Pete's eleven o'clock.

Pete held his tracking stick between the two tracks, measuring the distance between them, then straightened and asked, "Reed, Cap, either one of you come through here?"

Reed and Cap exchanged a look. Cap wagged his head. Reed answered, "I think I did."

"Let me see the bottom of your left boot."

Reed grabbed Cap's shoulder to steady himself and stuck up his foot.

Pete studied and measured the boot sole while Tyler pulled out a pencil and a preprinted diagram of a footprint. Pete dictated, "Okay, three-point waffle tread, section 4, thumbnail pattern on right side, center to lower right corner; section 10, sliver in lower right corner."

"It's him," said Don, looking at the track on the right.

Tyler drew the wear patterns on the diagram and labeled it "Reed Shelton."

"I suppose you were in a big hurry last night?" Pete asked.

"I was," Reed admitted.

"Well, it's you, all right. Thanks."

They moved farther into the trees, as far as the dog had gone. They could see his sign as Pete pointed it out—paw prints, a bent pine needle, a toe and claw mark on a rotting log—a trail left by a very hesitant canine who didn't know which way to turn next. This was the spot. Whatever was troubling Caesar had to have left something here.

Pete sank carefully to one knee and remained still, as if listening. His eyes began to sweep across the cluttered forest floor as he studied the twigs, the pine cones, the fallen needles, the scattered pebbles, the blades of grass and tiny, broad-leaved weeds. Reed saw his jaw tense. Then Pete pointed with his stick.

Tyler replied, "Yeah, you've got it."

Reed peered over Tyler's shoulder but couldn't see a thing except the cluttered, busy, infinitely detailed forest floor.

Pete removed his hat and went down on his belly, the side of his head to the ground, his open eye next to the ground, the other winked shut. "Yeah."

He raised up on his side and carefully pressed his thumb into the soil, leaving a small oval indentation. Then he went in close, his nose only inches from the tiny leaves and grass. "Yeah, maybe half a day old. Could've come through last night, easy."

Tyler whispered to Reed, pointing carefully with his tracking stick. "See the shine on that leaf right there? And the dip in the needles underneath?"

Reed looked a long time, but finally he saw it—he thought.

"Rear foot?" Don asked.

"I wanna see another one," Pete answered as he measured the impression with a tape measure. "Got about five . . . and one-half inches across. Whew! That makes him one for the record books. *Heavy* son of a gun too." While Don flagged the impression with a pink ribbon on a Popsicle stick, Pete pivoted the tracking stick forward, holding the handle over the impression and swinging the tip in a slow, careful arc. "C'mon now, let me see a heel print."

Pete—and so the whole group—inched forward.

Don pointed with his stick. "Got some snapped branches at one o'clock."

They all looked and saw the spindly, mostly dead branches on the lower trunk of a pine either bent or snapped in an uphill direction.

"Ehh, bingo," said Pete, selecting some tweezers from his pocket and plucking a long reddish hair from the jagged stump of a limb. The hair gave him pause. He handed it back to Don. "That look like bear to you?"

Don held the specimen up to the light. "Well, maybe. Kind of long."

Pete asked Reed, "What color is Beck's hair these days?"

Reed examined the hair Don held in the tweezers. "Reddish brown."

Pete exhaled a half whistle. "Hoo, lordy."

Don carefully placed the hair in a Ziploc bag.

Pete stood still, probing ahead with narrowed eyes. Finally, he let out a held breath. "Okay," he said, pointing. "We've got another one."

The body of trackers inched forward again.

This one was more visible, a roundish impression in some humus. To Reed it looked as though someone had knelt there and left a knee print.

Pete went on his belly again, eyeing the print carefully, then measuring it. He straightened up, still on one knee. He was troubled, eyeing the area between the two prints. "Where are the *front* feet?"

"We've missed something," Don agreed as he flagged the print.

"Well, we'll find 'em," said Pete. He stretched out his tracking stick to measure the distance between the two tracks, but it wouldn't reach. He chuckled. "Either that, or this bear has one heck of a stride."

They moved ahead, this time according to the length they'd found between the first two tracks. The third one, nothing more than a scuff on a rotting log, was where it should have been, the same distance from the second as the second was from the first. They had a pattern.

Sing crouched in the doorway of the sorrowful old cabin and took one last shot of the destruction inside. She was amazed. In her line of work, she'd photographed and reconstructed crime scenes involving hoodlums and vandals, domestic spats, drug-related murders, and meth lab explosions, but they were nothing like this. For one thing, the beast that made this mess was far, far outside the human category. Certainly, human scum could show this kind of disregard for property, but to snap support posts like toothpicks and tear whole walls open required an inestimable strength she had never encountered. For another thing—and this still felt a little odd to her—according to the rules out here, this wasn't even a crime scene but made perfect sense: bear gets hungry, bear finds food, bear does what is necessary to get it. Tearing the windows out of a building, smashing cots and shelves, and splintering a door were shocking, destructive acts to civilized perceptions, but to a bear's way of thinking, no different from clawing the termites out of an old stump.

It was frightening and fascinating, and not hard to understand.

If it was a bear.

"How's it going?" Jimmy, the conservation officer, called from the bridge.

He was obviously impatient, and she couldn't blame him. Agnes the dog handler had arrived with Caesar, and Jimmy and the hunters were ready to move, so the only thing holding them up was Sing's directive from Sheriff Mills. She'd photographed Reed and Beck's campsite, their food stash, the log bridge, and the littered area around the cabin. She'd paced off distances and made notes. Everything that was directly knowable she'd recorded on several pages. She'd worked expeditiously, but the process took precious time. Jimmy had somehow managed to defer to the sheriff on this one, but she could feel him breathing down her neck with each passing minute.

With great relief she called back, "I'm through," and stowed her camera and notebook in her backpack.

Jimmy immediately turned his attention to Agnes. "All right.

Let's get a scent and track that baby!" The hunting party, with sniffing Caesar in the lead, nearly stampeded off the bridge and down the trail.

They jostled past Sing as if she were an obstacle. She hurried up the trail, relieved with every step that put distance between them.

The other team members were now covering the surrounding area in widening quadrants. She could hear them calling to each other, maintaining voice contact as they worked their way among the trees like fleas in a hairbrush. At certain moments she spotted some of them, but she hadn't caught sight of Sheriff Mills to fill him in on—

"Sing! Up here!"

Ah. He was waving to her from the hillside above the trail. She selected a route up the embankment with sufficient footholds and branches to grab, and worked her way to him. At the top, Mills and Deputy Saunders were waiting for her. They were examining the campsite, two sleeping bags on a ground cloth, cloistered in a tight pocket among some trees. It wasn't an instant find; as Reed had warned, it was hard to see from the trail.

"Find anything unusual down there?" Mills asked her.

"Besides everything?" She looked down into the draw where Jimmy and his hunting party lurked near the cabin, waiting for Caesar to show them the way. "That bear was very hungry or very angry at being so hungry, or . . . Well, let's just say he was highly motivated."

"But no sign of Randy?"

She hated to tell him, "No sir."

Mills's expression was troubled as he scanned the forest in wide arcs, his eyes landing on the searchers below. "We need to find a body, Sing."

The deputy suggested, "Why don't we get Reed over here so he can show us where he saw it?"

"He won't leave the search for Beck," Sing cautioned.

Mills gazed at the rough map Reed had drawn. "We've located the campsite and the stash of food containers between the two trees . . . but this tree right here, the big cedar tree where the body is supposed to be . . . Well, maybe it's the right tree, maybe it isn't, but there's no body."

Then Jimmy cursed so loudly it startled them.

Agnes started hollering, "Caesar! Caesar, come, boy! Come, Caesar!"

Of course they had to watch. From up here the view was quite good.

Caesar was trying to run up the trail away from the cabin, and Agnes was hot on his heels, leash in hand. The dog stopped at her command, shied away again, answered her command again, then fidgeted, obviously wanting nothing but to get out of there. When Agnes finally snapped the leash onto his collar, he tugged at it, jerking in little circles, trembling and dribbling urine.

"What's his problem?" Jimmy demanded, rifle in hand but with nothing to shoot. "I said, *what's his problem?*"

"I don't know!" the handler shouted back. "I'm about to retire him! He's just never acted this way!" Her legs were getting snarled in the leash.

"Well, does he track bears or doesn't he?" Jimmy asked.

"He tracks bears! Black bears, grizzly bears, any kind of bears!"

"Well, he's not doing us much good now, is he?" Jimmy turned toward the marksman behind him. "What did you say?"

The marksman was not the kind to be intimidated. "I said, 'Maybe this ain't a bear.'"

Now Jimmy was simmering at a temperature even Sing could feel from the hill. He pointed his finger at the man. "Excuse me, Janson! If you're going to be on this team, you're going to handle yourself and your mouth with professionalism, you got that?"

"Yes sir, I got that."

Now Jimmy addressed all three people in a voice suitable for a hundred: "This is a rogue bear we're after. It's serious business. We're going to keep our minds clear and straight ahead so we get the job done without anyone getting hurt, is that understood?"

Janson nodded, the other hunter said yes, and Agnes just petted Caesar.

Jimmy leaned in on her. "Agnes, we need a dog that'll track this bear, and if your dog can't do that, we need another dog. Are we clear on that?"

"Clear enough." Agnes steamed a moment, then led Caesar back up the trail toward Abney. "C'mon, boy. We don't need any more of this!"

Caesar led her, only too eager to go.

Jimmy watched her go, then stomped around a bit, then conferred with his hunters, saying something about bait and bear stands.

The show was over. Sheriff Mills turned back to Sing and Deputy Saunders. "We'll give the searchers a few more minutes, and then we'll have to get Reed and Pete over here."

Sing thought it wise to remind him, "Sheriff, every other aspect of Reed's account holds up."

Sheriff Mills regarded the cabin below. "So you don't think one man could do that kind of damage to the cabin?"

She almost laughed. "Not even remotely. And if you'll remember, Reed's camera recorded pictures of the demolished cabin before it recorded pictures of Beck, alive and well."

Mills nodded but asked, "I don't suppose you've spotted any bear prints anywhere?"

She felt the strange sensation of thin ice under her feet—and maybe Reed's. "Well, it is loose ground around here, lots of rock,

lots of humus and pine needles that don't register a print, at least
to someone who isn't a tracker."

"We'll see what Pete says."

"Sure. We'll see what Pete says. But, sir . . ." She felt nervous.
"Reed never said anything about a bear. He provided no bear scenario. If there was foul play, if he had planned this—"

Mills held up his hand. "You don't have to sell me."

"I'm glad to hear it, sir."

Mills only responded, "But we'd better pray they find Beck."

Pete's team was picking up some speed now that they knew what to
look for. They'd worked their way up the hill another hundred feet
while two trackers, accompanied by the marksman named Thorne,
started crisscrossing their path a shouting distance ahead of them,
hoping to encounter signs farther up.

For Reed, it was all too tedious. Beck could die in the dirt
somewhere long before they would ever find her. Cap must've
sensed his mood, because he kept whispering, "Easy, now, we're
moving okay; we'll find her. Got to do it right."

"What'd this thing do, have its claws cut?" Pete muttered.

Then came a shout from one of the trackers far up the hill.
"We've got something!"

Pete told Reed and Cap, "Better stay here." He and his men
went on ahead.

Time stretched into an eternity, but Reed had no hurry left in
him. He could only stand there and take frightened, furtive
glances as Pete and his men disappeared into the forest. For a
long time—such a long time—Reed heard them pushing through
the limbs and brush as they spoke in hushed, clipped phrases and
moved in a wide arc. When they finally came into sight again,

they were far away, their outlines broken by a jittery web of branches and limbs. He could just barely see them approaching the other team members and whatever the object was.

Pete circled the object, then called out, "Come on up, Reed."

Reed drew a deep breath and wiped his eyes clear.

"C'mon," said Cap, touching his arm.

They pressed through the pines and firs, approximating the path the others had taken. When they finally emerged from the insistent, aggravating, view-blocking fingers of the forest, Reed could see the others gathered in a wide circle in front of a huge fallen log, the two marksmen warily standing guard. In the center of the circle was a blue backpack, not set there but dropped. It was dirty and the frame was bent—as if it had fallen over a waterfall. Every eye focused on Reed, waiting for the verdict.

FIVE

Reed's voice quavered though he tried to control it. "It's hers. She picked out the color."

"Don't touch it," said Pete, looking around the area and at his two flankers, visibly bothered about something. He asked Reed, "Do you know if there's any food in there?"

"We packed some granola bars, and she may have had some of her lunch left over."

Pete went down on all fours for a closer look, studying the pack on all sides. "If I were a camp-raiding kind of bear, I'd be interested in that. This one wasn't. This pack doesn't have a mark on it." Then he pulled out his tweezers again and probed at one of the flaps. "Got some more of that hair here, tangled up in the Velcro. Tyler? Let's get those medics up here with one of those . . . you know, those bags. We need to bag the whole thing up."

Body bags, Reed thought. Pete wasn't very clever at talking in code.

Tyler got on his radio.

"May I see the hairs?" Cap asked, leaning over the pack. Pete pointed them out and Cap looked at them closely. He even sniffed them, then sniffed the pack.

"Any thoughts?" Reed asked.

Cap backed away as if caught in an illegal act. "Oh no, no, no thoughts. Just curious."

"Got a pretty good toe print here," Don reported from near the log.

"We're on him now," said Pete, showing a hint of excitement despite himself.

Cap went to have a look, hands clasped behind his back, unobtrusive.

"Check that log," Pete told his guys. "See if he went over it." Then he sniffed the pack himself and made a face. "Reed? Come smell this."

Reed approached carefully, dropping to his knees, then all fours, crouching down to get his nose close enough to the blue fabric.

It was a defining moment he hadn't expected: a reassuring horror, a dreadful relief, an encouraging fear. He knew this odor; for him, it was the stench of Beck's abduction, the reek of the creature that had chased them and taken her. It had filled the air the previous night and become a suppressed and forgotten ingredient in what he'd taken for madness, a crazed illusion he'd come to doubt. But that was then. Now, among friends and objective observers in broad daylight, it was real—horribly, reassuringly real! "This is what we smelled last night. The smell was everywhere!"

"No wonder Caesar had a problem," Pete mused.

The flank men had reached the other side of the log and were checking the ground. "Got a heel print over here, deep compression," Don reported.

Tyler checked the top of the log, his head low, eyeing the aged, crumbling grain.

"What do you see, Tyler?" Pete urged.

Tyler looked at the heel print again, then at the top of the log again. "Looks like he jumped over."

That brought Pete to his feet. "Over *that*? Doggone, Tyler, I don't need any more surprises!"

Tyler explained, "We've got a deep push-off in that toe print and a deep compression on the heel over here, and nothing on top of the log."

Pete examined the toe print, then checked the top of the log with his light. "Don, I want you to tell me you've got some claw marks."

Don knelt and studied the print from several directions. "Can't say I do."

"No claw marks," Pete muttered, obviously fed up.

"That thing jumped," Tyler repeated.

Pete looked back. "And that's when Beck lost her backpack."

"We're missing something," Don objected.

"A bear would've torn some pretty good claw marks in this log going over, especially if it was carrying a . . . carrying somebody."

"What are you talking about, 'carried'?" Tyler said. "A bear doesn't carry a body; it drags it in its teeth."

Reed gave up trying to contain himself. "It didn't drag her. It carried her. I saw it lift her off the ground." They all stared at him, so he threw back a challenge. "Have you found any sign that says different?"

The trackers looked at each other, waiting for one of them to answer.

"We're . . . we're missing something," Don said again.

"No, we aren't," said Pete, and Tyler agreed with a wag of his head. "Nobody got dragged. The sign says what it says."

"And what is that?" Reed demanded.

No answer.

"Tell me!" he shouted.

Pete was thinking when his radio squawked, "Pete. Pete, this is Mills."

"This is Pete. Go ahead."

"We can't find a body up here."

Pete made a curious face. "Say again?"

Mills came back, speaking with forced clarity. "We cannot find a body. Do you copy?"

Pete looked at Reed, but Reed was dumbstruck. "Uh, we copy that you cannot find a body."

"We need you and Reed to come and help us out for a few minutes."

First one blow, then another! Reed shook his head.

Pete spoke into his radio, "We've found Beck's backpack. We could be close."

There was a pause, apparently while Mills thought it over, and then Mills replied, "Pete, hand off to your flank men, let Reed stay there, but give him a radio so we can talk to him, and you come up."

Pete checked visually with Don and Tyler. They were ready to take over. He reassured Reed, "You can trust these guys."

"I'd rather you were here," Reed protested.

Pete sighed and spoke into his radio again. "Can it wait?"

Mills came back immediately: "No, it can't."

Beck's head throbbed, her ankle shrieked, everything in between hurt, and it was getting hard to breathe with those huge arms squeezing her. She'd been hanging on to fistfuls of fur, ducking her head as branches swept close, and praying for an end to this for what seemed hours. The big female had climbed, galloped, strode, reversed course, run, reversed again, and run some more, penetrating miles of forestland and covering vast stretches of mountain slope to the point where Beck hadn't the foggiest clue where on the planet they were. Everything—trees, gullies, ridges, boulders—looked the same. She couldn't even be sure she was still in Idaho.

But the creature was hurting too. She hobbled and wheezed, swaying unsteadily as she walked. Beck had the uneasy feeling she was sitting high in a tree that was about to fall over.

She was right.

With her last feeble steps, the big female pushed into a scrubby clump of trees, spun a few dizzying turns, then collapsed like a condemned building imploding, her legs giving way beneath her, her nostrils huffing clouds of steam. She bumped on her behind, teetered there a moment, and then, with a long, breathy groan, slumped onto her side. Her arms wilted like dying plants and Beck rolled onto the moss and uneven rock. Her clothes were dampened with the creature's sweat, and she ached in every muscle, wincing from the pain in her ankle, and amazed she was still alive.

Her hair-covered captor sounded like a locomotive leaving a station, chugging and laboring for every breath, holding her side. Her eyes were watery, filled with pain and unmistakable fear.

Beck stared, unable to make sense of it. *The* beast *is afraid? What could a beast of such power and size be afraid of?*

The female looked back at her, never breaking her gaze, until her expansive rib cage began to settle into a quieter, more restful rhythm and her eyes softened from fear to a kind of resignation. With a deep sigh and a swallow, she pushed herself into a sitting position and began peering through the trees like a soldier in a bunker, scanning the expansive landscape below, the deep amber eyes searching, searching, searching.

Beck sat up as well and followed the creature's gaze. The view was spectacular from here. Below them stretched a vast valley under a thin veil of blue haze, and beyond that, so clear it seemed one could touch them, a range of granite peaks took a jagged bite out of the sky. It even *sounded* vast up here: dead quiet except for the all-surrounding whisper of air moving through the trees and the trickle of a stream nearby. If Beck wasn't so miserable, fearful for her life, and occupied with trying to think of the "right" thing to do, she could be enjoying this.

The right thing to do? She wanted to cry. The right thing *would have been* to stay home where she had a warm bed, a latte machine, fuzzy slippers, and a nice shower with brass handles. *This* was unthinkable!

The shadows were long now, the mossy rubble outside their hiding place almost entirely in shade. Not comforting. She'd learned the hard way what to expect in this weird, wild world at night, and she did not relish facing that alone and lost.

She looked at her smelly, unknowable, unpredictable host, who was still looking out over the valley as if expecting an enemy. What were her plans? *Had* she captured Beck for a meal? Beck remembered something she learned at a zoo once, something about gorillas being vegetarians. This creature seemed to like berries.

But so did bears.

Keep thinking, Beck; keep thinking!

Okay. What was it going to take to survive? Shelter. Water. Food. In that order.

She considered shelter. If she could move, if she had some tools, if there was anything with which to build a shelter . . .

Well, what about the next one? She hadn't had any water since last night, and that stream was calling to her. She craned her neck but couldn't see where—

Whooa! Hands wrapped around her like a big sling, and she was in the air again. No freight-train speed this time, though. As the creature ambled with smooth, bent-kneed strides through the trees, over rocks, and down a shallow draw, Beck felt a sensation much like floating over the ground on a ski lift.

They found the stream, sparkling and splashing over broken rocks and forming pools from which to dip water. The big female set her down on a large, flat stone and then squatted next to her, dipping up bucket-sized helpings in her hands, slurping them down. Beck watched, wondering if it was safe to move, to take a drink herself. She leaned over the water, then checked with a sideways glance. The creature didn't seem to mind; it may have been expecting it. Beck prayed silently, *Oh Lord, don't let me get beaver fever—whatever that is,* and then started dipping and drinking.

After only a few gulps, she heard a familiar whistle and froze to listen. Her furry captor heard it too and became alert, cocking her head one way, then another. When the whistle came again, she pressed her lips against her teeth and returned a whistle of her own. Its piercing sound made Beck flinch.

The whistle answered, closer this time, and now Beck heard rustling and saw movement in the brush on the other side of the draw. She backed away from the stream on one knee and two hands, looking about for a hiding place.

The beast reached with her inescapably long arm and pulled Beck in, half-dragging her, pressing her close against her furry, sweaty side. Beck felt like a trophy, a prize, a fresh kill about to be shared. Playing dead occurred to her, but the beast's big arm wouldn't let her fall down.

Across the stream, from somewhere in the trees and thick brush, a low whistle sounded, and then a pig grunt.

The beast whistled back and gave a soft pig grunt of her own.

There was an interval, a strange moment when nothing happened—no sound, no stirrings, no whistles or calls. Beck searched the bushes, but all she could see across the creek was a sea of leaves, motionless except for an occasional flickering in the breeze. She had the distinct feeling she wasn't just being watched—she was being *studied*.

Then, so slowly, so silently that it almost escaped notice, a gray, hairy dome rose like a dark moon out of the brush. Beck looked directly at it—

It vanished as if it was never there.

The big female whistled again and then made that strange guttural noise with the loud tongue clicking. *Tok! Tok!*

The gray dome rose again, and this time, two steely, amber eyes glared at Beck, narrow with suspicion.

Beck could only hang there motionless, expressionless, without the first thought of what she could do.

With its eyes darting from Beck to the big female and back, the second creature moved forward, only the head and shoulders visible above the brush, until it emerged, stooped over, stealing, sneaking, edging closer.

Beck looked it in the eye again. It leaped back several paces, almost vanishing in the brush, hissing through clenched teeth.

Don't look it in the eye, Beck thought to herself. *It doesn't like that.*

She looked down at the water instead and watched the beast's rippling reflection as it relaxed enough to approach again. It came closer, one furtive step at a time, until it reached the other edge of the stream, and then stood there, still making a nervous, hissing noise with every breath. Beck ventured a look at the feet. All five toes were up front, in a row, but the bone structure was somehow different from human. The feet had a funny way of flexing in the middle, conforming to the streambed, curving over the rocks.

Beck let her eyes move up a little more. The creature was standing nearly upright now, almost seven feet tall by Beck's estimate. It was another female, a mass of muscle covered in dark gray fur and a little thinner than the first one, although at the moment its fur stood out and bristled, making it appear larger and anything but friendly.

It uttered some pig grunts that could have been an inquiry. Beck's female gave some pig grunts that could have been an answer, then extended an open hand. The other female ignored it, eyeing Beck with vicious suspicion.

There was another stirring in the brush, and a third creature appeared. It was steely gray in color and, judging from its size, a youngster. It sidled up to the big gray, gripped her leg, and joined her in staring at Beck. This one appeared to be a male. Beck stole one quick little glance at its eyes; he was unflinching. He stood at least five feet tall. The face was pale, like a baby chimp's, and the hair on its head stuck out in wild directions. If she'd seen this thing in a zoo from a safe distance with bars between them, she probably would have thought it was cute.

She ventured one more look in its eyes—

"Roargghh!" The little beast exploded like a bomb going off, leaping into the stream, sending up a spray of water that doused her. Terrified, Beck squirmed, kicked, and tried to get free while the juvenile roared from the middle of the stream, arms flexing, fists clenched, fur on end, teeth bared in a vicious display. Then his mother got into it, roaring and putting on a horrific show of anger.

The big red female pulled Beck in close and turned her back to the onslaught. Beck was glad for the shield, but the female was cowering, and Beck could feel her tremble.

With just one eye peering through red fur, Beck saw the other female standing her ground on the opposite bank, teeth bared and growling, while the youngster, emboldened by his mother, splashed across the stream, grabbed up pine cones, and threw them. The hurled cones bounced off the big female. Beck leaned out a little too far and one glanced off her shoulder. It smarted. Another pine cone whizzed by her ear and she ducked.

The big gray stepped into the stream. In only a few long strides, she loomed over them, eyes burning with anger—particularly at Beck.

Shaking with terror, Beck buried herself against the red female's chest.

The female toppled forward.

"Nooo!" Beck cried.

Suddenly Beck was buried under an avalanche of muscle, fat, and fur, nearly smothering in the coarse hair, her back pinned against the rocks, in total darkness. On top of her, the mountain trembled and quaked, the heart pounding like a huge drum. Beck couldn't breathe. She couldn't move either. She cried out to God. Things got quiet. The mountain lifted slightly and daylight trickled in through the hair, along with breathable air. A pine cone bounced on the ground just outside, but it landed lightly, so it had to have been tossed, not hurled.

Beck heard feet sloshing back across the stream as the mountain sat up. She dared to peek. The youngster and his mother were returning across the stream. He clung to a fistful of fur on her side, and she stroked his head. He looked back over his shoulder as they left, bared his teeth, and huffed at Beck and her keeper.

With one parting, spiteful grunt, mother and son hurried into the brush, then barked one more loud insult before they vanished from sight.

So there were *three* of them.

Reed sat on the bed in Room 105, Beck's bent and soiled back-pack in front of him. Carefully, solemnly, he removed the contents, handing each article to Cap. As Cap arranged everything on the floor, Sing listed each in her notebook: dry changes of clothes, an extra pair of long underwear, rain gear, matches, dehydrated snacks, a first aid kit, a tool kit, a compact tube tent, a compass, a Swiss Army knife. Reed wept when he found two rolls of toilet paper and a small pouch containing makeup, but he kept going. He couldn't allow his emotions to keep him from this task. Next came a thermal blanket, some containers of food, and—Reed paused to look at it—a crumpled, bent book, *Wilderness Survival*, by Randy Thompson. Several pages were marked and paragraphs highlighted.

"She read it," he marveled. "She actually read all this stuff."

With so much precious time lost and Beck not found, Reed felt as if he were in a torturous limbo between faith that they would find her and cold reason that insisted she couldn't be alive. He dared not voice such things, for he wasn't ready to face them, not yet.

"I'm proud of her," he said, withered by emotion. "I'm really proud that she tried. You know she never finished a painting? She did finish one novel, but she was afraid to send it to any publishers. She was afraid of what they'd think."

"It was a great book!" Sing affirmed. "And listen, Reed, for the record, the survival vacation was a great idea. Sure, Beck needed it, but I think we all could have gotten something out of it."

"You did the right thing," Cap agreed.

Reed gazed down at the pack. It was empty now. Cap took it off his hands and he sat quietly, trying to fathom the day's disappointments. The two teams had returned for the night, some to stay at the Tall Pine, some to catch a few winks at home. What little hope there was, was fading. Reed wondered if they would all return the next morning. "They don't believe me, do they?"

"It's tough to get a read on some of them," said Cap. "I think Pete and the trackers are with you, but as for the others, there's some talk starting up."

Sing tried to reassure him, "You have to expect that, Reed. You know this business. It's all you can do to keep faith in people."

"I saw Randy's body. Beck saw it. We both *saw* it!"

Sing put out a hand to halt any more of that. "Reed, let's move on. Something happened to it. What—that's the question now."

"Pete did find the tree, right?"

Sing answered, "As near as we could tell from your map and directions. He thinks he found your and Beck's footprints around it, and that bush you say she fell into. That all lined up."

"But no body."

"No body. Anywhere."

"But no bear tracks either, right?"

"There may have been tracks—"

"But not *bear* tracks!"

"Pete wouldn't say one way or another."

"That's because this isn't a bear and he knows it!"

Cap objected, "He doesn't know it!"

"He found more of the same prints he found above the waterfall, am I right?"

Sing tossed up a hand. "He found some prints. Some of them could have been Randy's, and some of them were just—I'll tell you what I think: I think Pete does have some doubts about the bear theory, but he's waiting before he says anything."

"Nobody knows what the real story is here," said Cap.

"So what were you sniffing the pack for?" Reed said.

"What?"

"You were sniffing the backpack! You were looking at the hairs! What were you thinking?"

"Reed, I wasn't thinking anything." Reed and Sing locked eyes with him. "Well, nothing *serious!*"

Sing leaned toward her husband, emphatic. "We need to identify those hairs, Cap."

Cap looked cornered. "Why look at me?"

"You have friends at the university who can do it."

"They're not my friends!" They locked eyes with him again. "Well, okay, some of them are. They *might* be."

Sing reached into her backpack and pulled out a plastic Ziploc bag, sealed with red "evidence" tape. The hairs were in it. She tossed it to her husband.

He tossed it back. "I am *not* going back there! I *can't!*" He felt their gaze again. "All right, give me more reason and I'll think about it!"

It took a long moment of stillness before the big red female relaxed her grip and Beck could move a little. Beck allowed herself a small bit of relief, a calming breath or two, but her heart was racing and the trembling wouldn't go away.

A hand with the texture of a baseball glove wrapped around her face and forced her to look directly into the creature's face, mere inches away.

Beck couldn't even scream, her silent throat betraying her yet again.

With long, slimy strokes, a big pink tongue began mopping

the berry stains and blood from Beck's face. She raised her hand to push the big mouth away—*lick*—but then realized—*lick, lick*—that this disgusting, smelly, slimy act could be—*lick*—an act of kindness—*lick, lick*—and she'd better not mess with it.

The creature licked her some more, then inspected her face like a mother inspecting her child. Satisfied, she set Beck down and went to the stream for another drink.

Nauseous, Beck wasted no time crawling and hobbling to the stream, where she flopped on her belly and splashed water on her face. She could feel the slime on her skin, in her hair, on her neck, even in her ears. She kept splashing, frantically washing, longing for some soap and cleansing moisturizer, that wonderful, good-smelling stuff that came out of the quaint, decorative pump bottle by her sink in her nice, warm, clean house—

A string of slime hung from her fingers as she brought them up out of the water. When she stopped to stare at it, she heard an explosive spitting noise upstream.

The big female was drinking, then spitting huge, stringy mouthfuls of water. Apparently she wasn't too pleased with how Beck's face tasted.

Beck stopped, too insulted to continue washing. How could that disgusting monster find *Beck* disgusting?

The lady finished drinking, rolled back onto her haunches, and gave Beck a relentless, studious look, a gaze so unbroken it put Beck's nerves on edge.

A cold wind whipped across the mountainside, swaying the trees and leaching heat from Beck's body. The sun had dipped behind the mountain and a worrisome chill was moving in. So what to do? Was there anywhere she could curl up out of the wind? What if the other two creatures came back?

She eyed the big red female and tried to weigh disgust against wisdom. It seemed the big gal *was* intent on protecting her, something Beck couldn't figure out but had to consider. With night coming on, she might do well to reconsider that big, warm body.

She immediately looked elsewhere. There had to be another way.

The beast grabbed her again.

"Noo!" Beck screeched.

She pulled Beck close.

The smell was enough to make Beck gag, the fur was oily and sweaty, and there was still that frightful streak of blood.

But the body was warm.

The beast's big hands held her close, cuddling her. The coarse fur poked her in the eye and tickled her nose. The blood was turning sour; it gave off a smell like a dead mouse.

But Beck was warm. The cold wind would not reach her tonight.

She pushed the creature's hair out of her eyes, then tried to relax and, of all things, accept the situation—if she could only breathe.

Reed was right about one thing: the rules were different out here. How different? How would she learn them other than one mistake at a time, and what if a mistake turned out to be fatal? She wished Reed were here to help her.

A cold breeze interrupted her thoughts and reminded her that there were more immediate things to worry about—like staying alive right now. Cringing, she pressed in close to the odorous, furry body and drew in the warmth. The beast cradled her with a big arm. More warmth.

Not far south of Abney, in a small meadow about ten miles back on a logging road, Ted and Melanie Brooks, a couple in their twenties, were "roughing it," cooking up a meal over the open fire in front of their two-person tent. Several beer bottles lay empty in the grass, and they were working on two more. A boom box kept them company, preventing any unwanted quiet with the steady pulsing of bass and drums and the angry wailings of a lead guitar.

Ted was frying up the hamburgers. In the light of a camp lantern, Melanie was chopping up some bananas, apples, and melons for a fruit salad. Nearby was their camp cooler, the lid open, full of drinks, fresh eggs, and raw bacon for the morning's breakfast. They'd eaten lunch in the early afternoon and burned their paper plates, but the leftover McDonald's French fries and half of a Caesar salad still remained, resting on a stump, waiting to be part of tonight's meal.

"Hey, babe," Ted said, turning his face away from the heat of the fire. "You want to take a hike later? Nothing like a walk in the dark in the woods."

"I'm up to it if you are," Melanie teased back, her perfect smile lighting her face.

It felt good to get away from the big-city grind. Ted sang along with the CD now playing, a Hendrix tune he'd sung along with from his youth, as he flipped the patties in an iron frying pan.

"Almost done," he announced, excessively happy. He reached for another beer.

"Salad's about ready," Melanie answered, cutting crookedly as the beer metabolized.

A reflection appeared in the trees at the edge of the meadow. It glimmered, moved, then winked out. Ted *thought* he saw it. "What was that?"

Melanie looked up. "What was what?"

Ted took the iron pan off the fire and set it on a nearby stump where the grease and burgers continued to steam and sizzle.

Then he stood away from the fire, watching the darkness. "I thought I saw something."

Melanie stood very still, though a little unsteady. "I think I *heard* something."

Ted hurried over and shut off the boom box.

The sudden quiet was jarring, eerie. Except for the crackle of the fire and the steady breath of the camp lantern, there wasn't a sound.

Then there was.

Snap! Crunch!

Melanie grabbed Ted's arm, hard.

They both peered into the darkness beyond the reach of the lantern, frightened by the shadows—even their own.

A rustling and another twig breaking.

"Something's out there," Ted whispered.

SIX

"Did we bring a gun?" Melanie whispered in fear.

"No, no gun," Ted answered, eyes fixed on the darkness beyond the dimly lit trees. Something was still moving out there. He heard the thumping of feet on a log. "Hello? Hey!" he shouted.

"Don't yell. It might—"

The scream sent a shock through their nerves, jolting their muscles, turning their stomachs, quaking their hands.

"It's . . . it's a . . . there's a woman out there!" Ted blurted, his voice high and trembling.

The mournful wail was still going, rising, falling, rising again.

"Who is it?" Melanie asked no one in particular.

"Hello? Are you all right?" Ted yelled into the dark, then rebuked himself, "That's a dumb question." He stepped forward.

"Where are you going?" Melanie said.

"I'm going to see who it is."

"Don't go out there!"

Ted walked cautiously, shakily, toward the sound, just now falling away. "Hello? You hurt?" He ventured beyond the reach of the light. His form was dim, broken into segments by the shadows. He stumbled on some fallen branches he didn't see.

"Ted! Come back here! I'm scared!"

He turned to look back, his face illumined like a lone planet in the dark of space. "Can you see anything?" he said.

She could see only his face and his right shoulder.

Just beyond his right shoulder, two silvery-green retinas turned into the light.

Melanie screamed the scream of her life, backing away, hands to her face.

Ted spun around just in time to take a blow to his head that nearly snapped his neck. He tumbled like a rag doll out of sight. Branches snapped and Melanie heard hissing through the leaves.

"Ted!"

Something big was moving out there. It screamed like a woman being stabbed. Melanie found a rock and threw it into the blackness. It glanced off a tree.

"Melanie!" Ted's voice was muffled as if he was yelling into the ground.

The shadow moved that direction.

"Ted, run! *Run!*"

She heard him screaming, thrashing in the brush, moving right, falling again, screaming again.

The woman screamed just above him.

Melanie grabbed the hot frying pan with a pot holder and bolted crazily into the dark, her own shadow a black demon dancing on the trees before her. She caught a glimpse of Ted high-stepping, grappling, pushing through the woods on her right, trying to make it to some light.

"Melanie, it's behind you!"

She spun, swinging the frying pan like a baseball bat. The pan tilted vertically and contacted a black, furry mass with a dull *bong* and the hiss of hot grease.

The thing screamed and spun away. Melanie dropped the pan and ran toward the light.

Ted was ahead of her now, his body a silhouette against the camp lantern, his shadow a man-shaped tunnel through the campfire smoke. She ran down that tunnel, stumbling on the uneven ground.

The thing was behind her, screaming in pain and rage.

Ted had reached the car. "Come on, Melanie, come on!"

She got there as he started up the engine. She dove inside, slammed the door, then groped, slapped for the lock button until she found it and pounded it down.

Ted hit the gas and the car lurched forward.

The thing leaped through the headlights, its coarse, black flank absorbing the light, then glanced off the right fender. For an instant, Melanie saw a face in her window: crazed, glowing eyes, a gaping mouth, glistening fangs.

They roared down the logging road so fast that debris from the potholes and ruts hit them like flak.

Melanie twisted and looked through the rear window. The light of the camp lantern was quickly receding, and against that circle of light, in a backlit haze of campfire smoke, a monstrous, hulking shadow was ravaging their camp.

Arlen Peak stabbed two remaining slabs of beef brisket, lifted them off the open-pit grill, and dropped them onto a platter. "Okay, when they cool down, stick 'em in the freezer."

His wife, his daughter, and his two granddaughters were cleaning up dishes and tables after the barbecue buffet, the Tall Pine's contribution to the search effort. Most of the search crew had stuck around for the free meal, but it wasn't a festive occasion. The meal passed quickly, and now the courtyard and tables were empty under the floodlights, the haze from the barbecue thinning with the evening breeze.

Reed poked his head out of Room 105 and surveyed the courtyard and parking lot. Not too many folks still up and around. Most of the search crew had either gone home or were settling in for the night in the RVs neatly parked at the hookups across the parking lot. Satisfied, he stepped out, an empty plate and silverware in his hand. He'd eaten because he knew he had to, but he'd eaten in solitude. With a little luck, he could return his plate and utensils and maybe get some air without seeing anyone.

I'm acting just like Beck, he thought, wagging his head at the irony. This had to be how she felt most of the time: awkward, stared at, discredited for no good reason. No wonder she avoided people—as he was doing right now.

He'd often been asked, "How in the world did you ever get to know each other?" It wasn't easy. They first crossed paths in St. Maries, Idaho, when he was a well-established high-school senior and she was the new girl in school. He'd seen her at school but actually met her in church, which, he'd often reflected, was a good place to meet a girl. She was a shy, awkward, introverted newcomer to the youth group, devastated the first time the youth pastor called on her to read a scripture aloud, terrified of conversation, and slow to make friends. Nevertheless, he'd already eliminated most of the other girls from his field of interest, and though he could never explain it, he found her fascinating. Their first date was a movie—they just watched the movie and didn't have to talk. Then, after he promised that talking wouldn't be required, she took a pleasant afternoon walk with him along the St. Joe River. After that, he took her bicycling, which they enjoyed in silence. When he took her out to dinner, she pointed at what she wanted on the menu and he ordered for them both. The silence between them took getting used to, and he often caught himself babbling to fill the dead space. Nevertheless, it was in those quiet times that she could be amazingly articulate with her eyes and playful, even teasing, with the corners of her mouth.

Without a word, she had him hooked.

It was the evening they played Scrabble with her folks that he first heard her put an articulate sentence together, word after word, and he was astounded. When she was at home, in a safe and familiar world, her speech impediment nearly vanished. She won the game that night, and after that she started talking, in halting phrases at first, and later in fluid sentences, but only to him. It was like striking oil, a real gusher of information, her soul in words.

But she could only speak if she was comfortable, and that became *the* ongoing problem. At their wedding, her maid of honor repeated her vows for her and she nodded in agreement. His friends at the Sheriff's Academy never saw his wife, not even at graduation. She met Sing Capella only because Sing went out of her way to meet *her*, prepared with things to do and share without a word being spoken. The two were chattering with each other within a week, but talking with Cap took longer.

So Cap and Sing became their closest friends, but Beck still had *few* friends, and that was troubling. Cap, Sing, and Reed had often had their little talks in Beck's absence about what they could or should do to help her. If only Beck could get a little confidence, they'd said. If we could just help her come out of her shell and face life head-on, just a *little* . . .

Reed stacked his plate with the others in the kitchen pass-through and dropped his silverware into the big can of soapy water. Arlen's granddaughter looked at him, smiled a bit, and kept on stacking the dishes in the dishwasher. He passed two search volunteers on his way to the parking lot, but they didn't bother him; they didn't even look him in the eye.

Cap and Sing had already said their good nights. Sheriff Mills had left to catch up on loose ends at the department. Pete Henderson had gone home to crash, planning to start fresh at first light. And Jimmy Clark was . . . well, Reed didn't much care where Jimmy was so long as he was elsewhere, at least for the night.

All Reed wanted right now was a little space, a little air, a little time to think—or not think, which would be even better. A walk around the town might feel good—

He heard voices from the other side of the RVs, over in the picnic area.

"But did you see that cabin? One guy couldn't have done that."

"One guy with a good-sized hammer—"

"Oh, get real!"

Reed turned and drew closer, not sneaking, but not making his presence known either. From the shadows among the trees, he recognized two Search and Rescue volunteers sitting at a table, conversing with another man who leaned against a tree. The two at the table had worked with Team 1 at the cabin that day; the guy standing, with hair in a ponytail and so blond it was nearly white, was a newcomer Reed hadn't seen before.

"I've done search and rescue after a bear attack before, up in Glacier," said the newcomer, "and let me tell you two things: number one, the victim isn't drug very far, so it doesn't take that long to find him, and number two, the victim's dead. He isn't wandering off."

"That's how it's gonna turn out," said the bald guy.

"That's how it *should* have turned out, but it didn't. We're still here."

"Well, Jimmy's setting out bait tomorrow. We'll bag the bear, and that'll be the end of it."

"Hey, wait a minute!" said the younger man in the Mariners cap. "What if Thompson and Shelton's wife staged the whole thing so they could run off together?"

"You've seen way too much TV!" said the bald one.

They were laughing.

The newcomer wasn't laughing when he said, "What if Shelton turns up with another woman?"

Reed's hands balled into fists.

The other two quit laughing.

"You serious?" the bald guy asked.

"Why not?" The newcomer took a drag on a cigarette, the orange tip glowing in the dark. "Like that cop in Spokane who shot his wife and blamed some black guy that didn't exist. These things happen."

"But what about the cabin? You think Shelton tore it all up?"

"What if a *bear* wrecked the cabin and Shelton saw an opportunity? Took out his wife *and* Randy Thompson because Thompson could have been a witness?"

The two were silent as they thought about it.

"I guess Shelton's wife was a little strange, kind of a retard," said the bald one.

"Yeah," the young one agreed. "If he's got another babe somewhere . . ."

"So what'd he do with the bodies?"

"Put 'em where we'll never find 'em," said the newcomer. He took another drag and the smoke puffed out with his words. "That way nobody will find out how they really died."

"You're sick, you know that?" the bald one replied.

"Think what you want. My money's on Shelton."

Reed wanted to meet this guy, introduce himself, share a few words of understanding, and put him on the ground. Maybe he could even acquaint the man with the natural taste and crispy texture of pine cones stuffed in that big mouth. He took a step forward—

"Reed!" It was Cap, hollering from the inn. "Reed!"

Good old Cap. Reed hurried back across the parking lot with eyes and thoughts forward.

Cap was on the porch in tee shirt and jeans. His boots were still untied. "Reed, there's been another attack!"

Shock. Relief. Horror. I-told-you-so. "Where?" Reed breathed.

Sing burst out the front door in blouse and jeans, barefoot, her hair unbraided and billowing down her back, a handheld radio close to her ear. "Two campers were attacked an hour and a half ago, six miles up Service Road 19, north of Kamayah."

"Kamayah. That's—what?—about ten miles southeast of here?" Reed said.

"Ten miles southeast," Sing confirmed, "then six miles north up that service road . . . it'd be within four to six miles of the first attack."

Cap finished tying his boots. "That thing's moving."

"Does Sheriff Mills know?"

"He and Jimmy are on their way now," Sing answered.

"What about Pete?"

Sing traded her radio for her cell phone. "I'm going to rouse him out of bed."

Reed spun around, counting vehicles and RVs, trying to guess the number of available bodies still around. "We can't give up the search *here*!"

"We won't."

Cap was insistent, excited. "We've got to see this. It could explain everything!"

Reed looked directly, boldly, at the three men having their little whodunit discussion around the picnic table. "It sure could."

Flash! Sing, in warm coat and cap, photographed the empty frying pan lying facedown where the woods bordered the meadow. Cap was her light man; he held a strong floodlight so Sing could see what she was doing. It was close to midnight. Ground fog and campfire smoke hung along the ground and shrouded the trees in a ghostly haze.

Jimmy was shining his flashlight around the devastated campsite and counting the empty beer bottles scattered in the grass. From the breath and demeanor of the two campers huddled by the revived fire, there was no question in his mind where all the suds had gone. "Guess you've had a few beers, huh?" Jimmy said.

Apparently, Ted became obstinate and easily offended when drunk. "So what? We weren't driving!"

"You drove out of here, didn't you?"

Melanie, when drunk, became gushy and emotional. "Well, wouldn't you? Wouldn't you wanna get away if some big monster was coming after you?"

Flash! Sing captured the beer bottles, a shattered camp lantern, and a broken camp cooler.

Jimmy swept the edge of the woods with his light. "That the frying pan you hit him with?"

"That's it!" said Melanie. "He got the message!"

"I think he ate the hamburgers," said Ted.

"Looks like he ate a lot of things," Jimmy observed. "You had fruit salad lying out, hamburgers frying, eggs and bacon . . ." He walked to where the remains of a paper plate lay in the grass alongside scattered remnants of lettuce and tomato. "What was this, a salad?"

"My dinner salad," Melanie replied. "With French fries."

Flash! Sing took a shot to show the location of the ravaged salad in relation to the campsite.

Jimmy drew a breath, as if gathering patience. "Folks, you should know better than to have food like this lying around your camp. Fried foods, greasy foods, garbage like this putting out all that smell, it's a wonder you didn't attract every bear within fifty miles!"

"This-s wasn't a bear!" Ted countered, his voice slurred and unsteady. "It was a big, hairy thing! It was like K-king Kong or . . . something!"

Sing went blind in the dark. "Cap. The light."

"Oh. Sorry."

Flash! She captured a field of debris: a jacket, a paperback novel, a punctured thermos, shredded food packaging.

"What else have you had tonight?" Jimmy asked the two campers. "Any mushrooms, by chance?"

"Hey, whaddaya trying to—"

"Just be careful what you say. You don't want to get in trouble with the law."

Sheriff Mills picked up an edge of the flattened tent and looked underneath, probing with his light. Two sleeping bags were spread out; a hot rod magazine and a gardening magazine were undisturbed. There were no mushrooms.

Flash! As the sheriff held the fallen tent up, Sing captured the tent's interior.

Reed tried to keep his voice calm as he questioned Ted and Melanie Brooks. "Did it make a sound like a woman screaming?"

Their eyes got wide with the recollection. "Yeah," said Ted. "Scared us to death!"

"We thought it was somebody in trouble!" said Melanie.

"Did it walk upright?"

"Sure looked like it!"

Jimmy asked, "Was it about twenty feet tall?"

Ted and Melanie looked at each other, and then Ted answered, "Coulda been!"

"Big hairy hands?"

"I saw it using its hands, yeah! They were real hairy," said Melanie.

Jimmy nodded to himself, then called toward some flashlights sweeping and winking only a foot from the ground near the edge of the meadow, "Pete, you got anything?"

"Not yet," came Pete's voice through the murk.

"Sing, did you get a shot of this cooler here?"

"Got it," she replied, working her way toward the woods.

Mills met her with the punctured thermos in his hand. "Better bag this." The thermos had been nearly bitten in half, the tooth marks forming a jagged, saw-toothed rift.

Sing pulled a Ziploc bag from her pocket and dropped the thermos inside. "Mr. Teeth again, just like the can of beans I found at the cabin." She placed the bagged thermos in her shoulder bag.

Mills called, "Jimmy! Pete!"

"Yeah?"

"We're raising the caution level. Searchers go out in twos from now on, with at least one rifle or a sidearm between them."

"Understood," said Pete, his voice muffled by his nearness to the ground.

"You got it," said Jimmy, having a further look around. "Good idea."

Reed took hold of Jimmy's arm to get his attention. "Jimmy, you heard 'em, right? They saw the same thing we did!"

"Reed," Jimmy said, "didn't you hear the questions you were asking? You were leading the witnesses. Give me a break!"

"Jimmy! What's it gonna take to—"

Jimmy put his hand on Reed just to hold him steady—and quiet. "Reed, listen," he whispered, "you don't want to get lumped in with those people. They're drunk, they might be on drugs—"

"But they—"

"Reed! They're bad for you. They're two fruitcakes who did everything a stupid camper can do to attract a bear!"

"But it wasn't a bear!"

"Shh! *Don't!*" Jimmy looked around, clearly afraid that some-one may have heard that. "Reed. Look at me. I'm talking as your friend. This could be a real break. This has to be the same bear, which means we have a fresh trail. We might even be able to back-track from here and get some kind of lead on Beck. Now . . ." He put his finger in Reed's face to hold him in check. "Reed, I'm telling you—don't ruin it. We've got plenty of volunteers ready to work with us *as long as* they're good and clear on what it is they're doing. If there's a bear to be tracked down and killed, they're with us. But if you start going on about some big, hairy . . ." He looked around again. "They're talking already. Some of them are having some real doubts about what we're doing and about you, and you don't want that. You want them on your side."

Headlights illuminated the camp as a truck pulled up.

Jimmy searched Reed's face a moment. "Reed, am I getting through?"

Reed whispered hurriedly, "You don't believe me, do you?"

"What difference does it make as long as we find Beck?"

The blinding headlights obliterated anything and everything

behind them until the engine quit, the lights winked out, and four men walked into the dull orange glow of the campfire. All four were armed with rifles. The first two were Steve Thorne, the buzz-cut "marine," and a close partner Reed recognized right away, the man with the near-white hair, whose "money was on Shelton." Ol' White Hair had one of his picnic-table buddies with him, the kid in the Mariners cap, Sam Marlowe. The fourth was the hunter named Janson.

"Hey, guys," said Jimmy. "Probably won't need you till we get some light."

"Couldn't wait," said White Hair. "We brought the overnight gear. We can camp out here 'til morning."

Reed eyed him steadily but did not offer his hand. "I'm Reed Shelton."

The man just eyed him back with a wry smile on his face. "Wiley Kane, from Missoula. Glad to be along."

Reed shot a glance at Jimmy, then engaged Wiley Kane one more time. "Looks like it's happened again."

Kane nodded emphatically. "Oh, yeah. It's a rogue bear all right. I've seen this kind of thing before."

"Yeah. Right. A bear." Reed stole one more look at Jimmy, who returned his look approvingly.

"Reed?" It was Sing's voice, coming from behind Cap's light near the edge of the woods. "Can we see you a second?"

"Excuse me." He was more than glad to be somewhere else. He made his way through the grass to where Sing and Cap awaited him, dark shapes against the white, wiggling background of flashlight beams in the fog.

"Come on," said Sing, "and step where we step."

He followed them, his flashlight on their feet, as they moved through the grass in a single file toward Pete Henderson and the man helping him. Immediately to their left, peeking through the creeping fog and smoke, a trail of bent-over grass skirted the edge of the woods and then broke into clear ground.

Pete was on his knees and bent over, measuring a print while his assistant held a light at a low angle along the ground, bringing out the shadows. Without looking up, he said, "Reed, I think it's your critter."

They encircled a patch of bare ground next to a dry streambed, flooding it with their flashlight beams. When the stream ran during the rainy months, this patch of ground was a shallow eddy of standing water, the bottom lined with a thick layer of silt. The water had receded for the summer, leaving the silt in a smooth, moist state, perfect for registering a footprint—which it had done.

"This is big medicine," said the assistant, holding his light steady as Pete measured and sketched in his pocket notebook.

Pete looked up. "Reed Shelton, this is Marty Elkhorn. He runs the store down in Kamayah. The campers used his phone to call us."

Reed offered his hand. "Have you met Cap and Sing?"

Elkhorn nodded, his face grim, his wrinkles deep in the bouncing light of the flashlights. He looked up at Sing. "Pete tells me you're Coeur d'Alene."

She nodded.

"Shoshone," he replied. He gazed at the print that was starkly lit like a feature on the moon. "So you must know the warnings, the things our fathers taught us."

Sing gazed over Pete's shoulder at the print, her face eerily cold and statuesque in the weak light. "*Tsiatko?*"

Elkhorn nodded, the fear in his eyes chilling. "The wild men."

Pete looked up from his work. "Marty, I do appreciate your traditions, but this is an *animal*."

"No! Don't think that! The Indians didn't make up the *tsiatko*. They were here before we were! We knew about them before the white man came, and they have always been with us! Every tribe has its own name for them. *Oh-Mah*, the hairy giants. *Skookum*, the evil wood-spirits."

Sing offered, "And I believe the Salish word is *sess-ketch*."

Elkhorn nodded. "When the white man came, he pronounced it his own way: *Sasquatch*."

The mist crawled on their skin and the darkness closed in on them as every eye focused on the print, deeply impressed in the black silt. The heel was distinct, with clear dermal ridges, but the forward half of the foot had shifted in the track, leaving a smeared impression.

Reed was just as mesmerized as the others but had to be sure, at long last, that he could accept his own memories. "Pete, what in the world is it?"

Pete finished jotting down his measurements. "Fifteen inches long, six wide. It's not a perfect match with the other prints we found, but those prints were nowhere as clear as this one, so we might allow for that." He pointed. "Four clear toe impressions, and this dip here must be the fifth. No claws. I'm gonna figure he was at the cabin last night, and at the waterfall." He glanced toward the wrecked camp where Jimmy and the hunters were combing through the mess. "This ol' boy's temper is sure a match."

Elkhorn was getting more agitated the more they talked about it. He finally rose to his feet. "We can't stay here. This is big medicine. *Tsiatko* has taken this ground."

"It has my wife!" Reed objected.

"Of course it does! That's what *tsiatko* does when it finds men on his ground." He looked at the others, then pointed at the print. "And you think this is the only one? There are more.

They've come to these woods, and you won't see them either, not before they come in the night and take you!"

Sing tried to explain to the others, "Many of our parents raised us to believe that, if we weren't good, the giants would come and take us away." She added, as politely as possible, "For some of us, these traditions are ingrained in our thinking."

Elkhorn, all the more resolute and fearful, stood eye to eye, nose to nose with Reed. "It has your wife. What more do I need to say?" Suddenly, in what seemed an act of madness, Elkhorn dropped the flashlight, threw up both his hands, and shouted to the forest in a shrill voice, "Elkhorn is leaving! Do you hear me? Elkhorn will never set foot on this land again! His wife and his children will never set foot here! Do you hear me?"

Now the campers, hunters, Jimmy, and Sheriff Mills were looking.

Elkhorn bolted and ran across the meadow, through the tattered campsite, and to his old car. He opened the driver's door but stood to shout one more time, his arm upraised, "Elkhorn is gone, do you hear? He will never come here again!" Then, with his engine roaring and his wheels spewing gravel, he got out of there.

Jimmy hollered to Pete, "Where'd you get *him*?"

"Crazy Injun," said Kane.

"Pete! What are you looking at over there?"

"Prints," Pete answered.

"Okay," Jimmy said. "This bear's a regular camp raider. Tomorrow we put up some bear stands and put out some bait."

"Good idea," said the white-haired Kane. "I'll take the first shift."

"I'll back you up," said Thorne.

Jimmy rubbed his hands together briskly. "Okay, you two guys set up at the cabin. Janson and Sam, you take this site. We'll have both locations covered. It'll be a shooting gallery."

Pete waited, but Jimmy's attention was elsewhere. "Won't even look at 'em," Pete muttered. "Reed, maybe you can hold the light."

Reed picked up the flashlight and stooped down, once again illuminating the print in the silt. "Pete, what is it?"

Pete had to consider a moment before answering. "Could I please not have to answer that—at least 'til an answer comes to me? I've been tracking in and around this county for fifteen years, and I've never seen a track like this one. No question, though: whatever it is, it's one mean critter and we've gotta find it."

Sing snapped some photos and then said in an aside to her husband, "Cap . . ."

"What?" Then he wagged his head. "No, no, I'm not jumping to any conclusions—and neither should you."

"Conclusions about what?" Reed asked, impatient.

"I've seen how it works," Cap said. "People believe what they want to believe, and if they want to believe something badly enough, they can see things that aren't there or not see things that are."

"So what are you saying?"

"I'm saying . . ." Reed could tell that Cap was trying to be careful. "I'm saying we really, *really* want Beck to be alive. It's *the* driving force in our minds right now; it's dominating our emotions."

"So?"

"So . . . what if we just don't *want* it to be a bear?"

Now Reed stood to face him. "Now *you* think I'm seeing things, is that it?"

"Reed, maybe we *all* are because we *want* to. I admit, I really *want* to believe that something just picked Beck up and carried her off, because that opens up limitless possibilities, even fantasies that are a whole lot easier to handle than—" His sentence hit a wall. "See? I can't even say it."

Pete broke in, his hand outstretched. "Reed, I need that light."

Still looking testily at Cap, Reed slapped the flashlight into Pete's hand.

Sing intervened. "Cap, unless I'm wrong, you have it backward." He looked as though he would have come back with something if he *had* something. "You believe it, Cap, and not because you want to; you *don't* want to! You've been arguing with yourself ever since this whole thing started."

"Now I know it wasn't a bear," said Pete. He shone his flashlight farther up the dry streambed, illuminating a strange, lumpy pile. He approached the new discovery and they semicircled around him like a nature class, flashlights centered on a pile of fresh droppings—lobed lumps loosely connected in a chain by strands of leaves, grass, rodent hair, and paper food packaging.

"It's only a few hours old," said Pete. "But no bear leaves scat like this."

Sing looked at Cap and said softly, "Does it look familiar at all?" She gave him time to ponder while she aimed her camera and took some more pictures.

Cap studied the droppings. From the look on his face, the news was bad, and the longer he looked, the worse it seemed to get. The others fell silent, waiting for his answer.

Finally, after a fleeting glimpse at Sing, he asked Pete, "Can I get a sample?"

"Take the whole thing," said Pete.

Sing was already pulling out a Ziploc bag. The droppings were soft, loose, and messy; it was difficult to preserve their original shape as she spooned them up. "I'll get you those hairs as well. And I've got a thermos here you should take along. Saliva."

"Let me get some sleep and I'll leave for Spokane tomorrow— or is it today?"

"It's today," said Sing.

Reed was speechless for a moment, but finally he met Cap's eyes and said, "You're the one, Cap. Any help you can give us . . ."

Cap made sure the bag was properly sealed as he replied, "Well, it's a chance to sleep in my own bed again. But this is a long shot. They may not even let me in the door."

"Try the back," said Sing.

Cap weighed that a moment. "If they catch me, I'll tell them you said it was okay."

"You do that." She winked at him.

"So what do we tell Jimmy?" Reed asked.

"Aw," said Pete, rubbing his tired eyes, "just let him and his boys hunt their doggone bear. Cap's right; people believe what they want—but it's gonna be the weirdest bear they've ever seen." He shoved his notebook back in his pocket. "I gotta crawl into my truck and get some sleep. Don't let anybody mess up these tracks. And, Reed?"

"Yeah?"

"You're not crazy, so get to work."

"What do you want me to do?"

"Do . . . cop stuff. Find a pattern or something, one of those whatchamacallits . . . an MO. Any information's useful." Pete trudged on by. "It's time somebody else did some of the work around here."

Reed watched Pete disappear into the darkness and fog, and then met the eyes of Cap and Sing.

Cap looked away a moment, taking in the trashed campsite, the mysterious footprint, and the plastic bag in his hand, then met Reed's eyes again. "There *is* a chance you're not crazy."

"Far from it," said Sing.

Suddenly Reed had only a vague memory of feeling helpless and despondent in another time, another place. He could recall feeling like a liar even though he'd never lied, but now he had friends who believed. His mind began to turn over like an old car out of mothballs. "So . . . we really do have two occurrences, in two different places—No! *Three* attacks: Randy on Monday—we need to verify from Arlen Peak just when Randy went up there. Did somebody ask him that already? Then Beck on Monday night—and I can place that at about 11:30. Now we have this one, Ted and Melanie . . . ?"

"Brooks," said Sing.

"Brooks. Okay, you've got their contact information?"

"Got it."

"Cap, you'll stay in touch, right?"

"I'll have my cell phone," he answered, "or you can just leave a message at the house."

"If we all stay in regular contact, we can swap any new information. Sing, what about your mobile lab? Think we can use it?"

"We'll head home and I can bring it in the morning," she replied.

Reed was actually thinking, and it felt good. "Load it up. We need your computer, all your forensic stuff, and let's get a batch of GPS transceivers with peer-to-peer positioning, one for each of us."

Sing raised an eyebrow. "With satellite feed to a master console on a PC?"

Reed liked that. "That'll work."

Sing wrote it down.

Reed began to fidget and pace. "There might be a pattern here, something we can extrapolate both directions, past and future. We've seen three attacks, but there could have been more." He stopped abruptly, afraid he was getting ahead of himself. "Does that make sense?"

Cap smiled. "Just keep going, Reed. You're doing fine."

He needed that. "Okay. I'll get on it." He took off for the cars. "Can you drop me by the Cave Lake trailhead to get my car?"

Sing and Cap exchanged an arched look and followed close on his heels. "You got it," said Cap.

"Sheriff Mills!" Reed said.

Mills was finishing up, tossing garbage bags into the trunk of his car. "Yeah?"

"Is the office open? I need the computer."

Mills didn't ask why. Something in Reed's manner and tone must have answered that question. He just smiled the faintest hint of a smile, dug in his pocket, and tossed Reed the key.

SEVEN

Beck couldn't sleep. Lying against the beast's immense body provided plenty of heat, but Beck's slender rib cage, shoulders, and hips—not to mention her constantly complaining ankle—could only endure the bumpy, rocky ground for a minute or two before she had to wriggle, reposition, roll, curl, and search for some other way to get comfortable. The beast must have been uncomfortable too. She was squirming and rolling as much as Beck was, which gave Beck one more concern to keep her awake: making sure the big female didn't roll on top of her.

Finally, one brief moment of sleep came when the female lay on her back, her forearm over her eyes, and Beck found a way to lie against that big stomach with her head on the female's breast. Now, that worked—

Until the beast rolled and sat up, dumping Beck onto the ground again.

"Oww!" A rock jabbed Beck in her rump, her elbow took a gouge from another hard spot, and, of course, her ankle gave her a sharp reminder. Sitting there on the rocks, in the cold light of a half-moon, Beck whimpered. Anywhere else it may have seemed childish, but out here, who would fault her? Certainly not the ape, who seemed to be ignoring her anyway, lumbering over to a grove of young firs and inspecting them, first one, then another, then another. She tugged at their branches, sniffed them, yanked them hard enough to make their branches quake and their tops whip about.

She found a ten-footer she liked. With one hand and one lazy, apish move, she tore it out of the ground, looked around for a good spot, and flopped it down. She then probed and poked around in the grove like a woman at a yard sale until she found another one she liked. With no apparent strain, she plucked it up and laid it next to the first. Starting at one end, she moved along, removing the branches with deft little twists of her hands, and laid the branches side by side across the two tree trunks.

Beck watched in amazement—this big ape was actually building a nest to sleep on. Beck wondered why it had taken her half a night of sleeping on rocks to think of it.

Now the beast was gathering leafy limbs from surrounding undergrowth and laying them on top of the framework she'd made, mashing them down with her hands. She was quite absorbed in her work, which presented Beck an opportunity she knew would not last long. Of course, judging from the urgent signals she was getting from her bladder and bowels, she would not *need* long.

The squashed roll of toilet paper Beck found in her coat pocket was nothing short of manna from heaven. The two smooth logs, with a comfortable gap between them, lying in an enclosure of maple and syringa bushes, were like a tabernacle in the wilderness.

It went well. It was worth staying up half the night for. Never, ever in her life did she imagine herself doing such a thing, but now, as she began to unroll a length of toilet paper, she breathed a prayer of thanks.

The leaves rustled and she looked up.

The big female was watching her, head cocked in fascination.

Different rules, Beck reminded herself. *Different rules!*

The female came right in, pushing through the limbs and leaves and settling in front of Beck to see how the whole process worked. The toilet paper held special fascination for her. She reached out tentatively to touch it.

Beck tore off one little piece and gave it to her. She sniffed it, then put a corner on her tongue. Unimpressed, she tried to spit it out. It stuck to her tongue, so she tried again, then finally rolled it off against her upper lip and blew it away.

Having completed her task, Beck quickly pocketed the roll, reassembled herself, and rose gingerly. She hobbled out of the enclosure, hand-over-handing along the logs, expecting the female would follow her.

But the female didn't follow her.

Beck turned, curious, just as the bushes opposite the enclosure quaked, then parted, and the big gray female and her son burst headlong into the clearing like children after tossed candy.

How? She'd had no idea they were there, no indication, and—

And apparently Beck's female had not been the only one watching! Beck was mortified, and even more so to see how fascinated these creatures were with her most recent accomplishment. They probed and sniffed. They were almost fighting over it.

Since Beck was on their turf, and even the young ape outweighed her at least three to one, she backed off and gave them all the space they needed. Hopefully they would like whatever it was they were learning.

Then the juvenile's eyes darted elsewhere, his attention cut short by an eerie, faraway whistle. The two females became alert and silent, heads erect, eyes shifting. Beck was more than alert; so far, whistles had not brought good news.

From somewhere in the dark, far beyond the enclosure, an animal was calling, first in a low whistle and then in a low, guttural rumble like boulders tumbling.

The gray female answered in a whistle and then a low-pitched, subdued moan, chin jutting, lips pursed in a tight little O. When a rumbling reply came back, the three apes huddled, grudges apparently put on hold, eyes searching beyond the enclosure, anticipating something as they grunted and snuffed at each other.

For Beck, dread had become normal, changing only in degree. She peered through the trees, side-glancing at the others for any clues about which way to look. Part of her, like a hopeful child, wondered if it might be a team of rescuers come to take her back, but the rest of her knew better.

The forest on the mountainside was broken into smaller, struggling clumps of stunted firs and pines: black, saw-toothed cones against a moon-washed sky. A soft, distant rustling directed Beck's attention to a black mass of trees that swelled sideways until one tree separated from the others, walking, spreading in size as it approached. Beck perceived the shape of this new shadow from the stars and sky vanishing behind it: broad, lumbering shoulders; thick neck; high, crested head; huge arms, with hair like Spanish moss.

Like little kids caught in mischief, the females and the juvenile scurried out of Beck's makeshift outhouse, looking over their shoulders and panting little exclamations to each other. Beck's female, with typical surprising speed, swept Beck up in her arms, and Beck, in typical fashion, rode along, like it or not. They dove into the stand of young firs and sat on the female's nest as if they'd all built it, the other female overtly fascinated with her own fingernails; the juvenile cuddling up against his mother; and Beck's female doting on Beck, first dropping her onto the nest as if she could handle being dropped, then nudging her this way and that way as if to make Beck comfortable. Beck did not appreciate the poking and prodding. There was so much of it, it was sure to draw the big male's attention.

The big newcomer sensed—most likely *smelled*—something outside of normal before he even got there. He had been moving swiftly, silently, like a spirit through the broken forest and over the rocks, but now, just outside the grove of firs, he moved one careful, exploratory step at a time, sniffing and huffing suspiciously, looking about for whatever was wrong.

This had to be the daddy, all eight feet of him. He was covered in coarse black hair; his face was one big scowl in a leathery mask, and Beck had never seen such piercing eyes, each cornea reflecting the moon in a diamond of light. He carried a slain deer in his left arm, its head dangling on a broken neck. Preoccupied, he dropped it.

Beck knew what was wrong—*she* was wrong—but she hadn't a clue what to do about it. All she could do was cower behind the red female's big frame and—

That option vanished. Abruptly, the other female dropped facedown to the ground, bowing on all fours with her head low, rumbling and clicking her tongue in homage. Beck's female, as if reminded of her manners, dove to the ground and did the same. The young one, because he was a male, or because he was still a juvenile and not expected to know any better, did not participate in the ritual but sat where he was, glancing in Beck's direction as if to guide the alpha male to the proper target.

Beck, now on open display, had never felt so caught-and-in-trouble in her life. Her hand went unconsciously to her neck, as the images of both Randy Thompson and the dead deer flashed through her mind.

And she *was* in trouble. The male leaped backward in shock, eyes wide, a raspy huff gushing from his throat and his hair bristling on end. With steamy breath rushing through his nostrils, he glared at Beck and then at the two females, muscles tense, teeth bared.

He thinks I'm a threat!

Learning—fast—from the other two females, Beck flopped to the ground and bowed.

The thing didn't move. After three or four seconds, Beck was still alive.

The other female moved aside and enfolded her son, leaving the big red female to explain.

Beck's female rose to her knees and reached for Beck—

The male shot forward, took the female by the scruff of the neck, and threw her into a row of young firs, bending them over like field grass. She screamed, arms covering her face, white teeth glinting in the moonlight, as she slid down the bent trunks—

He grabbed her before she reached the ground and threw her again, this time into a larger tree that shuddered as she bounced off its furrowed trunk and thudded to the ground. She cried in pain.

Beck didn't have to think long or hard. There was absolutely no safety here, no hope of living. She pushed herself from the ground and hobbled and hopped out of the grove, dragging one foot while she jumped with the other, fleeing from one branch to another, stumbling from trunk to trunk, groping for anything that would bear her up and keep her moving. She could still hear the female screaming and the alpha male roaring; she heard the blows and felt the ground shake. It didn't matter that she had no idea where she was; the only thing that mattered was being else-where, anywhere but here. She pulled herself, pushed herself, counting the inches, desperate for distance.

The screaming stopped. Beck could easily imagine the big female's head nearly twisted off, her tongue hanging, her eyes rolling. So much for Beck's protector. Their strange, unnatural interlude was over, leaving Beck lost and unwelcome in a scratching, entangling, tripping darkness with nowhere to go that was anywhere.

She fell against a tree—she didn't find it; it found her, and it hurt. She remained still, just breathing, waiting for the pain in her ankle to subside enough for her to take one more step.

Now that she was quiet, she realized that the woods were not. Somewhere behind her came a crashing, a crackling, and the thudding of heavy footfalls.

"N-n-n-no . . . no . . ." She forced herself onward, tripped over a log, and rolled among fallen branches, clenching her teeth to stifle a scream. She reached, groped, tried to sit up and get her legs under her. Her good leg moved. The sprained one was stuck and punished her severely for pulling. She pulled anyway and couldn't help a whimper of pain. She was free.

The thing was coming closer, moving through the tangle with unbelievable speed.

Randy Thompson. This was how it was for him!

She tried to climb the tree but found no handholds. She lunged forward, leaping on her one good leg, groping for any branch, any tree trunk—

Huge hairy arms grabbed her around her middle and jerked her backward, knocking the wind out of her. She screamed, she kicked, she tried to wriggle free.

The arms were like iron.

Willard, Idaho, was a loosely arranged, quiet little town of red brick storefronts, older farmhouses on hillsides, and scattered modular homes on weedy lots. It was like many in Idaho, built in a day when timber and mining were sure to make money and folks thought there would be some point in living there. Today it survived as the Whitcomb County seat with a proud, pillared courthouse. Down this old building's tight corridors and behind its many doors with the frosted windows were all the entities that held the county together: the district court and judge, the prosecuting attorney, the county commissioners, Planning and Zoning, Disaster Services, County Assessor, Social Services, and on and on, enough to fill the building directory on the wall just inside the front door.

If someone wished to find the county sheriff, the directory would send that person next door to the newer building meant to serve as an expansion of the old one. This building was white concrete block, one story, plain and practical, intended for a specific purpose, which was to house the county sheriff's office and the county jail. Inside the front door was a reception counter; behind that were four desks, a fairly neat one for the secretary and three generally cluttered ones for the deputies; to the right was Sheriff Patrick Mills's private office, a separate room with a door he usually kept open. To the left and through an archway was the examining station for driver's licenses, complete with two testing booths, an eye chart, a camera, and two green footprints painted on the floor to show the applicant where to stand for his or her photo.

In a corner behind the counter and past the four desks was the computer station. There were other computers in the building, but this was the "department" computer, the one strictly devoted to law enforcement, available to any member of the staff for the performance of his or her duty. Some months ago, a flight simulator and a commando game had cropped up in a coded folder on the computer's desktop, but these were not openly discussed and only discreetly used.

Right now, with everyone gone but the night jailer and all calls forwarded to the central dispatcher, Reed sat at the computer in the light of a single desk lamp, the blue glow from the monitor on his face, an overlapped clutter of windows and boxes on the screen. He was tapping and clicking his way through the multiple levels and links of the National Center for the Analysis of Violent Crime, a networking tool used by law-enforcement agencies all around the country in tracking criminals and sharing investigative information. The program had subgroups for different categories of crime, regions of the country, and types of criminals, with subgroups under those, and side links from those. Sifting downward through all the levels could have been tough for someone who hadn't slept in more than twenty-four hours, but Reed knew what he was after and pushed away sleep as he pushed through the program.

Maybe Jimmy and the others—including bigmouth Kane from Missoula—did know the woods and had good reason for their opinions. They were outdoorsmen and Reed was a cop; so maybe Reed was a little out of his realm of competence.

He tapped the keys, hammered the backspace and tried again, clicking the mouse.

But then again, maybe they didn't know everything, and maybe he did know something. Just standing around and letting them tell him what to think wasn't going to resolve the question, nor was it going to expedite the process. Enough of that. Reed had a brain and skills of his own. He was going to do cop stuff, whatever it took to find Beck.

Was there a pattern? Whatever this beast was, had it attacked anyone else, anywhere else? If so, when? Where had it come from, and which way was it going? Was there anything more they could find out about it?

Reed finally clicked his way into a subgroup that linked and

compared known homicides with unexplained deaths, a program
intended to help law enforcement detect homicides that may not
have been recognized as such. In a few more mouse clicks, he narrowed the time frame down to the last two weeks, and the region to
his own and the three neighboring counties. The pickings were slim:
a hit-and-run outside a tavern, and a logging accident. The tavern
was far to the west, in another county, and took place a week ago.

The logging accident . . .

Reed read the entry again, carefully noted the location, and
then checked a map.

Ooookayyy. He clicked, nearly *banged,* the "print" command
and then fidgeted while the paper slowly rolled out of the printer.
By the time it had finished, he had his coat on. With the printout
in his hand, he turned off the lamp and got out of there.

With a slightly gentler drop than the last time, Beck landed back
on the nest in the grove, limp and despondent. She'd given up
trying to understand. The big red female, moving stiffly from her
own bruises, had brought her back and now hunched over her,
nudging, stroking, fussing.

Beck grunted and pushed her hand away. *I'm going to die anyway, thanks to you. What's left to fuss about?*

Her eye was on the alpha male as he shared the dead deer
with the other two just outside the grove. He slurped blood,
ripped flesh from hide, tore the meat with his teeth and hands,
and chewed, his mouth and chin bloodied. He looked her way
only once as he chewed, just long and intensely enough to send a
message of loathing, making sure she knew she didn't belong.
After that, for as long as Beck watched him, he paid her no mind;
he just kept eating.

Beck looked away. Maybe that was the end of it. Maybe for now, her captor "mother" had gotten her way and the male had relented—grudgingly, of course. But he'd sent his message loud and clear.

All things considered, this should be bearable. It beat being thrown against a tree or having her head ripped off. Beck glanced at her aching feet and the recent scratches on her hands from all those dry, prickly branches in the dark. This was the worst that had happened to her. She was alive for one more moment, maybe one more night. She should be glad.

She broke down and cried.

The big female sank onto the nest beside her with a quiet groan and pulled her in close, an act of affection that only worsened Beck's despair. Beck was too upset to say it; she could only think it: *Why can't you just let me go?*

The beast got a message—the wrong message. She immediately extended her hand toward the others and pig grunted.

They ignored her, so she grunted more insistently, rocking back and forth.

The male finally looked her way as if doing her one more additional, very troublesome favor, then regarded what was left of the deer. With indifference, he took hold of the head in one hand and the shoulder in the other, and wrenched the head and neck from the body. When the female grunted imploringly one more time, he tossed it to her.

It flopped at her feet, throwing blood. She picked it up, obviously glad to get it. With slow, lazy-fingered deliberation, she turned it over and over, sniffing and studying as if she'd never seen one before, and then, breaking the jaw open, she yanked out the tongue and bit the end off.

Beck looked the other way, feeling sick. How could God create such creatures? And even worse, how could He throw her in with them? She never asked for this. She wouldn't have been able to conceive such a horror to ask for.

The female grunted and nudged her. She winced and would not turn her head. The female nudged her again, grunting, and Beck ventured a timid look with one eye.

The ape was offering her a string of meat. Beck couldn't recognize where it had come from, which was a good thing. She shook her head, her mouth clamped shut.

The lady dangled the meat in front of her face and wiggled it so it thumped against her lips. It reminded Beck of when she tried to feed worms to a baby robin. The robin wouldn't eat and soon died.

Thump! The meat hit her face again. Beck reached up and took it as the female intensely, relentlessly watched.

It's a strip of bacon, Beck told herself. *It's like sushi. It's rack of lamb without the rack*, really *rare. It's steak on the platter right before the barbecue.*

Building up to the moment, Beck put the slightest tip of the meat between her teeth and nipped it off. As she pressed it against her tongue, the flavor came through, and really, it wasn't half bad. It was raw and tasted a little "wild," but it was meat. A little salt would have helped, she supposed, but . . .

She bit off another piece and chewed it slowly on one side of her mouth and then the other. She swallowed it, and then, of all things, she wondered if there might be more. She was hungry.

Her female captor was still working on the tongue but found a nice strip from the back of the neck and bit it off to give to her.

I'm eating, Beck thought. That was nothing unusual in itself, but it taxed her sanity to think she was taking part in this meal, in this setting, with these creatures. They were bloody, fearsome carnivores who were sharing a deer's head with her, but she was eating it. They had blood and grease on their fingers, but so did she. They were disgusting to watch, but she was gaining an appreciation for how hunger could supplant politeness; she could relate—sort of.

The female handed her another strip of flesh, and Beck received it gladly, chewing it down. That seemed to please the beast. She reached down and fingered the fringes on Beck's brown buckskin coat. Then with her index finger, she hooked and twirled a strand of Beck's reddish-brown hair.

Beck dared to take hold of the hand and give it a furtive stroke, an action she knew worked on dogs, cats, and horses.

It communicated. The lady gave a grunt, then another. The tone wasn't angry, but seemed comforting.

Beck couldn't speak it, but the big red lady—and her hot-tempered gray rival—reminded Beck of Rachel and Leah, Jacob's two wives in the Bible. Leah could bear children, but Rachel could not. Beck didn't know if that was the case here, but she felt sorry for the red lady anyway. She gave the hand a little pat and looked up into that quizzical, leathery face. "R-roo-Rachel."

"Hmmph," Rachel replied, rotating the deer's head in search of another bite.

Beck watched the others who were still eating, wolfing down the heart and liver and gnawing on the ribs. She'd made their acquaintance, she realized—they'd sniffed and studied her excreta and she'd eaten from their deer's head. Naming them would be appropriate. The other female's name would have to be Leah, the biblical Rachel's rival for the favor and attention of . . . Jacob. And the brat? Well, the biblical Jacob's firstborn son was named Reuben. It was difficult to give a name she liked to a creature she didn't like, but it would have to do.

As for what these creatures were, the time had come to settle on that as well. Like most anyone else, Beck had heard some snippets of the Bigfoot legend; she'd heard some of the stories, seen

a poster for a Sasquatch monster movie, even recalled seeing
Bigfoot as a cartoon character. In close-up reality, these creatures
were so different from their legend that it was difficult to relate
the two, but legend and myth weren't difficult to discard when
sharing a meal with the real thing.

These were Sasquatches—real ones.

Beck accepted another string of venison from Rachel's hand
and chewed on it thoughtfully, feeling just a little more ori-
ented now that she'd named and identified everybody. The
group almost felt like a big, hairy family, not entirely dys-
functional, but having some issues, to be sure, and Beck was
one of them.

Had she been observing all this from her own little world at
home, it would have been entirely too bizarre.

Wednesday morning, Jimmy Clark stood beside the sorry, splintered cabin and took a 360-degree look around the ravine, nodding to himself. "Yeah. He's out there, and we're gonna bring him
in." He unknotted the top of the black plastic garbage bag he'd
brought all the way up the trail from Abney and let the contents—four dozen day-old doughnuts—rumble and tumble into
the bottom of a sawed-off steel drum.

"Okay, let's mix in the scraps."

That was Steve Thorne's job. He, Jimmy, and Wiley Kane
had tossed coins that morning, and Steve was the odd man. That
gave him the privilege of packing in the bacon grease, kitchen
scraps, and dish scrapings from Arlen Peak's café, sealed inside a
five-gallon plastic pickle bucket. Steve poured the mixture in with
the doughnuts.

Jimmy spoke to the forest, "Okay, big guy, come and get it!"

"So what now?" Kane asked while Steve trotted in search of breathable air.

Jimmy pointed up the hill to a spot not far from where Reed and Beck had camped that first horrible night. "As long as the air's moving up the draw, you take that ledge. It'll make a good blind, and the angle ought to give you a clear shot through the heart and lungs. When night comes and things cool down . . ." He pointed to another high spot down the ravine from the cabin. "I'd set up in there and break out the night scope."

Thorne asked, "Aren't we gonna get relieved?"

Jimmy wasn't happy about his answer. "Some of the guys have gone home. I've got four hunters left to man the bear stands, and the sheriff has whoever's left going with the trackers."

Kane ventured, "It wouldn't have anything to do with all that 'Bigfoot' talk, would it?"

"What do you think? No man with better things to do wants to be out here day and night on a snipe hunt, and some of them think that's what this is."

"Should have brought a book to read," Thorne muttered.

"Well, the other two are no better off—no, they're *worse* off. That campsite's on level ground, so they have to sit up in a tree all day and all night, just the two of them."

"Well, all the more bear for us four," said Kane.

"*If* the search crews don't scare the thing off." Jimmy shook his head. "Well, that's none of your concern. Take turns relieving each other and sleep when you can. You've got your radios. Check in every even-numbered hour."

Pete and his whittled-down crew worked their way slowly up the drainage from the site of last night's camp raid, somewhat refreshed from a short night's sleep but not encouraged by today's progress.

They did have a plan: Joanie and Chris, with two armed searchers, were working the area above where they found the backpack, hoping to pick up a trail again. Pete and his crew were tracking backwards from the campsite, hoping to meet up with them coming the other way. If it worked, the two teams would have covered the creature's trail from the first location to the second. It was along that trail that they hoped to find whatever remained of Beck Shelton.

But the plan wasn't coming together. Some of the hunters had bowed out—for no good reason, as far as Pete was concerned— and because of the apparent danger and Sheriff Mills's order to carry firearms, the searchers who weren't comfortable with weapons had to stand down. Don, one of his key flankers, had called early that morning to express his disinterest in tracking "Indian legends" and to tell Pete that he was staying home. Medical personnel were on standby.

That left Tyler to help with the tracking, one searcher— Benny—to keep an eye out for any signs of Beck, and only one designated hunter, the bald guy named Max Johnson. Both Pete and Tyler had to carry rifles on their backs, which were becoming a real nuisance during the bending, crawling, and crouching that tracking required.

On top of all that, the trail of this creature, whatever it was, was unpredictable and rambling, cutting through thick serviceberry, syringa, and bracken fern that cluttered and confused everything. Sometimes the trail joined with established game trails, where it became obliterated by elk and deer prints. Unlike hoofed animals, this creature moved about on soft, padded feet that left little disturbance and no claw marks. An occasional impression in soft soil helped, but trying to find the next track, and then the next, and then the next, in constantly changing environments, was exhausting.

The searchers were feeling it too. Pete could tell by their conversation in the trees just a few yards downhill.

"Can't they make this hill any steeper?" Benny asked, puffing a little.

"I hope we don't have to go clear to the top," said Max. "I mean, just between you and me, we're never going to find her. She's table scraps by now."

"So what about the bear? How are Fish and Game going to bag that thing if we're up here chasing it off?"

Pete was wearing out from the tracking and wearing thin from the whining. "Gentlemen, let's keep the noise to a minimum, shall we?"

Beck didn't realize she was asleep until Rachel stirred, rolled, and woke her up. At first Beck groped for that same comfortable spot on Rachel's belly so she could rest her head there, but daylight hit her eyes and she realized it was midmorning. She and Rachel had slept quite a while, considering they were on the ground again and having to cope with rocks, bumps, and a limited menu of not-quite-comfortable positions. A few feet away, the rest of the family lay fast asleep on Rachel's nest, awkwardly entangled but clearly comfortable, enjoying the fruits of her labor.

Rachel rolled again, then sat up, alert, silent, sniffing the air and listening.

From the hairy, leggy mass on the nest, Jacob raised his head, eyes stern, nostrils flaring as he sampled the air. Whatever was bothering Rachel was bothering him.

Max said something funny, and Benny started laughing.

Pete straightened up, not wanting to be a babysitter. "Tyler, perhaps you can clue these guys in?"

Tyler faded back to have a word with them.

Jacob rolled off the nest with liquid grace, his hands and feet contacting tree trunks, branches, and the ground with a silent, cushioned sureness, bearing him through space as if he weighed nothing. Remaining crouched in the shadows of the grove, he peered down the slope, nostrils still sampling.

Rachel had found her own little window through the firs to the outside. She crouched in that spot, riveted to whatever was happening below. Beck copied her, finding another gap in the branches.

Was that a voice she heard in the valley? It could have been a coyote, or maybe a bird.

Or maybe a human.

Benny slipped on a smooth log and fell over, hollering as he went down.

Whoosh! Up the slope, a dozen finches fluttered out of a tree.

Beck saw birds flying just above the trees in the valley below. So that's what it was.

Unless something else had scared them.

Jacob didn't make a sound, nor did he move from where he was crouching; he only turned and, with long and powerful arms, reached and yanked Leah and Reuben off the nest and slapped the sleep out of them. Leah muttered and Reuben whined, but their first focused look at Jacob's face stung them silent.

Leah squatted, and Reuben leaped upon her back. She rose to her feet and followed Jacob stealthily, hurriedly, out of the grove.

Beck wasn't ready to leave, not at all. She pushed forward through the trees for a better view of the valley.

Rachel, seeing she was left behind, was so alarmed she couldn't remember how to pick Beck up. With a sudden lurch that knocked Beck's wind out, she grabbed Beck from behind and snatched her out of the trees.

Beck wanted to scream but struggled to breathe first. Rachel had her around the hips instead of her torso, and Beck, despite a frantic effort to remain upright, flipped over, head down, her legs kicking in Rachel's face. Rachel let go of Beck's hips to grab one kicking leg, fumbled that leg in her effort to grab the other, and finally dropped Beck altogether.

Beck landed in Rachel's nest and rolled right side up, her stomach reeling as if someone had punched it. Shadows of a blackout clouded her vision. *Rachel, you klutz!*

Rachel began to whine, rotating and stamping in one place, flustered.

Beck finally found a precious breath, then another. Not wanting to die of manhandling, she waited until Rachel turned her back toward her, then she grabbed onto fistfuls of hair and pulled herself up, pushing with her good leg, until she could get her arms around Rachel's neck as she'd seen Reuben do.

Rachel finally quit stamping and turning and bolted out of the grove, racing to catch up with the others.

Had Beck heard a human voice in the valley? Wondering about it would drive her crazy.

By now, Pete's crew had made enough noise to alert every creature on the mountainside. Pete paused to breathe, to rest and calm himself.

Tyler offered, "Well, it's not like we're actually hunting . . ."

Pete responded, "Not today, we aren't."

When Sing returned with her mobile lab—a thirty-foot motor home outfitted for remote forensic and crime-scene work—she didn't drive to Abney. Reed caught her on her cell phone while she was still en route from Spokane and gave her a new place to rendezvous: behind the Chapel of Peace funeral home in Three Rivers, a lumber town about thirty miles of winding highway to the northwest of Abney, just outside the national forest. The side trip took her an extra hour and a half.

She arrived in Three Rivers just as the whistle at the sawmill signaled the end of lunch break. She drove past the big yard where sprinklers sprayed acres of stacked logs, and the sweet smell of sawdust came through the RV's air vents. The funeral home was right where Reed said it would be, on the main drag, one block down from the grade school and kitty-corner from the Three Rivers Grocery and Laundromat. It was an attractive, cedar-sided structure with a shake roof, stained-glass windows, tall firs all around, and a decorative totem pole out front, obviously carved by a white man.

"Turn in where you see the brown hearse," Reed had told her.

She swung a wide, easy turn into the parking lot, coasted past the hearse, and came to a stop at the end of a long row marked on the blacktop with white paint: *FAMILY*. Had there been a funeral, she would have been first in the procession.

When she swung the RV door open, Reed was standing right there waiting for her, far more awake than he should have been. She couldn't imagine that he'd slept much, but he had obviously showered, shaved, and gotten into his uniform. He carried a Forest Service map in his hand and some big, exciting notion in his eyes. "Sing! You've got to take a look at this guy!"

She looked around. "What guy?"

Reed was already walking. Sing assumed she was supposed to follow, and she did. They were heading for the rear entrance. "Allen Arnold. He was a logging foreman working a clear-cut up Road 27 off Highway 9." Reed unfolded the map and stopped so abruptly Sing almost ran into him. "Look at this."

She looked as he pointed.

"Okay. Here's Three Rivers. Now here's Abney, right in the middle of the national forest, about thirty, thirty-five miles southeast of here. Here's the Abney trail up to the cabin, here's Lost Creek, and here's about where the cabin is. Now: Here's Kamayah, and here's the location of the young couple's campsite."

Sing easily followed the marks Reed had made on the map. "Right. The campsite is about six miles southeast of Abney."

"So check this out." Reed traced a line with his finger, moving northwest from the campsite attack, through the cabin attack, and to an X he'd marked near a squiggly, dashed line labeled 27. "Start at the campsite above Kamayah, go northwest ten miles, and you've got the cabin at Lost Creek. From there, go another eight miles northwest and you've got the logging operation where Allen Arnold was found dead—Monday morning."

Sing studied the map, tracing the line the other direction.

"Monday morning," Sing said, "Allen Arnold the logger is found dead . . . about sixteen miles southeast of here. Monday afternoon, by our best guess, Randy Thompson is killed at the cabin on Lost Creek, about twenty-four miles southeast of here. Monday night in the same place, Beck is attacked . . ."

Reed jumped in, "Tuesday night, the campers get raided another ten miles southeast. What do you think?"

Sing cocked an eyebrow and nodded, impressed. "Is Mr. Arnold inside the funeral home?"

"He is."

"Then I think we'd better see him."

Cap watched, smiling but impatient, as the brown capuchin—commonly recognized as an "organ grinder's monkey"—ran after the rubber baton and brought it back to Nick Claybuckle, the trainer, or rather, the researcher.

"Good boy," Nick exclaimed in a pet lover's tone of voice, handing him a grape through the bars of the cage. "That's my Sparky!"

The little monkey gobbled the grape down, shooting little side glances at his cage mate, a male of similar size, age, and appearance.

"Now watch this," Nick said over his shoulder to Cap.

He said to the second capuchin, "Okay, Cyrus, go get it! Go get it!" He tossed the baton to the far end of the cage.

Cyrus sat on his haunches, his eyes shifting unhappily from Nick to Sparky and back again.

Nick held out a slice of cucumber as an incentive. "Bring me the baton and you get a cucumber!"

Cyrus turned, walked away, and sat against the wall, pouting.

Nick looked at Cap, sharing the landmark moment. "Do you see that, Dr. Capella? Inequity aversion, pure and simple!" He straightened, beaming at the results, and grabbed his clipboard to jot some notes. "You know how it is with capuchins. Cucumbers are, ehhh, okay, but grapes, wow, they're to die for! Cyrus'll trade the baton for a cucumber if Sparky gets a cucumber, but if Sparky gets a grape, hey, *No fair. I'm not playing!*"

Nick, rotund and bespectacled, would have made a great nerd in high school. Come to think of it, he made a great nerd as a graduate student.

Cap smiled and hinted, "Should I have brought a grape?"

"Huh?" He caught on. "Oh, sorry. I was just, you know, the experiment, I was really into it. Yeah, I turned in your samples."

"And?"

Nick casually scanned the room, his fingers drumming his clipboard. Halfway down the row of cages, within earshot, a young female undergraduate was observing how a capuchin reacted to its reflection in a mirror.

Nick whispered, "Um, that's Carol. She's doing a perception analysis—you know, cognitive processing of nontypical sensory inputs."

Cap whispered, "So?"

"Does she know you?"

Cap stole another look. "I don't believe so."

"Eh, let's walk around anyway."

They turned and walked casually out of Primate Lab 1, went one door down the hall, and peeked into Primate Lab 2. This room was like the other—long, clean, and well lit, with a bank of cages along each side. These cages housed rhesus monkeys, some playing, some sleeping, some just staring through the bars. There were no humans in the room at the time, so Nick stepped inside and Cap followed.

When the door clicked shut, Nick took a CD from his pocket and handed it over. "The bottom line is the results came back inconclusive."

Cap winced. "That was quick."

"No, no, I think the lab really did the sequencing, but the sample was contaminated."

"Oh, come on! I brought a whole truckload of hair samples. There would have been more than enough DNA present—not to mention the PCR amplification."

"Hey, I'm a behaviorist. All I know is what they told me."

"Well, can I get the samples back?"

"They tossed 'em." Cap was incredulous. "Hey, Dr. Capella, come on, that's what they do!"

"I told you I wanted the surplus returned. Don't you ever listen? No. You don't. That's why I almost flunked you."

"Hey, I was having problems with Maribeth back then. You remember that."

"So is that your problem now, your love life?"

Nick brightened at the very thought of it. "Aw, no, it's just great. It's Susie Barton, remember her? She—"

"Did you tell them the samples came from me?"

Nick had to return to this world. "Well, yeah—"

"Nick!"

"They *asked* me. What was I supposed to do, lie?"

That cooled Cap's jets. "No. No, don't start doing that. There's enough of that around here."

Nick's face held that same imploring look Cap used to see in biology class, right around midterms. "Listen, Dr. Capella, it was primate poop. No question. I ought to know. I got my bachelor's cleaning out the monkey cages. I know my poop."

"That's quite a distinction, Nick."

"Proud of it."

Cap softened, smiled, and patted him on the arm. "I owe you one."

"Eh, you did a lot for me, Doc. I wouldn't have gotten into the graduate program without you. Hey. The droppings were diarrhetic. Did you notice that?"

"Yes."

"Your ape was ticked off about something."

"He has a bit of a temper."

"What are you working on, anyway?"

Cap patted him on the shoulder. "I need you to help me find out." He turned to leave.

"Are you spying on Burkhardt?"

That made Cap stop and turn. "Should I be?"

"Well, somebody ought to do something. I don't like having to cut back when he's—" He shrugged it off—poorly. "Aw, never mind."

"Never mind what?"

Nick backed away with a head shake of regret. "Nothing. Really. I mean, with all due respect, sir, if you're going to make a bunch of waves again, I don't want to get sucked into it. I've got a nice job here."

Cap cracked the door and looked to be sure no former associates would see him. "Well, I can't tell a lie either, and you deserve to know: there are going to be some waves."

EIGHT

"Dr. Arnold was well respected in the community, and certainly he had no enemies. I had no reason to suspect any foul play, but of course I had to be curious." Milton Tidewater was an amiable, older gentleman, soft-spoken, highly cordial, well suited to his profession. A man of proper procedure, he'd already put on his green apron and surgical gloves before opening the cold, walk-in storage locker.

The first thing Reed and Sing saw were the soles of Mr. Arnold's feet, jutting from under a white sheet on a wheeled worktable.

"Oh, dear," said Tidewater, readjusting the sheet, "I am sorry, Mr. Arnold." He said to Reed, "Could you take that side?"

Reed gave Tidewater a hand rolling the table out into the workroom.

"Mrs. Capella, you may help yourself to Mrs. Tidewater's apron and gloves, right over there."

Sing took a second green apron from a wall hook and put it on. She found a box of surgical gloves, size small, exactly one inch from, and parallel to, a box of gloves, size large, on the shelf above the work counter.

Tidewater carefully, respectfully removed the sheet from Mr. Arnold, fold by neat fold, revealing the remains. "Now, you understand that I've already begun some restoration, so you'll have to allow for that. Just imagine what he used to look like, right after the accident."

Reed didn't have to do a lot of imagining. It was a good thing this guy was going to be wearing a suit and tie. "How'd this happen?"

"A stack of logs rolled on top of him, just piled on top of him like jackstraws. It took his crew several hours to uncover him. Of course, he was long dead."

Sing spoke quietly, commenting as she observed. "Punctures and lacerations all along the front of the body. Bits of bark and pine needles embedded in the skin." She took hold of the left arm and lifted it gently. The upper arm bent as if it were made of rubber. "Fracture of the humerus."

"You'll find plenty of fractures," said Tidewater.

Sing rotated the arm for a closer view of some puncture wounds. "What do you think caused these?"

"Sharp rocks on the ground? Perhaps the jagged stumps of branches on the logs."

"Uh-huh. Any evidence of bleeding?"

"Oh yes. Certainly."

"What about these other injuries, these lacerations from the logs? Any evidence of bleeding before you cleaned them up?"

Tidewater was struck by his own answer. "Um, now that you ask, no, I don't think so. The blood was congealed for the most part."

Sing looked closely at a gouge on the left chest. "I don't see any bruising either."

"No, it's a little surprising."

"What about the lividity on his front side?"

"Hmm?"

"Well, the injuries tell me he was faceup when the logs fell on him. Was that the case?"

Tidewater fumbled. "Um . . . I believe he was faceup, yes."

Sing grabbed her camera. "Is it okay if we . . . ?"

"Oh, certainly," said Tidewater.

She handed the camera to Reed, who started snapping pictures, following Sing as she worked her way around the body. His first shots were of the puncture wounds on the left arm.

Sing pressed down on the rib cage with both hands. It sank easily beneath the pressure. "Rib cage is flailed." She pressed on the hips and made a painful face. "Iliac wings are entirely mobile! The pelvis is crushed!"

Tidewater wagged his head. "Oh, you don't know the half of it. It took hours to reshape him, and the rigor mortis certainly didn't help. The suit will cover a lot of it, of course. But the neck—that has me a little puzzled, especially the bruising. What do you make of it?"

Sing stood at the head of the table and gently cradled Mr. Arnold's head in her hands. She tilted the head this way and that, observing the neck. She pulled a little, and the neck stretched. She rotated the head to one side and the neck didn't resist; it just went *squish*. "I see what you mean."

"I've seen some broken necks, but nothing like this."

Sing felt along the neck, pinching, pressing, twisting. "No. It's a severe subluxation, a separation at the first and second cervical vertebrae. I would guess this hemorrhaging all around the neck is due to the vertebral arteries being severed." Her professional demeanor weakened as fear crept into her eyes. Reed wondered what it meant. She blinked the expression away and continued, "Of course, the spinal cord would have to be severed as well."

"Diffuse, circumferential ecchymosis around the neck." She held the head in an awkward, twisted position while Reed got some shots of the bruising on the neck, then she backed away, so troubled she couldn't hide it. She said to Reed, "Like Randy Thompson?"

Reed swallowed. "That's about how he looked."

She carefully returned Mr. Arnold's head to as near a natural position as the damage would allow. "Mr. Tidewater," she said, "this is what killed him, not the logs. The hemorrhaging and bruising around the neck are well spread. That means Mr. Arnold was alive when it happened. He still had a beating heart and blood pressure. The lacerations, the tears, and the punctures from the falling logs show no bleeding or bruising, which means there was no blood pressure when they occurred. Mr. Arnold was already dead.

"To make matters worse . . ." She pointed out large darkened regions on the man's chest and belly. "This discoloration you see is fixed lividity. When a person is dead, the blood settles by gravity to whichever side or part of the body is lowest. In this case, the lividity tells us that Mr. Arnold was lying on his stomach after he died, not on his back, the way he was found. The fact that the lividity is fixed—see here? When I press on it, it doesn't displace; the blood has congealed—that means he was dead at least eight to twelve hours before he was moved."

"So he died Sunday night," said Reed.

Sing nodded. "And the logs fell on him Monday morning."

Tidewater stood there, mouth half open, nonplussed. "I understand, but then again, I don't."

Reed and Sing did not discuss Mr. Arnold until they were alone at a picnic table near a playground on the edge of town.

Even though they were well out of earshot of anyone, Sing still spoke in lowered tones. "Those punctures on the left arm have the same arrangement and spacing as the punctures in that thermos from the campsite. This thing has teeth, and it isn't afraid to use them."

"It doesn't mind wringing necks either."

"No. In fact, I think it prefers it. The bruises on the head and neck weren't from teeth or claws, but fingers," Sing reviewed. "Somebody or something wrung that man's neck, just wrenched it, and then left the body facedown."

"And then someone else moved the body."

"And left it on its back, not on its stomach."

"And dumped the logs on him to make it look like an accident."

Sing shivered at the thought. "Which doesn't bode well for Cap."

"Excuse me?"

She waved it off. "Oh, just thinking out loud."

"But we have some patterns now, don't we? A line of attacks running southeast, two dead guys killed the same way, one hidden under logs, one . . ." Reed's voice trailed off.

"Hidden. We just haven't found him yet."

Reed nodded. "So I'd better get up to that logging site and see for myself. You took pictures of that cabin, right?"

"Took plenty."

"So did I. I want to see them. All of them, right next to each other."

Sing checked her watch. "Meet you back in Abney?"

Reed rose from the table. "Let's roll."

As Rachel plunged into the woods, barreled through pine and fir boughs, leaped over logs, and snapped off dry, obstinate branches, Beck found that riding on her back was a definite improvement over hanging, clinging, and dangling every which way in her arms. Rachel seemed perfectly suited to taking the brunt of the branches and limbs that whipped past. Riding her was much like riding a lean, well-bred horse.

So Sasquatches did have a practical and efficient way to transport their young. Rachel just needed someone to remind her.

Rachel and Beck were dropping down the mountainside into a shady draw where the trunks of ancient cedars and cottonwoods supported the forest canopy like pillars in a dark cathedral. Beck had no idea where they were geographically but guessed from the occasional flashes of sunlight that they were still heading south.

As they entered a boggy bottomland among the cottonwoods, Rachel slowed to a cautious, furtive walk, padding quietly over the black, rotting leaves, turning in quick little circles, looking this way and that, sniffing and listening. The fear was there again; Beck could sense it in Rachel's demeanor, in her eyes, in her movements, and in the fear odor that intensified when Rachel was alarmed. It made Beck wary, and she began rubbernecking in all directions, not knowing what to look for but wanting to be sure it wasn't there.

Rachel let out a soft whistle.

Another whistle came back immediately, and Rachel bolted forward, through the grove, through a stand of young cedars, and into a small meadow where sunlight showcased wildflowers and cattails grew in tall clumps at the edge of a pond.

Rachel sank to her haunches, disappearing up to her waist in the meadow grass. Beck alighted on the ground beside her. Taking one deep, calming breath, Rachel fingered the leaves of a dandelion, then plucked them up and put them in her mouth, her eyes scanning casually as she chewed.

She grunted, "Hmph!"

"Hmph!" came a reply among the cattails as a gray shadow came alive, moving but still hiding. Beck saw one coffee-and-amber eye gazing at her, then the other eye, then the first again as the breeze opened and closed the gaps in the leaves. Leah's gaze was icy and suspicious.

Rachel rose lazily, strode to the cattails, and with Leah's grudging indulgence, began fingering through them like a woman shopping for a blouse. When she found one she liked, she yanked it out, roots and all, and set it in the grass. She plucked up another, nibbled on it, plucked still another, nibbled on it, decided she preferred the first one, and put the second one back.

Rachel returned with her arms full and sat down, setting the plants between her and Beck, enough to get sick on. From past experience, Beck knew her future: she was going to have to bite off, taste, chew, and force down every raw, chewy, stringy bit while Rachel watched. And watched. And watched.

Rachel had already grabbed a cattail and was making quick work of it, chomping down the brown, cylindrical head as if it were a soft carrot and making it look delicious. She eyed Beck, waiting for her to do the same.

Beck followed her example and reached for one, wondering where she should start biting into it.

A whistle!

Leah was the first to reply, emerging from behind the cattails and whistling back. Then Reuben popped up out of the pond, streaked with slime and excited, mud flying from his feet. Even Rachel paused with a cattail hanging from her mouth and gazed toward the old cottonwoods.

Jacob emerged, looking tired from a long trek but still awesome in the light of day, his black hair gleaming, his sagittal crest a priestly miter atop his head. His hands and arms cradled something against his belly.

Beck actually felt glad to see him—he was carrying fruit! Apples and pears! Real food! *People* food! Nothing ever looked so wonderful!

Leah and Reuben were there in an instant, bowed low with hands outstretched, groveling like beggars before a noble, catching the luscious fruit as it fell from Jacob's hands.

Rachel stared and fidgeted, whining, clearly wanting to be invited to the party but too timid to ask.

Hey, come on! Don't just sit there! "Roo-r-Rachel!" Beck pointed at the fruit with one hand, poked at Rachel with the other, and gave a plaintive cry, as near as she could get to an apelike "Ooh! Ooohh!" The sound made her throat hurt.

Leah and Reuben bothered to send her a scowl and went back to consuming the fruit—an apple, a pear, another apple, not slowing, slamming them into their mouths, making them disappear with alarming speed.

Beck bounced up and down for emphasis, reaching toward the fruit and making whatever apelike sounds she thought would register. She felt ridiculous, but she was hungry.

Rachel lifted a lazy finger toward Jacob and grunted.

Jacob glanced her way and took several precious seconds to think it over. He looked down at an apple he held in one hand and a pear he held in the other.

Leah and Reuben had their eyes on the pear and apple too, their greedy hands outstretched.

Jacob reached a decision somewhat grudgingly and all too slowly took three steps toward Rachel. He tossed the pear and apple the rest of the distance. Rachel caught the pear with the skill of an outfielder. The apple bounced on the ground and Beck grabbed it up. Rachel chomped and mashed the pear like a fruit grinder until it was gone. Beck took a bite from her apple—

And then stared at it. *Wait a minute. An apple.* A domestic fruit from a tree someone had planted.

She lifted her eyes to Jacob, who was settling down in the grass for a much-needed rest. Then Beck scanned all around as if she might catch a glimpse, a clue, a hint of where Jacob had been.

Wherever he'd been, people had to have been nearby. It had to have been a farm, a homestead, an orchard, something owned and operated by people with roads, houses, and telephones.

She examined the apple again. *What kind was it? Was this kind of apple ripe in July, or did someone buy this at a grocery store? Where did—*

She didn't hear or see Reuben coming until his big, filthy fist appeared over her shoulder and grabbed the apple.

"Nooo!" Instinctively, in desperation, Beck clamped her hands around the apple, clutched it close to her body, and held on for sheer survival.

Reuben's grip was like an iron vise, and Beck's body was a feather as he flipped her on her back and tried to pry the apple from her hands. Screaming, hoping for help, wondering where in the world Rachel was, she slipped from his muddy grip, then wriggled and squirmed until she was on her belly, the apple under her.

Through the blades of grass, she saw Rachel come running,

screaming and displaying, until Leah, growling and showing her teeth, tackled her to the ground and pummeled her.

Reuben clearly felt no qualms. He took Beck by the hair and yanked her off the ground. She was twisting, dangling by her scalp, which brought a roar of pain from where she'd hit her head, but she didn't let go. Reuben groped for the apple, and Beck turned, holding it from him. She saw an opportunity and kicked him in the stomach with her good foot. The stomach didn't even give. Reuben dropped her, then grabbed at the apple with both hands. Beck tried to run.

One step and her ankle punished her. She screamed in pain, nearly fell, then recovered her balance—

So suddenly she scarcely saw it happening, the apple was gone. She yelped at the sight of her empty hands, and her eyes went immediately to the ground, searching, searching, darting everywhere.

But Reuben had left her, and she could easily see why. He walked away with a triumphant, head-high gait, his hand to his mouth. She heard the apple's flesh snapping and crunching deliciously between his teeth.

Leah punished Rachel with one more slap across her shoulders, and then she retreated, gathering up her thieving son.

Oh God, where are you? Beck cried. *How could you leave me like this?*

She collapsed to the ground, whimpering. It just wasn't fair!

She heard a familiar pig grunt above her, and for a moment a huge silhouette blocked the sun. Rachel sat beside her, sniffing, panting, and moaning little sounds of comfort. Leaning so close Beck could smell her breath—a scent of pear still lingered—she gently groomed the hair that fell across Beck's face and then, leaning back, offered Beck the only consolation she had: a cattail.

One chain saw was noisy. Four chain saws were very noisy. Four chain saws, a bulldozer, and an occasionally falling tree were more than enough to make conversation difficult. The clear-cut on Road 27 was going to be a noisy place, at least until the six-man crew quit for the day. Reed, wearing the required hard hat, felt a little silly yelling at the man who stood only a few feet away, but the new foreman, a beer-bellied man in his forties, yelled as if he was used to yelling, so yelling had to be okay.

"So where was the truck?" Reed asked.

A huge fir came down right on top of his question, and the foreman shouted, "What?"

"The truck! Where was the truck parked?"

The foreman turned his head to look toward the clearing, and that's where most of his answer went. "Oh, I theeni was ritovther supplace!" He was pointing to the center of the clearing, now a field of stumps, slash, dozer ruts, and sawdust.

Reed pointed to where the bulldozer was piling up a fresh batch of logs. "Was that where you found him?"

The foreman pointed at the pile and hollered something. Reed caught the words "Found . . . under there . . . morning . . . flat like a bug."

"Uh-huh."

"Duz mega bitta sense." The foreman finally turned and shouted in his face. "Those logs don't dump over that way, not without some real help. But you oughta think about this: that dozer had an extra tenth of an hour on it when we got here."

Another tree came down like an avalanche, sending a cloud of dust, pollen, and needles into the air. Reed waited for things to settle before asking, "Another tenth? Uh, could you explain that?"

The foreman turned his head to look and point at the bull-dozer as it came by, the stack rumbling, the treads rattling and shrieking. " . . . ev day we ridown thours . . ."

Reed hurried around to yell into his face. "You keep track of the hours on the bulldozer?"

The foreman looked at him as if he were dense. "Yeah, that's what I said. Clocked it out when we left Friday night, and when we came back Monday morning, Al was squished and the dozer had an extra tenth of an hour on the clock."

"So how do you explain that?"

The foreman shook his head. "Can't—'cept, if I wanted to dump over a pile of logs, I'd need a bulldozer to do it."

"You mean somebody could have purposely dumped the logs on him?"

"I dunno. None of us do."

"Well, if they did, how'd they get him to hold still?"

The foreman arched an eyebrow under his hard hat. "So *now* the police are interested, is that it?" He signaled Reed to follow and walked toward the road where the crew's vehicles were parked.

Reed came alongside him, relieved to get farther from the noise. When the foreman reached his old pickup, he reached through the window and brought out a jagged metal object.

It was a thermos, crushed and bearing a familiar pattern of teeth marks.

"Found that behind a stump near the truck, not too far from Allen's hard hat. Allen always liked to come up on Sunday night and stand by his truck, have a little coffee, plan out the week. And he always wore his hard hat. Whatever got him, got him over there. He wasn't anywhere near the logs."

🌲   🌲   🌲

Sing was only half her calm self. "We were looking for a pattern in the animal's behavior, but we weren't expecting *this!*"

Cap was listening over his cell phone while seated at a computer station in the University Research Library. From this spot in the library's Internet Center, he could see most of the main floor; if he slouched enough, the computer's screen hid most of his face. "Why would the perp dump all those logs but leave the thermos for somebody to find?"

"He didn't see it. It was thrown behind a stump."

"What about fingerprints on the dozer?"

"Obliterated. The dozer was handled and operated for two days after the incident."

"Sounds to me like you'd better be careful."

"*You'd* better be careful!" Sing said.

He smiled wryly. "Hey, I'm at an institute of higher learning, surrounded by knowledge's elite. What's to be afraid of?"

"That's not funny."

"It's incisive and satirical."

She chuckled. "We'll both be careful, won't we?"

"We will."

He said good-bye and folded his cell phone, feeling *careful*. Discreetly, he rotated his head and got a visual on who might be working—or lurking—at the other computer stations, and then eyed the flow of patrons on the main floor. Absolutely nothing appeared out of the ordinary, and he'd worked on this campus long enough to recognize ordinary when he saw it.

The University Research Library was a modern, inexhaustible depository of knowledge, six floors, miles of stacks, and millions of bound volumes. It was the haunt, the second home, of graduate students and doctoral candidates who created their own offices in the study booths along the walls and maintained a steady flow of traffic in the elevators. It was a quiet, somber place where great minds could meet and challenge new frontiers—as long as they did it quietly and brought in no food or drinks. There hadn't been any murders here lately—maybe a flasher or two up in the stacks, but certainly no spies or killers.

Cap relaxed and smiled to himself. *Okay*, he thought, *I've been careful.*

He directed his attention back to the computer screen, trying to sort out, make sense of, and interpret the "inconclusive" findings Nick had brought back from the Judy Lab—the campus nickname for the Judith Fairfax DNA Sequencing Core Facility. The files on the CD Nick had given him were burgeoned with row upon row of the same four letters—A, C, T, and G—in a myriad of combinations, all representing specific strands of DNA from the hair, stool, and saliva samples. These were the clues, the indicators that would tell him what creature the samples came from, if the specific strands could be matched with those of a known creature.

Fortunately, DNA sequencing had reached such a level of sophistication that, using Internet resources such as GenBank and the calculating power of a high-speed computer, Cap could access vast archives of known strands, request comparisons, and find a match.

At least, that was the way it was supposed to work. So far he'd found plenty of matches but plenty of confusion as well. To most anyone, including the folks at the Judy Lab, the data would have to be ruled inconclusive; Cap's samples had to have been contaminated.

Contamination was the classic "wrench in the works" as far as DNA sequencing was concerned. Even though much of the sequencing was now automated, eliminating most of the usual errors, contamination was one determined little gremlin, constantly waiting for a chance to mess things up. The field was full

of stories of misidentification due to foreign DNA somehow getting into the mix. DNA from a triceratops was once found to be
100 percent identical to DNA from a turkey, but the researchers
could never be sure whether the dinosaur was really identical to
turkeys or whether someone eating a turkey sandwich during the
sequencing contaminated the sample.

To most anyone, Cap's samples indicated that kind of contamination, foreign DNA somehow mixed in with known DNA.

To most anyone, that was the end of the matter.

For Cap, it didn't end there. Of course, he wished that it did.
It would have been so much better than having to deal with
another possible explanation and what that could mean.

Cap leaned back in his chair, hands interlocked in his lap, as
he stared at the screen. *What now?*

Well. A paunchy man in a sagging wool sweater walked into
the library's comfortable, chair-and-sofa study lounge.

Dr. Mort Eisenbaum, just the man Cap needed to see.

Eisenbaum was an unmarried, socially inept genius who preferred huddling and communing with organic molecules, amino
acids, and proteins to living in the complicated world of people.
He and Cap weren't close, but they'd often consulted on projects
and compared notes on particular students. This man was a pioneer in DNA sequencing and usually liked being consulted about
it. Cap had all the data laid out systematically on the computer. It
wouldn't take much of Eisenbaum's time.

Cap ventured out of hiding and into the study lounge.
Eisenbaum had settled into a favorite spot at a large oak table and
was leafing through a stack of research volumes, obviously on the
trail of something.

"Excuse me. Mort?"

Eisenbaum looked up over his reading glasses. A cloud fell
over his face. "Dr. Capella. How are you?"

"Pretty good, pretty good. I was working on something when I saw you come in. It's got me a little baffled."

Eisenbaum closed the volume he was reading, stacked it on top of the others, and rose from his chair. "I'm afraid I can't help you."

Cap groped for some words as Eisenbaum brushed past him. "Um, well, it's just over here on the computer. It would only take a moment, I'm sure."

Eisenbaum kept walking, not looking back.

"Well, what about—we don't have to meet *here*. What if we went someplace private, had some coffee or something?" Cap followed him, trying not to look desperate. "The agreement doesn't say we can't talk to each other, just outsiders—" He stopped. *I am an outsider.*

Eisenbaum went out the door as if he and Cap had never met.

Cap was disappointed. Eisenbaum had always struck him as a lone eccentric, not affected that much by department politics.

Back to square one. Cap returned to his computer station and slouched in his chair, staring at the computer screen in case God might send a revelation. Did these results really make sense in their own bizarre way?

Many of the sequences from the stool, hair, and saliva samples matched chimpanzee DNA, but there were just as many sequences that matched up with human DNA. At first glance, one would think that either the chimp DNA was contaminated with human DNA, or the other way around—except for an entirely distinct third group that seemed to be an odd hybrid of both. It closely matched chimp, and where it didn't match chimp, it closely matched human. Contamination couldn't have caused that.

To make matters worse, mixed in through it all were weird sequences that didn't match up with anything; they were "junk" DNA, unidentified contaminants with no explanation for how they got there.

Unless . . .

Cap saved all his findings to a fresh CD and tucked the disk away in his pocket with the CD he'd gotten from Nick. He had a hunch, but he needed someone to test it and hopefully tell him he was wrong. He needed someone who loved to tell him how wrong he was about virtually everything, someone who would pull no punches.

He immediately thought of just the person. Judging from the cold reception Cap got from Eisenbaum, it might be tough getting through to him, but no matter. Cap was desperate enough.

Pete set down his rifle, shed his tracking gear, and dropped onto a bench on the porch of the Tall Pine with a deep, tired sigh. He removed his hat, ran his fingers over his scalp, and allowed himself a moment of staring at the plank floor with his mind a blank.

Tyler had set his gear down near the porch rail. For some reason the young flank man still had enough energy to remain standing. "You guys want something to drink?"

"Coffee," said Max, lying on his back on the floor. "Nothing in it."

"I'll take a Coke," said Benny, plopping down next to Pete.

Tyler waited, but Pete said nothing. "Pete?"

Pete returned to this world long enough to answer, "Just some water. Thanks, Tyler."

Tyler went after the drinks.

There was about a three-second moment of silence, which was apparently all Benny could stand. "Well, we made it back. Still got about an hour of daylight left."

Pete could not be cheered. "There wasn't much left to do anyway."

Jimmy Clark walked over. He looked fresh enough. His clothes weren't even dirty. "Everybody down?"

Benny answered, "Yeah, we're calling it quits. Joanie and Chris have gone home already. They're the smart ones."

Pete took his turn after Benny—he'd been doing it all day. "The woods are clear. Your guys can have at it, and I really do wish you the best."

"Thanks, Pete, I appreciate it."

Pete rubbed his tired eyes. "I wanted out of there anyway. I don't want my crews up there in the dark when that critter has all the advantage."

"It'll all be over by tonight. I've got a feeling."

"Yeah, you'd better hope so," said Benny. "Not all of us are happy how things are going."

A voice called from across the parking lot. "Pete!"

"Speak of the devil," said Benny.

It was Reed, in uniform, coming from a big motor home Pete recognized as Sing's mobile crime lab. Pete gave a weak smile. The young man was brewing up something, he could tell.

"So where've you been?" asked Benny. "Out chasing Bigfoot?"

"Benny!" Pete's voice was strained. He then said quietly, "I think it's time for you to go home."

"Well, I'd just like to know what he's been up to while we've been busting our butts up there looking for his wife." He challenged Reed, "You *do* have a wife, don't you, or would you rather not discuss that?"

Reed smiled at him. "I appreciate all your hard work, but I think Pete's right—you need to go."

"Well, there's more going on here than meets the eye, I'll bet on that!"

Pete barked, "Go home, Benny!"

Benny glared at Pete, then at Reed, then grabbed up his gear. "I'm not coming back."

"I won't expect you," Pete said.

Benny stomped across the parking lot to his truck, muttering how he should have been paid, but no amount of money was worth it anyway.

Reed watched him go, strangely calm, then looked at Pete, the question in his eyes. Pete answered, "We didn't find her. Didn't find a thing."

Tyler returned with drinks in a cardboard holder. "Where's Benny?"

Max took his coffee and Pete took his water. Pete said to Reed, "Help yourself to a Coke."

Reed took it. "Sing and I would like a meeting with you over in the rig."

Pete was already interested before Reed even said anything. "You got it."

The sun was low and the ravine was in shadow. The forlorn, dismembered cabin was fading, becoming indistinct in a premature dusk. The white-haired Wiley Kane and Steve Thorne, the marine, had moved to the downwind location above the ravine, thankful for a change in the view and the tedium. They'd spent the afternoon bored out of their minds, whispering jokes to each other, expecting no action until darkness came.

Now, darkness approached, and as the light faded, their interest revived. Each checked his rifle one last time, sighting through the scope and drawing a bead on that half drum of doughnuts and greasy goo. Soon they would need the night-vision goggles. Wiley Kane, who would have the first shift, tried his out.

Sam Marlowe, the young Mariners fan, checked his watch. He hadn't slept much, but he'd gotten some reading done, and now it was time to relieve his partner. He rose quietly, rifle on his back, and moved out.

Janson carefully climbed down from the bear stand that was hidden among the limbs. They said nothing to each other. Marlowe simply gave Janson a pat on the shoulder and started climbing, limb by limb.

The bear stand was a device suitable only for the durable and patient. A precarious-looking platform clamped to the trunk of the tree about twenty feet off the ground, the bear stand was not much more than a foldable chair with footrests to keep the hunter's legs from dangling and a safety harness to keep him from killing himself should he doze off. Marlowe eased himself off the limbs and onto the platform and strapped himself in. The campsite of Ted and Melanie Brooks lay just below, deserted, but tantalizingly baited. Jimmy Clark had called for the old standby, a half drum full of doughnuts and bacon grease, but Marlowe and Janson had added their own enticements based on what the campers had been eating: a paper plate with a wilting salad and three fried hamburger patties on a small card table.

Come on, fella, Marlowe thought as he prepared his night goggles. *Let's get it over with.*

Sing's mobile lab was cramped, tightly furnished with two lab benches, drawers and shelves, flasks, test tubes, pipettes, cameras and tripods, a microscope, charts and maps, rulers and tape measures, a laser level, a drawing table, and now the radio and GPS gear Reed had ordered. Sing sat at her compact computer station, clicking and opening digital photos on her laptop while Reed and Pete, squeezed into two folding chairs, looked over her shoulder.

"Check this out," said Reed, finishing his Coke. "Exhibit 1. I took this picture when Beck and I first got to the cabin."

Sing opened the window on the computer screen.

It was a shot of the cabin interior, torn apart, shelves broken, with shredded packaging thrown everywhere and a white dusting of flour on everything.

"Huh," said Pete. "No tracks."

"I was shooting the area in front of me before I stepped on it," said Reed.

"And note this," Sing said, selecting and enlarging a detail with the mouse. "The shovel on the floor near the upper left corner."

"All right," said Pete.

"And now Exhibit 2," said Reed.

"I took this one the next day." She brought up another photo and positioned the two photos beside each other.

"Okay, right," said Pete. "That's how it looked when I was there." The second photo showed the same cabin interior, this time with several boot prints clearly visible in the flour, and another difference Pete saw immediately. "Hm. No shovel."

"And note the boot prints," Reed added.

Pete nodded. "Right. Two sets." He pulled some footprint diagram cards from his pocket and studied them one by one. "I recorded three different prints up there." He pointed at the tracks on the screen. "These are Reed's. Same size, same sole, same wear patterns. But these others, up in the corner where the shovel was . . . I thought they belonged to Randy." He leaned back, stroking the back of his neck. "But they sure don't."

Reed spoke what Pete had to be thinking. "By the time those other prints were made, Randy was dead and Beck and I were . . . having our trouble. Our campsite was hidden up in those trees. Whoever it was must have thought my prints were Randy's—until he found Randy dead."

"Our guess is our third person buried Randy's body, hoping no one would find it," said Sing.

"So we have two men killed the same way," said Reed, "and both deaths concealed. First, Allen Arnold was buried under a pile of logs, and then Randy Thompson was buried somewhere with the shovel from the cabin."

"The shovel was discarded, maybe hidden with the body so there wouldn't be any fingerprints or clues—out of sight, out of mind," Sing added. "This is all an educated theory, of course."

"What do you think?" Reed asked Pete. "Do you think we could be right?"

Pete leaned back and clasped his hands behind his head. "If you ever find Randy's body, you'll know for sure. Does Sheriff Mills know about this?"

"He will when he gets here tomorrow morning," said Reed. "I'm hoping he'll either buy our idea or come up with a better one, but *do* something either way." Reed drew a breath, his emotions close to the surface. "None of this says Beck is alive, but I'm still believing."

"And we're ready for new ideas, that's for sure," said Pete. "So what about Jimmy? You gonna let him in on this?"

"I'll leave that up to Sheriff Mills. Jimmy still thinks I'm crazy."

Pete stared at the computer screen. He ran a hand across his forehead. "As if that fool critter wasn't enough, now he's got helpers!"

There was something about the coming of night that changed things. As the sun turned bloody red, then winked out behind a distant ridge; as the sky faded from blue to black; as the night voices of the forest began to mourn, click, yelp, and chatter, Beck felt *another* fear returning like a slow-working potion, spreading through her in perfect cadence with the deepening of the night. Though she and Reed had tried to talk themselves out of it that first night above the cabin on Lost Creek, she now had a name for it—Night Fear—and believed in it, even trusted it. It never came invited, but it was there for a reason: there was something *out there* to be afraid of.

Strangely, chillingly, the Sasquatches seemed to feel it too. These wild animals, clearly capable of traveling and foraging at night, were afraid. Beck could sense it in the nervous darting of their eyes, the overcaution of their gait, their strange, stealthy silence, and, of course, the fear scent that thickened as darkness came. They were moving again, *fleeing* by the looks of it, winding and dodging through old-growth forest on a steep mountainside, stumbling and tired, short on sleep and hungry, driven by something *out there*.

They broke out of the cover of the forest to cross a vast field—*acres*—of broken, angular rocks. The sky was open above them, and directly ahead, Sagittarius and Scorpius twinkled close to the horizon. They were going south. The apes' soft, flexible feet conformed and gripped the rocks. With speed and silence, they made it across and back into the trees.

The clash in the trees was like a bomb going off—sudden, deafening, jolting. Beck lurched, gripped Rachel's neck, tried to see what was happening. It was too dark to tell exactly, but Leah had run into something, had disturbed something, or was being attacked by something. There was a terrible thrashing in the brush and branches. Leah screamed; Reuben bawled; Jacob roared.

Rachel, trying to look in every direction for what the problem might be, spun so fast she threw Beck from her back. Beck landed on one foot, hopped to favor the other, and stumbled backward into a thicket. She rolled, wrestled, tried to get up. Branches, leaves, vines, and twigs entangled her. She couldn't get her legs under her.

The ground was quivering. Jacob was still roaring. Reuben was screaming. Rachel was huffing, terrified.

Lost Creek. For a moment, Beck was back at the forlorn little cabin, hearing the same sounds, mad with the same terror. She let out a cry as her arms flailed in the thicket, trying to find a handhold.

Leah had encountered something big, powerful, and fast, but apparently she'd scared it. It was now smashing and crashing through the tangle to get away from her—and coming Beck's way. When the thing raced through a shaft of light, Beck saw an immense round body galloping toward her, leaping over logs and pushing through limbs. She knew immediately it was a bear. She also knew that in just a second or two, it was going to run right over her. She struggled to get up. She slipped, then tripped and got nowhere.

She screamed.

Was that Rachel? Just above her, something let out a roar so deep and loud she felt it in her chest. She wriggled and looked up just in time to see Rachel leap over her and land directly in the bear's path. Rachel's hair bristled like a brush, enlarging her outline.

The two huge bodies collided like a thunderclap, then rolled and grappled, impacting tree trunks, shattering limbs, throwing leaves and dirt, pounding and gouging the ground. Beck heard it and only partially saw it until Rachel stood in a shaft of ghostly moonlight, hefting the huge black mass as it kicked and flailed. With skill, quickness, and astonishing power, Rachel took the bear's head in both hands and whipped its massive body about until the neck bones crackled and the bear went limp. She whipped the body again. It hung like a sack of lead from her hands, motionless. She shook it to be sure, then dashed it to the ground, heavy, contorted, and dead.

Reuben was still bawling. Leah was moaning and clicking at him, no doubt trying to calm him down. Jacob huffed from somewhere close, pushing toward them through the undergrowth.

Rachel was still angry, her hair bristling, her nostrils steaming, her canines flashing in the dim light. She reached down, grabbed two handfuls of bear hide, hefted the bear over her head, and dashed it to the ground again. The guts tore loose with a mashing sound that made Beck wince.

Beck ventured only one look. She couldn't see the bear's eyes, only its tongue protruding from its mouth and glistening in the dim light, a row of white teeth—and the head grotesquely twisted and dangling, nearly severed.

Rachel breathed heavily as she came toward Beck, hands extended to gather her up.

Beck cowered, shied away. *Don't. Don't touch me.*

She'd heard terrible screams before and been terrified. She'd seen Randy Thompson's brutally murdered body and wondered what hideous monster could have done such a thing.

Now, looking up into Rachel's dark and wrinkled face, she knew.

NINE

The cold of the night was creeping into Sam Marlowe's feet, but since he was strapped into the bear stand on the side of a tree, there wasn't much he could do other than wiggle his toes and flex his ankles. The rifle was cold and heavy. Dew formed on the barrel, and his hands complained, threatening to cramp. He held the rifle in one hand while he flexed the other, then traded hands and flexed again.

The woods were alive; the night shift was on duty. Leopard frogs in the nearby streambed called each other at regular intervals; a crowd of coyotes howled and yapped in their usual, ghostly fashion, never *there* as much as *out there somewhere*. Every few seconds, a bat flickered like a giant, ghostly moth across the field of his night goggles.

Below him, the half drum of rotting refuse sent up its stench, but so far, no visitors.

Wiley Kane almost dozed off, but one tiny snore brought a quick elbow from Steve Thorne, the only one allowed to sleep at the moment. Kane lifted his night goggles long enough to rub his eyes, then went back to scanning the woods.

Movement down by the cabin caught his eye immediately, but he was disappointed. The half drum of grease and doughnuts had attracted its first visitor: a skunk.

Well. *Somebody* was bound to show up.

Beck held on, her arms around Rachel's thick neck, her legs wrapped around Rachel's middle, as Rachel hurried once again through the forest, floating in her strange, bent-kneed gait, back slightly stooped, long arms gently, silently moving tree limbs aside as they passed through. Leah strode about thirty feet ahead of them with Reuben on her back, a vague, cloudy shape in the dark that melted in and out of the shadows and hardly made a sound. Somewhere in the enfolding web of forest and thicket ahead of Leah, Jacob was leading, and somehow, Leah could see him. Where they were going, only Jacob knew.

They broke out of the forest and followed a dry streambed awash in cold, silver-blue moonlight. The path was littered with deadwood and crisscrossed with the weather-checked remnants of fallen trees. Mountain slopes formed black walls on either side, and directly above, Lyra twinkled beneath the Milky Way. Now Beck could see Jacob far ahead, a silhouette in light but invisible in shadows. He strode across the river rocks and leaped over fallen logs, maintaining a demanding pace the two females were expected to keep up with, even with heavy children on their backs.

The image was hauntingly familiar. Men. Always showing off. She could have named Jacob *Reed* instead.

Oh, Beck, such thoughts! Jacob was a bloodthirsty, flesh-tearing beast; Reed was a man, and what she wouldn't give to be home with that man right now! Sure, he was one-upping and offending her at every turn in the trail, but that was just his clumsy, male way of helping her grow. He'd pushed himself and her before, and she'd been offended before, but it was his way. He was a man who relished strength and youth, but still a boy tripping over himself trying to grow up. He meant well, and sometimes, like right now, she could see it that way.

She laid her head on Rachel's shoulder. She missed Reed, ached for him.

Rachel's pace, once steady, now slowed. Beck glanced ahead. Jacob had stolen to the opposite side of the streambed and become a dark extension of a dead snag's shadow. He remained still as Leah and Rachel, trudging and tired, caught up. Leah moved silently to where a tall hemlock and a hollow stump stood side by side and became one of them, standing still, dark, and massive. Reuben dropped silently from his mother's back and became a stump. Rachel located herself in a thicket and became a bush, blending her own outline with the shapes around her. Beck settled into the bushes beside Rachel and remained still, satisfied that the leaves would hide her.

Now only the forest made sounds—the barely noticeable whisper of the breeze, the occasional squeaking of a tiny creature under a rock, the faraway screech of an owl. As far as the forest knew, even as near as Beck could tell, the Sasquatches weren't there.

So what was happening? What was this all about? The only

information Beck could glean came from Rachel, who peered intently toward a clearing beside the streambed. Beck searched the clearing, shifting as stealthily as she could to peer through the leaves and branches.

Her heart quickened at the same time her mind balked with uncertainty. Just beyond the tops of some obscuring grasses, she saw a patch of bare ground, and in the middle of that ground, an incongruous pile of roundish objects.

It was fruit. Apples, pears, even some bananas.

So this was where Jacob was taking them. He had to have been here before.

But fruit meant humans, so what was this really? It was hard to imagine someone had placed all the fruit there just to be nice to animals. It had to be bait, and if so, for what purpose? Were hunters in the trees, waiting for some unsuspecting animal to walk into their gun sights?

The Sasquatches must have been wondering the same thing. They remained still, watching, listening, sniffing, wanting to know all there was to know about this place. If Jacob had been here before, it hadn't lessened his caution.

Should I call out? Should I make some noise?

She thought better of it. Silence and stealth were the rule now, and she was freshly aware that violating the rules could get her killed. Fear had become a given, never gone, seldom lessened, but she couldn't let it control her or make her do something stupid. She had to think, plan, learn, and wait. There would be another way, sometime, somewhere.

After another long moment of silent watching, listening, and smelling, Jacob finally broke off from his concealing shadow and moved forward into the clearing. Leah followed next, and behind her, like a half-sized copy, came Reuben.

Rachel sighed as if with relief and rose slowly from the thicket.

She took one more look and listen, then slipped into the clearing. Beck followed close behind her, limping but standing on her own, trying to step where Rachel stepped and be just as quiet about it.

The others reached the fruit first and wasted no time grabbing it up and gobbling it down. Rachel hesitated at the edge of the bare ground, then took a step. When she didn't get growled at or clobbered, she took another. Jacob tossed an apple her way, which she immediately grabbed up, but that was the only toss she got. She drew closer.

Hungry as she was, Beck was still more interested in the surroundings. She was unable to see anything amiss in the black wall of the forest. She heard no gun bolts sliding, no camera shutters clicking. She saw no blinking red lights from camcorders. Even so, this whole thing had to be a setup. Domestic, store-bought fruit didn't appear in the middle of the wilderness without some human with a plan.

Then she realized the ground under her feet felt different. Peering down, she saw that it looked different too. She reached down to touch it; her finger sank to the second joint in loose soil. The ground had been tilled and raked, much like a garden prepared for planting. Her boots sank in, making impressions.

It hit her.

Footprints. She and the beasts were leaving them everywhere—which was precisely the idea.

Rachel nudged her, but Beck paid no mind.

Footprints! She saw this once on a TV nature show, and now here it was for real. Some nature lovers were hoping to capture the footprints of wild animals. They'd prepared this site with loose soil and bait, and whether they were here now or would return later, they were keeping an eye on it! Beck looked for a trail somewhere, some path the humans had used to get here. She had to find it and remember it.

Rachel nudged her again, and Beck took a pear from her hand.

Footprints. Beck started stepping and limping around the site in any loose soil she could find. *Got to leave some footprints!*

Rachel followed her, offering her a banana and obliterating every footprint Beck left.

She took the banana and retraced her steps, trying to put her footprints back, but they were much shallower this time. Rachel kept following her, curious, flattening the impressions under her big, soft feet.

"Rachel, don't!"

"Mmm."

Beck stopped to eat the banana just so Rachel wouldn't follow. Rachel stopped and ate her apple.

While hurriedly eating the banana, Beck spotted some unstomped soil near the edge of the tilled circle. With the empty banana peel in her hand, she limped to the place. Rachel followed, protective and fascinated.

With her finger, Beck began scratching numbers in the ground. 2. 0. 8 . . .

Rachel squatted beside her and watched in the same way she watched everything Beck did, with utmost, unbroken attention. She reached down herself and ran her finger along the ground, leaving one furrow, then another, captivated by the activity.

Beck could only hope Rachel would remain distracted so she could complete the number. 9. 6.

She heard the others stirring behind her, rising to leave. *Please, just two more seconds!* 9. 2—

Jacob huffed. The party was over.

The banana peel tumbled to the ground. Beck's finger was still extended to write as she lurched into the air and flopped over Rachel's shoulder—Rachel's best attempt so far at loading up her kid.

"Nooo! L-l-l-leh . . ." *Let me finish!*

Rachel was already trotting out of the clearing, following the others. Beck hung on, gripping, grappling, trying to get right side up. She finally got one hand around Rachel's neck, then the other, and then her legs astride Rachel's middle, resting on the hips, as the whole family vanished into the woods again.

Hope. Beck hadn't gained as much as she wanted, but at least she had a start on it.

The gorilla was doing a clumsy line dance without a line, the tops of its running shoes plainly visible above its phony, slip-on feet. It carried a placard that read "Apes Have Rights," and from under the plastic ape-faced mask, a young man's voice chanted in a monotonous cadence, "Freedom for our brothers; freedom for the apes! Freedom for our brothers; freedom for the apes!"

He was one of about a dozen chanting protestors gathered for their Thursday morning demonstration outside the York Primate Center, an old but renovated brick structure on the Corzine University campus. The gorilla suit was a new feature Cap hadn't seen before.

On the other hand, Cap, in a loud, tropical shirt, straw hat, Bermuda shorts, and sunglasses, was a sight the *protestors* hadn't seen before. Not that he was that unusual; the protestors, most of them students with too few causes and too much time, liked to dress in outrageous ways to draw attention. Besides the gorilla, there was a cheap, K-Mart version of the orangutan from Disney's *Jungle Book*, an overweight Tarzan in a loincloth and fright wig, and a scientist in a white lab coat spattered with red paint. When Cap joined them and took up their chant, they were happy enough to count him as one of their own.

It was mostly during the summer months that these folks displayed themselves at the Primate Center's gated parking entrance, waiting for the "ape killers, torturers, and exploiters" to venture in or out. Any car arriving or leaving would have to run the gauntlet and endure the latest chant of outrage. Cap had driven this gauntlet on many a Thursday himself.

Someone had given Cap a sign to wave: "Where Have All The Primates Gone?" He held it high, utilized a few dance steps of his own, and tried to blend in as the chant broke apart and abated in the lull between cars.

"Hey! You're new here." He was being addressed by the group's leader, a brassy-voiced young woman with garish purple hair and enough metal in her face to set off an airport alarm.

"Not really. I used to work here."

"At the Primate Center?"

"Yeah, a little bit, but mostly in Bioscience. I taught biology."

Tarzan quit talking to the gorilla and they turned to listen.

"Why don't you work here anymore?" the leader said.

"I was fired."

"Cool," said Tarzan.

"How come?" asked the gorilla.

"I kept finding problems with Darwinism," said Cap.

The response was predictable: the little gasps, the incredulity, the wagging heads, the side glances and snickers.

"You're kidding!" the young woman in the lab coat cried. "I thought you were a biology prof!"

"Mm-hm, molecular biology."

"How can a biology prof have a problem with Darwinism?"

"How can a Darwinist have a problem with *anything*?"

"So what are you doing here?" She sounded just a little suspicious. "Do you care about our brothers?"

"You mean the apes?"

"*Yeah*, the apes! They're our brothers, our closest relatives!"

The gorilla added, "We're 98 percent chimpanzee."

Cap tried not to sneer. "*We* taught you that."

"So they have rights just like we do," said the woman, "and we're gonna stay here until those rights are recognized!"

That was a prompt. The others all cheered, "Yeah!"

"Rights for the chimps!"

"Set 'em free!"

Cap countered, "Have you ever been in there? The primates aren't being abused. This is noninvasive research, strictly behavioral. The worst they do is give the primates cucumbers instead of grapes."

Some moaned, others wagged their heads, some rolled their eyes. Tarzan even got hostile: "Hey, don't lie to us, man!"

"They're being held in cages, aren't they?" said the orangutan.

The woman got right in Cap's face. "That's what they want us to think! Sure, maybe the apes here on campus aren't being abused, but what about the ones they take *off* campus?"

"Off campus?" Cap asked. "How do you—?"

A girl decked out like a tree with a toy chimp in one of her branches—her arm—shouted, "Car coming!"

They scrambled into lines on either side of the driveway and took up the chant, waving their signs. "Freedom for our brothers; freedom for the apes!" The gorilla broke into his line dance; Tarzan yodeled a yell; the orangutan spun in circles, waving his arms; and the little tree swayed in the wind as the gate lifted and a car rolled through.

Cap bolted from the curb and stood in front of the car. "Hey! Hey, Baumgartner!"

The driver braked abruptly, then honked.

"You're gonna get arrested!" the little tree cried out to Cap.

Cap raised his sunglasses as he leaned over the hood of the car. "Baumgartner! It's me, Capella!"

The driver quit honking and stared through the windshield. Cap took off his straw hat.

"Cap! Michael Capella!" The driver rolled down his window and stuck out his head. "Cap! Are you crazy?"

Cap handed his sign to the gorilla and ran around to the passenger's side, shouting through the closed window. "We've gotta talk!"

Baumgartner anguished a moment, then reached over and opened the door.

Cap settled into the passenger's seat and closed the door behind him, blocking out the din of the chants. "Sorry for the getup, but they wouldn't let me in to see you."

Dr. Emile Baumgartner hit the gas. "Well, let's get out of here before anybody sees *you*."

Fleming Cryncovich, twenty-three-year-old, unemployed son of an unemployed miner, stood there and stared, his head wiggling back and forth in tiny, unconscious expressions of awe and amazement. His spidery hands shook, awaiting orders for an appropriate gesture from his stupefied brain. Words wouldn't come to his lips, only little gasps and *Ohhhhs*.

It was early morning. The shadows were still long, which brought out the footprints in stark relief. He'd been hoping for years to capture just one Bigfoot print, pressing on and wasting bait while the world laughed and his parents shook their heads. Sometime since yesterday morning, it all became worth it.

His hands shook so badly he had trouble pulling his camera from its case. He forgot for a moment how to turn it on. He nearly dropped it trying to focus.

Click! He shot from one side.

Click! He shot from the other.

Click! From high above.

ClickClick! Close-ups.

ClickClickClick! A montage he would paste together on his computer.

Click. A human print.

His finger froze on the shutter button. He stared over the top of his camera.

There wasn't just one, but several boot prints, some stepped on by a big Sasquatch foot, some on top of the Sasquatch prints, some by themselves. It was a small print, perhaps that of a woman.

He'd read about this, something about a missing woman up near Abney.

Arlen. He had to call Arlen! Fleming ran in a circle, excited, nervous.

Numbers. Those were numbers scratched in the dirt!

He yanked out his pen, dropped it, picked it up, wrote the numbers on his hand.

Then he ran up the trail, jamming his camera back into its case. He needed casting plaster too, and a ruler, and he had to call Arlen!

"We just need another day!" Jimmy was adamant.

"It's moving. It's gone," said Pete. "Doesn't matter how long your guys—"

"Listen! You've had your people tramping through the woods, stirring things up and making noise and leaving their scent everywhere. It's no wonder we didn't bag this bear!"

"I can't call the search off," said Sheriff Mills. "Not 'til we—"

"You've covered all eight zones. Where are you going to search next, the rest of the world?"

Pete, Sheriff Mills, and Jimmy stood nose to nose on the front porch of the Tall Pine, refreshed from some sleep and ready to lock horns.

Pete held up his hand, hoping to keep the floor for at least one complete sentence. "Whatever that thing is, it's moving south. It doesn't care about your bear stands and your doughnuts."

"You don't know that!"

"Well, Reed's worked up a pretty good theory—"

Jimmy rolled his eyes. "So you're listening to *him* now?"

"He's got a good case if you'd just listen!"

"I'd like to hear it," said Sheriff Mills.

"You'll lose credibility!" Jimmy warned. "You're losing people already, or haven't you noticed?"

Kane and Max stood to the side, having slept little and accomplished less. They weren't invited to be part of the discussion, but Kane spoke up anyway, "Sheriff, pardon me, but a lot of us need to know we're not wasting our time. Do we have a good, clear mission or don't we?"

Max piped in, "Are we still searching for somebody, or are we hunting a bear, or Bigfoot, or what?"

Jimmy jumped on him. "We're not hunting Bigfoot!" He returned to Mills. "See? That right there is the kind of fire I'm constantly having to put out, and I'm getting sick of it!"

"Just tell us what the mission is, once and for all," said Kane.

The sheriff looked at Pete. "Maybe you'd better tell me what's happening."

Pete had to admit, "It's been tough holding the crew together. Joanie and Chris cashed it in. Don's out. I had to let Benny go. The medical folks aren't waiting by the phone, we all know that."

Kane offered, "Nobody trusts this Shelton fellow, that's the problem. How do we know he didn't off his wife and he's just making everything else up?"

Pete bristled. "Kane, why don't you just shut up?"

"Well, I'm not the only one who thinks so!"

"Shut up anyway," said Sheriff Mills.

"Sheriff," Jimmy said with a sigh, "the search is over. Beck Shelton is dead, and so's Randy Thompson. We need to deal with the hazard that's still out there—we need to get that bear. It won't happen with everyone traipsing around."

The sheriff looked at Pete as if trying to read him.

Pete was struggling. "Sheriff, there *is* more to this. You haven't seen all the cards yet. You just have to trust me."

"What about the search? Are we done?"

Pete looked down at the ground. "I know some folks don't see much point in going out there again, and maybe they're right. I'm going back out there, even if I'm alone."

Jimmy sighed. "Pete, we all feel that way."

"Do we?" Mills asked.

"Patrick—Sheriff. You know the score here. I don't have to tell you the chances of finding Beck or Randy alive."

"So now I suppose you want some big decision from me."

Mills drew a deep breath and took a moment to weigh his words. When he had all four of them by the eyes, he answered, "It's easy enough to tell me—heck, even tell yourselves—that Beck Shelton is dead. But which one of you wants to tell Reed?" He didn't wait long for an answer; he just kept going. "When you can look Reed Shelton in the eye and tell him his wife is dead even though you can't prove it; when you're ready to watch his hope lie right down and die; if any of you can come away from breaking the heart of a friend and still call him your friend . . ." Now it was his turn to struggle. "Then, all right. I'll accept that and say we did our best."

They were silent and would no longer meet his eye.

"Sheriff Mills!" It was Reed, in hunting garb, bursting from his room.

Mills shot a warning glare at every one of them, and then he waited.

Reed strode up, papers in his hand: maps, charts, some blown-up photographs. "Good morning, sir. I have something to show you—" He noted the group. "What?"

"Reed . . ." Mills met Reed's eyes, then directed his attention toward Pete and Jimmy.

Reed looked at them. Jimmy drew a breath—

"Sheriff! Sheriff!" Arlen Peak burst out the front door of the inn, a scrap of paper in his hand. "Somebody's found her!"

Reed was all over that. "Where? *Where!* Is she alive?"

"No. I *mean* . . . I don't mean no; I mean, no, he doesn't know. Am I making any sense?"

Sheriff Mills looked about ready to grab the innkeeper by the scruff of the neck, but his tone was enough. "We're listening, Arlen!"

Arlen referred to his scribbled notes and tried to recap things in a logical order. He got a call from a friend of his—

"Who?" Mills demanded. "What's his name?"

"Uh, Flem Cryncovich."

"Come again?" said Jimmy.

Arlen repeated the name and told how he'd come to know the kid, then went on to explain the baiting site, the fruit, the soft ground—

"This isn't another nut case, is it?" Jimmy barked.

"Will you let him talk?" Reed scolded.

The footprints in the soft ground, the—

"Bigfoot?" Jimmy asked. He folded his arms over his chest.

Arlen ran a hand through his hair. "Uh, well, yes, if you really must know!"

Jimmy cursed and turned away. "I knew it!"

"But there were other prints!" Arlen went on. "Boot prints, uh, you know, people prints, a small size, like a woman's!"

Jimmy's face completed the transition from pale with shock to red with rage. "That is the most insidious, most despicable, most insulting pile of crap I have ever heard!"

"Jimmy," Mills cautioned.

"It's a hoax! This guy's read the papers! He's nothing but a sadistic wacko!"

"No!" Arlen insisted. "No, he's . . . he's a little different, but he's no wacko. He's honest. He tells the truth."

Reed was about to grab the paper from Arlen's hand. "I'm *waiting*, Arlen!"

Arlen showed him the numbers Fleming had given him.

"What are these?"

"They were scratched in the dirt right next to the prints."

Reed read them, then half cried, half laughed.

"What is it?" Sheriff Mills demanded.

Tears filled Reed's eyes. "That's . . . It's my cell phone number! The area code and the first four digits!"

They gathered around as Reed held the paper up for them to see.

"Beck's running around with Sasquatches and leaving her phone number?" Jimmy said, disdain in his tone. "Guys, come on!"

Mills had to cover the question: "Is there any way this Fleming What's-his-name could have had your cell number?"

Reed was trembling. "Are you kidding?"

Pete asked, "Where is this place?"

Arlen answered, tapping the paper. "Whitetail, up one of the gulches. I can take you there."

Pete nodded. "Whitetail. That's farther south, Reed. It's south of Kamayah."

Reed caught his meaning. "South! I'm outta here."

"Whoa, wait a minute!" Jimmy stood in Reed's path. "Reed, listen—"

"Jimmy!" Mills's big index finger filled Jimmy's vision. "Now *you* shut up." He followed that up with an arch of his eyebrow, and Jimmy held his peace. "The search crews pick up where they left off, and if they've covered the zones, they'll start over again at the first ones. Pete, give 'em their assignments, put Tyler on the tracking, and then grab your gear. Jimmy, if you want to come along on this—"

"No thanks. I've got a bear, a *real* bear—"

"Hunt your bear, any way you want. Pete, we need a fourth man."

Pete looked at Max, who shot a quick sneer in Kane's direction and said, "I'm in."

Pete tapped Reed. "Hey, maybe Sing oughta bring her mobile lab—" He halted when he saw the hope in Reed's eyes.

"What?" Reed asked.

Pete wished he could answer, but he had neither the words nor the time. "Nothing. Let's go have a look."

"Cap, it's impossible." Dr. Emile Baumgartner, jacket and tie removed and shirt collar open, sipped from his coffee cup, then smiled with amusement. "Oh, it's all very intriguing. It would make a great story, but it's impossible."

Baumgartner had driven them to his home, a comfortable Victorian on the south side of Spokane. They were seated at a wrought iron table on Baumgartner's patio, enjoying a latte while a timed sprinkler *chit-chit-chitted* in rainbowed arcs across the lawn. Cap's notebook computer rested on the table between them, its screen filled with the data from the Judith Fairfax DNA Sequencing Core Facility.

"Impossible?" Cap loved hearing that word coming from an evolutionist; especially Baumgartner, an esteemed anthropologist and research associate at the York Center. Over the years, he'd been Cap's kindest opponent in the evolution debate. They'd had many discussions in many places, some private, some public, at various volume levels, but still they managed to stay friends. "Are you sure you want to say that word?"

Baumgartner laughed. "I'm not afraid of it. I *think* it all the time."

Cap laughed along, out of courtesy. "And then you leave it to poor stooges like me to say it—or write it."

"That was your choice. But that's what amazes me now—that you, of all people, would think it possible when you've basically ended your career arguing that it isn't."

"Burkhardt thought he could prove it," Cap said.

Baumgartner rolled his eyes and snickered. "Still does, so Merrill thinks he can do it because Burkhardt says so, but I'm sure you'll agree, blind devotion to a theory sometimes supplants real science."

"*Merrill's* backing him?"

Baumgartner held up a hand. "Ah, tut-tut-tut. The agreement, remember. We go no further on that."

"All right."

"Suffice it to say, Burkhardt may be pitifully myopic in his area of expertise, but far-reaching in his ability to work the system. He has the respect of the scientific community; he has friends with money; he's published some amazing theories. The university brass dote on him as if he's the next Watson or Crick, and he may well be—if he ever, *ever* succeeds in proving anything he's proposed."

"Jealous?" Cap said.

Baumgartner sniffed a chuckle. "Of course. But he's starting with an entirely faulty premise, as you pointed out."

"Really? You're saying I was right?"

Baumgartner laughed. "Oh, come on! You're not always wrong, no matter what I've said!"

"But where am I right?"

"You want to hear it from *me*!"

"You bet I do!"

"All right, all right." Baumgartner took another sip of coffee and set the cup down, pensively watching the lawn sprinkler. "When you argued that an organism is much more than the sum of its DNA sequences, you were right. I agree with you on that."

"So you also agree that we can't find specific genes that govern particular behaviors like swinging from trees or preferring grapes to cucumbers."

"Or that make Homo sapiens walk upright or even read Shakespeare. Agreed."

"But Burkhardt seems to think you can."

"He's wasting a lot of money." The anthropologist caught himself again. "I didn't say that." He continued, "Anyone can lay human DNA beside chimp DNA and sort out the similarities and differences, even quantify them."

"As in, 'We're 98 percent chimpanzee'?"

"You can't embarrass me, Cap. I didn't coin that phrase, though I'd be a richer man if I did. But as you pointed out—and I agree with you—we can find patterns in the DNA. We can even ascertain what creature or plant the DNA came from, but we can't create the code in the first place, nor can we rewrite it. It's far, far too complex."

Cap was surprised to find Baumgartner so full of concessions. "Wait a minute. No argument in favor of site-directed mutagenesis?"

Baumgartner laughed. "Do I detect sarcasm?"

"You've argued for it, remember?"

"In *reverse*, Cap. *Reverse* mutations. If we can identify the mutation that knocked out a healthy gene, we can use site-directed mutagenesis to restore the original gene and rescue the mutant, returning it to normal. You've seen that for yourself."

"Okay. That's one for you."

"Thank you. For that you get a bonus." He lowered his voice as if enemies might be listening. "*However*: In all the years of mutating, we have never actually *improved* anything. We have never produced an individual more fit than the original."

"Another concession?"

"Delivered in private, in confidence."

"Well, given that, what about the argument that insects mutate and develop resistance to insecticides?"

Baumgartner glared at him in mock anger. "So this is how you return my generosity!"

Cap lifted an eyebrow. "You've used that argument on me in public. Now that we're off the record . . ."

Baumgartner took a prolonged sip of his latte, apparently trying to build up the willingness to say it. "You're right about that too. As long as the toxin is present, then of course selective pressure is going to favor those mutants that are resistant, at which point it's tempting to cut short all observation and conclude a beneficial mutation. But all you have to do is remove the toxin and keep observing, and you'll find that the resistant mutant has so many other weaknesses that it can't compete with the normal insects and it dies out. It's a bad trade, like someone with sickle-cell anemia being immune to malaria but dying from the anemia. There's no real benefit." He flopped back in his chair, smarting from his own words. "If you were still the least bit respected in the scientific community, I would never have given you that. But since no one will listen to you . . ."

"I've always appreciated your honesty."

Baumgartner relaxed, the worst over, then he said, "Tampering with DNA is like a child trying to fix a high-tech computer with a toy hammer. It's always an injury, never an improvement, and we have boxcar loads of dead, mutated fruit flies and lab mice to prove it."

Cap paused and watched the sprinklers for a moment himself. "You understand what you're saying?"

Baumgartner nodded. "Something I would never attempt to publish."

"That mutations are not beneficial?"

"No, that would be plagiarizing *your* work. I'm only saying that tampering with DNA would be injurious. If you try to alter the genetic code of a chimp, for example, you would get one of three results: a normal, unchanged chimp; a deformed, retarded chimp; or a dead chimp."

Cap was startled. "Why would you concede that?"

"Because we achieved all three." He sipped from his coffee cup, effectively hiding behind it.

For Cap, that was news. "You tried to alter chimpanzee DNA?"

Baumgartner squirmed as if he'd overstepped. "We tried it; we learned; and we abandoned the project. For professional and legal reasons, there's nothing more to be said about that."

"What about Burkhardt?"

"I won't go there either."

"I suspect he didn't abandon the project," Cap offered.

Baumgartner shot him a correcting look.

"Okay. Okay." Cap lifted his hands in the air.

Baumgartner finished his coffee. "By the same token, I have nothing to say about your DNA results, except to repeat my position: what you're suggesting is impossible—and I think we've proved that, at great cost."

"So would you care to comment on the scuttlebutt I got from the protestors—" Baumgartner laughed derisively. "Well, they said that some chimps were being taken off campus, away from the Center—"

"Cap. We can pretend that you never had a clue as to how things are run on that campus. We can pretend that you hung yourself in total innocence, that you didn't know the damage you could do to science. We can pretend you haven't noticed that you are now, for all intents and purposes, unemployable, but, Cap, make no mistake: I have noticed. All your former colleagues have noticed, and there is, of course, the confidentiality agreement. I can't help you any further."

Cap took the blow, then nodded. "It's a matter of survival, I suppose."

Baumgartner agreed with Cap one last time. "I suppose." Then he looked away, seemingly interested in the rest of the world beyond their conversation—his way of signaling that the conversation was over.

"I'm just trying to find out why my best friend's wife is missing . . ." Cap shrugged. He knew it was a low blow, but it was the best he had. He reached to close down his computer.

Baumgartner put out a hand and stopped him. "However, I might pose a rhetorical question—and it is only that, a question."

Cap left the computer turned on. "Pose away."

Baumgartner looked away again, as if he were talking to someone else. "What if you were Burkhardt, and you had Merrill breathing down your neck demanding results, because *he* had big backers breathing down *his* neck demanding results? And what if a certain Dr. Capella's published contention that 'evolutionists have no ultimate basis for being honest' is in fact true?"

Cap didn't know quite how to answer. If Baumgartner was

cutting him a break, he didn't want to ruin it. "Could you, uh, expound on your question just a little?"

Baumgartner would not look at him—apparently his way of having the conversation without really having it. "Well, just for the sake of discussion, if you were expected to, say, bridge that 2 percent gap between humans and chimpanzees to demonstrate how we originally diverged from a common ancestor through mutations, how many base pairs would you have to change, rearrange, correct, or mutate, in precisely the right order, using site-directed mutagenesis alone?"

Cap already knew the answer. He and Baumgartner had publicly debated this topic several times. "The human genome contains some three billion base pairs. Two percent of that would be sixty million."

Baumgartner nodded quietly, seemingly amused by the numbers. "Sixty million. That would be a lot of changes to make even if you had the four million years we all think we had, and of course every single change would have to be beneficial. Imagine how daunting that job would be to an ambitious anthropologist in his midforties."

Baumgartner finally turned his eyes to the computer screen as if to confirm something. "Given all this, if you were Burkhardt, would you attempt to cheat? Would you, perhaps, entertain the possibility of moving wholesale amounts of DNA, even whole genes, the quickest way possible?"

Suddenly Cap knew where Baumgartner was going, and it was so obvious it was embarrassing. He leaned toward the computer and began to see in those myriad, confusing lines a pattern he hadn't put together before. "Viral transfers."

Baumgartner pointed out some of the lines himself. "Your 'junk DNA' may not be the junk you thought it was." He leaned back in his chair again, acting aloof. "Then again, maybe it is.

Huge, horizontal transfers can get messy. You're never quite sure where the new information is going to land or how the organism is going to turn out."

Cap grabbed up his computer. "Emile, you just might be a real scientist one day, you know that?"

He waved it off. "I was only posing a *question*!"

TEN

For one fleeting moment, Beck felt a sweet happiness. She was home with Reed and they were talking and laughing with each other in whole sentences. Sunlight streamed into their living room through an open front door, and strangely, she felt no urge to close it. Whether someone was coming to visit or she and Reed were going to venture out for a walk, either prospect was just fine, maybe for the first time in her life.

But that fleeting moment was in a dream, and when she jerked awake under a dark canopy of serviceberry, the dream slipped from her, image, by image though she struggled to keep it, until nothing remained but a sad sense of loss.

It was morning again. She couldn't remember what day it was or how many days she'd been lost in this place, wherever this place was. But as she shook off sleep, one thing felt different, enough to make her look around the thicket, searching for old and familiar company.

It seemed she was alone.

She looked about discreetly, stealthily. She listened. Were they gone? Had they left her?

She felt her ankle, then put some weight on it. With a crutch, or perhaps a brace of some kind, she could walk on it—for a while. She was on a mountain slope. They hadn't traveled very far since leaving their footprints at that baiting site. If she could make her way down the mountain and find that dry streambed, it might lead her to the baiting site and from there, to people.

It was now or never.

She crawled quietly, pressing through the fine and brittle branches, looking about, hopeful. So far, the forest was silent, as if—

"Hmph," came through the tangle to her right as the ground heaved into a reddish mound obscured by needles and leaves.

Beck stopped crawling, closed her eyes, and sighed, her head dropping. So much for that little hope. *I can't outrun her.*

A quiet stirring beyond the thicket drew her eye, and she saw Jacob sitting with his back against a pine tree, eyes half-open. He looked rather smug. Leah was combing and picking meticulously through the hair on his head and neck, pulling out pine needles, leaf fragments, and an occasional bug, which she ate, a tip for the beautician.

With no escaping in her immediate future, Beck thought of her own hair. Just trying to run her fingers through it told her it was a mess. She pushed free of the entangling undergrowth and settled down on the soft humus, taking the folding hairbrush from her jacket pocket. She brushed slowly, finding snags, tangles, twigs, and needles, but it felt great, almost spiritual. It was something she could do for herself because she wanted to, a way to restore a small measure of order to her ridiculous world—and it was something *human* for a change.

Having brushed out the last tangle, she pitched her head forward to gather her hair into one strand and deftly tied her hair into a neat knot on top of her head. There! Neat, brushed, and out of the way.

She thought she heard Rachel gasp. An ape, gasping? She looked toward the bushes. Rachel stared at her as if she were a stranger with two heads, antennae, and one big eye in the center of each forehead.

Beck's hand went to her head. "Hmmm?" *What's the matter? It's just me.*

Not good enough. Rachel approached in a cautious, sideways gait, head cocked with curiosity and alarm as if she couldn't believe what she was seeing. Gently, but with the firmness of a corrective mother, Rachel took hold of Beck's head—

Beck screamed and fought back, squirming, kicking, swatting, trying to free herself, struggling for her life.

Rachel didn't kill her. She examined Beck's head and then, with a gentle but irresistible cradling embrace, pulled Beck in close, sitting her down, like it or not, scolding her with pig grunts.

Still alive, with head and neck intact, Beck put her screams and kicks on hold, but she couldn't control her trembling. In scurrying thoughts she reminded herself that Rachel had never yet harmed her. Maybe if she went limp and played dead, Rachel would be satisfied. Maybe if she remained calm, Rachel would calm down as well. Maybe if—

With Beck properly positioned in front of her, Rachel went to work, poking, pulling, and yanking the knot on top of Beck's head. It hurt.

"Oww!" Beck dared to reach up.

Rachel huffed and batted her hands away.

Beck reached up again. Rachel batted her hands away more

sternly, then picked her up and sat her down with a bump as if to say, *You sit still, young lady!*

There was nothing to do but grimace until Rachel undid the knot. Beck's hair tumbled to her shoulders.

With the issue resolved, Beck's terrifying brush with death was over. Rachel gave Beck's hair several gentle combings with her fingers and let her go. Beck hobbled away, hair untangled, groomed, and free in the breeze. She sat in the grass, trying to calm herself.

It wasn't easy. What was the big problem? If Rachel was so obsessed with appearances, she could certainly give a little more attention to her own appearance!

Beck took a slow, deliberate breath and tried to remind herself that these were animals, and animals just did what they did. Rachel liked Beck's hair the way it was, and as for the reason— Beck snickered bitterly—did Rachel even need one? Was she even aware of one? Maybe appearances *were* important to Sasquatches; maybe they were unsettled by change; maybe Beck was projecting her own feelings into these animals and was totally wrong about everything.

Feeling grumpy, Beck took out her hairbrush. If she couldn't wear her hair up, at least she could brush it again, her way of having the last word. She ran her brush through her hair with strong, anger-driven strokes, purposely turning her eyes away from Rachel and devoting her attention to Leah and Jacob.

Leah seemed in no hurry as she combed Jacob with her fingers. She deftly scooped out bugs with her fingernails and neatly arranged his coat one section at a time, all the while stealing an occasional side glance to see if Rachel was watching. Beck marveled at Leah's expression. She reminded herself again that these were animals, but the more she watched, the more she had to wonder—Was it possible for an ape to be *catty*?

A movement from Rachel drew her attention—and held it. Beck stopped brushing, the brush poised in her hair at the top of a stroke.

In her slow, lazy way, and with her eyes focused on Beck's right hand, Rachel was stroking the left side of her head with her big fingers.

Beck switched and brushed the hair on her left side.

Rachel clumsily stroked the right side of her head with her right hand, a hairy mirror image.

Beck felt Leah looking their way and shot a glance back. Leah immediately went to work as if she hadn't been watching a thing.

Now, this was intriguing. Beck looked down at the brush in her hand. Was Rachel mimicking, or was she asking?

She rose carefully, tentatively. While gently touching Rachel's chest to soothe her, she placed the brush against Rachel's head and passed it lightly through the tangled hair.

Rachel sighed and relaxed. She was all for it, like a dog getting petted.

Beck brushed a little more, and Rachel leaned into it.

Well. Okay, then.

Beck kept going, brushing out the tangles, combing with her fingers, cleaning Rachel's coarse, oily coat. When she stopped to pull twigs, bugs, leaves, and loose hairs from the brush, Rachel nudged her to continue. She returned to her work, parting Rachel's hair neatly down the middle, coifing the sides and teasing the hair to give it body, blending the head and neck hair with the hair on Rachel's back. She had to pause frequently to clean debris from the brush, but Rachel finally accepted that part of the process once Beck gave her first choice of anything the brush found.

Before Beck realized it, she was having fun. She started humming to herself, no tune in particular.

Rachel stared off into space and made a deep-toned noise of her own. "Hmmmmhmmmmhmmm."

Beck smiled and kept humming, working on Rachel's right shoulder. Grooming the whole body was going to be a big job, like brushing down a vertical horse, but the hair was mostly cooperative, sorting itself out and falling into place as the brush passed through.

Rachel watched, obviously pleased, as Beck brushed her right arm. "Hmmmmmhmmm."

Beck started whistling just to see what would happen.

Rachel cocked her head, apparently surprised.

"Woo-w-whistle!" Beck said, and did it.

Rachel had to think about it and then tightened her lips against her teeth and made her playful teakettle sound. Beck laughed and whistled with her. It was just like getting their dog, Jonah, to "sing" by making high, howling sounds. Beck whistled, Rachel whistled; Beck whistled, Rachel whistled. Now for that left shoulder—

"Rooarr!" Rachel flinched so violently she sent Beck tumbling.

Beck righted herself, poised to run, expecting to die, thoroughly, shakingly terrified. *I've broken the rules!*

But Rachel wasn't angry. She looked down at her left shoulder, gingerly touching the place Beck had tried to brush.

Still trembling, and making sure she had Rachel's permission for each step, Beck dared to come back.

Now that the caked blood was broken up by the brushing, Beck could see for the first time where the blood had come from. The wounds were recent and just beginning to heal—two large tears near the top of the shoulder with smaller cuts between and on either side. The curved pattern suggested the obvious: Rachel had been viciously attacked and bitten.

Beck backed away, the brush at her side, and stole a fearful glance in Jacob's direction. He was still sitting against the tree, basking in all the attention he was getting from Leah. He met her eyes only once, then looked straight ahead as if he didn't care to discuss it.

Cap, in billed cap and blue coveralls he borrowed from the caretaker's garage, carried a bag of garbage on one shoulder to obscure his face as he walked down an alley to check out the rear of a particular building. During the summer quarter, many of the labs and classrooms were not in constant use, meaning the lab he needed might be empty. At least the alley was empty. He tossed the bag into a Dumpster, looked around as casually as he could, then walked briskly up the alley to a back door.

This was Corzine University's Bioscience building, his old stomping ground, a modern, three-story structure with lots of glass, state-of-the-art labs and classrooms, and what used to be his office. Access through the front door would mean signing in and making his presence known, which would bring questions and permission denial, things he couldn't afford. This door in the back, known only to maintenance staff and professors trying to avoid squabbles with student protestors, required only a key.

He pulled a key from his pocket, the one he'd unknowingly left in another pair of pants when the administrator told him to turn in all his keys. He'd planned to bring it back or maybe just mail it. If things didn't go well today, they'd get it anyway.

The key worked. The door opened. He ducked inside.

He was in the combination office and locker room of the maintenance department. Against one wall was a row of lockers; opposite the lockers were the desk and cot of the head custodian, Louis. The desk calendar was filled with Louis's usual notes and reminders in blue felt-tip pen. Good. Things were still the same.

Hopefully, Louis kept the same schedule. He always arrived for work at eight in the evening, after everyone else had gone home—except for intensely occupied molecular biologists who had a habit of working late. He and Louis had gotten to know each other pretty well.

Cap even knew which locker was Louis's, and that Louis never bothered to lock it. Inside, he found the custodian's coveralls and, most important, an access card that operated the doors in the rest of the building. Louis lost that card once, and another time his youngest daughter had used it for making motor sounds in the spokes of her bicycle. Ever since, Louis kept it in his locker, strung on a lanyard.

Cap hung the access card around his neck. He checked his watch. Most of the staff and students were probably at lunch right now. This was going to be tight, but doable.

He hurried into the next room, where supply shelves reached to the ceiling and the cleaning carts were parked evenly spaced in a straight row. The trash cans on board were emptied and relined, cleaning solutions replenished, clean dust cloths in place, mops beaten and ready to go again. He picked a cart, added two more dust mops with big heads to the cart's broom rack—in case he needed to hide his face—and wheeled the cart up to the metal-clad fire door that stood between him and the rest of the building.

Without waiting to rethink this or bolster his courage, he swiped the card through the slot of the keypad. The lock clicked open, and he pushed through.

It felt odd sneaking into a place where he felt so much at home. He'd been up and down these clean, off-white halls and through these department doors so many times he almost knew this place better than his own house. He hurried down the hall, avoided the eyes of a few students who passed by, came to a T—

A man with perfectly coifed hair and wearing a tailored suit stood at the end of the hall to the right; he was straightening a few pages that had gone crooked in a notebook he carried.

It was Dr. Philip Merrill, formerly the department chair of Molecular Biology, recently promoted to dean of the College of Sciences. He was more than well entrenched in the system—he practically *was* the system—and he and Cap had never been on good terms.

Cap turned down the hall to the left, ducking around to the front of his cart and pulling it behind him, keeping his back to Merrill and the cart with the big mops between them.

He rolled past an informal lounge area with chairs, a couch, and some *Science*, *Nature*, and *Cell* magazines, and then through some heavy double doors marked Authorized Personnel Only Beyond This Point.

Immediately to the right was a door with a large glass window. A placard on the wall to the left read Molecular Biology Research Center, and under that was a blank space where his name used to be. Cap swiped Louis's card through the keypad, and once again, the lock clicked open.

Inside was a wondrous place, his former world. His micropipettes and PCR thermal cycler waited faithfully on the bench where he preferred them, although the electrophoresis gel boxes and power supply had been rearranged to someone else's liking. The reagents inside the glass storage cabinets were exactly as he'd left them, so they would be available if he needed them. Joy of all joys, the fluorescent microscope was still in place and operational, its video camera still interfaced with a computer.

There was no time to waste. Cap parked the cart against the door, adjusting the mop heads to block the window. Then he pulled the blinds on the outside windows. He reached inside his coveralls for a paper bag, and from the paper bag he pulled three plastic bags—one containing the rest of the hair samples, one containing the rest of the stool samples, and one containing the squashed thermos that still held dried saliva. The folks at the Judy Lab were good people, but Cap knew they also had professional considerations, especially where former biology professors were concerned. Holding back a portion of the samples and keeping them safely tucked away was a planned precaution.

He'd already made a trip back to the Internet, asked the right questions, and gotten a positive ID on that "junk" DNA. Now he knew what to look for, and he had a very good idea where to find it. The procedure would only take a few hours, and he could do it alone. If Baumgartner's not-so-subtle hint was correct, he would soon know.

As long as Beck was slow and careful, Rachel let her brush out the blood-encrusted hair around the wounds and even helped by licking the area with her tongue. It was tedious work, sometimes hair by hair—Beck didn't want to get decked again—but they made it through the task together. The perilous area groomed, Beck stepped back to clean her brush, admire her work, and enjoy the feeling.

Rachel grunted, reaching for the hairbrush. Beck let her take it to sniff it for treats while Beck removed her jacket. Rachel sniffed the brush and probed it with her fingers, but better treats could easily be found for less work. She lost interest.

"Hmm?" Beck prompted, her hand extended.

Rachel gave the brush back.

Beck worked her way down Rachel's expansive back and around her waist, nudging that big body one way and then the other so she could reach every side. Rachel was looking good, the dandiest Sasquatch in the forest.

She sent looks Leah's direction. *Hey, Leah!* I'm *getting* groomed! *What do you think about* that?

Jacob abandoned Leah, disappearing into the forest in his usual, mysterious way. With no source of glory, Leah sank against a tree and moodily examined her fingernails.

Rachel jutted out her jaw and wiggled it at her competitor.

Apparently, Leah reached some kind of limit. A plaintive expression came over her face; she actually fussed a little and then started to rise as if she would come their way.

Rachel lurched and barked at her, teeth bared, a display so abrupt and loud it made Beck jump. Leah sat back down, her eyes averted.

Beck wasn't sure she could believe what she saw. "M-my, my!"

Rachel snuffed in Leah's direction, an assertive postscript, then heaved a deep sigh and relaxed, looking lovely.

"Woo-w-well! It's about time!" Beck touched the side of Rachel's face and looked her in the eye, something only safe between friends. "See? You're not so bad." A cluster of mountain bluebells grew within reach. Beck plucked them up, twisted them together, and stuck them in Rachel's hair. "The ugly duckling is now a princess!"

Rachel pulled the bluebells from her hair, sniffed them, and ate them.

Oh well.

When Beck heard a sickening, ripping sound, she knew what it was—and who was responsible—before she leaped lopsidedly to her feet to look.

"No, noo!"

She'd wondered where Reuben was, and of course, all it took to bring him out of hiding were Beck's eyes averted and her jacket unguarded. He had her buckskin jacket in his teeth; he bit and yanked pieces of leather as if it were beef jerky. A sleeve was already torn off and lying on the ground by itself.

Beck limped toward him, yelling, screaming, waving her arms.

He found a pocket and pulled out Beck's precious roll of toilet paper.

"N-n-noo! P-p-p-!" *Please!*

She took one step too many toward Leah's child. Leah exploded from the ground and became a fearsome wall between them, teeth bared, hands ready to break Beck in half. Beck lurched away to save her life, and Rachel caught her, growling, but moving to their safe zone.

Reuben discovered that the toilet paper could unroll.

Beck wailed in anguish and disbelief. This couldn't be happening. God wouldn't let a thing like this happen. This was worse than losing the jacket.

When Reuben pulled on the streamer of toilet paper, the dwindling roll danced and tumbled. He leaped with delight and pulled it again, getting another loop of streamer as a reward.

Beck sank to her knees, defeated, insulted, and violated, watching the last vestige of her cherished world unravel in the hands of a savage beast.

With his body draped and looped in white streamers, Reuben grabbed the jacket again and, like a dog slinking away to chew on a treat, bolted into the woods and out of sight.

God, did You *make him do that? You couldn't allow me just* one *little comfort?*

And just when she was feeling better. She'd even spoken a few sentences.

It wasn't fair.

It was unbelievable, but the evidence was clear, recent, and right in front of them, not more than an hour's hike from Whitetail.

The roughly twelve-by-twelve patch of tilled and raked earth now abounded in tracks unlike any they'd ever seen before.

"Never in my life," said Arlen Peak, in total awe.

Fleming Cryncovich, still burdened with heavy bags of casting plaster and clanging mixing bowls, was the sort whose excitement went straight to his mouth. "Hey, forget Bluff Creek and the Skookum Cast, I mean, this is something, this is really something, this is four of 'em all at once! This oughta change some minds, don't you think? My mom and dad, you know, they don't believe in Bigfoot, but I always knew . . . It's patience, right? Patience is what it takes. Let's cast 'em, man, before they erode."

Sheriff Mills, unabashedly staring, visibly shaken, put up his hand. "Slow. Slow down. And stay back, please. We have no idea what we've got here, not even the half of it."

Fleming backed up a few steps, his impatience showing. Max Johnson and Arlen Peak stayed close to make sure Fleming wouldn't be a problem. That didn't mean they could keep him quiet. "I've tried to stick with local fruits, the kind that grow around here. But I guess somebody liked the bananas too. Listen, there's a running creek right over there. I can bring water for the plaster; it'd be easy."

Pete, with Reed at his shoulder, had worked his way around the perimeter, measuring boot prints near the edge and comparing them to a drawing he'd made near the Lost Creek cabin. He placed his tape measure in his pocket and looked one more time at his drawing. Finally, he reported, "It's her."

Reed exhaled a held breath and locked his knees to keep from collapsing. He couldn't hold back his tears, but he resolved he would remain standing, whatever it took.

Pete pointed as he spoke. "Same boot sole, same wear pattern. See there? She's favoring her right foot, putting most of her weight on the left. She's injured, but she's alive and walking. Can't explain it; can't explain any of this, but that's how it is."

"Well," Fleming piped in, "Bigfoot are not known for violence against humans, except maybe the Ape Canyon incident, but that's grown into a legend by now—but there have been reports that they don't like dogs very much . . ."

Sing kneeled on the opposite side of the tilled area, glasses perched on her nose, magnifying glass hovering over the largest print. "It's explaining itself, *if* we can believe it." She rested back, sitting on the grass at the edge, more shaken than Reed had ever seen her. She brushed some hair away from her face and looked at Arlen. "This footprint has a scar on the ball of the foot. It's an old injury that's healed, with the dermal ridges turned inward." She sighed, overcome. "Arlen, you know that casting you have back at the inn? That footprint and this one were made by the same animal."

Arlen was stunned, then beaming. He and Fleming high-fived each other.

Pete nodded. "Most likely a male." He turned to Reed and Mills, "The *alpha* male, if that's how these animals operate. We've got four of 'em: one big male, two smaller adults that are probably females, and one juvenile, can't guess what sex it is."

"And Beck," said Reed.

"And Beck," Pete agreed.

Sing was still looking at the big print. "This print's a full eighteen inches long, and—Pete, what do you make of this?"

Pete circled around, along with Reed and Mills, and knelt close. "Yeah, lookie there. See the outside edge of the print?" He pointed it out to Reed and Mills. "The dermal ridges—you know, the crinkles in the skin like fingerprints—they're running along the length of the foot, not across it, like human prints."

"So tell me what we're looking at," said the sheriff.

All eyes went to Pete. He scanned the prints one more time. "I may as well admit the obvious." He paused and gave a deep sigh. "I'd say we've got ourselves a Bigfoot." He cast a questioning glance at each of them.

Reed had thought so all along, and now he let his face show it. Sing nodded acceptance. Mills stared back, stern as a rock.

"Which one has Beck?" Reed asked.

"Not the camp raider." Pete pointed to one of the midsized prints. "I'd say this one here. It's the closest match with the size we found above the waterfall, and look at that pressure ridge in the middle of the print."

Sing was still amazed about it. "Right behind the midtarsal joint. These feet flex in the middle."

"That's how she fooled me. She pushes off from the whole front half of the foot. We couldn't tell what in the world we were tracking. But look there; figure that one out." He directed their attention to where the first digits of Reed's cell phone number were scratched in the dirt—two sets of prints seemed to be playing tag with each other. "When Beck tried to carve out your phone number, that big gal was following her." He sniffed a chuckle. "Looks like she even tried to write herself."

Sing grabbed the camera from her backpack and snapped pictures. Among her shots of the footprints, she also captured a few group shots, careful to include close shots of Fleming Cryncovich, Arlen Peak, and Max Johnson. She and Reed were compiling a record of every name, every face, no exceptions.

"How fresh are these tracks?" Mills asked.

Fleming blurted proudly, "I raked this area early yesterday. Found the tracks this morning."

Pete nodded. Apparently, what he saw matched that scenario. Still on one knee, his gaze sweeping slowly, he scanned the trail of tracks leading back across the coarse sand and into the streambed. "Could I have everybody stay put, and no noise, please?" He got to his feet and followed the tracks, taking one carefully chosen step at a time, staying well to the side. As the others waited and watched, the tracks took him clear across the smooth, dry river rocks of the streambed and to a narrow stand of river grass on the other side. Just beyond the grass, the forest began and the mountainside rose sharply, the trees rising one behind the other, tree above tree above tree, until the green mat of the forest ended abruptly against a jagged and near-vertical rock face. He stood very still in the grass, reading the sign, look-ing, listening, maybe even *smelling* for all the others knew.

Fleming piped up, his whisper loud and grating, "Can we do the casting now?"

Mills picked up his rifle as he answered, "When Pete gives the okay."

"I brought some more plaster," said Arlen, "but I don't think it'll be enough."

"I brought some too," said Sing. "We'll try to stretch it."

Mills looked at the field of footprints and gave his head a barely discernible wag. "Nobody's ever gonna believe this."

When Pete finally returned, his walk was brisk. He didn't speak until he was close enough to do it quietly. "They didn't follow the streambed." He pointed as the others gathered around. "They cut straight across and headed up the mountain. If they're still up there and we can push them up against that rock face . . ."

Mills nodded and whispered, "We can hem them in."

Reed got a grip on his apprehension by sheer force of will. His stomach was tight to the point of nausea, and even his whis-per quaked: "What if Beck's with them?"

They all exchanged nervous looks.

"If Beck's with them," the sheriff finally answered, "then we can't let them leave."

Max sighted through his rifle scope a little too calmly, as if he wasn't buying any of this.

Pete walked to his backpack and dug out some small plastic spray bottles. "Better spray this on. The air's moving up that slope like a brush fire." He tossed a bottle to each hunter. It was scent shield, rather unpleasant stuff that covered up human scent. They sprayed it on their clothing and boots, then smeared it on their hands and faces. "There're only four of us, but maybe that's better," Pete said. "No dogs, no mobs, no racket. I want to get close this time." He pulled his shirt open and sprayed his armpits. The others did the same.

"Can we cast the prints now?" Fleming nagged.

"You may," said Pete. He studied the mountainside as he addressed Mills. "If we push 'em, they're gonna break left or right. If I can get you and Reed to handle the left and right flanks, Max and I can sew up the middle."

Max seemed unconvinced. "So how do we even know they're up there?"

"Right now it's a good guess," said Pete. "But we're gonna find out real quick."

The big metal door swung open and Cap came through, shoving the cleaning cart ahead of him, brooms swaying, bottles sloshing. He checked his watch. Louis wouldn't be arriving for several hours. So far, so good. He pushed the door shut and wheeled the cleaning cart back into its parking place. Now. Which mops did he add? He pulled one out—

A key rattled in the back door.

I'm dead!

He never danced so quickly in his life as he spun and swivel-necked, trying to spot a place to hide.

Behind the carts. It was his only choice.

He yanked the cart out of its parking place, dove into the space behind, and pulled the cart in after him. It didn't fit all the way in, but maybe Louis wouldn't notice.

The back door opened and somebody big came in, work shoes thudding and shuffling heavily on the floor. It was Louis, all right. Cap knew that familiar whistle. The tune was "Georgia." Louis was a big Ray Charles fan.

And he was ever-so-inconveniently early!

Cap looked down and noticed he still had Louis's access card around his neck. *Oh, please, Louis, don't go to your locker.*

He heard the locker door open and the rustle of Louis's coveralls as Louis pulled them on.

Then the whistling stopped. Louis was rummaging around in the locker. The big footfalls went to the desk. Papers shuffled. A drawer opened and shut again.

The huge footsteps came into the supply room and stopped. Louis was looking around. The silence suggested he was being cautious.

I'm deader than dead. Louis had to weigh 270, 280 pounds, and he was all muscle. If he wanted to detain Cap—and that was put-ting it nicely—it would happen, absolutely.

Cap prayed, his heart pounding. *Dear Lord, don't let him worry about one of his carts being crooked—*

Louis came straight to the cart and pulled it out.

The light streamed in on Cap, cowering like a frightened mouse against the back wall.

Louis, a towering African American with a lineman's body and a shaved head, gawked at Cap for a protracted moment. Cap considered trying to explain, but this ridiculous situation and the sight of this huge man struck him stupid and he couldn't find the first word.

The big man sighed through his nose, rubbed his lips together thoughtfully, and finally asked, "Should I come back later?"

Cap struggled to his feet, never breaking eye contact and trying to smile. "Uh, no. I'm all through." Once on his feet, he still had to look up to meet Louis's gaze.

Louis reached and with one finger gave the card hanging from Cap's neck a little jiggle. Cap took it off hurriedly and handed it to him. Louis looked it over as if checking for damage, then put it around his own neck.

"You better get out of here," he said. "I got some crew comin' in, and I don't wanna be stuck explainin' you."

Cap inched around the big man's frame and made a beeline for the back door. "Louis, uh, thanks."

Louis followed him at a distance, watching him. "You get what you needed?"

Cap paused at the door, considering the question and the data printout he'd stuffed in his pocket. "I'm afraid so."

He got out of there.

Reed worked his way carefully up the incline, searching and selecting a firm, hopefully silent place to plant each step, weaving and dodging from tree to tree, his pulse pounding, his rifle slick in his sweating hands. The GPS receiver strapped to his left forearm showed him he'd come halfway up the slope; the four numbered blips on the moving map indicated he was maintaining formation with the others. They were moving up the hill in a semicircular arrangement, like the bottom half of a clock: Reed was at three o'clock; Pete was downhill and to Reed's left at five o'clock; Max was coming up the middle to Pete's left at seven o'clock; Sheriff Mills was directly opposite Reed at nine o'clock. The rock face was directly above them.

The GPS doubled as a two-way radio, and now Pete's voice whispered in Reed's earpiece, "The tracks are veering south a little. Let's add another ten degrees."

Reed spotted a big fir about fifty yards up the bank and ten degrees to his right. He headed for it. The blips on his map made the same correction. The half circle warped, lagged, caught up, overtightened, then loosened again as each man struggled with the terrain, but so far they were holding the dragnet together.

Reed held his rifle in one hand while he dried the other on his pant leg, then switched hands and dried again. Part of him—the part with the weak knees, pounding pulse, and sweaty palms—couldn't help dwelling on the flaws in the plan. There were only four hunters forming this semicircle, and they were spread out over half a mile. Any creature brave and wily enough could slip through the huge gaps between them and be long gone before they knew it. The success of Pete's plan rested on these animals being either very shy or very deadly. If they were shy, they would back away until the hunters could tighten the circle and hem them in against the rocks; if they were deadly, then at least one of the hunters was bound to encounter them sooner or later. Pete didn't mention how even shy animals could become deadly if cornered, but it did occur to Reed that, given what they were attempting, they were going to be dealing with a deadly wild animal either way. Pete's only admonition for whenever that happened was "Don't let them get past you."

Right. No problem. Those eighteen-inch footprints had given Reed a whole new way of looking at shadowy trees, obscured stumps, and breeze-rippled bushes. He'd already chambered a round. The safety was off. Thinking of Beck was the only thing that kept him pushing into this madness. Pete had said she was injured, limping most likely. Reed hoped it wasn't more serious. How had she managed to survive this long when two strong men had died at the hands of these beasts? That was the question no one had asked, and yet it bothered Reed. Was she living in a terror that far outpaced the hell he'd been living in?

There were only three blips on his GPS screen. "Sheriff Mills? I don't have you on-screen."

". . . I'm . . . on the . . . here," Mills came back, his voice breaking up.

Sing had returned to her mobile lab, parked next to a trailer-turned-tavern in the obscure, almost-town of Whitetail. She could see all four blips on her computer screen via the satellite dish on her roof. "The satellite's picking up everybody," she reported over her headset. "It's the peer-to-peer radio signal between the units. Sometimes terrain and distance can block it."

"Yeah, I'm down in a hollow," Mills reported.

"It happens. Max? Better add another ten degrees; you're drifting left."

"Ten more degrees," Max replied.

"Everybody, I copy you about a quarter mile below the rocks."

The blips kept moving, inch by inch.

"Whoa!" Max whispered.

Pete radioed, "Hold up!"

The radios went silent. The blips on the screen stopped moving.

Reed merged with an elderly hemlock, nothing moving but his eyes, and then, as slowly as the sweep hand on a clock, his head. The forest around him was thick enough to hide anything. Apart from the chirping of a bird somewhere, he heard nothing. No movement. No twigs snapping, no rustling. He waited.

Pete came on the radio, his whisper barely audible. "Max, I heard some movement your direction."

Max reported in a tense, hushed voice, "Yeah. There's something up there, my eleven o'clock."

Pete replied, "Any visual?"

"No."

Sing leaned toward her computer monitor, her hand pressing her earpiece against her ear, her mind leaping into the map she saw on the screen. The blips were motionless, still in a rough semicircle on steep terrain.

"Sheriff?" came Pete's voice.

"I heard it. My two o'clock."

Reed scanned the forest to his left, inside the semicircle. His gaze locked onto a brown mass behind some elderberry. It didn't move. After a blink, a look away, and a return, he saw that it was a stump.

He carefully stole a step, then another, then four up the hill where he merged with another hemlock.

"Yeah," came the sheriff's muffled voice. "There it was again, two o'clock."

Pete replied, "Sheriff, move up toward the rocks. Max, fill in. I'm up the middle. Reed, move left, close in, quick and quiet."

Reed separated from the hemlock and moved left, his eyes on the trees, the tangled brush, the ferns, the obscuring broad leaves. He stopped short at the sight of a shadow behind some devil's club. When he was sure it was an upturned root ball, he stepped again, carefully placing his foot on soft earth or solid log, anything silent.

"I'm getting closer," said Mills. "I can hear it moving, still to my right."

"Move in, everybody," said Pete. "Move in. Tighten the circle."

Reed checked the screen on his GPS. All four numbered blips were visible now, but the semicircle didn't look much tighter than before. He tried to move faster.

He froze. His finger wrapped around the trigger.

Something uphill, to his right, caught his eye. Something white, flickering, waving. A whitetail deer? No. It wasn't moving from that spot.

"Did you hear that?" Mills asked.

"Yeah," Max replied.

Reed checked his GPS. Mills was moving in, tightening the top of the semicircle. Max and Pete moved up the hill, flattening the pattern. He could see his blip still lingering out on the right flank.

The strange white thing was there, moving in the slight breeze. Reed quickened his pace, eyes alert, as he closed the distance. It appeared to be a ribbon of some kind, but what surveyor would have been clear up here?

"Heads up, heads up," Mills whispered. "It's coming down the hill."

"Max, eyes open!" said Pete.

A quick run across the open grass, and Reed came to an elderberry bush sporting the white ornament. It looked like—

He reached it, even touched it.

A string of toilet paper.

"I think I saw it!" said Mills. "Huh. I think it's a bear. It's black."

Reed did not remove the toilet paper from the bush but stood by it, surveying in all directions for any other sign. There! Only fifteen feet away, a small scrap of white lay like a fallen leaf on a patch of brown pine needles. Nervously, quickly, keeping an eye open for anything approaching, he entered his present location as a waypoint on the GPS. He was about to report when—

"I don't have it," said Max.

"I don't either," said Mills. "It's quit moving."

"Pete, Reed, where are you?"

Sing responded, "Pete's on his way, about a thousand feet at your five o'clock. Reed, how're you doing?"

"I've found something," he said. For some silly reason he didn't want to say he'd found toilet paper. "I'm going to—"

He heard it, and time stopped. His thoughts, his breath, maybe even his heart, stopped. That ghostlike cry of anguish, though echoing and distant, chilled his blood even more than when he'd first heard it in the dark near the cabin on Lost Creek.

Beck barely had time to flinch before Rachel grabbed her up and dove into a sheltering clump of elderberry and maple, huffing in alarm. Clamped against Rachel's chest, Beck looked backward over Rachel's shoulder and saw Leah crouching in the open, calling for Reuben with faint, high-pitched yelps, until the leaves closed in and she saw nothing.

She didn't have to. With the jolting surprise over and the

brush settling back to stillness, she heard the distant sound that so alarmed her captors. Her hands became trembling fists as she clamped onto Rachel's fur.

Reed was about to call, but Mills spoke first.

"It's her!" said Mills. "Reed, I can hear Beck!"

No. *No!*

"Sounds like she's hurting," said Max.

Reed tried to control his voice as he radioed, "It's not Beck! Repeat, it is *not* Beck. Do you copy?"

"Reed, you're breaking up," said Pete.

Faint in the distance, Sheriff Mills was shouting, "Beck! Beck Shelton!"

Reed broke into a run, ducking and veering around trees, thrashing through thick brush. He radioed as he ran, "Mills, get out of there!"

"Max, let's move!" Pete ordered.

The blips on Reed's GPS crawled steadily toward each other, tightening the pattern.

"I've got it," said Mills. "It's a—" A drawn breath. The squeak of leather, the rattle of metal. The sheriff was fumbling with his rifle. "Man, oh man, I don't believe it!" His signal cut out.

A rifle shot!

"Mills! *Mills!*" Reed cried.

Mills came back on the air, breathing heavily as if running. "Get up here; you hear me? Get up here!"

Another rifle shot.

Pete demanded, "Sheriff, are you all right?"

"God help me, that thing's *walking*!"

ELEVEN

For a microsecond, Reed forced himself to stop against every raging need to plunge forward. He gripped his rifle high, ready to sight down the barrel at so much as a squirrel if it dared to move. Between gasps for air, he listened for any sound, no matter how insignificant. Whatever Mills had encountered, it wasn't the only one.

Pete was yelling, his voice distorted in the earpiece, "*Mills!* Just shoot. Draw a bead and shoot."

"I can't see him!" Then came a scream of alarm. Another shot.

Reed was moving again, eyes wide open, rifle ready. He came to a clearing, swept it visually, and dashed across.

"Mills?" Pete called. "Mills! Max, do you see him?"

Max didn't answer. Reed checked his GPS as he plunged into the trees again. Mills was moving north, obviously running. Max's blip had stalled. "Max, Sheriff Mills is northeast of you. Move northeast."

Max finally answered, "I can't get there from here. I've got to go around—"

They heard a scream, first piercing, then garbled, then muffled—

Then cut short. Silent.

A second scream followed: the woman—that same invisible banshee of Lost Creek—screamed as if she'd been cut open, the echoes of her voice layering one upon the other as the barren rocks sent the sound back and forth, back and forth, back and forth across the valley. Reed froze in terror, his back against a tree, his eyes darting, his hands nearly dropping the rifle.

The nightmare had returned in daylight. From *out there*, a legion of demons answered the woman from their haunts and hiding places, their guttural howls long and mournful like ghostly sirens following one upon the other, rising, fading, notes clashing, echoing, echoing, echoing.

The radios were silent as every man went speechless. Reed was petrified, wishing he could meld into the tree at his back. These were no strangers; he'd heard this eerie dirge before, and it was no less terrifying now.

Beck clamped her hands over her ears and cowered, unable to squirm out of Rachel's iron grasp as the Sasquatch, head raised and jaws agape, howled with the power of a ship's horn. Rachel was trembling, stinking. Her eyes swept about the brush canopy as if death hovered over their heads.

I heard shots, Beck thought. But still the woman screamed. *What's happening?*

Just outside their hiding place in the brush, Leah crouched in the undergrowth and howled just as loudly, still anxiously looking for her son.

Reuben came bounding out of the trees, tattered shreds of toilet paper streaming behind him. Leah scooped him up; he clung to her, a frightened child, and Leah immediately plunged into the elderberry thicket, nearly trampling Rachel and Beck in her haste.

Pete called, "Mills? Sheriff Mills, can you hear me?"

No answer.

Reed checked his GPS. Max and Pete were moving again. Max would reach Mills first.

But Mills's blip wasn't moving.

Reed called, "Sing, are you getting anything from Sheriff Mills?"

Sing's voice was tight with emotion. "His GPS is still working and I'm getting his radio signal, but he isn't moving. He isn't responding."

Reed checked his bearings, dried his hands on his jacket, and plunged ahead, knees weak. "Hello, this is Reed. Somebody out there talk to me."

Pete came back, "We're closing on Mills. Watch yourself. That critter's still out here."

Reed was watching, all right. These woods were full of shadows and dark places to hide. His rifle barrel went anywhere his eyes went. A raven flew from a dead branch above him and he almost shot it.

Sing came on the radio. "Max? Are you all right? Can you talk to me?"

Max didn't answer. Reed checked his screen. Max was moving, so he was alive. He was getting close to Mills's location.

Sing asked again, "Max?"

Reed kept moving, pushing through the brush, clambering over rocks and logs, eyes darting, dread closing over him like a cloud.

Pete radioed, "I have Max. He's okay." Movement. Branches snapping. Pete's laboring breath and footsteps came over the radio. "Max? I'm coming up behind you." Pete's voice became strangely quiet, cautious. "Max, I don't see your rifle. Point it in the air for me, will you, bud? Okay. Good. Now just keep it there, okay? I'm coming up behind you. You see me? Max? Just look over your right shoulder. It's okay; it's me."

Now Reed heard movement ahead of him. "Pete? I'm coming your way from slightly uphill."

"I hear you, Reed."

"What's the story?"

"Stand by. I'm gonna check on Max. He's—"

Silence.

Reed didn't like silence, not now. "Pete?"

"Uh . . ."

Reed could see a small break in the forest canopy ahead of him. Light was penetrating to the forest floor. A few more steps through the undergrowth and he saw Pete, looking his way.

Pete waved at him, weakly at first, but then urgently. "Get out of those trees, Reed. We've got a casualty."

Those were the words none of them wanted to hear. Reed carefully chose some short leaps down the grade and broke into the clearing.

Max was sitting awkwardly on the ground, teetering as if he'd collapsed there, his face pale, his body quivering and palsied with shock, his eyes staring, then averting, then staring again. Reed thought he was injured, even shot.

Pete stood by Max, alert, rifle following his eyes as he continuously scanned the forest on all sides. He gestured for Reed to close in. Reed crossed quickly and stood by him, guarding Pete's back as Pete guarded his.

The question had only formed in Reed's mind when the answer assaulted him from across the clearing. He lurched, looking away, flooded with shock and revulsion.

"Sorry," said Pete in a hoarse whisper. "Should've warned you."

Reed forced himself to look again.

Sheriff Mills's body had been hurled against a tree and now lay wrapped around the trunk, crumpled and contorted like a broken doll. The earpiece lay in the grass, still connected by wire to the GPS on his left arm. Mills's rifle lay in the grass, the stock broken off. Except for a few remaining sinews and dripping arteries, the head was all but separated from the body.

Reed's mind was paralyzed, but only for a moment. Without a conscious thought, he positioned his rifle and turned his full attention to the surrounding forest.

For several seconds, with tendons tightened to their limit, sweat dripping down their faces, and every breath controlled, Reed and Pete rotated slowly about a common center, back to back, eyes, ears, and rifles on the dark, concealing forest that encircled them.

At their feet, Max slumped to the ground, vomiting and moaning.

"Max, shh," Pete whispered.

Max tried to finish as silently as he could.

Sing came over the radio. Her voice was frantic. "Pete? Reed? Please report."

Without taking his eyes off the forest or his hand away from the trigger, Reed spoke quietly, slowly, and deliberately, the way Sheriff Mills would have. "Sing, get hold of yourself. Sheriff Mills is dead, same as Allen Arnold and Randy Thompson." He thought he heard a faint "Oh *no*," but after that, nothing. "Sing? Acknowledge."

Her voice was controlled. "I'm here. Sheriff Mills is dead."

"Call Deputy Saunders. Tell him to evacuate all the search teams, every last one of them. And have him contact the Forest Service. No civilians go into the woods, not campers, hikers, anybody—and that's by order of . . . well, me. Guess I'm the county sheriff for now."

"What are you going to do?"

Reed kept his voice steady. "I want you to get hold of Jimmy. Tell him we need him and all of his hunters up here, and if he can scare up any more from the Forest Service, we can use them too."

"Reed, are you secure until they arrive?"

"Get us the medical crew, somebody to take Sheriff Mills out of here."

"Reed!"

He got firm. "Sing, are you copying this down?"

She was trying to. Her hand shook so badly her writing was nearly illegible. "Dave Saunders, evacuate the search parties. Jimmy Clark, relocate the hunters. Get the medics here to take out . . ." Emotion overcame her.

Reed's voice was so steady it was almost mechanical. "Remain where you are so you can meet them. I'll leave Sheriff Mills's GPS with his body so you can guide them in."

"Got it." She listened to several seconds of radio silence and finally asked, "Reed. What are your intentions?"

Reed exchanged a look with Pete, who gave him a slight but definite nod. "This is as close as we've ever been to finding her since Lost Creek."

"We'll be all right," Pete concurred.

Sing asked, "What about Max?"

Max lay on the ground, still recovering from shock and nausea. Discreetly, while Max wasn't looking, Pete crouched to examine the soles of Max's boots, quickly referring to the blue cards in his vest pocket. With a quick look and a barely discernible head shake in Reed's direction, he radioed Sing, "Max can come with us if he's up to it."

Max pushed himself off the ground and breathed a moment. He nodded at Pete and Reed, then slowly struggled to his feet. "I'm in." He was still shaking, and he kept his back toward Mills's body.

Reed and Max stood guard as Pete quickly found signs: scuffed earth, bent grass, broken twigs, one impression, and a few drops of blood. "He took off south again, uphill. If we can keep him up against those rocks, we'll have half the battle."

Reed radioed, "Sing, you got us on your screen?"

"Good to go," she replied.

"Pete, I'll check this out," Reed said. He showed Pete the waypoint he'd entered and told him about the toilet paper.

Pete shook his head in wonder. "Either Beck was there or something she had a run-in with. It'd be a good place to start; you're right about that." He then suggested, "If I were you, I'd duck downhill to that open country where you can make better time and get south of there. Then you can climb uphill again and close in from the south, maybe head 'em off. Max, you work your way from here, parallel to those rocks, and do whatever it takes to keep 'em up there." Pete nodded toward Mills's grotesque form. "It only took one of 'em to do this, so don't wait to shoot. I'll try to put the cork in the bottle, come in from the north. And, Reed . . ."

Reed knew what Pete was going to say. Pete eyed the mountains above. "Those footprints down below told a story, and I thought we had it right. But this . . ." He looked—unwillingly—at Mills's twisted body. "This is the real story. There's no mistaking this."

Reed was more direct. "You're saying Beck is dead?"

Pete glanced away a moment, waiting for words. "This might be more of a hunt than a search."

Reed weighed that, then replied, "So don't let them get past you."

Pete answered, "You neither."

That was enough for now.

Cap was considering, only *considering*, his next move, when Sing called and told him of Sheriff Mills's death. Her last words before "I love you" were, "Cap, we *really* need to know what this is. Please."

That locked his decision and his resolve. After a quick trip home to change into presentable clothing—black slacks, a plain almond shirt, conservative tie, navy sports coat—Cap drove back to the Corzine campus and went straight to the Bioscience building. He used the front door this time and walked boldly down the hall to the cherry-paneled office of Dr. Philip Merrill, dean of the College of Sciences, former depart-

ment chair of Molecular Biology, an ice sculpture in a suit—
and Cap's former boss.

"Do you have an appointment with Dr. Merrill?" his secretary asked.

Cap glared down at Judy Wayne, the same lady Cap had said
good morning to and mooched doughnuts from for the entire six
years he worked there. "Judy? You know I don't need an appointment. I need to talk to Phil."

She tilted her head condescendingly. "If it's about your sever-
ance package, you need to talk to accounting."

"What if I told you it's a matter of life and death?"

"I wouldn't believe you."

"Is he here?"

"I'm sure he's busy."

"You can tell him you tried to stop me." He skirted around
her desk and went to Merrill's door. She ran after him, of course,
protesting, citing policy, afraid for her job.

He knocked gently, then turned the big brass knob and opened
the door.

Merrill was still Merrill: hair combed straight back and in place,
suit jacket neatly hung on a wood valet in the corner, necktie conservative and tightly knotted under his Adam's apple. His desk was
a squeaky-clean battleship, and he was the admiral. He was on the
phone, which was actually a good thing because it forced him to
watch his language when he saw who barged in. His eyes went
frosty cold, but he held his demeanor, putting his hand over the
receiver. "Cap, you must know this meeting isn't going to happen!"

"I tried to stop him!" Judy squeaked.

Cap held up two fingers. "Two minutes. Please."

Merrill glared at him for a long moment, then spoke to the
phone, "Uh, got a snafu here at the office. Can I call you back?"
He hung up.

"Shall I call security?" Judy asked.

Cap gawked at her in disbelief but told Merrill, "Phil, this concerns you, not me. It's in your interest."

Merrill processed that, then waved Judy away. "Hold off on that. Just, uh, just leave us alone—for two minutes."

Judy walked out.

"And close the door."

She closed the door.

Merrill leaned back in his chair and silently gestured, *Well?*

Cap expended a few precious seconds taking a seat on the fancy leather couch. This wasn't going to be easy, but what the heck, he was already fired. "I thought you'd want to know that the Whitcomb County sheriff was just found up in the national forest with most of his bones broken and his head nearly torn off, just like a logging foreman from Three Rivers who died in exactly the same way on Monday morning."

Merrill showed no reaction. He simply said, "And why would I need to know that?"

"There's a trail guide missing, and then there's also a woman missing, a gal who's married to a friend of mine—a deputy sheriff. Sing and I have been trying to help out, trying to track down the *animal* responsible."

Merrill steepled his fingers under his chin. "I thought you said this concerns me."

"I ran a Fluorescent In Situ Hybridization on stool, saliva, and hair samples from the thing. I found chimpanzee DNA with human DNA present."

"Hm. Contamination. Too bad."

"The human DNA was juxtaposed with adenovirus."

Merrill processed a little more and then tried not to laugh. "You can't be going where I think you're going."

"I just thought you'd be interested."

"And you were hoping to get a reaction, I suppose."

"Considering what Adam Burkhardt's been working on all these years, and—hey, you know what? He isn't even around. I checked at his office and he's on sabbatical . . . again. How can he possibly make any money for the university when he's never here?"

Merrill's gaze was mocking. "By producing results, Cap. He produces results."

Cap nodded. "And that's why the department gets all that funding, all that money from those big corporations . . . uh, Euro-Atlantic Oil, the Carlisle Foundation—"

"So you've done some homework."

"American Geographic and Public Broadcasting's got their fingers in it too. He's worth a lot of money to you, isn't he? Come to think of it, you might owe him a debt of thanks for your promotion."

"Jealous?"

"Bothered, for the same old reasons: it's not *results* that get the funding—it's *correct* results. Give 'em what they *want* and they'll send the money. *Question* what they want and—"

"What they want is *science*, Cap. I could never get you to understand that."

"But science prides itself on being self-correcting."

Merrill looked at his watch. "I'm waiting for you to make your point!"

Cap leaned forward. "What if something went wrong? What if Burkhardt's results weren't 'correct'? What if people got hurt? What if people got *killed*?"

"I must warn you, if you are in any way considering a violation of your confidentiality agreement—"

"What do you suppose would happen to the funding—or even your job?"

That hit home—finally. An old, cold look returned to

Merrill's eyes. "As you may expect, I will not abide what you're suggesting, nor will I dignify it with a response."

Cap knew this man; he was familiar with Merrill's style of lying. He rose from the fancy couch and leaned closely over Merrill's desk. "Self-correcting. I've brought you data of great interest, I'm sure—if you're a *scientist*."

Cap had what he came for. He walked out, leaving the door wide open.

Merrill followed just a few seconds behind and watched him go down the hall toward the front door. The dean was not quite as poised as before.

Judy looked up from her desk. "Everything okay?"

"He's leaving."

Merrill returned to his office, circled behind his expansive desk, unconsciously checked his hair, then consciously checked his desk, his way of assuring himself that his world was still stable, predictable, and under his control.

His eye was immediately drawn to a void in the fastidious arrangement of calendar, telephone, desk caddy, and pen set on his desktop. An allotment of desk space was now empty where he usually kept—

He burst from his office. "Call security!"

Judy got on the phone.

Merrill was trembling with indignity, looking up and down the hallway. "That weasel just stole my master keys!"

Sheriff Patrick Mills's lifeless eyes gawked at the sky one last time as a paramedic placed Mills's cowboy hat on his chest and zipped the black body bag shut.

Jimmy Clark respectfully removed his own hat as two paramedics carried the body out of the clearing. Wiley Kane did the same, exposing his long white mane. Steve Thorne, looking tough and military as ever, watched grimly, camouflage cap in place. Young Mariners fan Sam Marlowe tried to concentrate on familiarizing himself with a GPS unit. Janson—no one ever asked Janson his first name—chose not to watch at all. Not one man set down his rifle for any reason.

Jimmy had already strapped Mills's GPS to his arm—a most regrettable task, but it had to be done. He carefully washed the blood off the earpiece with a handkerchief and water from his canteen, then put the earpiece in his ear and pressed the talk button. "Sing, this is Jimmy. How do you read?"

"Loud and clear."

Sing was at her computer in the mobile lab, watching the same GPS blips in a new arrangement: Reed was south of his toilet paper waypoint and doubling back; Pete lingered to the north, waiting to hear from Reed. Max was roughly halfway between them and a quarter mile below the stone face of the mountain. They formed a very large triangle, and each man looked pitifully, frighteningly alone out there. Jimmy, now represented by Mills's old blip, was still in the clearing where Mills had died, but that would change—soon, she hoped.

The hamlet of Whitetail had gotten busy. Two Forest Service vehicles, Jimmy's Fish and Game rig, a medical emergency vehicle, and two private cars were now clustered around Sing's mobile lab. A lot of firepower had gone into the woods, meaning there was a major chance something was going to come out dead. Sing was feeling hope and fear in equal proportions.

Another blip appeared on her screen right next to Jimmy's. A voice crackled in her headset: "Sing, this is Thorne."

About time!

"I have you on-screen, voice is loud and clear."

Steve Thorne was satisfied he'd figured things out. He positioned the GPS on the underside of his left forearm so he could read it while holding his rifle, and he was ready.

Sam Marlowe just did what Thorne did and he was ready in half the time. "Sing? This is Sam Marlowe."

"Okay," she came back. "You're number 6, on-screen, loud and clear."

Jimmy greeted the four armed forest rangers who had just arrived, then called via his earpiece, "Reed? Pete? We're ready down here."

Reed hurried up the hill through thick woods, homing in on his waypoint, eyes and ears wary. Under the circumstances, he was glad to hear Jimmy's voice.

Pete radioed, "Let's fill in the circle, guys, quick as you can. I think we can work within a quarter-mile radius; we're that close."

With all the grimness of a platoon leader leading his men into combat, Jimmy divided his hunters into three teams headed by himself, Steve Thorne, and Sam Marlowe. "Sam, you and your guys fill in around Pete's position; Steve, spread your guys along that west side and help Max. My team'll take the south end and do what we can to help Reed. We don't have GPS units for everybody, so the rest of you stay within earshot of your team leader. Let's go." As they dispersed into the woods, he radioed, "Sing, we're moving."

Beck tried moving once, just raising her head enough to peer out of the thicket, but Rachel held her back with a firm hand, clamping her like a child against her bosom and holding her still. Beck settled—for the moment—and became like Rachel, Leah, and Reuben: a shadow, a dark, indistinct area within the elderberry thicket, obscured by a web of stalks, branches, limbs, and leaves. This was hiding as Beck had never experienced it—as an animal: motionless, silent, part of the darkness. Like ogres in a dim, odorous underworld, they'd become as dead things while the forest lived, stirred, and chattered above them.

I heard shots.

Moving only her eyes, Beck tried to meet theirs. None would look back, but she could tell they knew what was happening: something terrible, something frightening—to them.

And hopeful—for her.

Maybe Jacob was in the middle of another grisly killing when he encountered something he wasn't expecting: Hunters. Humans. Big burly guys in camouflage, looking for a lost woman of her description, toting rifles and ready to blow away any hairy monsters that gave them guff.

Maybe someone found her footprints and made some sense of Reed's cell phone number. Maybe Reed was still alive and leading the search. Maybe, at long last, the rules were changing in her favor!

She had to know.

Fighting back a rising quiver of excitement, she tried to be still, like her captors, and hear what they might be hearing. The forest above was still speaking in its everyday way, in a language she didn't know. Were the birds concerned about something, or just gossiping? Was that quiet rustling a passing creature, the wind in the branches, or a hunter?

Then she noticed—and felt—something, only because it changed. Rachel's heart and the slow, steamy flow of air through her nostrils had quickened. For the first time, Rachel's head turned. The other heads turned. Beck turned her head.

The birds took flight, sounding alarms. Footfalls approached through the undergrowth—two feet, not four. There was a soft, rumbling grunt as they passed by and continued on.

Abruptly, and so typically, Rachel rose to her feet without warning and burst out of the thicket, heaving Beck over her shoulder. Leah, with Reuben on her back, followed directly behind. Beck hooked an arm around Rachel's neck and swung down into a manageable straddle, but she was looking back, to the sides, anywhere else she could catch a view of the forest. *Were there hunters out there?*

Rachel and Leah ran south in a nearly straight line as if they knew exactly where they were going, and then, so quickly Beck missed when it happened, Jacob was with them, leading the way. His gait was hurried and cautious, his hair bristling. His fear scent trailed behind him like smoke from an old locomotive, and he kept glancing over his shoulder, not at all the haughty kingpin he'd been before.

Beck was afraid to assume too much, to hope too much, but from all appearances, they were being chased. Jacob was leading a getaway.

Cap knew he wouldn't have much time and wasted none of it getting down a flight of steel stairs and into the subterranean world under Bioscience. The main hallway was narrow, its ceiling cluttered with conduit, plumbing, and ductwork. The walls were a monotonous gray, undecorated except for frequent red signs on imposing doors that shouted, Danger: High Voltage, This Door to Remain Closed at All Times, and Authorized Personnel Only. He came to a sign that read Blue Clearance Only Beyond This Point. He kept going, his shoes clicking on the bare concrete. He'd been stripped of his blue clearance badge along with everything else, but maybe no one would notice—if he even encountered anyone. So far, the whole floor seemed strangely deserted.

He did feel a pang of conscience, as if he were a spy or even a burglar, but he kept telling himself he was down here because (a) he was a scientist, (b) he had a theory, and (c) a scientist tested his theories through experimentation and observation.

Following up on Baumgartner's "question" and that second trip to the Internet, he'd used a fluorescent tagging method to check the human DNA in the samples for adenovirus sequences, and bingo! Knowing what to look for, he'd found them everywhere.

Adenovirus was a tool commonly used in gene splicing because, being a virus, it naturally spliced its own DNA into the DNA of a cell it infected, making it an ideal delivery system. It was a matter of using an enzyme to cut a DNA sequence from a donor cell, splicing that sequence into the virus, and then infecting the recipient cell with the virus. Once in the recipient cell, the virus spliced the donor DNA into the recipient's DNA along with its own, making the desired addition but also leaving its own detectable sequence.

In the case of the DNA from the stool and the saliva, meticulous rearranging of base pairs through site-directed mutagenesis—SDM—was clearly evident but, predictably, too slow for the genetic engineer's schedule. Whoever it was resorted to viral transfer, using adenovirus to transfer, splice, and mix human with chimpanzee DNA whole sequences at a time, a much faster process but haphazard. In SDM, the genetic engineer controlled what base pairs were being changed, switched, and moved. In viral transfer, the *virus* decided, potentially doing more harm than good.

So Cap had a theory to explain the strange sequences the Judy Lab had revealed: chimpanzee, human, and hybrid all in the same animal, laced with sequences from the adenovirus that did most of the splicing. It was no accident, and there was no contamination. The presence of human DNA was intentional.

But of course, it was still a theory, and incomplete at that. He had the *what* and the *how*; but he needed to confirm the *who*, and while the possible answer was a no-brainer as far as he was concerned, it was necessary to test that answer through observation.

That observation was going to begin on the other side of a plain door marked with nothing but a number: 102.

He pulled a small cedar box from his jacket pocket, a nice keepsake Merrill had received from the American Geographic Society in recognition of his contribution to the field of evolutionary biology. It bore his name and the society's logo, laser-etched on the lid. Cap flipped it open and took out Merrill's master keys to the department's labs and classrooms.

The third key Cap tried opened the door. With a quick glance up and down the hall—so far, he was still the only one here—he slipped inside, closing the door behind him.

He knew where to find the light switch because he knew this place well. This was the lab of Dr. Adam Burkhardt, the unsung and secretive pioneer—*poster child*, Cap had often thought deri-sively—of molecular anthropology. In Cap's early years at the university, and at the very strong suggestion of Merrill, Baumgartner, and other department colleagues, Cap had spent many hours in this room working side by side with Burkhardt, supposedly to restore Cap's faith in beneficial mutations and keep him on the right path as a professor of biology. If anyone could prove that mutations really worked as the mechanism for evolv-ing new species, it had to be Burkhardt. He'd spent his whole life trying—and as Cap kept pointing out, failing. That, of course, wasn't the conclusion Cap was supposed to reach. After two years of working together, their respective positions became so polar-ized that they parted company, Burkhardt to his secretive, high-priority research, and Cap to his role as the outspoken, question-asking department pariah.

But Cap had no time to dwell on unpleasant memories. Right now he had to deal with the fact that he was carrying stolen keys, would soon be caught if he didn't move quickly, and was standing in a lab that was, by all appearances, vacant. The workbenches, once cluttered with a dozen different projects in various stages, were now clear and unused except for a few cardboard boxes that were lined up near the door. The biology posters were gone from the walls, the specimen jars were gone from the shelves, the lab mice were gone from the cages.

Burkhardt's old desk was bare. Cap set down the box of keys and pulled out the drawers; they were all empty. The bulletin board above the desk carried a calendar still flipped to January even though it was July, announcements of events that had long passed, and a few snapshots held in place with pushpins: a pretty grad student holding a lab rat as she injected it; rats with mottled colors in their fur; four male students grinning as they held a tro-phy they'd won at a regional collegiate science fair. Burkhardt's

PhD diploma had been removed from the wall, but the square of unfaded paint still marked where it once hung. A "Teacher of the Year" plaque remained, dusty and forgotten. Cap remembered Burkhardt losing interest in teaching over the years, and now it seemed Burkhardt didn't care much for the memories either, nor for the young lives he'd influenced, considering he'd left their pictures behind.

Cap went to the cardboard boxes and folded back the top flaps of the first. Ah, here was at least one vestige of Burkhardt's presence. Inside, wrapped in several layers of newspaper to protect from breakage, were some of Burkhardt's glass specimen jars. Burkhardt always prided himself on his vast collection of evolutionary icons in formaldehyde, a display that once took up several shelves along the front of the room and caught the eye of anyone who dropped in. He'd bought, borrowed, and swapped with other biologists around the world to collect Galapagos finches with different-sized beaks, peppered moths both white and gray, coelacanths that were regarded as living fossils, bats whose wing bones bore a homologous similarity to the human hand, lizards that had supposedly evolved from snakes, and a boa constrictor that had supposedly evolved from lizards, all part of Burkhardt's sideshow of the dead. These remaining jars must have been the last ones packed, still waiting to make the move, wherever it was they were going.

Cap pulled out one of the jars and carefully removed the newspaper wrapping. He'd no doubt seen this specimen before—

No. He hadn't. This one was new, and from its appearance, Cap decided, Burkhardt hadn't bought or traded for it— Burkhardt had *produced* this one.

It was a lab rat floating in amber preservative, a pitiful animal with a twisted spine and—Cap counted them twice to be sure— six legs.

He pulled out and unwrapped the second jar. It was another lab rat, this one with mottled fur and no eyes.

The third jar contained a rat with no legs at all.

Cap felt his face flush and his stomach grow queasy. He rewrapped and placed the jars back in their box, not looking at the contents, trying to sell himself a foolish, vain hope that Burkhardt had gotten the message and stopped with rats—or at the very worst, chimpanzees. Burkhardt *was* a scientist, after all. Surely he knew how to read the indications of the data, especially at such a high level—

At the far end of the room, a solitary animal cage caught Cap's attention. He paused in wrapping the last jar and stared at the cage a moment, frozen in time, one hand on the jar and the other holding the box lid open.

He couldn't be seeing what he thought he was seeing. He wasn't ready for things to get worse.

He lowered the last jar into the box, then hurried down the aisle between the workbenches for a closer look.

The cage was similar to a large pet carrier, a rectangular box of tough plastic with a swinging, barred gate at one end. It had come on tough times. The opening all around the gate had been chewed as if by an enormous rat trying to escape. The slot for the latch was nearly gouged out. The gate was tooth marked and bulged outward as if pushed with incredible strength from the inside.

Whatever Burkhardt had kept in this cage, it was bigger than a rat; apparently—*hopefully*—Burkhardt had found a bigger, tougher cage.

"Dr. Capella!"

He'd stayed too long. Turning, he saw Merrill come into the room, flanked by two campus police in gray uniforms, the university's best and biggest.

Merrill was strong and confident between his two-man army. He extended his palm. "My keys?"

Cap nodded toward Burkhardt's empty desk. "They're on the desk."

Merrill retrieved them. "Cap, you have a choice: leave this campus immediately and do not come back, *ever*, or be placed under arrest right here, right now."

Cap walked slowly forward, hands half-raised in surrender. "Hi, Tim."

The first cop, lanky and bespectacled, said, "Hi."

"Kenny, how's it going?"

The second cop, arms crossed over his barrel chest, nodded and replied, "It's going all right."

Cap addressed Merrill. "Looks like more than a sabbatical. Looks like Burkhardt's pulled up and moved altogether."

"Which is no concern of yours."

Cap nodded at the damaged cage. "What happened? Did things get a little tough to contain?"

Merrill smirked. "A word to the *wise*, Dr. Capella—if that term means anything to you: we are all scientists here, and that means we deal in facts. You are a *creationist*, and now have the added liability of being a trespasser and a burglar. Before you say anything to anyone, please give careful regard to which of us has the credibility—and the power to destroy the other."

Creationist. Merrill used that word as an insult. Cap had seen this power trip before, and he was fed up with it. "Is this a *scientist* I hear talking?"

Merrill smiled. "In every way, Dr. Capella; in the eyes of my peers and, most of all, in the eyes of the public. I have my responsibilities, foremost among them, not allowing science to be undermined by detractors like you."

"Science? Wouldn't it be more accurate to call it 'the only game in town'?"

Merrill turned to his cops. "Get him out of here."

Rachel was in a full run, her legs blurring in a shock-free, fluid stride, her weight forward, her arms swinging in wide arcs. Beck hung on, head down, cringing close to Rachel's body and wincing as tree trunks and branches missed them by inches. She looked over her shoulder but saw no hunters, no friends, only rapidly retreating forest and distance building by powerful leaps. No hunter on foot could hope to catch them.

Though it terrified her, she looked down at Rachel's blurred feet, then the huge tree trunks that raced by, and tried to envision herself letting go, leaping into space, landing and rolling safely enough to live and limp away. What if she could drop into that clump of young firs? Would they soften her fall? Would Rachel realize she was gone? What if—

Suddenly, shockingly, Rachel dug in and lurched to a stop, nearly throwing Beck off.

Jacob burst out of the brush, stinking and huffing, so close he and Rachel almost collided. Leah followed, more frightened than Beck had ever seen her, carrying a whimpering Reuben on her back. The train was turning around. Rachel spun and moved into a run again, last in line. They were heading north, the way they'd come.

Beck looked behind and saw nothing but forest, but she'd read Jacob's face; something was back there—or some*one*.

Jacob turned down the slope, Leah and Rachel followed, and Rachel's fluid stride became a rocking, heaving lope as she leaped and landed, leaped and landed her way down the mountain.

Beck's stomach reacted immediately, and her grip began to weaken. She started sizing up landing spots again.

Rachel stumbled! Landing after a leap, she was trying to stop, heeling in, staggering, grabbing and snapping off branches. She danced several yards farther down the slope, finally gripped a tree trunk with one hand, and whipped around to a quick halt.

Beck couldn't have held on if she wanted to. She sailed backward, floating as the ground dropped away, then landing cleanly, tumbling through a struggling patch of Oregon grape until she found a stump to grab. It occurred to her not to stop, to keep going downhill. She let go of the stump and let herself roll until her feet came under her and she stood, bracing herself against a small pine.

Downhill and to her right, Leah clambered back up the hill with Reuben on the ground beside her, four-wheeling up the rocks. Beck veered left and half-limped down to the next tree, buying just a little time, a little more distance from Rachel.

Now she saw Jacob groping his way up the hill; he looked panicked, drooling and slow with exhaustion. Something had turned him back again.

A shock went through Beck like electricity. She caught only a glimpse, only a fleeting image through a gap in the trees far below, but she knew what it was.

A man's camouflage cap. Had it not been moving, and had she not seen one before, she would have missed it, but there was no mistaking it.

"Ohhh!" escaped her, a cry of hope *and* disbelief.

Rachel pounded down the hill toward her, snapping off branches and upsetting loose rock.

Beck hobbled downhill to the next tree and cried out again, not bothering with consonants or pronunciation but just making a noise, any noise she could.

A man's voice answered from far below, "Hello? Somebody up there?"

Beck had just opened her mouth to answer when Rachel caught her in midair, jarring her, stealing her breath, muffling her cry. Beck wriggled, squirmed, tried to get free. She screamed—

She saw nothing but fiery eyes, bristling black hair, flaring nostrils, and glistening teeth. Jacob never came this close to anything except to kill it. His throaty roar erased her brain; his foul breath paralyzed her will.

"Hello!" the man called.

Beck didn't answer.

Reed was closing in on his waypoint well ahead of Jimmy's team, when Steve Thorne's voice crackled in his earpiece, "I've got something above me! It's heading back up the hill!"

"Any visual?" he heard Jimmy ask.

"No, but I heard a woman scream."

"Max's team, tighten up!" Pete ordered. "Give us a wall down there!"

Reed looked at his GPS. He could see Max and Thorne tightening formation and inching uphill. Pete was moving south along the stone face, with Sam about five hundred feet below him. The other two guys were filling in between.

Reed got on the radio. "Heads up, everybody! Don't let the screaming fool you. That's not a woman! That's the target!" He didn't like the silence he got in response. "Jimmy, I've got you and Sam behind and below."

"Yeah, that's us," Jimmy replied.

"Can you get a man above me, between me and the rocks?"

"Give him a few minutes."

"Did everybody hear my heads-up about the screaming sound?"

Several answered that they had. Steve Thorne radioed, "You're sure that's not your wife?"

No, he wasn't sure and it was killing him. "Did she say anything?"

"No, she just screamed."

A hunt, and not a search. Reed fought down his fear. "Don't let that thing sucker you in. That's what happened to Mills."

"What the heck are we hunting, anyway?" Thorne asked.

Jimmy cut in, "I told you not to ask."

Reed paused to breathe deeply and gather himself. He glanced at his GPS. He was close now, only forty yards or so. The circle of hunters was closing in. Something inside that circle was going to be really ticked off.

Beck's world was a cruel kaleidoscope of blurred images—powerful, grappling arms, brush and tree limbs whipping past, her own arms and legs kicking and flailing, the total, choking darkness of Rachel's bosom. In quick, intermittent flashes between grabs, holds, slaps, and kicks, she saw Jacob leading, ascending the slope, his flexible feet grabbing the ground and his legs pushing relentlessly upward.

Rachel was just too strong, and Beck's ribs, arms, legs, and sprained ankle were sending her warnings: *Much more of this, and you're going to break something.* With a whimper muffled in Rachel's hairy body, Beck gave up the struggle, if only to live one moment longer.

The climb continued. Beck pushed herself up just far enough to look backward over Rachel's shoulder. More forest, thicket, and impenetrable tangle. How these beasts could pass so easily through that stuff, she couldn't fathom. No hunter could ever get through there.

Ahead, she caught a glimpse of Jacob as he plunged into a tangle of honeysuckle and elderberry that had formed a living dome over a fallen aspen. Leah and Reuben followed, dropping through the tangled web of leaves and into a hollow beneath. Without slowing, Rachel lowered her head and shoulders and stormed through.

It was like falling through a roof into a dark cellar, but the landing was soft—there were three hot, hairy bodies to cushion their fall. One of them, possibly Leah, gave a painful grunt on impact.

The hollow was tight and confining, stabbed through with limbs from the fallen aspen, obscured on all sides by vines and brush, packed solid with steaming apes. It got hot right away. Jacob's scent glands were working overtime.

They were hiding again, motionless, eyes intense, breathing in quiet puffs. Listening. Peering through the myriad tiny gaps in the leaves, vines, and branches.

It made Beck afraid, as if the monster were lurking outside and not on both sides of her.

She could see through the curtain, a slot here, a chink there, tiny windows blurrily framing puzzle pieces of the forest outside. Other than the troubled forest chatter, she heard nothing. Something moved, and she gasped before she could catch herself. She leaned closer to the tangle, peering through a vertical hole between twisting vines. Something white dangled from a nearby elderberry bush, moving lazily in the breeze.

They had come full circle. Obnoxious, raiding Reuben had already been here.

Of course, Reuben's escapade with her toilet paper was not going to help the Sasquatches' cause. A streamer of white toilet paper would stand out like a surveyor's ribbon. One of the hunters was sure to spot it.

Reed took a moment to listen and watch before taking another step toward the white ribbon. He had his bearings now. He recognized everything. He whispered via his earpiece, "Pete, I see the toilet paper."

"We're closing on you," Pete replied.

"Still moving uphill," said Max.

"I've got a man above you," Jimmy said.

Reed didn't move. Maybe Pete Henderson was rubbing off on him, or maybe he'd been in these woods so long he was growing a whole new set of senses, but he *felt* something.

Steadying his rifle with his right hand, he flexed and stretched his left, then reversed the procedure, flexing his right. *A search or a hunt?* He checked the progress of the other hunters on his GPS. It was a search right now but would definitely be a hunt in a matter of minutes.

As one, Beck *and* her captors alerted, their muscles tensing, their eyes shifting about. When they heard a second step, their heads turned the same direction, toward the south, the broken bits of light painting speckles on their faces, glimmers on their eyes. Beck peered through an opening, saw nothing but leaves, peered through another, saw only forest, peered through a third—

At the sight of her husband, her diaphragm involuntarily leaped and a squeal escaped her throat. Rachel's arm nearly collapsed her rib cage; Jacob shot her a glance and a warning hiss;

Leah's glaring eyes cut through the dark. Beck clapped her hand over her mouth.

Reed took another step toward them. Beck craned her neck to steal a tiny, partial view of him through a gap in the leaves, her hand squeezing over her mouth ever more tightly as her emotions defied restraint.

Reed stole forward, one step at a time, ducking branches, stepping over twigs, hands welded to his rifle. He removed the earpiece from his ear, putting aside the other voices. He only wanted to hear what was around him, right here, right now. Two more steps, and he reached his waypoint. He was standing by the white toilet paper streamer.

He was so close that Beck could see only his legs.

Rachel's body had turned to iron. Her hair was bristling, stabbing Beck in the face and arms. Jacob breathed slowly but deeply, building strength in silence, his hair on end, ruthless murder in his eyes.

Beck put her other hand over her mouth but could not steady the quaking breath rushing in and out of her nostrils.

They're cornered. They have young: Reuben—and me. If I make a sound . . . If Reed comes any closer . . .

Reed stood still again and scanned around him, occupied first and foremost with staying alive, but driven by one irrepressible longing: to see Beck, to hear her voice, to *know*, at long last, that she was alive. Maybe it was the *longing* that gave him the *feeling*; somehow—maybe it was that stupid toilet paper—but he felt she was close.

He remembered seeing another scrap of toilet paper the last time he was here, within sight of—

There! Fifteen feet away, the scrap of white lay on a patch of brown pine needles, right below a huge honeysuckle that grew over a fallen aspen. He took two small, careful steps. A leaf crackled under his boot and he froze.

Steady now.

One more step. Freeze. Listen. One more step.

A scent from an old nightmare reached his nostrils and his blood ran cold. Suddenly he wasn't just remembering that first horrible night; he felt he was *there*, hearing Beck scream and feeling helpless, so helpless. The *thing* was there too. Though he couldn't see it, he could feel it hiding, watching him.

Beck. He could think only of her and took one more step toward the terror.

It was one step farther than he'd ever gone before. One step ago, he was terrified. Now he was as good as dead, but he didn't care. His hands became steady. He had no urge to step back. This was his destination, exactly where he wanted to be, not just close, but *there*.

"Beck," he whispered. "I'm here, babe. I'm right here."

He could smell the *thing*. If he wasn't imagining that slow, steady, hissing sound, he could hear it too.

A search or a hunt? He'd come to do both. He swung his rifle about, daring that thing to move.

Reed stood just above the hollow. Beck heard a hiss crackling through saliva and teeth. Jacob's teeth were bared, his canines gleaming. He was crouching, poised, planning.

Reed, get out of here!

He didn't leave. He took another step toward them.

They're going to kill him. Honest to God, they're going to kill him!

TWELVE

Sing saw the circle tightening, closing in from the west, north, and south against the stone cliffs above. Inside the circle, toward the south end, Reed's blip wasn't moving. He wasn't answering his radio.

"Reed! Reed, talk to me! Jimmy, can you see him?"

"Negative," Jimmy whispered. "It's pretty thick in here."

"Do you have him on your screen?"

"Got him."

"Then what are you waiting for?"

Pete came on the radio. "Steady, everybody. Let's not get ourselves killed."

Reed could hear commotion from his earpiece. He replaced it, pressed the talk button, and spoke quietly, "This is Reed. I'm at the waypoint. I don't see the target, but I can smell it."

"Reed, fall back!" Sing cried. "Wait for the others."

"Negative. I'm not letting that thing get away again."

"Reed!"

He removed the earpiece.

Go away, Reed, Beck begged in her mind. *I love you. Please don't let them kill you. Go away.*

Jacob was waiting, ready to explode from the hollow. Beck couldn't even guess what would trigger him, but she knew the attack would only last an instant.

Reed moved slowly past the mound of vines, mentally mapping the area, looking for hiding places. An upended stump just below him could have hidden something. The fallen aspen looked suspicious, but could anything fit under there? Another step and he spotted an open space, just a little breathing room to his left. It might give him a half second more to react if anything charged him. He tried to catch that scent, tried to—

The sight made him jump. He calmed himself, looked around for danger, confirmed his grip on his rifle.

Brown leather.

At first he thought it was an animal, obscured by the wild grass and knapweed; then he thought it was a dead animal. It was bloody, torn, ripped.

Double-checking every direction, he carefully approached whatever it was, knowing what it was but not wanting to know.

Jacob eased back just a little, which eased Beck just a little, enough to think, *What can I do, what can I do?* No answers came.

She could see Reed through another gap in the overgrowth, moving into view in a small clearing. Apparently he'd found something, though for a moment she couldn't imagine what it could be.

Wait. Her jacket? She and the group had come full circle, back to where Reuben had raided her toilet paper. It might be her jacket.

Now her heart quickened with one spark of hope. If Reed found her jacket, he'd know she had to be around here somewhere. It would keep him looking, keep him hoping. It would be like a signal, a flare, a message in a bottle—

It *was* her jacket, or at least a piece of it. Reed picked it up, turned it over in his hands. Reuben had done quite a job on it, worse than a pup with a chew toy. It was chewed, shredded—

A foreboding hit her like a blow to the stomach; the fear—no, the certainty of death coursed through her like an electric shock. There was blood on that jacket, *Rachel's* blood from days ago. It was torn into pieces. It looked like—

A quaking, nearly dying breath passed through her lips as the words formed, "R-r-reed." *Don't think that, Reed. Don't think it. It's not my blood.*

The blood on the leather was days old by now, flaking and brown. The leather was tattered, tooth marked, and only a fragment of

Beck's jacket, a side panel and half of a sleeve. It spoke to Reed; it told him everything.

He sank to his knees, unaware of the forest, the search, the hunt, and even the danger. His rifle dropped to the grass. He gazed at the shredded garment and ran his thumb over the smear of blood. A shadow crept into his mind like black ink permeating a parchment, spreading, pushing away light and hope, stripping away every thought but one: Beck.

He raised his eyes. All he could see was Beck chewing on a cold sandwich and making a teasing face, a crooked, stuffed-cheek, half smile, while he took her picture. It was the last smile he could remember, and even as he tried to dwell on it, it faded, lost in the darkness of a night that would last forever. Though he tried to hear her laugh again, or even say his name, only silence answered.

If she screamed, he would die. She could only lie pilloried in Rachel's arms and watch in silent agony as Reed rose from the ground, weak as an old man, the tattered remnant of her jacket in his hand. He didn't think to pick up his rifle, but instead fumbled with an earpiece, his hand trembling, until he'd replaced it in his ear. She heard only the words, " . . . pulling out . . ." and then he started back the way he'd come.

Jacob tensed again. Reed would be passing by close.

Reed stopped, went back for his rifle, then passed by quickly, clumsily.

I'm not dead.

One last image through the vines: a trudging, wounded man, no longer alert or careful, in no hurry, stepping over a log, pushing aside a leafy branch . . .

I'M NOT DEAD!

He went out of sight. A quiet rustle followed, then the snap of a twig, then a very distant crunching.

Then there was no sound at all.

Sing threw open the door on her mobile lab and stood on the steps, gripping the handrail, watching the trail that climbed into the woods from the parking area. For the past forty minutes she had been not a human being but a stone, forbidding herself to feel, care, or cherish. There were hunters in the woods. Someone had to maintain contact and be their link to the outside world. Someone had to help them close up the circle in case the positioning signals winked out on their mobile units. She had to think of them, even while she watched one blip on her screen slowly make its way down the mountain, across the creek bed, past the site where Fleming Cryncovich found all the footprints, and back down the trail to Whitetail.

Now that the blip on her computer screen had reached the end of its journey, she expected to see Reed and Jimmy drawing near. When she did, she would release her heart. She would become a human being again.

But how she would ever bear the pain and loss, she didn't know.

Janson's voice crackled through her headset. "Hey, I need some help closing up the south end. A guy could drive a truck through here."

She shot a quick glance at her computer screen and replied, "Max? Steve? Do you have Janson's position?"

"No, I've lost him," said Thorne.

"He's bearing 135, about 800 feet. He's using Jimmy's GPS."

"One thirty-five, Roger."

"Janson, you're good. Stay where you are until they pick you up again."

Janson acknowledged grumpily.

And then she saw Reed and Jimmy emerge from the woods like tired soldiers returning from battle, eyes vacant, shoulders slumped, legs trudging, rifles slung on their shoulders. Jimmy stayed close to Reed, lending strength, as Reed managed to put one foot in front of the other. Reed caught her eye, but his face was hard to discern. He carried a bloodied piece of leather in both hands.

Now Sing's heart was free to grieve. Her hand went to her mouth as her body began to quake.

They met in the parking lot, embracing. Sing wept with no words. Reed seemed strangely empty, like a body without a spirit. He held her but did not cry.

"I'll, uh, I'll handle the radio," said Jimmy.

Sing watched him go to the motor home, recover the headset she'd left dangling by the door, and go inside.

When Jimmy's voice came over the radio, Pete had to turn down his volume. "Okay, guys, this is Jimmy. Just to let you know, Sheriff Mills and I had an agreement: as long as it was a search, the sheriff was in charge. When it became a hunt, Fish and Game would be in charge. Well, guys, like you've all heard, the search is over. We've got ourselves a full-blown hunt now, and that makes me the big kahuna. Thorne and Max, Reed and I are out of the game for now, so pull your line south and sew up the net before the big one gets away. Let's get ourselves a bear!"

Pete lost half his will to go on when he heard that Reed had pulled out. Now that it was clear there would be no finding Beck, he lost the rest of it. He checked his GPS. The north end was pretty tight now. Sam Marlowe was only ninety yards down the slope, with Wiley Kane and a forest ranger in between. They'd be able to carry on well enough without him. He got a bearing from his compass and started down.

Sing checked on Reed one last time. He'd shed his jacket and boots and left them on the floor by the bed, but he wouldn't part with the piece of Beck's jacket. He clutched it tightly as he lay on the bed in the back of the motor home, his face to the wall.

"I'll call Cap and let him know," she told him. "I've got some soup I can heat up. You need to have some."

He didn't answer. He didn't move.

"I'll be right here," she said.

Satisfied that he was comfortable—he would never be okay—she closed the door quietly and left him alone.

In the main room, Jimmy was at her computer, wearing her headset, still running things. "Pete, you need to move up the bank; you're slipping down too far. Say again?" He rolled his eyes. "Sam, head up the hill and push the other guys ahead of you. Close it up."

He looked over his shoulder at Sing. "How's he doing?"

"He's breathing. That's all I can tell you."

He stared at the rear bedroom door. "We were fools to let it go this long. I tried to tell him. I tried to tell Mills."

"But nobody ever listens to you." Her sarcasm was subtle but intentional.

"This isn't the time."

She picked up her cell phone. "No, it isn't."

"Have you called Dave Saunders?"

"I'm on it."

Jimmy turned to the computer screen, burying himself in the hunt. "Pete, can you hand off your GPS to Wiley on your way down? Thanks, guy, and hey, listen, we all understand."

Sing stepped out of the vehicle, closed the door behind her, and punched in a number. It was quiet out here—away from Jimmy.

She got Deputy Dave Saunders. "Hello, Dave? This is Sing Capella. Reed's calling off the search. Everybody can stand down." She listened to his question and fought back tears in order to answer. "No. Just a piece of her coat."

While he dealt with the news, Sing pulled herself together—for the moment. "Dave, are you there?" He was, full of condolences, wanting to help. "Reed would like you to contact the Forest Service; we have to close the woods to civilians until we hunt down the . . . until we get the problem cleared up. But, Dave, there's one more thing: the hunters have cleared out of the Lost Creek area, so you won't be in their way anymore. We still need to find Randy Thompson—I'm sure we're dealing with a body, or remains. If you could get a few deputies up there . . . Yeah, I know, but we have to try again, and this time, bring some metal detectors. You're going to be looking for a shovel."

Pete found Wiley Kane within minutes. All he had to do was follow the cigarette smoke.

"So," Kane said with a bit of a leer, "you've had enough, huh?"

Pete removed his GPS and handed it to him. "I was in this for Beck, not Jimmy."

Wiley dropped his cigarette and crushed it out in the dirt. He took the GPS and marveled at it. "Woo! So this has got all of us on there?"

Pete pointed out a few details: the available screens, the moving map, the zoom feature, and the various peer-to-peer blips. "You're gonna be me now, this dot right here. This one here is Sam, down the hill from you. You just put this earpiece in your ear and press this button to talk."

"Man, the toys these days!"

"Sometimes the terrain gets in the way and you wink out, but usually, as long as your unit's turned on, the other team leaders can see you and you can see them."

"Okay, my turn!" Wiley strapped it on his arm as he'd seen the others do.

"Just run that wire up the inside of your jacket. That'll keep it out of the way."

Wiley removed his jacket and started fiddling with the earpiece, trying to figure out where to route the wire.

Pete stayed at his back, acting as if he was helping, but all the while taking a good look at Wiley's boot print where he'd stamped out the cigarette. The print didn't match Pete's sketch from Lost Creek, but then again, Wiley Kane was wearing a brand-new pair of boots.

"Cap?"

"I'm here." No further words would come to him, but at the moment, he didn't care. It was enough for him to accept the news, bear the pain, and nurse the wound as he sat glum and alone in their living room in Spokane, the phone to his ear. The news didn't come as a shock, but more like the final, awaited outcome of a tragic story. From the outset, Cap and Sing knew it could end this way. Putting aside denial, a happy ending would have been more surprising.

"What are you feeling?" she asked.

He rested his forehead on his fingertips and closed his eyes. He was feeling so many things. "You mean, besides the sorrow? The loss?"

"I'm not sure what to do next."

"I got caught sneaking into Burkhardt's lab today. Merrill had me booted off the campus."

Now there was a silence on her end. Finally, "Is that it, then?"

He thought a moment, then answered, "Anger. I'm feeling anger; a close friend is dead and somebody's getting away with it."

"Do we have anything solid?"

"So far it's all circumstantial—and some of it could be imaginary. What about those photos?"

"I've photographed everybody within camera range. I took some more today when all the hunters came through."

"Why don't you e-mail those to me?"

"Will do."

"I've got one more lead I'm going to harass a little, and if that doesn't pan out . . . Maybe I should just get over there and, you know, be there."

"Reed could use you right now."

"Is he there?"

"He's sleeping."

"Oh. Well, give him my love, and get me those pictures, and . . . I'll take one more crack at it, for Beck's memory if for nothing else."

"You be careful."

"Oh, I think the worst is over—for me."

Sing closed her cell phone and climbed back inside the motor home. She found Jimmy still glued to the computer screen, not saying much and looking antsy. He nervously flexed his ankle with his toe planted, making his knee wiggle up and down like a jackhammer. It was a good sign he wouldn't be able to sit still much longer. She decided to let the tension build another few minutes before she said anything.

In those minutes, she used a second computer to go online through her cell phone, selected the folder containing her photos—some posed, some candid, some downright sneaky—of anyone and everyone who'd had anything to do with the search or the hunt. With a few quick taps on the computer's touch pad, the photos were on their way to Cap.

"How's everybody doing?" she asked Jimmy.

"Nothing so far." His voice was tense. "That south end was open a long time. The bear may have given us the slip."

"I can take over if you want to head up there again."

That turned his head from the screen. "You're sure?"

"Hey. You want to be stuck down here while somebody else bags that bear?"

He ripped the headset from his head, grabbed his coat and rifle, and went out the door, jamming the earpiece from Reed's GPS in his ear.

"You're welcome," she said, settling in front of the computer.

The first thing Sing noticed was Steve Thorne and Janson's GPS blips coming perilously close to Reed's waypoint, the place where he'd found part of Beck's jacket.

Jimmy's voice crackled in the earpieces, "Talk to me, Janson. What's happening?"

"We're at the location," Janson whispered back, "so everybody pipe down."

Janson stood guard while Thorne went first, keeping an eye out for any movement, any stirring. The streamer of white toilet paper was still there, hanging on the elderberry bush. It moved lightly in the breeze—as obvious and tempting as bait for a trap. Janson didn't like this place; there was just something about it.

Thorne moved slowly, carefully planting each step, sighting down his rifle as he checked out a dark stump amid a clump of young firs, a log within a thicket, a shadow under an upturned root ball. He was mindful that this was where the Shelton woman got chewed up, and he'd seen firsthand what happened to Sheriff Mills. He drew a sample of air through his nose. Didn't Reed Shelton say something about smelling the target? There did seem to be a certain odor about the place.

As a matter of fact, the odor could have been coming from a dome of vines that grew over a fallen aspen just a few yards away.

"Heads up," Thorne whispered, gesturing toward the dome.

Janson leveled his rifle at the mound. He nodded to Thorne. Ready.

Thorne approached slowly. The odor was getting stronger.

Sing watched intently. Thorne's GPS blip was dead centered on Reed's waypoint, apparently motionless, but probably stalking, sneaking. She couldn't imagine that that thing would still be there after all this time, but then again . . .

Thorne was close to the fallen aspen, and now he could tell that the tangled overgrowth had been disturbed, thrown open like a curtain and left to settle back in place. He shot a glance at Janson, nodded toward the tangled dome, held his rifle ready in his right hand, reached out slowly with his left, took hold of the vines, drew a breath, yanked the vines open—

Underneath the thick mat of vines, leaves, and branches was a dark hollow. A foul stench washed over him, making him flinch. His trigger finger tightened.

He relaxed.

Janson allowed himself to breathe again.

The hollow was empty.

The running, running, running finally came to an end in a secluded, soft-floored grove of pines and hemlocks somewhere in Idaho—or Montana, or maybe Canada for all Beck knew. Not that she cared anymore. When the adults finally stopped to rest and Rachel let Beck roll off onto the ground, Beck flopped and lay where she landed, face half buried in the moss and pine needles, too despondent to think about it.

Reed thinks I'm dead.

The image of him finding that tattered piece of jacket kept

playing, playing, and replaying in her mind. It wouldn't fade; it wouldn't turn off. It gave her no rest.

I'm alive and I can't tell him. He thinks I'm dead and that he can't save me.

I may as well be dead!

"Oooohhh!" She moaned and writhed from the pain and frustration, her voice muffled in the ground. *I may as well lie here until I rot, until trees start growing out of me. God hates me.*

Yeah. God hated her. He had to. Why else would He keep slapping her with nothing but lousy luck? Who else understood fairness enough to make sure she never got any good breaks? Who else could make her dead to the world and everyone she loved, and yet leave her alive to agonize in it? It was all too perfect. It had to be planned.

A rising anger gave her just enough strength to roll over onto her back, point her finger toward the converging treetops, and whine at God, "Y-y-yooo . . ."

Oh, right! She forgot. God gave her a stutter so she couldn't tell Him how ticked off she was!

She slapped the ground and growled at Him. Then she sat up and screamed at Him.

That upset Rachel, who'd been lying on her back in some maple bushes. She raised her head and looked over her belly. "Hmm."

Leah was half visible in another clump of maples, staring at Beck as she tore off the broad leaves and munched on them.

Beck just growled at them, waving them off. *I'm all right, don't trouble yourselves, don't get up, just leave me alone!*

Rachel's head sank to the ground again and she let out a tired sigh. Leah regurgitated a wad of chewed leaves into her palm and started eating them a second time.

Beck stared at the ground, angrily flicking tufts of moss with her fingertip. *What am I going to do? Everybody thinks I'm dead. They're not going to look for me anymore. They're going to get together and have a memorial service, and then they're going to eat chicken and potato salad and go home. Reed's going to cry for me every night, and I'm going to cry for him, and the only friends I have left are these . . . these . . .*

"Ooooohh!" Seething, she growled at Leah, who ignored her, and Rachel, snoring somewhere beyond those big feet and that round belly. She couldn't see Jacob or Reuben, but she growled at them anyway, wherever they were: *All right, so you hate me! Well, I hate you too! If you eat me, I hope you barf!*

Then she watched Leah, licking and nibbling her vomited wad as if it were coleslaw. These monsters *enjoyed* barfing! God thought of everything.

What am I going to do?

She sniffed derisively at her own thoughts. *Why do anything? God will only ruin it.*

She dug her hairbrush out of her pocket and began running it through her hair only because it made her feel better. Maybe God wouldn't notice and make all her hair fall out.

"Hmph." She heard a grunt from Leah. The big gray female was just finishing up her maple-leaf coleslaw and looking at her.

Beck looked back, angry enough to meet and match the gaze from those deep-set eyes. Direct staring was never polite in Sasquatch circles, and Beck could tell Leah didn't like it, but she stared anyway and kept brushing, not caring what Leah liked, disliked, thought, or wanted.

Leah swallowed the last of her green wad, licked her palm clean, and gave Beck's hairbrush her earnest, undivided attention. Then she extended her hand and grunted again. "Hmmph."

Beck quit brushing. She looked down at her hairbrush, then

at Leah, and the strangest and most unexpected thought came to her: *I have something she doesn't.*

It was uncanny. Had *God* thought of this yet? This huge, intimidating, massively strong animal could break Beck in half with no effort at all—but only Beck knew how to use a hairbrush, and Leah seemed to know it.

Leah's eyes glanced very quickly at the sleeping Rachel, then back at Beck, taking on an imploring expression, like a dog begging.

This is going to go wrong. Somehow, God's going to foul it up.

Then again, it could have been His idea. She looked toward the sky, didn't get an answer, and ventured a guess: *Maybe I'd better try it.*

She got up slowly, keeping her eye on Leah, who sat there next to the maple bush, eyeing her. Now she could see Rachel's face. "Mom" was asleep.

While the cat's away, the mice will play, is that it?

"Hmmph." Leah extended her hand again.

Looking around for Reuben and not seeing him, Beck stole forward, keeping the brush visible in her hand. She was about to enter Leah's space, so she hummed quietly, no tune in particular, and diverted her eyes from Leah's to be polite.

Leah sure looked big sitting there on her haunches, and those arms were all muscle, lots of it.

Beck came within a few feet—close enough to have her head swatted off—and thought of a safety tip: When approaching a Sasquatch, bow and try to make that low, guttural, rumbling noise. They seem to like that.

She bowed, knees bending, her hands almost touching the ground, and tried her best to make her throat rumble.

Leah looked puzzled.

Oh. Apparently, bows with rumbled greetings were only for the alpha male. Beck made a mental note.

"Hmmph," Leah grunted, leaning forward.

Beck reached out with the brush and touched Leah's head. Leah shuffled closer. Beck started brushing, stealing glances at the sleeping Rachel and feeling like a turncoat.

But she was doing Leah a service, maybe even gaining acceptance from Rachel's rival, and that seemed a smart thing to do. She continued, working more systematically, from Leah's head down to her neck and shoulders. Leah burped a green vegetation burp and sat still, looking pleased.

I don't know where this is going, but it just might keep me alive. After all, if Beck could be part of the group, maybe the group wouldn't eat her. Beck kept brushing, working her way down Leah's back, and Leah allowed her, letting out occasional hums of pleasure. Her gray hair was sensational, so soft and smooth, and once Beck got it all lying in the same direction, it became prismatic, reflecting a rainbow sheen.

So gross, and yet so lovely.

After that unfortunate death-flinch blunder with Rachel, Beck was careful to look before she brushed, and it was a good thing she did. Halfway down Leah's back, Beck spotted another anomaly and stopped brushing just in time.

Leah immediately noticed the pause and turned her head, grunting over her shoulder.

Beck hummed back at her pleasantly, finding a safe place to brush while she had a closer look.

Again, it was blood. Carefully parting the hairs, Beck recognized another bite wound, not as severe as Rachel's but just as recent. Beck gave a low, rumbling hum as if to ask, *What on earth happened? Did Jacob do this?*

Leah sighed, seemingly resigned to whatever the unfortunate situation was.

Beck kept brushing, carefully checking, then grooming Leah's ribs. She found a shallow gash under the right arm, possibly a bite that didn't quite land. Leah flinched when Beck brushed around it, but she didn't get mad.

As Beck thought about it, it didn't make sense that Jacob would do this. When Jacob punished Rachel the first night he saw Beck, he was brutal and unforgivably abusive, but he never used his teeth. Besides, Leah seemed to be the "alpha's pet" in this group; she could do no wrong. Maybe Beck was seeing the aftermath of a full-blown catfight between Leah and Rachel, with Leah the winner and Rachel the cast-down loser. Either that, or . . . she just couldn't imagine.

A shape moved through the pines, and Beck looked up to see Mr. Bad News himself, Reuben, approaching in a wide, tentative arc, head cocked in suspicion. He growled at her as if to say, *What are you doing with my mother?*

Beck looked him in the eye and kept brushing.

He stepped closer, then started sidestepping, left and right, left and right, making little waving, threatening gestures with his arms as he growled.

Leah pig-grunted at him, which set him back slightly, but he still wanted to fight about it and stared daggers at Beck.

Beck came to the brink of being frightened. She could feel her stomach starting to tense, her hands starting to tremble, her speech faculties starting to jumble—but strangely, surprisingly even to her, she went only to the brink and no further. Standing by Reuben's mother with her permission could have had something to do with it, but there was something else: for the first time in her life, her penchant for being afraid had worn thin. After several days of terror and dread, terror and loathing, terror and despair, she was tired of it.

And besides that, she was just plain mad. She'd lost her husband in a most enraging dilemma; she'd been a doormat to this snotty-nosed throw rug from the day they met; even God was picking on her and wouldn't give her a break. "Aaargh!" she growled.

She met Reuben's stare, held her eyes steady, and didn't turn away. She growled again and even huffed through her nose at him. *Listen, kid, I'm somebody too!*

Leah grunted more loudly at him, her displeasure obvious.

Beck seconded that with an angry bark, her weight forward.

Reuben bought it. He backed off, gave her a look that was half dirty, half perplexed, and shuffled sulkingly into the pines to mind his own business.

Well! To Beck's amazement, things seemed to be going the right direction.

Leah nudged her, wanting more. Beck returned to her brushing and enjoyed every square inch of it, right down to Leah's toes. She finished with a soft hum and a flourish, then backed away passively, eyes diverted, honoring the custom with confidence.

Back in her own personal space amid the pines, she settled to the ground by herself with no one bothering her, feeling strangely unafraid.

And strangely alive.

"She's not dead."

Sing and Pete looked up from the dining table at a man not quite risen from the dead. Reed stood, his frame filling the rear bedroom door, but he didn't appear well rested, to put it mildly. He was still clutching the bloodied piece of jacket.

Sing rose from the table. "Can I fix you anything? I have some soup."

Reed stood there as if he hadn't heard the question, a weird, catatonic look on his face. "Uh, yeah. Please. And how about a sandwich or something?"

Sing rummaged in the tight refrigerator. "I've got pastrami and turkey breast."

"Okay. Please." He sat at the computer and looked at the screen, now dark. "So what happened?"

Pete answered, his fingers curled around a coffee cup, "Hunters are back down for the night. They'll regroup in the morning, go back to using bear stands and maybe some dogs. They found plenty of sign that something had been up there, but it's gone now."

Reed broke into a delirious grin and chuckled. "So they didn't get their bear." He chuckled some more, enjoying a demented laugh at a sorry situation. Pete stared into his coffee, and Sing sliced bread until he'd finished.

"I'm sorry, Reed," said Pete. "I wish to God things could've turned out different."

Reed gave him a curious look. "We don't know how they turned out."

Pete looked at Sing, who only looked down at the open sandwich.

Pete found words first. "Reed. You know I have the deepest respect for your feelings on this, but we've got to face it. Three violent deaths in a row don't line up with Beck just tagging along with a bunch of creatures, alive and well and leaving footprints. Now that piece of her jacket, *that's* consistent with what we've seen. That talks."

"So you're with Jimmy?"

Pete winced. "Oh, man, don't put me in Jimmy's camp . . ."

"He thought the Cryncovich footprints were a hoax. He thought Beck was dead a long time ago. Is that what you think?"

"We've been talking about that," said Sing.

"We've been going around and around about it," said Pete.

Sing still had a touch of fire in her eyes. "I'd like to know how those prints could be so accurately formed, and just what creatures were doing all that howling when Mills was killed."

Reed focused on the tired tracker. "Do you have another explanation?"

Pete could only give a slight throw-up-his-hands gesture. "Like I was telling her, I don't know, but what if Fleming Cryncovich is as nutty as he looks and just wants attention? He's a Sasquatch fanatic; he would've known how to fake footprints. And as far as Beck's boot prints, he could've found a size 6 boot with a matching sole. A boot is a boot."

Sing jumped on that. "With the same tread pattern you noted at Lost Creek? You *did* sketch it all out on one of your blue cards, didn't you?"

Reed added, "With the same wear pattern?"

"And what about the cell phone number scratched in the dirt?"

Pete countered, "I don't have it all figured out. I'm just trying to see this thing from all sides, that's all. Reed, isn't it possible that Arlen Peak could have gotten your cell phone number?"

Reed saw his point. "Yeah."

"And he's a Bigfoot nut too, isn't he? And he and Cryncovich are friends?"

Sing's temper was starting to show. "You know what you're saying about Arlen?"

Pete drilled her with his eyes. "Why'd you take his picture then?"

Sing got flustered. "Just . . . there's this whole cover-up thing. We can't rule out any possible suspect—"

"Well, there might be a cover-up and there might not be."

Sing was ready to grapple on that one. "Allen Arnold was moved."

"And Randy—was he moved?"

"Possibly."

"But you don't know that."

"Not really."

"And that's my point."

Reed asked, "So, what has Cap found out?"

Sing's discouragement was obvious. "Nothing solid. It's all conjecture."

Pete let his hand come down forcefully on the table. "There! Thank you! That's the word I've been looking for. Conjecture! I conject, then you conject, and that's all Cap has is conjecture. Reed, we've been at this all afternoon, talking about whether Beck's dead or alive, or somebody's fooling us, or we're just fooling ourselves, or whether there really are Sasquatches up there . . ."

Reed answered quietly, "And whether Sasquatches are killers, and whether it's a bear like Jimmy says, and why in the world somebody would want to protect those monsters with a cover-up—if there really are monsters and there really is a cover-up."

That gave them pause.

"I thought you were sleeping," said Sing.

"I was until you two started in on each other. But I've been thinking too."

"So help us out," said Pete.

Reed lightly stroked the remains of Beck's jacket as he spoke in a quiet, tired voice: "Considering how much we don't know, it might be early to say how things turned out."

Pete looked out the window to mull it over. Sing busied herself with lettuce, meat, pickles, and tomatoes.

"It's kind of funny, isn't it, how much this whole thing's been about what people think they know: it's a bear, it's a Bigfoot; I'm a wife-killer, I'm a crazy victim; Beck's dead, Beck's alive; it was a cover-up, it was an accident."

Sing finished making the sandwich, put it on a plate, and handed it to Reed. "Still want that soup?"

"That'd be great. Thanks." He set the sandwich on the computer bench, truly hungry but needing to speak. "I just keep thinking of Beck and me climbing up that trail before this all started, and how much I thought I knew, and how much I really didn't. Here I was, telling Beck her world was too small and if she didn't get out and stretch a bit, she'd quit learning and growing, and all along, I didn't know how small *my* world was. It's been one tough lesson."

He considered the tattered piece of leather in his lap, looking it over as he spoke, "Anyway, I guess it's never a bad idea to let your world get stretched once in a while, to just humble down and admit there might be something right in front of you that you haven't thought of before. So on the one hand, Pete, you're right about Beck's jacket. It talks."

He held it up for them to see, tooth marks, bloodstain, and all. "This bloodstain is several days old, isn't that right, Sing?"

Silently, she examined the stain, and then she nodded, knowing what it meant.

Reed spoke what the others realized: "It means Beck died several days ago, probably that very first night." He folded the leather carefully, solemnly, and set it on the dining table in the midst of them. "There's no way she could have made those footprints."

Sing and Pete stared at that tattered remnant. It did speak, without words.

Sing finally said, "It still doesn't answer everything."

Pete tried to say it calmly. "It answers enough. The rest of it . . . Maybe we'll never know."

Reed replied, "So that's one thing we can agree on, that we don't really know."

Pete and Sing silently checked with each other, then nodded.

"But on the other hand, maybe it's okay to *believe* a little? Instead of just accepting the way things look, maybe there's still room to stretch what we're so sure of just one more inch."

He leaned forward, confronting Pete eye to eye. "Pete, you ever had a feeling you couldn't explain?"

Pete understood. He nodded.

Reed looked at Sing. "How about you?"

"All the time," she said.

"When I was up there at the waypoint and I found this" —he nodded at the remnant on the table— "everything I saw told me that I'd finally gotten the answer, that I finally knew. But there was a part of me that *felt* something, like she was talking to me. I had every reason in the world to think—maybe even know—that she was dead, but still . . . There was some part of me that wouldn't let go, that still believed." He leaned back, eyeing the remnant on the table. "I could say I *know* Beck is dead, but I don't, not really. And as long as we don't know for sure, I can *believe* she's still out there." Then he added, "And I *believe* there's one last thing we haven't tried."

"No, no, now listen, I said I didn't want to get sucked into it!"

Nick Claybuckle was enjoying a relaxing jog around Manitow Park. He passed the big duck pond and the geometric rose gardens, pounded over the beautiful stone bridge and under the spreading maple trees—

Until he was overtaken by another jogger who could outrun him. "You heard me, kid! Pull over!"

"Doc, somebody's gonna see us talking!"

"Not if you get off the road," said Cap. He pointed. "How about in there? Nice benches, lots of hedges, nice and private."

Nick was huffing and puffing anyway, carrying too much extra poundage to get away. He hung a right and they ducked into a pleasant grove, sending a brown squirrel darting up a tree. Nick collapsed onto an ornate concrete bench with a brass plaque commemorating the donor. He was soaked with sweat and his glasses were foggy.

Cap sat down next to him, not even breathing hard. "Nick, my needs are very simple," Cap began. "We all know Burkhardt's been shifting his operation off campus for years, and now he's moved off campus altogether. I need to know where he went. I need to find him and his lab."

Nick gasped a few breaths and then answered, "Dr. Capella, you're one of the main reasons he moved!"

"Nick . . ."

"They're going to know I told you!"

Cap nudged him. "You said your department's having to cut back. Where's the money going?"

"Now, how would I know that?"

Cap hooked a finger under Nick's chin and forced him to meet his eyes. "Let me tell you about my ape. Remember him, the one who's ticked off about something? He's been killing people, Nick. He's been breaking their necks." Nick tried to look away. Cap used his whole hand to hold his attention. "He's killed a trail guide, a logger, the Whitcomb County sheriff, and now . . ." Cap came closer, nose to nose. "He's killed Beck Shelton, a close friend of mine—lots of bites, lots of blood, ripping, tearing, the whole nine yards. So, Nick, you have to understand, now *I* am ticked off. I am *not* a patient man!"

Nick's face went white; he was paying attention now. Cap let him go. A question began to form—

Cap intercepted it. "Chimpanzees, Nick, maybe as many as four, spliced so full of human DNA they're a patchwork quilt. Now, how do you suppose that happened?"

"The Judy Lab said it was contamination—"

"It was put there using viral transfers. That means human intervention, which means somebody's responsible, which means somebody's going to be in big trouble when the law sorts this all out. So who are you more afraid of?"

Nick stared, struggling to process it all.

"Where's the money going? Is Merrill diverting funds?"

Nick thought it over one more second, then gave in, nodding yes. "I checked on it. The college budget's gone up the last ten years, not down, but all the departments are being cut back, including the York Center. Merrill's got some kind of pet project going."

"With Burkhardt?" Nick hesitated and Cap nudged him again. "With Burkhardt?"

"That's the talk on the inside. Merrill's hoping for a big payoff to make it all legit. I mean, you wouldn't believe the big people hovering around with grant money—"

"Like Euro-Atlantic Oil and the Carlisle Foundation."

"Yeah. And Mort Fernan."

Cap hadn't seen that name in his research. "The guy who owns the Evolution Channel?"

"Makes perfect sense, doesn't it? Whatever Burkhardt's working on, Fernan wants first dibs to put it on TV." He sniffed a bitter chuckle. "Must be pretty sexy stuff, a whole lot more exciting than inequity aversion in capuchins. But it's a gamble. The investors are holding back until they see results."

Cap nodded to himself. *Results.* There was that word again. "No results, no money."

"And Merrill will have some explaining to do."

"*Incorrect* results, no money," Cap mused.

"Same thing."

"So what about the chimpanzees being shipped off campus? Any truth to that?"

Nick nodded. "The York Center's turning away research proposals—which means we're turning away money—because we don't have new chimps. We have the old standbys, but they're getting too aggressive to be useful, and we're short on younger males."

"What about the females?"

"They're getting old too, and we don't have younger ones to replace them. The young ones get shipped out as soon as they're old enough to breed. Orders from Merrill's office."

"Where do they go?"

"Somewhere in Idaho. A place called Three Rivers."

That turned Cap's head. "Say again?"

Sing kept raking, loosening up the sand by the creek bank, cleaning out rocks and twigs that could prevent a clear footprint. Reed brought a gunnysack into the center of the tilled area and began setting apples, pears, and bananas on a short, sun-bleached log. Pete remained outside the circle, studying a map in the ebbing light.

"It's the right place," Reed assured him.

"Only if they come here," Pete answered, orienting the map to the surroundings. "They've got plenty of choices which way to go."

"But the food is here," said Reed, "alongside the same creek bed, and just a little farther south. If nothing else, Jimmy's hunters will drive them this way."

"We may have been driving them this way all along."

"That's what I've been thinking. If they were living in the forest around Abney all this time, why else would they move?"

"Then again, if they were living around Abney all this time, why haven't they attacked anyone before?"

Sing looked up from her raking. "I keep hearing the word 'they.'"

Pete grabbed up a second rake and directed a buddy's look at Reed. "It'll be 'they' as long as Reed wants it to be."

Sing smiled her gratitude at Pete.

"It won't be very long," said Reed, setting a few last items on the log. "I know this whole idea's ridiculous, but it's the only one I've got."

"Maybe just half ridiculous," Pete replied thoughtfully. "Look at it this way: Arlen and Fleming don't even know we're doing this, so if we get something this time . . ." He could only shake his head after that.

"It's either this or give up," said Sing. "So if you don't go through with it, I will."

"You write Beck a note?" Pete asked to make sure.

"I explained everything," Reed answered, taking long strides out of the circle, leaving a minimum of footprints for Pete to rake out.

Pete raked them all out, and then they stood there, gazing across a small circle of clear, carefully raked sand at what Reed had designated the Last-Ditch Attempt. It would be dark before they could make it back to Pete's truck, but they found it hard to leave.

"And I told her I loved her," Reed added. His gaze moved between his two friends. "Would you guys mind . . . praying with me? It would put my mind at ease."

Sing and Pete both nodded their consent. Reed put his arms around his two friends' shoulders and spoke softly. "God, wherever

Beck is, we know she's in Your hands. Hold her tight for me, will you? Keep her safe and bring her home soon. And . . . that's about it. Amen."

"We'd best get back," said Pete, and they grabbed up their gear.

THIRTEEN

Deputy Dave Saunders had spent Thursday evening on the phone, recalling any Search and Rescue volunteers he could find—four were ready, willing, available, and armed. Then he'd hunted around for metal detectors—two he borrowed from some hobbyist friends, one he rented, and one he bought with his own money. At first light Friday morning, he and his crew were at the cabin on Lost Creek. They would test Sing's theory by searching for something that was not necessarily there to be found.

"If you see, hear, or smell any belligerent creature in the area, I don't care if it's a bear or a Bigfoot or a raccoon on steroids, you get out of there," he told the faithful four. "If you find the shovel, then get on the radio and we'll all converge on the area. If there's a shovel, then chances are there's a grave, and that's what we're after. Any questions?"

The housewife, the fireman, the heavy equipment operator, and the machinist all looked back at him, silent.

"Okay, then, you know your quadrants. We'll take a snack break about ten. Let's go."

Cap drove east from Spokane. He planned to cut through Coeur d'Alene, Idaho, and then south into the timberlands. A highway map rested on the seat beside him, his destination represented by a small open dot.

"Three Rivers," he said into his cell phone. "I about fell off the bench when Nick said that. That's close to where Allen Arnold was killed, am I right?"

Sing replied, "Cap, I think you're heading into trouble."

"I remember Burkhardt talking about a vacation cabin in Idaho, and now Nick says the chimps are being sent to Three Rivers, right where all this trouble began, if the pattern means anything."

"That's exactly what I mean. I'd say call the police, but . . ."

"But what would we tell them?"

"Well, get something to tell them and then tell them!"

"Exactly my intentions."

"But tell me first—and be careful."

"Say hi to Reed."

Sing closed her cell phone and redirected her attention to the dozen camouflaged, rifle-toting hunters now gathered beside the mobile lab, planning, discussing, debating. Max Johnson, Steve Thorne, and Sam Marlowe were telling stories and expressing opinions about today's plan of action; Wiley Kane was having a smoke; Janson was repacking a backpack.

Jimmy and some forest rangers huddled around a map, pointing and muttering: "Set out bait here and here, but you can't have human presence pressuring from above," Jimmy said.

"How about a triangle? Just keep these guys in a triangle and make one big sweep," one offered.

"Dogs'll take care of that, really, if you want to wait," said a second.

Sing reached inside the motor home and brought out some briefcase-sized storage cases. "Here are the GPS units."

Jimmy was elated. "All right. I'll hand them out. Want to take the central command like yesterday?" He opened the first case and pulled out one of the units.

"I'll be here."

"Great. Now I need to know where Reed and Pete are."

Sing pressed through the huddle so she could see the map. She found the site of the Last-Ditch Attempt, along the same creek bed as the Fleming Cryncovich site, two miles south. "They're hiking back in there to look for any sign."

"Big footprints, I suppose?" Jimmy teased.

She only smiled. "We'll take anything we can get."

He gave her an encouraging pat on the back. Sing received it as such and stepped up into the motor home, settling in front of the computer.

"Okay, guys," she heard Jimmy saying, "here's the plan. Max and Janson, we'll start you guys up where Reed found that shred of jacket. You'll bait the area and then wait; you know the drill. Wiley and Thorne, I want you farther south, and take a look at the map here: Henderson and Shelton are in that area, so let's make sure we make contact with them and don't cross purposes; catch my drift?"

Jimmy's banter faded from Sing's awareness as she studied the computer screen, scrolling it south to reveal the terrain around the Last-Ditch Attempt. The map was clean—no activity.

"Hey, Sing?" Jimmy called. "We're short a GPS."

She called out the door, "Reed and Pete took it."

Reed and Pete were armed and cautious, working their way into the forest along a game trail that only the deer and elk used. There were no human trails here, no hikers, no trailside latrines, just thick, leafy forest and sun-starved undergrowth that swished and crackled despite their best efforts to keep quiet.

Pete led the way, setting his own pace, thinking, watching, moving stealthily, like an animal.

Reed's watch told him it was time to call in. He put a small handheld radio to his jaw and whispered, "Sing, we're half-way in."

Her voice came back, "Roger that. Jimmy's guys are moving in. Thorne and Kane are taking the south flank. They know where you'll be."

Leah sat on her haunches amid the Rocky Mountain Maples and wild roses, eyes half open as if she cared little about anything beyond her immediate, sweet little world, moaning and humming a song of pleasure.

Immediately behind her, Rachel hummed and grunted, busily, meticulously running her fingers through Leah's hair, making Sasquatch improvements in the grooming Beck had performed just the day before.

Immediately behind Rachel, Beck guided her brush carefully, maintaining the beauty of Rachel's full-body coiffure and humming quietly, constantly gauging how her behavior was being received and passed on.

The arrangement had fallen together spontaneously, like the revival of a forgotten routine. Rachel, as if desiring reconciliation, offered to groom Leah. Leah, having been groomed by the lowest member of the group, now seemed to find grooming from a slightly higher member acceptable, and allowed it. Beck, seeing a chance for just one more measure of acceptance—and possible influence—joined the party, and so it happened. She wasn't humming out of joy or pleasure, but to keep things calm and to keep appeasement flowing. This was a whole new social development, as precarious as a cease-fire between two mortal enemies, and she feared one wrong move could break the spell.

Either that, or one jealous little Sasquatch, obsessed with an ape's version of sibling rivalry. As Beck brushed, she kept a watchful eye on Reuben, fully expecting him to do *something*; she didn't know what. Right now he was sitting at a distance, his shoulder against a tree, contemplating his fingernails—a behavior he may have learned from his mother in a similar situation. Beck couldn't be sure just what it meant. He might be pouting or trying to act indifferent. Then again, he could be acting indifferent while plotting a vicious and wicked act. He was a wild card in this game.

He looked up, met Beck's eyes, and held the gaze—in this context, a challenge.

Leah gave a quiet, corrective grunt, and he looked down at his fingernails again.

Okay, Beck thought. *I just have to keep his momma on my side.*

As for Jacob, Beck didn't expect him to warm to her. He was a protector and provider, but every bit a beast, a cold and savage ruler. Even the gentle side she may have seen when Leah

groomed him seemed a thin facade in light of the beating he gave
Rachel and the brutal bite marks on his two women. The only
reason Beck was a part of this grooming chain was because he
wasn't around to render an opinion about it. If and when he ever
showed up—

Suddenly the bushes quaked. Jacob was returning. Beck
bolted away from the two females and hobbled to her spot in the
pine grove, pocketing the hairbrush and plopping down, trying to
appear passive.

Reuben was on his feet instantly, like a dog whose master had
returned.

The two females rose at the same time, looked into the forest, and then flopped down to their hands and knees in formal
greeting.

Beck got on her hands and knees as well, not wanting to challenge the patience of the king who now emerged through the
trees, light and shadow, light and shadow blinking on his face and
chest as he walked. He was clutching something against his stomach with his hands and arms.

Beck knew right away that he'd found more fruit, which
brought a volley of questions to mind: Was it a farm, an orchard,
or another baiting site? Were there humans around? Lastly, *Will
I get any to eat?*

Jacob came to a small gap in the trees, sank to his knees, and
let the fruit tumble to the ground. The selection was suspiciously
familiar: apples, pears, and bananas.

Another baiting site, Beck thought.

Reed knelt in the sand, staring, at a loss for words except to say,
"I don't know what to feel."

Pete was beside him, studying the huge footprints and needing a little time to become a believer again. "I've had my head turned around so many times it's about to come unscrewed." The similarity to recent horrors struck him. "Sorry."

"It's him, isn't it?"

Pete studied the tracks where they approached and then returned in a beeline across the creek bed. "It's him. Old alpha male, Mr. Scarfoot. He's still out there, like it or not."

"So Fleming's footprints weren't a hoax after all."

Pete didn't answer that but stood, scanning the area. "He took the bait, every piece of it."

Reed searched carefully around the perimeter of the raked ground. "*Every* piece?"

Beck held back, waiting to see what the rules might be this time around. Surprisingly, Leah and Rachel approached the fruit *almost* together, Leah first, but Rachel only a few steps behind. While Jacob sat back and watched without comment, Leah took an apple and allowed Rachel to take one after her. She didn't seem to mind Rachel sharing in the fruit as long as Leah chose first.

Reuben sidled up to his mother in his usual way and helped himself.

My turn? Beck wondered.

She waited, watching Jacob. He did not look at her, which could have meant a lingering hatred, prideful rejection, or total indifference. She tried to read his body language for any clues as to which it was, but she couldn't be sure.

She waited for Rachel to invite her, and after Rachel had downed two apples with the group's indulgence, she looked at Beck and pig grunted a call to supper.

Beck approached slowly, braced for some kind of reaction.

Jacob eyed her, his brow sinking slightly over his eyes, sending a warning, but just a warning.

She dropped her eyes and bowed slightly, trying to look small and submissive.

He glanced at the ground, scooped up a lump of his own dung, and popped it into his mouth, enjoying a fruit salad the second time around.

Beck came up behind Rachel, who moved over to give her room. Beck spotted a pear and leaned in to pick it up—

There was something lying next to it, and it was not a piece of fruit.

Reed found a crumpled shred of white paper snagged in a stunted pine. He carefully worked it loose. It had been chewed and was slimy with saliva, but he peeled the folds open enough to read what was left of his own writing: the last line of some instructions about batteries, the words "I love you," and his name. "I had this wrapped around the GPS with a rubber band."

Pete combed the surrounding ground with his eyes. "Well, obviously, it wasn't Beck who picked it up." He observed the chewed condition of the note. "Doesn't look good for the GPS, does it?"

Beck knew right away what it was. Reed, always the gadget nut, had shown her one in a sporting goods store. She'd managed to talk him out of buying it, but of course that reprieve only lasted a month before he brought home two. After they spent some quality time together learning how the gadgets worked, he put his in his car and she put hers back in its box.

But that was then. She felt no cynicism now, not the slightest tendency to brush it off as a "guy thing." That hand-sized device of yellow plastic with the LCD screen was nothing less than life itself. It spoke—no, it *yelled*—of Reed! This was so typical of him; he would have thought of this!

He's reaching for me! He hasn't given up!

Her hand trembled as she reached for it, reached for *him*—

Leah picked it up and sniffed it.

"Oh!" Beck stifled the squeal of alarm as soon as it escaped, her hand over her mouth. Leah shot a testy glance. Beck lowered her eyes—*Careful, careful, don't challenge her!* Now Jacob was watching, his piercing eyes focused on every detail, looking for trouble.

Beck tried to show interest in an apple, her hands shaking.

Leah went back to sniffing the GPS. She stuck out her tongue and tasted it.

Beck bit into the apple, trying not to look alarmed or interested, just letting her eyes pass over Leah without really looking. *Oh, please, Leah, please don't eat it!*

Reed and Pete stepped carefully, walking a square pattern around the baiting site, ten paces to a side, then twelve, then fourteen, probing and combing through the river grass, the flood-bent willows, and the knee-high pines, needing to know: Was it here? Did the beast pick it up and drop it? Eat it? Chew it and spit it out?

They needed to know.

The GPS fell to the ground, and Leah picked up a pear instead.

Beck reached—

Rachel was curious and picked it up.

Beck jammed her tongue against the roof of her mouth, blocking a cry on its way out. Eye contact with Rachel was allowed. She tried it, her eyes imploring.

Rachel didn't notice; she was too fascinated with the strange object. She sniffed it, turned it over a few times, and then popped it into her mouth.

This time Beck took the risk and made a sound, extending her hand.

Snap! The plastic cracked between Rachel's teeth.

"Noo!" Beck took hold of Rachel's arm and got half her attention.

Rachel spit it out, flipping it off the end of her tongue.

Beck caught it before it hit the ground, hoping, praying it would still work. It was slimy now, slippery like a wet bar of soap, but she hung on, clutched it against her heart. The case was cracked, but maybe—*Oh dear God—maybe* the electronics were still intact. She looked for the on button as she wiped slime away from the keypad—

A hairy hand flashed over her shoulder and the GPS shot skyward.

With a shriek and without thinking, Beck took hold of Reuben's arm, reaching and grabbing with her free hand. His arm was impervious to her weight, like a thick tree branch, and as he stood he lifted her torso off the ground so that her feet were dragging. She groped for a foothold. He twisted, whipping her about. She hung on, fighting to wrest the device from his fist.

Words were impossible; she shrieked, she yelled, she growled, she hit him on his arm.

The females were on their feet, growling and barking, but not at each other. They were two mothers scolding their quarreling children.

Beck locked eyes with Reuben. *I won't give it up. No, not this time! This is my life!*

She got both hands on the GPS and pulled. It could have been embedded in concrete for all the good it did.

Her eyes were closed in a grimace when the blow came, a stunning haymaker across her face. She no longer felt the GPS in her hands; she no longer felt her hands. She went numb and oblivious, the world spinning before her eyes in a blur of sky, trees, grass, light, dark—

She slammed into the ground but felt no pain, only nausea, as the earth reeled beneath her and her vision wandered, then went black. As if in a dream, she heard Rachel barking and protesting while Leah growled and snarled, but they sounded so far away, so very far away . . .

Reed and Pete had walked and combed a square of fifty paces, an area that now included the creek bed and roughly 150 feet of creek bank and adjacent forest. Now they stood at the edge of the creek bed, the dry river rocks under their feet, and reached a consensus.

"It's gone," said Reed.

Pete removed his hat, wiped his brow with his shirtsleeve, and responded, "It'll make one heck of a scat pile."

Reed felt so numb, so empty. He'd been hoping for so long, and had that certain *feeling* so deeply, that he now hung in emotional space with nothing under him and nowhere to go. He couldn't believe Beck was dead, but he'd expended his last hope that she was alive. For several minutes, he and Pete stood silently on the barren river rocks, waiting for the next course of action— not just in their search but in life itself—to come to mind while no water flowed past, no squirrels chattered in the trees, and no birds took an interest in the place.

Pete finally suggested, "We can probably track it."

Reed didn't answer for a moment, then asked, "Do you think those tracks at the Cryncovich site could've been a few days older?"

"Could've been, but I doubt it."

"So Beck could have been alive then, but then she was killed soon after. Or maybe the Bigfoot tracks were real, but Beck's were faked."

"I don't think it much matters. I just remember what Sheriff Mills said before he was killed: 'God help me, that thing's walking.'"

Several seconds passed before Reed replied, "Sort of says it all, doesn't it?"

"I would say so, yeah."

Now, as Reed felt weak and his knees feeble, he didn't fight it. He sat down on an old gray log. Pete joined him. As the forest went on living, not mindful of them, they sat motionless, staring at nothing in particular, their eyes landing on those eighteen-inch tracks just once in a while.

"I suppose we ought to track it," Reed said at last.

"It's your call. If you're finished with all this, so am I."

Reed took another minute to fish around in the feelings he didn't seem to have anymore and concluded, "I guess I'm finished."

Pete rose from the log and offered Reed his hand. "Come on. Let's get you home."

Pow!

The rifle shot echoed upon itself, stretching out into a clattering roar that rippled through the hills.

Pow! There it was again.

Beck awoke as if from sleep, head throbbing, mind dopey, the world crazily sideways. Through the swaying, blurring, sideways blades of grass, she saw the Sasquatches huffing and stirring, alarmed by something. That was nothing new. They were always alarmed about something. Beck guessed they were going to run again.

Yeah, they were going to run. Rachel hovered over her, panting and grunting, taking hold of her arm, yanking, trying to rouse her.

She thought she might have heard something.

Pete borrowed the radio from Reed and called in. "Sing? We heard some shots."

Sing came back, "Where have you been?"

"What do you hear from the hunters?"

"Stand by. There's so much chatter I can't make it out."

Pete waited, exchanging a concerned look with Reed.

Sing returned. "Better get over there. They're close to the creek bed, bearing 175, about half a mile."

"They're south of us," said Reed.

"What've they shot?" Pete asked Sing.

"Jimmy doesn't know. Whoever did the shooting doesn't have a radio."

"Okay, we're heading over there." Pete handed back the radio. "Lordy! If they bagged that thing . . . !"

Beck saw the ground fall away, then start moving beneath her. She watched the grass and the Rocky Mountain Maple whisk by, then the trunks of trees and more trunks of trees and patches of light and shadow on the plant-cluttered ground, but all the while, search as she would, she saw nothing made of yellow plastic, kind of cracked, kind of slimy, maybe broken.

Reed and Pete rounded a bend in the creek bed and heard the voices of two hunters uphill in the trees, laughing and talking it up, all caution and stealth thrown to the wind. One of the voices was Jimmy's.

"Doesn't sound like they shot anything unexpected," Pete muttered.

The knowledge brought Reed no joy, but on the other hand, he didn't care much anymore.

They climbed into the forest, came over a rise, and found Kane down in a hollow, looking like a wild-eyed, white-haired mountain man as he knelt by the biggest black bear either of them had ever seen. He was holding up the head by the scruff of the neck and striking a pose while Jimmy Clark, in an unusually chipper mood, snapped his picture. When Wiley saw them he whooped long and loud. "Can you believe this?"

Another voice came from higher up the hill. "You get him, Wiley?"

"I got him!"

A vague, camouflaged shape wearing a matching cap wove its way downward through the spindly trunks. Only when it came close did they recognize Steve Thorne, all marine, looking ready for jungle combat. His teeth stood out brightly against the green and brown greasepaint he wore on his face, which put them off balance. They'd never seen him grin before. "Now, that's a record breaker, my friend!"

"That it is," said Jimmy, snapping another picture.

Kane probed the thick black fur until he found a bloody spot on the flank. "Perfect heart-and-lung shot! He dropped like a rock!"

Jimmy spoke into his earpiece. "Okay, everybody. We have a confirmed kill. Wiley Kane gets the trophy. Good work, and many thanks to all of you!" He laughed at the chatter coming back through the earpiece and relayed it, "Everybody says congratulations." He spoke to the earpiece, "Sam and Max, you're closest. I'd like to get you over here to help pack it out. Yeah, it's a monster."

"Gonna dress him out?" Pete asked.

Jimmy grinned up at them, jubilant. "Yeah, he's too big to take out whole."

Pete set down his rifle and backpack, then spoke softly to Reed, "They're gonna find out they shot a bear for nothing." Reed answered, "I'd better stay here."

Pete nodded and stepped down into the hollow.

Jimmy extended a hand, and Pete grasped it. "You were right," Jimmy said. "It was moving south. Sorry to get the jump on you, but hey, Wiley saw it first."

Kane just grinned.

Pete gave Kane a courteous smile. "For a minute I thought you may have shot something else."

Wiley knew what Pete was talking about. "Not today."

Pete took hold of the feet, studied the pads carefully, then looked up at Reed with a discreet wag of his head.

Jimmy saw it. "This is your culprit, Pete. I'll bank on it."

Pete kept his voice down. "I think the culprit's gotten clean away thanks to all your noise." He forced a smile Kane's direction again. "But congrats on your bear."

Jimmy took out his hunting knife. "You're welcome to watch."

Reed wasn't the least bit interested and found a small log a comfortable distance away. Pete circled around to stand by Kane and Thorne as they watched Jimmy open up the bear's abdomen with quick sawing motions of the knife. In just a few minutes, with a few quick cuts and a yank, the stomach rolled out on the ground. It was bulging. Jimmy sliced it open with one clean pass of the blade and it blossomed like a flower, the contents sending up a stench that made Kane back away.

Jimmy probed through the contents with the tip of his knife. "Lots of berries." He snagged some aluminum foil and food wrapping with familiar golden arches. "Robbed a garbage can somewhere." Under the mass of berry pulp, seeds, and garbage, something caught on his knife. He pulled it up, letting the other contents fall aside. He lifted his gaze to Pete's.

Pete reached down and, with deft fingers, worked the piece of leather loose and spread it out. It was brown, with a row of fringe. It was unmistakable.

Deputy Saunders's crew had not given up hope even though Dave never had much to begin with. They combed the woods, four people working four quadrants, weaving back and forth according to compass headings, numbers of paces, and red ribbon markers, metal detectors sweeping the ground.

The heavy equipment operator's detector let out a squeal that made him jump—he'd never heard his metal detector actually find something metal.

The sound was so loud and the man was so close that even Dave heard it. He ran to the spot even as the man dug hurriedly with his shovel.

Clink! His shovel hit something.

He probed farther, scraped, pried, dug some more, and finally wedged up—

An old ax head.

He got to keep it. The search continued.

Sing called Cap to let him know the hunt was over. The news was such a foregone conclusion that it didn't shock or surprise him. It only strengthened his resolve.

"Well, it may be over for Jimmy and his crew, but not for us," he said. "Get over here as soon as you can."

Sing said good-bye, closed her cell phone, and stood by her motor home, watching the final exodus.

Jimmy Clark secured the last bungee cord over his gear in the back of his Idaho Department of Fish and Game King Cab pickup, gave Sing a good-bye tip of his cap, and climbed inside. The four rangers from the forest service were already in their pale green vehicle, the engine running. When Jimmy started out, they followed, easing down the road through the hamlet of Whitetail until their taillights vanished around a far bend in the road and all was quiet.

Wiley Kane had taken great care in rolling and wrapping up his bearskin, setting it securely in the back of his old pickup so that only the bear's snout showed from under the canvas. He was whistling happily as Sing approached him.

"I want to thank you for your help, young lady," he said.

"I'm glad for you," she replied.

"Thanks. But I am sorry. All in all, this is not a happy day for you and your friends."

"Thank you."

"What's, uh, what's Officer Shelton going to do now?" he asked.

Sing looked toward the forest where Reed had gone walking alone. "He'll go on living."

"You figure he's convinced now? I mean, he's not going to be out there searching for his wife anymore, or hunting for Bigfoot?"

"No one could ever know that."

Kane smiled and offered his hand. "It's been nice meeting you."

She shook his hand. "May I ask for one small thing?"

"Yes, ma'am."

"May I have just a portion of your bear meat?" He looked quizzical, so she explained, "It would be for a remembrance, like flowers."

"Got twenty dollars?"

Pete stepped out of the motor home, feeling weighted down, dispirited, and twenty years older. He'd lain down to rest but hadn't slept. He wondered where Reed was, and how he was—alive, hopefully, which was the most one could expect for now. He wasn't sure where Sing might be. Most of the vehicles that had been parked along the road were gone, and Whitetail was nearly its old, mostly deserted self.

Jimmy had left without saying a so-long. Pete leaned against the motor home and took a moment to regret the less-than-friendly departure. He and Jimmy had had a discussion, then a disagreement, and then a pretty good shouting match over that piece of Beck's jacket in the bear's stomach. To Jimmy, it settled every doubt and answered every question. To Pete—and Reed—it was just another piece of garbage the bear had found, attractive because of the bloodstain and gulped down after Beck was no longer anywhere near it. Of course, bringing in the alpha male's footprints at the second baiting site did not serve well in resolving things but only made them worse.

Pete sighed, deeply impressed with how badly things could go sometimes, no matter what he did.

Smoke rose from a small campsite back in the trees. He headed that direction and found Sing seated on a log near a fire pit. She was wrapped in a warm Indian blanket, tending a fire in which a piece of bear meat was burning and sizzling, sending up smoke.

Max Johnson was there, carrying on a one-sided conversation. "So really, there's not a lot of point in prolonging this. I think you and Reed and Pete just need to settle this in your hearts and get on with your lives." He spotted Pete as he approached. "Oh, hi, Pete! How're you doing?"

"Beck Shelton is dead," he answered, matter-of-factly, as he stepped into the circle of logs placed around the fire. "How should I be doing?"

"I'm so sorry. But it's for the best, isn't it—that you finally know? It's closure. That's what you've been needing for days, and now . . ."

"Max." Pete looked at Sing, who said nothing, only watched the flames. "I think this is supposed to be a private moment."

Max looked at Sing as if really seeing her for the first time. He nodded and, without another word, left them.

Pete found a few more chunks of firewood and carefully placed them on the fire, keeping the flames hot around the burning meat. He sat on the log beside her, as close as a good friend.

Before long, alive, safe, and silent, Reed returned from the woods. Pete and Sing greeted him with their eyes, but there were no words. Reed observed the fire and the burning meat, then picked up two more pieces of firewood and added them to the fire. He sat on the other side of Sing, and all three watched the flames together.

When the meat was almost gone, Sing closed her eyes, releasing a trickle of tears, and began a plaintive lament from the old traditions, rocking gently as the flames crackled. First she sang in low, mournful tones without words, expressing a sorrow that only the soul could know. Then sorrow gave way to pain and the song rose in volume and pitch, the anguish lofting like the smoke from the fire toward the mountains where a friend had gone, never to return.

Tears came to Reed's eyes, blurring the flames, as the song wrapped itself around his heart, carrying his sorrow as if he were singing it himself. The song spoke for him. *This is me, who I am and where I am right now.*

Pete removed his hat and looked toward the mountains, not thinking much, just wondering, feeling the same old *why* that always came at times such as this. The song spoke for the wondering too, and fit this place so well. Maybe the mountains had taught it to her.

The song had no ending of its own. When Sing was finished, when she had delivered in full her complaint to the mountains and the God who made them, when she had cried out her last farewell, the song came to a quiet rest, closing like a door on the past. Sing was weary and drained, but just a little closer to peace.

The bear meat was consumed by the flames. She opened her eyes and wiped the tears away.

"Thank you," said Reed.

"Where'd you learn that?" Pete asked.

"My grandfather sang it when my grandmother died," she said softly. "I don't remember all the words—but I remember the feelings."

Beck flopped to the ground once again, delivered there by her exhausted, frightened, adoptive mother in the same old way. The flight through the tangled forest was a perfect copy of the last flight through the tangled forest. Jacob led the group relentlessly, with Leah and Reuben following behind and Rachel last in line carrying Beck. Halfway through the long, frantic run, Beck recovered her senses and climbed around to Rachel's back to ride conventionally, so even that was the same. As always, Beck had no idea where they were or where they were going, only that it was *away* from rescue, *away* from Reed and all she held dear.

She rolled onto her face in the undergrowth with her arms covering her head, trying to block out the sounds, sights, and smells of a wilderness obsessed with no better cause than tormenting her. It was so unfair! She couldn't get away from her overly possessive "mother" even when she wasn't welcome; she couldn't leave a cell phone number in the dirt; she couldn't let her grieving husband know she was still alive when he was inches away from her; and now—*Of course! Pardon me for even assuming that I could!*—she absolutely could not make use of a GPS she was certain Reed had left for her to find.

It was all so un—

"N-no!" Beck opened her eyes and forbade that thought to play through her mind. *No more.* She'd spent enough time and energy on it and gotten nothing but more unfairness for her trouble.

And what was she doing, lying in the weeds and bushes, feeling sorry for herself again? She'd done that before and, judging from how things were going, could easily be doing it the next day, or the next year, or even for the next twenty years, in the same weeds in the same woods at the whim and mercy of the same smelly, dung-eating, barf-chewing, power-struggling, upright-walking, run-from-everything pack of apes.

She sat up. Rachel lay next to her, her once-lovely coat reverting back to a walking dust mop for every type of forest debris. Jacob was perched on a mound with his back against a rotting stump, keeping watch like a lifeguard, looking tired and irritable. Only Leah's left knee and stomach were visible above the undergrowth, her diaphragm laboring as she tried to catch her breath. Reuben sat beyond Leah, preoccupied with his toes.

So how about it, Beck? Want some more? Ready for another lap around the merry-go-round?

There was nothing like a dumb question to make things clear. *No more for me, thanks.*

But what could she do?

It would help to have some idea where she was. They may have headed north again, judging by the location of the sun, but as always, nothing looked familiar.

She once heard Reed say that going downhill was always a good idea: every hill eventually drained into a stream, every stream eventually flowed into a river, and every river eventually crossed a road, wound through a town, or flowed by a settlement. It might work, except for . . .

When she tested her ankle, then looked at Rachel, who looked back at her with those watchful, motherly eyes, the outcome of such a plan became as predictable as night following day.

It made her want to kill Reuben—another plan with a predictable outcome that instantly ruled it out.

But she did give him a second look. She thought he'd been playing with his toes, but just now she thought she saw a glimmer of yellow.

Acting as lazy, uninterested, and detached as possible, she rose to her feet, stretched, faked a yawn, and double-checked.

He wasn't playing with his toes. He was playing with the GPS, lazily batting it back and forth between his feet.

FOURTEEN

The Lumberman Café was Cap's third stop in Three Rivers. The folks at the local filling station hadn't heard of a Dr. Adam Burkhardt; the lady at the Ace Hardware store knew him as an occasional customer but didn't know where he lived. Mr. Dinsley, owner/proprietor of the Lumberman, knew just enough.

"It's up the Skeel Gulch Road," he said, scribbling a map on a napkin. "You go up there about two miles. You go over a bridge—it's one of those little ones, you know, made of logs? It goes over the Skeel Creek up there. Then the road takes a left turn, runs along the creek . . ." He drew it as he said it. "And it's up in there somewhere."

Cap studied the map—three lines for the roads, a squiggle for the creek, and a little box for the bridge—and asked, "Uh, any sign out front, you know, house numbers or something?"

Dinsley shrugged. "Well, Burkhardt doesn't like to advertise.

But you oughta try Denny over at Ace Hardware and Lumber. He's done a few deliveries up there. Adam was building a big old shop a few years ago."

"Denny's on vacation."

"Oh, you've already been there!"

"Yeah. Claire told me."

"Oh, well, I haven't seen Adam for a week or so. Did you try calling him?"

"Lost his number."

"Oh. Well, since you're good friends, I guess he won't mind you dropping in. He is a private sort of person, isn't he?"

"He's that way."

Cap put the napkin in his shirt pocket, paid for his coffee and cinnamon roll, and went out to his car.

Down the street, in a pricey Mercedes that didn't fit in this town, four men with specific orders watched Cap's every move.

Beck sat quietly in the syringa and snowberry, invisibly tethered to Rachel, who appeared to be sleeping. She was watching Reuben with quick, careful glances, never a direct stare.

If she did nothing, Reuben would eventually destroy the GPS, probably chew it to smithereens. Even if he tired of it, all she had to do was show the slightest interest and it would become important to him again. If she tried to take it from him—well, she'd already tried that.

By now the sun and shadows told her the group was definitely heading north, and of course this was the wilderness; there were no boundaries here. The Canadian border wouldn't stop them. They could keep moving as far as there was forest, which meant she could wander in these woods forever, be given up for dead, and never be found.

But she had an idea. It wasn't a sure thing, but considering how the future looked if she did nothing, a failure wasn't going to set her back that much. She hated having to be the one to change things, but for all she knew, she was the only player left on her team. Any change, for better or worse, was going to be up to her.

She reached for the hairbrush in her back pocket. It had gotten her close to Leah once. If Beck could buy just a little more favor from Reuben's mother, then maybe . . .

She made sure Rachel was asleep, held the brush up in a wide gesture so Leah could see it, then ran it through her own hair a few times.

Leah sniffed and sat up straight. She was interested.

Beck set out before fear could catch up with her, quickly working her way through the brush toward Leah, head down, body language submissive, eyes lowered. For good measure, she added some quiet, conciliatory grunts and a little hum, a carefree, meandering sound.

Reuben saw her coming and immediately took a strong, protective interest in the GPS, clutching it close and eyeing her suspiciously. She ignored him, obvious about it, and held out the brush to Leah.

Leah grunted pleasantly. Beck met her eyes for a quick inquiry and found no fear or animosity there.

She began brushing, smoothing out the hair behind Leah's left ear. Leah leaned into it. Beck breathed easier. This just might work.

Then Rachel woke up.

Beck could understand the displaying, crying, and commotion. After all, Beck and her hairbrush were the only unique claim to power or pride that Rachel had, and though Beck was by no means joining up with Rachel's rival, how could Rachel understand that?

What to do? Commotion and disgruntlement she didn't need, but she had to have Leah's sympathy, and this was the only way she knew to get it. She kept brushing.

She hadn't considered how Jacob might feel about it. His eyes had narrowed as she approached Leah, but since Leah wasn't bothered but interested, Beck thought he wouldn't mind. When Reuben got upset, Jacob's hair began to bristle, but Beck wasn't about to challenge Reuben and hoped Jacob would see that. Then, when Beck started brushing Leah, he grunted a warning, but Beck felt it was only precautionary.

When Jacob came thundering down at her, roaring and threatening, she didn't think, hope, or feel anything, but leaped and rolled through the prickly undergrowth toward Rachel's protective arms. A gust of wind blew past her, generated by a deadly swat of his hand that barely missed. Falling into Rachel's enfolding arms was like running into a fortress, and fortunately, it worked.

Having returned Beck to her rightful place, Jacob backed off and sauntered back to his spot against the old stump, satisfied that he'd made his point—whatever it was.

Beck was shaking, very glad to let Rachel hold her and desperate to understand the rule she'd broken. Jacob had always made it clear that he was unhappy with Rachel's adoption of a human, but having punished her for such a dumb move, he seemed to be tolerating it. Apparently his tolerance ended when it came to the human making any further alliances with his females. Whether out of jealousy or feelings of threat, he wasn't going to allow it.

Beck set to work right away, brushing and grooming Rachel to be sure their relationship was intact. Rachel was forgiving, her same old doting self.

As for assuring support from Leah, that idea clearly wouldn't work.

Dave Saunders surprised himself. When the concentrated effort of his search team found only a rusty hunting knife with the handle rotted away, a cluster of spent rifle shells, a canteen, and a set of car keys, he didn't get discouraged, just more determined, even angry.

"Widen the search," he ordered. "Same quadrants, double the size."

The searchers had never met Beck Shelton, but they felt they knew her. They didn't grumble or question, but went right to it.

Sing turned her motor home into the parking lot of the Tall Pine Resort, eased into the same place she'd parked before, and shut down the engine. With her chin in her hand, she looked through the windshield at the tired old lodge with the patched-together add-ons, the rambling, up-and-down porch, and the big, blackened outdoor barbecue, and mused on how she and Cap first came here to get away from the struggles, the pain, the disappointment.

Yet all three had followed them here, more real and present than ever.

Less than a week ago, they thought they would learn to survive. They hoped they would hear from God.

She sighed. Maybe they had. It all seemed too much like life to be otherwise.

She shook off the sorrow and the weakness. As Cap said, it still wasn't over—and that was like life too. She straightened her spine and took a deep breath. *Eyes forward,* she told herself. She would join up with Cap in Three Rivers. Maybe the answers were there.

She set the parking brake and got out of the driver's seat, eager to empty their motel room, settle up with Arlen, and get rolling.

She noticed her computer was still on, listening for GPS signals that were no longer there. She'd forgotten to turn it off, maybe on purpose.

She left it on and went out the door.

"So you heading out?" came a voice from a few doors down the porch.

Thorne and Kane sat on a bench, kicked back and enjoying a beer.

Sing was surprised and knew it showed. "Aren't you?"

Kane took a swig from his bottle and wagged his head. "Got my bear in Arlen's cooler. It'll keep."

"Thought we'd stick around and do a little more hunting," said Thorne.

Then Max stuck his head out the door behind them. "Oh, you going now?"

Sing studied the three men only a moment and then replied, "Can't wait."

They seemed satisfied with that.

Reed and Pete pulled up behind the motor home in Pete's old truck. They had nothing new to say to each other and just a nod to give to the men on the porch. Someday they would talk about how badly things had gone, but they both needed time. With only a handshake, they parted company, Reed to his room to gather his things, Pete to the lobby to update Arlen and thank him for his help.

Room 105 was still in the pitiful, panicky mess Reed had left after Arlen got the call from Fleming Cryncovich. His uniform was draped over a chair where he'd left it. His computer printout regarding the logger's death and the photos of the mysterious unknown footprints in the Lost Creek cabin lay scattered on the bed. Leaning in the corner, carefully reassembled by Cap and Sing, was Beck's backpack. Looking at it, Reed remembered so clearly the moment she picked out the color. He remembered helping her get her arms through the straps as she wriggled into it at the bottom of the Cave Lake Trail.

He tossed his sheriff's deputy shoes off a chair—and stared at his gun, his radio, his handcuffs lying on the bedside stand. He snapped open the black leather case that held the handcuffs and drew them out. They were small enough to fit in the pocket of his flannel shirt, so he put them there, if only as a reminder. For Beck's sake, he would be strong and forever stand between innocent people and those who would take away their loved ones. He sat down, letting his eyes drift where they wanted, mostly toward the backpack, and letting his heart feel whatever it needed to feel. No words, no thoughts, no answers. Just feelings. Sing would be heading out to join up with Cap. Reed would catch up later, in uniform if the situation called for it. But this moment he wouldn't rush. It had waited for him patiently—the grief. He would give it its due.

With Rachel's indulgence, Beck stretched the limit of her invisible tether and reached a tiny crease in the terrain where a feeble stream trickled among rocks, aging logs, and moss-covered windfall. Crouching on all fours, one hand on a tuft of wild grass and the other on a stick that bridged the stream, Beck sipped with her lips just touching the surface so as not to stir up the black mud on the bottom.

Survive, survive, survive, she thought. *Drink to live. Live to hope. Hope for a miracle.*

The stick under her hand shifted, and she sat up before it gave way and she got a face full of mud.

It didn't give way. It didn't crack either. With nothing better to hold her attention, she closed her fist around it and lifted. It came off the ground in her hand, about the size and weight of a baseball bat. She wielded it just a moment, thinking of Reuben and imagining what a good club it would make, but of course, she was only venting her frustration.

She let the other end of the stick plop into the streambed but still held on to her end, just for the feel of it. Thinking she should return to the group before Rachel got nervous, she almost let it go but didn't. Instead, she lifted it again, felt its weight, gave it a few small swings. She tapped it against a rock. The stick hadn't rotted. Years of sun had turned it hard and gray.

The stick had stirred up the bottom of the stream. She reached in with just one finger and spooned up a sample of the mud. It was fine and greasy between her fingers, like black paint. She smeared it along the top of one finger. It coated the skin evenly, turning it an impressive, smudgy black.

An outlandish thought crossed her mind: Displaying carried a lot of weight in Sasquatch circles, didn't it? Stomping, hollering, threatening, throwing things, banging on things . . .

She studied the grass under her other hand, closed her fist around it, and yanked it up. There was plenty of it. As a matter of fact, there was plenty of other loose material around here, like leaves, twigs, and moss. Her shirt was loose fitting. It could hold a lot of this stuff.

No! She shook her head at herself, at God. *No! I'm not the one to do this!*

As if God Himself were saying it, the thought came to her, *Of course you are. Who else is there?*

She caught her reflection in the shallow water. There was only one face, one person looking back at her.

She smeared the black mud over another finger. Now two fingers were blackened—she *hated* getting dirty!

But it wouldn't be enough. If she was going to put on a show, it had to be a big one, something no Sasquatch—especially Reuben—had ever seen before or even knew to expect.

She dug for more mud and blackened her whole hand, grimacing with disgust. It felt awful. But it looked awful too, and awful was good. Awful might work.

She probed around the immediate area, looking for more ideas—and stalling a bit. That was when she found a real prize: a fresh pile of Sasquatch droppings, most likely Jacob's. The scent of that stuff would be quite alarming. If it was Jacob's, it might even be confusing. Confusion was good. The more the better.

She scrambled around the area on hands and knees, then on two hands and one and a half feet, gathering leaves, twigs, moss, and grass. The process gave her momentum, enough to forsake her hygienic world and move to the brink of the stream once again.

A thin barrier of disgust held her back for only a moment, and then she made a choice. With a dangerous, reckless resolve, she dug into the mud, brought up a sizable blob, and smeared her face.

Sing made her last trip from Room 104, carrying her backpack and a toiletry bag out to the motor home. She piled them into the rear bedroom along with the other camping gear and a well-read copy of Randy Thompson's book, the last vestiges of the vacation that never was. Arlen Peak had been a neighborly sort: he only charged for the first night, not the several days of searching.

She stepped into the motor home's overcrowded midsection where the bulk of her lab and crime scene reconstruction gear was stowed, hung, stuffed, and folded. The last thing to fold up and put away was the computer, still running.

She pressed the *Menu* key, arrowed down to the *Shut Down* option, clicked on it, and got a box with the final question, *What do you want your computer to do? Shut Down* was the highlighted option.

She hesitated, the little arrow poised over the *OK* button. With a sigh, and feeling just a little foolish, she closed that window and left the computer running.

The computer map of the mountains came on-screen again, with no activity indicated.

She would be having a last, parting consultation with Reed as soon as he was ready. Perhaps she would shut down the computer then.

Jacob was probing the old stump for grubs, breaking off chunks of red, rotten wood with his fingernails and removing the white larvae with flicks of his tongue.

Leah sat next to an elderberry bush, indulging in the leaves from a branch she'd pulled down.

Rachel was picking through the hair on any part of her body she could reach, removing seeds, twigs, and small leaves, sampling each find for flavor and edibility.

Reuben was discovering how to regurgitate into his hand, but he still wasn't sure what to do with the dripping contents. The intriguing yellow object was beside him on the ground, no longer an object of keen interest but a matter of territory nonetheless.

All four were aware of the female human's presence on the other side of a thicket, near the tiny stream. None could see her, but they could hear her rustling about, raking the ground, often splashing in the little bit of water there was. She'd puttered about before, feeding, drinking, grooming herself. They'd grown used to her ways.

But then came a strange silence that bothered them. She'd never behaved in quite this way before, standing still as if hiding, lurking like a predator, even stalking in the bushes.

Jacob flicked a grub into his mouth and watched the thicket, curious but not alarmed.

Rachel looked over her shoulder, mildly curious what her "child" was up to, and puzzled to see Jacob still eating grubs from the stump when she could detect his scent from her "child's" direction.

Leah shot a protective glance at Reuben, wary of danger.

Reuben was paying attention to nothing other than the green goo in his hand and wasn't expecting—

"*Aaaaaaiiiiiii!!!*"

They all jumped, even Jacob, as if a cannon had gone off in the midst of them, and then they stared, mouths gaping, as Beck exploded from the thicket, running lopsidedly on a weak ankle, shrieking like a cougar, brandishing a club, face, arms, and torso blackened with mud except for wide white areas around her eyes. She'd stuffed her shirt, sleeves and all, to the bursting point with leaves, twigs, and moss, expanding her outline. Grass shot out like bristling hair from her waist, her collar, her shirt cuffs, her pant legs. She'd even fashioned a headdress from her handkerchief and long spears of grass, creating a sunburst of grass and blowing reddish hair around her face.

Startling to hear, shocking to behold, she even smelled frightening, smeared with a liberal coat of dung that made her reek as if ejected from the bowels of the alpha male himself.

It was all or nothing. No turning back. No fear. No gentle, timid world. No mercy, no compassion, no propriety, no fairness. If this was how matters were settled out here, then this was how she would settle them. She ran headlong, her club raised, her eyes crazed, her mouth wide open in a permanent scream.

She closed in on Reuben, so focused and intense that he seemed to react in eerie slow motion—shyly jumping to his feet, gasping, and raising his arms in a singular moment that went on and on.

She would never get a second chance for that first blow, that first desperate grab for advantage. As she passed on his uphill side, she swung the club in a wide batter's arc and broke it in half against the back of his skull. He reeled, stumbled forward. Beck dug in, reversed direction, lunged at him, swatted him again on his head and shoulders with the half club still in her hand.

He ran for his mother, who was on her feet, screaming with shock and indignity.

The GPS, that precious GPS, lay on the ground, ripe for the picking. She pounced on it, got her hands around it. Precious yellow plastic, hope from home—

Reuben pounced on her and, with one powerful heave of his arms, threw her, head over heels, into the bushes. She floated, mashed the branches, tumbled into the tangle until the thick stalks near the ground bore her up. Her head was swimming, her world spinning, but she kicked, struggled, stayed alive. Still entangled and suspended, not knowing which way was up or whether her body was intact or what she could do next, she screamed, yelled, thrashed, and displayed, doing anything her body could do to show anger, defiance, and strength.

Rachel was coming her way, trying to save her. No. She couldn't let that happen. She had to stay in trouble. With a violent kick, a twist, and several strong yanks, she got out of the bushes and onto the clear ground.

Reuben was hunting for the GPS. She saw it the same time he did, in the grass, still intact.

She crawled, then got to her feet. *No fear. Show him who's boss. Bluff if you have to!*

She leaped, screamed, beat on her bulky, grass-and-moss-stuffed chest, waved her arms, slapped the ground. Her hand found a rock and she threw it, hitting him in the hip. He roared in pain.

Her entire field of vision suddenly filled with gray.

Leah.

"Tell you what," said Arlen, his voice gentle, like that of a friend. "Those trophies are probably the last I'll ever see. I would say you've paid enough. The room's on me."

Reed smiled, admiring the four new plaster casts in Arlen's Bigfoot display case. He could understand what a treasure they must be to a man with Arlen's perspective. "I do appreciate it," Reed said. He examined the grainy photo of the big female striding along a sandbar. "Think they'll stick around after all this?"

Arlen's smile slipped. "Maybe not. They've never been hunted before. If I were them, I'd probably move on."

"I hope you're right. I might be the interim sheriff, but I can't keep the trails closed forever, especially for a reason nobody's going to believe." Reed turned to go.

"Reed?"

"Yeah?"

"If I may speak on their behalf?" Arlen looked down at the casts for a moment, drumming the countertop with his fingers. "I can't explain what we found up there, other than that your wife was with them and she was alive. I'd like to think it was the bear that killed her."

Reed would never believe that, but there would be no point in bickering. "See you later, Arlen."

He quietly closed the front door behind him, leaving a sad old man at the counter.

Leah snarled, displaying, baring her teeth, arms upraised as if to strike—and then she looked up.

A savage roar came from over Beck's shoulder. Beck hugged the ground as the truck-sized mass of red fur sailed over her and plowed into Leah, knocking her backward. Leah recovered in only two steps, then shoved, slapped, and punched as Rachel returned blow for blow. They faced off, mirroring each other, circling, hair bristling, backs arched, fingers spread like talons, hissing and foaming through their teeth.

With Leah occupied, Beck half-crawled and limped forward, searching for that glint of yellow.

It was in Reuben's hands. He was slinking away with it.

Beck got to her feet, yelling, displaying, then loping toward him. She leaped with her good leg, then kicked him in the side. It was like kicking a wall. He flinched a little but didn't even lose his balance. She landed on the ground, got up again, faced him—

The slap sent her spinning. Her headdress disintegrated, the blades of grass falling like winnowed straw. The world was a blur until her hair blinded her. She hit the ground, her nose dripping, her face burning.

With one eye above the grass, she saw Rachel holding her own, not backing down, getting slapped, slapping back, exchanging threats, and circling. Leah showed no weakness. As for Jacob, he sat next to his stump, surprisingly aloof, a spectator.

Beck pushed against the ground, her body aching, nauseous. The ground reeled under her. Drops of blood glistened on the grass. She got to her feet, bent over to clear the dizziness, and wiped her face with her hands, streaking the mud, smearing the blood. She wiped her hands on her shirt and left red streaks. She straightened slowly—

Reuben's foot caught her in the back and she went down like a limp toy, tumbling in the brush, arms flailing, until a tree caught her in the side.

Half conscious, she thought she would never breathe again.

Reed poked his head in the door of the motor home. "Everything okay?"

Sing sat at the computer, scrolling the map up and down, back and forth, retracing old possibilities, exploring new ones. The GPS system was its cold and cruel self; it had nothing to say. "It's hard to leave," she said.

Reed looked back at the inn, at the bench on the porch, the front doors, the door to Room 105. There wasn't a pleasant memory anywhere, only sorrow and finality. "We have to."

She nodded but didn't turn the computer off. She only closed the lid, then went forward to the driver's station and pulled out a map. "So what's the best way to get to Three Rivers from here?"

Reuben stood a few yards up the hill, snuffing at her, acting superior and victorious, clutching the GPS in his hands, his snarl warning her to stay away, to stay on the ground, to remain subservient.

Beck rolled a painful quarter turn away from the tree, drew her first full breath, and pulled her knees up under her.

The two females faced off, daring each other to make a move. It wasn't so much a fight as a game, a war of wills.

Beck straightened, got one foot planted, rose on one leg—

And fell again, hurting in every limb, every fiber. Reuben must have opened her somewhere; she was leaving a trail of blood on the ground.

He displayed again, snarling, stomping, coming closer. She knew he would hit her, and this time it would probably kill her.

She could barely keep the females in focus. They weren't looking her way but glaring at each other.

If only she had won some favor. If only she was accepted.

She cried out, the best series of alarm screams she could muster, and extended her hand, crimson with her own blood, their way.

Rachel, facing Beck, saw her first. With a loud howl, she bolted Beck's direction.

Leah opposed her—

Rachel could have been fighting the bear again. With ferocity Beck had seen only once before, Rachel forearmed Leah across the throat, knocking her back several steps, turning her. Leah leaned into a step, about to lunge, when her eyes followed Beck's scream and Beck caught her gaze. Leah hesitated. She stretched her neck for a better view, concern clouding her face.

Beck screamed again, her hand extended.

Time stood still.

Leah was wide open. Rachel hammered her with a right to the chest, then a left, pushing, pummeling. Leah covered her head, struck back once, then backpedaled, still staring at Beck.

Beck cried out again, hand extended. Leah moaned, pain filling her eyes.

Rachel pressed her attack, snarling, hurling another double-blow.

Leah ducked, arms over her head, as Rachel delivered a steady and violent drumming. Then, at long last, her will broken, Leah turned tail and ran into the shelter of some trees.

Reuben's bravado drained in an instant. He whimpered, looking at Beck, then up the hill toward his mother.

Finish it!

Beck noticed she was on her feet. It hurt like crazy, but she was standing. A good-sized stick lay only two steps away. She took those steps, grabbed up the stick, raised it high, and climbed the hill, closing in on Reuben one last time. He was looking for his mother when Beck brought the stick down on his shoulders, raised it, brought it down again. Again! Again!

He flinched, ducked, put his arms over his head, then started up the hill, retreating, ducking, whimpering.

Again!

The GPS bounced onto the ground and came to rest in the shards of a rotting log.

Reuben ran, disappearing into the same trees that concealed his mother.

Beck teetered but remained standing, her fist still clenched around the stick, not sure it was over. Her upper lip and chin felt cold and she tasted blood in her mouth. She wiped her sleeve across her mouth and it came away red.

Rachel was coming to save her.

No, please, not yet. Where's that GPS?

It was close enough to grab just before Rachel enfolded her in those huge arms. Rachel settled to the ground right there, cradling her, licking the blood and mud from Beck's face with her big tongue, poking with grave concern at the weird stuffing inside Beck's shirt, yanking and tasting the grass that protruded from Beck's sleeves.

Beck held that GPS close, trying to find the on switch in between swipes from Rachel's tongue. *Lick!* She found it. *Lick!* She pressed it. *Lick! Lick!* Nothing happened.

She almost felt a wave of despair, but another thought held it off: *Check the batteries.*

The licking had stopped. Beck tried to open the back of the GPS, but her fingers were slick with mud and blood, and now the GPS was smeared with it. She pulled her handkerchief from around her head and wiped her hands, then the GPS.

Rachel was poking her, humming with concern. Beck nestled in close to let her know she was all right and, using her fingernail, wedged the battery compartment open.

The batteries were there, the ends blocked with a piece of paper. Clever! A safeguard, no doubt, to make sure only a human could turn it on. Beck pulled the paper out, closed the cover, and pressed the on button again.

A little light came on. The LCD screen came to life.

Reed spoke into his handheld radio as he sat in his SUV just outside the Tall Pine. "Okay, 450 point 45. Hello?"

Sing came back from inside the motor home: "Gotcha loud and clear."

"All buttoned up?"

"Three Rivers, here we come. Oh. Sorry. Got one more thing." Sing set her radio in its rack on the dashboard and hurried back to secure the bedroom door. On her way, she remembered one more thing: the computer. Okay. It was time to turn it off.

She raised the lid and the screen came to life, the same old map of the surrounding forest with nothing showing but—

Something new caught her eye as her finger poised above the keyboard.

Was that . . . ?

No. It had to be dust on the screen, a bad pixel, the mouse pointer . . .

It was blinking.

She leaned in to make sure.

Yes, it was blinking.

She rolled out the computer chair and sat in it, digging her glasses from her shirt pocket.

The radio on the dash squawked, "Sing? Any problems?"

She put on her glasses and leaned close.

The blinking blip was labeled with a number 6.

"Reed . . ."

The radio squawked again. "Hello? Sing? You copy?"

"Reed . . . !"

Number 6. The GPS they'd left at the baiting site.

The Last-Ditch Attempt.

"Reed!" Sing bolted from her chair, ran to the dashboard, grabbed up the radio. "REEEEED!"

FIFTEEN

Cap drove up the Skeel Gulch Road, past quaint homesteads and run-down barns, freshly mowed hay fields, and a huge pond where a moose grazed on water cabbage. He found the bridge just as Mr. Dinsley had described it, a squatty rectangle of logs and rough-hewn planks with red reflectors tacked to each end. After the road took a left turn, Dinsley's directions ran out, and Cap was left to do the best he could with the man's broad-sweeping description, "It's up in there somewhere."

Cap drove two miles up the road, looking for anything that might be home to a scientist detached from reality. When he noticed recent tire tracks turning onto the road from a gravel driveway, he was desperate enough to check it out.

The driveway wound back through the trees for several hundred feet, then ended abruptly at a small, metal-roofed cabin. The parking lot was empty, so Cap felt safe pulling to a stop and climbing out for a look-see.

Just a few paces up from the parking lot, Cap could see past the cabin and into the trees beyond. The owner had added an outbuilding, a metal structure the size of an aircraft hangar.

Dinsley said Burkhardt had built a shop a few years ago. Cap may have come to the right place.

In an instant, Reed's entire universe had compressed to the size of a tiny blip on a computer screen. The blip was moving north, pulling the moving map downward across the screen pixel by pixel, blinking as it went, a little number 6 at its side. Reed didn't dare believe what it could mean; his nerves wouldn't be able to take it. "You double-checked?"

Sing, at the computer, was wiping tears from her eyes. "I cycled through all the GPS codes and every unit is accounted for, including this one: 1 through 5 are in their cases right here under the bench. Number 6 is out, and it's broadcasting—" Her voice tightened into a weeping squeak. She took a deep breath to clear it. "I tested it before you guys left it at the baiting site. This is it; this is the one!"

Pete, at Reed's side, couldn't have looked more intense if he'd been staring down a cougar. "You sure you wrapped those batteries?"

Reed was trying not to hope too soon. The whiplike reversal would snap his mind for sure. "I made double sure. Only an intelligent human being would have pulled that paper out of there and reset the batteries. This isn't an accident."

"What if it's a hiker who found it?" Sing ventured.

"The trails are closed," said Reed.

Pete pointed. "It's not on a trail. And look how fast it's moving. That's no hiker."

"ATV?" Reed suggested.

"Not in there. It's nothing but steep slopes, heavy forest, and no roads." He watched it a moment. "But something with eighteen-inch feet could move that fast."

Reed nodded, remembering that moment below the waterfall on the trail to Abney. "It's still carrying her."

Pete cautioned, "We don't know for sure."

"Right." Reed reined himself in. "What about radio contact?"

Sing replied, "I've tried to raise whoever it is, but the unit radio doesn't seem to be working. We've got GPS locating, but that's it."

There was a rap on the doorpost and Max Johnson stuck his head in. "Hey, we're all here!"

Reed went to the door. Max, Steve Thorne, Sam Marlowe, and Wiley Kane stood there, a firm set in their faces that almost overruled Reed's doubt. He still needed to be sure. "I need to know you guys are with me."

"I'm in," said Max. "Always have been. I want to finish this, Reed, and finish it right."

Reed wasn't satisfied yet. "Steve?"

"I don't care what's up there, and I'm not going to bicker about it," Thorne replied. "Whatever it is, if it comes between us and your wife, I'm prepared to take it out."

"Sam?"

Sam seemed so young, but the grim look in his eyes came from the heart of a man. "I know I'm the rookie here, but I'll give you my best and that's a promise."

Reed still couldn't address Kane by his first name. "Kane? Do you think I killed my wife and made up a story to cover it up?"

Kane sniffed a chuckle and wagged his head shamefully. "I'll wash my mouth out if that's what you want."

"I might."

"Fair enough." Kane grinned. "I just got me a record-breaking bear. Getting a big old Sasquatch, now, wouldn't that be something?"

Reed asked Thorne, "Think you can keep him in line?"

Thorne nodded.

"All right, then."

"What about Jimmy and the others?" Kane asked.

Max piped up, "We don't need the others. We know where your wife is."

"There isn't time," said Reed. He stepped back from the door to make room. "Come on in. Let's get organized."

The hunters climbed in and squeezed around the computer station, marveling at the sight of one little blip.

"So where is it now?" Kane asked.

"Four miles southeast," Sing replied. She zoomed in for a closer view of the terrain. "And it's coming our way."

The Sasquatch train was moving again, rushing through dense forest, brushing aside limbs, leaping over logs as they looked anxiously over their shoulders and gave off fear scent, pushing, pushing, pushing themselves to the point of exhaustion, an endless cycle. Only one thing had changed: Rachel and Beck were now second in line behind Jacob; Leah and Reuben brought up the rear.

The change was costly. Beck was sure she needed a doctor. The bleeding from her nose and mouth had gone from steady to sporadic, but it hadn't stopped. Her face felt puffy and her whole body ached, not just her ankle. With barely enough strength to hold on, she feared she had none left to survive.

She'd found a way to bind the GPS in the roll of her sleeve, leaving its antenna exposed to the heavens. Beyond that, she was living by faith. The case was bitten and bent in the middle, and she couldn't get the slightest hiss out of the radio. She could only hope the GPS part was actually working and that someone was watching.

Perhaps it was that person the Sasquatches were running from this very moment; hunters had encircled them before, and Reed was one of them. Beck cradled her head on Rachel's soft, furry shoulder, so tired, dizzy, wishing whoever it was would catch up and put an end to this.

Rachel's head turned, her leathery cheek bumping Beck's bruised face. It hurt.

"What?"

Rachel huffed and kept running, a new wave of fear quickening her step.

Beck raised her head, and through the rush of the wind and the snapping of passing limbs, she recognized a familiar, chilling sound: the cry of the banshee. The woman from Lost Creek was wailing again, her voice carrying like a faraway siren, following them like a distant shadow.

Wait. Following them?

Beck fought off her stupor and forced herself to think. All the Sasquatches were *here*, running together. She could see all four of them. Jacob wasn't making the noise; he was running from the noise.

She tightly clutched Rachel's fur as a chill went through her.

It was no hunter either.

She looked over her shoulder. There were so many trees, limbs, thickets, dark spaces. Anything could hide in there.

Max and Reed came to a wide-eyed, open-eared halt.

"Yeah, you heard it, and so did I," Reed said, answering the question in Max's eyes.

Reed faced south while Max faced north, both on high alert, watching each other's backs. They were working their way up the mountain slope above Abney, in a hurry and breathing hard, hoping they and the others could weave a net tight enough to catch a north-moving GPS and whatever or whoever might be carrying it.

Reed radioed, "Pete, we heard it to the south, down your way."

There was a pause before Pete replied, "It's north of me. It's in the circle, gentlemen—as soon as we get one."

Reed checked the screen on his GPS. He could see Blips 3 and 4, Pete and Sam, moving up the mountain to the south, but Thorne and Kane, sharing GPS unit 5, weren't on the screen. "Sing, you there yet?"

"We're at the drop-off point," she answered, just pulling the motor home to a stop at the end of Service Road 221, a road so old and unused that nature was taking it back. According to her Forest Service map, this would place Steve Thorne and Wiley Kane far enough to the north to intercept the blip *if* it continued on its present course and *if* they could get up the mountain in time to close up the circle.

Thorne and Kane were geared up, armed and ready, in the back of the motor home. Thorne had GPS 5 on his sleeve.

Sing killed the engine and set the brake. "Good hunting."

They jumped out the door like paratroopers and started up the hill.

Sing took her place at the computer station and scrolled the map to her present location. Zooming out, she found all the blips: Reed and Max, units 1 and 2, widening their position above Abney; Pete and Sam, units 3 and 4, farther up the mountainside a mile south, but swinging north to close in. And Thorne and Kane, unit 5, heading up the hill with a good climb ahead of them before they would cross the projected path of Blip Number 6. Because the radio on unit 6 wasn't working, only Sing could see the blip, via satellite. It would be up to her to guide the hunters to its location.

"Target is still moving north," she reported, "on a course roughly 355. Pete, bearing to target is 345, about half a mile; Reed, bearing to target is 110, three quarters of a mile. Steve, maintain your heading; at your present rate of climb you should intercept it."

It was like watching a fast-pitched baseball heading for home plate and hoping the catcher could put on his mitt in time to catch it blindfolded.

"I've found a sign," Pete reported. "It's more than one, maybe the whole family."

"So maybe they're going back home," Reed offered. "Back where this whole thing started."

Sing could see Lost Creek on the map just a few miles north. She wagged her head in absolute wonder and started trembling. She'd always believed the footprints at the first baiting station were real, and now being right terrified her. What had Beck gone through? If they found her, given she was still alive, would she even be the same person?

Cap had to know. Sing grabbed her cell phone.

Cap said good-bye and folded his cell phone, stunned, not knowing what to feel or think, except for one thing: he had to get inside this cabin.

He'd knocked on the cabin door several times and concluded

there was no one at home. Now he looked up and down the porch. Did Burkhardt have a particular habit when it came to hiding keys? From his two years as the man's unwilling protégé, Cap recalled Burkhardt liking overhead places: rafters, ledges, windowsills, light fixtures. He felt along the molding across the top of the door. Nothing. There was a hanging flowerpot next to the stairs. He reached and fumbled among the leaves.

A house key.

He stopped for one more cautious look around and then let himself in.

It was warm and homey inside, with pleasant, soft furniture, a bearskin rug, a stuffed deer head, a mounted trout with its weight and length proudly displayed on a brass placard beneath it. Fishing poles were mounted in a rack near the front door, and in a cabinet with glass doors next to the brick fireplace . . .

Rows and rows of glass jars containing Burkhardt's icons of evolution: the Galapagos finches with different-sized beaks, the white and gray peppered moths, the coelacanths and bats, the lizards and snakes, and on the top row, in a place of honor, four new additions—unborn chimpanzees, floating in a fetal position in the amber liquid, eyes half open, toothless mouths in a half yawn.

Baumgartner had listed three possible results of tampering with a chimp's DNA—a normal, unchanged chimp; a deformed, retarded chimp; or a dead chimp. Apparently, these were the dead ones.

Pete and Sam were moving north, following Sing's vectors while Pete spotted snapped limbs, bruised leaves, and soil depressions to cross-check their progress. From the sign Pete found, the targets were not moving in any lazy, meandering pattern that would

indicate foraging but were heading in a fairly straight line north-
ward, definitely on the run.

"How close are we?" Pete whispered in his radio.

Sing came back, "Still half a mile. They're moving just as fast
as you are."

Pete halted at the edge of some soft ground, scanned it for
prints, but found none. "Mm. We've veered off the trail somehow."

Sam stepped through and pushed ahead, peering intently in
all directions. "Why don't we bag this tracking stuff and just follow Sing's vectors?"

"I want to know what those critters are doing," Pete said, his
eyes searching the ground.

"Pete, come on, that thing's gonna pull farther away the
longer we stand here!"

Then Pete found a footprint in a bare patch of soft earth.

Sam's.

He dropped to one knee and produced a blue diagram card
from his pocket, quickly comparing.

When he looked up, Sam was watching him.

Thorne and Kane were pushing uphill, groping and climbing as
silently as possible through tightly spaced trees and limbs, following Sing's vectors, primed for a deadly collision.

"Veer to the right," came Sing's voice through Thorne's earpiece, "090."

Thorne whispered to Kane, about thirty feet ahead of him,
"Kane, move right. Kane!"

Suddenly Kane jerked to attention, whispered a curse, and
aimed his rifle uphill.

Before Thorne could caution him, the rifle went off.

Beck knew that sound and understood when Jacob turned on his heels and ran past, leading the group the opposite direction. Hunters. It was all happening again.

Thorne hissed at Kane, "What are you doing?"

Kane was nearly beside himself and had a tough time keeping his voice down. "I saw it! It was a Sasquatch—I am not foolin' you!"

Thorne caught up and put a hand on his shoulder to keep him calm—and corralled. "You weren't even supposed to be ahead of me. We were tracking with the GPS, remember?"

"I saw it! It was walking, standing upright. Man, it was huge!"

Thorne stared at him. "You're sure?"

Reed pressed his talk button and only half whispered, "Who fired a shot? What's going on?"

Blip Number 6 was heading south again, with Thorne's blip less than 500 yards northwest. "Heads up, everybody!" Sing said. "Target is moving south. Pete, Sam, it'll be coming your way!"

Pete answered, "Okay, moving north to meet and greet."

Sam reported, "I'll move uphill, spread out a bit."

Sing's eyes were glued on every player. "Reed and Max, it's going to pass you on the uphill side."

Reed answered, "We're heading that way."

Jacob lumbered to a halt, then barely stood, stooped and swaying, his breathing labored, his eyes darting about, his nostrils sampling the air. Rachel came up behind him, every breath a painful wheeze. Beck slid to the ground, barely able to move her arms. Leah trudged from behind, legs like lead, and plopped to the ground with Reuben still on her back. The forest floor became a hairy heap, huffing and steaming.

Jacob's gaze darted to the south, then to the north, then down the hill. He moaned, a mournful sound Beck had never heard before.

From somewhere up the slope, invisible in the forest, the woman whimpered, then snickered. She was closer, watching, waiting.

They were hemmed in.

Rachel lay on her belly, her body heaving with every breath, the wind from her nostrils wiggling the undergrowth in front of her face. Beck crawled to her and touched her shoulder. Rachel looked up at her through watery eyes, and Beck saw more than fear; she saw defeat.

"No. Rachel, come on, don't . . ."

Jacob sank to his haunches, still sniffing, still looking, his hair bristling. Reuben cowered behind his mother's prone body, and his expression was much like Jacob's. He was afraid, listening, sniffing, sensing the surrounding danger.

And then a searing awareness worked its way through Beck's pain and stupor: *It's me. I'm the cause of this.*

She struggled with her shirtsleeve and got the GPS loose. It appeared to be working. The map on the screen was now indicating a steep mountainside, and that's where she was. This thing was locating her accurately, and somehow those hunters out there were getting the signal.

Which meant . . .

She didn't understand what she did. It was the last thing on earth she wanted to do, but at the same time, it was the only thing.

She turned the GPS off.

The blip was gone.

Sing lurched forward. "No, no, don't do that!"

She radioed, "I've lost contact with the target. It just winked out. Does anybody see anything?"

Reed and Max had split up and spread out. Reed was alone now in timber so thick he couldn't see more than ten yards in any direction. "This is Reed. Negative contact."

"This is Max. Negative contact."

"Sam here. Still moving, still looking."

"Pete here. Sam, I'll wait for you to come up even with me."

"This is Steve. Sorry for the misfire. There's something wrong with Kane's rifle. We're checking it out."

Beck, what are you doing? Reed had heard of lost people getting so nutty in the woods that they actually hid from their rescuers. Was she afraid of being found? Either that, or . . .

Had she made friends with these creatures? Was she protecting them?

He radioed, "Everybody, keep closing on the last known position, steady and quiet, and be sure of your target before you shoot. Sing, let us know when you get the target again."

"Will do."

Reed wiped sweat from his hands and a drop of sweat from above his eye. He mentally reviewed the sight of the dead logger and the mangled body of Sheriff Mills. No more of that. Whatever Beck's mental state, the hunt would end differently this time.

Cap wasn't finding out much in the little cabin, other than Burkhardt was a fastidious person who always made his bed and put away his dishes. He searched and inspected his way to the back door and then gazed cautiously across the graveled alleyway to his next frontier: that huge metal outbuilding. It was time to get out there and take a look. He was pushing his luck beyond acceptable risk to take any longer in the—

The sound immobilized him. He was stunned, a statue in the small enclosed rear porch of the cabin. Yes, he'd heard Reed describe it, and Reed sounded like a nut case when he did. But Reed was right on the money!

From the big metal building, clear as day, Cap heard it for himself: the eerie wail of a woman in pain and despair, the cry of the banshee.

SIXTEEN

Kane's voice was getting loud. "*What* did you tell them? There's nothing wrong with my rifle!"

Thorne put out his hand. "That rifle's pulling to the left. Let me see it."

"You're nuts."

"Let me see it."

Kane handed it over.

Thorne peered through the sight. "Eh, it might be a little off. Did you drop it or something?"

Kane reached to grab it back. "We're wasting time!"

Thorne jerked it away, then raised a hand to calm him down. "Easy, Kane. You don't want them to know you saw that thing."

Kane worked on that a moment and finally caught Thorne's drift. "In case they get the kill first, is that what you're saying?" He got agitated again. "But if we stand around here, they're going to get it for sure."

"Take it easy. If the others see it, they won't be any better off. They'll be in the same mess you are."

That changed Kane's demeanor. "What are you talking about?"

The heavy metal door to the outbuilding was locked, but it had an electric locking mechanism with a numeric keypad. On a whim, Cap entered a number Burkhardt consistently used for locks, entry codes, and passwords: 1-8-5-9, the year Darwin's *Origin of the Species* was published. The mechanism whirred, then clicked. The door opened with a slight push.

At first, Cap was unsure if he'd entered a lab or a warehouse. The building was cavernous but well lit, with a vaulted roof supported by steel trusses and enough floor space to host a convention. A half-height wall divided the front section from the rear. From beyond that wall came the occasional stirring, banging, grunting, and hooting Cap had become familiar with at the York Center.

Chimpanzees.

Filling the front half of the building in geometrically arranged rows was a lab most scientists—and most major universities—could only dream of. Cap performed a careful walk-through, eyes and ears open for any human presence, which, at least for now, was strangely missing.

Adam Burkhardt's original basement lab had grown tenfold, dropped all superfluous décor and warmth, and taken on the appearance of an assembly line, dedicated to specific procedures executed efficiently and repeatedly: DNA and protein synthesis and analysis, DNA sequencing, viral transfer, site-directed muta-genesis, and in a large, dedicated section toward the rear, high-volume, assembly-line in vitro fertilization and cloning. The woman cried again, her wail coming over that half wall with the nerve-jangling volume of a fire alarm.

Cap saw an archway leading to that side of the building. Moving quickly yet warily, he made a beeline for it.

Thorne spoke reassuringly, the voice of reason trying to corral Kane's impulsiveness. "People can't handle this sort of thing, you know what I mean? They see something like this and they get all the wrong ideas. Sometimes it's better when *we* decide what they're going to know and what they aren't."

"I don't follow you!"

Thorne struggled a moment. "You just told me you saw a Sasquatch."

"You bet I did! It was huge, it was all black like a gorilla, and it was walking on two legs just like a man!"

Thorne chuckled and wagged his head.

"You think I'm crazy?"

"No, no, you're not crazy." Quickly, easily, Thorne leveled Kane's rifle at Kane's chest. "You're absolutely right."

He fired.

Reed got on his radio. "Who's shooting? Fill us in."

Thorne's voice came back, "Hey, we're sorry, we've got a problem up here. Kane's rifle's misfired again and now he's hit himself in the foot."

Reed winced. Kane. He should have known. "How bad is it?"

Thorne came back on, yet sounded distant as if he were addressing someone else. "No, try to stay off it. Yeah, just wrap it with something." Then, "Reed, he's okay, but I need to help him out of here."

Reed feared the hunt was as good as over. "Okay. Pete, Sam, any southbound traffic?"

Sam called back, "They're still in there, Reed, but after those shots they've got to know we're here."

"Max, can you swing north and fill in?"

"Will do," Max replied.

"Sing, let's mark a waypoint at Steve and Kane's last position so we can guide Max up there," Reed instructed.

"You've got it," she answered.

Reed scrolled his GPS over to Thorne and Kane's last position and marked that spot with a waypoint. Hopefully, he or Sing would be able to guide Max to that spot before there was no point in doing so.

Cap found a central hallway with doors to individual rooms on either side, much like a hospital ward. The place was well scrubbed and smelled of disinfectant.

The first door on his right was half open; some stirring from within drew his attention. He approached slowly and eased the door open.

Chimpanzees. Six of them, in six floor-to-ceiling cages. The chimp in the first cage immediately went to the bars and stood up, one hand gripping a bar of the cage, the other reaching through the bars toward him, her amber eyes meeting his imploringly. He knew that mannerism and expression and went to her, gently taking her hand and stroking it. Her eyes went across the room to a bin of oranges. He grabbed a few and passed one to her. She settled into the clean bedding and began to eat it.

From her bulging abdomen he could see she was pregnant.

The female in the next cage cowered in a corner, her arms enfolding herself. Except for one frightened glance, she wouldn't look at him. She was pregnant too. He rolled an orange toward her, and she reached for it but would not come out of her hiding place.

In the third cage, a female lay on her back in what appeared to be a drug-induced stupor. Her belly was shaved, and a large stitched incision crossed her abdomen.

The chimp in the fourth cage was the kind who liked to be friends with everybody. She had bright, expressive eyes and didn't amble up to the bars—she pranced. She looked him right in the eye and reached for the orange he offered. Her belly too was shaved, with an incision, but not as recent; the hair was growing back.

The female in the fifth cage was also pregnant, grumpy, and not interested in oranges.

In the last cage, an older female bore an old incision across her bulging belly. The incision had apparently been reopened several times; it was ridged with pink scar tissue that displaced the skin and hair along its length. She didn't acknowledge Cap's presence but merely sat on her haunches, endlessly counting her fingers.

Cap knew this mannerism too. She'd given up.

At the end of the room was a pulled curtain. On the other side of the curtain was a clean room divided into two well-lit cubicles, each with a stainless steel operating table such as veterinarians used, but with one troubling addition: leather restraints. Cabinets on each side were stocked with surgical instruments, dressings, gowns, caps, masks, and gloves.

Cap was getting a picture of how the process worked. When he opened the door to the walk-in cooler just past the tables, he got his confirmation.

On the shelves, in Ziploc bags that were labeled and dated, lay tiny, unborn creatures that could have been—should have been—chimpanzees. Two had legs, toes, and fingers so elongated as to be useless. One on the second shelf had gone the other way, with three-fingered stumps for arms.

On the bottom shelf, thrown into a tub, were four little females whose legs nearly matched human proportions and whose arms were intact. These must have shown promise—they were cut open and the ovaries were removed.

Beck huddled against Rachel, listening, watching, her body aching, her soul in turmoil, her finger poised over the on button. She and Rachel were pressed against a crumbling snag, blending with the redness of the rotting wood until they had become part of it. A short distance downhill, Leah and Reuben had found a way to blend and disappear within a sizable clump of serviceberry.

Only the top of Jacob's head was visible as he crawled through the underbrush toward the north, watching and listening, his eyes floating above the leaves. Beck had no idea what he was hearing, seeing, smelling, or even *feeling*, but she knew something had to have changed out there. Jacob wasn't in a hide or flee mode; he was planning something.

He stopped and became a big rock in the middle of the brush. Silence. Stillness.

When he gave a quiet sniff over his shoulder, the old snag and the clump of bushes became crouching, sneaking Sasquatches again. With stealthy moves and low postures, the group pushed north.

Beck slipped the GPS into her shirt pocket and buttoned the flap. The right time would come. It *had* to come. But not yet.

Sing saw Max's blip moving steadily toward the north, but he was moving far too slowly for her comfort. With Thorne and Kane on their way down the mountainside, the north end was wide open for the quarry to escape; with no GPS signal, Sing and the hunters would never know it. "Max? How's it going?"

Max's struggle came through in his voice. "It's pretty rough terrain in here."

"Kane's waypoint is bearing 024."

"Zero-two-four, okay."

She quickly scanned the other hunters' positions: Reed was to the west, trying to keep the creatures from running downhill, if he could even do that. Pete held his position to the south, supposedly preventing any escape in that direction. Sam was—

Where was Sam?

"Sam, I don't have you on screen."

No answer. No blip.

"Sam?"

With his eyes still fixed in horror upon the eviscerated bodies of mutant unborn chimps, Cap's nerves nearly melted when the cry of the banshee rose like a goblin over the partition walls.

He closed the cooler door and fell back against the wall to gather himself, take some deep breaths, talk sense to his mind, and make sure his bowels didn't let loose right there on the floor.

It was bad enough knowing that *thing* was in the same building.

It was far worse knowing he would have to find and identify it, which meant coming face-to-jaws with a savage, neck-wringing killer. He could only hope and pray it was in a cage *and* that the cage could contain it.

He looked around for anything he might use as a weapon. No crowbars or baseball bats were readily available. He crossed the hallway to what seemed the most likely door.

Careful, now. His hand shook as he grabbed the knob. He would open the door just a crack, take a look, then evaluate his next step.

The knob turned.

The door cracked open.

The banshee screamed in terror, anger, maybe both, so loudly, so piercingly, that Cap jolted back, slamming the door shut. The screaming continued, the sound of violent death knifing into every fear instinct Cap had. It was all he could do to stand still, be reasonable, and not create another window in the building trying to get out of there.

The screaming subsided to gasps and whimpers, and Cap noted that, as near as he could tell from the sound, it wasn't moving from one spot. Whatever it was hadn't stormed the door or come after him. Chances were good that it was confined.

He slowly opened the door again—

The thing screamed again.

He opened the door enough to look inside.

He saw another row of cages, larger than the cells that held the surrogate mothers.

At the sight of the first creature, he had to double-check not only his bowels but his stomach. In the first cage was a quaking, nearly hairless blob with blue-veined, leathery skin. On one end were stumps that should have been legs. On the other end was a head without a neck that turned only slightly when he approached.

Feeding tubes ran into the broad, flat nose, pumping in temporary life. It seemed only vaguely aware of his presence.

The next cage held a chimpanzee giant, grotesquely overgrown and suffering for it. Straightened out, it could have measured eight feet from head to toe, but this poor beast was bent and crooked like an arthritic old man, sitting painfully in the corner, its joints knobby, its fingers bent and useless. It tried to reach out to him, but the arm was a gnarled limb on a dead tree; it barely moved.

A shockingly white albino occupied the next cage, its cold pink eyes studying him with suspicion and loathing. It too was oversized, and judging from the crookedness of the fingers and feet, only slightly mobile. It huffed at him, then creaked and straightened to its feet to growl and threaten. The twisted legs buckled and it fell to its haunches again, resigned to making threats it could never carry out.

After what he'd seen so far, Cap thought he was ready for the next cage.

He wasn't.

At the first sight of him, the *thing* leaped at the bars, wailing and frothing—its eyes the crazed yellow orbs of a demon, its black fur bristling like a sooty explosion. It filled Cap's vision and he slammed against the opposite wall even before he felt the terror that put him there.

This was a malformation of the highest order, a creature far removed from a chimpanzee, but not better. Though smaller than Cap in stature, it had to outweigh him three to one, with muscles so pronounced they impeded its movement. It was deranged, drooling, out of control, and the cry from that throat— the scream of a madwoman!

It was urinating as it clung to the bars, tried to climb them, tried to bend them, tried to grab on with its feet, which only slid to the floor; the big, opposing toes looked to have been surgically removed.

Cap inched along the wall, maintaining distance from the huge arm that groped at him through the bars. Hoping to make it to a nearby exit, he passed the last cage, this one much larger—

It was empty.

The bars were bent, the sidewalls battered. Plywood was ripped from the back wall, and the two-by-six framing members were snapped aside like dry twigs. Foam insulation lay everywhere in broken pieces. The metal sheathing that formed the building's exterior was mangled and ripped open like a tin can opened with a hatchet.

The cage door was ajar, as if someone had already gone in to inspect the damage. Cap took one step inside, recognizing a familiar pattern of bite marks on the splintered lumber and a peppering of all-too-familiar diarrhetic droppings on the concrete floor.

Looking through the gaping hole in the rear wall of the cage, he could see no barriers between this building and the forest and mountains beyond.

Sing rebooted her computer, tweaked all the wires on the back of the satellite system, and double-checked her radio receiver. "Reed, can you hear me?"

He radioed back, "Loud and clear."

"I still can't find Sam, and now I can't raise Pete either."

"I have Pete on my screen."

"So do I, but he isn't moving and he isn't answering."

Reed called for Pete but got no answer. "Well, I sure won't buy this brand of GPS anymore. I'd better get over there." Then he asked, "What about Thorne and Kane? Where are they?"

"You don't have them on-screen?"

"No."

Sing sighed in exasperation. "Now I don't have them either. But they were almost back here."

"No number 6?"

"No. It hasn't come back."

"Max? Anything?"

Max answered, "Not yet."

Sing heard footsteps outside the motor home. The door opened, and Steve Thorne stepped up into the driver's area, his rifle slung on his back.

Sing was relieved. "All right. There's one warm body accounted for. We're having trouble with the system."

He broke into a tired grin. "So I hear."

She waited a moment, then asked, "Where's Kane?"

Her cell phone on the counter rang, Cap's special ring. She reached for it—

"Don't answer that," said Thorne, snatching it away.

She saw him raise a pistol and almost understood before the muzzle flashed and her awareness shattered into a starburst of fragments fading to black. Her body came to rest facedown against the bedroom door, a pool of blood spreading beneath her head.

SEVENTEEN

Cap hurried, his cell phone against his ear, waiting through ring after ring until Sing's voice-message system answered and gave him a beep. "Sing. I've located Burkhardt's lab and confirmed the source of at least one of the creatures. I'm ready to call the police, but first I have to get out of here. Tell Reed that—"

He'd only gotten halfway to the front door when the electric lock hummed and the knob rattled. He tumbled down behind a workbench as the door swung open, casting diffused sunlight about the room. Judging from the footsteps, three, maybe four, people came in, and they weren't little. He thought of the cell phone in his hand and frantically shut it off before Sing called back.

Now he heard Philip Merrill's voice. "Secure the exits—this one, the one in the rear, and the side loading doors. Then search every inch of this place."

By now Reed was praying, *Dear Lord, don't let me lose Beck again.* "Sing?" he radioed. "Any progress?"

She didn't answer, but Sam did. "Hello? Anybody hear me?"

Well, here was one source of relief. "Sam! You okay? We lost you, buddy."

"I'm fine. I was trying to swing around to cover the east flank, but now I'm worried about Pete. Have you talked to him at all?"

"Negative. I can't raise him. The whole system's breaking down. Have you talked to Max?"

Max came on: "I'm still scouting the north side. It doesn't look good. They may have gotten through."

"Sing?" Reed still couldn't get an answer. "Now *she's* cut off."

"We may have to call it a day, guys," Max suggested.

Reed wasn't ready to concede that. "Max, why don't you stay where you are. Sam, we'd better check on Pete."

"You got it," Sam replied.

Cap heard someone coming. He ducked around the end of a workbench just in time to avoid being seen. With a quick, one-eyed glance around the corner, he caught sight of Tim the campus cop, now in civilian clothing but brandishing a gun. It seemed out of character. Cap wondered what Merrill must have told him.

Slam! Clank! The rattle of a chain and a padlock. That had to be the loading doors on the side of the building. Cap wouldn't be escaping that way.

They were working their way through the lab, and it was only a matter of time before—

He wriggled around the corner to the backside of the bench and just missed being spotted by Kenny, the other campus cop. Now, that guy was not to be tangled with. He had an iron-jawed feistiness and the muscle to back it up.

Clunk! Rattle! There went the rear door.

Did these guys even know what was going on in this place? Did Merrill know? They were locking him in, but they were locking themselves in as well. Would they be all that happy with the idea once they encountered—

The thing screamed one of its best banshee screams yet, and just faintly audible under the screams and the rattling of the bars were the voices of men screaming in horror, running footsteps, more hollering, cursing—a frantic retreat.

Cap didn't smile outwardly, but some quirky part of him was enjoying this.

Now Merrill was in the mix, cursing, hollering orders nobody was hearing, trying to hold his band of thugs together. Cap caught the words, "Don't shoot it!"

Well. Imagine that. Merrill was surprised too.

Footsteps! Apparently they'd satisfied themselves—with a little help—that Cap wasn't in the rear half. The lab was going to get a thorough going-through.

There had to be a cupboard, a cabinet, a garbage can, anything he could hide in! He scurried on his hands and knees across an aisle, peeked around the end of a counter, scurried across another aisle, straightened to peek over a bench—

His shoulder upset a pair of forceps that hung over the edge. He tried to catch them but missed. They clattered to the floor.

The footsteps started galloping his direction.

There was only one place left to hide, and that was in a huge walk-in freezer built into the partition. He knew he was kidding himself, but then again, maybe he'd be able to hide in the cold just a little longer than they'd be able to search in it. He slinked across the floor, reached up, pulled the handle, slipped through the cracked door, and managed to click it shut just one nano-second before his pursuers rounded the corner.

It was dark inside, and yes, it was freezing. The cold was already working its way through his clothing. He rose carefully to his feet to look through the small window in the door and his breath fogged it. Nuts! He backed up, trying to get used to the dark—

He wasn't alone in here.

The first nudge of a hairy hand startled him like a jolt of high voltage. He jumped involuntarily; his arms flew outward and struck a hairy body on either side. Twisting, he saw two rows of four—no, six—no, *eight* glassy-eyed, deformed chimpanzees, some whole, some gutted, all staring back at him in the light from the window. Their eyes were vacant, jaws slack, faces and fur glistening with frost. They hung from two rails by steel hooks inserted in their ear holes, and now he'd set them swinging like bells in a bell tower, thumping against him and each other.

The first one rolled off the end of the rail and bounced off Cap's shoulder before thumping to the floor. The second followed, glancing off Cap and spinning as it went down.

The third bumped into the freezer door as the door swung open and flooded the room with light. The fourth dropped, teetered, and fell right in front of Kenny the cop, now silhouetted in the doorway.

Kenny hollered and jumped back but recovered when he spotted Cap.

Cap was on the floor, tripped up by the first two corpses and trying to wrestle himself out from under the third and fourth. Kenny reached down, not to give him a hand up but to yank him off the floor, nearly dislocating his arm.

Before Cap knew it, he was out in the warm, habitable lab, held fast between Kenny and a Kenny wannabe. A third guy in an expensive suit slammed the freezer door shut behind him. Tim stood before him holding a gun, and next to Tim was Dr. Philip Merrill, looking pale, his hair out of place, his tie crooked, and sweat glistening on his brow.

"Dr. Capella!" he said, winded and shaking. "You never should have come back!"

One more hour, Deputy Saunders thought, *and we'll call it a day.* His volunteers were getting tired, cold, and hungry, and they had to get back down before the light was gone. The last discovery, a rusty pocketknife, was over an hour ago, and expanding the search area to include the entire Inland Northwest didn't seem like a wise use of time and manpower.

"Okay, everybody," he spoke into his handheld radio, "one more hour."

They came back with muttered acknowledgments.

A metal detector somewhere in the woods replied with a loud chirp.

"Officer Saunders! I found it!"

"What is it this time?"

"It's the shovel! I found the shovel!"

Merrill and his men took Cap to an office in a corner of the lab, a simple cubicle made from sound-baffling dividers, and sat him down in one of two available chairs. Kenny stood in the entry, big arms across his chest, expression not firm but troubled. Tim leaned in the corner as if he didn't want to come out of it, the gun lowered but visible. Merrill took the chair behind the desk and smoothed his hair back repeatedly as if trying to compose himself.

The other two guys stood behind Cap's chair to make sure he stayed in it. Cap offered his hand to the one behind his right shoulder. "Uh, Mike Capella. Dr. Merrill and I know each other, did he tell you that?" The man gave him a cold stare. He and his partner were definitely on edge.

Cap checked around the room. Only one entrance. The walls were too heavy to knock over, too tall to jump over. The room was too small to avoid being grabbed if he made a move.

A snapshot push-pinned to the wall above the desk hinted that this was Burkhardt's office. It was a photo of Burkhardt, bearded and ponytailed, decked out in a billed cap and fishing vest and posing with a good-sized cutthroat trout. Burkhardt always had been an avid hunter and outdoorsman, which was ironic, Cap thought. Merrill loosened his tie, unbuttoned his collar, and finally reached a level of composure acceptable for conversation. "I suppose you've seen everything?"

Cap studied him—and his men. "Looks like you have too. Didn't you know what Burkhardt was doing?"

"We had an understanding." Merrill leaned closer. "Sometimes the greatest scientific breakthroughs have to be made in secret, away from prying eyes, politics, and boards of ethics."

"So how do you like his results?"

Merrill rubbed his face.

"I don't suppose your so-called scientific community will be too wild about them," Cap went on. "*American Geographic* isn't about to publish them, and forget about Public Broadcasting and the Evolution Channel."

Merrill's temper brought some of his color back. "Such steps are necessary—"

"To prove what? That random mutations work? Look around you, Merrill! Does all this look random? It's planned; it's monitored; it's carefully recorded, and it *still* doesn't work." He spoke to the men behind him. "Burkhardt's planting mutated embryos in surrogate mothers and harvesting the eggs from the offspring before they're even born—"

Merrill interjected, "To compress the amount of time between generations."

Cap spoke to Kenny and Tim, "—so he can further mutate the mutants, implant the mothers, and start all over again."

"And thereby replicate the natural process—"

Cap was so steamed up he had to stand. "Nature doesn't load the dice! You're using a lab here, Merrill! You're interposing intelligence into the process! You're—" The two guards sat him down again. "You're not only proving that random mutations don't work; you're proving that *purposeful* mutations don't work!" He spoke to Kenny and Tim again. "Did you get a load of those monsters in there? Nice improvements on the original, don't you think?"

Merrill tried to argue to his men, "Mutations are the mechanism by which—"

"So where is everybody?" Cap said.

Merrill wasn't in control, and it showed despite his effort to hide it. "I suppose it's their day off."

Cap felt sorry for this man. "Philip, come on. You've figured it out just as easily as I have! You know Burkhardt! He's not about to let somebody accomplish something when he's not around to take credit for it! The staff isn't here because he isn't here, and he isn't here because . . . ?"

Merrill sat there, cornered and seething.

Cap answered his own question. "Because his monster isn't here. You saw that hole in the wall, right?" He asked the guards,

"Right?" He pointed that direction. "There went the whole experiment, along with your funding, Merrill, into the great outdoors for the whole world to see. You think Burkhardt can live with that? You think he'd want you to find out?"

Cap could tell Merrill knew, but the esteemed college dean didn't offer to discuss it.

Cap spoke to the guards, "Burkhardt's gone after it."

Deputy Dave Saunders, the housewife, the fireman, the heavy equipment operator, and the machinist found the shallow grave only a few feet from where the shovel had been dropped. It was the equipment operator who first hit something with his shovel—a boot.

The housewife turned away.

The others dug carefully as the stench of a dead corpse rose into the air.

The fireman dropped his shovel and ran, bent over, and vomited.

Dave could hardly bear it himself, but he kept going, carefully moving peat and soil with his gloved hands until he found out what Sing and the others needed to know. Gasping for fresh air, he waved for a halt. "It's Thompson."

Merrill was desperate to make Cap the liar. "You can't possibly know where Dr. Burkhardt is or what he's doing! Of all the arrogant, outlandish—"

"Can I stand up?" Cap rose, testing the disposition of the two guys behind him. They didn't slap him into the chair again, so he knew he was making progress. Slowly, making sure they could see his every move, he reached into his shirt pocket and pulled out some folded sheets of paper, digital photos Sing had e-mailed him. He unfolded one and showed it to them. "Recognize this guy?"

They stared at it blankly.

Cap went to the desk, reached for one of Burkhardt's pencils from a desk caddy, and scribbled a beard and ponytail on the man in the photo. He held it up. "Now do you recognize him?" He directed their attention to Burkhardt's fishing photo on the wall. Cap saw the light of recognition in their eyes. "He's out there right now, lying to my friends and pretending he's helping them hunt down a Bigfoot! But we know what that monster really is, don't we? And so does he."

"You are a trespasser, Cap!" Merrill lifted his voice. "I could have you arrested!"

"Trespassing where? Care to show this place to the police?"

Merrill fell silent again.

"I'm guessing Burkhardt cut the big toes off his monster so it couldn't be arboreal and would have to evolve into a ground-dwelling, bipedal something-or-other. I'm going to guess that Burkhardt engineered that thing to compete with any other primates it encountered—that's the natural selection thing, you know, competing with other species and prevailing—and that includes human beings. Well, it's not evolving, but it *is* competing. It's responsible for the deaths of four people, one of them a dear friend and one of them the Whitcomb County sheriff!"

Merrill leaped to his feet, the veins showing in his neck. "You can't prove that!"

"Ah-ah-ah! The hair, stool, and saliva samples, remember? Now, the hairs don't reveal much, but that's okay. All the police have to do is match the stool and saliva samples with the saliva and droppings in that broken cage, and bingo!"

Merrill looked as though he'd swallowed a bitter pill. "I knew nothing about all this! I had nothing to do with it!"

"Ah!" Cap pointed at him. "You believe me!" He walked over to Kenny and looked up at him. "I'd like to go now. I need to warn my friends before Burkhardt gets a chance to do something really stupid."

Kenny locked eyes with him a moment, then exchanged a quick look with the others. Tim slipped his gun back into its holster. Kenny stepped aside.

"Thanks." Cap wasted no time getting out of there and called over his shoulder, "You might want to wait here for the cops—and show them that photo!"

Merrill bolted for the entryway, but Kenny blocked him. "Where do you think you're going?"

Merrill was dumbfounded. "You work for *me*!"

"Sit down."

Merrill backed away, rubbed his hand over his hair, approached Tim to try to reason with him—

He grabbed Tim's pistol from its holster and swept it around the cubicle.

The men shied back, hands raised.

Merrill dashed out of the office and across the lab and caught sight of Cap racing for the rear of the building. He aimed wildly and fired as he ran. The first bullet put a hole in a wall about twelve feet from the floor. The second shattered glassware on a workbench.

Kenny and Tim raced after him, hollering to stop, to simmer down, but Merrill was beyond that.

Cap ran down the hallway and ducked around the partition.

Merrill shouted, "Cap! The doors are padlocked! Give it up! There's no reason to call the police! We can reach an agreement!"

The banshee started screaming then—a perfect giveaway of Cap's location! Merrill hooked a sharp left and ducked through the doorway into the hall of monsters.

The beast in the far cage had already gone berserk, leaping and pounding the bars, spitting, screaming, groping, drilling into Merrill with murderous eyes. Merrill recalled how Burkhardt's creations felt about competing primates, and ran sideways with his back sliding along the opposite wall.

The last cage brought no comfort. Even before Merrill got there, he knew what the open cage door meant. Directly opposite the cage, he quit running and fell back against the wall in dismay.

Yes, all the doors were padlocked, but there was nothing beyond that hole in the rear wall but the wide outdoors.

"Sam? Sam, you there?"

Reed and Sam had been converging on Pete's GPS blip and getting close, but now Sam's blip had vanished again, and Reed couldn't raise him on the radio. Reed rested against a tree and called again, "Sam? Come in, Sam. Sing? Can you read me? Can *anybody* hear me?"

He took the GPS from his arm, checked the batteries, then recycled it. Pete's blip appeared again, but Pete still didn't answer his radio. As for Max, Sam, and Sing, he wasn't getting a blip or a radio response.

Guess I should have known. This gremlin-plagued GPS system had been playing a cruel game with his hope all along. He tried not to let it distract him as he pressed ahead through heavy forest, following a game trail, closing on Pete's blip, the one thing he could call a "known"—maybe.

Like an airplane popping out of the clouds, he broke into an open area where rocks and shallow soil stunted the trees and undergrowth. Grass found root and sunlight here, providing pasture for elk and deer. Hoofprints and droppings were plentiful, and there were obvious patches of flattened grass where elk had rested.

Ah! He got a visual. Pete sat against a tree in the middle of the clearing, his back to Reed. Reed blew a sigh of relief and gladness. After all the gadget failure, it was great to have direct human contact again.

"Pete," he said quietly as he approached, "I'm coming up behind you."

Pete nodded slightly.

"I guess you know your radio's out. The whole system's on the fritz. Maybe it's sunspots, I don't know—"

"Reed . . ." Pete's voice was weak, barely audible.

Reed double-timed and knelt beside him. "Pete . . ."

Pete's rifle was gone. His face was pale, drained of blood, and he was holding his side. Blood oozed between his fingers. It looked like a knife wound.

Reed didn't ask how it had happened. That wasn't important now. "Easy, bud. We're going to get you out of here."

"S-sam!"

"What?"

"Get down."

Reed saw the terror in Pete's eyes as they focused across the clearing. Not thinking, just trusting, Reed ducked.

A bullet zinged over his head and thudded into Pete's chest.

Then came the *Pow!* of a rifle.

Reed hugged the ground, looked up at Pete—

Pete's lifeless body slumped over, revealing a bullet puncture and a red smear on the tree behind him.

Reed held his rifle in a death grip. He had a general idea

where the shot had come from, but he dared not raise his head to make sure.

Sam. Pete said "Sam."

Why began to enter his head, but the why didn't matter, not now. *Not being killed* mattered.

Reed rolled behind a clump of rocks, disturbing some brush, a telltale sign of his location.

There was a puff of dust and the whine of a ricochet.

Pow!

The slope fell away just below Reed's position, providing a protective dome of earth between him and the shooter. He grabbed his chance and ran, crouching, down the slope and into the trees. Dropping behind a protective log, he peered back toward the clearing as he cycled the bolt on his rifle, chambering a round—

It didn't feel right. He opened the bolt.

The firing pin was broken as if someone had punched it in with a nail.

Max had offered to load Reed's rifle and Reed had said okay.

Max and Sam. The cover-up! Them? Why?

The questions would have to come later. For now, there was absolutely no sense in sticking around. Reed barreled down the hill, not navigating, just moving, ducking behind trees, zig-zagging, always looking for cover.

The GPS! He glanced at it. He could see his own blip, and now he could see Sam's, coming down the hill after him, homing in on his satellite signal!

Reed clicked off his unit. The LCD screen went black. No Reed. No Sam. No signals. He was alone in the woods except for the men trying to kill him, out of contact.

Hunted.

EIGHTEEN

It was like awakening slowly from an anesthetic, coming out of the dark, reentering the world from somewhere far away. She heard a voice but understood no words. The floor felt wet and sticky against her face, and it was reeling as if the entire motor home were floating on stormy water. A sharp pain hammered her skull with every beat of her pulse, and she smelled blood. She became aware of her body in stages, first her hands, then her arms, and then her legs, but somehow, through the morass of tangled, swirling thoughts that were half dream, half coherent, she knew that she must not move, she must not appear alive.

She heard a voice from somewhere, and in a few more moments and a few more painful pulse beats, she remembered whose voice it was.

Thorne. She recalled the last image she saw before her awareness came to a shattering halt: Steve Thorne, eyes as cold as a shark's, aiming his pistol at her. As near as she could determine from the pattern of the pain and the state of her body, the bullet had struck her in the head. Where the bullet was now she cringed to imagine, but she was still alive and beginning to think again, which astounded her.

"No, he's got it switched off," came Thorne's voice. He paused as if listening to someone and then answered, "I know, but just keep moving, keep the pressure on.

She sensed from the direction of his voice that he was behind her. Carefully, she worked one eye open. The floor of the motor home wavered and then came into focus.

The first thing she saw was a pool of blood. How she'd managed to regain consciousness she had no idea, but one thing was certain: whatever consciousness she had would be temporary at best.

Just a few more moments, she thought. *If I can gather my strength for just a few more moments . . .*

Reed rolled over a log, sank into the cover of some willows, and lay still, listening, thinking.

Encouraging thoughts were in short supply. For all he knew, there hadn't been anything wrong with Wiley Kane's rifle, which would mean Kane was dead and maybe Sing as well, both at the hand of Steve Thorne. That left him no friends and three hunters trying to track him down. If he could turn on his GPS and pick up their locations—

That was the problem. If he turned his unit on, the others would be able to see him just as he would be able to see them. He could guess that he was in the middle of a triangle with Max to the north, Sam to the south, and Thorne downhill to the west. They were no doubt closing in on him right now.

He wriggled through the willows and ran for a stand of firs—
A chip of bark flew from a trunk and nearly hit him in the cheek.
Pow!

Well, at least he was maintaining some distance.

Jacob halted again, turned in place, sniffed, and searched as he
grunted at his females, yanking them to keep them close together.
They were still working their way north, but in zigzags, quick
sprints, silent hidings. The woman was silent, unseen, but Beck
trusted Jacob's senses and understood why he was keeping the
group together: predators went for the stragglers, the strays,
those left alone. If they stayed together, maybe, just maybe . . .

Beck had heard more gunshots behind them. She couldn't
make any sense of it except to guess the hunters were trying to
signal her.

She felt the GPS in her shirt pocket. For now, surrounded by
the frightened, fleeing family, she left it off.

"Okay," Thorne was saying, "try to keep pace with him and
don't let him flank you. I'm all set to torch this place as soon as
you're done."

Torch. Fire. Now Sing recognized a particular smell that didn't
belong: gasoline.

She concentrated, then raised her head a hair's breadth, gritting
her teeth against the pain. *I must be a stone. Lord, help me not to feel;
help me not to hurt.* She raised her head higher. She tested the fingers on her right hand. From somewhere, she found strength.

She couldn't see Thorne but could paint a picture in her mind from what she could hear: four feet away . . . sitting at the computer . . . facing maybe a quarter turn away from her . . . looking down at the screen, and—*Dear Lord, please*—his weight on the forward half of the chair.

She wouldn't be able to test her strength or her ability to move. She would have only one chance to move at all.

She envisioned where the knife rack must be: very close, above the cutting board, near the bedroom door. One quick leap would get her there—if she was able. She envisioned the carving knife in her right hand, the one with the sharpest point. She reviewed her memory of the various knifing victims she had examined, which wounds had killed in the shortest amount of time.

"Is she dead?" Thorne was saying. "Are you kidding? I blew her brains out. You want me to do it again?"

I am a stone.

She pulled in a long, steady breath, then let it out slowly, silently. She pulled in a second breath, then let it out. Without motion, she tested her muscles.

Thorne was listening again, drumming his fingers on the counter. Hopefully, he would talk again; his ears would be filled with the sound of his own voice.

"Adam, come on, now. You're in this neck deep with the rest of us. Let's get it done—"

With every reserve of strength, of body, and of spirit, Sing flipped from her belly to her back and then to her side, closing the distance to the computer chair. Thorne's head was turning toward the sound and he was saying, ". . . and go home," just as her hands gripped the wheeled base of the chair, yanked, and upset it from under him. He fell away from her, grabbing the counter, trying to recover as the chair clattered on its side to the floor.

She pushed to her feet, reached with her right hand, grasped the knife from the rack—

Her head emptied of blood and she sank to her knees, head down, vision clouded, pain raging through her skull. Her hair and scalp were sodden and dripping. She held the knife in both hands.

Thorne was on his feet immediately. He came at her.

She raised her head and saw her target: the femoral artery near the top of his thigh. Her head was swimming, her strength departing.

He put his hands on her, tried to grab her arms.

With both hands, she plunged the knife into his thigh near the groin.

He screamed in pain and horror, releasing his grip, backing off. The knife slipped from the wound with a spurt of blood. His leg collapsed under him and he staggered backwards, tumbling over the fallen chair.

He was distracted, disoriented, on his back.

Her chance would never come again. Unable to rise to her feet, she lunged forward on her knees, screaming like a cougar, pouncing like a bear.

Just above the belly, just below the breastbone, at just the right angle—

With both hands and all her weight, she put the knife through his heart. He stared at her in disbelief, gasping, trembling, until his eyes went blank, his pupils dilated, and his head clunked against the floor. His arms, then his whole body, went limp. Near his head were the mobile lab's auxilary gasoline cans. He wouldn't be using them.

Sing rolled to the floor beside the man she had just killed, her scream becoming a loud sobbing from pain, fear, and horror.

Jacob and the females were moving swiftly, their articulated feet padding silently over deep humus and soft green moss, weaving up and down, under and around immense, ancient pillars of old-growth forest with seeming indifference.

But Beck was sure she knew this place. Hadn't she once compared it to a Tolkien or Lewis fantasy, a wondrous, otherworldly place where hobbits and elves, fairies and princesses, knights and ogres had their adventures and intrigues?

She'd been here with Reed only a week ago!

Hadn't she?

Painfully clinging to Rachel's shoulders, she looked for a trail, a ravine, a creek with a log bridge, an old cabin torn apart by a savage beast—frightening memories to be sure, but it was the nearest boundary of her world, the last place she'd ever been as a human being.

Rachel slowed, faltered, then turned downhill.

"Wha—?" Beck started to say.

Rachel kept going, loping down the slope even after Jacob stopped, turned around, and grunted a question at her; even after Leah barked in alarm and Reuben whimpered.

Beck pushed herself higher up on Rachel's back and scanned the forest on every side, wondering where Rachel was going, and why, and feeling anxious about being separated from the group. "Rachel! Hello? W-what are you doing?"

Beck looked over her shoulder. Jacob, Leah, and Reuben were huddling together, fidgeting and grunting. Rachel's side trip was not in their plans.

Rachel was sniffing, on the trail of something. Beck had never seen this behavior before, a Sasquatch sniffing *after* something rather than running *from* something it happened to smell. "What is it, girl?"

They came to an immense log that had once been a majestic cedar unnumbered years before. A web of tangled roots clawed the air at one end; the other end disappeared in the forest, covered over with young firs and cedars that had taken root along its surface.

Rachel sniffed the air again as if trying to be sure of something, then circled around the roots to the other side.

A loud fluttering startled Beck; she ducked behind Rachel's head as a gathering of birds scattered into the air: ravens, an osprey, two bald eagles. Recovering, and peering over Rachel's shoulder, Beck saw that the birds had been here awhile—the surrounding thickets, branches, and windfall were spattered with white droppings.

Rachel straightened in that certain way that let Beck know she could slide to the ground. Beck released her grip around Rachel's shoulders and slid clumsily onto a mound of red crumbles, the remains of a fallen tree. Her legs were weak; she collapsed to the ground.

Rachel took a furtive step, then another, looking at something amid the broken, dropping-spattered branches of serviceberry, until, with a mournful sigh, she sank to her haunches, her head hanging.

Beck struggled to her feet, eased closer, and caught a scent she'd come to know: raw meat and peeled animal hide, this time with a reek of decay. From behind Rachel's slumped back, she peered into the broken bushes and saw a rib cage almost picked clean by the birds, the blackening meat showing red where it had been freshly torn by their beaks. Eyes widening with horror, Beck saw an arm, half eaten, half covered with reddish-brown fur, with an ape's hand—five fingers and a thumb.

Beck moved from Rachel's right shoulder to her left for a better look.

The innards were almost completely gone. The spine was visible through the empty chest cavity, and Beck saw that the neck had been violently twisted and broken. Lying crookedly, almost separate from the body, was the rotting head of a Sasquatch child, one eye closed, one eye gone, the face pecked and gouged.

The little female was Beck's size. The mouth was smeared with huckleberries, and the hair—the long, magnificent hair—was reddish brown, the same color as Rachel's.

"Sh-she was yours, wasn't she?"

Rachel's body began to quake as air rushed in and out of her nostrils like . . . sobs? Beck, already in a state of shock, was further astonished. Was Rachel . . . *crying*? Was it possible?

Tears flooded Rachel's eyes, overflowed, and ran down her face, something Beck had never seen or imagined in the great ape.

"Rachel . . . sweetheart . . ."

Beck touched her, patted her.

Rachel threw back her head and howled, a loud sound that rippled through the forest and carried for miles.

From above, Leah began howling and Jacob barked a warning. The forest was filled with the noise.

Beck covered an ear with one hand, stroked Rachel's shoulder with the other—

She recalled the bite marks on that shoulder, the patch of blood that had soiled Beck's leather coat, the howls she and Reed heard that night—not vicious howls of predation and threat as they'd thought, but howls of struggle and loss, pain and remorse, the same as she was hearing now.

Then, like a loathsome reminder, a third voice joined Leah and Rachel's from *out there*. The wailing woman, the demon of Lost Creek, began to answer the howls with her own eerie cry, matching them volume for volume.

The ghostly chorus from that night on Lost Creek was complete.

Beck *had* been in this place before.

Reed was not terrified when the howling voices floated his way through the forest, layer upon echoed layer. For him, it was an awakening of hope. He knew those voices well, and judging from the sound, the beasts were still within reach—if he could only live that long. He took a measured risk and raised his head from his hiding place between two moss-covered logs, scanning the forest all around. He saw no telltale movement behind the trunks of trees and the tangled stalks of bushes; he heard no snapping of twigs or crunching of leaves to indicate his enemies had found him.

Not that it mattered. They were hunters. They would be doing all they could to remain unseen and unheard. The last two bullets had whizzed by his head before he'd seen or heard anything else.

But he'd heard the beasts, and if they were nearby, Beck could be nearby, and if, on the outside chance that she'd decided to send a signal . . .

He turned on his GPS and the screen lit up. He could see Sam almost straight uphill from him—and knew Sam could see him. Max was still to the north and moving farther that way, not interested in Reed at all but going after the beasts—and maybe Beck. He last saw Steve Thorne's blip approaching Sing's motor home near the end of Service Road 221, but it was off the screen now, which could be the worst of news. Only Sing could update him on Blip Number 6, *if* Beck's unit was turned on and *if* he could raise Sing on the radio, and *only if* Sing were still alive—

A weak and faltering voice came through his earpiece, "Reed, I see you on my screen. Can you hear me?"

Reed felt as though he'd reconnected a lifeline! "Sing! I was afraid you were dead!"

"Almost. Steve Thorne shot me in the head."

He couldn't have heard that correctly. "Say again?"

Sing was slumped over in her computer chair, pressing a bloodied towel to her head, trying to view the screen sideways and work the keyboard with one free hand. Sometimes she could think clearly, and sometimes she felt she was dreaming. "It was a glancing blow." She touched the wound and winced. "It feels like a shallow depressed fracture, nonpenetrating." She looked at the bloodied towel. "The bullet missed the temporal artery, but there's still a mess."

"Have you called the medics?"

"Thorne smashed my cell phone and I can't find the police radio."

"Where is Thorne now?"

"Steve Thorne is dead."

"Did you say Thorne is dead?"

She looked at the corpse on the floor for a moment, her focus wavering. "I'm pretty sure. I severed his femoral artery and stabbed him through the heart. He isn't moving."

"Sing, Pete's dead too. Sam killed him. Do you copy?" She heard the anguish in Reed's voice, as if he were hearing the news himself for the first time.

Her wound pulsed out fresh pain in a faster rhythm. "Did you say Pete is dead?"

"Yes. Sam shot him, and now Sam's trying to kill me."

She rested her head on the counter, weak with shock and grief. Maybe she *was* dreaming, and this was a bad dream. It felt like one.

"Sing? Are you there?"

"The cover-up," came to her mind and out her mouth.

"We need to find Beck. Can you see her on your screen?"

Sing blinked and forced her eyes to focus on the screen. "Reed . . . Sam is coming down the hill, coming close to you." Sam's blip winked out. "Oh no, he's not—"

Ping!

Reed had just turned to scramble out of the logs when the bullet hit and chips flew only inches away. He ducked, rolled, plowed into some bushes, found a tree to protect him.

"Sam?" Reed called into his GPS radio. "Sam, you don't want to do this."

No answer. Reed looked at his screen. That's what Sing meant: Sam had turned off his unit. He'd gone invisible.

Well, it could work both ways. Reed switched off his unit. He knew Sam was heading down the hill from the south. Hoping to flank him, Reed started up the hill toward the north.

Beck heard the shot and searched that direction but saw no movement, no camouflage jackets or caps. She thought of shouting, but no, not here, not where they would find Rachel.

As if Rachel were not giving them plenty of noise already. She was still howling inconsolably, her head thrown back, her right hand beating her chest.

Beck tried to calm her, quiet her down. "Shhh, now! Shhh! Rachel, don't do this! The hunters will find you!"

Rachel shrugged her hand away, and Beck shied back a step, stricken by the tableau of a grieving mother and her dead, mangled child, incredulous at the revelation in the child's reddish-brown hair: "I was *her*! You thought I was *her*! No wonder you wanted my hair the way it was."

Ka-wump! As if he'd dropped from the sky, Jacob came leaping over the log and thudded like a falling timber right next to them. Beck jumped with a yelp, but Jacob paid her no mind. Growling and scolding, he yanked Rachel to her feet and shoved her against the log, trying to knock some sense into her. She quit howling but kept crying. He pushed her from behind, herded her, swatted her, got her moving around the log.

Rachel did not look back to find Beck. She just went around the log, still whimpering, with Jacob huffing at her to be quiet.

Beck stood there. Alone. Amazed. Nonplussed.

Rachel didn't look back.

When they reappeared on the hill above the log, Jacob was hurrying her along, pushing and grunting. She obeyed and climbed the slope in front of him, her soft feet taking hold of the ground with sure steps, her head hanging as she wiped her tear-stained face. They disappeared behind a tree, reemerged, passed behind another tree, then two, and then the forest shrouded them like a closing curtain and Beck saw them no more.

Somewhere in the deep forest, out of sight, Rachel quit whimpering and Jacob fell silent.

Beck backed up a step, and noticed that she could. She looked over her shoulder, down the hill, and realized she could go there. She looked up the hill. No Jacob. No Rachel. No group.

What about the woman? Beck listened carefully, rotating a full circle. The woman was silent, which could mean she was gone, or lurking, or stalking, or trailing the Sasquatches . . .

There was no time to fret about it. There was no option but

to get moving, to find a landmark or trail, to get that GPS turned on and make sure the hunters found only her.

She ventured One Small Step downhill, slowed by the pain in her body, her ankle complaining but carrying her. Other steps came after the first, from tree to tree to ledge to stump to tree to fallen log, farther down and still farther down, always peering ahead, always hoping to sight something familiar emerging through the ever-changing curtain of trees.

Just one more time, she looked back. The Sasquatches were gone. She was no danger to them.

She pulled the GPS from her shirt pocket and pressed the on button. The LCD screen lit up.

Sing just had to accept it. She couldn't explain it; she wasn't expecting it; she could hardly comprehend it, but there it was: Blip Number 6.

"Reed . . . I have Beck on my screen."

The screen faded to black; her thoughts disintegrated into nonsense and she began to dream.

She didn't know how much time had passed before she jerked awake, forced her eyes open, and brought the screen back into focus.

"Reed, Max is heading for Blip Number 6. He can see where Beck is. Reed? Reed, do you copy?"

No answer.

Beck studied the screen on her GPS as she hiked a meandering, limping course down the mountain slope, heading for what looked like a stream on the moving map, hoping to find another human being.

"Hello! Is anybody there?"

She was alone, and she knew it. She was a stray, a straggler, and a perfect target for a predator. No wonder Rachel never let her wander off.

"Hello! I'm Beck Shelton! Is anyone there?"

Keep moving, girl; keep moving. Find those hunters.

Was *she* making that noise? She stopped. The rustling she heard continued. It came from up the slope, back among the trees where anything could hide.

"Hello!"

No answer—just the snap of twigs, the rustling of some brush.

Reed crouched in a thick cluster of young growth, not sure enough of where he was to keep moving. He may have slipped by Sam on his way uphill, but there was only one way to be sure.

He pressed the on button.

The screen told him he was a little upslope and a little south of where he wanted to be. "Sing? Do you read?"

Her voice was weak but tense with excitement. "Reed, I have Blip Number 6, bearing 342, close to Lost Creek. Max is closing on it!"

Something in Reed came alive again. He zoomed out on his screen to find the creek, to orient himself to the bearing.

Sam's blip appeared like a ship out of the fog, closer than ever.

The bullet hit with a loud *whack!* Reed spun and went down with a cry, grasping his shoulder.

"Reed, Sam is coming uphill toward you!"

Reed had to grab a breath before he could answer, gasping with pain. "Sing. I've been hit."

Beck quickened her step. A human would have answered when she called. She moved downhill, ducked behind some trees, froze, and listened.

The sounds were following her, moving down the hill: a thump, a dragging, another stick breaking.

She leaped and limped to the next tree and listened again. She may have heard more noises, but now the gurgle of a creek was making it difficult to tell.

A creek?

She limped to the next tree and peered around it.

A ravine. A creek. It had to be Lost Creek!

Thump! Drag. Thump! Drag.

She ducked behind the tree and peeked uphill.

Through the spaces in the trees she caught a flash of black hair, a patch of yellowing flesh.

Whatever it was, it was walking.

Beck only whispered, "Jacob?"

The woman screamed in reply, so close Beck could hear the rattle of phlegm in her windpipe.

Beck spun, tried to run, but her legs were weak and she fell headlong.

The cry of the banshee blasted over her, around her, so close and so loud it hurt.

Thump! Drag. Thump! Drag.

NINETEEN

Reed disappeared from Sing's screen. "Reed, don't do this to me! Be alive, please!"

With a few fumbling tries, she zoomed in on Sam's blip. He was shifting back and forth as if searching.

Reed ducked and wove around trunks and undergrowth as quickly and silently as he could, mimicking the stalking techniques he'd seen Pete use, half-guessing his bearing, hoping, praying for enough time to live, to stay ahead of Sam, to get to Beck and end this. His GPS was off. For now, he would have to be invisible.

Beck rolled to a stop, righted herself, looked up the slope—
Thump! Drag.

It emerged from behind an ancient fir, thumping on one crooked leg and dragging the other, still raw and bleeding from a bullet wound. It wavered, grabbed at one tree and then the next with long ape arms to steady itself, wheezing hoarsely, teeth bared and canines glistening. It was every bit as large and powerful as Jacob, but bent, twisted, deformed. Its black hair was sparse and patchy, bristling like quills from its jaundiced skin. The wrinkled head was nearly bald, and one half of the face was peeling, blistered and scabbed from a recent burn. When it saw her, it glared with bulbous yellow eyes and screamed a scream Beck could *feel*.

It came after her, hobbling on uneven legs, careening, its long arms guiding it from tree to tree as it descended the slope.

Beck leaped aside as it rumbled past. It planted a hand on a tree and spun around, fell, rose again, and crawled up the hill on all fours, thumping and dragging, grabbing and pulling, a crooked, arthritic hand clawing to reach her.

Beck screamed as she turned to escape up the bank, her strength ebbing, the humus crumbling and giving beneath her feet. She screamed again with all that was in her as a huge hand swung close enough to strike her foot but not grab it.

Thinking like an animal, Beck wailed a Sasquatch wail of alarm, loud and throaty, again and again, grabbing roots and small bushes to pull herself away from those hands, those teeth, those glaring eyes.

Reed heard the screams—Beck's screams; he'd know her voice anywhere—and it was all he could do to keep his cool, stay smart, and not break into a blind run. Sam was still a factor, and Reed would never be able to outrun him.

He found a hiding spot behind some rocks and collapsed there, taking off his hat, struggling out of his jacket. *Hang on, Beck!*

The thing fell on its face as its legs buckled; it writhed and flailed until it was moving again, hobbling on twos, walking on fours, stumbling on threes, shoulders uneven, knuckles skinned and bleeding. It lagged behind long enough for Beck to break into a clearing where patches of maple and elderberry grew through a crisscross of wind-fallen trunks. She came up against a wall of brush and fallen trees with no way over or around.

The creature broke into the clearing, huffing and wheezing, froth on its chin, eyes crazed. *Thump! Draaaagg. Thump! Draaaggg.*

Beck turned, her back against the brush pile, her arms and legs tangled in an explosion of shoots, leaves, and branches. She cried out again, looking for a way out, over, under, *anywhere.*

The thing bared its teeth, reached out—

Boom! The left shoulder jerked violently as blood and flesh exploded out the creature's back. It cried out in pain and horror, afraid, wondering.

Boom! The right arm jerked and twisted, the bicep punctured and spurting red, the bone beneath snapping.

Boom! The creature reeled backward, a puncture in its chest.

It stood, glaring at Beck, teeth bared, reddening saliva seeping through its teeth.

Boom! With another blast through its chest, its breath became a gargle. It teetered and swayed, choking, its eyes locked on Beck with murderous intent until they slowly closed in sleep and the creature fell with a *wump!* that shook the ground.

It lay still. There was a momentary, unnatural silence.

Beck could not comprehend that the danger was over. She pushed farther into the thicket, tried to get a foothold on the log, slipped and fell into the elderberry branches.

Then she saw someone. A hunter in camouflage came into the clearing, stepping cautiously, rifle leveled at the creature.

Beck couldn't move. She couldn't speak. She could only stare through the leaves.

He went to the creature, now spread flat on its back on the rough ground. He poked it with his rifle, then pointed the rifle directly at the thing's head.

Beck turned her head away.

Boom! One last shot.

The hunter glanced around the clearing. "Hello? Beck Shelton?"

He spotted her through all the helter-skelter limbs, and he appeared a little puzzled. "Beck? Beck Shelton?" Why was he staring at her? "It's all right. The creature's dead."

Language had left her. "Whoo . . . hoo . . . hoooo . . ."

"Who am I?"

She nodded.

"I'm a friend. My name is Adam Burkhardt."

Reed lay among the rocks, unable to move. He switched on the GPS and spoke in a weak, trembling voice. "S-sam. Sam, why are you doing this? Why are you trying to kill me?"

For the very first time, Sam replied. "It's nothing personal, Reed. It's something I was hired to do."

"I don't understand."

"It's not that complicated. Just call it survival."

Sing saw Reed's blip on her screen, but it wasn't moving. Sam's was, changing course and heading directly for him.

She mumbled into her headphone, "Sam . . . Sam, I can see you on my screen. I'm a witness."

There was an ominous silence as the blip kept moving closer to Reed's position.

Abruptly, Sam radioed, "You've got a hole in your head, so I figure I've still got a pretty good chance of catching up with you later. Reed? You still with us, buddy?"

Reed's voice was barely audible. "Please don't kill me."

Beck pushed a few limbs aside. She studied the man, unsure about him. He was suddenly preoccupied, listening intently to the device in his ear. She could see a GPS on his sleeve.

Sam Marlowe got a visual: Reed Shelton down, propped against a log, hand against his chest as if he were having trouble breathing. Sam steadied himself against a tree, sighted Reed's back through his scope—"Sorry, pal"—and pulled the trigger. The body lurched with the impact, then remained still, flopped over the log.

He sighed with relief. "About time."

Keeping his rifle ready, he stepped carefully into the open, approaching his target. He could see a good-sized hole through Reed's jacket. He spoke into his radio, "Boss? You there?"

"Go ahead," Burkhardt answered.

Sam reached the body. "Heard you doing a lot of shooting. Did you get what you were after?"

"Uh, yeah, so far."

"Well, I just got Reed, so let's close this up and get out of here. We've still got Thorne's job to finish."

"Uh, roger. I'll get back to you." Burkhardt's voice didn't sound too sure.

Adam Burkhardt set his rifle down, removed the earpiece from his ear, and turned off his GPS. "I guess that's that." He looked at Beck, who was still hiding in the bushes. "Don't be afraid. It's all over now. I, uh, I spent quite a few years studying these creatures."

For some reason, she couldn't move.

Sam shook his head. Burkhardt sounded as though he was having doubts again, which wasn't good. Burkhardt set this whole thing up, and now he was becoming the weak link! Never send a boy . . .

Sam grabbed Reed's body by the shoulder and flipped it over.

It was Wiley Kane, dressed in Reed's jacket, his white mane stuffed inside Reed's cap.

Reed could move now. He aimed his rifle from his hiding place in the rocks, only fifteen yards away. "Sam, drop that rifle!"

Sam's face flushed with surprise. He raised his weapon—

Reed shot him through the heart, knocking him backwards. He dropped like a limp puppet.

Reed rose only enough to make sure Sam and his rifle landed separately, then got on the radio. "Sing? It's Reed. Can you hear me?"

Maybe being shot in the head had something to do with it: Sing was still hearing Reed's voice. "Reed, are you *alive*?"

"I had to do some playacting. Sorry to scare you."

"Sam . . . Sam's close!"

Reed stood over Sam's body and double-checked. "Sam is dead. I shot him with Wiley Kane's rifle." He looked about cautiously. "Do you have Max on your screen?"

"No. He's gone now. But I still have Beck."

"Get me there, Sing."

Sing was fading. Her answer came in disjointed pieces. "Head for . . . um, Lost Creek. The bearing is . . . 340. Less than a quarter . . . mile."

Adam Burkhardt sat on a log, wiping his close-shaven brow and staring at the grotesque, bleeding beast at his feet. "This creature was an experiment that went terribly awry." He laughed. "Makes me sound like a mad scientist, doesn't it?" He quit laughing abruptly. "Maybe I qualify. This is a terrible thing, just terrible."

Beck ventured to the edge of the bushes, eyes probing this man and the hairy, misshapen creature that had almost killed her. "Did it kill . . ." She could not recall the man's name.

"Randy Thompson?"

She nodded.

"Oh yes. It's killed several people. We thought it had killed *you*." His face was sad, and yet he seemed to marvel. "It was bred that way, bred to prevail—even though it can't reproduce." He pointed, almost proudly. "But did you notice it was trying to walk upright? We removed the big toes so it couldn't live in the trees and would have to navigate mostly on the ground. We may have confirmed our theory, but then again, the knee and hip joints are unsuitable for bipedalism, so it's hard to draw any conclusions."

She stared at him blankly.

He shook his head. "I'm sorry. This does take a bit of explaining, doesn't it? Well, have you ever heard how we're all 98 percent chimpanzee?"

Reed ran, ducked, swerved, jumped, ran some more, jamming more cartridges into Kane's rifle as he went. He still didn't have Blip Number 6 on his screen, but he had to be getting close. He'd entered a familiar stretch of old-growth forest; the terrain descended toward Lost Creek.

Sing's eyes were so heavy she could hardly keep them open. "Too far downhill. You want . . . 355."

Reed's blip changed course, but its progress seemed agonizingly slow.

"Sing, is Beck moving at all?"

Sing closed her eyes. The motor home was rocking again, heaving like the ocean. She was getting nauseous.

"Sing!"

She opened her eyes. "Uh, now it's, uh, 350."

"Anyway," said Burkhardt, replacing his hat and eyeing Beck with a strange look of pity, "what we've taught people to believe, we have yet to prove, and now . . ." He indicated the beast at his feet. "Some could even say we've proven the *opposite*, which would be very difficult for us, to say the least. We wouldn't want that fact to become too, uh, noticeable. Am I making any sense?"

Beck could only shake her head.

He stood, wringing his hands, obviously agitated, nervous. It made *her* nervous. "Well, here's the situation: many, oh, at least half of the search party, thought it was a bear, and when they shot a large bear, they thought they had the villain, and they all went home. That was excellent! That took care of half the problem!"

He stepped closer to her, his hands out in front of him as if gesturing. "And then there was a really wonderful hoax by some Bigfoot fanatics—oh, you should have seen it, footprints and everything! It provided an excellent dismissal of that contingent as crackpots that no one would take seriously!"

He came so close that Beck took a step backward.

"But then there were the people who actually saw our *creature* but were not killed—people like your husband, Reed . . . and you." He grimaced. "If you just hadn't been in the woods, things could have been different! As it is, you and your husband became a liability, and now, with your husband no longer a factor, that leaves you."

Beck pressed backward into the tangle, dismay becoming

dread, and dread becoming terror. *Reed no longer a factor?* What did that mean? Then it occurred to her—she was not back in her own world. This was not a human being come to save her, but an articulate, educated beast. She could see in his eyes what she'd seen only moments before in the eyes of his creature.

He was there to kill her.

She turned and bolted into the bushes.

He dove, grabbed her by her collar, and jerked her backward, off her feet. She fought, striking and flailing, as he dragged her out of the thicket by her collar, by her hair. "I'm sorry, I'm sorry," he kept saying.

Reed heard a scream, very close. He checked his GPS.

He was picking up Blip Number 6, uphill, bearing 005, not more than 200 yards through dense, young growth. "Sing! I've got her! 005! Can you confirm?"

Sing saw both blips on her screen, with Reed converging. The image was fuzzy, fading in and out of her awareness, becoming meaningless to her. "Go to her, Reed."

She backed her chair away from the computer and put her head between her knees. The pain made her whimper. She checked the towel she'd been using, and fresh blood dripped on it the moment she lifted it from her head.

She didn't remember toppling to the floor. She only remembered seeing the ceiling as high as the sky above her and hearing the faint sound of a helicopter before she fell asleep.

Beck was facedown in rocks, needles, and grass, trying to squirm free, flailing her arms at nothing, struggling for breath as Burkhardt's knee pinned her to the ground. He clamped his hands on either side of her head; she peeled them loose. He gripped her forehead and the back of her head and began twisting. "I'm sorry," he said. "I don't want to do this."

She grabbed, clawed, kicked, but couldn't resist his strength. Her neck twisted, twisted some more. Her scream became a gargle. He was going to snap her neck, kill her like all the others, carry out what his beast couldn't. Abruptly, his grip forced her head backward, and then—

He was gone. His weight lifted from her body as if a huge eagle had plucked him up. She got her arms and legs under her, ready to dig in and get away—

The sky was blotted out by blackness that moved, roared with anger, and held Burkhardt aloft as if he weighed nothing. With long, tree-trunk arms, the monstrous shape hurled Burkhardt across the clearing.

Burkhardt hit the ground, tumbled, struggled to right himself—

He looked up—*way* up—and the sight paralyzed him.

Beck was amazed, relieved, and terrified.

It was Jacob, vicious and defensive, taking position between Beck and Burkhardt with black hair bristling, fangs bared, and arms ready to dismember.

Burkhardt's rifle was only a few feet beyond his reach. He noticed it, tried to ease toward it.

Deputy Dave Saunders had an iron grip on the wheel and a determined set in his jaw as he drove his squad car through Abney, lights flashing, and veered onto Service Road 221. Behind him came another squad car carrying two more deputies, a squad car carrying two Idaho State patrolmen, an ambulance with four paramedics, and behind that, a light-green rig carrying three shotgun-toting forest rangers.

Cap rode in the squad car beside him, hand on the dash, eyes intent on the road. "How far?"

Dave got on the radio. "Chopper Oh-9, we are entering road 221 at Abney. Any fix on the motor home?"

High above, piloting a National Guard helicopter on loan to Idaho Fish and Game, Jimmy Clark eyed the old road that snaked through the rolling, forested terrain. Two sheriff's officers rode with him. Where the road began to fade from brown dirt to green weeds, Jimmy spotted the silver rectangle he was looking for. "Car 12, I have the motor home, about four miles up the road. No activity, but we'll stick around. Drive safe, everybody."

Dave drove as fast as "safe" would allow, the wheels pounding over ruts and potholes, the car nearly bottoming its springs. The other vehicles stayed right behind him.

Burkhardt had just grabbed his rifle when Jacob plucked him off the ground by a wad of his jacket. The scientist dangled in the air, legs kicking, face stretched with horror, trying to chamber a round, trying to aim his rifle. Jacob didn't wait for Burkhardt to resolve such issues but threw him into the brush, where he tumbled and thrashed out of sight in the tangle.

Beck was suddenly surrounded by reddish-brown hair as huge arms enfolded her and pulled her in. She fell against a familiar bosom, felt a sweaty heat, inhaled a disgusting stench, and for the first time in a week, felt perfectly, wondrously safe.

"Mmm!" Rachel grunted, looking down at her. Beck had seen that expression before, when she awoke in Rachel's arms in a patch of huckleberries.

Jacob tromped halfway into the brush, watched Burkhardt's still body for a short time, growled a last word, and then he was satisfied. He stomped out of the bushes and started to leave, but not without an obligatory glance in Beck's direction.

She wanted to smile, to thank him, to give him a hug, but of course, he would not understand such things. She only hummed her thanks, looking just below his eye line.

He huffed back at her as if to say, *This doesn't mean I like you*, and vanished into the trees.

Beck tried to relax. She had to deal with Rachel somehow, had to—

Rachel tensed, her arms closing tightly against Beck. *Danger*. Beck could read it clearly in Rachel's manner. Was Burkhardt still—

The brush across the clearing opened, and Beck gasped audibly. Her legs weakened and her hands began to shake.

It was Reed, hard-run and sweating, holding a rifle, suddenly motionless at what he saw.

She couldn't express what she felt in words, only a Sasquatch sound, a long, mournful cry as she hung in Rachel's arms, trying to believe.

TWENTY

Reed was prepared to confront anything, but the scene before him was impossible to fathom. It was as if time had folded back on itself and he was below the waterfall again. The creature he never quite saw that night stood across the clearing plainly visible, a reddish version of Arlen's photograph, but so much bigger in real life. Just as before, it held Beck—but what had happened to her? The pitiful woman in that creature's arms was dirty all over, smeared with mud and . . . it looked like manure! Her face was bruised, and one eye was puffy. Grass and weeds hung from every chink in her clothing, the front of her shirt was stained with blood, and now she was making sounds like an animal.

In the center of the clearing lay a grotesque, fly-infested corpse that shattered all of his previous assumptions.

*   *   *

Rachel growled low in her throat and began to back away.

Beck shot a hand toward Reed and cried out like a Sasquatch, pleading, "Ohh, oh-oh-oh, Reeeeed!"

Rachel hesitated, huffing air through her nostrils, her arms like steel, on the verge of fleeing. But something held her here; maybe, just maybe, she recognized this stranger.

Beck detected Jacob's stench. He hadn't left.

Reed didn't move, but he had a round in the chamber and his finger on the trigger.

Beck had cried out his name. He said hers, very quietly. "Beck."

"Look at me," she said, her hand extended toward him. "Don't look at her; look at me." Beck was *talking*!

"Are you all right?"

The big red beast was huffing, nervous, spooked, ready to attack, or ready to run—Reed couldn't tell which it would be, but he would shoot either way.

He heard a low growl coming from the trees behind the beast and recalled the multiple footprints, especially those of the alpha male. He forbade himself to be afraid, but his hands were getting icy.

"Reed," Beck called quietly, "you have to bow. You have to show them you're not a threat."

Reed had to be sure he'd heard her right. "Bow?"

Beck sensed that Rachel was warily checking out this intruder, which was a good sign. In a different situation, Rachel never would have stuck around at all. Beck kept her hand stretched out to show friendship and connection, hoping Rachel would read it that way.

"Bow, Reed." She pantomimed a slight bow. "Bow down."

Reed bowed only a few inches, his eyes taking in his target, his rifle pointing only slightly away.

"Yes, yes, that's right." He looked up. "*Don't look at them; look at me!*" He dropped his eyes and met hers. "We have to show them we know each other. Just look at me—and don't smile!"

He wasn't smiling anyway, but he relaxed his expression as best he could. "Good, good, good. Don't show your teeth; that's a threat. Now maybe you'd better put the rifle down."

No way. "Can't do it, Beck."

There came that growl from the trees again. Reed saw something moving back there—if that was the top of the thing's head, it was a lot taller than Reed would have expected.

Beck made that weird guttural sound again, reaching out with both hands, "Ohhhhh, oh-oh-oh!" Then she clicked her tongue. "*Tok! Tok!*"

Now what was he supposed to do?

"Reach out to me, like I'm doing."

Reed cradled the rifle in his left hand and slowly reached with his right, an eye on those trees.

"Look at me, Reed!"

How far do I trust her?

The big red creature huffed, eyeing him with obvious suspicion as the trees behind her quaked.

Come on, Big Red, he thought. *You know me. We've met before.*

Beck pushed to get free of Rachel's arms but was held tight. As for Jacob, Beck recognized his breathing from the last time Reed came too close. "Reed? Reed, listen to me. I don't think they're buying it."

He tightened his grip on the rifle.

"No! No, just put it down."

"Can't do it!"

"They've seen hunters before. It scares them."

Reed had to trust Beck or shoot. He looked into Beck's eyes one very long, final time.

"Reed . . ."

He found her. He finally saw, under all that filth, the Beck he'd known was there all along—the confident, competent woman he'd grown to love. He slowly stooped over and set the rifle down.

"Stay there now," she said. "Stay bent over. Don't look up."

He bent low, eyes to the ground, every bit of common sense telling him this was death for sure.

The growling behind the trees stopped.

Beck forced herself to relax. She looked up at Rachel and hummed in as calm and happy a tone as she could. Rachel gazed down at her, then cocked her head, eyes troubled.

Beck reached for Reed again, not pleading this time, but expressing happiness. "Hmmm . . . hmmmph."

Across the clearing, Reed sank to all fours.

Rachel's arms relaxed. "Hmm."

Beck told her, "Friend. My friend. Hmm. *Tok! Tok!*"

Rachel eyed Reed for a long, careful moment, as if she was finally sorting out where she'd seen that strange creature before.

"See?" said Beck, patting Rachel's arm. "You know him. You've seen him before."

Rachel quit huffing and just stared.

Reed stayed on the ground but was poised to grab his rifle if anything went wrong.

Rachel drew a deep breath, sighed it out, and slowly relaxed her arms. Beck stepped down, limping slightly, one hand holding Rachel's, one hand toward Reed. "Look at me, Reed." He lifted his face to hers, and she could see hope flooding his eyes. "Don't get up. Let me come to you. I have to come to you."

She gazed back at Rachel one last time. Rachel seemed perplexed and troubled, but when Beck let go of her hand, she withdrew it, letting it fall to her side.

Beck turned toward Reed and limped across the clearing, passing by the fallen monster. She could muster only a quick, fearful glance in its direction.

It was the longest wait of Reed's life, but he kept to the rules, watching Beck come closer, stepping and limping over rocks, easing through grass and low brush. When she was only ten feet away, she said quietly, "I think you can get up now."

He rose slowly, meeting her eyes, careful not to look at the—

She fell into his arms.

He embraced her as she held him, kissed him, clung to him, stinking like a sewer but totally, wonderfully Beck. He was still cautious, checking the area over her shoulder, almost dancing with her as he scanned a full circle, wondering what became of Max Johnson, checking the location of his rifle, wondering what the Bigfoot might do—

The Bigfoot. He stopped and stared.

Beck turned. "See, Rachel? He's—"

It was as if a dream had ended. The creature was gone. The brush and trees were motionless as if they'd never been disturbed.

Cap pressed his fingers against Sing's carotid artery. The pulse was weak but steady. "Sing! *Sing!*"

She opened her eyes. It took her a moment before recognition settled, but finally she smiled. "Cap, you're all right."

"So are you," he lied. He kissed her gently, almost imperceptibly on the cheek, afraid he might snuff out whatever spark of life remained.

"Hello," Sing said to all the wonderful people in uniform who were stepping around Steve Thorne's dead body to get to her.

The medics went right to work, assessing her vitals. One shined a light in her eyes. The pupils responded.

She pointed to the wall beside the computer station.

The medics were too busy saving her life to look. Cap and Dave followed her direction and found a thin spattering of her blood and some of her hairs on the wall. In the center of the pattern was a bullet hole.

Dave took a penlight from his pocket and shined it into the hole. He smiled. "The slug's in there."

The medic tending her wound smiled. "Pretty good scalp wound, but no penetration of the skull. She'll make it."

"Sing," Dave asked, "what about Reed and Pete?"

"Reed's looking for Beck." She gasped. "And Max is still up there!"

Cap told Dave, "Adam Burkhardt."

Dave eyed the computer. "Can you show us where?"

"Lost Creek." Sing tried to rise but couldn't. She gestured toward her computer. "Help me up there."

Reed gave Beck a kiss, giving no thought to the mud, blood, and filth, then immediately turned his attention to her battered face and bloodstained shirt. Her nose and mouth had been bleeding, then apparently wiped and smeared with a dirty rag. "Are you . . . what happened?"

"I got in a fight."

"Somebody *hit* you?"

"My snotty little cousin."

"But you're, you're all right? Nothing broken, nothing . . ."

"I've been worse. But I'm with you now, and—"

She gasped, her eyes looking in horror over his shoulder.

Reed spun, then froze.

Max Johnson emerged from the brush, limping, in pain, his shaved head scratched by branches and bleeding. He sighted down his rifle at them.

Reed spoke quietly, without moving a muscle. "Max, it's over."

He wagged his head, his eyes burning. "I'm sorry, Reed. I have to survive."

Beck whispered, hiding behind Reed. "He made the monster."

The pieces flew together in Reed's mind. "Survive as what? You want to end up like your creation? A killer?"

The man was trembling. The barrel of the rifle oscillated in erratic circles. "It's a natural process. It's been going on for billions of years."

"Max—"

"Burkhardt!" he spat. "Professor Adam Burkhardt!"

"Okay," Reed lowered his voice. "Professor Burkhardt. You see? You have a name. You're a person, a *man*; you're more than that thing you made."

The faint sound of a helicopter grew louder, coming closer.

Reed never broke eye contact. "And now, just look at yourself. Is this Professor Adam Burkhardt standing here? Is this something he would do?"

Burkhardt was shaking. "I don't *want* to do this! But I have to survive!"

Reed insisted, "As what?"

Burkhardt glanced at his creation.

The sound of the helicopter grew louder and then appeared from the southwest, heading directly toward them.

"Professor. When that chopper lands, what are they going to find standing here? A man, or a monster?"

Burkhardt could no longer sight down the rifle. His eyes

strayed, looking far away, filling with tears. The rifle drifted to one side and then sank as his resolve melted.

At last, his gaze fell and he began to quake, weeping.

The chopper rose overhead, circled, and began to settle toward a landing site beyond the trees.

"Professor. It's over."

Burkhardt sank to his knees, sobbing in shame and remorse.

Reed reached into his shirt pocket. The handcuffs were there, for this moment. He pulled them out. "Professor Burkhardt, you're under arrest." He took the rifle from Burkhardt's weak and trembling hands and handed it to Beck. "It's my duty to advise you of your rights. You have the right to remain silent . . ."

He cuffed Burkhardt's hands behind his back.

Jimmy Clark and the two sheriff's officers were aghast when they first arrived, and Jimmy had not yet recovered even as he snapped photos of the scene and of Adam Burkhardt's monster.

Click! Click! Click! The clearing from several compass directions.

Click! The location of the monster in the clearing.

Click! The monster, wide shot.

Click! The apelike feet, missing the opposing toes.

Click! A close-up of the burn injury on the side of the head, compliments of Melanie Brooks and her pan of hot hamburger grease.

Click! A close-up of the bullet wound in the leg, compliments of Sheriff Mills.

Click, click, click! Jimmy lowered the camera and shook his head—something he'd been doing incessantly since he and the officers arrived.

Reed had just finished using the chopper's first aid kit to

clean Beck's wounds and prepare a cold compress for her face. Now he came over to take one last look before they left for the chopper.

Jimmy gazed at him, struggled for words, and finally came up with, "I guess you've made your point."

"Well, next time—" Reed smiled and waved that one off. "No, we don't want a next time."

"No, we sure don't."

They shared a laugh and then a handshake.

The two officers had Burkhardt between them. Burkhardt wouldn't look at his monster; he wouldn't look up at all.

Jimmy hollered, "Okay, let's get these people out of here."

Beck sat in the coarse grass, holding the cold compress against her face with one hand while pulling itchy, prickly grass, twigs, and moss from inside her shirt with the other.

When Reed and Jimmy came over to help her up, Jimmy shied back from the filth. "*Eeesh!* What did you do to yourself?"

"Hey!" She got to her feet without any help and looked him squarely in the eye. "Just for your information, this is my family scent. It tells everybody who I am and what I've been eating and how I'm feeling about things."

Reed and Jimmy stared at her.

"It even tells you whether I like you or not, so read it and weep—"

"Beck," Reed began.

"—unless you can't read plain Sasquatch!"

"Beck?"

She turned toward him, her dignity reclaimed. "What?"

"What happened to your stutter?"

The question stopped her cold. Plainly, she hadn't noticed until this moment. "Uh . . ." She glanced toward the woods. "Maybe God took it."

He gave her a special smile and then pulled her in close. She clung to him unabashedly. "Ready to come home?" he asked.

"Anywhere with you."

He gave her his arm to lean on. "Come on. Let's get you to a hospital."

The chopper was parked on a rocky knoll a short hike up the hill. As it rose above the trees, Beck watched out the window and marveled: the mountains really were as vast and mysterious as they seemed.

Almost immediately, Jimmy started circling as Reed tapped her shoulder and pointed.

They passed over a deep, meandering ravine with a creek running down its center. Because of the thick forest, Beck could only catch a few quick glimpses, but it was enough for her to recognize a natural log bridge across the creek and the square, split-shake roof of a forlorn little cabin.

EPILOGUE

"What in the world were they thinking?" A week later, Reed still couldn't get over it. "I mean, how were they going to explain all the dead people lying around? Didn't they think somebody would start to wonder?"

He sat at one of Arlen Peak's best tables at the Tall Pine Resort, debriefing and remembering with Cap, Sing, Dave, and Jimmy while they waited for the best barbecued steak dinner Arlen could whip up.

"The problem got away from them, literally," said Cap. "Even if Burkhardt and his crew had a containment plan, it had to be trashed the moment Beck got grabbed. These guys were desperate."

"Nice pictures, Jimmy." Sing, wearing a head bandage and a modified hair arrangement, was once again glued to her computer. "But Thorne cut us a nice break, right, Reed?" She was hinting. She still hadn't heard the full explanation.

None of them had. Reed had a rapt audience. "I figured Thorne had to leave Kane's gun with him so people would think Kane died from a self-inflicted gunshot wound. I had a waypoint in my GPS marking where Kane and Thorne left off, so I used that to find Kane's body—that and some lucky guessing."

"A mighty long shot, Reed," said Jimmy.

Reed shrugged. "That's all I had left."

Jimmy patted his shoulder. "It was brilliant. Pete would've liked it."

Reed, along with the others, fell into a somber moment at the mention of their old friend. "It does sound like something he'd do, doesn't it?"

Dave had plucked a cracker from the basket in the middle of the table and said with his mouth full, "So what were they going to do with that monster's carcass, let the birds eat it?"

"Bury it, I suppose," said Sing.

"Well, it's in a cooler now," said Jimmy.

"Just like Burkhardt," Reed quipped, and got a laugh.

"He and Merrill could end up being bunkmates," Cap ventured.

"Tell them about your job," Sing prompted her husband.

Now Cap had their undivided attention. "Well, it looks favorable. I don't know whether the university's had a change of heart or whether they're just trying to save face, but . . ."

"But you can't argue with Right," said Sing with an overacted pat on his hand, "and that's what you are!"

Arlen swept through to take drink orders. "And by the way, it's not such a bad idea to let the birds and the bears and the coyotes eradicate a carcass. They can make quick work of it, let me tell you." He directed his next sentence at Jimmy. "Which is why nobody's ever found a Sasquatch skeleton. Nature has a way of erasing things."

Jimmy smirked good-naturedly, hands lifted in surrender. "Whatever you say, Arlen."

"Didn't Beck find a skeleton up there?" Dave asked.

Reed put up a hand of caution. "That's a sensitive area."

Cap interjected, "But remember, Jimmy: Those hairs from Beck's backpack turned out to have clean DNA from a creature not yet catalogued. Nobody mutated that animal; it was the real thing."

Sing peered closely at her computer screen. "And you might take a look at this, Jimmy, especially since you took these pictures."

They all rose and gathered around Sing's computer. She scrolled through the photos as they murmured, reacted, and pointed. They'd seen these before but were more than eager to see them again. Sing clicked and enlarged one of Jimmy's wide shots of the clearing. "See those two fir trees and that bush between them?"

They did.

She scrolled to a medium shot of the monster's corpse on the ground. The two fir trees were visible in the background. She clicked and dragged over the fir trees and zoomed in on that area.

"Take a look, gentlemen. Take your time."

At first there was silence as they studied the blown-up image of two fir trunks with a splashing of green, yellow, and red leaves between them.

Green, yellow, and red.

But red only in one area.

"I think I see it," said Reed, as he traced it with his finger.

Sing clicked and dragged, enlarging the image until the saw-edge of the individual pixels began to appear.

Jimmy's eyes narrowed, glued to the screen. "I took this picture?"

They could all see it now: a domed head, a red brow, two

amber eyes, and a flat nose—a face peering through the leaves, keeping an eye on all that was happening in the clearing.

"That's her," said Reed. "That's Rachel."

"Beck needs to see this," said Cap.

"Where is she, anyway?" Jimmy asked.

Reed put out a hand to calm them down. "Outside."

"She okay?" they all wondered at once.

Reed nodded. "She'll be right back. She just needed to say good-bye."

Beck had not gone far, just enough of a walk up the Lost Creek Trail to stand still and silent among the trees, out of sight of her world, just barely within the boundary of *theirs*.

The swelling in her face was nearly gone, reduced to bruised patches of yellow, purple, and blue. Her cuts were healing. Her ankle was back to business as usual.

Her stutter had not returned. She could still lapse into shyness, but for the first time in her and Reed's marriage, she was answering the phone.

She'd gotten that shower and shampoo she used to dream about the first several nights in the woods—plenty of showers, as a matter of fact. Her skin was bathed, moisturized, and perfumed.

Nevertheless, the Sasquatch stench still lingered—in her memory.

She'd come to this place to wonder, she supposed, just wonder, and for how long, she couldn't guess. One moment, one night, one lifetime might never be enough to finish what felt so unfinished.

If only . . .

She listened for the voice of the forest. The birds were

singing their closing number, but there weren't too many. A light breeze moved through the treetops, but so gently that other sounds could still be heard.

She didn't feel foolish when she whistled; she only thought about how to achieve that particular, teakettle-like wavering in the main part and that curious warble at the end. The first attempt was only fair. The second was better. The third was delightful, almost exactly the way Rachel did it.

Then she stood quietly, listening, knowing how unlikely it would be, thinking she would never tell anyone, wondering if her whistle would carry far enough.

The voice of the forest continued to speak, but it had nothing to say to her.

Yes, it was a bit foolish. The mountains were so vast, the forests so deep. The wind could be wrong.

She turned to start back—

Somewhere out there, so far away, a teakettle whistled.

She held so very still, not breathing, straining to hear it again.

The teakettle whistled, wavering in the main part, warbling at the end—and so much better than Beck could do it.

There was nothing after that—only the breeze and the last verse of one bird's evening song. Beck cried a little, deeply happy and not having to wonder quite so much. She started back down the trail while she still had light to see her way.

It could have been a bird. It could have been the bugle of an elk or the squeaking of one tree swaying against another. She couldn't be sure.

But it was enough for now, and maybe forever.

acknowledgments

It's not so easy finding capable people who can get excited about somebody else's book when they have their own projects and commitments. These guys are special, and I thank them profusely for making this whole story such a pleasure to tell:

Jonathan Wells, postdoctoral biologist and senior fellow at the Discovery Institute, whose book, *Icons of Evolution*, first got my creative wheels turning, and who helped me clarify my main story idea over a pleasant lunch.

Dr. David DeWitt, director of the Center for Creation Studies at Liberty University, who, besides being a brilliant scientist and technical advisor, is quite an imaginative story crafter in his own right.

Dr. Paul Brillhart, my family physician, who loves to tell stories and went beyond the call of duty to provide me with medical details.

Nick Hogamier, a real, honest-to-goodness tracker, whose knowledge and fascinating stories became the model for the character Pete Henderson.

Thanks to all of you for making *Monster* such a great adventure!

Frank E. Peretti
April 2005

An excerpt from *House*

ONE

J ack, you're gonna kill us!"

His mind jerked out of a daydream and back to the lonely Alabama highway in front of the blue Mustang. The speedometer topped eighty. He cleared his mind and relaxed his right foot. "Sorry."

Stephanie went back to her singing, her voice clear if melancholy, her inflection classic country. *"My heart holds all secrets, my heart tells no lies . . ."*

That one again. She wrote it, so he never criticized it, but those awful lyrics, especially today—

"Jack!"

The speedometer was inching toward eighty.

"Sorry." He forced his foot to relax.

"What's the matter with you?"

"What's the matter—" *Easy now, Jack. No fuel on the fire.* "A little tense, okay?"

She smiled at him. "You should try singing."

His grip tightened on the steering wheel. "Yeah, that's your answer for everything, isn't it?"

"Excuse me?"

He sighed. He had to quit taking her bait. "Sorry." Always apologizing. He looked her way and forced a smile, hoping she would believe it.

She smiled back in a way that said she didn't.

She was beautiful, enough to capture the next man just as she'd captured him—blond, youthful, a real credit to those jeans—everything the guys in the lounges and bars could want in a country singer. No doubt those blue eyes could still sparkle, but not for him anymore. Right now they were hiding behind fashion-statement sunglasses, and she was craning to see out the back. "I think there's a cop behind us."

He checked the rearview mirror. The highway, which had narrowed to two lanes, curved lazily through late-spring forest and farmland, rose and fell over dips and rises, hiding and revealing, hiding and revealing a single car. It was gaining on them, near enough now for Jack to recognize the light bar atop the roof. He checked his speed. Sixty-five. That should be legal.

The police car kept coming.

"Better slow down."

"I'm doing the speed limit."

"You sure?"

"I can read the signs, Steph."

A few seconds more and the cruiser filled Jack's mirror as if he were towing it. He could see the cop's iron-jawed countenance behind the wheel, reflective black sunglasses obscuring the eyes.

Highway patrol.

Jack double-checked the speedometer, then slowed to sixty, hoping the cop wouldn't rear-end them.

The sedan inched closer.

He was going to rear-end them!

Jack smashed the gas pedal to the floor, and the Mustang shot ahead.

"What are you doing?" Stephanie cried.

"He was gonna hit us!"

The car fell back ten yards. Its red and blue lights flashed to life.

"Oh, great," she muttered, turning and flopping back against her seat. He could hear the blame in her voice. Always the blame. *But you're the one who walked away, Steph.*

The cruiser veered into the oncoming lane and pulled up beside them. The uniformed officer turned his face to Jack. Met his eyes. Or so Jack imagined. Black glasses. No expression. Jack forced his eyes back to the road.

The two cars were side by side, locked in formation at sixty miles an hour.

"What are you doing, Jack? Pull over."

He would if he could. Jack strained to see an opportunity. The forest, a thick tangle of maple, oak, and birch draped with kudzu, encroached like an advancing wall. "I can't. There's no shoulder. I can't just . . ."

He slowed. There had to be a turnout somewhere. Forty miles per hour. Thirty. The cruiser matched his speed.

Jack saw a break in the foliage, a sliver of a shoulder, just enough room. He began to veer off.

The cruiser surged and left them behind, lights blazing in silence. Fifteen seconds later it was a dot on the road between the towering trees, and then it was gone.

"What was that about?" Jack asked, checking his mirrors, rubbernecking, and easing back onto the highway. He wiped a sweaty palm on his jeans.

"You were speeding." She fixed her gaze on the highway, fumbled with a map, avoided his eyes.

"He didn't pull us over. Why was he so close? You see how close he was?"

"That's Alabama, Jack. You don't do things their way, they let you know."

"Yeah, but you don't ram someone in the tail for speeding."

She slapped her lap, a release of frustration. "Jack, will you please just get us there, legally, in one piece? Please?"

He chose silence over a comeback and concentrated on the road. *Save it for the counseling session, Jack.* He wondered what she'd been saving up, what new claims she'd unload tonight.

She shook out her shoulders, put on a smile, and started humming.

You really think it will work, don't you Jack? You really think you can save something you just don't have anymore?

If smiling and singing could bring back those days, he would laugh like a fool and even sing Stephanie's lyrics, but he was fresh out of illusions. All he had were the memories that stole his mind away even as his eyes remained on the road: her arms about his shoulders and the excitement in her eyes; the inner dawn he felt whenever she entered the room; the secrets they shared with a glance, a smile, a wink; all the things he thought life and love should be—

The accident changed everything.

He imagined himself sitting in the counselor's office, being honest about his feelings. *I'm feeling . . . like I've been had all my life. Life is pointless. If there is a God, He's the devil, and . . . What was that? Oh, you mean Stephanie? No, I've lost her too. She's gone. I mean, she's here, but she's checked out . . .*

He couldn't put away the idea that this whole trip was only a formality, another nail in the coffin of their marriage. Steph would sing her way to Montgomery and back and still get the divorce she wanted, go on her merry way.

"Jack, you're lost."

I sure am.

"Jack."

With a start, he returned his attention to driving. The Mustang purred along at sixty-five, gobbling up the highway. The forest was breaking up now, giving way to crude homesteads and stump-filled pastureland.

She was scanning the map, studying all those little red and black lines. Did she say *he* was lost? Right. *She* was holding the map, but *he* was lost.

He caught the sarcasm before it escaped. Hurtful words came so easily these days. "What do you mean?"

"Didn't you see that highway marker? It said 5."

He glanced at the mirror, then twisted to see the back of the receding sign. "5?"

She studied the map, tracing a route with her finger. "We're supposed to be on Highway 82."

He leaned and tried to read the map. The car swerved. He shot his eyes forward again, corrected the wheel.

"We're going to be late," she said.

Not necessarily. "You see Highway 5 on there? Where does it lead?"

She dragged her finger over the map and stopped about three inches out of Montgomery. "Not to Montgomery, unless you have a week to sightsee. How could you possibly have gotten off 82?"

Dare he defend himself? "I was a little distracted by a cop eating up my bumper."

She pulled her cell phone out of a cup holder and checked the display clock. "There's no way we'll make it."

Was that hope in her voice? He checked his watch. If they turned around now, maybe—

"I cancelled a gig to go to this appointment with you." Stephanie hunched in the seat, arms folded.

There it is again. My fault. She started humming. *There it is again.*

Red and blue lights flashed up ahead.

"Oh great," said Stephanie. "We *really* don't need this."

Jack slowed as they approached the patrol car parked just

beyond a turnoff. Orange cones and a sign blocked the road ahead. "Repaving Operation. Highway Closed to Through Traffic," Jack read. "Well, we have to turn around anyway." Jack pulled onto the gravel shoulder but had a second thought. "Let's ask. Maybe there's a faster way."

Jack eased the blue Mustang forward, up to the turnoff, and stopped a few feet behind the patrol car. The cruiser's door swung open and an officer—the officer—stepped out, aviator sunglasses still hiding his eyes.

THE OATH

10TH ANNIVERSARY EDITION

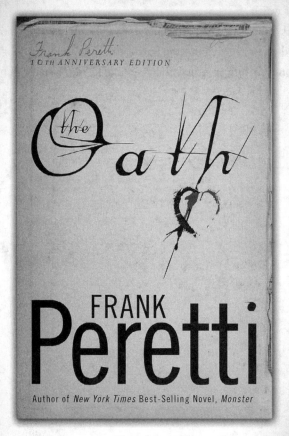

Featuring:
Author's signature on special hard cover
Exclusive interview with the author
Letter from the publisher

AVAILABLE AT BOOKSTORES EVERYWHERE

The Veritas Project series!

FRANK **Peretti**

Watch your locker.
Watch your back.

Watch your soul.

hangman's curse

THE VERITAS PROJECT VOLUME

nightmare academy

THE VERITAS PROJECT VOLUME TWO

About the Author

Frank Peretti, whose books have sold more than 12 million copies, is the *New York Times* best-selling author of *Monster* as well as the international bestsellers *The Oath*, *This Present Darkness*, and *Piercing the Darkness*. Peretti lives with his wife, Barbara, in the Pacific Northwest.